DELLIA

The Ever-Branching Tree

Episode One

THE EVER-BRANCHING TREE

DELLIA

DAVID SCIDMORE

Meerdon Publishing
Verona, Wisconsin

David Scidmore / Meerdon Publishing, Inc.
P.O. Box 1234
Verona, WI 53593
meerdon.com

Publisher's Note: This is a work of fiction. Names, characters, places, and incidents are a product of the author's imagination. Locales and public names are sometimes used for atmospheric purposes. Any resemblance to actual people, living or dead, or to businesses, companies, events, institutions, or locales is completely coincidental.

Front cover image by Elena Dudina
Front cover layout by JD Smith
Book layout by David Scidmore

Dellia (The Ever-Branching Tree, Episode One) – 1st Edition
Library of Congress Control Number: 2019908155
ISBN 978-1-64571-000-4

To Brenda, my one true love

Acknowledgments

It would be an understatement to say that without my wife Brenda this story would have been impossible. It isn't just that she had to live with my absent-mindedness, distraction and late nights while I worked on it. No, she is a part of me in so many ways that it would be impossible for them not to influence this story. We have always shared a love for science fiction, fantasy and storytelling in all its many and varied forms across the globe. Even more profound is that because of her I know what it is to fall in love and to be loved. How could that not find expression in these pages?

It is likely that without my brother Rob, I would still be working at a desk and have little time to think up crazy stories.

Every page of this book has benefited, in ways big and small, from the professionalism, kindness, skill, knowledge and diligence of Christopher Noel and Susannah Noel at Noel Editorial.

I knew that Elena Dudina was an amazing artist when I asked her to create the cover artwork, but the result continues to astound me every time I look at it. With the addition of Jane Dixon-Smith's brilliant lettering the cover truly captures the spirit of the story.

Lastly, thanks to the many musicians in Spock's Beard, The Flower Kings, Yes, Squackett, Kate Bush, The Enid, Coldplay, and many others whose work were, for me, the soundtrack to the story in my mind.

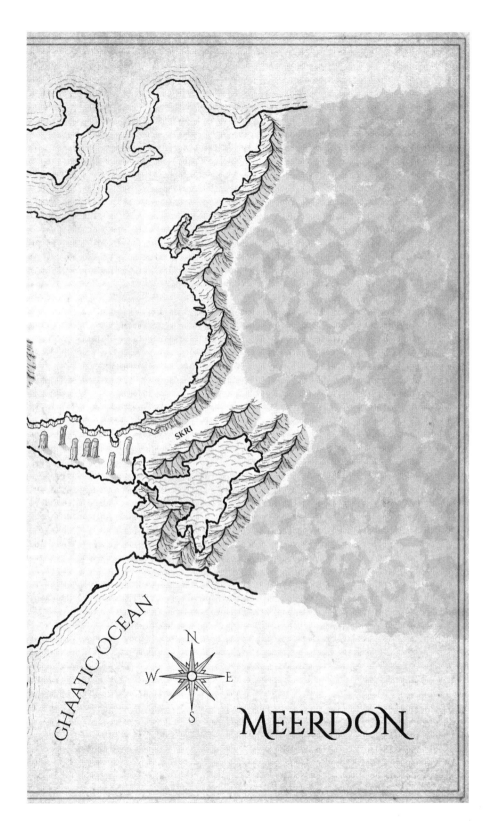

SKRI

GHAATIC OCEAN

MEERDON

Contents

they zipped by. He was too preoccupied, trying not to be distracted by thoughts of Megan as he plotted what to do about this absurd promotion mix-up.

Jon rushed through the open door into a bright white office. He shielded his eyes from the light pouring through a large picture window overlooking a lush, grassy yard before a small wooded area.

Spotless and undecorated, the severe look of the space matched Robin's plain clothes, short black hair, and businesslike appearance. Situated behind a barren white desk with a small monitor, she glanced up through her clunky, black glasses while Jon closed the door. As he charged over, she ceased her pecking at the keyboard.

He halted next to a white, plastic rolling chair. "You know, I never accepted any promotion. It's not fair that I have to go around avoiding people just so I don't have to keep explaining your mistake."

Robin looked up at him with a startled expression. "Good morning to you, too."

Not in a mood for pleasantries, Jon simply waited for her response.

She leaned back in her seat and eyed him for a moment. "It wasn't a mistake."

He gave a quick shake of his head. "What?"

"And I'm not accepting your answer."

"Huh?"

She motioned to the seat next to him.

Shocked at the casual indifference with which she had discarded his wishes for his own career, Jon absentmindedly rolled out the chair and plopped down into it.

Robin waited for him to seat himself before continuing. "Jon, why do you work here?"

Thrown by the question, he shrugged his shoulders and

stuttered out a hesitant reply. "You … pay me?"

She dismissed his words with a wave of her hand. "No. I mean, why did you become a physicist?"

"What does that have to do with this whole promotion thing?"

"Just answer the question."

Jon gave a bewildered shake of his head as he leaned back in the chair. "I'm good at math, I guess." He pondered the question for a few seconds more. "Trying to make sense of the way the world works has always been fascinating to me."

Robin made a hasty "continue" motion.

"I guess I've always been curious. When I see something inexplicable, my mind just latches onto it, and I can't let go of it until I understand it."

Robin sent Jon a self-satisfied look. "From what I've been told, you studied to excess in college. You had no family, spent little time with friends. That's not simple curiosity, it's an obsession."

Taken aback by her assertion, Jon looked down at the immaculate desktop. It was a bit of a mischaracterization, actually. He had friends. And as for family, his biological mom thought it was more important to protect the world than raise her son. So, she died overseas in the military, leaving him with a stepfamily in which he had never been welcome. It would be pointless debating all that now, so Jon simply lifted his head and shrugged his shoulders. "Okay, so I'm obsessed with understanding how things work."

Robin leaned forward in her chair as she eyed him. "Yeah, but why negative energy?"

Jon shrugged again. "It's thought to be necessary to holding open a stable wormhole."

Robin gave another dismissive wave of her hands. "So what?"

Surprised that someone who worked in a physics lab could know so little of his research, he straightened. "Are you serious?"

She nodded.

"Wormholes could allow travel to the nearest star or let us cross billions of light-years. They could be a gateway to different universes, different times." Jon leaned forward in his chair as his passionate words began to flow. "Think of the possibilities—space travel, time travel. They might even open up whole new worlds, allow us to see different cultures, encounter new life forms. My little experiment is nothing. It's just a tiny little proof of concept, to show that it's possible to create an energy density less than zero. But someday, with vastly more power, it could become a passage to wonders we can only begin to imagine."

As he finished, Robin pointed at him with a smug look on her face. "See, that's what I'm talking about."

Confused, Jon gave a rapid shake of his head. "What?"

"Listen to yourself. I feel inspired just hearing you talk about it. You want to know why I announced a promotion before you accepted it? I'm determined to push you into it."

A bit panicked at the notion of being forced into a situation that was the polar opposite of what he could handle, Jon snapped back. "But that's not your call. This is *my* life."

Robin placed both hands on her desk and leaned in further. "Look, we have many bright, highly educated people here. Among them, you are one of the most passionate, persuasive, articulate, personable, and focused. Those are all excellent qualities for someone who leads a team of researchers." She shook her head. "Sitting in your lab, alone, with your one experiment, is a waste of human capital."

Even more uncomfortable with her characterization and annoyed at being referred to as "human capital," Jon fired back. "You're delusional! I don't know who you're talking about, but that's not me."

He paused for a second, realizing his argumentative posture was only serving to polarize the situation. He let out an exasperated sigh. "Look, I appreciate the kind words, but the reality is, the world you're trying to force me into is not a place where I fit."

"What is that supposed to mean?"

"Trust me, I would love to be the guy you described, but if you want to watch explorers crashing and burning on some brave new world, just put me in charge."

Robin folded her arms and leaned back in the chair. "I don't agree."

From her tone, it was obvious that further discussion would be counterproductive. So Jon jumped to his feet. "Really? So you're not going to retract your announcement?"

"No."

He turned and marched to the door. He had misjudged the situation, and apparently, now, he would have to find another way to deal with this whole mess. He barged out into the hallway and as he hurried down the shiny white floor, he shook his head and muttered under his breath, "Unbelievable."

Jon's hands clung to the steering wheel as he cruised down a well-worn city street. Cars rumbled past in the approaching lane while behind them spread a seemingly endless row of old but well-maintained two-story shops and restaurants. Across the street, a hillside rose up from the sidewalk to meet a ridge that ran the length of a huge, long park. A garbage truck roared past, but the noise barely registered. Even the loud bang of a backfiring car couldn't pierce his thoughts as he stared down the bustling road.

It had all been a colossal waste of time. The corporate offices were some distance from the lab, in a clean, modern office building. He had hoped a trip there might help clear up the whole promotion issue, but it had only seemed to further cloud it. Human resources reported directly to the chief operations officer, but the man had been entirely too busy to deal with him. He seemed generally confused by the concept of turning down a promotion that had never been offered. And when he finally did begin to grasp the situation, he had been dismissive, making comments about how inappropriate it was to go over Robin's head and how he had faith in her judgment. In the end, he had given up and headed back to his lab.

As the sandwich shop approached where he had planned to grab lunch, Jon found a parking spot. The aroma of savory food only intensified his hunger as he pulled up to the curb across from the King Chi, a clean, modern-looking Chinese restaurant.

As the car rolled to a stop, a loud gunshot rang through the open window.

Jon went rigid, his hands twisting on the steering wheel until his knuckles turned white. His breath came in short bursts as images from long ago flashed through his consciousness: his stepsister's terrified face, the sound of screams and moaning, and the smell of blood.

An overwhelming wave of guilt and shame hit, and his head whipped over toward the source of the gunfire. He gasped as he spotted a man at the top of the ridge with a rifle. It was as if an oppressive weight had slammed into his chest as his eyes fixed on the terrified expressions of two teenagers with the weapon aimed at their heads.

Without a moment's pause, Jon flung the car door open and flew into a sprint. In a terrified haze, with all his attention focused on the gunman's back, he slipped and stumbled his way up the hill.

As he approached, Jon lowered himself to the ground, and when he reached the top, he leaped. His hand smashed the rifle out of the way and the full weight of his body careened into the gunman, sending him sprawling.

The man tumbled to the ground with a loud grunt and a cry of pain.

Jon's head whipped up at a chorus of gasps. There, behind a line of yellow tape, stood a crowd of bystanders, watching with shocked expressions. He halted in confusion when his eyes met a young woman in front of the tape, filming the scene with a camera on a tripod. Overwhelming horror and embarrassment struck as he realized he had apparently just tackled an actor performing a scene.

The two teenagers flew to the gunman's side as the stunned crowd stood gawking.

Jon stumbled to his feet as a woman in the crowd called out, "Is he okay?"

A man's voice shouted, "What an idiot" as the assemblage broke into a tumult of hushed comments.

The woman stepped out from behind the camera. She glared at him and shouted, "What the hell do you think you're doing?"

Jon froze, unsure whether to help or flee in humiliation. "I'm sorry. I heard a gunshot. I ... I thought ..."

The complaints and derogatory remarks of the crowd grew to a rumble.

The camerawoman yelled, "Get out of here!" and started to march toward Jon.

Mortified, he turned and spoke quietly over his shoulder as he hurried away. "I ... I'm sorry." He sped up, ignoring the crowd as he scrambled back down the hill.

He glanced up, and a much deeper and more personal wave of shame and humiliation struck as his eyes met Megan and Nichole, standing outside the door to the King Chi, staring with stunned expressions.

Nichole's piercing dark eyes remained fixed on him as she shook her head in disbelief. Megan made some comment to her and motioned for her to go. Nichole sent one last disparaging look, then tore her eyes from the scene and headed for her car.

As Megan moved to the curb, her gaze remained fixed on the stream of cars, searching for an opening to cross the street. When she looked up, their eyes met, and Jon's head whipped down, avoiding her gaze.

Still shaking, and his breathing labored, he approached the sidewalk and seated himself on the dry, short grass. Too dazed and embarrassed to look her in the face, he kept staring downward and listened for Megan's footsteps as she approached.

Then came her voice. "What the heck, Jon? You were just going to go get a sandwich."

He never lifted his eyes. He had been too ashamed to mention his trip to corporate. In a shocked trance, he peered down at an ant crawling into a crack in the sidewall as he heard his weak words drone out as if they weren't even his own. "Why does this kind of thing always happen to me?"

Megan came to rest beside him. "Because you ran toward the gunshots, you idiot. Most people have the common sense to run the other way." She placed a hand on Jon's trembling shoulder and looked into his face. "Are you okay?"

He nodded. "But I don't think I should be driving."

The two sat for a moment as the sounds of the bustling midday traffic echoed down the park. Still too stunned to think straight, Jon stared out across the street at the customers hurrying in and out of restaurants.

His eyes began to tear up as his thoughts went back to his step-sister, and he absentmindedly said, "For a minute, I was right back there."

"Back where?" Megan sought out his gaze.

He shook his head as a profound sadness took hold. "It's nothing. … It's just, sometimes I don't feel like I fit into this world. Like this isn't the life I was meant to be leading."

Megan perked up. "I know, right? I always thought my life would be super exciting. Like I'd be a mixed martial arts fighter, or a race car driver or something. Instead, I work in a dingy lab with no windows." She smiled and once again sought out his gaze.

Thrown by her remark, Jon took a deep breath as he fought

back his ghosts. He turned his head and smiled. "I don't know where this conversation took a wrong turn, but you and I are not talking about the same thing."

Megan nodded, and her gaze became sympathetic. "I know. I know." She looked him in the eye. "It's not nothing. Ever since I've known you, you've been running from something. You're a friendly guy. Yet, you preferred to study instead of being with friends. You throw yourself into your work like it's some kind of protective shield. You're not dealing, Jon, and it's holding you back."

Feeling a bit less shocked, he took a deep breath. "We should really get back to work."

Megan smiled. "Right. Look at me." She laughed. "Prying into your life like some kind of girlfriend or something."

Her casual words struck him to the core. The thought of them together took his breath away, and for a moment all he could do was stare at her.

Then he pulled himself out of it and motioned to the car with his head. "Can you drive?"

She gave a crisp nod of her head, and the two rose and headed down the hill.

For so many years he had hoped she could be part of the simple life he wanted. He had stayed by her side and waited for any sign while he tried not to dwell on what might never be. But now, as they returned to his car, and even on the drive back to the office, a notion gathered focus in his thoughts. Because after the easy way with which the words had slipped from her mouth, he could think of nothing else but Megan.

Jon slid through the door into Ryan's office. The dimmed lights always made it seem like he was stepping into some kind of high-tech prehistoric cave, complete with writing on the walls. Scribblings and multicolored diagrams lay scratched out across a set of oversized whiteboards, illuminated by the soft glow of monitors and equipment.

Ryan's narrow face with its neatly parted brown hair peered around a pair of flat-screens that crowded his desk. The gentle staccato of keystrokes stopped, but he didn't utter a word when Jon approached. He simply scooped up his mug, leaned back in his chair, and took a sip of his early afternoon coffee.

The dramatic pause wasn't something Jon had planned, but it suited the occasion. So he hung on to it awhile as he leaned against the wall, waiting for the right melodramatic moment.

He took a slow deep breath. "I think I'm going to ask Megan out today."

Ryan didn't speak right away, preferring to take another sip of his coffee first. "You still doing those negative energy experiments? Quantum optical squeezing, lithium niobate lenses, super-high-speed rotating mirrors? Very cool stuff."

"Did you hear me?"

"Yeah, I heard. And I might be excited, too. If it wasn't so ludicrous. You've been obsessing over this girl for ten years, and you're just now going to ask her out?"

Jon gave a small shrug. "Yeah, but she's always going out with someone else, or getting over them, or it was finals, or she was on vacation. It's just never been the right time."

"For *ten* years? It never came up? Isn't that a clue she might not be interested?"

Jon hesitated. After all, Ryan was right. Not to mention, it was a bit hard to explain. When they'd met in his second year of college, she was part of a larger group of friends. He had casually asked her out many times, but there always seemed to be something going on that made her reluctant to say yes. Yet her emphatic concern that he understand her reasons for declining made it seem as if she wasn't simply brushing him off. Even so, over time he'd stopped asking, and decided to be content that she just wanted him as a friend.

After he graduated and moved away, they stayed in touch. And when Megan needed a job, she pushed to find one working with him. When she made up her mind, she could display the most incredible determination and enthusiasm.

Even though they'd been friends the whole time, it wasn't until they were both strangers in a new city that he'd truly gotten to know her. In that time, they'd become closer, and maybe Ryan was right, maybe she had no interest in him in that way. But it was also possible that she would be open to something more.

Jon glanced down. "Maybe, but how else am I going to find out if I don't ask?"

Through the dim light, Jon studied Ryan's reaction. He didn't seem satisfied. In fact, he was eyeing Jon as if the conversation were some kind of chess game and he were contemplating his next move.

Jon snatched the Rubik's Cube from the small collection of toys and puzzles on the corner of Ryan's desk. He fiddled with it while Ryan retrieved his mug and took another sip.

"So," Ryan said, "what if Megan isn't interested? In theory, if you love her, then you'd want her to be happy. What if being happy means not being with you?"

Jon recognized the sound of Ryan baiting him. He tinkered with the cube and shook his head, resisting the urge to skewer Ryan's argument. But when he glanced up, Ryan was staring at him, waiting for an answer.

Skewering it would be. "I don't buy the premise of your question."

"What's not to buy?"

"People want what they want. At some level, love is always about what the other person can do for you. For example, theoretically, what if Hitler were married to … I don't know, Gandhi. Then by your ration—"

"Well, first off, neither of them is gay. So, nice example."

"Okay, then what about Hitler and Mother Teresa?"

Ryan winced. "Nice. Thanks for that image."

"If they were in love, then by your rationale, she'd want him to be happy. So she'd want the Nazis to dominate the world. And if he wanted *her* to be happy, he'd have to … I don't know, kill himself?"

Ryan shook his head. "Ever hear of reducto ad absurdo … whatever? It means your argument is crap."

"Reductio ad absurdum. I know what it means, but you can't use it to write off someone's argument like that. To do so is a form of propaganda, a glittering generality. You're insisting it's invalid to carry an argument to its logical conclusion so you can avoid having to explain why."

"Fine. Can we get off the topic of Hitler's love life and back to negative energy experiments, warp drives, cool stuff?"

Jon leaned back against the wall again, eyeing Ryan as he took a deep breath of coffee-scented air. Okay, so maybe staying on topic would have been a good choice. Yet, how could he describe the feeling he got every time he imagined a life with Megan? How he dreamed of waking up to her smile each day, of laughing with her as they shared stories over dinner, or of curling up on the couch at night while they watched movies together? What words could express the way he felt about her? Or how he longed to hear her say she felt the same way? Even if he knew exactly what to say, Ryan would never understand. He'd just see him as some pathetic dreamer.

Having created a pattern that amused, Jon finished messing with the cube and left it with each side a solid color except for the square in the center. He placed it back among the baubles on Ryan's desk and peered down into his face. "Look, I know what you think about Megan and me, and I can't say you're totally wrong. But how can I not at least try? So we've known each other forever. Maybe that just means we have a great basis for something more. Truth is, I can't stop thinking about her and how amazing a life with her would be. How can I not at least ask her if there's a chance?"

Ryan set down his mug and leaned back in his chair. "I think you're nuts, but far be it from me to rain on your parade. I truly think you should ask her out, put an end to this madness. Just don't get your hopes up is all I'm saying."

Jon labored diligently in the muted light of his lab, surrounded by the warm glow from computers and equipment scattered around the room. He stood hunched over a table full of lasers, mirrors, and metal, making his last-minute checks.

It was a thing of beauty, the way the brilliant, blue beam ricocheted here and there across the surface, then passed through a lens of lithium niobate. The lens resonated, turning the beam into a series of imperceptibly short pulses of alternating positive and negative energy. The resulting blue thread bounced around the table through more mirrors, then into a super-fast rotating mirror that split the pulses, creating two beams, one of positive energy and the other of negative.

Jon turned to one of the two cameras on tripods that hunched over the table like a pair of Martian invaders. It had occurred to him that the component-level tests and calibration were unlikely to reveal any real problems. So, if he moved up the schedule for the full-blown demonstration, he could show progress today. It was a risky proposition, but if it worked, it might give him a bit more pull with management in deciding his own career path and show everyone he didn't need a team to make progress.

He made a small adjustment, re-aiming the camera so that it was ready to record anything that might happen. As he finished, the door closed, and Jon glanced up from his work. There stood Megan, quietly watching him with a somber expression that was uncharacteristic.

With her arrival came the realization that the moment he had planned was close at hand, and a sudden fog of apprehension clouded his mind.

Jon waved her over. "Just starting. Can you check that?" He pointed to the computer where the video and sensor recording system needed to be verified.

Megan had assisted with countless experiments and knew precisely what needed to be done. So, he turned back to the table, rechecking it, while Megan skated over to the computer. She slid down in front of it and her eyes fixed on the screen as she softly clacked away on the keyboard.

After a moment, the key clicks stopped. "Jon?"

He looked over at her. "Yeah."

"Uh … never mind." She turned her attention back to the computer screen, and the quiet clicking of keys resumed.

Her words barely registered. He gazed at the table as his mind swirled around the prospect of asking Megan out. Should he be blunt and honest, or pour his heart out? No, that might put her off. Unless she felt the same way. Was that possible? Could this be the day everything changed? Or would she brush him off again?

His mouth dry and his heart thumping in his ears, Jon glanced over at her, then glanced again. He stopped and stared at her so focused on her work. Perhaps he was worried about nothing. After all, she was sitting here now because she had gone out of her way to get a job working with him.

He turned back to his work and pretended to be making casual conversation. "Hey, I was thinking—"

Megan never looked up. "Well, that is what they pay you for."

"What I mean is, you know, maybe after work, we could go out."

"Sure."

"To a nice restaurant." Jon's words hung in the air while he waited for any sign from Megan.

She raised her head. "Wait, you mean like a date?"

He tried to sound nonchalant. "No, not *like* a date. An *actual* date, you and me. What do you think?"

Megan stood up and turned around, staring at Jon across the table of bright lasers and mirrors. Bars jumped up and down on a large monitor behind them while another switched between camera views of the table.

Megan shook her head. "Yeah, that's not happening. Ever."

Jon's heart nearly stopped. "What?"

"Look, I like you, as a friend. Never as a boyfriend."

"But we're perfect for each other."

Her manner was blunt and matter-of-fact. "Not even close. It's not happening."

"But whenever you're going out with another guy, you're always saying how you wish he was more like me."

"Yeah—nice like you, but someone that actually wants to make something out of his life. Someone responsible. An actual grown-up, who doesn't turn down a promotion because he doesn't want to do performance reviews."

He stepped back and stared for a second as his frustration welled. "Any other criticisms? Keep 'em coming. How about I'm a coward? Or too much of a geek? Or maybe just a big idiot for thinking I could ever have a chance with you?"

"God, you can be so insecure sometimes."

"Oh, excuse me, I forgot to throw in insecure."

"And don't put words in my mouth. It's infuriating."

Jon looked down, staring at the bright blue lasers, shaking his head in disbelief. This didn't even sound like Megan. She could be direct, sure, but this was downright hurtful. "Fine, so all these years I was wrong about you sending me signals?"

"Sure, I might have been nice to you. Because we're friends, and you were always helping me."

"So why are you being so mean now?"

"Because I don't want there to be any misunderstanding."

"Well," Jon barked back, "too late for that."

He waited for her next crushing retort, but her eyes flew wide open, and she stared at him. Then she pointed to something. "Uh, Jon, what's that?"

Jon followed her finger. He straightened and gasped.

There, above the table, hovered an irregular swirling ball of liquid darkness about the size of a fist. It was utterly impossible. Yet there it was.

As Jon stared at its wet, undulating surface, it became clear it wasn't exactly dark. It was more like he was looking through a piece of liquid glass at something dark and unrecognizable. Its surface moved and rippled, and it spun just fast enough that it was hard to make out anything but darkness.

Jon's mind raced, searching for any theory, any explanation, no matter how far-fetched.

He shook his head. "I have no idea."

It had almost doubled in size. Suddenly, the implications flooded his mind. Whatever this was, it could be historic, epic.

His gaze shot over to Megan. "Wait, are we recording this?"

Megan raced to one of the two cameras and quickly checked it over while he checked the other.

Jon glanced at the irregular, spinning patch of fluid darkness, now the size of a soccer ball. His attention snapped back to Megan. "The computer, is it logging this?"

She flew back and began typing madly. For a moment, Jon followed her fingers as they zipped across the keyboard. But the pull of the unknown became irresistible, and his gaze was drawn back to the spinning ball of darkness.

He peered into it, studying it, mesmerized by the sight. It had doubled again, swirling, pulsating, growing. But there was something more. It was like he was looking through it at something, or some-*where*. As if he were staring at a distorted image of stone with flashes of metal swirling by, viewed through a fluid, whirling chunk of glass.

A gentle tugging sensation yanked Jon out of his trance. "Wait, do you feel that?"

Movement caught his eye. His head whipped over, and his gaze followed a set of paper clips as they slid toward the mass, then acceler-ated into it.

Pens flew out of a mug and rocketed into the blob.

The mug itself began to rattle.

A book flew from the desk and smashed into it. The mug shat-tered, sending fragments tumbling into the dark ball.

A chair rolled across the floor on its own and clattered into the table.

Jon's heart jumped into his throat at the sudden realization: it had some kind of pull, and it was growing.

Hysteria took over, and he barked out, "We need to leave, now!"

Megan reached for her purse, but it slid away from her. She lunged at it again, barely missing it as it flew into the darkness.

Suddenly, her feet began to slide across the floor.

Jon could almost feel the panic seize her.

Her terrified eyes pleaded to him, and she yelled, "Jon!"

She clutched at the rim of the desk until she caught hold, then dragged herself along its edge. She grabbed the handle of a file drawer next to it, but it yanked open.

Piles of documents scattered from the surfaces of desks and out of the open drawer, flying up into the lab. The air filled with paper, swirling around the room and into the mass.

An overhead light dropped, and sparks crackled from broken wires.

Large pieces of equipment and computers began shuddering. Then one after another, they flew from the walls in bursts of sparks.

Megan twisted out of the way as they whizzed by her, barely missing her as they rocketed into the growing mass.

In a panic, Jon struggled against the inexorable pull, dragging himself around the table, headed for Megan, desperate to reach her. He dodged a lamp and a series of books that flew into his path as they screamed by him into the hole.

He reached for her hand, but the file cabinet tipped, causing her to stumble and lose her grip.

She let out a gut-wrenching scream that twisted its way through his stomach. Her frenzied breathing—short, uneven, nearly hyperventilating—caught in his ears.

The sound of fingernails against metal raked through his mind as Megan, frantic to save herself, clawed at anything near.

He reached out again, powerless to stop her from being dragged screaming into the darkness.

As an abrupt silence fell, Jon braced himself against the crushing pull, his mind a frozen haze.

Time seemed to slow around him.

He stared at the spot where she'd been. This couldn't be happening.

Through his panicked breathing came a faint remnant of Megan's familiar scent. In that moment, somewhere deep inside, horror turned to resolve.

He took a couple of deep breaths while he steadied himself against the relentless tug. Then he let go and dove headfirst into the swirling patch of darkness.

Chapter Two

SUNLIGHT AND DARKNESS

The early rays warmed Dellia's skin as she gazed out her bedroom window, watching a handful of birds pass across the morning sun. The light streaming into her room brightened the warm colors of the small chamber she called home. She loved this time of day, the sun on her face, the smell of the air, and the light breeze blowing through her hair. It always seemed like a time of new beginnings.

She smiled at her good fortune. She had a beautiful home, with a location and a view that was the envy of her peers. It was a stone's throw from the majestic, circular Shir Courtyard outside the council keep. So during the rare times when she was home, she would unwind by going for an evening stroll among the plants and trees, or relax in the sun while she enjoyed her lunch.

The irony was, she'd gotten the room because nobody wanted it, partly because it was the smallest home in the row, but also because it sat at the edge of a plateau, and a tree had grown up from the rock face blocking the view. When she'd expressed interest, the council leader, Kayleen, had agreed to let her have it, even though it was intended for much more important people. A few years later, the tree had given up clinging to the rock face, and all of a sudden, she had a soaring view from hundreds of feet above the base of Mount Karana.

If she poked her head out the window and looked to the right, she could spy the very edge of the city of Shirdon, nestled at the foot of the plateau. To the left, trees dotted the base of the mountain, and straight ahead, the sun was rising over the hills of Erden.

A soft rapping came from the door, and Dellia glanced over as Kayleen entered. To look at her simple robes, gentle, hazel eyes, or dirty-blond hair chopped off at the shoulder, you would never guess she was the leader of the Ruling Council of Meerdon, the most powerful force in the three realms. She never put on airs or wore anything ostentatious, save for the long blue crystal that hung from an ancient silver thread that always adorned her neck. Yet her simple way and calm manner hid a persuasive tongue and sharp mind that could read people and situations like they were an open book.

She smiled when she met Dellia's gaze and strolled over to join her at the window. They stood together for a moment, admiring the view.

Kayleen closed her eyes and took a deep breath of the clean morning air. "It's beautiful, isn't it?"

"Yes."

Kayleen turned to Dellia and placed a hand on her shoulder. "I hate to pull you away, but we need you. There's been some kind of disturbance in the veil, at the far southern edge of the Illis Woods. We need you to investigate."

"A ride in the woods. I think I can handle that." Dellia brushed it off, but there had to be more to it or they wouldn't be sending her.

"It's more than that. It was unusual. I've never experienced anything exactly like it. I don't know what caused it, or what you'll find. So, I need someone who can think on their feet, figure out what's happening and deal with it."

"You know me. I love this kind of thing." Dellia smiled. "It's an adventure."

Kayleen gave her a stern look. "If anyone else had said that, I'd be worried that they weren't taking the risks seriously. Sometimes I think you love this job a little too much. Promise me you'll be careful, all right?"

"Always." Dellia rested one hand on the hilt of her sword and the other on the haft of her dagger.

Then she noticed that something was disturbing Kayleen. It was impossible to know if it was this mission or something more profound. Even so, she felt the compulsion to reassure her, to explain.

Yet, what could she say? It wasn't as if she *liked* rushing into the unknown. After all, she was cautious by nature. It was just that this was who she was. She was the one who faced the unknown so others didn't have to. Because it was her duty, her calling. It was what gave her life purpose and meaning. And she was good at it. There was nothing more satisfying than waking up each morning and looking forward to the day because she was doing good, she was making a difference.

Kayleen held out a small, red, round spire stone, about the size of a marble. "We want you there quickly. So you'll have to use the spires."

Dellia had only used the spires a few times and only in cases of extreme urgency. It was said the powerful enchanter Varish had constructed them over a thousand years ago. Part of his master plan to leave a legacy of quicker travel through the three realms. The story was that his ambition exceeded his life span, and he had died before he could fully realize his vision. So there were only a handful of towers. You could travel from any spire to any other spire, so long as you possessed a spire stone tuned to your destination. Over the years, so many stones had become lost that those that remained were precious and rare.

To be entrusted with one was an honor and bestowed a solemn responsibility not to lose it. The council didn't hand them out merely to investigate some minor unknown occurrence. Dellia stared down at the smooth, round sphere. This was no simple mission. The council suspected something. They thought this disturbance might be of critical importance.

Dellia held out her hand, and Kayleen dropped the little red stone into it.

"I'll leave right away." Dellia gave Kayleen a hug.

Kayleen eyed her as she let go. "May Adi watch over you."

Dellia bowed to her. It was odd to hear Kayleen offer any sort of blessing. Like most in Shirdon, she had never shown any sign of belief in anything. That she would do so now was surprising. Or perhaps yet another sign that this mission was of some concern to her and the council.

Dellia turned and walked Kayleen to the door, and as she stepped through the doorway, Dellia swung around to have one last glimpse of her home, bathed in the warm rays of the morning sun.

Her eyes fell on the small collection of items arranged on her dresser: the ancient dagger discovered on her first mission, the little carved wooden horse Cholta had given her upon rescuing the boy's father, and the pinecone Tilla had decided was a toy during the brief time she was her dog. Each of them was a little piece of her life, a fragment, a memory of a place or a person she'd met in her travels. As she closed the door, Dellia smiled and wondered what memories she would bring home this time.

Jon crashed to the ground, landing with a sort of metallic thud. He lay sprawled out on his back, mind racing from the adrenaline coursing through his veins. His panicked breathing slowed as he stared up at a glowing, liquid mass still hovering over him.

It was undoubtedly the same phenomenon as in the lab. Except, like a window out of a bright room at night, light from his lab was pouring into the darkness. As the mass moved and rippled, that light moved with it, reflecting off the mirror behind it and dancing across the nearby wall. It played and flickered all around him, like some kind of strange disco ball.

A rustling sound startled him, and Jon's head whipped around. Relief flooded in, washing away the adrenaline as there, next to him, sat Megan, the light flittering across her familiar face and through her long hair.

He squinted through the dim light. "Megan? Are you hurt?"

"I don't think so."

He gazed up at the mass looming over him. Looking past the surface light show, he peered deep into it, studying it. Despite the bending, shifting, and distorting of the image, it slowly became recognizable as the inside of his lab. Details started to solidify: his desk, his bookshelf, and the laser table. The table seemed to rattle and shake, becoming more and more violent. With a sudden jerk, it broke free and headed straight for him.

Jon twisted around, grabbed Megan, and flung her over, rolling both of them out of the way, just as a half ton of metal came flying out of the swirl and crashed down next to them. In an instant, the irregular, glowing mass vanished, leaving only the darkness and the soft rustling of paper settling around them.

Then came Megan's tentative voice. "Jon?"

"Yeah."

"You're laying on top of me."

He rolled over and sat up. The air was damp but not clammy, and the place had a kind of dank, musty odor to it. As his eyes adjusted to the darkness, the surrounding debris became recognizable as the familiar contents of his lab, in shambles, scattered across the ground. Then it hit him. It was too dark. The LEDs and displays on his equipment should be enough to produce some light. Many of them ran on batteries. Yet every piece of equipment was dead. Jon fumbled for his smartphone and discovered it, too, was dead. Oh man. Megan would not do well without her phone. Her life was on that thing.

He glanced over at Megan again. She seemed so shaken up. "I'm so sorry about all of this."

"It's okay," Megan said, but they were just words, something that came out automatically because the shock of the experience had left her too upset for his words to register.

Jon shook his head. "No, it's really not."

If only there were something more he could say or do to make her feel better, but there wasn't. And fussing over her because he felt guilty wasn't going to help.

After a moment, Jon's eyes had adjusted enough to reveal that the floor under and beyond his equipment was a sea of gold, silver, glass, and copper. They were sitting on a bed of ancient-looking coins, jewelry, weaponry, and ornamentation of astounding variety. It was as if they'd fallen into some kind of treasure room, like something out of a movie.

"Where are we?" came Megan's voice.

Jon glanced over, and she was staring down at the glittering carpet beneath them. He reached down and brushed his fingers across the surface of a jewel encrusted circlet between his legs. "I have no idea. No physics I know of can explain what just happened."

Still, Megan's question was a good one, so Jon gathered his wits and began to survey their surroundings with greater care. Behind them, where the swirl used to be, stood a large mirror. Beyond that, a granite wall extended out in every direction until it disappeared into blackness. In front of them lay a shorter, jagged wall, perhaps ten feet high, that curved away near the top, and a hundred feet above that, barely visible in the darkness, was what appeared to be a massive stone ceiling.

"I think we're in a cave. There seems to be light coming from over there." Jon pointed to a passage between the granite wall and the curved wall where the pathway gently angled off to the left, and the light appeared almost imperceptibly brighter.

Megan stood up and steadied herself. Then she extended her

hand to Jon. "Well, if you're going to get us back home, then the first thing we have to do is figure out where we are. And we can't do that sitting here."

Metal and glass crinkled and crunched underfoot as they made their way to the granite wall and fumbled along it. The wall somehow didn't seem as cool to the touch or as damp and clammy as expected.

The curved wall kept getting higher as they moved through the pile of coins, jewelry, and weapons, then off onto solid rock. They worked their way down the path, and as it gradually turned to the left, the light became brighter. Around the edge of the curved wall, they spotted light reflecting off the floor far in the distance.

Way up ahead, the cavern narrowed to an opening, and beyond that lay a passage where the rocky ground inclined upward. The path appeared to be illuminated by a bright light, perhaps from an entrance farther uphill.

Jon halted in his tracks, staring at the curved wall ahead as it moved out a few inches to obstruct the light, then back in again to reveal it. Then out again. Then back in again. And with the brighter light glancing off the wall, it became clear it wasn't so much jagged as it was covered with overlapping rows of large, black, metallic scales.

A chill ran through his body.

Megan glanced over at him, then back at the wall. She pointed. "What is that?"

As he watched the surface expand and contract, his voice became a whisper. "Oh crap, I think it's breathing."

In an instant, the wall right beside them began to move forward, then accelerated. His head whipped over to face it and he stepped back as a fresh surge of adrenaline shot through his veins. He stared wide-eyed at the light glinting off the metallic scales as they raced by, like a freight train, inches from his nose. The breeze from it blew across his face, and he froze in terror.

Megan broke into a sprint.

Jon gasped. Oh no! What if it could see movement? "Megan," he called in a loud whisper.

A gust of wind blew through his hair, and he ducked.

Something huge, long, and covered with dark scales swung out from behind him and over his head. At a frightening speed, it whipped out over Megan and slammed down in front of her with a tremendous thud that echoed through the cave.

Jon's heart stopped, the ground shook, and dust flew into the dimly lit air as she screeched to a halt. She stood there, frozen, trembling, only inches from a massive tail that blocked her way. It lay in her path, extending well past her, ending in a giant ball of spikes, some as tall as Megan herself.

The tail swept back around her, the spikes scraping across the ground. It dragged to a stop behind her, surrounding her, trapping her. She looked back at Jon with fear and desperation in her eyes.

His heart hammered in his ears. Dust swirled around him and into his lungs with each rapid breath.

Through the chaos of debris and darkness, the curved wall twisted and turned, becoming a long body attached to the even longer tail. In a rumble of noise that reverberated through the cave, the enormous torso rose up onto a pair of massive, heavily muscled legs.

The legs lumbered toward Jon, each footfall slamming down with a deep thud, sending a fresh gust of wind and dust all around them. The sound of sharp, metallic claws raking across the stone floor sent shivers down his spine. His instinct was to run, to use the dust for cover, but there was no place to hide.

Something enormous whooshed past him, a mere foot or two from his head. It swung out in front, blocking his way.

Jon stood there, shaking and paralyzed, while the nostrils of a gigantic head came within inches of his face. It stopped in front of him, light glinting off its razor-sharp teeth as it stared. The piercing gray eyes seemed to scrutinize him, examining him, like a scientist observing some new species of bug.

He stood with his feet frozen to the ground. His stomach wrenched, and he couldn't help imagining a cat chasing its prey here and there, oblivious to the frenzied terror of the mouse.

He jumped as it snorted, and its hot breath blew back his hair. Then the beast let out a disturbing, low moan that reverberated throughout the cavern.

The wing of what now looked very much like a dragon extended over Megan and Jon and then snapped back to the body again.

Another gust of wind blasted them, followed by a burning sensation that ran down from his head through his body and into his feet. In the distance, a light glow ran across Megan's skin, then vanished.

The head whipped around and leered at Megan, looking her up and down. It began closing in on her.

Jon jumped and flew toward her.

The head snapped back toward him and let out a short, sharp grunt.

He slammed to a stop and froze in place.

The enormous head seemed to keep one eye on Megan while it glared at him with the other and growled under its breath, as if to say, "Don't you dare." The head turned slowly back toward her and eyed her for what seemed like an eternity.

Nausea burrowed its way through the pit of his stomach at the thought of all the horrible things it might do to her.

The huge eyes drifted down to a glint of dark metal dangling from something caught on Megan's belt. They rested there while she glanced down, yanked it from her clothes, and pocketed it.

At that, the beast let out a deafening roar that blew back her clothes and hair and caused her to cringe and shrink away. She hunkered there, wide-eyed, while the sound hung in the air for what seemed like an eternity, echoing off the cavern walls.

Then, in a single, slow movement, the tail rose up out of her way, as if the creature were inviting her to leave.

Jon shouted, "Megan, run!"

She broke into a mad sprint, heading for the light. She looked back at Jon.

"Go!" Jon yelled out.

The massive head turned back toward him and began to close in on him. Megan's labored breath grew distant as she scrambled over rocks, disappearing up the incline into the light.

Jon's eyes darted everywhere, searching for some new place to hide, some fresh path of escape.

Then, out of the gigantic head came a voice. It spoke with slow deliberation, in an impossibly deep but breathy tone that sounded distinctly female.

"Be ... still," she said.

Chapter Three

ISLA

Garris danced out of the way as his opponent slammed into the ground right where he'd been standing. He smiled at how skillful he'd been in dodging the lizard man's move just as a large, green tail smashed into his head, sending him staggering.

His head still stinging from the blow, he dove behind one of the trees that made up a small forest atop a mountainous pillar of stone. The Neri Mountains weren't so much mountains as they were massive pillars of rock shooting up thousands of feet from the canyon floor. Trees topped each and sprang from every ledge and crevice, appearing to cascade down the pillar like a living waterfall.

Garris shook off the blow to his head. Damn lizard and his extra appendage.

Elt rolled out of the way, turned, and leaped at him, slashing downward, putting all his weight behind a single stroke of his sword.

Garris raised his blade and braced himself, straining against the inevitable blow. The sheer force of it sent him staggering backward, and his hands stung from the shock.

The sound of clashing swords rang through the crisp mountain air, and the sun hung low in the sky as Garris and his opponent crashed through the forest in a brutal dance of fists, feet, and metal.

With grim determination, he slammed the lizard man against a sturdy tree and wrested the sword from his grasp.

Elt swung around and kicked Garris. Then with a lightning

flick of his tail, he sent both swords clattering across the rocks.

Redoubling his efforts, Garris charged him, punching, kicking, dodging, blocking as the pair flew through and around the trees and rocks of the forest. He kicked the lizard man, sending him smashing into a tree, nearly dislodging a large, rotted branch that teetered above him. He grabbed a nearby stick and rocketed it upward, sending it crashing into the limb with a crack. The branch broke loose and plummeted down toward his opponent's head.

The scaly combatant flung himself onto his back and kicked the heavy log with both feet, sending it flying into Garris's chest.

His opponent leaped as the decayed limb shattered, sending Garris to the ground. In an instant the lizard was on him, kneeling on his chest, a knife to his throat.

Elt leaped to his feet and stood over Garris, sturdy and muscular, his dark scales smooth and shiny in the late-day sun. "Nice try. You almost had me."

Garris lay on his back, still catching his breath. "No. I was off today, but don't expect me to take it so easy on you tomorrow."

Elt extended a clawed hand. "Well, I'm sure in a real fight you could just tell your opponent you're having an off day and they'd go easy on you."

As Elt helped him up, Garris shook his head. The condescension really wasn't necessary; he wasn't born yesterday.

Fifteen years ago, Elt had brought him to a small log cabin in a wood on top of a towering column of stone and proposed he stay there with him. Having grown up in the city, the idea of living in such an isolated place seemed ludicrous, and he laughed in the lizard man's face. Elt's response was to puff out his chest and in his typical pretentious manner suggest he was only offering because Garris was in such dire need of instruction. At the suggestion, Garris broke down laughing hysterically. The lizard man simply smiled and proceeded to thrash him within an inch of his life. Having taken Elt's point, and with nowhere else to go, he had agreed to stay.

So for fifteen years, Elt had been his friend and instructor, and for fifteen years, he'd wondered why he put up with all the arrogance and condescension. Over time, he had come to suspect it was just Elt's nature. After all, the Skri had a reputation for being both. Then again, it often seemed like Elt was trying to cultivate the image of a wise instructor imparting pearls of wisdom to his naive student. Though Garris was hardly naive. A jaded old warrior still clinging to a code that had long ago ceased to make sense, perhaps—but hardly naive.

He snatched the two swords from the rocky ground and passed one to Elt. "You know, it's a thing of beauty the way you've turned condescension into an art form."

Elt ignored the jab. "About tomorrow, remember when I agreed to train you, I told you there would come a time for you to leave?"

"Oh, so the student has finally surpassed the master?"

Elt shook his head. "No, you still fight like crap, but fate won't wait long enough for us to fix that."

"Great, more of your mystic jibber-jabber."

"Okay, then let's call it a test, a part of your training. There's someone you need to help and protect."

Garris halted in his tracks and turned to face his mentor. "What kind of someone? And where?"

Elt's response was hesitant. "Meerdon."

The part of the question Elt had avoided could only mean one thing.

Garris folded his arms and glared at him in defiance. "No. I'm not traveling that path again. No way. You know what happened last time. You know what it cost me."

"I ask you to go to a place where you could be hunted like a dog, and your biggest concern is history repeating itself?"

Garris stood still and unmovable as he stared at Elt.

Elt tried again. "Look, this is important to you. It is something you need to do, for *you*."

Garris took a deep breath, and as he exhaled, he closed his eyes and nodded his head. "Fine."

The pair began, once again, to work their way back to the small cabin in the woods.

After a moment, Garris granted Elt a sly smile. "So they need my help?"

"We just covered this. I said it is *you* that needs to help *him*."

"Fine." Garris shook his head. Elt couldn't even allow him a single moment of self-importance.

"You should leave right away. It's in the Illis Woods. I'll show you where to go and when." The tone of Elt's voice was all too familiar. It meant he believed he knew something or sensed something, but even he wasn't sure of the specifics. Or, if he was, he remained determined not to share them. So it was pointless pressing for details. Besides, even if Elt did have some special insight, he'd just wrap it in that pseudo-mystic crap he loved to spout.

A fleeting notion sprang into Garris's head. If he really was going to leave, he'd miss that crap. He quickly banished the thought.

Elt turned back to him. "One more thing. I know your desire is for revenge, but you can only satisfy it by letting go of it."

Garris hated that. It wasn't revenge, and Elt knew it. It was justice. Even so, he wanted to make sure he understood. "So to get my revenge, I just have to stop seeking it?"

Elt glared at him. "It's not letting go if your entire motive for doing so is to get revenge. Wow, I can't be even a little cryptic with you. Look, there will come a moment when you have a choice between revenge and … let's just call it a higher purpose. Revenge won't get you what you seek. Set it aside, choose the higher purpose. Have faith that the universe will balance the scales."

Garris clapped his hand down on Elt's scale-covered shoulder.

"Oh yeah, that's much clearer."

He peered out across the Neri toward Meerdon, watching as the setting sun headed for a collection of massive pillars in the distance. His trips back to his homeland were always turbulent. And they often ended in a tumult of disaster, bloodshed, and despair. The pair clambered over the forest floor, back to the rustic cabin nestled in the small woods atop the giant pillar of rock. And as Garris stared off toward his destination, he couldn't help but wonder what sparkling new disaster awaited him this time around.

For a moment, Jon stood there, unsure what he'd heard. Maybe it was just some noise distorted by the acoustics of the cave. Maybe he'd just imagined he'd heard words. After all, why would this enormous creature talk to him at all? Was it in the habit of conversing with its food?

His mind struggled through a haze, trying to make sense of things as he stared at the the massive dragon's head, its sharp canines only a few feet from his face. Each hot breath of the carnivore on his skin caused him to flinch, and he trembled at the sounds of the massive beast moving restlessly in the dust and darkness.

Then there were those enormous, steely eyes. They peered down at him with an eerie air of intelligence, following his every move, watching, expectant. Those eyes seemed to be waiting for a response.

Jon squinted and cowered. "Are you going to kill me?"

"Hmm." The dragon let out a low grunt that he could swear had a hint of annoyance to it, and for a moment he felt like a child asking a stupid question.

"I … am … Isla," the creature said, her voice even slower, deeper, and more breathy than before.

Then, it hit Jon. "Wait, you speak English?"

She let out a low rumbling breath, and when she spoke her words seemed stilted, as if she had to inhale every few syllables.

"No. … I gave a gift … of understanding."

His fear and frustration bubbled over. "This makes no sense." He shook his head. "This is crazy. You're a dragon. They don't exist, so how could I even know what you are?"

"You … are not … the first."

Jon stood, digesting the words, and through his panicked haze, a seed of understanding took root. Of course. If others had been here and returned, they would've brought back stories and drawings. That might explain why dragons appear in so many cultures. But, more than that, it implied there was a way back, a way home.

Jon glanced all around the cavern, searching for anything that might get him away from this menacing beast. But all he saw was that the creature was blocking his every path of exit, and it seemed likely this wasn't by chance.

He gulped. "If you're not going to kill me, then why won't you let me leave?"

Isla reached over with a claw at the joint of her wing and, with nimble movements, plucked a small metal object from the pile of silver and gold. She dangled it by its chain, a foot or so from Jon's chest.

"A bargain," she said.

"I don't understand." He reached out and accepted what appeared to be a medallion the size of his palm.

Isla's breathy voice echoed through the cavern. "Three realms … three parts … find them … reassemble it. … I can send you … home."

All of Jon's fear washed away with those last words. "You can get us home? How? Where are these three parts? What do I do?"

He turned the medallion over, examining the light chunk of metal. It was an almost white shade of silver and had three leaf-shaped spots where it seemed like three pieces might fit, as if someone had removed them.

He lifted his eyes, staring into the beast's dark face. "What about Megan? Can you send us both?"

"Either … both … same time … different times … your choice."

"Then tell me where to find the pieces. I'll do it."

The dragon reached out with the tip of a razor claw in the center of her wing and scrawled a crude outline in the dust and dirt of the floor before Jon.

He stared at it, trying to memorize the shape of what was most probably some kind of map.

She scribbled out a pair of lines that divided it into three parts and pointed to one after the other as the echo of her low breathy voice resounded all around. "Ruled by one, … Meerdon is … three nations, … three distinct realms. … Each has … its own race, … its own ways, … its own gifts."

It was the second time Isla had used the word "gift," and the emphasis she gave it made it seem like she was using it to mean some kind of ability or talent. Jon nodded as the beast gently tapped the leftmost section.

"The first leaf lies … among the warriors … of Talus, … governed by the five … elected … Ephori. … You will find it … at the top … of the ancient … Recluse Tower."

Jon nodded as he endeavored to embed the relevant names in his memory. "Talus. Recluse Tower. Got it."

The right half of the map was divided into two parts. The ground rumbled as Isla brought herself up higher. She peered down at him as she tapped the southern half. "In the kingdom … of Erden, … ruled by the Rhanae, … the gold leaf is entombed … under the streets … of Mundus, … beneath the Temple … of Knowledge, … in the Andera … Catacombs."

Again, Jon repeated the meaningless names, struggling to burn them, and the map, into his memory. "Erden. Mundus. Temple of Knowledge, Andera Catacombs. Understood."

The beast let out a low grumble that reeked of skepticism. She eyed Jon for a long second, then tapped the last section of the map.

"In the city … of Kanlu, … in the Empire … of Elore, … solve the riddle … of Kita Pass. … Find … the oracle room. … The last leaf … will reveal … your path."

He nodded some more as he repeated, "Elore, Kanlu, riddle, Kita Pass, oracle room."

What this riddle was that he was supposed to solve, or how he was supposed to find this oracle room, or even what the heck it meant to reveal his path, he wasn't sure. More pressing questions crowded his mind. "Okay. But how will I find these places? What do I do with the leaves when I get them? What do I do with this"—he looked down at the medallion—"after I assemble it?"

Isla raised herself up higher and moved out of Jon's way, making a clear path to the light. "The rest … is for you … to find. … This is all … I ask. … More … I will not say."

Jon glanced up at the massive beast towering high above him. She could crush him like a bug. He turned his attention to the light reflecting off the path ahead, and his sense of unease returned. She had said it herself. She would not tell him more.

He began to walk under the dragon's head and toward his path of escape. After a few steps, a deep scraping reverberated through the stone floor. Then Isla's rumbling, low voice halted him. "A warning. … Keep your own counsel. … Tell no one … where you are from, … what you can do."

The words barely registered as a renewed sense of urgency crowded every other thought out of his mind. Jon began again, only faster now, scurrying toward the lighted floor ahead. It seemed like an eternity, each step, waiting to see if it was just the dragon's cruel way of toying with him.

His heart leaped at a rumble of movement from behind and he sped up again. Yet even as he raced forward, trembling and terrified, his mind was drawn back to the obvious. Dragons were a physical impossibility. The surface area of a wing required for flight grew exponentially with the mass of the beast. That meant the theoretical flight limit for anything made of flesh and bone was no larger than a medium-sized dog. Yet this dragon was larger than any beast that ever roamed the earth. Perhaps Isla was made of more exotic stuff. Or maybe she couldn't fly. Maybe the wings were vestigial, or used for some other purpose. Yet still …

Then there was his phone and all the equipment from his lab. It seemed odd that all those battery-operated electronics would be dead. Perhaps they had been damaged in passing through the phenomenon, or maybe some massive interference existed here. Yet something as simple as their power LEDs shouldn't be so easily affected. One thing was certain: the probability that every single one of them would fail simultaneously was as astronomical as flying dogs … or dragons.

All thoughts flew from his mind at the low breath and rumble of the beast moving in the darkness behind him. It was an instant reminder that he was not yet out of danger. With a renewed sense of urgency, he pressed forward, and not just to escape what lay behind. Somewhere in the light ahead was Megan, and beyond that lay their path home.

It looked like a simple stone, like any other stone, like the kind she used to skip across the surface of a pond as a child. Kayleen could almost picture the ripples in her memory as the stone dashed across the water. It was only about the size of her palm, round, flat, black, and unpolished, with three straight lines scratched into its surface. Yet, like all the artifacts in this room, it was said to possess tremendous power. The ripples it could create held the potential to collapse civilizations and end empires. But it was also considered to be a relic of the past, and all those with the ability to wield that power had long ago turned to dust. Even so, it stayed here, safely kept from the public, in a display carved from the wall of the council chambers.

The sound of footsteps echoed through the marble hall, interrupting Kayleen's thoughts. It was a sound she knew well. She'd heard Braye strut across the chamber's smooth marble floor a thousand times. His countenance was indelibly etched in her mind: short, bald, and pudgy, with his chin always coated in a layer of salt-and-pepper stubble. His eyes, often warm and welcoming, never betrayed the shrewd mind whose intentions she could never quite fathom, even after two decades of observation. And then there was his gait. It had an intensity about it, a sort of driven march that suited his demeanor.

Without even looking, she could trace out his steps as he walked through one of the many marble columns and arches on either side of the hall. He skirted the long table with nine chairs where the council would meet and debate, then headed toward another archway where she stood.

Kayleen had been absentmindedly toying with the long, blue crystal dangling from a silver thread around her neck. She stopped as Braye grew close and quieted her anxious heart. Staring down at the black stone, she showed no sign of recognition as the footsteps halted beside her.

It was a blatant game, the kind she always found so distasteful. But it was also a reality that not all debate occurred at the council table. The subject she needed to discuss with him was one that filled her with apprehension, and this might be her last opportunity to steer things down a better path—but she needed to set the right tone. So she waited, letting Braye speak first.

Eventually, he did. "Are you contemplating the Stone of Syvis again, or just staring into space?"

Kayleen took a deep breath before speaking. "Have you ever thought about artifacts like this, and why, like all gifts, they are so often suited to destruction rather than creation?"

Braye paused, which was a good sign. It meant he might be giving her question some due consideration. "They're just a part of nature, aren't they? And like so much in nature, their tendency is to destroy."

Kayleen turned to face Braye. "But nature is power, raw and uncontrolled. Because it's so much harder to create than destroy, that power, like all power, tends to find its expression in destruction rather than creation."

"So, what's your point?" Braye said, seeming impatient.

"The council has enormous power. We should respect that, use our power lightly, with restraint."

"If I believed that, then I'd leave the council. The council is not some mindless force. It's directed by our insight, our intelligence. We exist to serve people, to protect them. Why would we want to limit our power to do that?"

"Because we can't always know the damage we do." Kayleen sighed. The discussion was futile. She'd steered them straight into an old argument. One they had never agreed on, and there was no reason to believe this time would be different.

Braye had always been such a black-and-white thinker. Either a thing was good for the people, or it wasn't, and if it was, he'd advocate for it on the council. So he was always seen as the champion of the people. He could point to all the things he'd done and tell everyone he was behind them. Which only reinforced his belief that he was right and she was wrong.

What he never seemed to understand was that every action the council took came at a cost. Every law they passed had the potential to harm someone innocent. Every soldier they conscripted to enforce that law took someone from their family. And every time that law required them to send that soldier to some faraway place, someone paid for it; it took food from someone's table and clothing from someone's back. So she had always advocated that the council act with restraint, and it was much harder to see the good in what the council *hadn't* done. Which meant that even though she was council leader, she was less popular. This was an old argument and one on which it was certain they would never agree.

It appeared Braye felt the same way. "I thought we'd stopped having this debate over a decade and a half ago. Once you got over the excitement of being on the ruling council and figured out how stubborn I can be." He smiled. "What's really eating you?"

Kayleen looked over at the stone. "I think you know. It's this disturbance."

Braye glanced down at her neck.

She'd been unconsciously holding the long, blue crystal of her necklace again. She dropped her hand. "We have sent a protector into a perilous situation without adequate information and no more instructions than to 'handle things.' "

"That's what protectors are for, handling things."

"No, it's not. Our artificial sense of urgency is clouding our judgment. We should be sending scouts to assess the situation so we can devise a careful and appropriate response."

"Our sense of urgency isn't artificial. It's real. What if the situation demands immediate action?"

Kayleen shook her head. "This is most likely the dragon's doing. What if Dellia confronts it? That could kill her and spark a war with untold other dragons. What if this is a trap laid by an unknown foe? What if it's a breach or incursion and something horrible and malevolent awaits her? What if this is a prophecy we know nothing about, or even worse, one we *do* know about? Who knows what havoc she might wreak? We are determined to bring the full weight of the council to bear when we have no inkling how calamitous the repercussions might be. It is irresponsible and dangerous."

Braye eyed her with a solemn expression. "I've never known you to lack faith in Dellia's ability."

Kayleen shook her head. It was like he wasn't even listening, and to use her affection for Dellia in such a transparent ploy was shocking. "I would applaud letting Dellia use her judgment. But the council has no such intent. She'll report back, and you'll tell her what to do. You only care about the might of her sword arm."

"Are you suggesting the judgment of one little girl is better than the collective wisdom of all the nine council members?"

She wanted to say yes. She wanted to point out that Dellia would be better informed and better equipped to make those judgments, that a single person is often more levelheaded than a frightened group—but it would be pointless.

Instead, Kayleen took a deep breath and stared Braye in the eyes. "I can't shake this sense of foreboding, the feeling we are inviting tragedy through our incessant need to control events. We should be cautious and strategic. We need to reconsider."

"You know we have an obligation to protect the people. To manage whatever situation is evolving."

"And you know I have always opposed using force in circumstances we know nothing about. We wield the power of the protectors like a blunt instrument, and like the Stone of Syvis, that power has a tremendous capacity to destroy. And I know firsthand how quickly events can spiral out of control."

Braye rested his hand on Kayleen's arm and gazed at her with the sympathy of an old friend.

She peered into his face, trying to discern if the look of concern was genuine or just the artful move of a practiced old politician.

Braye smiled. "What happened fifteen years ago was a tragedy. Nobody doubts that, and we all regret it. But this is different."

The painful memory came rushing back. All those years ago, Braye had set a hand on her arm and gazed at her, just as he did now. She could still recall the note of regret in his voice as he relayed his sympathies for the death of her sister. In one incident, she had lost the two people she loved most in the world, and it shook her to the core to have her pain and loneliness used so casually in a political debate.

Still, she needed to remain poised. So, Kayleen simply patted Braye's hand. "What is truly tragic is that you still can't see how we caused that tragedy. Because here we are repeating the same mistake. Only this time it has the potential to destroy many lives and not just my own."

As Jon started up the incline toward the light, Isla's words rang again in his head, her low, breathy voice seared into his memory.

"A warning. … Keep your own counsel. … Tell no one … where you are from, … what you can do."

But what did that mean? What did she imagine he could do, and what did she expect would happen if he told someone? Yet it didn't seem like a good idea to dismiss the dragon's advice. She seemed intelligent, wise even, and she appeared to have a vast understanding of this world. Or perhaps his bias was showing. Perhaps he was assigning her human attributes just because she could talk.

Then again, keeping it to himself seemed the smart move. In fact, what could be gained by telling of dragons and medallions, or of ancient towers, catacombs, riddles, and oracle rooms? The very words sounded insane in his head. Isla's warning implied there would be someone to tell, but who knew if a lynch mob would string him up at the mere mention of a dragon? No, only an idiot would run around telling complete strangers "the dragon made me to do it." It was clear Isla's words were wise, and he would heed them. He would keep his own counsel and tell only what he must, *when* he must.

Everything was becoming brighter as Jon hurried up the incline. He looked over at the rough stone walls. The streaks of blue against the dark granite seemed almost to glow as he hurried past them. The path was broad and the floor smooth where Jon was walking, yet rough at the edges, as if worn through repeated use. With the Archard equation, he might be able to figure out how long it took the dragon to wear down a path like this. He just needed the strength of the stone—okay, well, maybe the weight of the dragon. … Uh, yeah, well … it must have been a really long time.

The passage was becoming brighter still from light pouring down the passage from a broad opening way up ahead. A warm breeze brushed across his skin, and as he caught a whiff of fresh air, his optimism began to return. Perhaps they'd get out of this in one piece after all.

Jon smiled at the thought of getting to the top and finding Megan waiting for him. She'd be worried, and he'd have to tell her all about his discussion with the dragon. She'd make fun of him, and they'd both laugh, and then together, they'd set about finding their way home.

A faint noise jarred him out of his ruminations. He slowed, straining to hear.

Then it came again, this time louder: the distant sound of horses snorting and hooves pawing the ground reverberating down the passage.

Terror ignited at the realization that Megan wasn't alone.

"Megan!" Jon shouted as he shot to a run.

As he raced up the path toward the entrance, the light became brighter, and he was forced to shield his eyes. Unable to see, he slipped and staggered his way over the polished, uneven floor.

Then another sound: arguing voices. But between the echo of the cavern and his own clatter, he couldn't make out a single word, and he didn't dare stop to listen.

He pushed harder, but he stumbled and skidded along a stretch of floor, then fell flat on his face, banging his knee.

The voices halted.

Jon scrambled to his feet to the sound of horses breaking into a gallop. In pain and limping, he pushed still harder, breaking into a frenzied race, desperate to reach Megan.

His breathing was labored, and his legs burned as he careened through the entrance and flew out into the tall waving grass of a clearing.

The blinding sun forced him to cover his eyes. There was no sign of Megan anywhere. Jon spun around, squinting and peering through his fingers, his gaze darting everywhere, searching the clearing for any sign.

The clearing was surrounded by woods, and panic welled up. If the riders had her and they hit the woods, he'd never find them.

Jon stopped to listen.

There, above the whistling of the wind and rustling of grass, came the rumbling sound of horses' hooves.

He whirled around toward them and started moving in their direction, faster and faster as he squinted and strained.

Then, up ahead, a pair of horses came into focus, galloping away at breakneck speed. Their hooves pounded the ground as they flew through the tall grass toward the woods.

Jon broke into a frantic sprint, racing after them, still limping, half-blind, barely able to see. The grass stung where it whipped him as he flew through the clearing. He stumbled over the uneven ground as he strained through the glaring light, trying to spot any sign of her.

Suddenly, there she was, as plain as day. Megan, seated on one of the horses, in front of its rider with her ginger hair fluttering behind her. She looked back at Jon, then pointed at him. She yelled something at the man, then punched him in the arm as the horses flew into the woods and disappeared.

A wave of nausea burst into the pit of Jon's stomach. Questions whirled through his mind. Why did they take her? What were they going to do to her? This was his fault.

He was gasping for breath when he hit the edge of the woods. In a frantic haze, he raced around, looking everywhere, but there was no sign of her. He darted here and there, calling out, searching in every direction, straining to catch any glimpse of her, or the horses, or the riders.

Exhausted and heaving from exertion, he staggered to a large fallen tree and sat, attempting to catch his breath. He glanced back to the entrance of Isla's home or lair or whatever it was, trying to get his bearings. He turned and stared in the direction the horses had gone, peering deep into the lush green of the forest.

Nothing.

He was thoroughly out of his element. He was lost in the wilderness, for crying out loud. No civilization, no phone, nobody to call, and no way to get anyone's attention. But he had to do *something*. He had to sort through his options and come up with a plan.

Maybe the smart thing would be to stay put, to sit here and wait for someone to come by. Perhaps they'd help. But that hope seemed forlorn. This was a wild area, after all, and near a dragon's lair, and it was unlikely that many people would venture near, at least not by choice. Most likely, he'd never encounter another soul and he'd die of thirst in three days. That's what they said on those television shows: you can go three weeks without food but only three days without water.

Then again, if someone did come by, they'd most likely steal his stuff and leave him for dead, or worse. It'd be just like *Deliverance*. No thanks.

His desire was to strike out after them on foot. He wanted to chase after her, to do anything to reach her. But he'd never catch them. And even if he could somehow outpace the horses, his complete lack of ability to track meant he'd most likely get lost and wander for three days. Or he'd go in circles, and wind up back here dying of thirst, because he also had no idea how to navigate. Television shows about people lost in the wilderness never ended well.

He could try to forage. He could try to find food and water. But his television education really didn't prepare him to identify edible

49

plants in a strange world.

The more he examined the situation, the more he was forced to come to grips with reality. All of his options ended with his likely death. And with that realization, a crushing despair took hold. He would never have wished this on Megan, and if there were one thing he would change, it would be to send her out of the room, or home, or whatever it would have taken to make sure his stupid experiment didn't drag her into this. Her screams were something he was unlikely ever to forget. But her being here, his not being alone—it was the one thing that gave him a reason to keep going. And now he'd never find her, never catch them.

Jon watched the pattern made by the sunlight as it filtered through the fluttering leaves and scattered across the ground around him. Oblivious to the sound of the gentle breeze waving through the grass of the clearing, or the songs of birds echoing through the forest, he sank deeper and deeper into despair. He shook his head and buried it in his hands, certain he would never see Megan or his home again.

Chapter Four

JON'S GIFT

Dellia could almost sense Ulka's excitement the moment she entered the stables. With his ears forward, his soft brown eyes in that beautiful gray-and-white face watched her, excited and expectant. Those eyes had almost certainly read the signs and knew this was a full-fledged expedition rather than a short outing for exercise. Ulka's hooves pawed the ground in anticipation while Dellia slung the blanket and saddle over his gorgeous, soft, white-and-dappled-gray body. Yet he stood motionless while she grabbed a chunk of gray mane and mounted.

Dellia buried her face in that mane as she hugged Ulka and drew a deep breath, inhaling his heady scent. Then she urged him out of the stables and down the long ramp to the outskirts of Shirdon.

The Shirdon Spire stood at the base of the mountain, near the city but in a small wooded area that shielded it from view. As soon as it came into sight, Dellia pulled Ulka to a stop and paused for a moment, marveling at it.

She had always found the spires fascinating. Their platform was perfectly flat and circular, broad enough to fit a small caravan yet carved from a single piece of stone. And strewn across its surface lay mysterious and intricate symbols whose meaning had long been lost down the rivers of time. Three massive, curved stone pieces rose up from the base, arching over it, their surface white and smooth like polished ivory. They were fashioned like the long teeth of some gigantic and ancient creature. They ringed the base, jutting upward as they arched inward, way above Dellia, over the platform, above the treetops, curving in until they almost converged over the center.

She often wondered how those ancient architects had fashioned such massive pieces of stone, how they'd been transported and wrestled into place, and what held their tremendous weight aloft. But they had stood for hundreds of years and showed no sign of decay.

Some unseen force repelled you if you attempted to enter the platform without a spire stone, or if someone at your destination had already entered with a stone for your spire. A precaution to prevent two groups from using them at the same time.

As Ulka stepped up onto the platform, a shimmering circular portal crackled open high above Dellia, at the peak of the spires. Its surface appeared almost wet, as if it were a reflection in a pool of water. Only it was the reflection of a different sky, the sky above the spire at her destination.

Without a second spire stone, the trip was only one way. So Dellia made certain Ulka, her supplies, and all she needed were inside the spires before using them. Then, when she was ready, she touched the round, red stone to a circle on one of the spires, and the portal began to descend.

It expanded as it fell, following the edges of the three spires. As it passed down over Dellia, her hairs stood on end, and there was a sudden smell, like the air after a storm. When it passed over her eyes, the view changed from secluded woods outside of town to the wild beauty of flower-strewn, green fields and nearby woods. The portal continued down to below the platform and disappeared. No longer was she in the spire outside Shirdon; now she stood in a different one, in a large clearing near the western edge of the Illis Woods.

From there Dellia struck out along the Eastern Trail, a simple dirt road used by travelers and merchants carrying goods to and from the cities to the east and west. Kayleen had described the disturbance as being near the dragon's lair on the southern edge of the Illis Woods. So, after a brief ride eastward, she left the road, heading south into the heart of the forest.

Paths tended to avoid places dragons were known to reside. The giant, winged beasts seemed to prefer to steer clear of humankind, and most people were more than happy to oblige. So she'd never seen a dragon. She'd only seen drawings and heard stories, and the impression they gave was that good things seldom happened when men and dragons mixed.

The hours passed by quickly as she trotted through the peaceful green of the forest. Sunlight streamed through the canopy above Dellia's head, scattering across the forest floor, making the entire world around her seem to glow green. A light breeze brushed across her skin, and it made a peaceful rustling sound as it whispered through the leaves of the trees.

At first, she relaxed to the familiar plodding of hooves and the rhythmic movement of Ulka beneath her as she worked her way through the Illis Woods to the dragon's lair. But as she neared her goal, Dellia became more vigilant, scanning the area, listening and watching, alert to anything that might be out of place. Not to mention signs of any dragon. She was running out of forest to search, and she had yet to encounter a single sign of anything unusual.

Then, a clearing appeared up ahead, and if she wasn't mistaken, this was where the dragon was said to live. With nothing beyond but an impenetrable mountain range, that would spell the end of her search. If so, then perhaps there was nothing here to find after all, despite the council's conspicuous interest. So she'd stay and do a few passes, searching the area, and once she was satisfied, she'd head back.

A flash of color caught her eye. Dellia turned toward it, and as she approached, the view cleared to reveal a man sitting on an old fallen tree. The sunlight through the trees dappled the ground all around him, and a grassy clearing spread out behind him, back to the broad mouth of a cave. It looked like something out of a painting, except for the man himself. He didn't seem peaceful or content, and his clothes were all wrong.

He wore a simple black shirt, tight fitting and different from any she was used to. On it was a strange, curved rune above a beautiful image. What surprised Dellia was the intricacy of the pattern and the vividness of the colors. And scrawled out below it was what appeared to be writing in a strange and foreign script. The pants he wore fit tightly, too. They were pale blue and worn, with detailed stitching as elaborate as any finery she'd seen.

His look, his well-kempt blond hair, his smooth, clean face—everything about the man seemed utterly out of place, a stark contrast to the natural, green beauty of his surroundings. Now there was something unusual, something worth checking out.

The man never acknowledged Dellia's approach, never even lifted his head as her horse came to a stop. He simply stared into space, as if in a profound daze. It was clear that something traumatic had happened, something deeply disturbing, and he was utterly lost. She couldn't help but feel sympathy, even as she kept a cautious eye on him and slipped quietly down off her horse.

"Bad day, huh?" she said.

At first, she wasn't sure if the man understood her or if he was even aware of her presence.

Then he spoke. "Worst of my life," he said, looking ahead as if still in some kind of stupor.

"Must be a good story, considering you're out here miles from anything. Alone, with no food, no water, no weapons, and what is that you're wearing?"

Finally, the man lifted his eyes to hers, and his expression surprised Dellia as much as the rest of the encounter. He gaped at her as if he'd never seen a woman before, as if *she* were the one out of place.

There was a long pause, as if he was trying to figure her out.

Eventually, he spoke again. "You forgot the part where Megan, the girl I've been in love with for the last ten years, stomped on my heart. Just before my work blew up, and I was transported to … well, let's just say I'm very, very far from home."

The emotion in his voice was infectious, and a fresh wave of sympathy washed over Dellia. He was worried about something, too, the dragon maybe, or perhaps the girl.

As much as she needed to know his story, her instinct was to reassure him. He certainly seemed to need help, even if he didn't realize it, and perhaps she might learn what she needed just by being a friend.

Dellia strolled up in front of him and looked down into his bright blue eyes. His face was different but pleasing, and there was kindness there and a certain softness in his manner that made it easy to give in to her instinct to be as comforting as she could.

Dellia crouched before the man and looked straight into his eyes. "I didn't want to mention the heartbreak." She placed her hands on his. "Or that you seem more lost than I think I've ever seen. And you're worried, too. About what?"

The man unexpectedly pulled his hands away, as if recoiling from her. But he stared straight back into her eyes.

She glanced down at his hands, then back into his eyes. There was that look again. The one that made her feel like she was the one out of place. Who was this man? Why did he react so oddly to her attempts to reassure him? Dellia peered into those blue eyes, searching for answers.

The man eventually tore his gaze from hers and glanced over at the mouth of a cave that bordered the clearing. It had to be the dragon's lair.

He peered back into her eyes. "I … I was in the cave."

"The cave with the dragon?"

"Yeah, Isla. She's fine. It's Megan I'm worried about."

"You're on a first-name basis with the dragon?"

"You're not listening," the man protested. "When I came out of the cave, a couple of men rode off with Megan. They took her."

"Are you sure they took her? Maybe she *wanted* to go with them."

"No. I know Megan. They must have taken her. I have to do something, go after them, rescue her."

Dellia stood up and took a step backward. This man was either delusional or desperate. "Let me see if I understand this. You're going to rescue the woman who just broke your heart, with no horse, no food, no water, and did I mention … no weapons?"

There was that instinct again, telling Dellia to help this man before he got himself killed. Then again, perhaps she should. She'd been sent here to investigate, to look for something unusual, and this man and his missing friend definitely qualified. He claimed he'd come from far away, that he'd been transported here. If he'd been snatched away suddenly, without warning, it might explain why he was here in the middle of the woods unequipped for even the short-est trip. Perhaps the disturbance Kayleen mentioned was caused by whatever snatched him away. Maybe that's how he got here.

"What's your name?"

"Jon."

"I'm Dellia," she said as she remounted her horse.

Jon gave her a peculiar look. "Deelia?"

Incensed at the butchering of her name, Dellia scowled. "Come on, I'm not the one with the strange name, *Jon*." She deliberately dragged out his name to emphasize its foreignness. "And what kind of a name is Deal-ee-uh? It's Dell-*yuh*."

Jon nodded and said to himself, "Dell-ee-uh."

Dellia smiled and gave a crisp nod. "Listen, there's a farm a cou-ple of miles from here. What do you say we go get you a horse and supplies, Dragon Boy? Then, we'll both make sure your Megan is safe."

At her words, Jon's expression transformed, and Dellia couldn't help but be touched by the hopefulness that lit up his face.

"You'd do that?" he said.

Of course I would, Dellia thought, but she simply extended her hand.

Jon grabbed it and held on like it was some kind of lifeline while she yanked him up behind her on Ulka.

He made a clumsy attempt to position himself behind her, then proceeded with various attempts to put his hands on her waist without actually touching her. It was sweet and amusing, and Dellia rolled her eyes. Oh, this was going to be some adventure.

She didn't want the story to include "and then he fell off my horse," so she grabbed Jon's hands and wrapped his arms tightly around her waist.

"Say, have you seen anything unusual around here?" Dellia turned Ulka back the way she'd come.

"Just my whole day," Jon replied as they trotted off into the scattered light and green beauty of the forest, leaving behind the dragon's home and the gentle breeze sending waves through the tall grass of the clearing.

Hooves pounded the ground as Garris raced across the sturdy wooden suspension bridge and onto a narrow path that wound its way through the Neri Mountains and into the sunset. The cool evening air was exhilarating as he barreled down the pathway at full gallop. To his left, the path hugged the edge of the canyon, and to the right lay a sheer drop, hundreds of feet down into the rocky bed below.

Kyri loved to run, and the night air seemed to invigorate her. So he hadn't stopped her when she'd decided to careen down the path at this breathless pace. She was a flashier horse than he would have liked, covered with large, torn patches of rust over white and a black mane and tail. But Kyri was sturdy and fearless, and he couldn't have hoped for a better partner all these years in conquering the treacherous mountain terrain of the Neri. So it was comforting to know she'd be his partner again on this new sojourn.

Garris glanced to the right as they passed one of the gigantic columns of stone and spotted a familiar grove of trees springing from a ledge in the rock face. He had clambered up those trees a few years back when instructed to climb that "mountain." The reasons for this were never made clear. Merely another of Elt's enigmatic tests. Who knew, perhaps on some future day his life would depend on scaling some impenetrable wall, and he'd think back and thank Elt. Or, more likely, Elt would think back on his climbing that thing and laugh his butt off.

It was just like Elt to spring this on him at the last minute, with an absurdly long distance to cover in a ridiculously short time. It was almost certain the lizard man had done it on purpose, merely to annoy.

It was idiotic to be leaving at sunset, but he had little choice. Because of Elt's timing, he needed to cover a lot of distance before he made camp for the night. He wasn't even sure why he was going. Perhaps he'd just gotten used to doing every eccentric little thing Elt asked. But then again, if he was being honest, he knew it was more than that.

The Skri Gift of Knowing, some called it. It was considered exceedingly rare, yet Elt was reputed to have it. Some claimed it was the ability to sense when something needed to be done, or "the rightness of a thing," or some such nonsense. Garris had never been able to tell if Elt possessed some secret insight the rest of the world didn't have, or if he simply made enough guesses that some of them were bound to be right. Even if Elt possessed this Gift of Knowing, he doubted the value. The future was too full of unknowns. Even if you knew most of the picture, the parts you didn't know would ensure that what you expected would be miles away from what actually happened. He'd learned that firsthand.

Garris pulled Kyri up short. She danced in place as her heavy breath shot through quivering nostrils. He patted her and drew a deep breath of brisk evening air. Then he brought her around and gazed back at the place he'd called home for so many years.

It had been his home for over a decade, and he was never quite sure why. Though a better question was why Elt had stayed with him. Especially when his people, the Skri, lay so much farther east, past the Neri. He and Elt had holed up in that small cabin for so many years, living off the land and training. Lots and lots of training. And for what? For reasons he never quite knew. Though Elt always seemed to act like it all had some deep meaning.

Perhaps he'd stayed and trained because he let Elt's certainty infect him. Or maybe it was because he had nothing better to do. Or it had just become a habit. Or perhaps there was a deeper reason, one tied to the reason for this trip, for going when Elt said go. Despite how remote the possibility that this expedition would amount to anything other than a colossal calamity, it gave his life something that had been missing for a very long time, something he'd often yearned for: a purpose, a direction, some reason for all those years spent training. Garris shoved the thought aside. That was exactly the kind of idiotic thinking that could set him on a path he'd vowed never again to travel.

He turned back down the road. The sun was just slipping down behind a collection of massive stone pillars that flanked the path off in the distance. He reached into his shirt and pulled out the chain around his neck. Garris eyed the shiny, polished, silver fragment of metal that hung from it. It had been given to him by someone he cared deeply about, as part of a dying wish, and he'd promised to pass it on. It had been passed down from grandfather to grandfather hundreds of years back.

A legacy like that was no small burden. And it hadn't escaped Garris that he was growing old, with no children to pass it on to and no prospects for any in the future. So perhaps that was what this return to the three realms was really about: a chance to fulfill a promise hundreds of years old. Life had a nasty habit of taking away his chances, so he resolved that while he was there, he would find someone to pass it on to. And he'd give them the message that had been entrusted to him so many years ago.

The amber rays of the setting sun spilled into the valley, giving the whole world a strange, golden glow. A reminder that those rays would soon be vanishing.

Garris gently urged Kyri forward, and she shot to a gallop. Surrounded by enormous towers of stone, he felt insignificant, like an insect racing down a winding path into a fiery sunset. He needed to cover a lot of ground before he stopped for the night. It was the only way he could reach his destination in time and discover the reason for this return to a place where tragedy seemed to hound his every move.

Jon stood on a stone and gravel path, pondering a bird. The pathway wove through what, at first glance, appeared to be an ordinary cottage garden. Yet a closer look revealed a little fantasy world filled with plants and flowers of every imaginable shape and size. It was a breathtaking work of art, planted, arranged, and tended with meticulous care to be pleasing while also seeming unplanned and natural.

Dellia had left to barter for a horse and supplies, and with little else to do while he waited, Jon had taken to poking around. It was only after he'd started examining individual plants and flowers that he realized that almost none of them were familiar. They presented a range of scents that were both intoxicating and familiar, and they resembled flowers and plants he'd seen before. But each varied in color or shape or size from something he recognized. And then there were the birds.

Jon puzzled over one of those birds as it hovered like a hummingbird in front of a deep-throated red flower. It didn't make any sense. Hummingbirds were small, and their hollow bones made them light. Their wings flapped up to eighty times a second, which allowed them to hover in place. The bird Jon had been pondering appeared to be much larger, much heavier, and its wings didn't flap anywhere near fast enough. Gravity seemed the same here, which meant the bird should fall to the earth. But there it was, inexplicably hovering, defying the laws of physics.

It was like most of his day, like Dellia, in fact—a contradiction. He pictured her standing in front of him in her soft brown leather armor, a sword and a dagger hanging from her waist. She looked like she was ready for battle, and everything about her said she could take on anyone or anything. But instead of acting tough or callous or battle worn as he'd expected of a warrior, there was a quiet calm about her, a relaxed self-assuredness. As if she knew she could handle anything and felt no particular need to prove it. And when she knelt in front of him, her long, brown hair framed a face full of kindness, and her soft blue eyes gazed with genuine concern. She was a contradiction, like the bird, yet it seemed certain that if anyone could help get Megan back, it was this Dellia.

Jon checked down the stone path, past a patch of blue flowers, through the giant, overgrown pergola into which Dellia had disappeared. But there was no sign of her return. He drew a deep breath of air sweet with the scent of flowers and turned back to the strange bird, studying it as it drifted from flower to flower.

During their trip from the clearing, Dellia had seemed content to travel in silence. And despite her being a stranger, the silence hadn't felt strained or awkward at all. Jon even welcomed it, not sure he was capable of a decent conversation after all that had happened.

They'd traveled through what must've been several miles of forest, and he was beginning to wonder where a farm could be in all of this when they broke into a large open area. Spread across it lay several farms, each with its own elaborate fairy-tale garden. They passed by several on the way, and each was impressive in its own unique way, with their carefully orchestrated ponds and fountains, hills and valleys and waterfalls. Eventually, they arrived at this one, with its startling flowers and puzzling bird.

Jon glanced again down the path, and there, under the pergola, laden with greenery and white flowers, he spied Dellia returning.

She'd left with one horse but was returning with two. The new horse was similar to Dellia's but with patches of soft, smooth gray over white. The two made a beautiful pair, and there appeared to be a familiarity between them as one nuzzled the other and nibbled its fur. Dellia seemed to be chatting with the new horse, carrying on quite the conversation. The whole scene was sweet and charming, and more touching than he thought possible.

The gentle clip-clop of hooves against the stones of the path ceased, and Dellia stood in front of Jon adjusting the reins on the new horse.

He glanced all around at the meticulously arranged plants and flowers. "This garden is amazing."

"Yes, it is." Dellia pointed back to the small farmhouse beyond the garden. "Her owner Yavani, it's her gift, knowing what the plants need, how to make them grow."

"Oh," Jon said, even as he wondered what she meant.

"She believes that old story that the Illis Woods has some kind of effect on plants and trees, that things grow faster and bigger and stronger here. I suppose if anyone could sense it, it would be her."

"Huh," Jon said, not at all sure how to respond.

"Anyway, she seems like a nice horse." Dellia passed the reins to

Jon. "Her name is Enna."

He took the reins as he stared at Enna. "Are all horses gray like this?"

"No. It's really quite rare, but my horse was bred here, too. It was kind of strange, actually. I told Yavani Enna was too valuable for a simple trade. But she insisted. Said it was 'meant to be,' whatever that means."

Jon stood, admiring Enna, not paying much attention while Dellia patted her horse and mounted. Enna was a gorgeous horse, white with the softest patches of gray, some darkening almost to black on her rear legs. He smiled and gazed at her placid face of white and silver as she flicked her ear. He brushed her face with gentle strokes, and it was soft and warm under his fingers. He had never been this close to a horse before, and she seemed to be a true thing of beauty.

Jon glanced over at Dellia, and she was gazing at the two of them, smiling.

He turned to the task of mounting the massive beast. He looked up at the saddle and stopped short. He had no clue what to do. Oh boy. And he'd missed the opportunity to see how she had done it.

He glanced at the saddle, then at Dellia, then back to the saddle again. He approached it with trepidation. It seemed so high up, and he wasn't sure if his clumsiness might somehow spook her.

Enna appeared to grow calm in the face of his anxiety. She stood still for him to mount and turned her head away, as if telling him it would be okay.

Jon tried holding the stirrup with his hands while he put his foot in it. He missed, stumbled, and almost fell, hopping on one foot a couple of times before he caught himself.

"Don't tell me you've never ridden a horse before," Dellia said.

"Okay, but can you just tell me quick which side to mount on?" Jon said, trying to joke away his discomfort.

He took a deep breath and put one hand on the saddle. The sturdy leather felt cool under his fingers. He concentrated, studied it, hoping he'd somehow figure it out and avoid further embarrassment.

All of a sudden, everything around him slowed down and came to a stop. Dellia, the horses, the bright flowers waving in the breeze, the wings of the bird hovering in front of him—they all came to a halt, and everything stood suspended in an eerie stillness.

The frozen world dimmed and gained a sort of gossamer haziness. Jon turned and looked around, trying to figure out what fresh new horror had befallen him.

Suddenly, a shimmering, translucent scene appeared overlaid on top of the world. It was a man tanning leather, complete with the sounds of him working. It was astonishing and beautiful, and from somewhere deep inside came a feeling, a distinct impression, that this was the leather of the saddle he'd been touching. He was seeing it being made.

In front of Jon stood a rack made of branches with a skin stretched over it. The scientist in him wanted to understand every minute detail of how this phenomenon worked, how such a thing was possible. But that part of him was overtaken by the sheer wonder and awe of it all. He hesitated, then stepped forward and reached out to touch the skin, like a child at his first 3-D movie, but his hand passed right through it.

No sooner had Jon wondered what more there was to see than the scene began to speed up, slowly at first, then faster and faster until it became a blur.

Then it slowed again, back to real time, to a scene of a woman absorbed in her work, stitching together pieces of leather in the shape of the saddle. It seemed as if she sat right in front of him. And when she looked up, he waved his hand, trying to get her attention. He snapped his fingers where she couldn't help but see. But she just took a deep breath, readjusted her position, and returned to her work, never showing the slightest sign she'd seen anything. Someone called from the next room, and the woman got up and started to leave. She was obviously the maker of the saddle, which made Jon wonder about its owner.

The scene accelerated again, becoming a blur. When it slowed down, it was to a man on horseback, galloping through the woods. Jon watched the heavy muscles on the horse ripple while it ran in place, right in front of him. Trees and brush flew past his eyes, and he reached out his fingers to touch them, but the glittering images passed right through as they raced by.

Jon shook his head, and the scene vanished. In an instant, he was yanked back to the exact position he'd been in when the world froze. The experience left him disoriented, and he shook his head again as the real world brightened and began to reanimate.

Without thinking, he put his foot in the stirrup and mounted with practiced ease. Then he guided Enna around next to Dellia as if he'd been doing it his whole life.

Jon looked down at the reins in his hand with a mixture of shock and disbelief. What the heck just happened? And why did he have this sudden confidence he could handle any horse with skill and ease?

Dellia stared at him for a moment, seeming equally baffled. He looked at her, and she let out a laugh. "Very funny," she said.

Still disoriented, all he managed was, "Uh, yeah."

"We'll have to pick up the trail back where I found you." She spurred her horse on.

He nodded and followed.

The sun hung low on the horizon as Dellia worked her way back along the simple stone path. Still staring down at the reins in his hands, Jon guided Enna after her. And as they left behind the small wonderland of birds and flowers, a thousand questions spun through his mind. He was a physicist. Which meant he was supposed to have at least some understanding of how things were supposed to work—but this was mind-boggling.

He had suspected something when every battery-driven device that came through the portal was dead. His suspicions had grown when he saw the dragon and inexplicable bird. Even Dellia and Isla's use of the word "gift" was noteworthy, but not extraordinary. But this. This was a whole other level. Nothing like it had ever happened to him, nor could he have ever dreamed it was possible. To see three-dimensional images? To view past events? To gain the ability to ride a horse in an instant?

No, there was something seriously wrong with the way this world worked because there was no way he could ever reconcile the physical world he knew so well with the impossible phenomena he'd just experienced.

Chapter Five

MEGAN'S RESCUE

Dellia felt sorry for the poor fellow. Jon seemed out of his element in every imaginable way. Dusk had hit the forest when they started searching for a spot to rest for the night. As the horses plodded along through the dwindling light, Jon had been quiet and withdrawn, as if lost in his own mind. So when he showed signs of life again and started suggesting spots to make camp, she had found it encouraging. But then she had to explain that this spot was too low, that they'd get washed out if it rained. And this other spot offered no protection. And this one was too close to trees for a fire. Each time, at her words, she sensed his hopelessness only deepen. Until eventually he shut down again, glazed over, and withdrew back into his own thoughts.

And so it went with every little task, from making camp, to tending horses, to building a fire, and even collecting firewood. Jon attacked the job with eagerness. He even looked like he knew what he was doing, kicking through the underbrush and with great deliberation selecting just the right pieces. But it turned out he'd collected green wood along with the drier twigs and branches she needed. And every time she tried to explain what he'd done wrong, he clammed up again, no matter how gently she tried to break it to him.

By the time they'd stopped, it had grown too dark to hunt anything for dinner. So their meal consisted of a few strips of dried meat and a chunk of hard bread from their supplies. Jon was appreciative enough and ate eagerly, but it was obvious something was still pulling at his attention. Even before he finished, he was slipping away again, retreating into his own thoughts, staring into space.

Having finished the meal, they reclined against a moss-covered fallen tree, bathing in the warm glow of the campfire. Dellia reached out and plucked another log from the pile, then tossed it onto the flames. Sparks crackled and drifted up into the night sky as the forest beyond disappeared into a veil of darkness, lost for a time in the blackness of the night.

Dellia glanced over at Jon, watching the firelight flicker across his face. Poor man was troubled, and he seemed so lost in thought. It was obvious what he was doing. She had seen it many times before. He was withdrawing, trying to cope with what had befallen him. But it was also true that as much as he wanted his solitude, if she could perhaps gently coax him into talking, it would help. And it also couldn't hurt to learn a little more about this situation with this woman he was so desperate to find.

"So ten years, huh?" Dellia ventured. "You must have really thought Megan was the one."

"Yeah, I guess I really did," Jon replied, as if his thoughts were still far away.

"Did you see an oracle?"

"Huh? Oh … an oracle?" He stumbled over the words as he snapped out of his daze.

"Yeah, to see the future, tell you whether you were fated to be together."

"Yeah … I don't think I believe in that stuff," Jon said, then seemed to catch himself. "Wait, is that … common?"

"In Erden, yeah, some parents even use an oracle to help find a spouse for their children."

"Like an arranged marriage?" Jon said. "That's barbaric."

"Really? So how do you find the right person where you come

from?"

"You just meet someone, I suppose. Oh, and there's computer dating."

"Huh?" Dellia stared, thrown by the unfamiliar word.

"A machine. It matches people up."

"A machine?" She continued to stare in puzzlement. There were machines for grinding wheat into flour or spinning wool into thread, but how could a spinning wheel know what made two people suited for each other? "So this machine, it can know what's in two people's hearts? It can see them together and understand how they would be perfect for one another?"

Dellia could see Jon's expression of certainty transform into one of bewilderment, and he stumbled over his words. "Uh ... yeah. Well no ... I mean, sort of."

Dellia gave a small smile. "So, it's barbaric to have someone who can see the future help choose a mate, but a machine ..."

"See, now you're just making it sound foolish." Jon smiled back.

"Sorry. So this machine. It works? It finds your one true love?"

"One true love? What does that mean?"

Dellia peered into his face. It was curious how puzzled he seemed by her question. Especially for someone who professed to have been in love with the same woman for ten years. She had never been in love. Yet she knew the answer like the back of her hand. She had known since she was young.

She turned her head and gazed into the fire as her thoughts drifted back. "Someone you fall madly in love with. You wake up every day, and you can't wait to see them. Someone that sees all your flaws and wounds and weaknesses and accepts them, even loves them. And helps you heal them. A best friend, a lover, for the rest of your life."

Jon paused for a moment, as if taken aback. "And there's only one?"

"If you find the right person, you only need one."

"Wow. Do people even believe in that kind of love anymore?" he said as if thinking aloud. "I mean, so many relationships go bad before they even get to marriage. And something like half of all marriages break up. I don't even think I believe in that. I mean sure, that's what everyone wants, but it's not realistic. You're just setting yourself up for disappointment."

Dellia poked the fire with a stick. It settled with a rush of crackling, and a fresh batch of sparks leaped into the night sky.

"Hmm," she said.

"What?" Jon asked.

"It's just a puzzle. You say you were in love for ten years, but then you seem sure love won't last." Dellia hesitated. Then she added, "Plus, it makes no sense. To give up on something you want in life because you'd be disappointed if you didn't get it."

Jon gawked at her for a moment, and his bewildered expression returned. "Can we just change the subject?"

"Sure," Dellia replied, but it was clear he wasn't going to let this go.

"What about you? I suppose you have the perfect relationship."

"No. I'm a protector."

Jon stared at her with a blank expression.

"A protector. I serve the council."

He gave her a questioning look and shrugged his shoulders.

"Huh, you really have no idea what I'm talking about. How can you not know about the Ruling Council of Meerdon?"

"I told you I'm not from around here," Jon said. "My home is really far away."

"Are you in the habit of traveling places you know nothing about?"

"No," he said, seeming flustered. "There was ... and then ... Look, can we just change the subject?"

"Sure, but we're gonna run out of things to talk about."

Jon barged ahead. "I don't understand, what does working for this council have to do with it?"

"It's not just working for them," Dellia said, her passion spilling over into her words. "I swore an oath. I've dedicated my life to serving and protecting the council and the people. There's no higher calling, and there's no room in a protector's life for romantic entanglements. Nothing that could take my attention away from my duty."

Jon seemed to think about that for a moment. "Hmm. Now *there's* a puzzle."

Dellia tilted her head. "What do you mean?"

He eyed her and smiled, seeming a bit smug. "It's just the way you talked about love. It was beautiful and heartfelt, like you're this big romantic. But then you speak of your duty to the council with such passion. Even though it means never having love."

She turned toward the fire, staring into its warm glow. Jon hadn't said anything she didn't already know. She'd understood what it meant to be a protector and what she'd have to give up, and she'd never regretted it. She loved her life and would never consider trading it for anything. Not even for a moment. If her apprentice or Kayleen had said the same thing, she would have brushed it off without even thinking about it. So why did Jon's words bother her so much?

"Well, we should get some sleep." Dellia scooted down. "We'll want to be well rested when we catch up to them tomorrow."

She turned away and settled her head on her bedroll. From the sounds coming from his side of the fire, she could tell Jon spent a long while watching her before he, too, lay his head down for the night. She took a deep breath and stared into the fire as she considered the day's events, watching the flames dance and flicker while she waited for sleep to take her.

Jon was shaken awake. It was cold and dark as he opened his eyes.

From the faint light, it seemed like dawn had barely broken, yet there kneeling over him was Dellia, awake and alert. So it hadn't all been some kind of nightmare, after all.

An abrupt "Let's go" was all she said.

He wasn't used to sleeping on the ground, so he rose stiff and sore and began slowly following her lead in getting ready.

How Dellia had managed to wake at precisely the right time, in the dark, with no clock and no alarm to jar her out of her slumber, was a mystery. Jon wanted to inquire about it, but he was held back by a sense of awkwardness over his less-than-gracious words of the night before. He'd let his impulse to one-up her goad him into saying things he shouldn't have, and judging by the abrupt ending to the conversation, he had struck a nerve. He'd been callous and unthinking, and now he was left with a sense of shame and the wish that he could take it all back.

With scarcely a handful of words between them, they ate, packed up, and started off just as the first amber light filtered through the trees. And with those early golden rays, the world of the forest came to life, the stillness of night replaced by the gentle rustling of leaves and the distant sounds of birds echoing through the peaceful green of the forest floor.

Dellia had been gracious enough to provide Jon with what he imagined was less conspicuous attire, for which he was grateful. He'd felt out of place already without people staring at him and commenting on his clothes, as Dellia had. The items were loose fitting but comfortable and a little like something you'd find at a renaissance fair.

When he tried to mount Enna, Jon discovered that the riding skill he'd acquired in the garden was gone, so he placed his hand on the smooth leather and focused on the saddle. He was trying to trigger another episode, but for whatever reason, he couldn't. Luckily, the experience had taught him something of how to ride, and though it still seemed clumsy and unnatural, he was able to mount and handle Enna without embarrassing himself too much.

No sooner had they set off than Dellia went to work while Jon watched with fascination. She was amazing. Scanning the forest while moving at a decent clip, she could spot the tiniest broken twig, disturbed pile of leaves, or trampled patch of grass. From indistinct smudges in the dirt and mud, she explained, she had identified two sets of hoofprints. She followed their path unerringly for hours, making it seem effortless. Yet to Jon, it was just endless miles of trees and brush that all appeared the same.

The sun had risen higher in the sky and the air had warmed considerably by the time Dellia caught sight of their camp. Well before Jon could make out anything, she pointed at the tiniest bit of movement way off in the distance and signaled him to hush.

As they crept up behind a stand of tall trees, their goal came into view. There, barely visible through the brush, were a man and two women. They'd set up some kind of camp below the twisted branches of a massive, gnarled old tree at the water's edge. It towered over them like some ancient sentinel, its leaves nearly dipping into the stream behind them. One of them, a short, thin woman with long, straight black hair, was tending to the horses, while the other two rested on the contorted roots that writhed along the ground from the tree's enormous base. Jon couldn't be sure with her back to him, but the other woman seemed to have Megan's wavy, ginger hair.

He tried to catch what they were saying, but all he got were little snippets. "Who knows how much is even true?" the man said. Next came some inaudible bickering, then, "There's an old saying: history is written by the victor." Followed by something that sounded like "written by the vanquished." A few more muffled barbs flew back and forth. Then came a loud, angry response. It was sharper than the tone he had heard in his lab, yet instantly recognizable.

"I'm not worried about *me*," Megan said.

Dellia leaned over and put her mouth to Jon's ear, her lips brushing against it as she spoke in the quietest of whispers. "I'm going to go talk to them. You stay here."

Suddenly, the situation seemed much more real than it had a second ago. Jon's stomach turned queasy at the thought of what these people might do. This was his mess, and the idea of someone else getting hurt because of it seemed worse than his fear of being the one who got hurt.

"You don't need to do this," he whispered back.

"Do what? I'm just going to talk."

"But what if they don't want to just talk? This isn't your problem. It's mine."

Dellia shot him a stern look. "It's my job."

"Yeah, that's what my mom thought. It got her killed."

"What are you talking about?"

"Nothing, just—"

"Look, it's too dangerous for you, and I can handle those two." She motioned to the encampment. "Now just stay here. All I'm going to do is talk."

From the tone of Dellia's voice, it was clear those were her final words, and it was a command, not a request. So Jon waited and watched while she stepped out from behind the stand of tall trees, hands up, and strolled across the rough, uneven ground toward the camp.

The woman near the horses caught sight of Dellia first and whirled around. "A protector!" she yelled.

Chaos broke out as the man flew to his feet and whipped around. He was tall and thin, and like Megan and his companion he was possessed of an Asian appearance. His stance along with his sinewy arms and short, unkempt, jet-black hair made this look like a scene from a martial arts movie. His eyes locked on Dellia, and he and the woman charged.

She seemed shocked at their reaction. She whipped out her dagger and readied herself for the attack.

As they dove at her, she sidestepped and spun out of the way. She slammed the woman in the back and put out her arm, catching the man in the chest.

Both opponents crashed to the ground.

All of a sudden, dust, debris, and leaves whirled into the air as Dellia's feet left the ground.

Jon stared dumbfounded while his queasiness turned to shock, horror, and panic. He followed Dellia's gaze down to Megan.

Eyes fixed on Dellia, Megan stood tall amid the gnarled roots of the ancient tree. Sunlight glanced off the ripples in the water behind her. Dust and debris swirled from the ground around her and whistled up through the twisted branches.

Megan's concentration was intense, her arm outstretched, aimed at Dellia, as if holding a doll in the air. *She* was doing this.

Jon charged out from behind the trees. "Megan," he shouted. "Wait. Stop. Don't hurt her."

Her eyes flew wide open. "Jon, you have no idea what's going on. Run."

He bolted, startled by the urgency in Megan's voice. He turned and raced straight into the tree behind him. The blow caused his vision to momentarily go dark, and he staggered backward and almost fell. Dazed, he shook his head and glanced over at Dellia, still floating in the air, helpless.

She looked down at him with an expression he could swear was more concerned about him than herself. "Can you fight?"

"No."

Dellia looked at Jon's hand and tossed her dagger. "Protect yourself as best you can."

He failed to catch the weapon. The hilt glanced off his hand, and the dagger spun, blade first, into the dirt at his feet.

Having regained their footing, the pair of attackers stood eyeing Jon and the weapon, seemingly uncertain what to do.

He reached down and snatched the dagger from the ground.

The two charged, but all he could do was stare down at the blade in his hand, wondering what the heck he was supposed to do with it. Suddenly, everything around him slowed to a crawl, then froze: the charging men, the leaves and dust whirling around Dellia, Megan's hair blowing in the wind, even the ripples on the water all stood utterly still, suspended in time.

The world became hazy and dim, and a new shimmering translucent scene appeared before Jon: a smith hammering a blade. It was déjà vu all over again. Only this time, he'd had a chance to consider the incident with the saddle. On a level he couldn't quite explain, he knew he'd learned to ride from the scene with the rider in the woods. It wasn't something he reasoned out. It wasn't some logical process of deduction. He just understood, somewhere deep inside, that he'd seen the rider who owned the saddle, and somehow, he'd absorbed the man's ability to ride.

He wasn't sure how it worked or how he triggered it, and the effect didn't last, but he was seeing the weapon being forged. And if he wanted, he could end here and go make his own dagger.

Jon looked over at the two charging figures, and an idea struck him. He focused on the attack he'd just witnessed, and the scene before him sped up, spinning faster and faster until it was a blur. When it slowed again, the scene played out just as it had moments ago, the attackers racing at Dellia, her sending them plummeting to the ground. Jon shook his head and snapped back to the exact position he had been in when the world had frozen.

Everything began moving again, and the two attackers resumed their reckless charge.

Precisely as Dellia had done, Jon sidestepped and spun out of the way. He slammed the woman in the back and put out his arm, catching the man in the chest.

Both his opponents crashed to the ground, exactly as they had before.

Jon turned to face Megan. Why was she doing this? She was going to hurt this woman whose only crime was helping him. It was his worst fear. This was why he'd wanted to talk to them instead of Dellia. He knew it wasn't rational, he knew it didn't make sense, but the thought of someone getting hurt because of him—it terrified him.

He broke into a sprint, racing at Megan. If he got to her, grabbed her, and shook her out of it, maybe he could stop her.

She turned toward him and aimed her arm at him.

Dellia crashed to the dirt, landing with a thud.

Megan flicked her wrist, and leaves and dust leaped from the ground in a line and raced toward him. Her expression turned to shock and horror; she'd reacted without thinking.

Jon was yanked off his feet and flung backward through the air, slamming into one of the tall trees. A sharp pain stabbed the back of his head as Megan raced toward him, her hand over her mouth. The world began to spin as his vision went hazy. Then everything went dark.

Garris rode hard that first night until it was too dark to see the path, and then for several hours more, plodding along by the flickering light of a torch. He left the Neri, camping at the eastern edge of the Erden Plains outside a sleepy little town named Durgun. In the morning, well before dawn, he made an unwelcome call on Trishan, a man known for dealing in certain unusual herbs, powders, and potions, most of them hard to get, some recreational, and a handful forbidden by law.

A few threats and a little bullying garnered him a rare powder that he mixed into Kyri's feed. Something that would allow her to run much farther and faster without getting tired. If he was right, and he always was, it would shorten the trip from three or four days to one long day.

Garris struck out from Durgun at first light, riding fast and hard across the flat, barren landscape of the Erden Plains. He had never been one to go all weak in the knees at the sight of some showy magic. But the wind on his face while the landscape raced by at an astonishing speed was exhilarating. It was the dry season now. The bulk of the rainfall on the Erden Plains came in torrential bursts during the early spring. And the dry spell that followed lasted the rest of the year. So Garris watched while the hard, dry ground and brown, scrubby vegetation gave way to town after town as he hurtled past them.

He flew by Indare and Wardhal, driving south of the holy city of Mundus at midday. Even though he'd grown up in Shirdon, he was of Erdish descent. His black hair and golden skin would easily blend in with the locals. Even so, his large size and leather armor would make him stand out, and thus he preferred to stay somewhat out of sight. So instead of joining up with the Eastern Trail beyond Mundus, Garris rode parallel to it, past Akolah and Dule, all the way to the eastern edge of the Illis Woods, arriving shortly before dusk.

He stopped for a brief time to rest and eat, then struck out into the Illis Woods at dusk, hoping the darkness would mask him from traveling strangers. He raced down the Eastern Trail with nothing but the light of the half moon to guide his way. The pounding of hooves and the sounds of the forest surrounded him, and the brisk air left him chilled. He rode on in the near darkness until exhaustion overtook him. He camped late, a short distance off the path, falling quickly into an uneasy slumber.

With little rest, Garris dragged himself out of bed in the darkness of night, broke camp while half-asleep, and set out into the woods at dawn, heading straight for his destination.

It was a little past midday when he arrived. He recognized the spot by the magnificent old gnarled tree by the water's edge, exactly as Elt had described. He rode straight toward it, scanning the area for any sign of a man. Then, he spotted a body lying motionless on the ground next to a towering tree.

Garris shook his head. Oh great. *Wouldn't it just be typical for the guy I'm supposed to be helping to turn up dead?*

As he pulled to a stop next to the man, Garris froze as he got his first good look at the face. He'd never seen anyone quite like him. Yet there was an inexplicable familiarity in his neatly cut hair, soft skin, and blemish-free features. One that filled Garris with a sense of foreboding. He took a step back. What the heck had that blasted lizard man gotten him into this time? He shook the feeling off. He was most likely imagining things. Besides, if this man was still alive he would need assistance, and there was no way he could leave him here.

Garris slipped off his horse and knelt on the rocky ground next to him. As he did, it became apparent the fellow was still breathing. Well, at least there was that. He felt all over for injuries, and apart from a nasty bump on the back of his head, he seemed fine. He closed his eyes and shook his head. Of course, why on Earth would he expect the man to be conscious? This was Elt, after all.

Garris stood and surveyed the area, trying to sort out what had happened. Yup, this had to be the guy. He'd expected something unusual, and the pattern of disturbed debris and leaves told him it wasn't a typical brawl.

He didn't want to move or shake the man without knowing if there was some hidden injury. So, with nothing to do but wait, he plopped down and leaned back against a tree, soaking in the warm air and familiar sounds of the forest. He watched the man for a minute or two before he closed his eyes and drifted off into an attentive sleep.

Garris's eyes flew open at the sound of the man stirring. He looked down at him, then scooted over, positioning himself so the man could see him.

The man opened his eyes, not yet seeming to be all there. "What happened?" he said as he dragged himself up to rest on his elbows.

Garris watched for a few seconds, waiting for signs of lucidity, then bounced to his feet. He pointed to the remnants of a fire and numerous footprints down by the old tree at the water's edge. "Best as I can tell, there were three camped down there. Two of them charged your partner here and got taken out." He pointed out the pair of tracks coming from the camp to where they collided with footprints leading from the tall tree. "Then there was some big disturbance. The two charged you about here." Garris traced out the tracks running toward the man. "You disabled them, then you charged down toward that old tree." He pointed along the tracks leading toward the camp.

Garris paused, trying to come up with some other explanation, but barged ahead when none offered itself. "Then something threw you all the way back here, against this tree, and you landed here." He pointed to where the fellow lay. "Then they took your partner and your horses and rode off."

For the longest time, the man stared at Garris with a blank expression, as if he'd stumped him. Finally, he spoke. "It was a lot more confusing being in the middle of all that."

Garris nodded. "It usually is."

"Like, you left out the part where my longtime friend, Megan, told me to run from her. Then she used some power she's never had before to levitate Dellia and toss me into a tree."

"Dellia, huh?" Garris quickly scanned the area for any signs of the protector.

"Yeah, they took her, and I'm worried they might hurt her."

80

"So, what are you going to do?"

"Go get help?" the man ventured.

Garris took a step backward and eyed the man. "Exactly how many times did you say you landed on your head?"

The man stared back, clearly not comprehending the idiocy of his own suggestion.

Garris sighed. "Look, sure, you could do that, and maybe in a few days someone would be back here trying to pick up a very cold trail."

The man glanced away, seeming unsure what to say or do.

Garris looked down at the rocky ground as he rolled the prospect around in his head. It was a backward sort of proposition, really, rescuing a protector. They were the ones who were supposed to do the rescuing. Yet, doing so might gain him some small goodwill with Dellia, and from what he knew of her, she was nothing if not fair-minded. The man seemed in dire need of decent suggestions, and it might be worth the risk.

"So what's your name?" Garris asked.

"Jon," the man replied.

"Huh. Unusual name. Well, Jon, I'm Garris. What do you say we go together to get Dellia back?"

The man brightened visibly. "You'd do that?"

Garris extended his hand to help Jon up. "Here's the thing, Jon. You don't look like you've ever held a weapon, yet you took down two attackers with little fuss. If we're going to work together, I need to see what you've got. Maybe show you a thing or two. I need to know what to expect when we confront the ones who took Dellia."

He unsheathed his sword and presented it hilt first for Jon to take. "Hold this sword like you're defending yourself."

Jon took it almost absentmindedly, like Garris's words hadn't sunk in yet, or he couldn't make sense of them. He held the blade out with a distinct awkwardness, as if he'd never touched one before.

Then he seemed to snap out of it, grasping the weapon more firmly and repositioning his feet so they were spread apart with his left foot forward. He stared at Garris, as if seeking approval. Which was disheartening because his stance looked abysmal. Garris walked around him, uncertain where to even begin.

"Your form is horrid." Garris shoved Jon's shoulder, causing him to lose his balance, stumble, and almost fall.

The man didn't seem surprised, which was a good sign. Garris pretended to hold out a sword and positioned himself correctly. "Like this."

Jon tried again. His attempt to copy Garris's stance was notably less horrid. Garris nodded and kicked Jon's feet, nudging them into an even less dreadful position, and rebalanced his weight.

"See how that feels better?" Garris shoved Jon's shoulder again. This time, his stance held, with only a slight movement of his feet. Garris scowled. "I've seen six-year-olds with better form, but it's a start."

Jon seemed to take his verbal jab well. Another good sign.

"Now let's work on how you're holding that sword."

Garris carried on instructing this strange man he was supposed to help. Under the leafy, green canopy of the forest, he pushed and shoved, challenged and taught, and for all his efforts, he started to see a glimmer of improvement. And with it, he began to feel something he hadn't felt in a very long time: a sense of pride and a feeling that all those years spent training might have found a reason.

Then he quickly reminded himself he wasn't going to get caught up in this. He had no idea where this path would lead, and although he'd follow it, for now, he didn't like how this had started, much less where it seemed headed.

To the left of Jon, the brook gurgled as it poured over rocks and stones, masking any sound of their slow and stealthy advance. With apprehension, he peered ahead at the three figures sitting with their backs to him. They were resting on a rock outcropping at the brook's edge, where it twisted and turned as it wound its way through the soft green of the forest floor. The sunlight streaming through the trees cast a spotlight on Dellia while she sat propped against a nearby tree, hands tied with a bag over her head. Swords drawn, he and Garris crept toward the group, one slow, careful footfall at a time.

Meeting Garris had been a jarring experience. He awoke to find a hulking stranger's golden brown face hanging over him. The man was heavily muscled, with broad shoulders, unevenly cropped, jet-black hair, and amber eyes. A scar on his upper arm, and the patch-work of dark, heavy leather that mostly covered his chest, wrists, and torso, gave him away as some kind of fighter.

Upon opening his eyes, he had been groggy, his head hurt, and he was confused. But when he asked what happened, instead of introducing himself or explaining he'd been knocked out, Garris painstakingly recounted the entire encounter, most likely from tracks he'd seen. When he offered to help, it'd been a tremendous relief, and he expected to rush off after Dellia and Megan right away. But instead, this man had launched into a lesson in swordplay.

Now, sword in hand and a mere few feet from the backs of the three, Jon was beginning to see the wisdom in that lesson. He looked down at the sword in his hand, and the gnawing in his stomach returned. A warning that this could lead to violence, that someone could get hurt because of him. And with it came the fervent wish that the lesson had consumed just a little more time.

They halted, and Jon glanced over at Garris. He stood silent and confident, his sword to the back of the strange woman while Jon's was poised inches from the man's neck. Garris motioned with his head, telling Jon to go ahead.

He summoned his calmest, most nonthreatening voice, and

over the quiet sound of the brook and the wind through the trees, he said, "Megan, we need to talk."

The three startled and snapped their heads around, eyeing the swords at their backs. With slow and deliberate movements, all three rose and turned toward Jon and Garris.

The man spoke first. "Whoa, whoa. I know how this looks, but we meant you no harm. We were just trying to help Megan."

"Is kidnapping protectors a part of helping?" Jon shot back. "Go cut Dellia loose."

The man remained unnaturally calm, his voice determined and steady. "I cannot do that. She will try to arrest us all, and I cannot let that happen. So we will have to stop her, and someone will get hurt. Let us take our horses and leave. Then you can cut her loose."

Jon's stomach wrenched. Whatever happened here was his doing. And the idea it might lead to Dellia or even this man or woman getting hurt, or worse … Jon put it out of his mind. "You're bluffing," he said.

Nervous and uncertain, he glanced over at Garris, who was eyeing the man up and down. "No, he's not, and neither is she. If you cut Dellia loose, it won't be pleasant."

"But they kidnapped Megan and Dellia."

"Please, Jon, just let them go," Megan said.

Garris gave Jon a solemn look. "It's not my decision to make." He motioned to Dellia with his head. "Dellia can't let them go, but you can. Tough choice."

Jon eyed the man and woman. "No, it's not. I can't let anyone get hurt because of me. Okay, you can go, and I promise Dellia won't follow you. You have twenty-four hours. But Megan comes with me."

For an instant, Megan looked alarmed. Then her expression fell, and her voice became soft and quiet. "I can't go with you."

"But why?"

"You have no idea how much I just want to grab you now and

go away with you. Away from all this." Jon could swear Megan's eyes were beginning to well with tears.

"Then let's go," Jon said.

"I know how confusing this must be. But I can't explain. Please, just trust me and understand that for now, my path can't be yours."

As Megan turned and started walking away, Jon scrambled to pull the medallion out of his shirt. "I might have a way home. If I find the parts to assemble this." He thrust the medallion forward for her to see.

She turned and peered at it for a moment. Then she stared into Jon's eyes, her voice becoming strong and passionate. "If you want to go home, then you find a way. Don't let anyone or anything stop you, not even me. I will find a way to follow. Don't wait for me. Promise me."

Confused beyond words, Jon simply nodded.

The man and woman mounted their horses. Then the man reached out and grabbed Megan's hand, swinging her up on the horse in front of him. He turned his horse to leave but stopped halfway, his focus on Jon as he spoke. "I know you have no reason to trust me. But this I promise on my life: No harm will come to Megan. Not by my hand or by any other."

He kicked his horse, and the three rode off. Jon stood watching as Megan disappeared, lost once more to the sunlit, emerald world of the forest. He turned and sauntered over to Dellia, still leaning against a tree, bathed in sunlight. As Jon examined her bindings, Garris tapped his shoulder and handed him a knife. Jon used it to saw through the ropes.

Dellia reached up and yanked the hood off her head. She tore the gag out and flew to her feet. Anger flashed across her face, instantly settling into hard calm.

Jon reflexively took a step backward.

Dellia flew at him and slammed her palm into his chest.

It was a more powerful blow than seemed possible, and Jon staggered backward, his chest stinging, and he almost lost his footing.

He glanced at Garris, but he just put his hands up and stepped back, watching the whole scene unfold.

"You promised them I wouldn't follow?" Dellia spat out the words. "What were you thinking?" She smashed her hand into his chest again, sending him stumbling backward. "What in the world made you think I even needed your help?"

Jon struggled for words. "I … just—"

Dellia shoved Jon backward a third time. "You act like you can't ride a horse, then suddenly you can. You say you can't fight. Then you use my moves … *my* moves."

"I'm a visual learner?"

Jon glanced over at Garris again, hoping for a little support, but he was just standing there, arms crossed with a smirk on his face. He was enjoying this.

Dellia shoved Jon again, sending him slamming into a tree. She drew her dagger and leaped at him like a tigress springing onto her prey. She pinned him against the tree, her blade to his throat. "And you lead me into a trap? Against your friend. You never mentioned she has a gift. And a powerful one. Like I've never seen."

Jon stumbled over the words. "I … I didn't know. I never lied to you. She's never done anything like that before—honestly."

Dellia seized his arm and shoved him into the brook.

He stood there, the frigid water running over and into his shoes.

Dellia raised her arm, pointing her finger at Garris. "And who is this?" she demanded.

"Just someone who helped me."

"And you don't even know who he is. Well, you'll just let any-one help you."

"I let *you* help me."

Dellia shot Jon a hard stare. "Does he have a name?"

Jon glanced over at Garris, who was pulling his fingers across his throat in a frantic effort to signal Jon to keep quiet.

"Garris?" Jon ventured.

The hulking warrior shook his head and rolled his eyes.

Dellia pointed at Garris again, addressing him directly now. "No," she said, sounding quite sarcastic. "I know this can't be *thee* Garris. No way can this be *thee* Garris. Because if this were *thee* Garris, I'd have to arrest him. Because *thee* Garris was banished."

Garris calmly replied, "Clearly, I'm the other Garris."

"Well, this is just great."

"Nice to meet you, too," he quipped.

Jon had reached the end of his rope. His frustration bubbled over, and the words tumbled out. "Look, I'm sorry for everything. This isn't my home. Nothing here works like it should. My friend just left with two complete strangers, and she won't even tell me why. I just want to go home."

His last pleading words hung in the air while Dellia and Garris both stared at him. Perhaps it was the desperation in his voice or perhaps she'd simply calmed down with time, but for whatever reason, Dellia seemed to soften visibly.

"And this medallion, it will help you do that?" Dellia said, her tone much more even tempered.

Jon nodded. "Yeah, the first part is in Talus."

She seemed to think for a long moment, calming even more. "My mother is one of the Ephori, the rulers of Talus. Her home isn't far. I'll take you."

Jon decided it might be safe to step out of the brook now. His chest hurt where Dellia had hit him, and water squished in his shoes as Dellia fetched Enna and Ulka and they all headed back toward Garris's horse. On the way, Garris leaned over and whispered to Jon, "That went better than expected."

A powerful urge struck to punch Garris in the arm for not warning him that he expected it to go badly, but he took a second look at the bulky muscles of the warrior and decided that might not be wise.

Once they reached Kyri, Dellia handed Enna's reins to Jon without ever looking him in the face. He turned his attention to Enna, and as he looked up at her, he stopped for a moment, comforted to see her placid face again. Despite still having two companions, the experience of Megan leaving and Dellia attacking him had left him feeling even more alone and isolated than ever before. He patted Enna, then leaned his head against her body and in a quiet whisper said, "You're still my friend, aren't you, girl?"

As Jon mounted, he noticed Dellia watching him and realized he hadn't whispered quietly enough. The three brought their horses around and splashed across the brook, heading back through the forest and toward Dellia's home.

Chapter Six

TALUS

Jon's shoes were still wet and his feet uncomfortable and shriveled when they finally found a place to make camp for the night. They'd traveled in strained silence, broken only by the gentle sounds of the forest and the quiet thumping of hooves. Garris seemed at complete ease with the lack of chatter, plodding along under the canopy of green, past towering trees and loose brush, with that calm expression that never changed.

Dellia was a different matter. It seemed as if the whole experience had left her oddly troubled. Maybe it was the abduction, or maybe something had happened to her while in their hands. Maybe it was him. Maybe he'd broken her trust. But then again, he couldn't see why he'd matter that much to her. Whatever it was, Jon sensed a distance between them that seemed as if it would never be bridged.

Their confrontation was etched in his mind: Dellia repeatedly shoving him across the uneven forest floor, her frustrated tone, her angry questions, and that blade to his throat. But what had been even more disquieting than the knife was the realization that he deserved her wrath. He knew how it all looked. He'd hidden things from her. He was lying to her. But Isla's words still echoed in his thoughts, *"Tell no one ... where you are from, ... what you can do."* So, despite the urge to explain everything, to mend fences, Jon remained silent and let the rift between them fester.

The trip had only taken a couple of hours, but it seemed like forever. It was all so unreal. Everything required so much time, so much patience. A trip that would have taken minutes by car had taken a day. There were no videos to watch, no web to surf, no texting friends, and no Facebook status to change to "abandoned by my friend in a foreign world of terrifying dragons." And with no conversation, there had been nothing to distract him. He was alone with his thoughts, and dwelling on them only seemed to amplify his awkwardness and confusion.

At first, Jon kept replaying his conversation with Megan over and over in his head. But no matter how many times he went over it, it never made any more sense. Eventually, he put it out of his mind. This was what she wanted, and as much as it made no sense, he needed to accept it. She was apparently okay and protected, and that was what really mattered. Still, it left him despondent and unsettled.

They stopped well before dusk in a protected area shielded by several moss-covered boulders and thick brush. Without so much as a word, Jon set about collecting firewood. Dellia made herself conspicuously absent, going off to tend the horses. A process that seemed to involve having a little chat with them.

Garris shouldered his crossbow and, with an unusual degree of cheer, announced he was going off to hunt something for dinner. Jon shook his head. That man liked killing things just a little too much. He returned to his search for kindling while Garris ducked through the underbrush and disappeared into the dwindling light of the forest near sundown.

Dellia was busy starting a fire when Garris returned a short time later. He held up an oversized rabbit with an arrow through it and smiled as he approached. As he passed Jon, he dropped a large berry and a leaf in his hand. Then he pointed off into the woods and gave Jon a hearty slap on the back, propelling him off in that direction.

Despite the fading light, Jon had no trouble locating the

berries. There were tons of them in a broad patch of thorny canes growing in an open area. The leaves were harder to find, but after a while, he managed to locate them a short distance away, on a dense patch of small plants hidden among a plot of flowers.

He couldn't resist tasting both. The deep red berries smelled fruity and were tart but flavorful, and the leaves were green and sweet, like sugar. He held up his shirt to form a container in which he gathered handfuls of the tiny fruit and fistfuls of leaves. When he returned, he dumped them onto a cloth that Garris had laid out. Garris picked through the berries and mixed them with the leaves, reserving most of the mixture to eat. The rest he mashed up and used as a glaze for the rabbit already roasting over the fire.

The result smelled and tasted delicious, and Jon ate with eagerness. Garris and Dellia appeared satisfied with their portions, as if they'd had an ample meal. But Jon always seemed to finish feeling hungry. Dellia and Garris ate far less than he did and seemed to accept it as normal. Perhaps he was just used to supersized meals, with milkshakes and jumbo fries, and with time he'd get used to it, too.

The rest of the evening played out in awkward silence, broken only by the sounds of the forest and the crackling of the fire. It was a stark contrast to his talk with Dellia the night before. There had been something intriguing and appealing about that discussion. Perhaps it was the way she seemed to know her own mind and was able to explain it with so little effort. Or the way she called him out on his nonsense, dismantling his statements with relative ease. Or perhaps it was how she never seemed to take offense, at least until the end when he'd put his foot in his mouth. If only he'd remembered to curb his enthusiasm and measure what he said.

Despite the hard ground beneath him, Jon was quick to fall into a sound slumber. Near morning, his sleep became more restless, filled with ghastly visions of being chased through an endless forest by a giant rabbit covered with berries.

Garris shook him awake early, at the crack of dawn, and after a brief meal, they broke camp and headed back out into the forest just as it was beginning to come alive with morning activity.

Dellia took the lead, while Garris rode in back: placid, expressionless, and quiet. Maybe it was the rest, or maybe the experience of a quiet ride through a peaceful, green forest at sunrise, but Dellia's mood seemed brighter. The way their last exchange had ended, Jon considered it best to keep his distance and let her deal with him on her own terms. He glanced over a couple of times and swore he caught a slip of a smile. But it drifted away as soon as she noticed him watching. At several points, Jon even had the impression she was about to talk to him, but then the moment passed.

They'd ridden for what must have been several hours when they finally broke from the trees amid a group of a dozen or more horses. They stood quietly grazing on thick grass that spread out beyond them like a soft, green carpet rolling out to meet the silhouette of distant mountains.

A mare bolted, flying right past Jon. Chaos erupted as the rest followed, converging behind her, their hooves thundering as they raced past. They charged out across the open planes and around a lone tree. There they stopped, eyeing the travelers from afar with a layer of wispy clouds hanging over them set against a brilliant blue sky.

Jon watched the horses for a while in awe as the tree line receded and the closed-in feeling of the forest melted away. He raised his face skyward and took a deep breath, relishing the warm sun as it spilled over him and the gentle breeze that brushed across his face.

He reached down and gave Enna a hug. How was it that in a world so distant from his own, this beast who moved rhythmically under him felt like more of a friend than anyone else? "It's beautiful, isn't it, girl?" he whispered in her ear. He was so busy soaking it all in, he never noticed Dellia drop back next to him.

"You're still upset, aren't you?" she asked with an unexpected note of concern in her voice.

Jon released Enna's neck and sat up as he searched for the right words, trying to put a name to what it was he felt. "No, not exactly. Confused, maybe. Overwhelmed … definitely. Intimidated, oh yeah. And not just by you."

"By me?" Dellia seemed incredulous. "I'm just—"

She halted when Jon sent her a glance that said, *Really?*

"Okay. Yeah, I guess I deserve that. Can you forgive me?"

"Sure. Besides, it's more this whole thing with Megan."

"Well," she said, then seemed hesitant to continue. "I shouldn't say this, but from what I saw back there, I wouldn't give up on her."

"You know, where I come from we have a name for someone who keeps after a woman who's clearly said no. We call them stalkers."

"Yeah, around here we have a name for that, too. We call it asking to get the crap kicked out of ya." Dellia seemed totally serious, but Jon found it impossible not to laugh.

He shot back, "Yeah, I guess you deal with things a little differently here."

Jon gazed ahead as a butterfly fluttered past in the light breeze. Its brilliant orange and black stood out against the pale blue silhouette of far-off peaks. His mood seemed to lift as he soaked in the warm sun and open spaces.

"But she's a friend, too, right?" Dellia asked, snapping Jon's focus back to their discussion.

"Yeah, exactly. My best friend, really, and I don't want to screw that up. And she was pretty clear that it was never going to happen."

"Are you sure? Maybe you misunderstood."

"Well, 'not happening' were her exact words. Twice. She said she wanted someone who was an actual adult. Someone that wanted to make something out of themselves."

"Huh," Dellia said. "I don't see it. All I've seen is someone who knows exactly what he wants and who helps people even when he's afraid. I know what I'd call that."

Jon couldn't help but smile again. Boy did she have him pegged wrong. "No, that's not really me. I think you're confusing helping people with being terrified that something I did might hurt them."

Dellia gave him a sideways glance and shook her head as if he were a child uttering complete nonsense. She smiled and urged her horse on.

"What?" Jon called after her as the slender rider surged ahead through a field of flowers, her sumptuous brown hair tossed by the light breeze. With the backdrop of green fields and faraway mountains, she seemed like something out of a painting. He smiled and urged his horse on after her.

As Jon pulled up alongside Dellia, she glanced at him, then back at the edge of the forest growing smaller behind them. "Well, I thought you might want to know. That tree line back there, that was the end of the Illis Woods. This is Talus, my childhood home."

"So you grew up here?"

"Until my thirteenth year. That's when I moved to Shirdon. When most protectors begin their training."

"At thirteen? And your parents were okay with that?"

"No." Dellia gave a small shake of her head. "My mother didn't want me to go, but in the end, she accepted my decision and made sure I knew that she'd be with me."

Jon stared at her as he tried to recall what he was like at that age. "I don't think I was even equipped to make that kind of decision at thirteen."

"I don't know that you're ever really ready," Dellia said, her voice becoming distant. "At least not until you wake up one day and realize this is what you were put here to do."

"Wow. So you think there's some grand design? That we're all

94

put here for some reason?"

"I didn't say that. You can't look to someone else to give your life purpose. Whatever meaning your life has, that's your choice."

Jon turned his attention ahead while he considered the implications of her words. "Yeah," he said, "that's not intimidating at all."

Dellia smiled and gave him a good-natured shove. "Well, anyway, trust me, my mother made sure I understood what I was doing."

"You haven't mentioned your father."

Dellia flinched and her face clouded over. "He died when I was very young." Her words were short, and she glanced away, as if acutely uncomfortable with the topic. "I never knew him."

Jon studied her as he puzzled over her reaction. Still, it would be impolite to dwell on a subject that seemed to be a source of discomfort. So he proffered the only thing he could. "Oh, I'm sorry."

She seemed to shake it off. "It's hard to miss something you never had." She turned back and granted him a mischievous smile. "Although, perhaps if I grew up with a father, I'd understand *you* a little better."

"Yeah, because I'm so mysterious. It's you I can't figure out."

"I go for long rides in the forest and hit things with a sword. What's not to understand?"

Unsure where to even begin, Jon just smiled and gave Dellia a sideways look as he shook his head. Then, he urged his horse on, trotting out ahead.

"What?" Dellia said as he pulled away.

Garris stared out over the grassy plains, squinting through the bright sun as several birds soared through the skies way out ahead. The weather had been good so far, and the cool breeze that had persisted since they'd reached the plains had been a welcome change. He checked the Alundeer Mountains off in the distance, trying to keep a watch on his bearings. They'd been traveling cross-country so far, but if he wasn't mistaken, they were about to cross one of the many small roads that branched off the Eastern Trail, meandering through the plains like the tributaries of some mighty river.

This was the land of many bloody tales. It was on this very spot that the final battle of The Persecution took place. The combined forces of the other three realms had pushed the Talesh army back through the Illis Woods and converged here to put an end to the Battle of Aima and thirty years of bloody war. It was the last gasp of a corrupt Talesh empire bent on subjugating the world through a rich tradition of slavery, deceit, manipulation, and sheer force. It was the beginning of The Reformation.

While their armies had been off waging war, a swarm of giant, insect-like creatures had descended from the mountain to overrun the capital city of Katapa. The Talus center of commerce, Lanessa, lay behind it and became lost in the carnage. With the fall of their two most important cities, weakened by decades of war, and having earned a reputation as the most despised people in history, the Talesh had been eager to embrace Ellira and her message of a better way.

Garris squinted again, peering at the birds, observing the pattern of their flight with more care. Then, he realized the birds weren't soaring; they were circling. An almost certain sign that some miserable creature had expired and scavengers were now picking it apart. Well, he'd see soon enough.

For a while, the journey had been quite civilized, each of them carrying out their roles in silence, with a minimum of fuss. He had been able to enjoy the trip and focus on the essentials: food, water, shelter, and keeping a close watch for any sign of danger. Sure, there had been a certain awkwardness between Jon and Dellia after she … well, let's call it what it was, after she threatened his life. But these things happen, and it would have blown over … well, actually, it *had* blown over. … If only it had lasted longer.

Since reaching the Talus Plains, that pair had subjected him to hours of nonstop chatter. Dellia grew up here. Jon was clueless. I get it. Could we please, for the love of all that's good and decent, just have a little peace and quiet?

For now, it seemed his bet was paying off. Dellia may not have been grateful as he'd hoped, but she hadn't tried to arrest him, either, which was for the best. Garris knew her to be a fair and honorable protector and had no desire to embarrass her or tarnish her reputation by evading her attempts at capture. She seemed content to let him lend his considerable expertise. So he'd play this out, see where it led.

Garris sat taller in the saddle, ignoring the ceaseless babbling as he squinted through the bright sun. Far off in the distance, below the circling birds, something lay on the ground, obscured by the grass.

"Of course it's beautiful," Jon said. "But I don't know. It's kind of unnerving at the same time. I mean what if you need help out here? There's nobody around for miles."

Garris breathed a heavy sigh as he hunched lower in the saddle. Aw, crap. He kicked hard, and his horse shot forward.

"Well, you're not—" Dellia hushed as Garris blew past her at a gallop.

He raced out ahead of Dellia and Jon. The pounding of their horses' hooves sounded behind him as they broke into a sprint. As he flew toward the scene, he began to make it out in greater detail. Below the birds lay the bodies of people and horses, motionless on the ground.

Carrion birds scattered from the area with a rush of flapping wings as Garris pulled up short and flew from his horse. The odor of death wafted through the soft breeze as he stood, surveying the gruesome scene. Jon and Dellia pulled up beside him and dismounted, appearing shocked and nauseated.

Scattered across the bloodstained grass lay the bodies of a man, a woman, and their two horses. The man's neck was torn open, and jagged teeth marks and ripped flesh covered his throat and chest. The bite marks were those of a carnivore with huge teeth with pronounced canines. Part of the man's leg had been stripped to the bone, as if something had clamped on and pulled hard enough to rip the flesh off.

The woman's neck was twisted into a grotesque and unnatural position, and she lay in a crumpled pile. Her back seemed bent and broken, as if she'd been shaken by a force powerful enough to snap her in two.

A short distance away lay the bodies of the horses. Their legs and necks were riddled with bite marks and blood. From the way the tracks and bodies lined up, it appeared as if they had been pulled down first and their riders thrown clear, then caught in a desperate flight to escape.

Garris had seen grizzly scenes before. He knew how to shut off the sick feeling in the pit of his stomach and focus on what needed doing. But this was almost as disturbing as anything he'd ever witnessed.

"Oh, Adi," came Dellia's quiet voice.

Garris shook his head. The divine had little to do with this unholy scene. He glanced at Jon and Dellia.

She was upset, but managing to handle it. Jon was another matter. He turned pale, staggered away a short distance and bent over, as if on the verge of retching. Garris slid over next to him and placed a hand on his back. To his credit, Jon managed to stifle the impulse and get himself under control.

Garris turned back to the carnage, pushing down his feeling of revulsion, looking past it to piece together what had happened. Dellia followed suit, and the two set about their work with a detached efficiency.

"Wolves," Dellia said as she leaned over the body of the man.

"Extremely large ones."

"Blood Wolves?" Garris asked as he surveyed the mangled bodies.

"They don't come this far from the Alundeer."

"I know, plus they're familiars; they never travel alone."

Dellia scanned the bloody chaos. "Still, I think you're right. The paw prints are definitely canine, and Blood Wolves are the only thing large enough and aggressive enough to do this."

"I count five sets of tracks." Garris turned to Dellia.

She nodded. "If they're this far east, then nobody on the plains is safe. We need to get to my mother. As one of the Ephori, she can send word to Commander Prian, to warn people."

Garris gave a sharp nod, and the two proceeded to make a hurried, but more detailed, assessment of the slaughter. They noted supplies, examined the pattern of the wounds, and checked out the tracks and signs.

Something gnawed at him as he scanned the whole scene.

Then it hit him. He looked down at a set of paw prints leaving the scene. He walked along their path, following them for several steps. He stopped, but kept following them with his eyes, then raised his arm along their route. He glanced back at the sun, then down the path again, estimating where the tracks might lead.

Garris turned to Dellia. "They're headed into the Illis Woods, even farther from the mountains. Where did you find Jon?"

"At the southern edge of the woods."

Garris groaned. *Oh crap, I hate when I'm right.* He motioned with his head and said, "Look where the wolves are headed."

Dellia walked up next to Garris, following the tracks with her gaze. She looked at the sun, then back in the direction of his arm.

"This is bad," Dellia said, half to herself. A flash of revulsion and horror crossed her face. Her head whipped around and she stared at Jon.

Garris glanced over as Jon's expression turned pale and sickly again. Apparently, he understood the implications, too. Those wolves were looking for *him*.

The respectful thing to do would be to bury the bodies, but people's lives were at stake, and they couldn't afford the delay. It was disagreeable, but Garris knew what he needed to do. He spun around and returned to his horse. Fishing through his pack, he located the small, silver, metallic vial. He held it up so Dellia could see its distinctive vaselike shape and the tiny vines etched in its surface. She nodded, so he marched over to the bodies, bowed his head for a moment, then sprinkled a few drops from the vial on each, including the horses.

No sooner did the drops hit the bodies than tiny lime-colored vines began to grow from them. They rooted in the flesh, growing and multiplying, writhing across the bodies, spreading with frightening velocity. Garris had had little chance to use this concoction, and the sight of it still impressed. He glanced at Dellia to see her head bowed in solemn reverence. Jon seemed stunned and a bit nauseated as he watched the rampant growth.

Garris nodded to the expanding vegetation. "It's called Priyal's Pyre."

"Pyre?" Jon asked.

"Just wait."

The vines had nearly covered the bodies, twisting, tightening, thickening. Roots dug deep into the flesh and poked through the other side.

Sprouts shot straight up. At first just a few, then more and more, like a tiny forest rooted in dead flesh. The ends of the shoots arched over, and round pods formed at the tips. The pods grew and matured, turning from lime green to bloodred. They popped open to reveal the most intense vermilion flowers.

A ruby-colored powder dropped from the flowers, and where it settled, it burst into an intense violet flame. Garris glanced at Jon, who still stood staring, his expression one of intense fascination.

"We don't have time to inter the bodies," Garris said. "This is an alternative, but not widely used because it's said to draw its power from necromancy."

"Necromancy?" Jon asked.

Garris stared over at him for a second, not entirely surprised that he would ask. "Yes, a gift. It draws power from the living to spread death."

Powder fell, and the flames grew and spread, covering the entire body, vines and all, raging into an inferno. Flames leaped up taller than Garris, like a strange, bright, violet funeral pyre.

Jon glanced over at him and Dellia as if he were expecting an answer to some unspoken question. Garris just shrugged. Jon glanced again and took a tiny step forward. He reached out and, with tentative care, inched his fingers into the flames. It seemed he'd noticed the lack of heat. The violet inferno enveloped the surrounding vegetation, which, instead of withering and burning, seemed to grow darker and more lush.

The flames became more and more intense, burning with an alarming fury. They leaped and danced, casting a violet hue all around them. The blaze consumed the bodies down to ash. Ash sprang to the sky, spiraling upward twenty, thirty, fifty feet above them, continuing to burn as it danced in the breeze. The fire consumed the swirling ash completely. Until all that remained was a dense, dark-green spot where the bodies had lain.

Garris returned to his horse, and the three mounted and set off again across the plains. The sun was still bright, the breeze refreshing, and a handful of birds still circled through the sky as the three traveled on in silence once more. He had wanted things to be quieter. He'd wanted a little less chatter, but never like this. Because, this time, it wasn't the awkward silence of before, but a silence born of the horrific scene they'd all witnessed and the disturbing suspicion that the wolves' aim may have been to deliver a similar fate to Jon.

Dellia reached down and fetched her water skin, then lifted it to her lips, taking a short drink of warm water. She patted her horse as she put her water back in place and gazed out over the open grassy plains, scanning for signs of her childhood home. She checked the sun, now hanging low in the sky, partially hidden behind a light layer of red clouds. It was nearing evening, and she hoped to be home soon and see her mother's welcome face.

It had been a long time since anyone had mentioned her father. Most who knew her avoided the subject. The tragedy at Githeo was beyond her remembering, but she grew up in a world of those who had lost loved ones due to her father's selfish actions, and it had made her a pariah. With few friends and surrounded by smiling faces that hid deep-seated feelings of resentment, the choice to serve as a protector had been all the more appealing. At least in Shirdon she could find redemption and regain some small sliver of honor.

From behind Dellia came the quiet thumping of Jon's horse's hooves, and farther back Garris's, but curiosity compelled her to check on them nonetheless. Jon was clinging to Enna, his face solemn, still appearing shook-up from the grisly scene he'd been forced to witness. Garris sat tall in the saddle, calm and controlled, his face as unreadable as ever.

A vague sense of unease had followed her ever since the wolf attack. Her instinct was to embrace it, to *use* it. Instead, she tried to shake it, but it stubbornly refused to give way. So she'd frittered away the hours attempting to distract herself with thoughts of returning home. Her mother standing in the yard welcoming her with open arms while her giant wire-haired dog, Tilla, greeted her like a long-lost friend.

DELLIA

She imagined waking up in her old bed to the aroma of Mom making breakfast. Or her mother stifling a laugh while she chastised Dellia for slipping Tilla tidbits from her plate. She could almost see the two of them laughing as they played a game of *chelchi* across the kitchen table. Or sitting in front of a warm fire sharing the latest gossip, with Tilla's head heavy in her lap.

There wasn't much she would change about her life if she could, but seeing her mother more often was one. Family was paramount to her, as it was to most of her people. She tried to get home every chance she could, but opportunities were rare, and many months had passed since she'd seen her.

Dellia took in a deep breath of fresh air while she scanned the green fields, searching for one of the signposts that marked the edge of her mother's land. She caught sight of one up ahead, near a patch of scrubby brush. They were easy to recognize by the symbol of a stone tower painted on the surface. A mark signifying the importance of her mother's position in the realm's government.

As Dellia passed the signpost, she looked out across the open fields of green grass and flowers she used to play in as a child. She'd spent endless hours there chasing down wild horses, juggling sticks and stones, or having mock sword fights with a group of local dogs. Sometimes she would sit on the front porch as night fell and watch the fireflies float up out of the grassy field and drift through the darkened sky.

Yielding to her impatience, she sped up as the large stone house came into view with its nearby guesthouse and stables. They were just as she remembered them. All three constructed of light-colored cut stones of varying shapes and sizes and topped with overlapping wooden shingles. Several fireplaces adorned the two houses, and their stone chimneys were quite distinctive. They poked up well above the roofline, giving the impression of little towers.

In the yard, garbed in her distinctive burnt-umber leather over a deep-green robe and leaning against the well, stood Rillen, Dellia's apprentice. Although it probably wasn't fair to call her that anymore. Ceree, one of the council members, had taken a particular interest in her, often sending her on missions of which Dellia had no knowledge. It appeared this was one, too, because Dellia wasn't expecting her, at all. A sudden flash of irritation struck at the realization that the council had most likely sent the girl to check up on her. As if she needed monitoring—and by her own apprentice, of all people! She tried to put that out of her mind and not let it spoil the moment.

As they rode up, the door to the main house swung open and her beautiful mother, Sirra, ambled out, a broad smile on her face. Her favorite shawl of rose was draped over a long white chiton that trailed behind her as she raced out across the yard. Tilla followed, pacing and circling her mother as she strolled up to greet them.

Dellia slid off her horse and raced up to her mother. Sirra's smile grew even wider, and she opened her arms wide. Dellia stepped forward into her mother's strong embrace. She stayed there a moment, letting the feeling wash over her.

When Dellia let go, her mother stepped back, and Tilla took her turn. She slid between them and leaned against Dellia. Her mother placed a gentle hand on her daughter's cheek and smiled as she gazed into her eyes, as if trying to memorize the moment.

"I missed you," Dellia said, barely managing her composure.

Sirra grabbed her again, embracing her even more firmly.

When she stepped back, Sirra turned to Garris and smiled. Then she strolled over to him and gave him a brief hug. "Garris, I wasn't sure I'd ever see your sour face again."

Apparently, he knew Mom. A fact he'd neglected to share. Not that it was a surprise. He didn't seem like the sharing type.

Garris smiled, and Dellia stared in shock. This man, who'd scarcely said a word the whole trip, suddenly seemed charming.

"Well, I couldn't let a little banishment stop me from seeing you again, Sirra," Garris said, acting nonchalant.

Sirra smiled. Then her expression turned serious. "Elt?" she said as if it were some secret code word between them.

Garris nodded.

Dellia straightened in surprise. What was that about?

Sirra turned to Jon. She planted her hands on her hips and eyed him with suspicion, looking him up and down quite thoroughly.

Dellia watched as a feeling of dread filled her mother, as deep as any she could recall. She was practiced in ignoring her gift. The Gift of the Heart, it was called. To sense what other people were feeling was a tremendous responsibility. From the time she was a little girl, she had learned to guard against its abuse, and the easiest way was to tune it out. To pay little attention to what her gift told her about other people's feelings. Besides, a lifetime of experience had taught her that eavesdropping on her mother's emotions rarely ended well. Only this time, her reaction was too strong to ignore.

Dellia waited for some explanation, but after a moment, Sirra seemed to shrug it off. She turned back to Garris, flashing him a skeptical look.

He simply shrugged his shoulders and smiled, but when he noticed Dellia and Jon gawking at him, he snapped back to his normal unreadable expression.

Jon, who'd witnessed the whole exchange, seemed as baffled as she felt.

After a moment, Dellia glanced around and realized *everyone* was staring at her. Of course. She was being impolite for not making the customary introductions. "Um … Jon, this is my apprentice, Rillen, and my mother, Sirra. Mom, this is Jon. I'm helping him. I was hoping he could stay here for a few days."

Sirra nodded, then addressed Jon. "I'll show you to the guest-house while Garris puts away the horses. You two can stay there as long as you like." Sirra glanced over at her daughter. "Dellia can have her old room with Rillen."

Garris gathered the reins of the horses and strolled off toward the stables while Sirra ushered Jon to the guesthouse. Dellia wished she could eavesdrop on that conversation. Perhaps he would ask Mom how she knew Garris or why she'd given him such a thorough looking-over. But there was no time. Dellia grabbed Rillen and let her annoyance flood back as she marched her toward the main house. They were going to have a little discussion.

Chapter Seven

RECLUSE DEBATE

Jon struggled to keep up as Sirra rushed him toward the small, stone guesthouse. He was exhausted and sore from the long day's journey, not to mention the two days of insanity before that, and he had to wonder what the hurry was. Maybe Sirra was just one of those people who rush through life with a certain sense of urgency, as if she wouldn't know what to do with herself if she weren't perpetually busy. Or maybe she was eager to talk to him. Something to do with that uncomfortable looking-over she'd given him.

Sirra scurried up onto the wide, stone steps and flung open the front door, waiting for Jon to enter. As he hurried past, he glanced over at her. The family resemblance was unmistakable: rich brown hair, blue eyes, slender, and her face similar to Dellia's, though older, obviously. And there was also that air of quiet confidence that seemed to follow Dellia, the impression that nothing could ever alter her sense of who she was.

As he stepped into the guesthouse, a single, large room greeted him, dimly lit by the late-day sun peeping through the cracks of the closed shutters. Two sturdy, wooden beds lurked in the shadows at either end of the room, each accompanied by its own modest table and dresser. And between them loomed a broad, stone fireplace.

Jon stepped aside, and Sirra brushed past. He rushed to follow her as she marched across the smooth wooden floor. The door clattered shut behind them as she arrived at one of the three small windows set around the room. She yanked the shutters inward, and the amber rays spilled into the room, brightening the stone walls of warm yellow mixed with rose and gray.

The new light revealed a mantle strewn with colorful flower petals and dried seeds, probably responsible for the faint fragrance of lilac and spices that hung in the air.

Sirra turned her head, addressing Jon behind her while she lashed the shutters to the wall. "So, Jon, where are you from?"

"Hard to describe. Can we just say I'm from far away?"

"Hmm ..." There was a certain judgmental quality to her tone that was disquieting. She hurried around him on her way to the second window. Without looking at him, she asked, "So what brings you here?"

"I'm trying to get home. Dellia said she'd help."

"Hmm ..." Sirra said again as she swung open the second set of shutters and fastened them in place. There was that tone again. She turned, staring straight at Jon, her silhouette dark against the sunlit yard visible through the window. Her expression was cold and her voice flat and matter-of-fact. "Don't take this the wrong way, but I don't like you. And if my daughter hadn't promised to help you, I'd show you the door."

Sirra took off toward the last window as Jon stood there, stunned. After an awkward moment, he recovered. "Gee, how could I take that the wrong way? What have I done?"

Sirra paused, as if struck by Jon's words. She took a breath, then pulled the shutters open. "Most likely nothing, but there's something going on here. Garris isn't here by accident, and Dellia's job isn't helping strangers find their way home. Whatever's happening, it's probably big and dangerous, and you're going to get people killed."

"What?" Jon said as he stared in astonishment. "Me? That's the last thing I'd ever want ... ever. Trust me."

As she was passing him, Sirra stopped and drew close. She

stared at him with hard eyes, and her voice had a disturbing edge to it. "Then stay away from Dellia and Garris."

Jon stood there dumbstruck while Sirra marched to a simple, wooden cupboard, yanked it open, and snatched a neat stack of bedding. Her reaction was way over the top and her explanation not entirely convincing. To elicit such acute fear, there had to be something more substantial than just the presence of Garris and Dellia.

Even so, her distress was real and the compulsion to explain eventually took over. "Look, I'm not stupid. I know something is going on, but I couldn't begin to tell you what it is. I haven't been able to make sense out of much since I got here. Honestly."

"Hmm ..."

"You keep saying that."

Sirra placed the stack of bedding at the base of the bed. "Whatever's going on, it involves the council. I don't like them or trust them."

"Wait. I don't get it." No sooner had the words left his mouth than he regretted them.

Sirra halted and moved uncomfortably close again. "What don't you get?" she asked, the edginess saturating her voice.

"Sorry, it's none of my business, forget I said anything."

"Spit it out."

Jon spoke with reluctance. "Well, you don't trust the council, yet you let Dellia go work for them, at thirteen?"

The question seemed to strike her with unexpected force. Her brusque facade faded, and the judgmental tone was absent from her halfhearted response. "You've seen her. Do you think I could stop her?"

"You mean she was like this at thirteen?"

Sirra turned and slumped onto the unmade bed. She sat for a moment staring into space, then glanced up at Jon with a mournful look in her eyes. "You know her job. Protectors die young. Chances are I'll outlive my daughter. No parent should outlive their child. She'll probably never fall in love, never have children. You think I wanted that for her?"

Jon's remorse was profound. He turned and lowered himself next to her on the bed. "No, I just—"

"But Ellira teaches us that family is all. That we are honor bound to put them first. So it was my most important job, my sacred duty, to make sure she was ready to face the world, to accept how the world works, to be strong but kind, to stand on her own two feet and make her own decisions. So how could I stop her when that's exactly what she did?"

"I'm sorry, I didn't mean anything. Really."

"Hmm …" she said again, only this time there was no judgment at all in her tone, just a hint of sadness.

Jon lowered his head, studying the wear marks on the floor as he considered how to reassure her. He glanced over at Sirra sitting next to him on the small bed. Then he leaned forward so he could gaze up into her downturned face. "Look, if there's danger to face, I'll face it alone. I meant it when I said I don't want anyone getting hurt because of me. *Never again.*"

There was a finality in those last two words that must have caught her off guard. She eyed Jon for a moment with a puzzled look on her face. Then her expression softened, and she managed a smile as she patted his hand and gave him a gentle nod of her head.

Dellia barged through the door of her old room. She stormed across the worn wood floor, past her small bed and simple dresser, both right where they should be. In fact, her whole room appeared neat, well cared for, and precisely as she had left it. Under any other circumstances, it would have made her smile, but not now, not today.

She paused at the small wooden table under the window,

admiring its elaborate inlay of a galloping horse, crafted from various types and shades of wood. She loved that table, and it was wrapped up in so many warm memories, but even that couldn't lift her mood.

It had been difficult enough sneaking off to communicate with the council without Jon catching her. Now with Garris, who'd wake at the slightest disturbance, it was frustratingly impossible. The whole situation with him was like walking a burning tightrope. It would sabotage her mission to arrest him since she'd have to lug him around or haul him in. And it would be wrong, on so many levels, to kill him or to get hurt trying. Besides, she remained convinced he had a valuable part to play, and she'd learn more by letting things play out.

So she'd held off mentioning Garris to the council. But now with Rillen here, the whole situation had become a tangled mess. She didn't need someone watching her every move and informing on her to the council so they could berate her for doing everything wrong.

Dellia spun around as her protégé strolled through the door. As aggravating as Rillen could be, the same qualities that made her annoying also made her an extraordinary apprentice and sparring partner. She was as much a contradiction as the abalone hair clip that held back her golden-blond hair but also doubled as a deadly weapon. Capable of being shy and demure or bright and bubbly one moment, in an instant she could turn lethal. She was skilled in many fighting styles so it was impossible to tell where, or when, or how she'd strike.

Dellia's young apprentice stepped aside and leaned back against the stone wall, calmly waiting. Somehow, her placid expression was even more annoying.

Dellia jerked the pack off her shoulder and flung it into the corner behind the small table under the window. A small sigh drew her attention. When she glanced up, she caught Rillen shaking her head and staring up at the wooden planks that spanned the ceiling. She noticed Dellia and ceased. Her gaze drifted down from above, and she smiled as her deep blue eyes stared at Dellia, acting innocent and attentive.

"I'm getting enough pressure from the council without them sending you to spy on me," Dellia said as she stormed back across the wooden floor.

"Nobody's spying. I was sent to help."

"Help with what?" She continued strutting back and forth. "Escorting a harmless, heartbroken guy around Talus? Yeah, that requires two protectors."

Rillen replied in a bored monotone, as if reciting her orders. "I'm supposed to help you in any way I can. And see if you've learned anything about Megan before I try to track her down."

Dellia shook her head. "I don't even know why they want me to stay with him. There's nothing here."

Rillen darted into Dellia's path, interrupting her pacing. "Hey, what's up with you? You wouldn't be this upset over a pointless mission."

Frustrated, Dellia glared at Rillen. Was she asking to have that calm expression wiped off her face? Dellia took a deep breath while she studied Rillen's earnest countenance. The reasons for her disquiet were not to be found there.

Dellia lowered her head as her irritation faded and her mood softened. "They know the people of Talus," she said. "They know our code. How could they ask me to violate that?"

Rillen put a hand on each of Dellia's shoulders and gazed into her eyes. "I don't know what you're talking about, Dellia, but nobody has a better grasp of right and wrong than you do. Ignore the council. Do what you think is right."

Dellia shook her head. *Well so much for being a great mentor.* She glanced out the small window at the quaint guesthouse across the yard. Her dilemma was beyond anyone's ability to help. It was a question of conscience and duty, and Rillen had no part in it.

Dellia managed a small smile and chided her softly. "As my apprentice, I find your grasp of the whole chain-of-command concept appalling."

Undeterred, Rillen continued, "I know you think you have to follow the council's orders to the letter. You always have. But there's power in being right. Do the right thing. The council will have to accept it."

Her sincerity was touching, and Dellia gave her a brief hug. "Thanks," she said, pulling back. "I appreciate what you're trying to do. I just don't know if it's that simple."

It seemed odd being indoors again after several days on the road, and Jon wondered if it was like this for Dellia all the time. Sirra had whipped up a small supper for the travelers, which they'd devoured at the kitchen table in the main house. They all seemed tired, and the meal went by with little chatter. Evening had settled in by the time they parted, each destined for their respective rooms.

Headed for the guesthouse, Jon stepped outside, and the sight before him stopped him in his tracks: thousands of fireflies drifting up off of the field and into the night sky. Garris just grumbled some offhand remark about bugs as he passed, then marched off across the yard.

Jon plopped down on the cool, stone porch, staring out over the fields. He'd seen fireflies before, but these were composed of several colors, all swirled together: emerald green, amber, and fuchsia. He let himself relax, enjoying the brisk night air while he soaked in the croaking of frogs and the chirping of crickets. He lingered there for a long time, gazing at the flashing curtain of swirling light as it drifted through the evening sky. It was the first time since he'd arrived in this upside-down world that he felt calm and at peace.

When Jon finally strolled through the guesthouse door, Garris had already made his bed and was crouched at the fireplace arranging logs and kindling with care. The temperature outside was cooling off at a rapid pace, and it seemed likely that before long, a fire would be welcome. Jon strolled to his bed and snapped up the rather large pile of bedding. He placed it on the nearby table and set to work making his bed.

After a moment, Garris struck up a conversation. "So now that we're in Talus, how do you plan to find this piece you're looking for? Talus is a big place."

"Oh, I know where it is. It's at the top of some place called the Recluse Tower." Jon was so focused on his task he hardly noticed the man freeze and drop what he was doing.

Garris slowly turned to face Jon. "The Recluse Tower?"

"Yeah, sounds like a hermit lives there or something."

Garris strolled over to the bed and stared at Jon. Slowly and with a distinct emphasis, he said, "I doubt it. Since nobody who goes in there ever comes out."

Jon stopped and looked up at Garris, and his face had a deadly serious expression. It was a bit scary, actually.

"Nobody?" Jon said as he stood and faced him over the bed.

"Nobody."

"So you're saying if I go in there, I might die?"

"No. You *will* die."

Garris's certainty hit like a sledgehammer, and his heart dropped through the floor and into a deep, dark pit of despair. The tower was his only chance to get home, and Garris was sure it was impossible. Jon felt his entire world crumbling. This couldn't be. His mind raced. Why would Isla set him on this path? Was she unaware of the danger? No. She was intelligent, wise even. Why would she send him to his death? How would that possibly benefit her? Could it all be just a cruel joke?

Suddenly, through the swirling chaos of questions, Megan's words echoed through Jon's thoughts: *"If you find a way home, then don't let anyone or anything stop you."* He pictured her in those final moments in his lab, her screams as she was dragged into the dark mass. He had made a decision then, to follow her through. Even if it killed him. So how could he give up now? How could he strand her in a strange world of unknown dangers without even trying to get her home? If there was even the slightest possibility that Isla was right and Garris wrong, he had to take that chance.

Jon leaned in toward Garris. "It doesn't matter. I have to go."

"Well, then you're a fool because you're going to find it pretty hard to get home when you're dead."

Jon glared at him, only vaguely aware of Dellia slipping through the door or drifting to the end of the bed, drawn in by the tense exchange.

"You don't know that. I could be the first."

"You're right," Garris said, his voice dripping with sarcasm. "Everyone's been going about this all wrong. How stupid. They've been sending their fiercest and most capable warriors when they should have sent an incompetent dimwit."

"Call me whatever you want, it doesn't matter. I'm going."

"Why should I try to stop you? If your life means so little to you, then why should it matter to me?"

"No, getting *home* means that much, and this is the only plan I've got."

"What *plan*?" Garris shot back. "To be a *plan*, you'd actually have to have some clue what you're doing. As it is, it's just foolhardy, reckless, and idiotic. But far be it from me to pass judgment on your irresponsible and boneheaded *plan*."

"Wow," Jon said. "Do you work at that vocabulary or do just have a natural talent for insults?"

Garris smirked. "It's really more of a calling."

"It fits your personality, combative and caustic."

Garris's hard stare returned. "Now who's slinging insults?"

"Compared to you I'm an amateur."

"No, you're just making it easy."

Jon stood studying Garris's annoyed expression, their debate at an apparent standstill.

Dellia leaned over the bed, and both Jon and Garris turned to her. She eyed the two. "Not that this torrent of insults isn't amusing, but what are we talking about?"

Garris seemed more than happy to explain. "Jon here, of minimal fighting skills, wants to go to the top of the Recluse Tower."

Dellia shook her head. "Well, that's not happening."

Jon threw up his hands. "Why are people always telling me that?"

"That tower's killed everyone who's gone into it for the last seven hundred years." Dellia motioned to Garris. "It's killed people far more skilled than Garris."

"Or *you*," Garris chimed in.

"Well, let's not get carried away," Dellia shot back.

"So that's it," Jon said. "No discussion. No concept of free will."

"Well, in human society we generally frown on suicide," Dellia said.

Jon reached inside his shirt, yanked out the medallion, and shoved it forward, holding it out for Dellia to see. "I need to reassemble this, and the first piece is in that tower. It's the only way I can get me and Megan home."

"No. No. The answer is no. I can't let you face it alone, and I won't watch you die in there."

"I'm not asking you or anyone else to go with me. In fact, I don't want you there. This is my life, and I should be able to do with it as I see fit."

Dellia put her hand on the hilt of her sword. "What part of no is unclear? You're not going. End of story."

Jon whipped around and stormed out of the room, out into the crisp night air. The sound of crickets chirping and frogs croaking drifted in from the nearby fields as he gazed up at the night sky, trying to get a handle on his frustration. This was completely unfair. It was his life. What gave Dellia the right to tell him what he could and couldn't do? He wasn't a child.

The door opened and closed behind him, and footsteps approached across the lawn. He sensed Dellia was standing right behind him. His instinct was to say something, to convince her, but he bit his tongue. He didn't want to polarize the situation further. He didn't want to say something out of frustration he'd regret later.

Eventually, Dellia spoke. "You're going to die ..."

There was a pleading quality in her voice that tugged at his heart. He closed his eyes, fighting back the temptation to tell her whatever was needed to make it okay. He turned to Dellia and faced her.

The concern that filled her face made it all the harder, but Jon responded with all the calm he was able to muster. "I know you think that, Dellia, but I know I can do it. I'm going do it."

"How? What makes you so sure?"

"I wish I could explain. ... Look, your mother, she could have stopped you from becoming a protector, but she didn't, even when she was afraid it might kill you someday. Because she raised you to stand on your own two feet, make your own decisions."

Dellia seemed moved by his argument, but she just shook her head. "I'm sorry. I'm not that strong."

With that, she turned and walked off, and all Jon could do was stand and stare. A thousand bright fireflies flashed and drifted through the night sky behind Dellia as she strolled back to the main house and disappeared.

Jon closed his eyes and breathed a deep sigh. There was no

escaping what he needed to do. But he hated it. They were the only two people he really knew in this world. And they had helped him, asking nothing in return. He hated the very idea of it, of ignoring Garris and defying Dellia, but he had no choice.

Chapter Eight

THE TEETH OF BLOOD

Faint light spilled from her room, down the hall, and into the darkened kitchen, casting long, angular shadows through the table and chairs. Dellia lingered in that kitchen trying to untangle the small knot in her stomach. It was past the time for her to check in with Kayleen, and the compulsion to do her duty pressed upon her. But with Rillen in her room, this was one of the few places where she could be alone with her thoughts.

She slumped into one of the chairs, staring into the shadows, searching them for answers. The Recluse Tower, of all places. She shuddered. It was ancient, having once been the southernmost watchtower for the great city of Katapa, back when it stood as the thriving capital of the Talesh empire. But that was before the city had been overrun and abandoned.

Its makers had erected the stone edifice at the base of the Alundeer Mountains. And the speculation was that something dark and hideous from deep within had taken up residence and would kill anyone who dared venture inside. The only stories that survived were from observers some distance away when a poor soul entered. They told of awful noises and screams that reverberated along the mountain base.

If only she could make Jon see. He was acting like a reckless child, blithely ignoring everyone's warnings as he drove headlong to his inevitable doom. What part of "suicide" wasn't sinking in?

Except, to be fair, Jon hadn't exactly *ignored* the warnings. It was clear he was afraid, petrified even. He was just irrationally determined. At another time or place, or in another person, she might have admired the bravery. But this wasn't bravery; this was foolishness. She had to stop him.

Words were not going to do it. Her quarrel with Jon had only served to strengthen his resolve. Perhaps if she told Kayleen, the council would have her arrest him. That would stop him. Or at least buy time so she could get through to him ... if he didn't hate her too much. It bothered her, the notion that he might hate her, but she could live with that if it saved his life. It was worth a try, and with her report to Kayleen overdue, now would be the time.

Dellia took a deep breath and rose from her chair. Then she hurried down the narrow hall, back to her small room.

Rillen's deep blue eyes looked up from her book as Dellia barged through the door. She'd been resting on the floor, propped against the wall, reading by the soft glow of a small, glass sphere resting on a nearby table. She thought she'd recognized the dark ball on their arrival. It was sitting out on the surface of the porch, collecting daylight. Now the sunstone was giving it all back, splashing muted sunlight all around her old familiar room, creating a sharp contrast of soft-lighted stone jutting out of deep shadow.

Rillen set down her book on the worn wood floor and watched with interest as Dellia stormed to her pack and rifled through it. In it, she found the smooth, shiny metal rod, about the length of her arm, and snatched it up. She carried the Window of Rhina over to the small table under the now-shuttered window and positioned it with care, lengthwise on the table's surface. She stopped for a moment to admire the inlay of a galloping horse as she ran her fingers over it, caressing its smoothness with her fingertips.

Dellia turned her attention back to the bar, adjusting its position. "He wants to go into the Recluse Tower."

"What did you tell him?" Rillen asked.

"I said no, of course, but he's no fool. If he wants to go, he'll find a way. I can't watch him forever."

Rillen grinned. "A little while ago, you were saying you didn't even know why you were watching him at all."

Dellia glared back. "Not helping, Rillen."

She leaned over the table and exhaled onto the rod. It seemed to draw in her soft breath, then release it. The breath rose from the bar's silver surface, like a delicate mist. The mist became denser and denser, forming a sheet that drifted up off the bar, dissipating an arm's length above it. A faint smell, like the air after a storm, wafted through the room as a hint of an image appeared out of the fog.

Rillen moved closer, drawn in by the scene gathering focus in the coalescing haze. As it solidified, the image became recognizable as the inside of Kayleen's austere chambers. Dellia sat and adjusted her position, centering herself in front of the image. Then she waited, anxious and impatient, while it clarified, becoming like a reflection in a shimmering sheet of water hovering over the bar.

The sound of approaching footsteps emanated from the scene, and Kayleen appeared. She promptly seated herself and spoke first. "So, have you learned any more of Megan's whereabouts?"

"No. I still think Jon's telling the truth. He doesn't know where she is." Dellia paused for a second, waiting for Kayleen's next orders, but when none came, she forged ahead. "There's something new. We found a man and woman set upon by what appear to be Blood Wolves. Sirra is having Prian alert people in the area, but the wolves seemed headed to where I found Jon."

Kayleen glanced away, and her reply was drawn out, as if digesting Dellia's words. "Interesting, but not surprising."

"There's more." Dellia rushed the words out. "Jon seems determined to go into the Recluse Tower. There's something there he believes can get him home."

Kayleen responded with casual indifference. "Well, I guess if he did, it would end all debate over which of the two to focus on."

Dellia straightened. "This is a man's life we're talking about."

"I know, but what would you have me— Wait. Don't tell me you're considering helping him."

"No. No. I …" A sudden inspiration struck Dellia.

"Good." Kayleen nodded, then tilted her head and stared.

Dellia lowered her gaze as the thought began to organize itself in her mind. There was a distasteful deviousness to the scheme, but it might save a man's life. And with that seed of a plan, her small knot unwound, just a little.

She turned her attention back to Kayleen. "I may have an idea. Perhaps there's a way to dissuade him."

"Very well, do whatever you think is best." Kayleen waved it off as if it were a trivial matter. "Is there anything else?"

Dellia shook her head.

"Thanks." Kayleen got up from her seat. "I don't think any of this changes anything, but I'll have to discuss it with the council." She pushed in her chair as if preparing to leave, then stopped and smiled. She gazed at Dellia with the fondness of a cherished friend. "And Dellia, take care of yourself, okay? Don't go and do anything foolish."

Dellia forced a smile as Kayleen's hand passed through the shimmering scene. The image shattered into myriad tiny, colored droplets that splashed across the table and floor, where they rapidly faded into nothingness.

Dellia shook her head. "I swear, she'd just as soon he died because it would solve her problem."

"You're just now seeing that?" Rillen said.

"I have an idea how to stop Jon, but I'll need you to find me an oracle." Dellia granted her a mischievous smile.

A questioning look spread across Rillen's face as Dellia motioned her to come closer.

Kayleen's footsteps echoed around her as she marched along the colorful marble floor, down the long hallway toward the council chamber. She had sent word to Braye and Ceree to meet her there before the rest of the council arrived. In this matter, they would be the two most influential members. And if she swayed them, so that all three presented a unified front, the rest of the council would almost certainly fall in line.

Kayleen gazed past the rows of glowing lanterns that lined the hallway at this time of night, watching her shadows dance backward along the wall as she pushed forward. The way they flittered away more quickly the faster she rushed ahead seemed a reminder of the struggle that lay before her.

It had scarcely been a couple of days, with barely a hint of what might be unfolding. Yet already the impatient on the council were clamoring for action. All because of a shortsighted obsession with controlling the uncontrollable. With managing the playing out of an enigmatic, old prophecy that most likely didn't even apply here.

No, a few arcane scribblings were not what mattered now. What mattered were the concrete actions the council was contemplating and their very real consequences. And those actions were a repeat of the same lack of restraint they had displayed fifteen years ago, which had led to her sister's death. Not a day went by that she didn't feel the hole in her heart where Leanna used to live.

And Leanna wasn't the only casualty. She had sent her ambitious young protector into just such a situation, where there was no clarity on what forces might become entangled in the affair. Yet, the council had been determined they could control events, and when they were proven wrong, they had been incapable of seeing their actions as anything but necessary. Unable to comprehend that they were to blame, they had to find a scapegoat. The terrible image of that young protector's pained face was indelibly seared into her memory as she was forced to banish a man whose only aspiration had ever been to be a hero.

The fear that history was repeating itself had haunted her since the moment Dellia had reported the presence of this mysterious pair. And the prospect that one she regarded as a daughter might suffer the same fate as her young protector filled her with dread.

How could the council not see how reckless this course could be? Her sister Leanna had spent her youth researching just this type of situation and she was sure of two things: every human on Thera was descended from those who came from another world, and gifts were always the strongest in the newly arrived. Myths often have some basis in fact, and her beliefs fit the Erdish ones around a world they called Prith. If true, that meant Megan's gift was extraordinarily dangerous, and they weren't even sure yet if Jon possessed one.

Even more treacherous were the Blood Wolves. They meant that unknown forces, of unknown strength, with an unknown intent, might draw these two into a maelstrom. Left to her own devices, Dellia was capable of navigating those currents, but the council had already ordered her to spy on a man of unknown power, and protectors can't use their better judgment with the council directing them to march into the heart of a storm.

Equally precarious was that someone or something with an unknown agenda had set Jon on a path with unforeseeable repercussions. Dellia had reported that he was being highly secretive about it all, but with time, her sincerity and compassion would gain the man's confidence, and she would learn what she must. The council's arrogance in directing her to betray the man's trust was frighteningly shortsighted and self-indulgent. It endangered the only relationship the council had that could give them insight into all that was unfolding.

So here Kayleen was again, fighting the rest of the council, struggling to buy Dellia more time, to let things play out in the field, to see where events took them. With time would come clarity. And with two protectors involved, she remained confident they would handle whatever might happen. Braye, in particular, was much less trusting. He was never one to grasp the subtleties of a situation. He'd want to eliminate variables and control things. Or simply club the problem into submission. Convincing him would be the challenge.

As she flew through the last of the stone archways into the council chamber, Kayleen spied Braye and Ceree settled at the long, marble table. The pair were leaning over its dark, polished surface engaged in a quiet, yet animated discussion. This was bad. They might arrive at some undesirable consensus before she even got there. If they ganged up on her, it could polarize the discussion, making her task much more challenging. She'd have to play her cards with care. Get them to question their current plan, then hit them with the news.

As she approached, their hushed conversation ceased, and they looked up at her. Ceree smiled that warm smile of hers that matched her gracious heart. She always appeared so soft and innocent with her long, mahogany braid draped over one shoulder. Yet behind her matching dark brown eyes lay a sharp intellect and will of steel.

"I wanted to speak to you before the full council arrives." Kayleen paused as she eyed the pair. "I've just spoken to Dellia."

"Is Rillen still there?" Ceree asked.

"Yes. I saw her. I don't know if she's learned anything from Dellia, though. Dellia is convinced Jon doesn't know where Megan is."

"Then did you have Dellia arrest him?" Braye interjected.

Well, that clarifies his agenda. Kayleen smiled and said, "No, the timing didn't seem right. And I wanted to consult with the council first."

"Why take chances? Have Dellia arrest him. Bring him in right away. We can deal with Megan later."

"I agree," Ceree added.

Well, there was the consensus she dreaded. This was going to be tricky.

Kayleen gave a shake of her head. "While he's a guest at Sirra's house? She's one of the Ephori, one of their leaders. And she's not going to take kindly to us snatching her guests from under her nose. She could turn many in Talus against us."

It was a valid point, but not terribly persuasive. Still, it might soften their view a little.

"So what?" Braye said in his arrogant tone. "People have short attention spans. So they'll be upset for a while. Until the next controversy appears. And if none appears, we can create one."

Kayleen cringed. He was right. But it was a blatant political game, and it bothered her that anyone on the council would advocate taking advantage of the public. She sent Braye a disapproving stare and continued.

"What about the Verod? They could use this to damage the council."

Braye scoffed. "Please. Why would any of us take an impotent resistance movement seriously?"

"Have you also forgotten the Augury? They are far from impotent. They speak with the authority of oracles. Theirs is an almost religious influence. If they were to involve themselves, they could cause untold damage, turn most of Elore against us. And that won't just blow over."

A pause ensued as Ceree studied her reflection in the table's polished surface while Braye stroked the salt-and-pepper stubble of his chin.

"True," he said.

"But that's not why I wanted to speak to you," Kayleen continued. "I came to tell you that Jon seems determined to enter the Recluse Tower. He seems to think there's something there that can get him home."

There was another long pause and more chin-stroking while Kayleen let the implications sink in.

"Interesting." Braye nodded his bald head. "That could clarify things considerably. If he really has no idea where Megan is, he's of little use to us, and when he fails, we'll have one less thing to worry about."

"And if he succeeds?" Ceree asked.

Braye almost chuckled as he spoke. "Where dozens of others have perished?"

Kayleen smiled. "Then he goes home, and half our problem is solved."

Braye gave a dismissive wave of his hand. "I say, let him try. We can revisit this after he leaves Sirra's house."

Ceree looked thoughtful. "Agreed."

Kayleen granted the pair a decisive nod. "Then we are all agreed."

And there it was. With these two on her side, the outcome was all but assured. Kayleen wanted to smile. It was precisely the consensus she'd hoped for. It was the wisest possible course, given the perilous path they had already set for the people of Meerdon. But she didn't want to betray her sense of satisfaction. Instead, she adopted her usual dispassionate yet cheerful exterior as she turned and seated herself in the large, straight chair at the head of the table. She smiled to herself as the sound of footsteps echoed through the hall and the remaining council members filtered in.

Jon lay alert and still in the darkened room, studying every crack and feature of the pale stones that comprised the wall. Heat from the dying embers warmed his back, their settling the only sound breaking the near silence as he listened and waited.

At first, he had lain motionless, straining to catch every minuscule noise coming from the bed opposite him, waiting for sleep to take Garris and all movement to cease. Then, he waited several minutes more, alert to any sign of snoring, but none came. So he shifted his focus to Garris's breathing. It had slowed now, becoming shallow and regular. If he wasn't asleep, it was an exceptional imitation.

Tense and alert, Jon began inching his way out of bed, careful to avoid even the slightest sound. With excruciating slowness, he pulled himself up and placed one bare foot, then the other, on the cold, wooden floor.

Straining against the tiniest creak, he shifted his weight, little by little, from the bed to the ground until he was standing. Then, footfall by painstaking footfall, he crept across the floor. Without a sound, he lifted his bag and gathered his clothes and shoes. Then he slunk to the door, eased it open, slid outside, and inched it closed.

As soon as his hand left the door, all the tension drained from his body, and he began to breathe normally again. The night air was nippy, and goose bumps prickled his skin as he set down his bag and slipped on his clothes.

Jon glanced around the yard, getting his bearings. The houses and stables were lit by the soft glow of an almost full moon, and everything around him stood eerily still. He quietly scooped up his bag and headed for the stables. The dew on the grass left his bare feet cold and wet as he stepped across the yard.

He paused at the stump that served as a chopping block and sat to don his shoes. He rested a hand on the cold metal of the axe next to him, buried in the stump. Moonlight bathed the rustic stone house as he stared at it, imagining Dellia slumbering within. A wave of guilt washed over him. These people had helped him, without hesitation, when he desperately needed it, and here he was slipping away with no thank you and no goodbye.

Bathed in the stillness of the moonlit night, Jon lifted his head and looked up at the thousands of stars that littered the night sky, questioning the sanity of this move.

He had no real idea where to go, and he'd seen firsthand how adept Dellia and Garris were at tracking. His only hope was to find a nearby village, tonight or early tomorrow. Before they got a start. If he hid out there and luck was with him, he just might evade them. If he managed that, then he'd still have to locate the tower and hope he didn't find someone waiting to pick him up when he arrived. He shook his head. The chances of his plan working were pitiful, but staying here meant no chance of getting home.

Jon took a deep breath of cold night air as he closed his eyes and summoned his courage. He reached into his shirt and pulled out the medallion, then stared down at it while he caressed the smoothness of the metal surface. It served as a reminder of the task he had undertaken, of what he had to do. Somehow, seeing it, touching its warm surface, helped give him courage. He took another deep breath and slipped it back into his shirt.

Jon stood up, and as he turned toward the stables, he froze at the thud of restless horses pawing the ground and the faint sound of whinnying. He glanced around, and out of the corner of his eye, he caught movement. His head snapped toward it, and there, materializing out of the darkness, appeared the outline of a massive wolf.

Jon's heart jumped. This had to be one of the wolves that had ripped that couple to shreds. The beast was unnaturally large with deep, bloodred fur and bright, amber eyes that bobbed in the night as it trotted straight at him.

He glanced at the door of the guesthouse, then back at the wolf, estimating speed and distance. With the wolf at forty miles an hour and him at maybe thirty … oh, who was he kidding—twenty. His heart sank at the inevitable conclusion: he had zero chance of making it inside.

Terror took hold, but he stifled the instinct to call out, afraid it might hasten the attack, and he needed every millisecond.

Jon reached down and yanked the axe from the stump. He began slinking backward in a hasty retreat toward the hitching post in front of the stable wall.

All of a sudden, the lone wolf morphed into three when two more veered off from a line that had been hidden behind the first. The three trotted across the moonlit yard with effortless ease, closing in on him with a terrifying sense of purpose.

Images of the attack on the plains raced through his head: wolves hanging from the panicked horses while they dragged them to the ground, jagged teeth rending flesh from the man's throat, the woman being shaken until her screams halted with a crack as the wolves broke her in two. He shoved the visions out his mind.

Jon hit the wall of the stable. The cold, sharp edges of the stones scraped against his back as he slid along it toward the hitching post. Pain erupted in his foot, and he almost fell when he stumbled over a pitchfork leaning against the wall.

He reached down and yanked it from the dirt, holding the axe in his left hand and the pitchfork in his right. The heft of the implements somehow eased his fear.

One wolf veered off from the others, heading around him, giving him a wide berth. The other two slowed their approach as Jon slid behind the hitching post.

There was something unmistakable in their purposeful movement and posture. It screamed at him, telling him they were hunting him; they intended to kill him. Yet something in their curled lips and flattened ears told more. Then it dawned on him. He wasn't mere prey to them; they *feared* him, and their eyes held a malevolence, something dark and cold and threatening. *These were not ordinary wolves.*

Jon searched the area, desperate to devise some kind of plan. The hitching post was no real cover, but the axe and pitchfork were. If he kept them between him and the wolves, like a lion tamer with a chair, maybe he could hold them at bay. He flipped the axe so the blade end was down with the sharp edge facing the wolves.

A chill ran down his spine as he watched the two wolves slink toward him, their heads down, leering at him. As he peered into their cold amber eyes, a black dread crept into his soul, like nothing Jon had ever experienced. A dark hopelessness took root.

He averted his eyes and shook it off.

The wolves seized the opening and lunged.

Jon swung the axe and pitchfork over, blocking the wolves. Then he realized: that stare, the feeling of dread and hopelessness—it was their ability. It was a tactic.

A fresh new panic gripped him. How could he fight something he couldn't even look at?

Jon tried staring past them, keeping them at the edges of his vision. He caught motion as the wolves flew at him. He jerked and jabbed, blocking where he sensed movement. It worked.

He tried to call out but was cut short as the wolves lunged again and again. They charged and flew at him, their bright eyes a blur in the dark night, enormous jaws of glistening teeth snarling, snapping inches from his legs.

The wolves began shifting farther apart, and his heart jumped. They were working him, like a pack surrounding a helpless fawn.

Then it hit him. That's what happened to the man. One would grab his leg, the other his throat. Then they'd yank and tear until it was over.

Jon glanced at the door, desperate for someone to save him. One of the wolves seized the opening and slipped around the pitchfork, grabbing at the axe handle.

He lunged forward and stabbed the pitchfork at the wolf's side.

The creature let out a yelp as the tines ripped its skin. It shook its head as it backed up, blood oozing from the tear. The wounded beast growled and shot Jon a blistering stare while the other wolf continued its unrelenting assault.

The bleeding wolf scrambled away, disappearing around the jagged edge of the stable.

Jon quickly scanned the area and spotted the third wolf watching from the farthest edge of the yard. He turned all his attention to the remaining wolf before him, staring it in the eye. A sudden wave of hopelessness gripped him once again, and the morbid dread flooded back.

Jon broke his gaze, and it flew at him like a streak. He wrenched the axe into it, and the blade nicked its skin. It shook its head and dove back at him, time and again.

Heart pounding, he dodged and stabbed, petrified that any instant the wolf would fly around the corner in a last furious charge.

A shudder shot down his spine at the sound of claws scraping against the wood shingles of the roof. Oh, crap.

Jon glanced up, in dread of an attack from above. The wolf before him seized the opening, lunging at him over and over, its amber eyes flashing through the dim light, jagged teeth slashing a hair's breadth from his leg.

He glanced up again.

A massive, dark red wolf loomed over him, its angry eyes leering down as it crouched at the edge of the roof, ready to spring.

Jon swung the pitchfork with one arm and jabbed upward with all his force. There was a sickening resistance as the dull tines sank into the wolf's neck.

He yanked back, hard. The pitchfork screeched against the edge of the roof as the wolf planted its feet. He yanked again, and in a rush of scraping, the wolf's feet broke free.

Jon dropped the axe. He reached up and seized the pitchfork with both hands.

The wolf below darted at his leg. He jerked it back, but the wolf caught the edge of his pants and dove backward, almost wrenching Jon's legs out from under him.

Jon yanked out and down.

The wolf below choked up on his pants, getting closer to his leg.

The wolf above began sliding off the roof, and Jon heaved forward, throwing all his weight into the pitchfork.

The wolf below choked up on his pants again, its teeth now scraping against his skin.

The wolf above hurtled off the roof, headfirst, accelerating toward the ground.

The wolf below scrambled out of its way as the huge bloodred head slammed into the dirt with a heavy thud. Jon winced at the loud yelp and sickening crack as the wolf's neck broke and it fell into a twisted mass.

The remaining wolf raised its head to the moonlit sky and let out a pitiful howl.

Sounds and barking erupted from the houses as the remaining wolf attacked again with frightening vengeance.

Jon yanked the pitchfork out of the crumpled pile of wolf and poked and thrust, repelling the remaining wolf's attack.

With blistering speed, the wolf skirted the pitchfork and dove at his leg.

He jerked it back, but the wolf snagged his pants again.

This time, he heaved the pitchfork down, right through the wolf's muzzle, pinning it to the ground.

The wolf screeched and struggled, frantic to free itself.

Jon snatched the axe and lifted it high.

The doors of the houses clattered open, and people scrambled into the yard.

He swung the axe downward with all his weight. It sank deep into the wolf's back with a nauseating thunk, and all went eerily quiet.

His breath was labored, and the world seemed to move in slow motion as Jon glanced over at the third wolf. It was still watching from the edge of the yard, but on catching his gaze, it turned and raced off toward the mountains, disappearing into the darkness. He slumped to the ground, resting his back against the cool stones of the wall, and steadied himself.

Jon stared out into the moonlit yard, vaguely aware of Dellia and Garris racing toward him and Rillen traipsing across the yard with an astonished look on her face.

First Garris, then Dellia flew to Jon's side and knelt next to him, checking him over.

"Are you all right?" Dellia sounded panicked herself.

Jon attempted to gather his wits as he looked into the worried faces of the two crouching before him. "Yeah, I think so." He raised a shaky hand and pointed his finger at the dead wolves. He forced a smile and in a quivering voice said, "But you should see the other guys."

Garris's concerned expression broke out into a broad grin. He granted Jon a nod of approval and clapped a heavy hand down on his shoulder.

Dellia closed her eyes and let out a deep sigh of relief.

Garris glanced at the two implements lying on the ground next to Jon. "Did you just kill two Blood Wolves with nothing but a pitchfork and a chopping axe?"

"I was just trying to stay alive." Jon glanced over at the limp pile of deep red fur, with Rillen in her dark leather and forest-green robe standing over it, staring at it … right next to his … *Oh no, the pack.*

He jerked his eyes away and stared at Garris and Dellia. If they saw it, they'd know he was planning to run. Maybe they wouldn't notice.

Garris eyed him with suspicion. He glanced straight back to

where he'd been looking, then back at Jon again. He stood up and stepped backward. With casual ease, he sauntered over to the wolves and scanned them, as if examining them.

As he strolled past the pack, he knelt, and his eyes never left the wolves as he scooped it up. His subtlety was impressive.

Jon tore his eyes from Garris and glanced back at Dellia to find out if she'd noticed.

She eyed him and tilted her head, then glanced back at Garris and down at the pack.

Jon averted his gaze. *So much for* my *subtlety*.

Garris stopped staring at the wolves. He marched back to Jon, grabbed his arm, and hoisted him up. "I'll settle Jon. We can deal with the bodies in the morning." He yanked him toward the guesthouse.

Still looking alarmed, Dellia nodded as the two rushed by.

Rillen, now crouched before the body of a slain wolf, glanced up from stroking its fur as they hurried past.

Up at the house, Sirra watched, her strong silhouette gracing the doorway while Tilla's sweet and curious face peered around her.

Jon took a slow, deep breath as he trudged across the yard. He raised his head to the thousands of stars scattered across the night sky. And in this strange place, far from home, a rush of relief and gratitude washed over him. Because by some inconceivable miracle, he had managed to survive.

Chapter Nine

IMPLICATIONS OF AN ORACLE

Dellia struggled against an invisible force in a frenzied attempt to reach Jon. Wolves circled him, flying at him, vanishing and reappearing, lunging from every angle. Blood oozed from countless gashes and teeth marks. It splattered across the desolate ground until its odor permeated the air.

Dellia raced toward him in a reckless dash, but the harder she pushed, the farther away he drifted. A wolf seized Jon's leg, yanking it out from under him. He toppled to the ground. Dellia stumbled to her knees, crying out, reaching for Jon.

A wolf clamped down on his throat and another on his arm. Joints cracked and twisted as all three braced their feet and yanked and tugged in different directions.

An unseen force dragged Dellia down into the ground. Jon thrashed in agony but could hardly move. He tried to scream, but no sound would pass with the wolf crushing his throat. She dropped through the earth, watching Jon's last seconds as she fell away from him.

Dellia bolted awake to the sunlight streaming into her cozy room. She sat motionless for a second, trying to shake off the horror and confusion. After a moment, she began to look around. Judging by the color of the sunlight, it was early morning, and at the base of her bed, Tilla lay across her legs, head down, quietly watching.

Dellia rose, and as she hurried through her morning rituals, much of the horror left over from her nightmare dissipated, leaving an uncomfortable, uneasy feeling. It was the same one she'd had after encountering the carnage of the wolf attack on the plains, only multiplied.

She set about a variety of morning tasks—from tending the horses to cooking to gathering supplies—in a fruitless attempt to take her mind off the attack and that horrific dream. They'd all agreed to let Jon sleep in after his ordeal of the night before. But amid her tasks, Dellia was drawn back to the window, watching the guesthouse almost compulsively, waiting for Jon to emerge.

She spied him straggling into the yard about midmorning, squinting against a bright sun hanging in the crystal-blue sky. He raised his head and paused for a moment, seeming to bask in its warm yellow rays. Then he scanned the yard and located Garris on a small, sunburnt patch of bare ground in front of the stables.

Dellia stepped back into the shadows of the kitchen and watched as Jon sauntered across the yard. Garris must have seen him approach because he looked up from his work of lashing a set of tree branches together to make a pair of sturdy frames. He smiled and announced they were going to tan the wolf hides.

Last night, after Garris had seen Jon to bed, she could hear him toiling late into the night, skinning the wolves. Tanning the hides was a brilliant idea. Blood Wolves were known to vanish shortly after death. It was believed they were summoned creatures and returned to the place from which they had been called. It was rare to encounter them at all, rarer still to kill one, and unheard of for them to have been in the world long enough to become anchored to it. The large size of the wolves and their rarity meant the oversized pelts would be exceedingly valuable on their own, but these were quite possibly the only Blood Wolf pelts in the world.

Garris treated Jon to a full explanation of how he intended to preserve the hides. Careful not to be noticed, Dellia watched from the dim recesses of the kitchen while Jon soaked it up with rapt attention, as if Garris were revealing the secrets of the universe. Jon was certainly one of the most curious and bright people she had ever met.

Garris pointed to the frames and explained that it would be Jon's task to stretch the hides over them. Garris would return later and start a fire, which would melt away any remaining fat from the skins. It was a novel method, but it wasn't hard to see the wisdom of it. It avoided the risk of cutting through the hide while scraping them and allowed the fat to be collected for use in cooking or torch making.

His explanation over, Garris directed Jon to the kitchen. Dellia had whipped up a batch of cold porridge earlier. She hurriedly scooped some into a bowl and slid it onto the table for Jon to eat. Then, she scurried off to her room and busied herself while keeping one eye on him as he ate.

Never one to overlook an opportunity for food, Tilla crowded him at the table, pretending to starve while she waited for any little crumb. Jon eventually succumbed to her pleading eyes and shared fingersful of porridge as he ate.

Once finished, he strolled back out into the bright, sunlit yard. Tilla, having now become his best buddy, bobbed along behind him and plopped down at his feet, basking in the midday sun while Jon worked.

Dellia gazed from the darkened kitchen window as he strung the wolf hides to the pair of wooden frames. She should have breathed easier after he had proved he could defend against the wolves. Instead, she found herself watching his every move, hovering over him like a mother hen with her chicks.

She was contemplating which task to distract herself with next when Jon finished. He stood back for a time, admiring his handiwork.

Then he motioned to Tilla, and the pair struck out along a small path that meandered through the flower-dotted fields beyond the house.

Dellia rushed to the door and barged through it, hurrying out across the warm, grassy yard, anxious that Jon not go for a walk alone. He must have heard because he turned and looked back. He smiled when he spotted her and waited as she caught up.

Before she could reach him, a man appeared, approaching on horseback. He was tall and thin, wearing a long black robe with a hood that obscured his face.

Jon must have noticed her staring because he turned and watched the rider grow near. Dellia ran up alongside Jon, and they strolled out to meet the man together.

The serene, middle-aged man pulled his horse to a stop. His dark eyes evaluated Jon from beneath his jet-black hair, shrouded in the darkened hood of his robe. And under the garment, he wore an embroidered silk shirt of black and jade green, a sign of influence and prestige that was entirely unexpected.

He slipped off his horse and pulled back his hood. As he turned to Jon, a smile spread across his serene face, and he granted him a gentle bow of his head. "I am Tsaoshi, an oracle. I have come from the Augury on other business but felt obliged to travel here to speak to you and to Dellia."

Dellia wanted to smile. The secretive and enigmatic Augury was the mouth of prophecy, the home to which all oracles were believed to belong. To mention it by name was a nice touch.

Jon turned to Dellia with a questioning look, apparently expecting her to decide if they should talk to the man.

She motioned to the path ahead. "You can join us if you like."

The three turned and continue their walk, with Tilla forging ahead and Tsaoshi's horse trailing behind.

Jon eyed Tsaoshi with intense fascination. "An oracle, huh?"

Dellia smiled. There was that curiosity again.

The oracle gave him another small smile.

Jon acted like a kid with a new toy. He skipped out ahead as he jammed his arm behind his back. He flashed a mischievous grin and walked backward, hiding his hand as he quizzed Tsaoshi.

"Okay, how many fingers am I going to hold behind my back?"

"Not really the future," Tsaoshi replied as if he'd done this before.

"Okay, then tell me, what am I going to have for dinner?"

"It doesn't work like that."

"How convenient."

Seeming satisfied for the moment, Jon scooped up a stick and eyed Tilla as he teased her with it. She bounced a few times before Jon hurled it out across the fields of thick grass and toward the pale blue mountains in the distance. Dellia smiled as Tilla raced after it, bounding out beneath the warm sun and clear sky. Jon turned and walked abreast Dellia again. It was gratifying that he found this so fascinating and amusing, but it wasn't getting her anywhere.

Tsaoshi remained placid and his words gentle. "I understand. You are a skeptic."

"Look, it's just that I refuse to believe our future is cast in stone. I believe we have free will." Jon pointed to himself. "That *we* decide our own future."

"You think you have free will?"

"Of course," Jon said as he absentmindedly took the stick from Tilla.

Tsaoshi watched with a tranquil expression as he asked, "Could you kill Dellia here in cold blood, or decide to fall out of love with someone, or say nothing as your friends are led to their slaughter?"

"Oh man, no. Why would you even put those images in my head?"

"To show you that in so many ways, the idea of free will is partly an illusion. We are all bound by who we are, by our beliefs and ideals, and therefore in the things that matter the most, we are all predictable."

Jon baited Tilla with the stick, and she raced away, anticipating the throw. He flung it over her head, far out across the green field again. As soon as the bouncing bundle of wiry fur spotted it, she tore after it with joyful abandon. Dellia smiled, but her patience was growing thin. This wasn't where this conversation was supposed to go.

"But that doesn't make the future predictable," Jon said.

"No, it does not."

"So you can't predict the future."

Tsaoshi remained unfazed. "If I told you what you were going to eat for dinner, you could simply change it to prove me wrong. The fact that I am speaking to you now could change your whole future."

Dellia's patience at the limit, she pointed to Jon and blurted out, "What about going into the Recluse Tower?"

He stared at her with a quizzical expression, as if the question were out of left field. Which it kind of was.

Tsaoshi turned and addressed Dellia. "Ah. Good example."

"Huh?" Jon exclaimed.

"What if I told Jon he was going to die in that tower?" Tsaoshi said. "It might not stop him, but it could make him more afraid. It could result in his death."

"But—"

"And what if I told him he would live? That could make him careless. And that could result in his death."

"But—"

"What if the only prediction I can make that keeps him safe is that your fate and his are intertwined? That for your sake as well as his, you must stay with him, protect him, keep him safe?"

The conviction with which Tsaoshi uttered his proclamation was entirely too convincing, and Dellia stood for a moment staring. "Wait. Is that a real prediction?"

"Is that not what you wanted?" Tsaoshi replied.

"Is *that* a real question?"

"Perhaps it is the real answer."

Jon gave a quick shake of his head. "I think I'm getting a headache."

"Look." Tsaoshi eyed both of them. "I did not come here to give you answers. I came to give you both a warning."

"A warning?" Jon said.

"Yes. The wolves are just the start. They have your scent. They will follow and multiply, and I fear before the end, they may threaten all."

Impressions from her nightmare flooded back, and Dellia stared at Tsaoshi as she blurted out, "Why would you say that?"

His placid expression never changed, and his only response was a slight bow of his head before he turned to leave.

"That's it?" Dellia eyed him in disbelief. What just happened? That couldn't be it. This wasn't how this conversation was supposed to go.

"I have said too much already." Tsaoshi mounted his horse, then turned and trotted off.

Dellia stared after him, hardly able to believe what she'd heard. Flustered, she turned to Jon. "Could you ..." She motioned to Tilla. "I'm just gonna ..." She pointed to Tsaoshi. "I'll see you later, okay?" She spun around and marched off after him, but his horse galloped away and disappeared around the edge of the guesthouse.

Behind her, Dellia heard Tilla bark and Jon rifled the stick out across the sunlit field. Tilla bounded after it, the pair blithely unaware of her frustration.

Dellia veered off the meandering path, striding across the fields, and headed straight for the corner of the guesthouse where Tsaoshi had disappeared. The ground flew by under her as her mind raced, struggling to make sense of what had just happened. Had Rillen screwed up? Were her instructions unclear? Was this Tsaoshi just incompetent? Did he not understand it was a matter of life and death? It was unnerving, watching him act in such a cavalier manner when a man's life hung in the balance.

Dellia stormed around the corner of the stone guesthouse and into its shadow. There, by the well, stood Tsaoshi with his horse. He was cranking a bucket of water up to the top as if nothing were wrong. She burst out of the shadows, glaring at him as she charged across the yard to where he stood.

She seized his arm and spun him around to face her. Water sloshed from the bucket in his hands, barely missing her as it splashed across the ground. Tsaoshi appeared startled for a moment but quickly regained his calm facade.

Dellia glared at him. "What the heck was that? Rillen paid you to play an oracle, not blabber incoherent nonsense."

Unruffled, he smiled, and with a hint of sarcasm said, "Oh, I thought that is what oracles do."

"You were supposed to tell him not to go into the tower. Not give *me* advice."

"Could you not see? That was never going to work. I am a stranger. What would make you think I could convince him where you could not?"

"Because that was the point." Dellia gestured back toward Jon. "You were supposed to be able to see his future."

He remained serene in the face of her frustration. "You saw how much faith he put in that. Did you really think me being an oracle was going to persuade him?" Tsaoshi turned and dumped the bucket of water into the trough.

Cool droplets splattered Dellia's arm, and she studied the ripples as his horse drank. As much as she didn't want to admit it, he was right.

Her gaze fell. "Well … you weren't supposed to make it *worse*."

And with that, her plan came crashing to a halt. As if it ever had any chance of working. Jon remained too skeptical, and his stubbornness was beyond all reason. And now she had no way to stop him from blundering headlong to his death. Suddenly, she felt very alone in all this. The council couldn't care less whether he died. Garris might, but he insisted his argument with Jon was the end of it. She was the only one who cared enough to actually do something about it.

"What am I supposed to do now?" she said.

Tsaoshi stared at Dellia for a moment and his face filled with unexpected concern. "I wish I could tell you it is all going to be okay —"

Her head flew up, and she glared at him. "I don't need people telling me it'll be okay. I need Jon to be … I mean, I need to stop a man from getting himself killed."

Tsaoshi paused as if choosing his words with care. "For what it is worth, I planted a suggestion. The idea that he needs you to protect him. Maybe that will be enough to stop him from going without you."

With that, he bowed his head once more, then turned and mounted his horse. Dellia stood in the sun-drenched yard, watching him ride away, wondering what to do next. But when she turned to head back to the main house, there in the doorway stood Sirra with a look of disapproval on her face. She'd overheard the entire exchange.

Dellia let out a soft sigh of dismay. *This day just keeps getting better and better.* Her mother snapped around and disappeared from the doorway. Dellia stood staring after her for a moment before she dragged herself off toward the house and the inevitable lecture.

Sirra was seated at the table, still and quiet, as Dellia trudged through the kitchen door. She hesitated for a moment in the doorway, reluctant to face her disapproval. Taking a breath, she steeled herself and trudged over to the table.

Dellia stood across from Sirra, studying her mood. Her face was calm and her manner patient, as always. But her disappointment hung heavy in the air. Her mother's anger or frustration or worry, even her sadness at seeing Dellia go—those she could handle. But that particular type of disappointment that sprang from not being the person Mom expected, that was the worst. It always had been.

"Sit." Sirra motioned to the chair across from hers.

Dellia dragged the chair out and plopped down into it. She set her hands on the kitchen table, and Sirra reached out and put a hand on hers.

"You know what you're doing is wrong," Sirra said in a gentle tone.

Dellia pulled her hands away and rested them on her lap. She glanced to the side, studying the pale stones of the kitchen wall. "Can we not talk about this, Mom?"

"You have a gift, Dellia. To know what other people are feeling, that's an immense power and a tremendous responsibility. So we live—"

"By three simple rules." Dellia said it in unison with her mother. "I know. We don't use our gift to hurt people. We don't expose other people's feelings—"

"And we don't manipulate emotions," Sirra finished, giving her words particular weight and emphasis.

Dellia closed her eyes and hung her head. She'd heard those words hundreds of times, as far back as her memory stretched. There was the time when she witnessed a meeting of the Ephori and started telling her mom how each of them felt about her speech. Or the time members of the Council of Meerdon had visited. She'd gotten angry and informed Nomusa that Ukrit wasn't really attracted to her, that he was just using her. Always, her mother was appalled, and every time came that disappointment, and a lengthy lecture, and those same words.

It was a part of her soul, and she didn't need her mother to remind her of the crushing guilt and shame that gripped her every time she considered what she was doing. What she *had* to do.

Her gaze still averted, in a quiet voice Dellia said, "I'm under orders from the council."

"Then what they're asking is wrong. The council and I often don't see eye to eye, and this kind of disregard for people is why."

Dellia shook her head and looked up into her mother's face. "It's not that simple."

"Right and wrong are usually very simple. It's people who complicate them with elaborate rationalizations for doing what they know is wrong."

"There's a lot more at stake than just my integrity."

"That's what worries me." Sirra leaned over the table. "Do you not remember Ellira's words? Nothing is so important as who we are. If we lose sight of what is right and wrong, then we see folly as wisdom, we think cruelty is kindness, and our strength becomes our greatest weakness. Then we will have earned the wrath that inevitably follows."

These words too were indelibly etched in Dellia's mind, and she understood the truth of them. But how could she explain that this was different?

"I'm doing my best, Mom."

"Are you?" Sirra straightened in her chair. "You've been here barely more than a day, and you're trying to trick a man into doing what you want."

"For his own good."

"Then forbid it, and deal with the consequences, but this kind of subterfuge is not how I raised you."

"It backfired anyway."

Her mother sighed as she leaned back in her chair.

Dellia started to get up, but Sirra swayed forward and grabbed her wrist. She needed no gift to sense her mother's concern.

She peered into Dellia's eyes. "You have feelings for him, don't you?"

"I do not," she shot back, faster than she could even think. Too fast, she realized, for someone who didn't care.

"I'm worried about you," Sirra said.

"I know. So am I."

"Please. Promise me you won't go into that tower. I can't lose you."

She was torn. The council didn't want her to go, and her mother's concern was so heartfelt and sincere, but how could she let Jon go alone? How could she stand there and watch him die?

Then, as she gazed into her mother's eyes, it all became clear. She couldn't go with Jon. And not just because of her mother, or Kayleen. In fact, Kayleen had never actually forbidden her from helping him. But that wasn't the point. The point was, she'd worked and struggled, since her first day of training, to become the best protector she could. Someone the council could rely on. That was her life. That was her calling. And being the best meant she had an obligation, a duty, to serve not just the council's orders, but their will. She couldn't go against their wishes in pursuit of one man's foolish quest. She had to be strong.

Dellia nodded. "I promise."

Jon sat on the floor, reclining against the cool stone wall, staring into the flames as they danced along the logs in the fireplace. The day had been long and exhausting, and the heat from the glowing embers spread out across the room, bathing his sore muscles in a relaxing warmth. He inhaled deeply and leaned his head back against the wall, enjoying the simple act of zoning out in front of the warm fire.

The day had been an eventful one. He'd learned Garris's own

unique method of tanning hides and even had a small hand in it. Garris had given him his daily lesson in swordplay and seemed quite proud of the fact that Jon now "conducted himself as well as some ten-year-olds." And he'd met a rather strange man who claimed to see the future. They were all fascinating new experiences, and he found he relished them far more than he might've expected.

As he stared into the glow of the embers, he found himself wishing he'd seen more of Dellia today. He enjoyed her company almost as much as he enjoyed the new experiences. There had been that brief, if not bizarre, encounter with her and the oracle, but that wasn't the same as actually getting to talk to her.

A sudden loud pop from the fire jarred Jon out of his contemplation. The embers shifted, and from across the room, their warmth on his skin intensified. Another loud pop startled him again, and a spark shot out across the hearth. He followed it with his eyes and caught Dellia standing silently in the doorway, surveying him.

Jon smiled and motioned her to come sit next to him. She strolled over and slid down right by his side. They both sat in silence, enjoying the warmth of the fire and the gentle flicker of light playing across the stone walls of the room.

After a long while, Dellia turned to him and rested her hand on his leg. "Are you sure I can't talk you out of the tower?"

Jon took a deep breath, rich with the sweet scent of flowers from a vase stuffed with grape-colored blooms that had appeared on the mantle.

He turned to Dellia, watching the firelight reflected in her eyes. "It's the only way home for Megan and me. The only way back to my life. And I know some people think it wasn't much of a life, but it was to me. I had this plan, you know, a simple life, with few responsibilities. And I had someone I wanted to share it with. Just me and her. Plenty of time to do things together, go for walks, talk, you know, just be together."

She peered into his face, her gaze distant, as if caught up in his vision. "That sounds like a beautiful life."

As Jon stared into her eyes, a slip of a thought crept into his mind. How easily he could let himself fall in love with her. He shoved it aside. How stupid would that be? Even if the situation weren't impossible, it would almost certainly wind up being a repeat of Megan. Horrified at the prospect of Dellia rejecting him too, he pushed the feeling down deep and buried it.

Jon smiled and said, "How in the world did someone like you ever get to be such a big romantic?"

Dellia turned away and seemed deep in thought for a moment as she stared into the fire. "Well, I suppose it goes back to this silly childhood dream I had." She gave a quick shake of her head. "I don't really talk about it."

Jon sought out her eyes. "No, really, I want to hear."

"It's nothing."

"It's obviously important to you. Please."

Dellia sighed. "Well, when I was young, when I still lived here, for the longest time, every night, I'd have this dream. About a man. He'd appear riding a dragon." She lifted her gaze to Jon's, her earnest eyes seeking his. "Only, it wasn't even about that. You know how some dreams are more about a feeling than about what happens? Well, when he appeared, I felt this warmth and happiness and over-whelming love. And, well, he swooped down and rescued me."

Jon smiled at the charm of her story and her hesitancy in telling it. "On a dragon."

She glanced away. "I told you it was silly. Childish. Especially since people don't ride dragons. I mean, trying to ride one, that would be extremely foolish. ..." Dellia turned back to him, catching his gaze. "But I think it was the feeling that really stuck with me. It's hard to let go. And after a while, it just became a part of me."

"That's not silly or childish." Jon smiled. "Of all the people I know, I can't imagine you ever needing anyone to rescue you. But when I was in that forest alone and lost, with no idea what to do, you came along and swooped down and rescued me. How could I ever see that as silly?"

Dellia smiled. Then suddenly, that smile drifted away, and her expression became serious. She tore her eyes from Jon and stared down at the floor. "Well, it's taken a lot of courage to talk myself into this, but if you have to go into that tower, I have to let you. I won't stop you." She looked into his face and shook her head. "But I can't be there this time to rescue you."

He simply nodded. He didn't have the heart to tell her he didn't want her there anyway. He couldn't stand the thought of her getting hurt because if him. "Thanks, but I don't even know how to get there."

"My mother can get you there. You'll have to ask her about it."

Dellia slid her hand into her pocket and produced a coin. She stared at it for a moment, as if it were a distant memory. It was about the size of a half dollar, having eight sides and an elaborate dragon motif on the surface. The intricate beauty of the design was breathtaking. Jon looked down at it in her hands, watching the flickering light play off its shiny gold surface.

"Promise me something." She handed the coin to him. "Take this with you. It was my grandfather's. He believed it brought him luck. I think it also gave him courage. I hope it brings you courage as well."

"Oh. I can't take this. It's from your family. It means something."

"It would make me feel better. Please."

Jon signaled Dellia to wait and pulled his bag over to him. He fished through it and produced a silver bracelet. Its design was a simple one, reminiscent of delicate, intertwined vines with a few tiny leaves. He'd picked it because it possessed a quality that seemed ancient and beautiful.

He offered it to Dellia. "I won't take it unless you take this. I was going to give it to Megan. I know it's not the same, but I want you to have it."

She drew a short breath of wonder and surprise as her gentle hands lifted it from his. It glittered as she held it up to the firelight, examining it. She seemed far more taken with it than he'd expected.

"I've never seen anything like it." She turned her eyes to his. "I can't take this."

"Please."

Jon dropped the coin in his pocket as he watched Dellia slip the bracelet on her wrist and admire it. He smiled at her and gave her shoulder a playful shove with his. "So, does this mean we're going steady?"

She shoved him back, only much harder. "Yeah. I have no idea what that means."

"It means we sit together at the school cafeteria. You have a date for the prom."

Dellia grinned. "No dating. Still a protector, remember. Well, I could court you, but then I'd have to kill you."

Jon couldn't help but laugh.

Chapter Ten

IN THE GRAY OF DAWN

Nervous about being alone in the dark and chilled from the night air, Jon rushed through the darkness. The sky had turned overcast at dusk, with a thick layer of clouds that made the entire world seem gray and gloomy. And now, in the fullness of night, he strained to catch sight of the main house while he hurried across the blackened yard.

Though the wolf threat seemed over, for now, the attack of last night lingered in his memory. And Tsaoshi's warning wasn't helping, either. No matter how much his rational mind told him he was safe, that no predators were stalking him from the blackness of night, every other part of him wanted out of the dark as quickly as possible.

Jon nearly collided with the rock wall of the main house as it burst into view. He felt his way along it, around the corner and down the wall. The front steps arrived before he expected and he collided with them. He bumbled his way up them, fumbled for the kitchen door, and stumbled through.

As Jon clattered into the room, a pair of heads whipped over, startled by the sudden disturbance. Sirra was seated at the table, a steaming cup between her hands, while Tilla lay sprawled out across the worn, wooden floor at her feet. A flame flickered in their eyes from a candle burning on the windowsill. Its light cast a soft glow over the room as the two remained frozen like statues, eyeing him as if expecting an explanation.

Jon pointed over his shoulder at the door and stammered, "It was dark out ... and I just ... you know ... the wolf."

Content to see it was merely Jon, Tilla lay her head back down on the floor's smooth surface.

Sirra took a sip from her cup before motioning him to sit.

He strolled over to the chair across from her, pulled it out, and dropped down into it. For a moment he sat there, catching his breath as he stared past Sirra, working up the courage to ask her about going to the tower.

She beat him to it. "I suppose I should thank you for killing the wolves."

Jon shook his head. "I don't deserve your thanks."

"Why? You eliminated two of those who threaten my people."

"Because you were right."

Sirra glanced at Jon sideways. "Right? About what?"

"The wolves were probably looking for me. That means that couple on the plains died because of me. You said it yourself. Whatever is going on with me, it's getting people killed."

She tilted her head and in a sympathetic tone said, "Jon—"

"Listen." He rushed the words out. "I need to go to the Recluse Tower. Dellia says you can get me there. But I want to go alone."

A flash of what seemed like fear disrupted Sirra's usually calm exterior.

Jon stiffened a bit, more alarmed than ever about the prospect of the tower.

Her look of fear vanished as quickly as it had come, leaving a stunned expression. She gazed off into space as she shook her head and in a quiet voice said, "I can't do that."

He closed his eyes and sighed in resignation. It was as he'd feared. She wasn't going to help him, and he couldn't really blame her.

"Okay. I understand." Jon rose, and as he turned away, he caught

Sirra staring at him with a torn expression. Her concern seemed more profound than a simple desire not to help. He hesitated, wanting to ask her what was wrong, but instead he took a deep breath and started to leave.

"No. Wait," Sirra called out.

Jon turned back, and she seemed even more torn. She stared at him as if his eyes held the answer to some inner dilemma. Then she let out a sigh, and her reluctance seemed to melt away.

"I can take you. I'll open a portal to the tower, and you can go in ... *alone*," Sirra said. "But I have to go to the tower with you so I can open a portal back here when you're done. And it's dangerous there so I'll need as much protection as I can get."

"A portal?" Jon asked.

"Yes, that's my gift. As long as I have a recent memory of a place, I can open a portal to it."

"Oh. Okay. Thank you." He was curious about this "gift," but now wasn't the time to pursue it.

"We can go in the morning." She motioned to the seat across from her.

Jon sat back down and closed his eyes as his frustration melted away and an intense sense of relief flooded in. Finally, he would be on his way home again.

Sirra's hesitant words drew his attention back to the conversation. "Jon, do you ... I mean, is this what Dellia wants?"

"No. But she said if I had to do it, then she wouldn't stop me."

"You know you could be asking me to deliver you to your death?"

He nodded.

"You see why that's complicated, right?"

"Yeah." He nodded again. Then he stopped himself. "What? I mean, I guess so. ... I can imagine. ... But why do you think it's complicated?"

"For the same reason that it's complicated to warn you to be wary of the council."

Confused, Jon paused for a moment. Then it dawned on him: Dellia worked for the council, so of course it was complicated. In a way, Sirra was warning him to be wary of her own daughter.

He gave a slow nod. "Oh. Yeah, I see what you mean."

He stopped again and stared as his confusion returned. Her explanation did little to clarify why it was complicated to take him to the tower. Then again, it probably wasn't worth pursuing, so he let it go. Besides, her mention of the council might be the perfect opportunity to learn more about them.

Jon took a deep breath, catching a scent reminiscent of heavily spiced tea. He glanced at Sirra sideways. "You don't seem to like the council much. Why?"

"*So* many reasons," she said, her voice adopting the cadence and strength of a skilled orator. "They have no honor. They pass laws and edicts and believe they've accomplished great things. But they have never *once* toiled or slaved or sacrificed to accomplish them. That duty they *force* upon others."

She stared with a fire in her eyes. "They treat our people like children, believing their vision for our lives is far superior to our own."

Sirra leaned in toward him, her passion becoming infectious. "But most of all, they take our children. *Our children*, Jon. We raise them to be the best warriors in the three realms. In part because we instill in them a code of honor, to use their power fairly and with compassion. But the council cares *nothing* for those beliefs. They see only their might. So they take our best warriors and send them to the farthest reaches to enforce their will, whether it *violates* their honor or not."

The strength of her diatribe caught him off guard, and all he could manage was, "Surely it can't be all that bad."

Sirra wrapped her hands around her mug, and her tone became more casual. "For the most part, they do good, and that's the part Dellia sees. As one of the rulers of Talus, I see the other side. I see the problems they create. I see how their disregard for our beliefs has sown the seeds of discontent, and they are so certain they are right they can't even see it. Their heavy hand has even spawned a resistance, the Verod. Yet they are blind to their part in creating it."

"Have you tried talking to them?"

She raised her mug to her lips but paused before taking a sip. "To what end? Theirs is a world of ideas and talk. What do they understand of the world of deeds?"

"Hmm," Jon said.

During the exchange, Tilla had raised her head. She peered into her master's face, curious about what had prompted the impassioned outpouring. Sirra finished her drink, then reached down and petted Tilla, reassuring her.

Jon sat for a moment, watching the pair as he considered her strong words. After a moment, he pushed back his chair and rose. For a second, he stood there, unable to shake the impression that there was something he was forgetting. As he turned to go, Sirra's words echoed in his thoughts. "Strong children," she had called them. And she was the mother of one of those "best warriors." That might make her the perfect person to provide a few words of advice on handling the tower.

Jon turned back to Sirra again. "Say, you raised Dellia, and she seems like she could handle anything. Any advice?"

"So you want me to give you a lifetime of advice and instruction in a few minutes?"

He smiled. "Well, if it's not too much trouble."

"Okay. Yeah. Well, don't end up dead." She smiled back.

He suppressed a laugh. "Right. Good point. Consider it done."

Jon turned again, ready to leave, but Sirra's solemn words drew him back. "Fear is your biggest enemy. You can't stop it, but you can control it."

"How?" He slid back down into the chair.

"Watch what you tell yourself. Focus on being fearless for your friend. Tell yourself that you have to be."

Jon considered her words, and they had a ring of truth to them. Perhaps he could learn more. "I don't suppose this stuff is in some book I could read."

"No. Mostly passed down, generation to generation back to Ellira."

"Ellira, huh? You've mentioned her before."

Sirra's expression became far away, and pride filled her voice. "There was a time, long ago, when we saw our gift as a curse because it was abused by a few among us. Those few could learn anyone's most secret yearnings and exploit them. In so doing, they made our people distrusted, feared, and despised. She changed all that. She gave us the three rules, so our gift became our strength. She taught us to cherish family and raise strong children. She showed us how to use our differences to become the best warriors. She saved us."

Jon grinned. "Can we invite her along?"

Sirra shook her head. "She died hundreds of years ago."

He sat for a long moment, staring at the pattern of long geometric shadows against soft, candlelit stone, while he considered all that she'd told him.

He got up to leave, but this time Sirra rose up, too. She strolled around the table and put a hand on Jon's shoulder, and her earnest face stared into his. "But if she were here, right now, I have an idea of what she'd say."

"What's that?"

"She'd say, if you are going to do this, don't let me or Garris or Dellia tell you that you're going to die. Fight like your life depends on it, but always know you'll make it home. Okay?" And with that, she hugged him. He stood for a moment, shocked at the sudden show of affection.

"Okay," Jon said, then hugged her back.

Garris lifted the lantern and slid the handle over a hook that hung from one of the giant beams spanning the rough ceiling of the stables. The warm light flooded the center of the room, creating shadows of huge timbers against the crude stone walls.

Kyri stirred in her stall, softly nickering as Garris walked along the row of doors to where she stood. She greeted him with her head bowed, and he reached out and scratched behind her ears.

She and Elt had been Garris's only companions in his exile. And of the two, Kyri had always been a good deal more companionable. The thing is, she had not left the Neri for many years, so he'd been worried about stabling her and turning her out in strange surroundings with unfamiliar horses. And to ease his concern, he'd taken to checking on her often. His concern had turned out to be well founded, because when they first arrived, Kyri had refused to drink the water. He had tried every trick he knew, until Sirra suggested he put a handful of grain in the water bucket, and that had done the trick.

So tonight, it was a relief to find his horse peaceful and content, with her front hoof back and her head down over the stall door. She stood motionless while Garris scratched, and the moment he stopped, she took a deep breath, turned her head, and watched him with soft eyes.

It had been an eventful couple of days, and despite his many faults, Jon was growing on him. In fact, he quite enjoyed teaching him. And not merely because he got to shove him around, and hit him, and ridicule him, although that was a big plus. It was also because after a few lessons, Garris could already see the man had strengths. What he lacked in aptitude, which, to be honest, was pitiful, he more than made up for by being smart, inquisitive, and eager to learn. Jon didn't just want to know what to do; he always had to understand *why*. And he worked very hard to apply what Garris had presented. Even after a lesson concluded, he would stay and keep tinkering with what he'd learned.

It would be nice to believe that his couple of lessons had something to do with Jon dispatching the wolves, but that would be ridiculous. He wasn't anywhere near that accomplished. No, from what Jon described, that had more to do with having an uncanny ability to read the wolves and know exactly what to do to keep them at bay.

The last few days had been gratifying, in so many unexpected ways. So it was with a heavy heart that Garris had decided it was time to end this misadventure. Ever since he'd seen Jon's foreign, yet familiar face, his sense of foreboding had only grown. It had bloomed into outright concern following the two wolf attacks. They had all the earmarks of something dark and sinister lurking farther down this twisted path. And after he'd attempted to talk sense into Jon about the tower, it had become abundantly clear that this was all a colossal mistake.

Why was he here anyway? What was the point? When it came right down to it, he didn't have the slightest idea. He was just hanging around hoping to find out. And going into the tower was precisely the kind of foolish heroics that had led to his banishment. There was no way he was going in there. Least of all on something as flimsy as Elt's word he needed to help someone. And if he wasn't helping Jon, then why was he here, risking capture or death by returning to a land that had exiled him?

There was something disturbing and uncomfortable about the idea of leaving, but it was the smart move. He had already pushed it staying here as long as he had. And the longer he dallied, the greater the risk that Rillen or Dellia would be asked to arrest him. Then he'd be forced to do things none of them wanted to see. So first thing in the morning he'd make his goodbyes and head back out across the three realms to home.

As Garris scratched Kyri's neck, her ears pricked up and swiveled toward the stable entrance. Garris followed her gaze, and there, materializing out of darkness, came Sirra. She approached through the broad stable door as she eyed him with a somber expression. He continued to stroke Kyri's neck as she strolled over.

Sirra came quickly to the point. "I thought you should know, I'm taking Jon to the tower tomorrow. I'd feel better if you were there to protect me."

He sighed. So Jon had dragged Sirra into his delusional scheme. He shook his head. "Well, I've made my views known. If he still wants to go through with his idiotic plan, then—" Garris stopped at the sight of Sirra's impatient expression. "Sorry. Yeah, I'll come along, protect you."

He bowed his head. *So much for my plan of leaving.* He couldn't even make a decent exit plan without getting it screwed up. Now he'd have to stay, at least long enough to be there when Jon met his death in that tower, something he'd hoped to avoid.

Expecting Sirra to leave, Garris returned his attention to Kyri. Instead, Sirra strolled up to a rickety old stool nearby, pulled it over, and plopped down on it. She leaned toward him and cocked her head. "Garris, why are you here?"

He turned back to Sirra. "You know Elt. He says I need to help the man, and I go. No point in asking for details."

"Just like that?"

"Just like that."

Sirra didn't seem satisfied. She eyed him with suspicion and waited, as if expecting him to explain further.

Garris studied the pattern of hoofprints on the dirt floor as he considered the question. Then he raised his eyes to Sirra's. "I don't know. I guess being in the Neri, day after day, month after month, year after year—it lacks a certain ... sense of purpose. When Elt told me I needed to go help a man, it just felt right ... still does, actually. Like I'm doing some small good." He glanced away into the starlit night. "Without getting sucked into that whole saving-the-world thing again."

Garris's last words sounded bitter and cynical, even to him. It appeared his tone wasn't lost on Sirra. She straightened on her stool, staring at him, seeming surprised. "Wow. You've changed. What happened to the young man I met when I took Dellia to Shirdon? The one who went out of his way to make me feel better? He was sure he was destined for great things. He was going to change the world, be famous."

Garris shook his head as he stared at the ground. "He was an idiot. He grew up. ... In Erden, they'd call it karma, I guess." He looked up, catching her eyes again. "Truth is, I was always more in love with fame, and well, myself really, than I was with doing good. I guess I learned that doing great things can have a cost."

"Like being banished?" Sirra asked.

Despite Garris's attempt to keep his cool, a flurry of emotions flooded back. They struck him like a hammer: affection, pride, pain, anguish, sorrow, and the intense anger that fueled his desire for vengeance. He knew better than anyone how tragically wrong things had gone, and he understood in excruciating detail every calamitous step that had led to his exile. And as torturous as it had been, he had made his peace with it. No, it wasn't his banishment that had earned his rage. It was the gruesome fifteen-year vendetta that had followed.

"Oh, and so much more." Garris smiled, determined to make light of it. "But thanks for dredging up painful memories."

He waited while Sirra considered his words. She looked him straight in the eye. "So you're not going into that tower?"

"No. Are you kidding me?" Garris shot back. "With my luck, I'd have the wrong guy and be following him to my death."

He stumbled as Kyri nudged him with her giant head, and he realized he hadn't been stroking her for a full ten seconds. He gazed at her soft rust-and-white face and his tumult of emotions melted away. He resumed scratching her and turned his attention back to Sirra.

She sat looking away, staring out into the darkness. This wasn't like her. In fact, she seemed restless and preoccupied, a state he'd never seen her in before. Something was troubling her, but if she wanted him involved, she'd say something, so Garris waited.

After a while, Sirra spoke. "I'm scared, Garris. It's all happening just the way he said."

"Who said?"

Her frightened words tumbled out. "An oracle. A few weeks ago, he came to me, paid me to take him to the Recluse Tower. And I was there when he put his hand on the tower. And his eyes kind of glazed over. And he turned to me, and he said ..." Sirra gulped. "He said, 'Either your daughter falls in this tower, or all humankind falls.' "

Garris stared for a moment. "Wow."

"And the moment I saw Jon, I knew he was the one. He was going to lead her in there. She's all I have. I can't lose her."

"Have you told her?"

"No," Sirra barked out, her voice tinged with panic. "The oracle said if she learned of this then both would fall. You're the only one I've told. You can't mention this to anyone. If it made it back to Dellia ..." Her eyes widened.

"Sirra, you can't trust oracles and prophecies. They never turn out the way you think. Don't do this to yourself."

"He said one other thing. He said, 'Trust your heart, do what's right, have faith. It's the only way through.' So that's what I'm trying to do. But how can I even know what's right when my daughter's life hangs in the balance?"

Garris shook his head. "You're letting this mess with your head. Look, this oracle, he gave you two impossible choices. So don't make those choices. Take each moment as it comes, and do the right thing in that moment. And have faith that things will work out for the best. That's all any of us can do."

Sirra forced a smile. "You know you just said what the oracle said."

"Well, apparently he's not a total idiot."

Garris strolled over and crouched before her. He gazed up into her concerned face. "Look, Dellia is a grown woman, with her own mind. And she's already decided not to go into that tower. So maybe there's no choice for you to make here."

"Hmm." Sirra lowered her head, seeming to think for a moment as she digested his words. Then, she rose from her stool and gave him a quick nod of her head. "Thank you, old friend. I'll see you tomorrow then, bright and early."

And with that, she whirled around and marched off, passing back through the wide opening of the stable entrance, disappearing into the blackness of night.

Jon stepped out of the guesthouse under a dark rolling blanket of clouds. As he strolled across the wet grass, distant lightning flashed on the horizon, a reminder of the storm that had passed in the night.

Sirra was already standing on the lawn, waiting, when he arrived, her rich brown hair blowing in the gentle breeze. She greeted him with a dagger strapped to her waist and a lantern hanging from her hand.

Jon strolled up in front of her and stood with her. With a mixture of anxiety and impatience, he watched and waited for them to gather under gray skies, in the early morning hours on the Talus Plains.

Garris strolled up a short time later, silent and expressionless. It did little to ease Jon's fear to see the seasoned warrior armed with enough arrows and throwing daggers for a small army.

The mood was as gloomy as the weather when Dellia and Rillen straggled in. Neither of them said a word, and there seemed a distinct awkwardness and a reluctance to look him in the eye.

The moment they all assembled, Sirra set down her lamp on the still-damp lawn and raised her arm, putting her palm forward in front of her. She closed her eyes, and an expression of calm concentration washed over her. A mist formed in front of her palm, growing larger and larger as it became more and more dense. A hint of an image formed on the surface, barely visible at first, but growing more and more distinct as the mist solidified into a shimmering portal.

Its liquid surface was not unlike the phenomenon in his lab, only it was as if Sirra had the power to control it, to stretch it and constrain it into a flat, round shape. Through the portal appeared a stretch of rocky ground leading to an old tower, looking like a reflection on a circular pool of water. The surface rippled in the breeze while the plaintive cries of distant animals echoed along the mountain base behind it.

Without thinking, Jon stepped toward the portal.

Sirra snapped out of her concentration and flung her arm out, blocking his way. After scooping up the lamp, she stepped with care through the portal. She glanced around, apparently checking out the area. When she was satisfied, she motioned to Garris to follow, then Dellia and Rillen. One at a time, each passed through and took up positions around her.

Finally, she motioned to Jon. As he stepped into the water-like surface, static electricity prickled his skin, and there was a faint odor of ozone. He turned to look back at the portal, and there were no ripples, a sign of the complete calm in the air here. It was a mystery how one side could ripple but not the other, but his musings were interrupted when the portal dissolved into a colored mist that drifted away in the air.

He turned back and looked out across a couple hundred feet of open rocky ground at the enormous stone tower. It loomed above him, massive, tall, and square. Nearly two hundred fifty feet high by his estimation and framed by the dark, gray clouds of morning. The small group gathered around him seemed so insignificant compared to this towering edifice standing at the foot of the majestic mountains.

Jon gulped and took a deep breath. He scanned the sheer rock wall that rose up behind the tower with the mountain peaks climbing into the clouds. The air stood in eerie stillness, and carried on it were the disturbing cries of some bird or creature that seemed to come from a small wooded area off to the left.

He stepped forward, standing next to the other four as he searched for the entrance. He spotted a large door separated from the central tower by a short hallway.

In an instant, his anxiety flared as it all became far too real. He was going through that door and into that tower that had killed so many. All of a sudden, he was back in Isla's cave with the tower looming over him like a dragon twisting in the darkness. His chest tightened and his breathing became short as his fear bloomed into full-fledged panic.

I have to be fearless, for Megan, he told himself. It helped, and his dread eased just a little.

Sirra turned and looked him over, much like she had done when they first met. "Jon, are you crazy? See Garris here." She waved her finger at the sturdy warrior with his two swords, his crossbow and quiver bulging with arrows, and his harness jammed with rafts of throwing daggers. "He's not even going inside, and he's *under*prepared for what you're doing. Sirra unhooked her belt and held it out for Jon to take. "At least take my dagger."

Only half-aware, Jon took it and slung it around his waist. He found it gave him some comfort to have a weapon, even if he wasn't sure how to use it.

He turned again to the tower and took another step toward it, trying to master his fear.

A gentle hand rested on his shoulder, and Dellia stepped up beside him. He calmed at the warmth of her so close to him, and his fear eased at her reassuring touch.

Jon kept staring ahead. "I'm so afraid, Dellia."

"Then don't do it," she pleaded. "Stay."

"I can't. If it was just me …" He shrugged his shoulders. "But it's not. I dragged Megan into this, too. And I know what she said, and I know she doesn't blame me." Jon shook his head. "But none of that matters." He turned to Dellia. "This is about doing what's right. And right now, that means going into that tower and finding a way to get my friend home."

She turned to him and nodded. There was sadness in her eyes, and she reached out and hugged him for a long moment. When she let go, she slid her hands onto his shoulders and gazed into his eyes. "Listen, you have to manage your fear, you understand? That terror you're feeling, it will paralyze you, get you killed. Just take a few deep breaths, okay?"

Jon closed his eyes and breathed in, filling his lungs with clean, crisp air, the kind that lingers after a storm. And when he exhaled, a tiny amount of his fear was expelled with his breath.

As he took a second deep, slow breath, Dellia nodded. "That's better. Do one more thing for me. Please. Make some kind of plan. Something that makes you feel like you can handle this. Like you're in control."

Jon nodded. "Okay."

The dagger Sirra had given him was strapped around his waist. So he reached down and wrapped his hand around its cool, smooth hilt. He closed his eyes and concentrated, and as he willed it, the world slowed, then froze and turned dim.

"A plan, huh?" Jon muttered to himself.

A shimmering scene appeared before him, this time already moving at a blur. It gradually slowed to the moment Sirra had opened the portal minutes before. Jon walked up to the portal and around it, staring at it as she stepped through to the tower.

Jon shook his head and was yanked back to where he'd stood when the world dimmed. The translucent scene vanished, and the world brightened and started to move again.

He stared up at the tower again, and his fear was still there and almost as intense, but now he had an escape plan, and it did make him feel more in control. He turned to Sirra, and she handed him her lantern.

He took a step forward, then turned around to face Dellia and Garris. "I can't thank you both enough for getting me this far." Then he turned, took another deep slow breath, and marched off toward the tower.

It loomed above him larger and larger as Jon approached it, no longer seeming small next to the soaring mountains. Gravel crunched under his feet. Distant lightning flashed against the gray skies, and eerie cries echoed from the nearby forest.

Garris and Dellia were talking behind him. Garris said something about his "idiotic plan," but Jon was way beyond feeling anything about his opinion. He was consumed with keeping his fear at bay.

He reached the entrance and pushed against the heavy wooden door, harder and harder until it gave way, but all he could see inside was darkness.

"I have to be fearless … for Megan," Jon whispered, then took another deep breath and slipped through the door into the tower.

Dellia's stomach twisted in knots as she watched Jon walk away toward the massive, stone edifice. She couldn't shake the sense that she was losing something valuable and precious, something she would never get back. A compulsion tugged at her to run after him, to do anything to help him, or to stop him, and it took all the discipline she possessed to just stand and watch. She was a protector, she told herself, and this was her duty.

She glanced over as her mother stepped up to her side. She needed no gift to discern the concern written on her face. Only Sirra's concern was not for Jon, but for her. She had only sensed such an intense apprehension in her mother a few times in her life. Dellia couldn't fathom how she could be concerned about her when Jon was the one facing certain death.

Then her mother spoke. "You want to go, don't you?"

Dellia's stomach twitched, and she steeled herself against the urge to go, telling herself that it was her duty to stay.

"Kayleen asked me not to." Dellia's voice sounded cold, even to her.

Garris spun toward Dellia, staring at her. Clearly, her remark had struck some kind of nerve. She suppressed the temptation to pry into his feelings.

He glanced at the tall, gray tower, then back at her, then at the tower again, and she needed no gift to sense what he was feeling. The determined expression that filled his face said it all.

"Well, crap. Then I guess I'm going." Garris struck out for the tower.

A sudden twinge of guilt hit her as Dellia realized it might be her words that were urging this man toward his death. She yelled after him, "You'd risk your life for someone you just met, simply because the council doesn't want it?"

He turned back to her and seemed to think about it for a second, then said, "No, that's just part of it. They say life is about choices, Dellia. Well, what are mine? Do nothing? Go back to the Neri and spend the next fifteen years wondering what's the point of me? Well, maybe *this* is the point. If I die in there, at least I will have done the right thing. I will have protected a good man when he ..." Garris paused. "When he ..." He paused again. "Oh, who am I kidding? What he's doing is still idiotic."

Confused, Dellia could only stare.

After a moment, he tried again. "Look, truth is, I just can't let him die in there alone. I thought I could ... but I can't." Garris spun around and marched off again, even more resolute.

Lightning flashed in the mountains, high above the peak of the massive tower. Distant thunder followed, rumbling along the mountain base.

"So ... what?" Dellia shouted after him. "You'll be dead, and for no good reason?"

He swung about and walked backward while he yelled. "Protecting him is reason enough. Besides, apparently, I have other reasons."

She gave a questioning tilt of her head.

"And as soon as I figure out what they are, I'll let you know."

Garris snapped around and hurried off.

"Take care of him for me," Dellia said under her breath as he rushed away toward the tower.

Sirra must have heard because her head whipped over, and she eyed Dellia for a long moment as her troubled expression dissolved into one of sympathy and concern.

"I told Jon to leave you alone," she confessed.

It took a moment for her words to sink in. Dellia turned to her mother. "You *what?*"

"I know. I thought because of the council and Garris there must be something going on, and I didn't want you getting hurt by it. But I was wrong. It was your decision, not mine, and I was wrong to try to make it for you."

"It's all right. Kayleen doesn't want me to—"

"And I do?"

"I'm sorry, Mother, I didn't mean—"

"You still don't get it. You're not a slave, Dellia. This is your choice, not mine, not the council's."

Dellia stared down, studying the ground, wrestling with her conscience as the plaintive cry of some distant bird echoed across the rocky terrain. A flush of shame overcame her, and the words tumbled out. "I think the council would just as soon he die. It would solve their problem."

"Figures. But the council's not here, are they?" Her mother's gentle hand raised Dellia's chin, and her eyes peered into her daughter's. "They don't know him. You do. What do you think?"

"I don't know."

"Look, Dellia, you have a gift. As strong as any in the realm. You know what's in Jon's heart. Garris doesn't have that, and neither do I, and you have such a great heart. What is it telling you?"

Tears began to well in Dellia's eyes. "That I'm letting a good, sweet, kind man, that I care about, die in there because I'm too afraid of what it might mean to me."

Sirra grabbed her, hugging her tight.

A deep longing pulled Dellia's gaze toward the tower.

Her mother let go. "Come back to me. I couldn't bear to lose you."

"I promise," Dellia said, then turned and ran off toward the tower.

Chapter Eleven

THE RECLUSE TOWER

Jon slid through the massive stone tower door and silently slipped it closed behind him, afraid that any sound would call out to whatever terror awaited within. He turned and scanned the entryway. Having come from the soaring mountain landscape outside, the blue-gray granite walls felt oppressive and claustrophobic. His attempt to quell his fear not entirely successful, Jon's quickened heartbeat thudded in his ears as he set the lamp down on the rocky floor.

Dull, overcast light filtered through a pair of narrow windows high up on either wall but quickly dissipated, leaving the end of the hallway shrouded in complete darkness. His mouth dry, Jon stiffened as his eyes followed the floor a short distance to where the ground vanished, as if swallowed up by the darkness. His fear beckoned to him as he imagined all manner of death that might lurk in that black recess.

He snatched a torch from his pack and, with trembling hands, lit it on the flame from the lamp. He thrust it forward and crept down the hall, each step fearing that any noise would draw some deadly peril out from the shadows. As the darkness danced away from the flickering torchlight, the top of a staircase materialized that descended into blackness.

Jon slowly crouched, then bent over and thrust the torch into the darkness. It gave way to show a stairway that delved down a full flight of steps to a short walkway. And at the end stood a gray stone wall with another heavy stone door, much like the one at the entrance.

The ceiling followed the stairs down, blocking his view of the top of the door at the end of the hall. Jon descended a few steps and crouched lower still. The shadows above the door fled from the torch-light revealing a giant spider clinging to the upper right corner of the wall. Its body was brown and hairless and ended in a large bulb the size of Jon's head with a violin-shaped dark spot on its back.

His fear blossomed again, and under his breath he mumbled, "I have to be fearless, for Megan."

As if it heard him, the spider twitched and jerked around. It stopped and stared at the flickering light with dark beady eyes.

Jon startled, and his heart jolted as the creature skittered down the wall. He reached for the dagger Sirra had given him, but his hand missed the hilt. He reached for it again but caught only air.

He jumped at the sharp click of a crossbow and the whistle of an arrow whizzing by his ear. He froze as the arrow pierced the spider dead center, and it dropped to the floor.

"Ugh. Spiders. I hate spiders," came Garris's voice from behind him.

Jon whirled around and startled again. His hand flew up over his heart at Garris looming above him, leering over him down the hallway.

Jon made a fist and raised it to punch his arm but thought better of it and withdrew his hand. "I don't want you here. What if something happens to you? I can't be responsible for that."

Garris gave him a scornful look. "Well, aren't you full of your-self? Maybe I just strolled in here on my own. Who says you're not helping *me*?"

Suddenly touched by what Garris was attempting to do, Jon smiled. "You know you're annoying even when you're trying to help."

Garris grinned and patted his shoulder. "It's one of my better qualities." He scooped up the lantern he'd brought with him, and they crept down the steps together.

After a step or two, Jon stopped and turned back to Garris. "Thank you."

Garris's only response was a dismissive grunt.

Something bright caught Jon's attention, and he glanced up at a brilliant ball of light slipping through the tower entrance. He froze, gawking, as there by the door stood Dellia. She was surveying her surroundings by sunlight that poured into the hallway from a sunstone that hung in a loose net from her belt. Jon's astonishment must have been apparent because Garris turned and stared at her, too.

Jon's surprise transformed into exasperation. He shoved past Garris, nearly knocking himself over as he marched back up to the top of the steps. He stood staring at Dellia, subtly shaking his head. "What part of 'I need to do this alone' was unclear to you guys?"

"Just go." She motioned down the hallway.

"But your mom is going to kill me if anything happens to you."

Garris chuckled, and it suddenly struck Jon how childish his words sounded.

He glared at him and said, "Oh shut up."

"I can handle my mom," Dellia said.

"When you're dead?" Jon protested. "That'll be a neat trick."

As she approached, Garris's face adopted a sudden look of realization. "Oh my, how the mighty have fallen. Can't you see it? She has feelings for you."

"You're really asking to have your butt kicked, old man," Dellia shot back.

Garris beamed a huge smile. "Oh, sensitive. I must have hit a nerve."

"Oh, grow up."

"Old man? Grow up?" Garris said. "You need to make up your mind."

Jon butted in. "Am I going to have to separate you two?"

Both Dellia and Garris stopped and turned to face him, staring at him with incredulous looks.

Suddenly feeling defensive, Jon held up his palms and stepped back. "I'm just saying, can we not stand around bickering while we're in an actual death trap?"

"Good point," Dellia said while Garris grumbled agreement.

They turned and began down the smooth, stone stairway once again, Garris graciously allowing Dellia to lead while he protected the rear. Silent and alert, they crept down the narrow hallway toward the door.

As much as Jon appreciated Garris, and particularly Dellia, trying to protect him, in so many respects he was even more frightened than before. Because now, instead of just fearing for himself, he was terrified his venture might get one or both of them killed.

They reached the end of the hall, and Garris pushed the dead spider out of the way while Dellia signaled them to be quiet. Then, while Garris kept watch, she and Jon slowly forced open the large carved door. She peered through the opening, then slipped through, and Jon followed.

He stepped out onto a large stone landing as Garris quietly pulled the door shut behind them. Jon stood for a second, stunned and terrified by the spectacle before him. He crept to the edge of the landing and stared down into a gigantic, jagged hole that consumed the entire center of the tower floor. The air drifting up from the depths was warm and had a foul stench. And mixed in was a familiar smell Jon couldn't quite place.

Garris and Dellia joined him, peering into the pit, the flutter of the flame from his torch the only sound breaking the silence. He thrust it over the black opening, but its light never reached the bottom.

The three raised their heads, staring upward into the vast cavity above. They stood at the base of a heavy stone staircase that wound its way up the inside walls of the square stone tower, disappearing into the darkness. Garris pointed to a spot high overhead where the stairs had crumbled and broken away and a section was missing.

Jon's head whipped over as he caught movement in the shadows. A second spider darted out into the flickering light, scurrying across the bottom of the stairway above them. He jumped again at a crossbow discharging and an arrow whistling by his ear, hitting the spider.

It fell, headed for the opening of the pit below them. Dellia lunged out, nearly losing her balance as she snatched the arrow out of the air. It dangled from her fingertips as she teetered at the precipice, staring into the cavern below.

Jon reached for her, but Garris had already grabbed her shoulder and was steadying her.

She turned around and let out a long, slow sigh of relief as she silently set the spider on the floor. She eyed Jon and Garris and raised her finger to her lips, signaling them to keep quiet. They both nodded.

Light from Jon's torch flittered across the dark gray of the tower walls as they crept up the staircase in their slow, silent ascent. He jumped at every little drip or scuffle of feet, unable to stop imagining what terror must lie hidden in that dark pit, what monstrosity could have killed every living soul that dared enter the tower.

They reached the crumbled section of stairs and discovered that nothing remained but a few stones still clinging to the tower wall, jutting into the air like jagged, broken teeth.

Jon stared into the empty space where the stairs should be, waiting for the announcement that this little adventure was over and they were turning back. Then, without warning, Dellia flattened her back against the wall and stepped out onto the first small stone that hugged the tower wall.

Jon reeled backward, certain his heart would stop. She stood there, back plastered to the wall, with only a few tiny crumbling stones between her and a fall that spelled certain death. This was madness; she was going to get herself killed. But he didn't dare make a noise for fear of attracting a grisly death.

Little by little, Dellia tested each stone as she worked her way across, and each time Jon held his breath, unable to turn away, but afraid to watch.

Finally, she reached the other side and stepped over onto a small landing formed by the corner. She turned and motioned Jon to come. He stepped back, and his eyes opened wide. *Oh boy.*

Garris signaled him to hurry up.

Jon handed him the torch as he stepped up to the edge. He looked down through the hole that used to be stairs, summoning his courage. Then, he smashed his back up against the wall and was about to step out into space when Garris grabbed his arm, steadying him.

Clinging to him for support, Jon stepped out onto the first stone, then the second. Then, Garris became too far away to help, so he had to let go. He glanced down at the third step, and he was dangling in space with nothing below him except unending blackness.

Distracted, Jon stepped out and missed, landing on a smaller loose stone that broke free and tumbled away into the darkness. He fumbled for footing and caught the third stone, but it was too late, he'd lost his balance.

He gasped in sheer panic as he slowly began falling forward toward the pit with nothing to stop him.

Suddenly, Garris lunged way out and shoved him with alarming strength.

Jon's forward descent halted, and he lurched toward the far side. He reached out for it, but it lay well beyond his grasp.

He flailed at the ledge as he fell past it, frantic to snag it.

Then something grabbed his wrist with a viselike strength.

His feet slipped from the rocks, and in an instant, he was dangling in space.

Jon glanced down at the fallen stone as it clattered across the walls of the pit, the sound echoing through the tower.

He stared up into Dellia's determined face as she reached down with a second hand and clamped onto the same wrist. With both arms, she yanked him up where he could grab the ledge, then hoisted him over and onto the landing next to her.

Her face turned to alarm. She jerked Jon forward, and he scrambled to his feet. He turned to see what could surprise her so, and there was Garris, sprinting toward the cavity where the stairs should be.

At a flat-out run, he held the torch in one hand as he snatched up the lantern with the other and sprang into thin air. He landed on the first stone, then leaped and dashed his way across the ledge stones like an acrobat. Each jump he leaned a little farther out, then with one last, long push, he vaulted through the air to the land on the corner next to Jon and Dellia.

He stumbled and fell backward, but Dellia was ready and grabbed hold, stopping and steadying him. He turned and nodded to her, then mouthed the words, "We need to hurry."

With a more pressured pace, the three continued their soundless climb, hurrying upward along flight after flight of stairs.

Suddenly, a bloodcurdling screech broke the careful silence, echoing up from the blackness below. The companions redoubled their pace again, no longer soundless as they dashed up the stairs.

Another screech reverberated through the tower, this time much closer. They halted, then peeked over the edge as a much larger spider the size of a person burst into view, clambering up the tower walls at a terrifying pace. Chasing behind was a massive swarm of smaller spiders the size of the two before.

Jon's heart leaped at Dellia's sudden worried expression.

Without skipping a beat, she turned to Jon, reached out, and gripped his shoulders. "I'll hold them off. You get to the top. I'll follow. Now go."

Before he could say a word, she turned and bolted off. She yanked out her dagger with one hand and her sword with the other while she charged down the staircase toward the oncoming horde.

Jon spun around and began dashing up the stairs. He looked back as Garris planted himself, shouldered his crossbow, and fired at the larger spider. The arrow ricocheted off its back as it skittered around Dellia and on up the wall.

Jon raced around the corner and up another flight. He looked back again. Garris stood flinging daggers as fast as he could, piercing spider after spider, covering Dellia as she flew into the swarm.

Jon stopped, mesmerized by the display.

She was a blur, all reflexes and instinct, both blades whistling through the air as she kicked, punched, slashed, and stabbed, dispatching spiders at a dazzling pace.

They turned and swarmed after her, surrounding her. They skittered and leaped from every direction while Dellia hacked and pierced, obliterating them without even looking at them.

Whenever she didn't get one, a dagger would rocket in and smack it out of the air, as if Garris knew precisely what she was going to do.

He must have heard the footsteps stop because he jerked his head around, glared at Jon, and shouted, "Move! Go!"

"Who *is* she?" Jon yelled back.

"She's a protector. Now go."

Jon broke into a run, glancing back again as the huge spider scurried past Garris and headed for the top.

He reached the top of another flight of stairs and stopped again as a rumble of fluttering wings reverberated through the tower.

Jon looked down at Dellia still fighting furiously and backed up against the upper edge of the missing section of stairs. His fear blew into full-blown panic, and once again he repeated to himself, "I have to be fearless … for her."

Dellia turned to leap across to the stairway below just as a stream of some type of flying lizard blew by her in a rush of flapping wings, whirling its way up the tower. One of the creatures caught in her hair just as she sprang, causing her to twist badly.

Dellia fell short and missed the far side. She slammed into the edge of the crumbled stairway with her stomach and banged her head against the wall. Reeling from the blow, she clawed at the crumbled stonework as she slipped lower, fighting to hang on until she went limp and fell.

"No!" Jon shouted as he thrust his palm out toward her.

A shimmering, liquid portal flashed into existence below Dellia, and she plummeted through. In an instant, the portal turned to vapor and scattered as a falling spider plunged through the remaining cloud of colored droplets.

"What the—" Garris yelled, and his head jerked around to see Jon with his palm outstretched.

"No time," Jon shouted back.

The horde of flying creatures pummeled his outstretched palm. Jon jerked his hand back, but one of them smashed into the back of his hand, leaving a dark streak.

He recoiled back to the safety of the wall.

Flying lizards swirled through the air in a chaos of noise, obscuring the huge spider as it descended toward Jon suspended by a thin, silvery thread.

He glanced back, hoping Garris would help him, but he was entirely preoccupied, backing up the stairs, fighting madly against a swarm of spiders swirling around him.

Jon grabbed Sirra's dagger and jabbed at the huge spider, shocked to find he wasn't terrible. With some struggle, he kept the spider at bay while he backed down the stairs away from it, his dagger glancing off its impenetrable shell.

Garris and Jon backed into one another.

"I need a weapon!" Jon bellowed over the flapping of wings.

"You have one," Garris yelled back.

"Something owned by the best fighter you know."

"What?"

"You heard me," Jon insisted.

He sheathed his dagger, and Garris handed him a sword from his left hand. "Elt gave this to me." He drew another blade.

Jon concentrated on the weapon, slowing and freezing the swirling chaos around him. He found a moment of a strange lizard-like man attacking Garris with the sword and focused on the blade.

As things started to move again, he turned to a blur himself, startled that he just seemed to know what to do. He slashed and pierced several spiders while his blade pushed the huge one back up the thread.

Garris looked back, and his face brightened when he spotted Jon attacking like a berserker.

Just as some small degree of hope blossomed, there came a deafening roar from the depths below. Jon glanced down, and through the blizzard of flapping wings, a new terror appeared.

A massive scaly creature that almost filled the middle of the tower clambered up the center toward them. Its mouth, much larger than a man, was lined with rows of dagger-like teeth, like some kind of subterranean shark.

With massive claws, it snagged the stairs on either side of the tower, using them to propel itself upward. It roared again, burying the sound of flapping wings and the screech of the huge spider.

"Well, it was nice knowing you, kid," Garris said.

The words of surrender chilled Jon more than the new threat. Still struggling against the huge spider, he cast his gaze everywhere in a frenzied search for some way out, some shred of hope.

Flying lizards whirled through the air, spiders swarmed all around, and another bellow echoed up from below as his mind raced. He sensed there was something he was missing, but what?

The black, glistening streak on the back of his hand caught his eye, the one left where the lizard had hit. Then he realized what that familiar smell was, and a rush of hope filled his heart.

Between parries, he swiped the dark streak with a finger of the hand still clutching the torch. He rubbed it between his fingertips, and it was slick and slimy, as he'd suspected. He tried to recall the flash point of crude oil, but there were too many variables. *Aw, forget it.*

He jammed the torch to a black patch on the side of a dead spider at his feet. He lunged and stabbed and slashed at the huge spider with one hand while he held the torch steady with the other, but nothing happened. As the seconds passed, hope faded.

Then suddenly, the spider burst into flames.

Jon kicked the flaming spider down the tower, and it landed on the scaly creature with a splat.

He smashed the torch onto a large black spot on the giant bulb of the enormous spider. It screeched in pain and dodged away, then leaped to the wall.

Jon tossed his sword to his torch hand and unsheathed his dagger. He slammed it through one of the spider's legs and into the crumbly mortar of the wall, pinning it.

As the spider struggled to free itself, he dove forward and jammed the torch to the slick black spot.

Garris's sword whistled through the air around Jon, covering him while he held the torch firm. Fire from the remains of the massive, scaly creature danced through the whirlwind of flapping wings as the behemoth lunged ever closer.

Suddenly, the huge spider burst into flames and let out a

horrifying screech of pain. Jon hacked through several of its legs.

It leaped to the thread. Jon severed it and kicked hard. The huge flaming spider hurtled away down the center of the tower.

Garris smiled as he watched the enormous, screeching ball of flame soar by.

Its screams of pain abruptly ended as it collided with the enormous scaly creature with a deep thud.

The beast lost its grip and roared as it slipped back. It bursts into flames, letting out a deafening roar of pain.

Fire from the monstrosity engulfed several smaller spiders near it, and they burst into flames as they scrambled away.

The scrambling flames spread as they ran, turning the wall into a scurrying sheet of fire.

The blaze licked the flying lizards diving near it, and several of them burst into flames. The flames leaped from flying lizard to flying lizard, turning into a flaming whirlwind.

The heat caused Jon and Garris to recoil to the wall and cover their faces as burning creatures hurtled into them.

A rain of fiery lizards fell, pummeling the scaly monster. It slipped with a loud scraping, then slipped again, roaring in pain.

Through the intense heat, Jon dove for the edge of the stairs and thrust his palm forward.

An enormous shimmering liquid portal formed below the flaming, scaly creature as it slipped one last time and fell.

It vanished through the portal in a roaring, screeching mass. A deluge of smaller blazing lizards followed it through until the heat caused Jon to recoil, and the portal dissolved into vapor.

Burning lizards fell through it, scattering the vapor as they plummeted down into the pit.

The few remaining smaller spiders scurried away.

"What just happened?" Garris asked.

"No time," Jon shouted back. "It's going to get very hot and smoky in here, fast."

He turned and raced up the stairs. As they hurtled toward the top, Jon looked down at the distant dots of fire as they scattered across the floor of the pit.

They reached the top, and Garris slammed into a hatch in the ceiling. It flung open, and Jon dove through.

He clambered out of his way, and Garris flew through the hatch behind him into a gray stone room with a window in each of the four walls. His breathing labored, Jon's lungs filled with sweet clean air as the hatch clattered shut behind him.

A distant screeching, punctuated by loud roars, greeted them from outside the tower. He rushed to the window, and Garris joined him. High above the tower, a flaming mass plummeted down from the heavens, set against dark, cloudy skies. Trailing it, like a shower of comets, were the fiery remains of dozens upon dozens of smaller creatures.

The screeching, pained cries and the roar of flames grew louder as the burning mass fell downward, passing only a hundred feet or so from where they stood. Jon and Garris shielded their faces from the heat as the roaring comet hurtled past, set against the peaceful silence of the mountain behind it.

As it passed from above to below, the pitch of the screams lowered. Then it all suddenly halted as the blazing pile slammed into the earth with a thunderous rumble, spattering across the rocky ground outside the tower. The floor shuddered, and they braced themselves as the impact shook the tower. A hail of smaller flaming remains pelted the earth, becoming a roaring pyre near the base of the tower.

Jon and Garris stood for a while, staring at the stunning scene of destruction.

Garris turned to him and beamed a huge smile as he slammed a hand down on his shoulder. Almost laughing, he said, "That was brilliant. You portaled it into the clouds."

"Well," Jon said, "I figured it would reach terminal velocity in about—"

Garris stepped back and turned his sword on Jon, glaring at him with a disturbing seriousness. "Who the heck *are* you?" he demanded. "You fight like a maniac."

"No, I don't," Jon shot back.

"You open portals like Dellia's mother."

"No, I don't."

"You think on your feet as well as anyone I've ever seen. And you're smart."

"No, I ... okay, that's not really me, either," Jon said.

Garris sheathed his sword. "This isn't the time or place, but when this is over, you and I are going to have a very long talk."

He turned his attention to searching every stone of the walls and floor, presumably for some sign of the metal piece or its secret hiding place.

Jon rushed over to a decrepit skeleton propped in the corner and knelt next to it, examining it. He'd never seen a real skeleton of an actual human being before, and it was thoroughly disgusting. Remnants of tattered clothes still clung to the fragile, ancient bones, and it had an odd, flat, wood and metal chest slung over one shoulder, like a backpack. A rusted metal chain encircled its waist and secured the chest. It appeared as if it must hold something valuable, and right now, the most valuable thing he could imagine was the piece that could get him home.

Jon reached through the bones with his knife and began prying open the old chest. Garris glanced over and stopped for a second, shooting him a disapproving stare. "Hey, have some respect for your weapon." He scowled even more deeply. "For *Sirra's* weapon."

The chest was desiccated and frail and yielded to little pressure. It popped open, and a few gems and several books tumbled out. The books fell a short distance then jerked to a stop, dangling by chains that secured them to the chest. An acrid odor of dusty bone and ancient tomes assaulted his senses as Jon stared at the chains in bewilderment.

Garris must have noticed his confusion because he said, "Protection against book thieves."

Jon puzzled over it for a moment. In a society without electronic publishing, or even printing presses, books would have to be made by hand. Perhaps that would make them valuable enough to worry about theft.

As he snatched up a few gems, he noticed a carefully wrapped bundle in their midst. Although the piece of leather tightly wrapped around it appeared tattered, it seemed tidy and well cared for. Someone must have deemed it valuable.

Curiosity got the best of him, and Jon plucked it from the debris. Then he gently unwrapped the soft leather piece that enshrouded it. Inside, he found a leather-bound book, neat and well preserved. He gently opened it and thumbed through a few pages. They seemed old and fragile. He picked a page and began reading aloud: " 'And as Undara breathed her last, I felt such love in her heart. When I told the ambassador of his wife's devotion, he broke down crying, and I realized this gift for which we are so widely despised is a power for great good.' "

Garris stopped his searching and stood, caught up in Jon's words. Jon glanced up, then continued reading. " 'But that good is seldom seen because a few among us feel entitled to abuse it. They cheat and swindle as if it were their right. They learn people's most secret desires and bribe them. They expose people's feelings to embarrass and discredit, or merely to amuse. They manipulate friends, lovers, and enemies alike. They start wars and ruin lives, and then we wonder why we must suffer The Persecution. Our people need rules to employ this gift with wisdom. We need to shout them from the rooftops and teach them to our children until that for which we are so despised becomes our greatest strength.' "

As Jon reached the part about rules, Garris sat down hard on the stone bench. He landed with a grinding noise and reached out to steady himself, as if the seat had moved. He looked down at the bench, then back at Jon with an astonished expression. "It can't be. ..." He reached out, and with delicate care, Jon handed him the book.

"What?" Jon asked.

Garris paged through the book, scrutinizing it. "Those sound like Ellira's words. And it looks like a journal."

"I thought there was nothing written by her."

"There isn't. Or wasn't. Until now." He glanced over at the smoke beginning to seep through the hatch in the floor. "It could still be a fake. Take it. Keep it safe." He gingerly handed the book back to Jon, who rewrapped it with care and placed it in his pocket.

Garris rose and felt around the edges of the seat of the stone bench. He gave it a shove, and it moved with a grinding noise of stone against stone. Jon knelt next to him, and together they heaved against the slab of rock.

It slid out of the way, and inside they found a small, silver box with an impression on its cover of three leaves arranged in a circle. Garris plucked it out of the bench and set it on the floor in front of him. He fished through his pockets and produced a set of lock picks, which he jammed into the lock.

After a little persuasion, the lock gave way, and the chest popped open with a small click. Resting inside, in the center of a velvet cushion, lay a polished, silver piece of metal.

Jon grabbed it and popped to his feet. He yanked the medallion out of his shirt and slid the chain over his head. As quickly as he could, he tried fitting the silver piece into the three empty spaces on the medallion, rotating it various ways to see if it would fit. He stopped, unable to find a spot.

He stared at it, trying to figure out how this could be. This was the tower. He was at the top of the tower, just as Isla described. This should work. Then he noticed that the edges along one side were smooth and polished, but the other half was jagged, as if it had been torn in half, like a piece of paper.

Jon tried again, fitting the fragment in various spots until he found one where it fit neatly in half the space. It was obvious: it had been broken in two. It even *looked* like half of a leaf. Perhaps he'd find the other half later in his journey.

He looked up, about to explain, but Garris was backing away. His eyes were wide and his face covered with a look of shock and disbelief. Jon found it more than a little unnerving. Garris never looked shocked.

"What?" Jon said, half expecting another swarm of spiders or flying lizards.

Garris reached in his shirt, plucked out a chain, and yanked something off of it. Then he held it out, a polished silver piece, exactly like Jon's. Jon held out his piece with the rough edge facing Garris. Garris brought his fragment over, holding it next to Jon's. The jagged edges were a perfect match.

Jon jumped when the two edges suddenly burst into a blue flame. The two men both dropped their pieces. They landed near each other and slid across the floor until the two torn-looking edges touched.

Jon and Garris looked on as the two fragments melted and fused, sputtering with a blue fire as they merged. The flame ceased, and the melted metal smoothed out, becoming a single seamless piece. Polished and flawless, it had the shape of a perfect, silver leaf, almost as if it had never been in two parts.

Jon reached down and tried to pick up the piece. He jerked his hand away when he touched it, expecting it to be searing hot, but it wasn't. He reached out again and snatched it up, then held it out for Garris to see. "It's completely cold."

He brought the piece near the medallion and jumped yet again when it flew out of his hand, shooting into its space on the medallion with a clank. A blue aura surrounded the medallion. Some of the aura dripped onto the floor, forming a pool. Then it disappeared as quickly as it had formed.

Jon and Garris stared at each other for a moment in amazement. Then Jon shook it off and looked over at the hatch, smoke now pouring up from it. "I think we better go."

He pictured the tower entrance, then thrust out his palm and willed it. A mist formed in front his hand, coalescing into a shimmering water-like portal. And through it appeared Dellia's body, rolled up against the entrance door.

Jon stepped through first, kneeling to scoop her up. She was warm, and he felt her breathing in his arms.

He glanced back as Garris strode through the portal, smoke rolling across the ceiling above him. He stepped around Jon and wrenched the tower door open, and they both stepped out into the sweet morning air of the Talus Plains.

The first rays of the morning sun were peeking through the clouds in the distance as the tower door closed behind Jon. A gentle breeze blew Dellia's hair, and it brushed against his arm as he gazed down at her, making sure she was okay. Flames and smoke poured from behind the tower, disrupting the majestic view of the mountains as he and Garris walked away.

Sirra turned nearly white when she spotted him carrying Dellia with Garris at his side. She shook her head and began racing toward them with Rillen following behind. When Jon glanced over, Garris was nodding and trying to signal Sirra that her daughter was okay.

Jon lowered her to the ground, cradling her in his arms as Garris stepped out to meet a breathless Sirra. He spoke to her in a hushed voice. "I think she's fine. She hit her head. She fell in battle, just like ... you know. But Jon—"

DELLIA

Garris stopped as Dellia opened her eyes, and when she looked up a faint smile appeared as she spotted Jon's face. Sirra stepped around Garris to Jon's side.

"What happened?" Dellia asked.

Before Jon could even think of what to tell her, Garris jumped in. "Jon saved you. I hacked my way down to you. He threw you over his shoulder and carried you out."

Dellia's face lit up, filled with a look of surprise and admiration. She stared into Jon's eyes. "You saved me?"

"Well ... I did the hacking, remember?" Garris said.

Jon smiled at Dellia and shook his head. "No, you were amazing. I've never seen anything like it. The way you fought. *You* saved *me*. You saved us *all*."

As he looked down at her, still cradled in his arms, she smiled, and her soft, blue eyes returned his gaze. For a moment, the world disappeared and all he could see was her. She seemed like the most beautiful and amazing thing in the world, and he wanted nothing more than for time to stop so he could stay in this moment forever.

Then he realized time hadn't stopped, and everyone was staring at him. Jon tore his gaze from Dellia's and set her down.

She suddenly seemed self-conscious and looked away as they both stood up. "So, the mission failed?"

Garris blurted out, "No, we got the fragment."

Dellia stared at Garris, appearing puzzled.

Suddenly, Jon found himself very curious to see how Garris was going to explain this.

"Well," Garris said, "see, there was this skeleton."

"Yeah," Jon chimed in, "a skeleton."

Dellia seemed puzzled. "I didn't see any skeleton."

"Oh, well, it was there," Garris said. "And it had this pack. And in it was the metal piece. I simply reached in and grabbed it before we took off. It was the darnedest thing."

Garris turned his face away from Dellia, toward Jon, and grimaced.

Jon noticed Sirra glancing over at the flames and smoke pouring out from behind the tower. She subtly leaned in toward him and
whispered in his ear, "Smooth. Very believable."

He never looked up. His gaze remained fixed on Dellia, trying
to discern her reaction. She puzzled for a moment, then seemed to
accept it.

Sunlight broke through the clouds, flooding the area around
them. Dellia rose, standing with the tower and flames at her back.
Smoke and ash rose into the air, drifting past the mountains behind
the group as Sirra turned and held out her hand. And slowly a shimmering portal began to form in front of her.

Chapter Twelve

ON THE EMBERS OF DUSK

Jon closed the book and bowed his head, staring down at it between his legs as he sat on the cool steps of the porch. It was an astonishing story. So full of wars and political intrigue, prejudice and hatred—it was hard to believe it had all really happened. This was an accounting of someone's actual life. But it was so much more than that. It was a story of a devastating war and its aftermath. And how one lone woman, with no real power or title, stood against a treacherous cabal, a warlike empire, and their enemies, to transform an entire civilization. And not by defeating one side or another, or by trying to make them realize they were wrong. But by making them see that free people inspired to accomplish a common goal would prosper far more than they ever could through oppression, slavery, and conquest.

With reverent care, Jon wrapped the journal in the old tattered piece of leather. He raised his head, staring out across the quiet green plains, lit by the late-day sun, and in that scene before him, he found a whole new appreciation for this place, its history, and its people.

He glanced over as Sirra plopped down beside him. And he realized there was a newfound closeness to her, too, an understanding of her and a kinship with both Sirra and Dellia he'd not had before. Not one born out of blood or common ancestry, but out of a shared reverence for, and appreciation of, a people and their beliefs. He wanted to ask her a thousand questions about this land, and her people, and the things he'd read. But he just sat with her, gazing out across the landscape, enjoying her company while a herd of wild horses grazed in the distance, set against far-off mountains.

Sirra glanced at him, her voice tentative. "It's possible I may have judged you more harshly than you deserve."

Jon kept staring off at the horizon. "You weren't wrong. They went into the tower for me. And it could have easily gotten them killed."

He glanced over at her, and she was gazing past him, her calm replaced by the distant look of a painful memory. "Outside that tower, when the screeching started, then the roaring, and the fire … I was terrified."

Jon closed his eyes, recalling the events, and it seemed incomprehensible that it had only been a handful of hours ago. "Trust me, it wasn't any better inside." He turned his head and looked Sirra in the eye. "But you should know that Dellia, she took them all on, so we could get away. She saved us."

Sirra shook her head. "My daughter doesn't have the power to do what I saw, and neither does Garris. The only—"

"Neither do I, really. Sort of. I mean, it's complicated. It's like it wasn't really me. I just … reacted."

"Well, I never felt more alone, waiting outside that tower. I was sure I'd lost her. Then you brought her back to me…. Thank you."

Jon gave a small nod, and the pair returned to staring off at the pale blue mountains. He remembered the journal and glanced down at the leather-wrapped tome in his hands. He breathed a small sigh. "We found something in there."

She glanced at him, then down at the worn bundle in his hands. Jon held out the journal, offering it to her. "This really belongs to your people."

She gently took the package, turning it over in her hands, examining the ancient wrappings. She unwound them with care, and her eyes widened as she stared at the cover. When she opened it, her hand flew to her mouth. And as she gently flipped through a few pages, she began to read.

" 'I was at the Battle of Volus today. It was like a hundred other battles I've seen in this cursed war. A war that has spanned my entire life. I felt the terror in the enemy's heart as they struggled on the battlefield. I held one of the fallen in my arms as the last shred of hope slipped from his heart and his last breath left his body. I felt the unendurable anguish and heartbreak of the widows and the children. And I resolved that I must find a way to make my people see: there is no honor in war, no glory in winning. The honor is in avoiding the fight.' "

Sirra pulled her eyes out of the book and stared at Jon, apparently speechless.

He motioned to the bundle. "Those are Ellira's words, aren't they?"

She simply nodded. She looked over at Jon, then down at the well-preserved journal. "It's unbelievable … but here it is. We must present this to the Ephori. They will find a place where everyone can see it. It will be studied and treasured by my people. Jon, your name, it will be remembered."

A sudden inexplicable stab of anxiety struck, and he stiffened. "No, not mine. That would be wrong. Without Garris and Dellia, I would have died. Promise me *their* names will be remembered."

Sirra studied Jon for a long moment.

He averted his gaze. Perhaps his reaction might have been a little over the top.

"Jon, you can't have it both ways," Sirra said. "You can't blame yourself for putting them at risk, then take no credit for finding this."

"Well, then just tell the truth, warts and all, okay?"

She thought for a moment, then nodded. "The truth then."

He looked away into the distance. He wanted to ask so many questions. But he just glanced down and said, "I read some of it."

"And?" Sirra asked.

Eager to share his impressions, his animated words rushed out. "It's amazing. I feel like I've met her. And it makes me understand Dellia better."

"But? ..." Sirra said.

"There's no 'but.' I mean, there was this one part that surprised me."

She handed him the journal. "Which part?"

Jon paged through to find the section. " 'Elona believed as I do. And so at the end of the battle, when she had a chance to finish it, she took pity and let them retreat, hoping her show of mercy would pave the way for peace. But in their hearts was only venom and anger, and what Elona saw as an act of kindness, they saw as a sign of contempt. They gathered reinforcements and attacked with such vengeance and hatred that Elona was forced to wipe them out to a man. What started as an act of mercy and restraint ended in a massacre that cost the lives of many of her best. The experience strengthened my belief that if you must fight, be powerful, swift, and decisive. There is mercy in ending it quickly.' "

Jon closed the book and looked over to see Sirra watching.

"You don't agree?" she asked.

He handed the well-worn journal back to her. "It's just a little disturbing, you know. I mean, she's advocating wiping them out."

"What if your survival, or the survival of your people, is at stake?"

"But to call that mercy? Don't you think there's mercy in, I don't know ... being merciful?"

"What about the wolves?" Sirra eyed him with a solemn expression. "You had to kill them or they'd kill you. Then wasn't it merciful that you ended it quickly and decisively?"

"I suppose, but they're not people. Maybe I just have a hard time with the idea that any fight is inevitable."

She smiled, as if gratified to hear his words. She rested her hand on Jon's, and her voice became strong and passionate. "That's good. Hold on to that belief. Never stop searching for another way. But if someday, after you truly have tried everything, the moment comes when you're forced to fight, don't let that desire hold you back. Fight or don't fight, but never fight halfway."

He stared at her for a moment. She had a way about her, and it was in moments like this that he glimpsed the wise leader making impassioned speeches.

"Is that another saying from Ellira?" Jon asked.

Sirra nodded, and he returned to staring across the beautiful green plains. The horses were still there, grazing, and a pair of them, most likely youngsters from the look of it, were racing around frolicking.

He was on the verge of laughing when she pulled his attention back to the conversation. "Are you sure you won't accompany me to the meeting of the Ephori? I know they'll want to meet you."

His uncomfortable feeling returned. He had no desire to gain any attention, much less be the center of attention. His eyes were drawn to the dark horizon to the east, back the way he'd come a couple days before. He had done what he needed to do here, and it was time to leave, but the thought made him a little sad. He'd miss this place, and he'd miss Sirra. But how could he say that, and to what purpose?

Jon drew a deep breath. "I think, for now, my path lies elsewhere."

"Hmm. Yes. Perhaps that's best. So where will you go next?"

"I think it's best if I keep that to myself." He turned back to Sirra.

"I think that'd be wise. And a word of advice, do not tell anyone where you come from. And whatever power you used in that tower, tell no one."

Jon stared at her, stunned by her particular turn of phrase and its eerie similarity to the warning Isla had given. "Why would you say that?"

"Call it a hunch. And one more word of advice: talk to Dellia."

He sat up taller. "About what?"

"I could be wrong, but it seemed like you had feelings for her, and she for you."

"No," Jon said, shocked at the suggestion. "Why would she have feelings for *me*? She's beautiful and amazing, and I'm just simple plain old … me."

"If I'm wrong, then you can both have a laugh at my expense. But if I'm right, then I don't see how this ends well for either of you. So talk to her."

Jon sat staring at Sirra for a moment, then nodded. "Okay, I will."

She turned her attention to the precious bundle in her hands, staring at it with a sort of reverent awe.

He got up, his mind still preoccupied with her outlandish suggestion. It didn't make any sense. Dellia was a protector, and even if she weren't, why would she be interested in him? But Sirra was right about him, and he knew it. He kept telling himself to set aside his feelings, not to think about her, because there was no way it could end well. But in a way, even doing that only seemed to validate what he was feeling.

Jon turned to go into the house, but a sudden and inexplicable urge struck. He had always imagined what it must be like to have a real mother, someone who actually cared about him, someone to talk with. And he realized that these moments with Sirra, her concern for him, her advice, and his newfound affinity with her—this was as close as he was ever likely to come. He turned back and gave her a firm hug. She looked up at him in surprise and smiled as she patted his arm. He let go and hurried in the house.

DELLIA

Dellia stormed to the window for the seventh time in as many minutes. She leaned over the small table and gazed out at the lush green yard. Across the way, the late sun was dropping behind the stone guesthouse, heading for the distant mountains, but she barely noticed. She was too busy rehearsing what she'd say to Kayleen. Yet everything she tried sounded wrong, or awkward, or—even worse—confrontational. And she had no desire to create a rift between her and Kayleen. Still, her mother was right. She had been entrusted with a rare and precious gift—the greatest gift anyone could possess: the ability to know what's in another's heart—and what they wanted her to do with it was perverse and wrong.

So she had done her best to carry out the council's wishes without using her gift, but she knew in her heart she hadn't succeeded. She was only fooling herself, and the guilt was eating her alive. She had to find the words to convince Kayleen, to make her see how wrong this was.

Dellia pushed off from the rough windowsill and scurried over to her well-used pack. She rifled through it but couldn't locate the Window of Rhina. Then she recalled finding it earlier and realized she'd been clutching it in her hand the whole time.

She rushed back to the small table under the window and stopped to admire the beautiful wood inlay of a horse. It had always made her smile, but not this time. With care, she set the smooth metal bar on its surface and breathed on it.

She paced, staring at the worn boards of the floor as the mist grew and deepened and coalesced into the familiar, shimmering, water-like curtain. Then she stood and fidgeted as she looked down at the bare walls of the sparse chambers reflected in its liquid surface.

Minutes went by before Kayleen appeared in a rush and plopped down into the chair in front of Dellia. Her apprehension was palpable, and Dellia stared for a second, wondering what was wrong.

"Listen," Kayleen said, "we aren't satisfied with the current situation. The council believes we need to be much more direct. Here's what we need you to do."

"Can I just—"

"We want you to ask Jon directly if he and Megan are from another world and then tell us if he's lying."

Stunned by her directness, Dellia reeled backward and shook her head. Until now, Kayleen had only hinted at using her gift. This was an *order* to use it.

"I already told you, he isn't from this world."

"But we need to be sure. And we want you to tell him Megan's life may be in danger—or no, better yet that she's near death. Tell him that you need to get to her."

"What?" Dellia could hardly believe the request. "This is ridiculous. I told you he doesn't know where she is. Don't you trust me? I suppose that's why Rillen is really here, to check up on me?"

"Of course I trust you, but you know the prophecy. You know what it could mean. We have an obligation to protect people. We have to be certain."

Suddenly, it became clear. Kayleen's apprehension was over this. She knew what she was asking was wrong, and she was doing it anyway. All of Dellia's frustration came rushing to the surface. She couldn't take it anymore, and the words poured out, sharp and cold. "Look, you asked me to get close to Jon. Well, fine, I've done that. You asked me to be sure he doesn't know where Megan is, and I've done that, too, and more. I've intimidated him, threatened him, nearly beaten him up, manipulated him, lied to him, pried into his feelings, betrayed his trust … and it's gotten me nowhere. And now this? Now you want me to lie and say Megan's life is in danger?"

"I know, and we wouldn't ask unless—"

"He's been hurt by her. When he says he doesn't know where

she is, he's telling the truth. I'm not the council's personal lie detector."

Kayleen's eyes widened in surprise.

Jon stood in the dim light of the kitchen at dusk, staring down the darkened stone hallway, wrestling with indecision. Sirra was right. He needed to tell Dellia how he felt. But it seemed incomprehensible that she would have feelings for him. And even if she did, what was he supposed to say? "Dellia, do you love me?" That sounded super dumb. And what if she laughed? What if she thought he was stupid and pathetic? Even worse: What if it was like Megan all over again?

He turned away. He couldn't go through that one more time. He couldn't take it, especially not with Dellia. Maybe it was best to just leave things as they were. What could possibly be gained by encouraging his feelings? What would it change? Jon began to walk away.

Then, he spotted Sirra still sitting on the porch, and he froze. Could she be right? Was he just being a coward? He had to at least take a chance.

He inhaled a deep breath and turned around. In a distracted haze, he shuffled through the kitchen and down the hall toward her room. His mind raced. What would he say? What would he do?

The sound of voices from Dellia's room ahead yanked him out of his thoughts, and he halted. He shouldn't eavesdrop on a private conversation. That would be wrong.

He turned to go. But a woman's voice caught his attention. "Of course I trust you, but you know the prophecy."

He had trouble making out the rest, but a notion compelled him. What if this was about him? What if this answered the hundreds of questions he had about Megan and Isla and everything? So he turned back and moved to right outside the door.

"We have to be certain," the woman said.

Then came Dellia's voice, loud and clear, but her tone was harsh and cold. "Look, you asked me to get close to Jon. Well, fine, I've done that. You asked me to be sure he doesn't know where Megan is, and I've done that, too, and more. I've intimidated him, threatened him, nearly beaten him up, manipulated him, lied to him, pried into his feelings, betrayed his trust … and it's gotten me nowhere. And now this? Now you want me to lie and say Megan's life is in danger?"

Jon slumped and put a hand on the wall to steady himself. It was as if his heart had been ripped from his chest. He couldn't stand to hear any more. He couldn't bear it.

He turned and trudged down the hall, using the stones of the wall to prop himself up. Head spinning, half in a daze, he nearly collided with Rillen as she dodged out of his path, passing him on her way to Dellia's room.

Jon could still hear the voices behind him. "I know, and we wouldn't ask unless—" the woman said.

"He's been hurt by her," Dellia said, her utterances fading behind him. "When he says he doesn't know where she is, he's telling the truth. I'm not the council's personal lie detector. Wait … is that why you sent me?"

The words rang in his ears, but they barely registered. He couldn't think. He couldn't function. Maybe he misunderstood. Maybe he had it all wrong.

Jon passed through the doorway into the kitchen. It was like he was back in the lab with Megan telling him all the ways he was broken, all the ways he could never be with her.

No, he understood perfectly, and this was far worse than Megan. Dellia had used him, taken advantage of him. Deliberately. Because he was her *job*. And with that realization came a sudden and overpowering urge to flee. He had to go, this very second. It didn't matter where, as long as it was far away from here, away from it all.

Jon moved faster and faster as he barged through the kitchen door and onto the porch. He flew past Sirra, still sitting quietly, staring out across the green plains at the mountains in the distance.

His feet accelerated across the plush, green yard. He thought he heard Sirra calling to him, "Jon, is everything okay?"

He just kept going. He had only one thought, to get out of there. He slammed through the guesthouse door. Garris's head popped up, and he stared at Jon like he was a madman.

"I'm leaving," Jon said as he rushed over to his pack.

"I'll grab my gear," came Garris's instant reply.

Jon snatched his pack up off the floor and slammed it down onto the wooden table. He grabbed the few pieces of loose clothing lying around and shoved them in it. He yanked the bag closed, jerked it off the table, and stormed out the door, with Garris right on his heels.

Dellia glared at Kayleen through the shimmering image on her small table, her frustration boiling over as she recounted all the horrible things she'd done to Jon. All the ways she had hurt and abused and taken advantage of this poor man.

"And now this?" she said. "You want me to lie and say Megan's life is in danger?"

Kayleen tried to get a few words in. "I know, and we wouldn't ask unless—"

"He's been hurt by her," Dellia interrupted. "When he says he doesn't know where she is, he's telling the truth. I'm not the council's personal lie detector. Wait … is that why you sent me?"

Kayleen seemed flustered by the question. But her response was unflinching. "That might have been a factor, yes."

All of Dellia's fury and resentment came bursting to the surface. They had used her. As if she were some mere unfeeling thing for the council to play with. They understood with absolute clarity what they were asking, yet they didn't care. As if no longer in control, her words poured out, powerful and passionate.

"This is so wrong. My people live by three simple rules: we don't use our gift to hurt people, we don't expose other people's feelings, and we don't manipulate emotions. And you've asked me to do all three. And foolish me, I went along with it. You've gotten me to do terrible things to a good-hearted guy who's not out to hurt anyone. Well, that's on me. But now it's over. Enough, I'm not doing it anymore."

Kayleen tried to respond. "If I knew of another way I'd—"

"There is another way. We protectors exist because you need people who can act on their own judgment. How about trusting me to use mine? I'm telling you something is wrong here, and it's not Jon. So you're just going to have to trust me to figure it out and do the right thing. Now if you don't mind, I'm going to go do my job."

Dellia slashed her hand through the image of Kayleen, and it disintegrated into a rain of colored drops that vanished as soon as they struck the table and floor. She leaned over the table, trembling as she buried her head in her arms and tried to calm herself.

She took a deep breath and managed to regain some small degree of composure. What had she done? She'd never spoken to a council member like that before.

She uncovered her face and looked over at Rillen's calm countenance, watching her from the soft yellow and gray stone of the doorway. "Nice speech," she said, "very passionate."

"I've never actually told the council 'no' before. I just hope I haven't broken their trust."

"I hope you didn't do this because—" Rillen stopped when she saw Dellia's eyes go wide with disbelief. Rillen slumped onto the bed, her hand to her cheek. "No. Why would you listen to me? You know I say foolish things in the heat of the moment."

The words she'd spoken came out of guilt, frustration, and anger. They had barely come from her, much less Rillen. Dellia shook her head. "No. No, you were right."

"Well," said Rillen, "I just wonder how much Jon heard."

A sudden wave of panic hit Dellia. "What?" She took a step backward.

"He was standing in the hallway listening when I came up."

All of a sudden, everything was spinning out of control. First the council, now this. ... All Dellia could manage was, "Rillen, go ... do something."

This was beyond a disaster. If Jon knew. ... A sudden compulsion seized her. She had to get to him, to talk to him, to make him understand.

She flew down the hallway, through the kitchen, and out onto the porch. Her mother looked up with an expression of deep concern, an expression that confirmed all of her worst fears.

Dellia's gaze shot everywhere. Then she spotted Garris leading two horses out of the stables, and one of them was Enna.

"No, no, no, no, no," she mumbled to herself as she raced across the yard.

The sun was slipping below the horizon behind Jon and Garris, painting the clouds shades of yellow and orange as Dellia raced up behind them. Jon had his back to her and was tightening the girth on his saddle.

He stopped but kept his back to her as she spoke. "I know you heard me speaking with the council. And you have to believe, I would—"

He swung around to face her. She could feel his hurt and pain, but he simply smiled, and his expression was soft and gentle.

As he gazed into her eyes, nothing but affection showed on his face. "Listen, Dellia, I appreciate everything you've done for me. I don't know if you were ever really my friend, but from—"

The words were like a dagger in Dellia's heart. She blurted out, "No, I was always your friend."

"From the start, all I've wanted is just to go home. And you were there for me when I was lost, when I had no friend in the world. I'll never forget that. But I just don't … I mean I can't—"

"Jon, please," Dellia said, her panic turning into wild desperation. "I need to explain. There's this … prophecy—"

She was stopped by his gently taking her hand. His pain was intense, almost more than she could bear, but he simply smiled as he gazed at her.

"Goodbye, Dellia. I wish you all the happiness in the world. Take care of yourself."

All of a sudden, it became clear. All of that pain, all of Jon's pain, it belonged to her. This was the price for violating the three rules. She had done this to him and to herself. And *she* would have to live with that, not him. She couldn't ask that of him. She couldn't ask him to stay. She watched, paralyzed and helpless, as he and Garris climbed onto their horses, turned, and rode off across the plains— and out of her life.

Chapter Thirteen

HONOR AND DECEPTION

Torchlight flickered across the white marble walls as Kayleen sped down the hallway toward her inevitable confrontation with the council. The clamor of voices echoing up from the chamber grew louder as she approached, but she barely noticed. She was too busy contemplating her impending report to the council. The situation was ugly. Her options were narrow, and her possible avenues of defense nonexistent. Yet hurrying somehow made her feel better, more in control, despite being at an utter loss for how to argue her way out of what had just happened.

She had been pushing Dellia too far, and she knew it. The evidence was present at each meeting and in every aspect of her face and body. Countless years of debating and discussing had led her to rely on her ability to read people. And lately, that ability had been screaming at her, telling her that what she had been compelled to ask of Dellia was too much. Yet with each new request to push it just a little further, the stress kept building. Who knows how much that inner conflict had already affected Dellia's gift, and what critical details she may have missed? But what choice did she have? The council's decisions were clear, and there was no way she could ease her way into asking Dellia to do something morally repugnant.

So as disastrous as tonight's blowup was, it had not been unexpected. She had even gone so far as to work out what to tell the council should this happen. But now, in the aftermath, all her carefully considered words seemed inappropriate. She'd have to rely on what she always did: her wits, her ability to read the room, and her knowledge of the council members.

Braye remained a lost cause; he wouldn't like anything. So was Aapri since she frequently sided with him. Idria was ambitious but too caught up in procedure and protocol to pose a significant threat. Tealus wouldn't challenge her; he fancied himself an idea man, and Ceree seemed too obsessed with Rillen and tracking Megan to care. So it came down to Jiam, Lyceran, and Shaon. Any of them could be swayed, especially Jiam, who was one of the more rational thinkers. All she needed was a cogent argument and half the council would be on her side.

Kayleen burst through the archway into the well-lit council chamber to the rumble of discussion echoing off the polished marble walls. She sized up the table as she approached, and all that greeted her were faces eager for news. This was going to be tough, seeing as how Dellia had cut her off before she could gather any.

As she surveyed the table, an awful feeling of déjà vu hit, and with it the stabbing pain of guilt and regret. Here she was again, facing the council, trying to justify the actions of her protector. Actions the council had precipitated by their incessant need to barge in and control everything. Just as with Garris fifteen years ago, the situation was in the process of blowing up in their faces. Yet they were incapable of seeing their own part in it. She had failed all those years ago. She had failed Garris, and she had failed herself. Horror and dread gripped her at the very real prospect that she could fail Dellia in the same way.

As Kayleen approached her empty chair, she steeled herself. This was not the time for self-doubt. She had spent fifteen lonely years, missing the two people that had been at the center of her whole world. Since then, Dellia was the only real friend she'd had. There was no way she was going to let it happen again. Not with

Dellia. Not this time.

Kayleen summoned her most poised and confident demeanor as she stopped at the head of the table. She decided not to seat herself, preferring to lean over the dark, shiny table as the din of voices subsided and all eyes turned toward her.

She rested her hands on the smooth, cool surface and leaned in, scanning the members' faces, making sure she caught everyone's full attention.

In her most confident voice, Kayleen began. "I've spoken with Dellia, and there's been a change of plans."

Kayleen left a momentary pause for dramatic effect, but before she could continue, Idria's crisp voice chimed in. "A change of plans?"

"Wait, first, what about the tower?" Braye said.

"Yes, I take it he's still alive," Ceree added, "and there have been reports suggesting something happened in that area."

"I don't know, we didn't discuss it," Kayleen continued, brushing aside their questions.

A tumult of impassioned voices broke out at the table, and Idria's calm, strong voice rose above the racket. "Didn't discuss it? Then what *did* you discuss?"

Kayleen stood tall and straight as she continued. "She is absolutely certain they are from another world and that Jon doesn't know where Megan is. She felt our course of action was a waste of time and that there was nothing further to be learned by *abusing* her gift in the manner we requested."

She gave just the right degree of weight to the word *abusing*, and just as expected, a round of murmurs swept the room. She slowly scanned the table again trying to make eye contact with each member. "In fact, she objected strenuously to using her gift in that way."

The murmur grew to a clamor, and Kayleen interrupted, raising her commanding voice. "Fellow council members, her objection is valid. We would never send a general to war, then require them to give us daily reports so we could give them a blow-by-blow strategy for how to conduct each battle."

Nods of agreement spread around the table. Pleased with the reaction, she continued. "And since when does this council concern itself with such an insignificant matter as what tools a protector in the field uses to get the job done?"

"That's true," Aapri chimed in.

"In so doing," Kayleen continued, "we hamper her effectiveness, and right now we need her to be as effective as she can be."

"But," Tealus said, "the fact remains that she is substituting her judgment for that of this council."

"Just as a general would do when conditions change. And conditions are changing on a constant basis. Dellia needs the freedom to pursue this as she sees fit."

Aapri spoke up, addressing the other council members. "Perhaps Kayleen is right."

"I don't like it," Braye said quietly.

"It's as I've been saying all along." Ceree addressed the other members. "We need to shift our focus to Megan."

"We can do both," Braye said.

Kayleen closed her eyes and breathed an imperceptible sigh of relief. This was the direction in which she'd hoped to steer things. She straightened again, reminding herself the subject was far from closed.

"Are there any other protectors we could put on finding Megan?" Tealus asked.

"Sure," Jiam said, "but we gave the only Window of Rhina to Dellia, so she could report to Kayleen. Without that, we'd have to send runners to bring them in. It would take precious days."

All around the table, council members began talking among themselves. Kayleen stood for a moment, listening to the murmur of discussion echoing through the columned marble hall.

Then, suddenly, Ceree's lone voice rose above the din. "What about Rillen? Has she left yet to find Megan?"

The murmurs ceased, and all eyes turned to Kayleen, waiting for her answer.

"I don't know," she said.

The table broke into an uproar, and it was disturbing to see so many heads shaking in disapproval.

Then Braye's loud, annoyed voice caught everyone's attention. "So the situation is completely out of hand, and you're just fine with that?"

Kayleen struggled for a moment, trying to come up with the perfect answer, but before she could, Idria jumped in.

"Kayleen, even if we conceded you're right on every point you've made, the proper course of action would have been to carry out our orders while we take her objection into consideration. As it is, our orders have been willfully disobeyed."

"For good reason," Kayleen shot back. "Our orders didn't make sense to her, and she thought there was a better course of action."

Braye jumped in. "What good is having soldiers if they discard any order they disagree with?"

Her worst fears were being realized. If she didn't cut this off now, it would turn into a feeding frenzy, with everyone attacking Dellia like sharks at the smell of blood in the water.

Kayleen leaned over the dark table, addressing Braye directly. "We asked her to violate her beliefs. Can you blame her? And she didn't disobey. She asked us to let her figure out how to handle the situation."

"Asked?" Idria said. "That's not how you described it. It sounds like it was a demand. Or are you suggesting you gave her permission to run off on her own?"

"It still amounts to the same thing," Braye continued. "We told her to do something, and she refused."

Kayleen never acknowledged Idria, continuing to focus on

Braye. "So, if the council told her to murder your son, she should do it without objection? Even if she knows he's innocent?"

"It's not at all the same thing, and you know it," Braye shot back. "Jon and Megan are a threat to this institution. And asking her to get close to Jon is not the same as murder."

"So it would be okay to have her murder your son if he posed a threat to this institution?"

Idria jumped in, her voice strong and insistent. "You're making false comparisons, we never asked her to do anything close to murder."

Unable to ignore her any longer, Kayleen shifted her attention to Idria. "You're wrong. It is to her. We asked her to violate deeply held beliefs about how to use her gift. And we did it *knowing* it violated her beliefs."

"We still need to know," Idria insisted. "Did you okay this, or did she willfully disobey our orders?"

"She's not a soldier," Kayleen said. "We train protectors to use their minds. We expect … no, we *demand* that they do so. She's doing as she was trained, deciding how to act in our best interests."

The instant Idria's annoyed expression appeared, it was obvious Kayleen had pushed it too far. She could feel Dellia's fate being decided in those pale blue eyes.

This time, Idria was loud, slow, and insistent. "Did you or did you not give her permission?"

The entire table froze, seeming taken aback by her strong reaction. All eyes turned to Kayleen as they waited for her answer.

There was only one way out now. If she told the truth, the council would consider Dellia to have disobeyed a direct order, and in a matter of this gravity, where the fate of the three realms stood in the balance, it would be a blow from which she'd never recover. If they didn't dismiss her outright, she'd never be given a mission of any importance again. And working for the council leader would be out of the question. Worse yet, if things went particularly badly, as they had with Garris, she'd be charged with treason.

Her heart broke at the idea of Dellia bearing a stain like that. All those years ago, when she had defended her protector, she had played the idealist. She'd been truthful, and it had crushed the dreams of the man she loved. For fifteen lonely years, she had lived with the remorse over what she had done to Garris. No power on Earth could make her repeat that again with Dellia. This time, she would choose differently.

"Yes," Kayleen said, her voice strong and bold. "Her objections made sense to me. So I told her to handle it how she saw fit."

Braye seemed incredulous. "We decided. We voted. And you're telling me you just decided to discard our voices in the matter?"

Now it was all about saving herself. Kayleen brought herself up taller. "Things get messy in the field, and sometimes you have to improvise. So yeah, if blame is what really matters to you now, then look no further."

"You've taken the power to decide out of our hands," Braye said, "so finding blame is the only course left to us."

"Has she cut off communication?" Ceree asked.

Kayleen paused. The answer was bound to make matters much worse. So she stood in silence as she struggled with what to say.

Before she could formulate an answer, Idria's slow, strong voice jumped in. "When do you think you'll hear from her next?"

Kayleen struggled again as her prospects for salvaging the situation evaporated. "I don't know," she said, not truly hiding her frustration. "When the situation changes, and she has something to report."

Grumbling and disagreement erupted all around the heavy black table, the clamor resounding through the spacious white chamber. Kayleen stood by, powerless, having completely lost command of the situation.

Suddenly, Idria's voice rang out again, strong and clear. "Thank you for your honesty, Kayleen. I think we understand the situation. Now, if you don't mind, the rest of the council would like to meet and discuss how to proceed."

Again, the entire council seemed shocked and surprised. Kayleen waited, and nothing came but silence. Not a single objection, and not a single member rose to her defense.

"You're dismissing me?" Kayleen said.

Idria gave a crisp nod. "For now."

She turned and quietly walked from the crowded table. The whispers and hushed voices echoed from behind her as she strolled across the polished floor, but she barely noticed. She was too busy calculating the enormity of what had just taken place. Her friends and colleagues on the council had dismissed her as if she were some petulant stepchild. And sure, she had protected Dellia for the moment, but now, nothing stood between her and the council. Who knew what they might ask of Dellia next, or how she might react? And for the first time in two decades, Kayleen realized she was powerless to influence what happened next.

As Sirra's homestead disappeared behind them, and the sun slipped farther below the horizon, Jon fell deeper and deeper into a muddled haze. For once, he was grateful that Garris was not the talkative type. With only the light of the almost full moon to guide his way, Garris led them in silence across the vast, grassy expanse. Minutes passed into hours, the thudding of hooves and chirping of crickets carrying on the cool evening breeze as they pressed onward.

Eventually, out of the darkness appeared an enormous, lone tree, rising above the plains like a dark behemoth, reaching for the star-filled sky. Garris adjusted his heading, aiming straight for it. As they came to a stop under its sheltering branches, Jon slipped off his horse and began to sleepwalk through his tasks. But Garris grabbed him and directed him to the base of the tree, motioning for him to sit. So Jon plopped down on a gigantic root and stared into space as Garris tended the horses, built a fire, and found something they could both eat for dinner.

Jon didn't have much of an appetite, so he spent more time picking at his food than actually eating. Eventually, he finished and settled before the fire, watching it dance and flicker.

Garris stirred it with a stick, and the embers settled with a burst of pops and snaps. Sparks flew into the night, and Jon followed them up, watching as they drifted through the massive branches that twisted and wound their way up into the darkness.

He sighed and turned his gaze outward, beyond the fire, as the night wind rustled through the leaves of the tree. He had hardly been able to form a decent thought since leaving Sirra's house. He was spent, his mind a muddled mess.

Who wouldn't be, hearing Dellia speak so casually of lying to him and manipulating him? How could he have been so utterly wrong about her? How could he have felt such a strong connection where nothing existed? And when he announced he was leaving, she seemed genuinely distraught. So much so, he found himself feeling sorry for her, despite everything she'd done. How could he be so deeply grateful to her, and yet so deeply hurt, all at the same time? Just another in the litany of ways in which he was broken. And perhaps someday he'd work it all out and find a lesson in all this pain. But right now he just felt burned out, used up, unable to think.

Garris snagged another log and lobbed it onto the blaze. The campfire roared again, and a new batch of sparks leaped from the flames, swirling up into the gnarled old branches and toward the starlit sky. Jon glanced over at his water skin and scooped it up. He opened it and raised it to his lips.

"Yup," Garris said, "it's gotta be a lot more fun, us two out here alone, instead of sitting around a fire, just you and Dellia."

Jon choked on the water, coughing and sputtering. That was deliberate. He turned his head and threw him a blistering glare. "Every other time it's impossible to pry two words out of you, but now you want to chitchat?"

"No. No. We can just sit here and stare into the fire and brood, or pout, or whatever it is we're doing."

Jon wanted to punch Garris ... or something. But he just continued glaring at him. "Good," he said, then turned back to the fire.

A pang of guilt struck. After all, none of this was Garris's fault. Quite the opposite: the man had left immediately and followed him without comment, question, or complaint. And he'd waited patiently for an explanation while doing all the work. Whatever his reasons for helping, Jon was grateful for it, now more than ever.

"Anyway," Garris said, "good thing we left before morning, so we didn't have to sleep in those nice soft beds."

Jon turned his head toward him. "Sorry, I couldn't stay." Even to him, the words sounded overly dramatic.

"Care to tell me why? All I got out of that was, 'I'm leaving.' Then Dellia standing there like she'd just shot her best friend's puppy. Then you saying goodbye."

Jon sighed. "The council asked her to spy on me, get close to me, manipulate me. Something about a prophecy."

He waited for a few sage words of support or sympathy, or at least a grunt of indignation. Instead, Garris became quiet and thoughtful, as if mulling over possibilities Jon had yet to fathom.

"Oh, man, poor Dellia," Garris said, half to himself.

Jon stared at him, hardly able to believe his ears. "Excuse me? 'Poor Dellia'?"

Garris returned to poking the fire with a stick, and when he spoke, his manner was calm and reasonable. "Yeah. You'll get over it, but her kind, they have this code, an almost religious conviction about not misusing their gift. A bunch of rules, and my bet is the council got her to go against them. She won't forgive herself for that."

"What are you talking about? What gift?"

He turned to Jon. "She can sense feelings. You didn't know?"

"No. Really?" Jon raised his eyes, staring at the firelight as it flittered across the enormous branches above. "Well, I mean, I guess I should have suspected, especially after reading Ellira's journal." His attention flew back to Garris. "Wait, you're talking about the three rules?"

"Yeah, they take them pretty seriously."

Jon faced the fire again, peering into the flames as he tried to reconcile the two incompatible versions of Dellia. There was the manipulative agent of the council who had coldly recounted her betrayal, and the sympathetic friend that Sirra would have raised to never misuse her gift.

"Oh," he said as the implications cascaded through his mind. So every time he and Dellia talked, she could tell what he was feeling. It was like she'd been spying on his innermost thoughts. What kind of person violates you like that, all the while pretending to be your friend? And with that thought came another: Did it really matter what her motives were? The fact that she may have been pressured didn't change the reality of what she had done. Or the fact that she'd still be doing it if he hadn't caught her.

"Still, I mean, how can I trust her?" Jon said.

"You shouldn't," Garris shot back. "She works for the council."

Jon stared at him, puzzled by the seeming contradiction.

"Look, I wasn't going to tell you this, but the council's most likely up in arms over this nonsense called The Prophecy of the Otherworlder. No doubt they're scared it's you or your friend, and that's why they sent Dellia."

"Is that the prophecy Dellia mentioned?"

Garris nodded.

"Well, what does it say?"

"Nothing good." There was finality in Garris's tone that said he wasn't going to reveal more.

Jon stared. "So you're just not going to tell me?"

"Look, it's not important. It'll only mess with your head. The minute you give up your free will because you think you know what some idiotic prophecy says, your life is over." Garris glanced away into the fire, his normally calm expression replaced by the distant look of a troubled soul. "You'll end up like me."

Jon continued to gawk as he puzzled over what could have happened to elicit that kind of reaction from a man who seemed impervious to everything.

Then the sturdy warrior seemed to shake it off and returned his attention to the conversation. He took a deep breath. "No. I'm not going to tell you because you need to live your own life. Not let a few meaningless words make your choices *for* you."

Jon shook his head. "Fine. But you really haven't told me anything new."

Garris gave him a stern look and his voice became strong and insistent. "Then let me be crystal clear. The council and their obsession with this idiotic prophecy should scare the crap out of you. Those are the people protectors like Dellia work for."

Jon leaned away, taken aback by the man's unusually powerful words.

"Nothing against Dellia," Garris continued in a more even-tempered tone, "she's got a reputation as a fair, decent, and compassionate protector. And she's done nothing to convince me otherwise. So it's—"

"Yeah, well, she didn't threaten you with a knife and then use you for information."

Garris waited until he'd finished, then stared at him a few seconds more, as if to say, "Are you done now?" Apparently satisfied, he continued. "Point is, it's not her, but the council you need to worry about."

Jon lowered his head and grumbled. "Yeah, well, what she did to me didn't feel particularly fair, or decent, or compassionate."

"Look, as you may have overheard, I was banished. Dellia could have arrested me, or reported me to the council, or even tried to kill me. But she didn't. I'm not saying you should trust her. Just don't judge her too harshly."

Jon lifted his eyes, and for a time, he watched the crackling blaze as he considered Garris's words. "All I know is, she's someone who I thought was my friend—who went out of her way to befriend me—and it turned out it was all a lie."

"I get it. Besides, who am I kidding? I'm the last one who should be giving anyone relationship advice."

Incredulous, Jon shot back, "*What* relationship?"

Garris raised both hands and shook his head. Then he turned away and laid his head down on his bedroll. And just like that, the discussion was over, whether Jon had more to say or not, and Garris went back to his usual stoic self.

Jon punched his bedroll and slammed his head down onto it. He stared into the fire, trying to take his mind off everything that had happened. Because if he didn't, it was going to be a long, sleepless night.

Chapter Fourteen

THE CONSCIENCE OF THE COUNCIL

Many times, Kayleen had strolled the winding pathways of the enormous circular Shir Courtyard. And she'd seen many a sunrise like this one, listening to the songbirds as she wandered among the immaculately maintained trees and shrubs. Often, her aim was to relax in the peaceful garden as she contemplated an issue that had been weighing upon her conscience. But today, it was not the debate of the day that occupied her thoughts but the repercussions of her reckless actions of the evening before.

How had it come to this? She had always striven to be honest with the council. From her first day, she had felt it essential, because only when armed with the truth could they make the best possible decisions. And how many times had she been uncomfortable with the council's casual relationship with the facts? How often had she found herself standing as the lone conscience of the council, advocating for honesty where the others argued for some "small lie"? A lie, they reasoned, that would enhance their power today, allowing them to do even greater good in the future. But she had seen enough history to know that future never came, only more and bigger lies.

Yet, after two decades of advocating for truth, last night she had told a bold-faced lie herself. She had covered for Dellia by misleading the council. And even now, the weight of that decision plagued her. This had not been one of her carefully considered plans, made with a clear view of all the options. It had been an act of desperation, made at a point of vulnerability. That moment's weakness had cost her—and not just the ability to keep Dellia safe, but the ability to serve as the conscience of the council, at a time when they so desperately needed one.

It was becoming clear that even if the Otherworlder were not Jon or Megan, something or someone lurking in the shadows of this vast world thought they were. History told her that if events were to careen down that path, it could drive all of Meerdon into the heart of a tsunami that may cost countless lives. Cool heads, patience, and prudence were needed to avoid catastrophe, and she feared those attributes were the last thing on the council's collective mind. And she also feared what course they might take without the common sense she provided.

As a couple approached along the broad pathway, their discussion came to an abrupt stop. Kayleen averted her gaze, staring off at a cluster of flowering trees reflected in the still surface of a small pond. No sooner had they passed than the woman glanced back at her, and quiet whispers flew between her and her companion.

It was not the first time she had endured the conspicuous silence or the fleeting glances and hushed words. News of her removal had no doubt spread, and now she was the subject of rumor and speculation. Kayleen sighed. Long ago she had gotten used to being the center of unwanted attention. It was simply a part of being on the ruling council. Yet somehow, this time, everything seemed different.

She stopped and inhaled deeply, savoring the sweet scent of her favorite patch of warm, yellow flowers. She shielded her eyes from the golden sun, just beginning to reach above the row of stone archways that ringed the courtyard. As Kayleen glanced up, Ceree passed through one of them and headed straight for her. She smiled as she marched down the pathway, and there was a crispness in her gait that said she had sought Kayleen out.

She couldn't muster a smile for Ceree as she approached and pulled up alongside her. And as the two strolled the sunlit garden together, Ceree's manner took on a distinctly serious note.

"Well," she said, "you've certainly stuck your foot in it this time."

Kayleen glanced over at her and smiled.

Ceree took a deep breath. "You know, almost nobody believes you agreed to let Dellia handle this on her own ... except for Idria."

"Idria." Kayleen shook her head. "Were we ever that anxious to prove ourselves?"

Ceree smiled her warm smile. "Oh, you were worse. But you never would have thrown another council member to the wolves like that."

"I don't blame her."

Ceree sent Kayleen a sly look. "Why? Because you didn't really tell Dellia to go away and not report back?"

Kayleen paused for a moment along a sturdy rock wall, and turned to enjoy the sunlight stream through the soft rose petals of the large flowering tree next to them. "Does it matter? She was right. What we were asking was wrong."

Ceree joined her in admiring the glow of the petals lit by the early morning rays. She appeared to ponder Kayleen's words for a time, then motioned, inviting Kayleen to continue their walk.

As they strolled, Ceree's dark brown eyes turned downward, staring at the pathway in front of her. "You know, Braye would disagree. He would argue that there is no absolute right and wrong. That it is for the council to decide, and therefore what we ask can't be wrong."

"Yeah, well, he's an idiot," Kayleen said. Ceree stifled a laugh as she continued. "He thinks just because something is popular it's right, as if right and wrong were a matter of opinion."

"Yeah, we all know how easily people can be misled."

"It isn't just that." Kayleen halted their walk, turning to face

Ceree. "Remember the Talus slaves?"

Ceree thought for a moment. "You mean when the Ephori gave them the vote to pacify them?"

"Exactly. For a hundred and twenty years, they never had the votes to end slavery. All because the majority could lead easier lives off the sweat of the slaves. Yet they insisted their society was a free one because nobody was denied a vote." Kayleen moved closer to Ceree to emphasize her words. "By Braye's twisted logic, slavery was right because people voted for it."

"I remember," said Ceree. "And it took Ellira and her reformation to end slavery."

"Exactly."

Kayleen turned back down the simple stone path, and they resumed their walk.

After a moment, Ceree nodded. "I understand your point, and I agree. Just because the council ordered it doesn't make it right. But don't you think that the potential good that the council could do is worth asking Dellia to do a small wrong?"

Kayleen eyed Ceree. "Asking or ordering?"

"Hmm. Well, I didn't come to debate. I get enough of that in the council chamber."

Kayleen smiled, and they walked for a moment in silence. The sun warmed her skin, and the sweet smell of flowers wafted on the breeze.

As they passed a large, rust-colored boulder at the side of the path, Ceree stopped and motioned for her to sit. Kayleen nodded. *Well, I guess I'll find out what she's really up to now.* She turned and seated herself on the flat surface of the boulder, facing Ceree.

Ceree caught her eye. "I know the council considers this to be a grave matter. Grave enough that I fear a consensus that someone be held accountable."

Although the notion of the council acting against her had

occurred to Kayleen, it was a surprise to hear the councilwoman actually give it voice. She straightened slightly and focused her all her attention on Ceree.

"So, I've done a little informal lobbying on my own." Ceree sent her a solemn look. "I think if you were to say that you were just trying to protect Dellia, the matter would be over, and you'd be back in the chamber to debate this."

Kayleen glanced away, somewhat shocked by the notion. For a moment, she stared off at the bright flowers and dense shrubs that lined the path ahead. Then, she faced Ceree again. "So, throw Dellia to the wolves?"

"Look," Ceree said, "if you are covering for her, then it's not you that's done this. She's done it to hersel—"

"So our insistence that she violate her beliefs played no part? That's exactly what's wrong with the council. We never see ourselves as causing the problem."

Kayleen half expected Ceree to come back with some kind of biting retort, but instead, she calmly said, "Look, the bottom line is you hold a lot of sway. With you in that chamber, it may be possible to steer this to a peaceful solution. Without you, I fear what the council may do to Jon and Megan, and what might happen with Dellia."

It was not hard to see the truth of Ceree's words. Dellia was an idealist. Maybe even more so than Kayleen was in her early days. And she had done everything possible to prevent the reality of council politics from tarnishing Dellia's romantic view of her role in this world. But if Dellia were to sound off to Braye the way she had to her, it would have been the end for her. And the thought broke Kayleen's heart.

She noticed Ceree staring at her neck, and she realized she'd been tinkering with the long blue crystal of her necklace again. As she dropped the crystal and looked down, it dawned on her. She was no better than the council. How many times had she been critical of their willingness to commit some small wrong to enhance their power to do good in the future? Yet here she was trying to convince herself that by turning on Dellia today she could hang on to power and help her in the future.

And with that realization came the hidden truth in her own thoughts; the question of whether or not she had sanctioned Dellia's actions was irrelevant. It was a technicality, based on the fact she'd never had a chance to stand with Dellia. Well, here was Ceree, offering her that chance, and all that really mattered now was what she did with it.

She took a deep breath and looked straight up into Ceree's face. "I appreciate what you have tried to do here, Ceree, and I won't soon forget it. But I can't do as you suggest. Because the truth is, I agree with Dellia, and I trust her to do the right thing."

Ceree nodded. "I figured as much … I mean, given the past. But I had to try."

Ceree turned and marched off. And as Kayleen stood watching her retreat, it was as if an enormous burden had been lifted. As events had unfolded over the last few days, her sense of foreboding had only grown, and the need to find her way back to the council table had grown more urgent than ever. Only from there could she influence events along a course that avoided disaster. But it set her heart at ease to know that her seat at that table would not be purchased at Dellia's expense.

As the peaceful feeling of the courtyard at sunrise washed over her, all the tension and conflict washed away with it. And she could finally relax in the cool air and warm morning sun. She had taken a stand. She had done the right thing. And, for now, it was out of her hands.

Garris was pulled out of an uneasy slumber by movement and the sounds of Jon's preparations to leave. Soft chittering and the scraping of claws against bark drew his gaze to a squirrel scrambling across one of the contorted branches of the giant, lone tree. *Good meat on a squirrel—tender, nutty, and sweet.*

Pulling himself upright, he stretched his stiff neck and stared up into the leafy green canopy, set against the deep blue sky of sunrise. Anxious to get off the plains and out of the open, where he might be recognized, Garris rose and joined Jon in his hurried work.

This morning, he seemed edgy and withdrawn, fumbling around with a dour expression and reacting to the slightest frustration. Garris recognized that mood all too well. So he pushed him to do a little practice. Jon appeared reluctant at first and set about it with a distinct lack of enthusiasm. But Garris assigned him a couple exercises that required hitting a low branch with a rather large stick. Then, he pushed him with an unrelenting barrage of goading, and before long Jon was throwing himself into it with reckless abandon. The intensity with which Jon tackled the drill was exceptional, but his form was abysmal. More importantly, though, when he finished, his mood seemed improved.

They set out at a good pace, heading away from the lone tree and out across the Talus Plains. By midmorning, a layer of billowy clouds had moved in, throwing gigantic shadows that drifted far out across the nearly flat countryside. With them, the stillness of dawn had been replaced by a gusting wind that swirled through the plush green grasses.

The bulk of the trip was a quiet one. Jon seemed to stew for lengthy periods, then throw out some encounter with Dellia or Megan and ask how he had misread things or where he had blundered. They were always questions Garris couldn't possibly answer, and he found himself wondering what made Jon think he had any special insight into women, or people in general, for that matter.

Eventually, Jon made a few last, offhand remarks about being hopeless, then seemed to withdraw completely, settling into a cloud of quiet brooding. If it had been about fighting a demon or storming a stronghold, he would have kicked Jon's butt for his self-doubt. But these were women he was talking about, and it would be the height of hypocrisy for him to criticize. They spent the remainder of the crossing in silence, plodding along with only the sound of hooves and the swishing of grass that accompanied each burst of wind. Their good pace continued, and they made decent time, managing to reach the Illis Woods by midafternoon.

Once surrounded by the quiet green of the forest, Jon seemed to grow anxious for a practice session. He never asked directly, but he'd glance at a sturdy tree trunk, then hint at his desire with frequent questions about what Garris had taught. Not inclined to discourage him, Garris made for a nearby clearing, deciding they'd had enough travel for the day and it was as good a spot as any to make camp.

Once they dismounted, Jon became more direct, insisting on a short practice before they set about making camp. In return, Garris pressed for that little chat about what had happened in the tower. Despite seeming quite glum, Jon agreed.

So, as they searched through the underbrush for a sturdy stick to use as a practice sword, Jon divulged, in exceptional detail, how his gift worked and what he had done in the tower. What was as surprising as Jon's gift was his explanation of something he called a "flash point." From what he described, the key to surviving in that tower hadn't been his gift at all but his ability to recognize that he could burn the creatures.

By the time he set to practicing, Jon's shadow had become long in the late-day sun, stretching far out across the grass of the clearing. Garris studied him as he worked, scrutinizing his every move. Jon gripped the stick and swung it back and forth above his head with tremendous energy as he danced in and out, whacking one side then the other of an old rotted tree trunk. It looked … not great. But there was a deep sense of satisfaction in seeing his intense concentration and the way he could throw himself so completely into it. He'd made tremendous progress in the handful of days they'd worked together. But then again, this particular session was more about Jon having an outlet for his frustration.

Entirely too sympathetic to his plight, Garris found he was unable to tell him how tragic his performance was. So, he merely stared and nodded, trying to act interested.

The rapid whacking of Jon's stick against the decrepit old tree resounded across the long grass of the clearing and deep into the forest, as Garris stood and contemplated what he'd heard. Jon's gift was unique, unlike anything he'd ever heard of or seen. And as he stood in the still air of evening, watching and nodding, a deep sense of shock took hold at how this unremarkable man wielded such a dangerous power.

"So if you wanted," Garris said, "you could just do whatever it is you do and gain all the skill of the sword's prior owner."

"Yeah," Jon said as he dove forward and back, "but I don't like to use it."

"Good," Garris shot back. "It's a crutch. You can gain their skill, but not their wisdom in using it. You need to learn to handle yourself without it."

"Yeah, it just feels like cheating. Like it's power, and something in the back of my mind says that kind of power always comes at a cost."

"It's not just that. I've seen what power can do to the people that have it."

Jon glanced over between blows. "I'm not worried about that."

"You should be," Garris barked back.

His reaction was a bit strong, and Jon stopped and faced him. "I'll be fine."

Garris glared at Jon. "This is serious. With power comes the ability to affect other people's lives, and the greater the power, the greater that effect. And the greater the harm when things don't turn out like you planned."

Jon glared back. "I don't want the power to affect other people. I don't want that kind of responsibility."

This time it was Jon's reaction that was a bit strong, and Garris stared in silence as Jon returned to swinging the stick around, whacking the dead tree. After a moment, he walked over and grabbed Jon by the shoulders. He looked straight into his face, making sure he had his full attention. "One last thing. And this is very important. Never reveal to anyone how your gift works. I mean it. Not Dellia. Not anyone. In Erden they have a saying: knowledge is power."

Jon nodded.

"Your ability allows you to do things that seem miraculous. That mystery has a power of its own. It is also a secret that could be used against you."

Jon nodded again. "That makes sense."

Garris motioned to him and then crouched and positioned himself with his fist to the ground, ready to charge. Jon whipped the stick up to his shoulders, grasping it with both hands. Then he lowered it, twisting his hands around the end until his wrists crossed. He aimed the tip into the dirt below the long grass and took a solid stance. Which, to be honest, didn't look half-bad.

Garris charged, and Jon swung the stick up to his shoulders and braced himself. The stick jabbed Garris in the chest, right where it would have pierced his heart. It was fluid and well aimed, but Garris waited to smile until Jon turned and walked back. Then he crouched again, poised to rush Jon, and they repeated the exercise.

As Garris walked back the second time, Jon said, "What about that metal piece around your neck? Are you going to tell me what the deal is with that?"

Garris turned and crouched again. "It was given to me a long time ago. It's been passed down for hundreds of years. And just like every other owner back those hundreds of years, I had to promise to pass it on with a message and a vow. I had to repeat the words exactly. That was important."

Jon cocked his head. "What was the message?"

Garris charged, but Jon fumbled, and Garris didn't stop. He slammed into him, knocking him back. Jon stumbled backward through the thick grass and began to fall, but Garris grabbed his shoulder, steadying him.

Then he stared at him, and his words were clear and strong. "Help the one that needs it find their way home."

Jon stared back in apparent disbelief. "What? Wow."

"You needed it. That someone is you."

Garris let go and strolled back to his starting point. But Jon was still stuck pondering. Half to himself, he said, "But that means someone hundreds of years ago knew I'd need it, and they knew who to pass it on to so that it would eventually get to you, and then me. That's crazy."

"Yet you were there," Garris said as he crouched.

Jon readied his stick. He got a sly look on his face and smiled at Garris. "So you made a promise to help me get home."

Garris stopped and stood. "Don't get all excited. Only a fool would put too much faith in this kind of mystic mumbo jumbo. Like, apparently those people hundreds of years ago weren't exactly gifted enough to foresee my banishment."

"Is that a problem?"

The question was thoroughly idiotic, and he glared at Jon, trying to perfect his look of the impatient tutor.

"Okay," Jon said, "stupid question. How *much* of a problem is that?"

"Well, we're headed to Mundus. That's a big city with guards, and city officials, and such. Any of which might feel a particular obligation to arrest me or kill me."

All Jon managed was a simple "Oh."

" 'Oh' is right. And it gets better. The Andera Catacombs—which, by the way, they'll never let you enter—are under a temple that's smack in the middle of the city."

He realized Jon was no longer paying any attention, which made it a perfect opportunity to provide an object lesson. He bolted straight at Jon, who still seemed to be mulling over Garris's words. He smashed into him, sending him tumbling backward across the clearing.

"You're not focusing," Garris barked.

Jon jumped up and brushed the dried grass off, looking quite annoyed. He repositioned himself, the tip of the stick to the ground, in a rock-solid stance that was actually rather impressive. He glared across the still grass of the clearing with an angry and determined expression as he braced for the next attack.

Garris ducked lower, then charged.

There was no way she could sleep, so Dellia lay in bed staring in silence at the four stone walls of her childhood room. And there, alone with her thoughts, it became increasingly difficult to avoid confronting the crushing hopelessness of her predicament. So she got up and stared out the small window. But all she could see across the darkened yard was the guesthouse, now lifeless and vacant.

The pull of despair tugged at her heart, and she needed to do something, anything, to take her mind off her troubles. She glanced over at the stables, standing quietly in the moonlight, and decided what that something would be.

She spent the next several hours feverishly cleaning every nook and cranny of the stables. But every time she'd glance over at Ulka, all she could see was that Enna wasn't there in the stall next to him. The two had taken to one another almost at once. And when they were turned out to pasture, she had often spotted them grooming one another or simply grazing together. Now the empty stall stood as a reminder that the two would most likely never see each other again.

Dellia ran out of steam a couple hours before sunrise and dragged herself out into the dark, grassy yard. Exhausted and drained, she sat and leaned back against the rough stones of the stable wall. There, wrapped in the stillness of predawn, she spent what seemed like an eternity staring at the skyline as it brightened and the birds began to chirp. But the longer she sat, the more her sense of despair took hold. So, eventually, she straggled inside and threw herself onto the bed, falling instantly into a troubled sleep.

Dellia rose in the early afternoon and spent most of the day in a frantic haze, performing mindless tasks in a futile effort to take her mind off her dilemma. Then, after a quiet dinner with her mother, when she was too spent to tackle anything more, she retired to her room. There, with the late-day sun splashing across the stone walls above her, she sat on the floor with her back against the wall, petting Tilla as she lay quietly next to her.

After a while, her mother, most likely tired of watching her mope, came and sat across from her. For the longest time, Dellia stared at the floor, as her mother sat in silence.

After a long while, Sirra spoke. "I've seen you suffer setbacks before, Dellia. This isn't like you at all."

"Setback?" Dellia said, still staring at the floor. "I failed completely."

"Listen, I know how badly you must feel, but what you're doing now, it's not helping anyone, especially not yourself."

Dellia looked into her mother's face and said, "It seems like I've screwed up my whole life."

"Only if you sit here doing nothing," her mother replied.

"Doing nothing? It's over. I don't have a choice. I guess you'll get your wish. I won't be a protector much longer after telling off the council."

"They don't care about words. They only care what you do for them."

"What I do?" Dellia stared at her. "Mom, Jon's gone, never to speak to me again. I can't fix that. And I made such a big deal out of telling the council I would handle things, and now I can't."

Dellia returned to staring at the floor.

After a moment, Sirra bent lower so she could peer up into her daughter's downcast face. There was understanding in her eyes, and when she spoke they were the gentle words of a troubled mother. "Maybe you need to stop focusing on what you can't do and ask yourself what's the right thing to do."

Dellia had tried to do as her mother suggested, to come up with the right thing to do. And she knew she needed to do *something*. But it always came back to the same intractable problem. She had been emphatic in telling the council she'd handle things, but after what she'd done to Jon, that was impossible.

"I wish I knew," Dellia said.

She could see her mother grasping for what to say, but it was hopeless. After a moment, Sirra sighed. "Well, right now there's a man out there that probably needs your help, whether he knows it or not. And you've hurt him. Even more than that, you violated him. He didn't offer you his feelings, you took them and used them for your own purposes—"

Sirra stopped when her daughter glanced up and in a weak voice said, "I was there, remember?"

Her mother's concerned look deepened, but she halted only a moment before continuing. "And you have a duty to the council to make good on your promise."

Dellia shook her head as she returned to staring at the floor. "I can't do anything about either of those."

Sirra sat in silence for a long moment, then suddenly straightened. "Are they really two different things? What if Jon knew everything?"

Dellia recoiled from the thought. The council would never condone telling Jon everything. But then again, she'd already told them off, insisting she'd do what she thought best. But was telling him everything really the best course of action? How would that make any difference? How would it change anything? And yet somehow it felt like the right thing to do. Dellia raised her head and stared at her mother, puzzled and encouraged.

"Huh?" she said. "Why would he want me around if he knew I was reporting his every move to the council?"

Sirra perked up. "Because he knows you. The council's not going to lose interest in him because you're not there. Would Jon want someone else coming after him?"

The wisdom of her mother's words was undeniable, and Dellia felt her mood begin to brighten. "Yeah, that's true. I would be on his side with the council. And his only desire is to get home. I could help with that."

Sirra seemed encouraged, and she barged ahead. "See? Maybe you can serve the council and help Jon at the same time."

"I don't know, Mom. At some point, I might have to choose."

"Well, isn't that better than now, when you have no choice?"

Then, all of a sudden, Dellia's guilt and shame rushed back as she remembered what she'd done to Jon. And with that realization, it all evaporated, and Dellia returned to staring at the floor.

"It sounds like a nice dream, but Jon is done with me."

Her mother leaned in toward her and smiled. "Well, imagine for a moment that you are the most stubborn, determined, strong willed, and amazing person in the world. What would you do?"

Dellia simply shook her head. "I don't know."

"Okay, what if Jon's life depended on it? Because it could."

Fear suddenly gripped Dellia, and her gaze shot away. It took only an instant to see that her mother was right. He was hunted by creatures that frightened her. Yet he seemed unequipped to handle even simple, everyday life. She stared at the fading sunlight playing across the warm, yellow walls as she let the implications of Sirra's question sink in. What would she do to protect Jon?

Dellia turned back to her mother. "Honestly, I would do almost anything."

Her mother smiled, and she seemed to Dellia to be quite encouraged. With an edge of excitement, she asked, "What would you do first?"

"I guess I'd go to him and make him listen to me. Beg. Plead. Whatever it took. Ask his forgiveness. Make him see how truly sorry I am. And make him understand that I was always his friend."

"That would be a good start."

"But it isn't that he doesn't want me around. I can feel that. It's that I hurt him. Badly enough that he can't risk being hurt again. I don't know if I can fix that."

Sirra reached out and placed her hand gently on her daughter's shoulder. "Forget the council for a moment. Forget the rest of it. If he's a friend and you've hurt him that badly, isn't it your duty as a human being to do all in your power to fix it?"

"I guess so," Dellia said.

"Focus on that. Make that your duty. Do that and the rest may just take care of itself."

Dellia turned and looked out the window at the rapidly fading light of evening. She thought of Jon out there, how badly he needed her help, and what that help could mean to him.

She turned to her mother. "You know you just talked me into leaving right away?"

As Sirra rose to her feet and prepared to leave, she smiled at

Dellia. "Well, you were just bringing down the whole mood of the place, anyway. Now go. And may Adi be with you."

Dellia smiled back.

As Sirra briskly walked away, Dellia raced to her bag, snatched it from the floor, and hoisted it onto the small table under the open window. And as she began jamming items into it, faster and faster, her thoughts turned to the quickest way to catch up with Jon and Garris.

Chapter Fifteen

SPIRE DEFENSE

For Jon, the journey from Talus to Erden seemed slow and the days difficult. Slow, because without the protection that Dellia's presence provided, Garris was forced to stay off the beaten path, meandering back through the quiet green of the Illis Woods, using a rambling labyrinth of trails only he could decipher. The hours passed in near silence, broken only by the breeze through the sunlit branches and the gentle sound of hooves plodding through the underbrush.

As calm and unreadable as Garris seemed, Jon had begun to pick up on a sense of wariness that followed him everywhere he went. At times, he reminded him of a lion's prey, vaguely aware that it's being stalked by some threat hidden in the tall grass but never quite certain where that threat was or when it would strike.

Jon spent most of the trip in a self-indulgent funk. It was a state well known to him when women were involved. He was gloomy and troubled. And usually, if he indulged his tendency to withdraw into a cloud of melancholy, it helped him get past it. But this time, it wasn't helping. Perhaps because as much as Jon had wanted to flee Dellia and everything that came with that whole situation, he was beginning to realize how much he missed her.

Several times during the trip, he had tinkered with his gift, trying to use the saddle again as he mounted Enna. But despite numerous attempts and intense concentration, he could not trigger another episode. Still, he kept trying, unable to shake the impression that with enough time and focus, it might be possible to use the same object twice. There were other questions to explore, such as using a second object owned by the same person. But in his present state of mind, he lacked the will for anything more than a passing curiosity.

During the extended silence, his mind often wandered back to the nearly endless list of physical laws he saw being broken on a daily basis. Defying gravity, seeing the past, instantaneous travel, empathic ability—these were no small things, nor was the energy needed to power them. Even something as simple as time slowing around him and coming to a stop was a blatant violation of Einstein's special theory of relativity. That such a basic and well-proven theory would be so casually violated was mind-boggling, and there was only one conclusion he could summon: this was not the universe he knew.

The laws of physics didn't just change from one world to the next or one time to the next; they were constants, universal and unchanging. So this had to be someplace outside the known universe, a place where at least some of the physical laws he knew so well had been warped or shifted. The specifics of those changes mattered little, but the synchrony of these new phenomena had made one thing clear: whatever impossible new gifts he and Megan now possessed, they were tied to this place and would almost certainly vanish the instant they returned to their world where the laws of physics prohibited them.

A couple times each day they would stop, and Garris would goad him into another of his lessons. The sessions themselves had adopted a strange intensity, with Garris pushing him into a frenzy nearly every time. Yet as much as he would drive him past the point of exhaustion, there was a sense of release afterward, and in those few moments each day, Jon felt a little less alone, as if he had at least one friend in this world.

It wasn't until the forest thinned out into the sunburnt plains of Erden that the constant gloom that clouded his mind melted into a sort of resignation, an acceptance of the fact that he was completely out of his depth when it came to women. And with that newfound acceptance came the recognition that he was not blameless in all this, that both he and Dellia were victims of a situation that neither had asked for. And that although he could've perhaps handled it better, their parting was for the best, for both of them.

Along with the barren expanse had come another change: Garris had actually started talking. He explained how in Talus they had once believed in a pantheon of gods, and how they had adopted the belief in Adi, a single god. That in Erden, they also believed in a divine but with many faces, born of its many incarnations. And that in both places, family held great importance but in very different ways.

He also described how Talus was ruled by an elected five Ephori, but Erden was a kingdom where offspring must marry before they could inherit the throne and become Rhanae. According to Garris, the prior Rhanae's only son, Katal, had left after a dispute over marrying. Then, one day, after being gone for months, he surprised everyone when he reappeared with a bride and claimed the throne.

Jon found he enjoyed the new Garris, but as the day wore on, he realized the man wasn't just making idle chitchat. He was preparing him, helping him see who these people were that he would soon be dealing with.

Late in the day, they stopped to make camp some distance from an enormous monument Garris called the Mundus Spire. It towered in the distance, a truly massive, circular, stone platform ringed by three enormous "teeth," rising up out of the desolate landscape. The three spires arched upward over the platform, reaching out to touch the deep blue sky. He explained that it was some type of transportation device, and that with the use of a special stone, it could transport large numbers of people and equipment in an instant to any of a handful of similar spires spread across the three realms.

After the obligatory lesson, they settled in front of a small fire and ate a simple meal of dried meat and fruit. Jon sat basking in the warm glow, enjoying his newfound sense of acceptance, when the topic turned once again to the spires and the millions of questions that pricked his imagination.

After all, for near-instantaneous travel to be possible, you'd need a wormhole, or perhaps a folding of space, or access to other dimensions. None of those were concepts Garris could help him with, but he could explain the mechanics of how the thing worked.

Jon gazed past the crackling fire and Garris resting opposite him. Out across the dry, scrubby brush and barren ground, the rays of the setting sun glinted off the three massive spires in the distance. And as he studied them, he rolled the prospect around in his head: How did one group of people avoid being transported into the space another occupied?

He looked up at Garris. "So, these 'spire stones' you told me about, they're different colors depending on what spire they send you to?"

Garris nodded. "Yeah."

"And when you step onto the platform with one of them"—he pointed upward to the sky— "it opens a portal above you to that destination?"

"Yup."

"And when you touch the spire stone to a symbol on one of the spires, the portal falls and sends you to the destination?"

"Yes," Garris said with a single crisp nod.

Jon tilted his head. "Then what if someone's already on the platform at the destination when you're sent there?"

The question seemed to confound Garris, and he stared for a while. "Oh, you mean they both try to use it at the same time? They can't, you need a spire stone to enter."

"What if they both have stones?"

"When the first one enters, it stops the other from entering, even with a stone."

"Even if one of them is going to a third spire?"

Garris raised his eyebrows, then shook his head. "You ask too many questions."

Jon puzzled for a second, trying to figure out the logic of how it all worked.

"Yes," Garris said. "I believe it does."

"Okay, but then what ... if ..." Jon's voice trailed off as he spied a horse and rider appearing around the edge of the distant spire.

A plume of dust swirled behind them, wafting far out along the desolate landscape. His heart stopped as he realized in an instant who it was. It was impossible to make out the rider, but the horse had to be Ulka.

Garris turned to watch as Jon stared dumbfounded. A quiet nickering sound caught his attention and Jon glanced over at Enna. She stood watching through the fading light as the pair raced across the arid ground toward them. A rush of feelings overcame Jon: affection, apprehension, indecision, but most of all, an unexpected sense of completion, as if Dellia arriving now gave him a chance for some sense of closure.

The two waited as the pounding of hooves grew louder and the horse and rider rushed toward them. Dellia raced up near them, sending a plume of dust drifting out across the glowing red horizon. She tugged on the reins, turning Ulka sideways and bringing him to a halt right beside Jon and Garris. As the horse moved restlessly, Jon stared up at Dellia in surprise; she was a stunning sight.

Dellia sat tall in the saddle, but her usual self-assured manner had been replaced by an unexpected tension. She patted Ulka rhythmically, looking unsure what would come next.

Jon looked to Garris, half hoping he would provide some clue as to what to do or say. But he just glanced back and forth between Jon and Dellia, as if he expected some kind of explosion.

Jon shot her his sternest possible look and in his most disapproving voice said, "So you just show up out of nowhere. ..." Then he flashed a broad grin. "After all, the chores have been done. Where were you when we needed the horses tended?"

Garris paused for a moment, then smirked and eyed Dellia. "I gotta admit it's pretty suspicious."

Dellia seemed shocked for a second, then smiled and acted innocent. "Timing is everything."

Jon leaned in toward Garris. "Well, she'd have probably spent most of the time talking to the horses, anyway."

Garris nodded. "Well, to be fair, they are probably better company than we ..."

His words trailed off as he stared past Jon and into the distance. "Guys, something's coming," he said as he rose to his feet.

Jon leaped up, and he and Dellia both turned their eyes to the southeast, following his gaze.

At first, Jon couldn't make out what it was; it just looked like dust and movement in the distance. But then they appeared, many pairs of amber eyes, bobbing up and down in the dim light of sundown. Blood Wolves. Huge, deep red, a dozen, perhaps more, loping across the plains, headed straight for them. And among them, half as many of some other kind of gangly, hominid-like creature.

Horror seized Jon's heart, and he turned to Dellia. "You brought the Blood Wolves with you?"

She glanced back the way she'd come, the opposite direction from the wolves. Then she gave him an annoyed look, her voice dripping with sarcasm as she nodded. "Yeah, that makes sense."

He wanted to defend himself, to say something about not thinking straight when panicked, but instead, he glanced all around as his mind raced.

"We have to run!" Jon spat out the words.

"Where?" Dellia fired back. "They can outrun us."

He spotted the enormous stone teeth in the distance and pointed. "What about the spires?"

Garris shot back, "Without a spire stone we'll be trapped outside with the wolves."

"I have a spire stone," Dellia said.

"That's good." Jon nodded. "That could work. I have a plan."

She stared at him in disbelief. "*You?* Have a plan?"

Garris smiled and slapped Jon's back. "Hard to believe, I know."

Jon shook his head. "Just head for the spires."

Garris raced for the horses as Dellia shot her palm out from atop Ulka. "Take my hand. You can ride with me."

"I'm not falling for that again," Jon said, without thinking.

Dellia gave him a look of incredulity. "Really?"

He glanced at his horse. "I'm not leaving Enna."

"Garris can get her."

"It'll be faster if I ride her."

"Not the way you ride," Dellia said.

"Ouch," Jon said. "Come on, I'm not that bad."

Garris pulled up with Enna, and Jon reached up to mount her but stopped. He stared at her, confounded, with no idea how to mount with no saddle.

Dellia shot Jon an "I told you so" look.

A flush of annoyance struck, but he turned and thrust out his hand, grabbing hers.

She yanked him up behind her on her horse, and he gingerly placed his hands on her waist.

Dellia seized them and wrenched Jon's arms around her. "I thought we'd gotten past this."

Ulka shot forward, with Jon clinging to Dellia. "Ever hear of pushing it?" he asked.

Hooves thundered against the barren ground as Garris, Kyri and Enna raced up aside Jon and Dellia. The group flew across the dry, crumbly brush of the plains toward the enormous white spires.

"Well," Dellia said, "excuse me if I was more worried about you falling off. You know, into the mouths of the wolves."

Jon glanced back at the huge pack loping toward them, then down at his arms. He squeezed her tighter, plastering his head up against her back.

The spires loomed closer and closer, rising higher and higher into deep blue sky. But every time Jon looked back, it seemed as if the wolves had gained on them.

He stared up at the spires towering above him. The horse heaved beneath him as it sprang onto the immense, circular, stone platform. All three horses landed in a clatter of hooves accompanied by a brief crackling sound and the appearance of a beautiful, shimmering portal high overhead.

The three screeched to a halt and flew off their horses.

They turned and looked across the plains as the cluster of deep red wolves approached across the darkening expanse.

"You know," Jon said as he peered ahead, "Tsaoshi said the wolves had my scent, that they would multiply and follow."

Dellia turned to him and in a meek voice said, "Jon, Tsaoshi was a ruse. I hired him to talk you out of going into the tower."

"What?" He turned and glowered at her. "Was anything real with you?" As he stared into her hurt face, everything else in his world ceased to matter.

"I was afraid for you," Dellia said. "That was real. The council asked me not to go into that tower, but I went anyway because I care about you. That's real."

He shook his head, ignoring Garris's anxious face.

The burly warrior's eyes darted back and forth between the approaching wolves and his two companions. "Guys, this really isn't the time—"

Jon continued as if Garris didn't exist. "I'd convinced myself that you were just a good person in a bad situation, and I could trust my judgment with you, but now—"

"You can," Dellia pleaded.

"But now I don't know," Jon finished.

Garris's pressured voice jumped in. "Quick tip, Jon. Let's not kick the one with the spire stone out of the group. You know, the stone that's gonna somehow magically save all our butts."

"Right," Jon said.

"Look," Dellia said, "I spent the last couple of days thinking about nothing else but what I'd say to you. But then when I saw you, I realized there's nothing I could say to make what I did right. So at least give me a chance to tell you what's happening. Because you deserve to know."

He felt torn. There was so much he needed to know, so many answers only Dellia could provide. And he wanted to say yes, but the wounds of their parting were still fresh.

She rested her hand on his arm. "You need to know."

"Fine," Jon said, "when this is over, we'll talk."

He glanced at the pack of massive wolves, barreling down on them with frightening speed.

"Great," Garris said, looking alarmed. "Now that that's settled, can we please get back to the life-and-death situation?"

Jon thrust out his hand. "I need the spire stone."

Dellia reached into her bag and fumbled around, producing a small red stone the size of a marble. She dropped it into his open hand.

He held it up between his fingers. "I'm going to throw it outside the spire. They won't be able to enter without it, and you can pick them off."

Garris snatched a smaller crossbow and a quiver with a few

arrows from Kyri and tossed them to Dellia. "What makes you think we won't be expelled into the wolves?"

Jon held up the stone. "It doesn't work like that. You aren't expelled at the destination."

"Because you still have the stone." Garris chucked a pile of arrows on the ground next to him and started to load one into his crossbow.

"But the stone doesn't work at the destination or it would open a portal when you get there." Jon pointed to the foreign sky above them.

Garris gave a skeptical shake of his head. "That's pretty thin, but I guess we're gonna find out. Toss it already."

Jon readied himself, poised to throw the stone. "I want them to see it. If they go for it, you can pick them off."

Now nearly upon them, he could see the gangly creatures with more clarity. They were dark, scaly, and hairless, except for a single bloodred stripe of fur that ran the length of their backs. Their narrow, sticklike arms were twice as long as their legs and ended in three long curved claws, allowing them to amble across the ground semi-upright, like some scale-covered, spindly version of a gorilla.

Dellia shouldered the crossbow and glanced at Garris. "I'll aim left. You aim right."

He gave a curt nod of his head.

The lead wolf leaped, then three others, right as Jon chucked the stone out past their heads. Jon was too late and the lead wolf flew onto the platform and sprang toward him.

An arrow whizzed past it through the eye of the wolf behind, then it smashed into an invisible barrier, along with the two trailing wolves. With each collision, a flash of blue light spread across the barrier, and they crashed to the ground with a splash of blue aura sprinkling down on them.

In a single fluid motion, Dellia yanked out her sword and

swung it up in front of Jon with tremendous force. It whooshed by him, lopping the head off the wolf in midair, inches from his face.

Jon spun out of the way as the body careened past him and crashed to the ground, its head tumbling along the platform.

Two more arrows whistled by and into the skulls of the wolves at the barrier as they dragged themselves up from the dirt.

Garris and Dellia both shook their heads, seeming disturbed. "Whoa. What the heck was that?" Garris said.

In a flash, Jon recalled the dread he'd experienced when holding off the wolves outside Sirra's stables. "Oh yeah, don't look them in the eye." He shuddered. "It's bad."

"Great, so fight them without looking at them?"

"It can be done."

Three of the gangly creatures scrambled for the spot where Jon had lobbed the stone.

Like some kind of crazed machine, Garris reloaded and fired into the group. An arrow whooshed by Jon and into the scale-covered chest of a creature. With blistering speed came another arrow. Then another pierced the trailing creature's head, and all three crashed to the ground with a thud and a billow of dust.

The wolves backed off and began circling the spires, crossing each other back and forth. Jon strained to follow them in the dust and dwindling light of sunset.

Arrows arced over his head with Garris and Dellia continuing to fire into the wolves, as they widened their circle.

Two more wolves went down in a cloud of dust. Then an arrow wounded a third, and it took several more to finish it off as it attempted to drag itself out of range.

Garris and Dellia stopped, their arrows no longer able to reach the wolves. Then Garris's eyes went wide and his gaze fixed somewhere off to the northeast. "Oh crap," he said.

Jon's gaze snapped over. "What?"

Garris pointed. "See that light in the distance? Someone's coming."

Jon strained, then suddenly there it was, a light approaching across the barren expanse. He panicked and blurted out, "We can't reach the wolves anymore, and they'll tear whoever that is apart. It's my fault."

"You didn't invite the wolves," Garris said.

"But they're here for me." Jon readied himself to run.

Dellia eyed him with shock. "What are you doing?" she said with a note of panic in her voice.

"I'm going outside. You pick them off as they go for me."

"As bait?" Dellia nearly shouted. "That's insane. You won't be able to get back in."

"I'll find the stone," Jon said in as confident a tone as he could muster.

Jon started to run for the edge of the platform, but she snagged his arm. "What if you can't find it?"

He stared at her hand on his arm, and she let go. "You got a better plan?"

"Fine, just … be careful," Dellia said.

Before she had finished, he was sprinting for the spot where the stone had landed.

As he leaped from the platform, all half dozen wolves and several of the gangly creatures turned in a swirl of dust and tore straight at him.

Jon hit the spot and began scrambling through the dimly lit undergrowth, searching for any sign of the red orb as the pack of enormous wolves and menacing creatures bore down on him.

Arrows streaked by him as he fumbled through the brush, frantic to find the stone. An arrow whistled by and a heavy thud sounded right next to him. A dead wolf body tumbled across the ground in front of him as he plucked the stone from the dust.

He leaped to his feet.

Another arrow whizzed past his ear, and a wolf body slammed into him, catapulting him to the ground. He landed with a painful thud, and the stone flew from his grasp.

On hands and knees, trying to ignore the snarling wolves racing at him, he scrambled after it as it rolled away.

Jon snatched the stone again and sprinted for the spires. He leaped onto the platform with a crackling sound as the portal opened above. He turned and lobbed the stone out past the wolves charging toward him.

The wolves leaped, and a whoosh resounded from above as the portal evaporated.

Jon startled as an arrow flew by him into the skull of a wolf as it collided with the barrier in a flash of blue, inches from his face.

All three of the remaining dark creatures scrambled for the stone. One grabbed it, and they all turned and raced toward Jon.

He stood his ground as they flew toward him, their long, curved claws reaching for him, ready to rip him apart.

"Jon, run!" Dellia yelled.

The creatures lunged at him, and blue flashes surrounded him as the animals smashed into the barrier, inches away.

Two arrows screamed by Jon into the chests of two of the creatures. They crashed to the ground and the blue aura splashed across their bodies.

"They don't have the real stone," Jon yelled to Garris and Dellia behind him. "I rolled it off at my feet."

The last creature and three wolves turned and fled, but Garris downed the last of the gangly creatures as it scrambled away.

Jon stared after them, and panic welled again as the three gigantic red wolves veered off and headed straight at the approaching light.

Garris flew onto his horse.

Dellia followed onto hers, and the two thundered past Jon and out after the wolves.

Jon jumped down off the platform and snatched the spire stone. Enna trotted past. With no idea how to mount but desperate to stop the wolves, he dove across her bare back. He landed on his stomach with a guttural grunt and a chunk of mane in his hand. He yanked himself around to straddle Enna and clung to her neck as she bolted to a gallop.

Hooves pounded the hard ground as Enna heaved and jolted under him. He was sure he was going to be thrown off any second as she raced across the desolate landscape. The spires shrank behind Jon, and he clung onto her dapple-gray neck as he flew past Garris and Dellia.

Dellia looked over in shock as she saw him race by, riding bareback. Despite how fast he was going, the wolves were pulling farther ahead. The horse and rider bearing the bright light turned and raced away.

Jon panicked and began yelling at the top of his lungs.

One of the wolves glanced back, then pivoted. The other two followed, and he found himself ahead of Garris and Dellia, flying toward the wolves as they tore at him with breathtaking speed.

Jon tugged on Enna's mane.

Nothing.

He panicked yet again as he realized he had no idea how to stop her. He tugged several more times, glancing back and forth between Enna and the wolves. Desperate for help, he looked to Dellia behind him, but she seemed more alarmed than he felt.

Jon yanked the mane to the side, and finally Enna pulled up short. He flew from the horse and by some miracle managed to land on his feet.

Enna turned and raced away as Dellia and Garris landed on either side of him. Garris tossed Jon a sword, and he positioned it as Garris had instructed him, hilt at his side and hands twisted with the tip in the dirt.

Dellia and Garris shouldered their crossbows as all three wolves sprang into the air. The crossbows twanged as arrows whistled away and into two wolves on either side.

Jon yanked the sword up, blade forward and hilt to his shoulder. The tip slid into the wolf's chest as it hurtled down on him. Pain wrenched through his shoulder as the force yanked him backward and slammed him to the ground.

The wolf's body careened down on top of him with a heavy jolt, then rolled away.

A sudden pain seized Jon's chest, and he gasped for air, unable to breathe.

Dellia was on him in an instant, checking him over. "That was brilliant and terrifying and stupid and amazing."

Garris rolled his eyes. "Don't encourage him."

"And don't ever do anything like that again."

Jon heaved as he tried to inhale. "Can't … breathe …"

"You just got the wind knocked out of you," she said. "You'll be fine in a minute."

After a few seconds, his breath returned.

Dellia extended her hand and helped Jon up. He looked at the wolf carcasses scattered around them as Garris plucked a couple arrows from their lifeless flesh. Jon stared back the way they'd come at the moonlight reflecting off the enormous, arching spires. They would almost certainly have fallen prey to the wolves if not for that monument and a simple red stone. A stone that they would not have had if not for Dellia arriving at precisely the right moment to save them.

The torch fluttered quietly as Jon lifted it higher. Its warm, flickering light spread across the field of fallen wolves, their remains strewn along the dry ground and brush at the feet of the Mundus Spire. He stepped around a body and plucked an arrow from the dust. He glanced over toward Garris, hoping to hand it to him, but he stood some distance away yanking an arrow from the chest of the creature beneath him.

Jon glanced the other way to catch Dellia, nearby, bathed in torchlight, with the massive, moonlit teeth of stone rising above the barren landscape behind her. He let his gaze linger there for a moment. She was so intense and focused as she scoured the area for arrows. Her clothes were dusty and her hair disheveled, yet even those imperfections seemed to have a beauty about them, and to Jon, the vision before him seemed to be among the most magnificent he'd ever seen.

She paused to glance over her shoulder. He followed her gaze to a rider approaching from the northeast, with a bright light held aloft. It appeared to be the same rider who had approached during the attack and been chased off by the remaining three wolves.

Dellia caught Jon watching and smiled.

He yanked his gaze away. This was one of the reasons he had left her behind in Talus. He had to keep his distance and not get caught up in the moment.

In a quiet voice, Dellia said, "That's probably an official from Mundus sent to investigate. They'll want answers, and I'm not sure what to tell them."

"The truth?" Jon offered, trying to sound nonchalant.

"Good idea. Now if I just knew what was going on."

He smiled and nodded. "I see your point."

As the rider approached, Jon began to make out a striking woman sitting tall in the saddle, with jet-black hair and golden-brown skin that was slightly darker than Garris's. She was draped in clothing and armor of azure blue with a metallic-looking bow at her side. The gnarled stave she held aloft was fitted with some kind of spherical, glass light source. In its glow, Jon could see the full carnage that lay before him.

A huge gray-and-white cat a couple of feet tall appeared out of the darkness, leaping over the fallen bodies as it trailed behind her. The sound of hooves stopped as the woman pulled up in front of the group, surveying the scene with a quiet intensity.

She glanced back at the cat and called out, "Chatin."

The cat followed up and sat regally beside her.

"I am Antar Gatia from Mundus," she said, addressing Dellia alone. She motioned to the dozen and a half bodies scattered before her. "Am I correct that you are responsible for slaying all of these?"

Dellia adopted a formality Jon had not yet seen from her. "I have heard much about you, Antar Gatia. I am Protector Dellia."

Gatia glared at her, seeming quite annoyed. "I am aware, Protector. But I must admit to being somewhat shocked. Is it no longer fashionable for the council to show us the respect of sending word when its operatives will be interfering in our domain?"

"I'm sorry, Antar. They didn't know I was coming. And neither did I."

Gatia's hard stare softened to an intrigued curiosity. "Oh, interesting."

"Yes, we are responsible. We were beset by a pack of Blood Wolves."

"A pack? Here? Even more intriguing."

Dellia placed her hands together before her and gave a small bow.

Gatia motioned to Jon. "And is this the man that called off the three that were chasing me earlier?"

"Yes," Dellia replied.

Gatia faced him. She smiled, placed her hands together, and gave a deep bow of her head. "I am in your debt."

Jon had no idea what might be the appropriate thing to say in such a circumstance, so he remained quiet and simply smiled.

Gatia raised her head, and her brow furrowed as she surveyed the blood-soaked field, strewn with the corpses of wolves and creatures. She faced Dellia again and took a deep breath.

"This is of grave concern. The Parishad must hear of what has happened here. It could have implications for the security of our people."

Dellia gave a short bow. "May I ask that I alone address them? I can speak for these others." She motioned to Jon and Garris.

"I can introduce you alone, but it is not for me to decide if that will satisfy them."

"Thank you, Antar."

Gatia smiled. "No need for titles. You may call me Gatia."

"Thank you, Gatia, and you may call me Dellia."

Gatia surveyed the whole group. "Now, I'm afraid I must insist that you collect your belongings and accompany me back to Mundus. You will all be my family's guests while Dellia waits to be heard."

Gatia agreed to resupply all the lost arrows, which seemed to please Garris greatly. It appeared the fletchers of Erden are renowned for their work. So the group left at once, plodding back to the camp where they gathered their belongings then headed on to Mundus.

The trip was a longer one than expected, the group trotting across the dark, arid expanse with only the sound of the horses' hooves to break the silence. The spires receded in the distance until nothing remained but flat, dry ground as far as the eye could see. Eventually, the outline of the city appeared out of darkness, growing larger and larger until it became a sea of mostly two-story buildings lining a network of crude brick roads.

As they strolled through the stillness of the dark and deserted streets of Mundus, the clip-clop of hooves seemed amplified, reflected by the buildings that crowded either side of the lane. Jon stared about, feeling a bit like a tourist in a foreign country, trying to take in every morsel of the unusual ambiance. The houses were larger than he had imagined and their architecture more elaborate, with many arched windows and openings. Ornate terraces and gardens graced nearly every home, complete with intricate carvings and statuary. In the bright glow of Gatia's glass orb, each seemed to become its own little world.

After leaving the horses behind at the stables, the group strolled down the dark, still streets on foot. They turned the corner through a small gate into a peaceful garden in front of a modest mansion that seemed to be made of some type of dry, hard bricks. Gatia led the way down a path of flat, pale-pink stones that led beside a quiet pond and up to a set of brick steps. They climbed the steps to the porch then went through the front door and into the house.

Gatia escorted them up another staircase to a little corner room that, she explained, Jon and Garris were to share. Across and down the hall sat the room where Dellia would stay. From a few offhand remarks, Jon surmised that it wouldn't have been proper for Dellia to share a room with them, especially with children in the house.

He had forgotten how good it felt to sleep in an actual bed again, and, exhausted after the evening's ordeal, he fell quickly to sleep. But in those few moments between wakefulness and slumber, when his thoughts were no longer truly his own, his mind wandered back to that image of Dellia strolling among the fallen wolves. And even though she was surrounded by death and carnage, in that moment none of it existed, and all he saw was her face in the moonlight.

Chapter Sixteen

SHADES OF THE PAST

Dellia descended the staircase in her reluctant search for Jon. As she stepped onto the landing, halfway down, hushed voices greeted her. She glanced to the right, toward their source. In a small alcove, off the main room, two women knelt before a familiar elephant-headed statue, a flame flickering on a platter next to them. Their Vedic verses mingled with the scent of incense and breakfast, wafting up the stairs to greet her.

They were comforting sights and smells but did little to ease her apprehension over the discussion she knew was coming. She had convinced Jon to let her stay by promising to explain the circumstances surrounding his arrival. But her true motive was not to inform him at all but to persuade him to let her stay with him for good. And in that sense, it was yet another deception of the kind she had hoped were in the past.

As she turned the corner and started down the second flight, laughter and playful voices burst from the kitchen on her left. She slowed and ducked her head, peering into it, basking in the affections of a young couple who toyed and teased one another as they cleaned up after breakfast. Nothing brought peace to her soul, and clarity to her gift, quite like the sight of such love between two people mated for life.

Dellia stopped on the stairs and smiled. There at the large dining table, with his back to her, sat Jon, still lingering over his morning meal. Across from him lounged the most adorable little girl, draped in shades of fuchsia and amethyst. It was almost certainly Aishi, Gatia's young niece. Dellia renewed her descent, only slower and more quietly, eager to eavesdrop on their conversation.

Aishi stared at Jon, her big brown eyes scrutinizing him from beneath her midnight-black hair.

He leaned in toward her and with a hint of mischievousness said, "I am fascinating, aren't I?"

Aishi gave the cutest of smiles and nodded her head. After a moment, she looked up at Jon, puzzling over him as she picked up fingerfuls of a colorful yellow rice dish and stuffed them into her mouth.

Behind her, Chatin, the cat from the night before, slunk around the chair, then rubbed her huge head against Aishi's thigh.

After she'd chewed and swallowed, the girl gazed up at Jon again and in a quiet voice asked, "What's wrong?"

Dellia smiled at the innocence of the question and Jon's surprise at the asking.

"What? Nothing." He glanced around at all the people in the kitchen and alcove. "It's nice here. So much family all in one house. And so much color."

Aishi looked as thoughtful as a little girl can.

As surprising as it was coming from someone so young, Dellia could understand the question. Jon was more at ease here than she was used to seeing him, yet below the surface, hidden deep, probably below his own ability to recognize it, was turmoil, as if two things he desperately wanted were in fundamental conflict. Such feelings were all too common, but even if he was aware of the dissonance, it was doubtful he could put it into words.

Aisha eyed him with a puzzled expression. "Are you from beyond the veil?"

Having reached the front door, Dellia had a clear view of the sheer surprise on Jon's face, and she had to stifle a giggle.

"I'd tell you if I knew what that meant," he replied. "What made you ask?"

"Your aura, it's muddy … funny."

He bugged his eyes and donned his most astonished expression.

This time Dellia couldn't stifle her laugh, and Aishi turned and stared at her.

She smiled at the girl, then motioned for Jon to join her.

Aishi's eyes bugged, too, and she turned back to Jon.

He leaned in toward her, as if to share a secret. "What do you think? Should I go talk to her?"

She leaned in toward him, too. "I think she likes you."

"Let me guess. Her aura?"

She giggled and nodded.

Jon stood and strolled over to join Dellia, then waved goodbye to Aishi as the two slipped through the front door.

Outside, Dellia stepped out onto a large brick porch that led down to a lush garden area surrounded by a low fence. She led Jon down to the right, to a small bench in the corner under a large tree, surrounded by vines heavy with ruby-red, trumpet-shaped blooms. There, they sat at either end of the bench, facing a small pond rich with water lilies, their butter-yellow blooms reflected in its motionless surface.

Surrounded by the sweet scent of flowers, she sat there fidgeting, unsure where to begin. She glanced over at Jon, and he was staring into the street beyond the pond, watching as brightly clothed people passed by. She watched with him for a moment, until her attention was drawn to the sound of children laughing and playing in the yard across the street.

She had rehearsed what to say over and over on her way to catch up with Jon, but now that the moment was here, all her carefully considered words seemed empty and self-serving. In so many ways, her whole life, everything she had ever worked for, depended on this moment. On staying with him. Yet the problem remained: she had misused her gift and misled him. And here she was, trying to find some way to convince him to let her stay by him so she could take advantage of him some more.

"You can tell if I'm lying, right?" came Jon's voice.

His words took a moment to register, and Dellia turned to catch him staring at her, waiting for an answer. "Um, I try to tune it out sometimes."

"Don't. Not around me. I want you to know what I'm saying is the truth."

"I can't always tell," she said, her head not yet fully in the conversation. "There has to be some anxiety or guilt or something. Some people can lie and feel nothing. And some convince themselves a lie is the truth."

A flash of surprise crossed Jon's face. "And you think I'm one of those people?"

Dellia reached out and set her hand on his arm. "No. No. I know you're *not.*"

He seemed put off by the gesture, so she quickly withdrew her hand. But she scooted over a little closer and faced him. "Look, when I found you, my only mission was to investigate a disturbance. It wasn't until the end of the next day that I found out what the council suspected."

"Something about a prophecy?" Jon seemed reluctant to look her in the eye.

"Yeah. There's a prophecy, hundreds of years old. It's called The Prophecy of the Otherworlder. It says that someone will come from another world with a unique and powerful gift, and they will become a leader, but they will lead us to disaster and the end of our civilization."

A spark of fear flashed in his eyes, and in his heart, at the mention of becoming a leader. His gaze flew down to the wooden bench below them, lingering there for a few moments as the apprehension seemed to fade. Then he shook his head and raised his eyes to Dellia. "Wow. So you think I'm from another world?"

"Oh please," she blurted out, incredulous that he would even try to put up the pretense.

He winced, seeming contrite. Then he looked away, staring into the yellow, lily-strewn waters. "Okay, so I'm from another world." He turned back to her, his eyes questioning. "But still, you think that's me?"

"That's just it, nobody knows. Not the council and certainly not me. But you don't have a gift, and the whole disaster part is all wrong. But the council was worried about Megan; she has a gift, and it's a powerful one."

"But, Megan wouldn't hurt anyone," Jon blurted out.

Dellia cocked her head. "She hurt *you*, even though I know she didn't mean to. Anyway, that's why the council asked me to … to get close to you."

At her last words, his gaze shot away, and he peered into the street again.

She leaned in toward him. "But you have to believe, I never—"

"Yeah, well, stupid me, I fell for it. What's wrong with me? First Megan, then you. I keep falling for the wrong women."

His words hit with a jolt. She pulled back and turned away. "Falling for … What?" She stared into the distance, her mind racing. "How could I miss that?"

Dellia was too preoccupied for Jon's reply to sink in. "I was trying to deny it, I think, bury it. I still am, I suppose. I mean, even if you weren't just following orders, I'm going home, you're a protector. How stupid would that be?"

Dellia fidgeted with her bracelet, staring at it, going over every moment with Jon in her head, trying to understand how her gift could have failed her so completely.

She was too lost in thought to notice him turn to her, scrutinizing her, searching her face for some feedback, some hint of validation. "So I was really just a job to you?"

His accusation struck her like the hilt of a sword, and her head whipped over. "No. No. It wasn't like that. Ever. You have to believe me. I don't help people because it's my job. I wanted this job because it was my way to help people." She put her hand on his arm again. "I only ever wanted to help you."

Jon pulled away from her touch. He rose and strolled to the edge of the pond. Lilies spread out along the water at his feet as he looked out across the street again at the children laughing and running and playing.

"Look," he said. "I want to believe you because the alternative is I can't trust my own judgment."

"For what it's worth, I never believed you were the Otherworlder. And I told the council so. It's just—"

Aishi burst through the door, startling Dellia. She swung around and watched the young girl race down the path, across the street, and plop down with a group of girls playing gutte. One of them handed Aishi a stone which she tossed in the air then snatched two pebbles from the dirt before it fell back into her hand.

She turned back to Jon to catch him standing there staring at the ground at her feet, reluctant to confront whatever burden weighed on his heart.

"There's a much bigger reason I can't be this Otherworlder," he said. "You see, my mother, she was a soldier, like you. She always said she wanted to protect the country, keep everyone safe. Well, she died keeping everyone safe and left us alone."

Dellia looked up into his downcast face. "Oh. I'm so sorry," she said, but her words did little to assuage his sense of abandonment or his resentment of a mother he loved.

Jon took a deep breath, then trudged back to the bench and lowered himself onto it. He sat close to Dellia, but his gaze remained down and his eyes unfocused and far away as he spoke.

"A few years later, my dad remarried. Days after the wedding, I was in class with my new stepsister when we heard this loud noise. So the teacher went to investigate. And she told me to keep everything under control." He tensed and gripped the edge of the bench. "Well, pretty soon, we started hearing shots, and these terrible screams and cries for help. Most of the class wanted to escape, down the hall to the stairs, then out of the building." He shook his head. "But I was so smart, I was going to save them all."

Jon lifted his head and peered into Dellia's eyes. There was a pitiful pleading there that tore at her heart. "So I insisted everyone stay put, because, that's what you do, right? Shelter in place? I even quoted statistics … oh god."

He faltered. He looked at her, his eyes reflecting his fear and regret. She reached out and placed a hand on his. He glanced down at it then away, staring into the yellow reflections on the pond.

"So we stayed there, hiding behind a few desks, for the longest time. Then we heard footsteps and the sound of shots just down the hall. My stepsister freaked out. She kept saying how we were going to die, that we should have run, that it was all my fault—" Jon's voice cracked. "I told them it would be okay, I'd fix it, and I ran out into the hall. I was going to lead them away. Instead, I ran right into the two of them. They just laughed at me, like I was this big joke." He closed his eyes and lowered his head. "They told me to run. So I did. And they shot at me and laughed until I tripped and fell down the stairs."

He halted and took a breath as if to compose himself. "I must have gotten knocked out, because when I came to, I ran back to the room and found them, eleven of my classmates, including my stepsister, all dead."

Jon turned to Dellia and stared at her with anguished eyes. "If they'd run like they wanted, they'd still be alive, but because I told them not to, they're dead."

She struggled to find the words. "Jon ..."

He looked away, as if the demons of his past were reflected in her eyes. "My stepmother and stepbrothers, they never got over it. I'm sure they blamed me ... *I* blamed me. And ever since, I panic at the thought that something I might do could hurt someone. And the idea of being in charge of anything. I don't want that, ever again."

Dellia studied his face for the longest time. To *hear* a shot ... to cower in a room when under attack ... it all seemed so foreign to her, but Jon's trauma was unmistakable. She imagined the poor young boy standing over the bodies of his fallen friends and family, his heart torn open by the guilt of feeling he was responsible. She wanted to ease his burden, but all she had were mere words against such a horri-fying reality.

Still, she tried. "You know you didn't kill anyone, right?"

His head jerked up, and she pulled her hand away. Anger flashed in his blue eyes. "Didn't I? How would you feel if your mother got killed while you were protecting her?"

She knew the unassailable truth of his words, even as she knew he was wrong. "I understand, I do, but—"

"This Otherworlder prophecy"—Jon shook his head—"it can't be about me. You see, me being a leader, having people's lives depend on me ... that's insane to me. It's the last thing I'd ever want." His gaze drifted from her face. "Never again."

The mention of her mother brought Dellia back to Sirra's reas-suring words. This frightened boy in front of her was utterly unequipped to face the world that was against him. He needed help. Whether he knew it or not. And not just help from Garris, a banished ex-protector as much in danger as he was. She had a duty to fulfill, and she would. But he needed her, and if this prophecy truly wasn't about him then that need was even more dire. She had to find a way

266

to help.

"Then let me help you prove it," Dellia said.

"Trust me, I want your help. It's just—"

Dellia leaned in toward Jon. "No, *you need* my help."

"I know." He pulled away and rose from the bench. "And I know I'd be a fool to turn it down. ... So I guess I just need to get past this." He turned back to her, and his soft eyes gazed into hers. "Just give me time. Okay?"

Relief flooded her at the realization that he'd just agreed to let her stay with him and help. All the lies had ended, and all the shadows of the past had been illuminated. They both knew the truth, and despite it all, she would still be able to do her duty. At least there was that. Even if her position with the council was still as precarious as ever.

There was so much more Dellia wanted to ask, so much more to say. She yearned to know more about the feelings he had for her and whether she had put an end to them through the unforgivable way she had treated him. She wanted to ask if that was the reason he was so reluctant to accept her help when he so freely admitted needing it. Her duty compelled her to discover how he had come here and where he had learned of this path home he was pursuing. She needed to speak of all this and more, but Jon stood before her, and all he had asked for was some time. So she nodded her head.

He turned and meandered around the pond and down the path. Then, without looking back, he passed through the gate and headed out onto the street. She feared for him. He might become lost in this strange city, or word of what the council suspected could get out, or any manner of mischief could befall him. He had no training and no gift. So she should follow and watch over him, protect him. But she had given her word. So all she could do was watch as he disappeared into the busy streets of Mundus.

Kayleen had decided to spend the afternoon reading in the large alcove carved of stone. It had become one of her favorite spots. It sat halfway down the broad, stone steps that wound their way from Shir Courtyard above to Shirdon far below. It was distant enough from the courtyard and Shir Keep, where the council met and its members lived, to serve as a refuge from the pressing issues of the day. Yet it was not so far down that the sights, smells, and sounds of the busy Shirdon Market below were a distraction.

It was the perfect place to get lost in the pages of a book, and today, of all days, Kayleen needed a distraction from the intolerable waiting. And waiting for what? To find out what reckless course the council may have already concocted? They seemed oblivious to the danger inherent in the powers they were trifling with. So who knew if it was already too late to talk them out of whatever rash plans they had made and into a saner course of action? She needed to be back in that council chamber. This was the most critical time in over a decade, and only from that chamber could she influence events, only there could she keep the council from acting out of fear and arrogance and doing irreparable harm.

A shadow passed over the ruled and handwritten page of Kayleen's book, and footsteps stopped in front of her. She closed and latched the cover, adorned with gold and set with jewels, then rested it on her lap.

She glanced up to find Idria towering over her, her outline framed by the immaculate Shir Courtyard high above, and beyond it the peaks of Mount Karana. The long climb in the stiff mountain breeze must have disagreed with her, because she stood glaring down at Kayleen with those unusually pale blue eyes, her short silver hair disheveled, her face harried, and her manner impatient. "You didn't make it easy to find you."

Kayleen motioned to the long, winding stairway, carved from the side of the mountain, and smiled. "Did you climb all this way for me? I'm sorry. Why didn't you just send for me?"

Kayleen's attempt to be gracious seemed to irritate Idria, and her words were curt. "It's fine. I won't take much of your time."

Kayleen gave a deep bow of her head, showing Idria the respect she was due, then motioned to the bench, inviting her to sit beside her.

Idria thrust out her palm and shook her head, declining the invitation. "I've come to let you know the council has expended a great deal of effort reviewing your handling of this whole affair."

Kayleen smiled, half-amused, and in as calm and cordial a manner as she could said, "Let me guess—they all think they could have handled it better."

Though Idria strived to hide it, the response seemed to make her even more irritated and defensive. "This prophecy could spell the end of this council and all the good it could do. Our only goal was to manage the situation, to control things. And yet here we are days later with no word from Dellia and the situation decidedly out of control."

"And what would you have done differently?"

"The minute you knew Jon existed, you should've had him detained."

Kayleen smiled, and her tone was calm and measured, as if explaining to a child. "With Megan missing and Jon willing and eager to help find her? Don't be foolish."

"And what about when Dellia had them both together? Why didn't she detain them both?"

"I see." Kayleen nodded. "In your mind, she should have detained them while she was bound and gagged? By the time she was free, Megan was gone, and it was either stick with Jon or follow Megan and risk losing them both."

"And how does a protector get taken in the first place?"

"She saw Megan's gift and realized her abduction was an opportunity, a way to stay near her and listen in on their conversations. She had no reason to believe Jon would free her."

No longer appearing to hide her agitation, Idria said, "And when Jon rescued our valiant protector, she should've arrested him on the spot."

"Why?" Kayleen said, still striving to remain patient and amiable. "So we could bring him here and try to get information out of him? How forthcoming is he going to be after we've arrested him? Unless you're suggesting torture?"

Idria's frustration was apparent in her voice. "Nobody suggested—" She stifled her protestations as a couple passing by on the stairs caught her strong words and glanced over to see what had caused all the fuss. Idria grabbed Kayleen's arm and led her to the railing, where the two continued their discussion as they peered down the overlook to the bustling town of Shirdon far below.

"Nobody suggested torture," Idria said in a loud whisper.

"So then you agree," Kayleen said, this time a bit more emphatically. "It was the right call to let him stay with Dellia while she found out what he knew."

This time Idria did not whisper. "All the excuses in the world won't change—"

Kayleen glared at Idria. "Excuses? Perhaps I should've explained in simpler terms. It was a well-thought-out, well-executed strategy that yielded disappointing results."

"The fact remains, you let a protector with a conscience problem talk you, a veteran politician, into cutting the council out of the process, leaving us uninformed and with no control."

"And we have yet to see if that was the right call."

"I didn't come here to rehash this," Idria said. "I came to tell you the council voted, and you've been removed as council leader."

Stunned, Kayleen stepped back and stared. "What? You can't do that."

"I'm sorry, but it's done."

She knew the council disapproved of her handling of things, but to be removed? "But we believe in the same things," she said. "We all see the council as a force for great good. And I am as determined as any of you that the prophecy not threaten that."

Now it was Idria's turn to be calm. "Yet it is you who have undermined us. So you are suspended from participating in all debate. At least until this Otherworlder situation is resolved."

Still reeling, Kayleen turned away, hiding her reaction. She wandered a handful of steps away as she struggled to come to terms with the disturbing turn of events. Removal as leader required a unanimous vote. Were they all that terrified of this prophecy? Did she not have one single friend on the council, not one member who would side with her? No. She couldn't accept that. She knew them, and it didn't make any sense. Or, perhaps getting rid of her was part of a larger, more reckless course of action. But what could that plan be?

Kayleen calmed herself and turned back to Idria. "So, twenty years on the council and I'm shut out, just like that."

"Not completely. There's a suspicion on the council that you may be covering for Dellia. So we're leaving the Window of Rhina with you, as long as you agree that if she contacts you, you will convince her to bring Jon in." Idria took a step closer, and her manner was sincere. "Nobody is closer to Dellia. So, if anyone can reach her, it's you. Do you think you can persuade her?"

Suddenly, the pattern emerged with crystal clarity, all the puzzling pieces fit, and it all made perfect sense. This was the plan. And a clever one at that. It had all the earmarks of Braye's deviousness. But she needed to hear Idria say it.

Kayleen donned an expression of innocent curiosity. "Of course. But if you think I'm lying, why trust me?"

Idria seemed to contemplate the question. "Dellia is fond of you, and if you can convince her to bring Jon in, or better yet, get her to convince Jon to come in on his own, then perhaps this whole unfortunate affair can be forgotten and your position restored."

It was precisely as she suspected. Kayleen feigned surprise, then strolled back to Idria. She granted her a sly smile. "Shrewd. You're bargaining that Dellia's concern for me and my removal will put pressure on her. But your scheming is unwarranted. Dellia lives to be a protector. If I order it, she will do almost anything."

Idria flashed a perfunctory smile, then whirled around and marched off up the stairway. Kayleen watched for a few moments as the brisk mountain wind tousled Idria's hair and clothes. Then, under her breath, she muttered, "Regardless of the cost to herself."

Jon strolled down the street, marveling at the massive houses that lined either side. They were quite distinctive, with their flat rooftops and rows of arched windows and doorways. They were like little estates, each with its own spacious gardens, patios, decks, and porches, replete with elaborate carvings and artwork. Brightly clothed residents dotted the roofs, balconies, and yards. Their gold and brown faces with their serene smiles and pleasant manner only served to remind Jon of his difficult conversation with Dellia.

He had told her things he had never expressed to a living soul, not even Megan. Yet it was not his words that troubled him but the prospect of spending time with her. Not because he didn't want or need her help but because he wanted it too much. He had just told her how he felt, so it seemed pointless continuing to deny it to himself, but it was clear from her reaction she did not feel the same. And regardless of how much she might want to be a friend, or how sincere her desire to help, it didn't change the fundamental truth that he was her job. And he'd be a fool to imagine ever being much more.

DELLIA

It was difficult to be around someone he had feelings for and know they could never be returned. He only knew one way to cope, and he was well practiced in it after his many years with Megan: Don't indulge those feelings or dwell on them; set them aside. Be a good friend, but also be disciplined and keep focused on the task before him. If he hid in the refuge of his work, with time, those feelings would fade.

Right now, his task was to locate the Andera Catacombs, whatever that was. For that matter, he wasn't even sure what a catacomb was, other than that it sounded like a twisty little maze, all dark and creepy. Isla had described them as being under a place in Mundus called the Temple of Knowledge. So far, he hadn't seen a single structure that had the remotest resemblance to a temple.

Jon stopped and spun around, scanning the street, memorizing where he'd been while trying to figure out which way to go next.

A woman eyed him as she approached, moving gracefully down the street and draped in shades of emerald and canary yellow. She stopped, and a smile adorned her cheerful, tanned face. "You look lost. Can I help?"

"Um, I'm looking for the Temple of Knowledge."

The woman smiled again and motioned for Jon to follow. She led him to the next intersection, only a couple dozen feet from where he'd been standing.

As he approached the corner, signs of a temple began to appear from around the two-story houses. First, a set of four spires poked above the rooftops, followed by a massive, rounded dome that towered above the city.

The woman pointed way down on the western side of the street where a set of broad stone steps drifted down to meet the avenue. "You can't miss it." He must have still looked puzzled because she quickly added, "Look for the mandapa with all the yali."

With no idea what the heck a mandapa was, or a yali, Jon just smiled and thanked her. He continued in the direction she'd pointed, shaking his head, hoping the reference would somehow become clear once he saw whatever it was.

As he approached, it became apparent that the stairs led to a pillared area and that the spires and dome that lay beyond were all part of the same enormous structure that stretched way back off the street.

Jon paused at the base of the series of stone steps as broad and as tall as some houses. He gazed up it at an even larger open pavilion. Its architecture was simple, just a square stone roof supported by an array of carved columns. But every surface seemed to be covered with the most intricate three-dimensional carvings. If this wasn't a temple, it was a pretty decent imitation.

He ambled up the deep steps, spinning around and gawking like some kind of tourist, searching for something that looked like it could lead to catacombs. He had no idea what that might look like, but he'd probably know when he saw it. He continued to scour the area as he reached the top and stepped out under the massive stone roof, where the gentle scent of orange and incense wafted through the air.

As Jon wandered further into the pavilion, an elderly man strolled up to greet him, swathed in robes of soft orange. He had a quiet air about him that made it seem as if he belonged there. He came to a stop in front of Jon and cocked his head, as if making a quiet offer of assistance.

"Is this the Temple of Knowledge?" Jon asked. "I was told to look for the mandapa with all the yali."

The man smiled. "You are standing in the mandapa. This pavilion serves as the entrance to the temple. As for the yali ..." He peered up at something above Jon's right shoulder. Jon turned his head and jumped as his eyes met the open mouth of a massive lion's head, its smooth, carved canines inches from his face.

He stepped back and stared at it. The head was crowned with a pair of giant horns that swept far back over its mane, and out of its spine grew a pair of gigantic wings. Though huge compared to a real lion, the carving was surprisingly realistic and intimidating, and a shiver ran down his spine.

"Nasiri carved them," the man said, as if the words carried a meaning Jon could not fathom.

"Looks like a lion with horns and wings."

"I am Umata." The man placed his palms together in front of him and bowed his head. He turned and looked up at the lion's head, admiring it with Jon. "Yes, this one is a lion with the horns of a ram and the wings of an eagle. But in other temples, the yali may contain the trunk of an elephant, the body of a horse, or the tail of a snake, whatever Nasiri thought would best protect the temple."

"Protect? Like a gargoyle?"

Umata cocked his head. "I do not understand. Nasiri was an artificer."

"Artificer?"

"Yes. Varish created the spires. Rhina created many artifacts for saving voices and seeing over a distance. And Nasiri created these." Umata motioned to the inside of the temple, and Jon realized all the pillars featured the same kind of carving, some lions and others lionesses, and each in a slightly different pose.

He stopped gawking and turned his attention back to his search. "They are impressive, but it is really the Andera Catacombs I came to ask about."

Umata tilted his head once more. "Why would you wish to know about them?"

"I need to know where they are."

Umata motioned to the floor of the pavilion. "They are under your feet. They are carved from the caverns that run beneath this part of the city."

"Thanks," Jon said. Well, at least he was in the right place.

Umata's curiosity suddenly seemed to turn to suspicion. "I'm sorry. I cannot allow you to enter the catacombs. Now if you'll excuse me, there are others in need of guidance."

He placed his palms together again and gave a curt bow before drifting off toward another group of people strolling through the temple.

Despite Garris's warning that they'd never let him enter, being rebuffed like that was discouraging. Still, he had to find a way in, and even if he had been thwarted for now, he could at least find out where the entrance was. So Jon resumed his survey of the pavilion, marveling at the multitude of intricate carvings and the way the architecture and sculpture seemed to blend into one another, making it impossible to tell where one ended and the other began.

He arrived at the westernmost end of the pillared area where a set of short steps led to an open doorway. He peered through the entry into another large, square area further into the temple. It was enclosed, but the warm morning sun poured into it through a series of windows near the ceiling, giving the whole room a sort of soft glow. It had even more pillars, also covered with intricate carvings, and every wall was an artwork of sculpture and dioramas.

Jon turned to the right and there, a short distance from the steps leading upward, stood another set that led downward, underneath the temple. Perhaps those stairs led to the catacombs. He headed toward the stairway, but as he passed one of the carved pillars along the way, an intriguing thought occurred to him.

He halted and turned to stare at the carving on the column next to him. His footsteps echoed through the pavilion as he strolled around to the front. He stood for a moment, gazing up into the face of the massive lion as it loomed over him. Then he reached out and ran his fingers over the smooth surface of the lion's chest.

"Yali," Jon said.

A bolt of movement streaked by the corner of his eye. His head jerked over and a blur of orange and silver flashed by. He swung around to the glint of shiny metal flying at his skull. A sharp crack and a stab of pain jerked his head back. Then he was falling as the world faded away.

Chapter Seventeen

BLOOD IN THE SHADOWS

For some time, Dellia remained on the small bench in the corner, under the graceful branches of the tree. Surrounded by the scent of brilliant red flowers, she stared into the street, watching the passersby and the children playing as she considered her predicament.

Her fate depended on handling a situation rich with questions and few answers. She remained more convinced than ever that the prophecy simply couldn't be about Jon. Even without that awful childhood story, he was too delicate a soul to be some kind of great leader, much less the source of anyone's harm. Yet, all her instincts were ringing alarm bells, telling her something was going on, something was off. But how could she get to the bottom of a thing she couldn't even put into words?

A falling leaf drifted down, coming to rest on the still waters of the pond. Dellia watched it as it floated on the reflective surface. Perhaps that was what she needed, to be like that leaf on the breeze. To stay by Jon and help him, however she could. And with time and patience, answers would come. Then she would do what was needed. No matter what, she would prove to the council they could trust her, that having faith in her was the right choice.

Dellia startled at the sound of someone clearing their throat. She tore her gaze from the reflection of yellow lilies on glistening water and glanced over to find its source.

Off to her side stood Gatia, with a small smile on her face. "I didn't want to interrupt you," she said. "It seemed like you and Jon were discussing something important. I held off so you two could talk in peace."

Dellia shook her head as she rose and turned to Gatia. The urge to explain their discussion tugged at her, but all she could think to say was, "It's complicated."

Gatia brought herself up straight, standing at attention, and her manner took on a sudden formality. "I thought this matter might be left to the Parishad, but it appears I am to escort you to the audience hall to see the Rhanae."

"Oh." Dellia quickly checked herself over, trying to decide if she would be presentable to royalty.

Gatia led her through the small garden, past the gate, and out into the warmth of the sunny streets of Mundus. The lane was lined with the huge, sprawling houses that exemplified Erden. They were like little communities with several families, grandparents, aunts and uncles, cousins and offspring all living and working together. It was one of the hallmarks of their culture. It was admirable, but it was not the way of her people. The people of Talus were much too independent, and the responsibility to spouse and children too fierce and personal. It was not something to be entrusted to others, not even when those others were brothers and sisters.

For a short time, Gatia led them down one dusty, stone road after another in silence, surrounded only by the sounds of the city streets as its residents ambled through their morning activities. But soon she began to quiz Dellia, pushing to learn every detail of the wolf encounter. Dellia explained how they had used the spires as a shield and baited the wolves. Gatia took a particular interest in the tactics and seemed shocked to learn Jon had been behind much of them.

"What is it about him?" Gatia said.

"What do you mean?"

Dellia

Having come to the end of a long strip of desert garden, she led the way up a flight of steps to the audience hall. "If I passed him on the street, I wouldn't give him a second thought. But then he does … I mean … there's just something about him." Gatia stopped and stepped to the side of a huge, open doorway, then motioned for Dellia to pass.

Dellia considered asking Gatia to explain but fell silent as she entered into the enormous, well-lit hall. The beauty of the elaborate interior was startling, and she slowed and stared upward, gawking at the stunning high walls and arched ceilings. As they strolled through the hall, they passed through beams of sunlight that spilled from numerous long, narrow windows high up on either wall. Light from them blended with the intricate architecture of yellow and gold, giving the whole room a warm glow.

Gatia directed Dellia to the audience area, where the entire end of the room was raised a few steps to form a massive dais. The gentle scent of flowers filled the air from rows of vases stuffed with sprays of heavy magenta blooms that lined the back of the platform.

There, at the top of the handful of steps, sat a man dressed in shades of saffron and ocher. Reclining on a regal-looking couch of golden yellow, he evaluated Dellia with quiet detachment as she approached. His tawny skin, his intense brown eyes, everything about him said he had to be Katal. Sprawled out next to him, a large Bengal tiger purred and licked its paws as it ignored the entire proceedings.

Katal placed his palms together and bowed his head. "Respect, Protector."

Dellia replied in kind.

His manner remained formal, but his words were soft and kind. "Perhaps you could clarify, are you here in an official capacity?"

"Yes, but why would you ask?"

He sent a fleeting glance behind him. She followed his gaze to a veiled woman she hadn't noticed before standing motionless near the back.

Katal crossed his arms and took a deep breath. "It is known that you take your orders from Kayleen, but a rumor has reached us that she has been removed from the council."

Dellia stood for a moment in stunned silence before a sick feeling overcame her. Was this her fault? Had she cost Kayleen her position on the council? She lost her balance for a moment as the enormity of her actions hit her. And with that disturbing revelation came a sudden urge to run off, this moment, and talk to Kayleen. To find some way to set this right. But what good would that do? Whatever was done was done. There was no taking it back, and the path she had set for herself now remained the only way out. It was more imperative than ever that she prove herself, because now Kayleen's reputation and position depended on it.

Dellia brought herself up taller, trying to master her feelings of horror and guilt.

The woman stepped forward. Wrapped in lush shades of lemon that flowed down to tangerine, she eyed Dellia from beneath a soft, yellow veil as she drifted to Katal's side. She lifted it and tilted her head, eyeing her with genuine concern. Then came her voice, filled with compassion. "I am so sorry, Dellia. Did you not know?"

In an instant, she realized it was Asina, and a flush of shame caught her at her weakness in front of the rulers of all Erden. Dellia bowed her head. "I'm sorry. I am no diplomat, Rhanae."

Asina smiled and sent Katal a sideways glance. "As you know, Katal and I rule as one, but if it would set you at ease, let us discuss this as friends."

Relieved, Dellia pressed her palms together and gave another brief bow. "Thank you, Rhanae. I would very much appreciate that."

Asina strolled over to her and lowered herself down, sitting right in front of Dellia at the top of the steps.

Katal leaned forward to the edge of his seat, and his voice took on the tone of a concerned friend. "I'm sorry if this news has upset you."

"How certain are you of this rumor?" Dellia asked.

Asina tilted her head. "I'm sorry, Dellia. We are quite certain."

"You can see our predicament," Katal said. "As you know, relations between Erden and the council are often strained. Kayleen would only be removed over a matter of great significance. If that matter were to involve your visit here, it could put us in a … difficult position."

"I assure you." Dellia rushed the words out. "I may answer to Kayleen, but I serve the whole council."

Asina smiled again. "You misunderstand. We must report your presence to the council. And we cannot go against them should they request that we take action."

It took her a moment to realize that Asina was talking about action against *her*. And with that realization, her hopes of completing her mission faded. There would be no helping Jon and no restoring the council's faith in her and Kayleen.

"I understand." Dellia lowered her head. "Thank you, Rhanae."

Asina rose to her feet and gazed off into space, appearing thoughtful. "However, the fastest our courier could get to Shirdon and back is a day and a half. And as of late he has been most unreliable." She flashed Dellia a sly smile. "In fact, I feel certain he will not leave for another half a day, which should give you a full two days."

A deep sense of relief washed over Dellia as she realized that the rulers of Erden, for no reason other than concern for a stranger, had just granted her a reprieve. She reached down and touched Asina's feet. "Truly, I see the divine in you, Asina."

Katal gazed at Asina in adoration. "Then you see even as I do every time my eyes fall upon her."

Asina returned his gaze and, for the first time, it hit Dellia. There was a reason she hadn't recognized her right away. The love between her and Katal should have been obvious, her gift should have told her. Without that, she had assumed the woman meant nothing to him, and that meant she couldn't be Asina. But more importantly, it meant that for the first time in her adult life, she couldn't count on her gift.

Katal leaned back on the couch, reclining in the warm sunlight with a cloud of magenta blooms behind him. He became somber and heaved a heavy sigh. "And then there is the matter of the Blood Wolves. We don't know whether to thank you or blame you."

"Blame me?" Dellia couldn't hide her surprise.

"We understand this is not the first you've seen of these wolves," he said.

"May I ask how would you know this?"

Asina threw him a quick glance. "Rumors travel quickly."

"Am I to be judged on the basis of a rumor?"

Asina shook her head. "There is no judgment here. Only a concern that your presence within our city brings with it a threat."

Dellia bowed her head. "I understand. You wish us to leave."

The purring of the tiger tugged at Katal's awareness, and he absentmindedly reached out, stroking it as it lay next to him on the golden cushion. "We cannot force you to leave, but it was our hope you'd share our concern and wish to protect our people as much as we do."

"Of course." Dellia gave a single definitive nod. "We will leave at once."

Asina shook her head. "Such urgency is not required. Given the timing of the last attack, it seems likely you have at least a few days, but we would be appreciative if you left the city by sundown tomorrow."

Dellia stared in surprise. "The timing? That's a remarkably precise rumor."

Asina smiled. "As all our rumors tend to be."

There was a finality in those words and in Asina's manner that said this audience was over. Gatia placed her hands together, and Dellia followed her lead. Then, they both bowed and turned to go. Dellia breathed a sigh, taking one last sweet breath of flower-scented air before marching away, leaving the pair behind her on the bright, sunlit platform.

Things had just gotten impossibly complicated. She had less than two days to find the answers that would restore the council's faith in her and in Kayleen, and she had no idea where to begin, much less how she intended to do it.

Jon stared up at the dense, wispy haze drifting through the air above him. It was impossible to tell where he was. No sound met his ears. No walls or ceiling surrounded him, and there was no feeling of the floor beneath his back, only the dark fog that spread out all around. Yet some undefinable quality of his senses informed him he was lying on the ground.

As he gazed upward, the wisps above his feet grew brighter. He propped himself up on his elbows, staring, as the vapor swirled into a clean, white mist. The ethereal fog seemed to grow brighter and denser until it came together to form a real, living woman. Tall and regal, she stood at his feet, draped in a pristine white robe.

A faint light seemed to emanate from her as she peered down at Jon with gleaming silver eyes. "You are unconscious. I had thought to come to you in a dream, but your present state suits what I have need to convey."

"Unconscious?" He pulled himself up to a sitting position.

"Yes. I have come at the behest of Megan, with a message."

"Megan?" Jon sprang to his feet. An abundance of questions had been stirring in his consciousness about where he was, what he was doing here, and the nature of this mysterious woman, but the mention of Megan drove them all from his mind, and his entire being became focused on this messenger and what she had to say.

The woman nodded. "She beseeched me to let you know she is unharmed and safe."

"Where is she?"

"I will show you." The lady in white motioned him to come.

As he stepped up to her side, the dark haze on all sides wove itself into swirls of bright green and earthy brown. They drifted together, turning solid, and suddenly they were both standing in a sunlit wood that wound its way around the jagged walls of a large, craggy hill. The distant caw of a crow rose above the buzz of cicadas and the chittering of animals from the rocky fields and woods that spread out around them, and barely visible beyond were mountainous cliffs that rose up to form a giant backdrop of stone.

The air was warm and still as Jon looked down at the greenery poking through the crumbling remains of a long-forsaken brick roadway, only a few feet in front of them.

In the distance, the now familiar clip-clop of hooves approached from where the ancient path disappeared around a rocky hillside.

The woman touched his arm. "You are still unconscious, but I have brought your senses here, to the Seteepta Valley, so you could know that I speak the truth."

Her words brought a notion to mind. Perhaps this was all a hallucination or a dream, or some elaborate illusion. Before he could fully entertain the thought, a man on horseback appeared around the edge of a cliff. The face was indelibly etched in his mind as the one Megan had gone off with. A moment later, Megan herself appeared, plodding along with a bored expression.

Jon lurched forward at the sight of her and called out, "Megan!"

The woman touched his shoulder. "She cannot hear you."

He spun around to face the mysterious lady. "Is this real?"

She looked at him with the earnest expression of a mother reassuring a child. "Yes. This is where she is, right now. The man with her is Aylun. They do not believe the prophecy could be about either of you. Out of a desire to protect you, she has separated from you."

He watched as Megan approached down the ancient stones of the long-abandoned roadway. His concern for her had been a constant nagging in the back of his mind, and a tremendous sense of relief flooded in at seeing her face again. Even so, he needed to temper his enthusiasm: it still might not be real, it might not be her.

As the pair neared, Megan stared at the heavy moss clinging to the side of a stand of trees. "Are you sure you know where you're going?" She reached out to touch the dense green carpet. "How can anyone make out where they're going in this ... stuff?"

Aylun's response seemed exasperated, as if he couldn't quite hide his irritation. "The path can only go one place, Lanessa. We have been over this."

Clearly irritated by his remark, Megan wrinkled her nose and bobbed her head as she mouthed the words, "We've been over this" to Aylun's turned backside. Then she stuck out her tongue.

Jon stifled a laugh as all his doubts vanished. Now *that* was Megan.

She put on a sarcastic bubbliness. "And we just have to make it there and search the whole city before sundown. Sure, piece of cake, no problem."

As he passed directly in front of Jon, Aylun sighed. "Not the whole city. I told you." He twisted around in the saddle to face Megan. "Has anyone ever told you you are kind of a negative person?"

Reins in hand, Megan planted her fists on her waist. "Oh, that's rich coming from Mr. Sunshine."

The mysterious woman touched Jon's shoulder a second time, and they shot upward toward the rolling clouds drifting through a brilliant blue sky. He watched beneath him as Megan and Aylun became distant, then vanished in a sea of vegetation.

They stopped high in the sky, yet it felt like they were standing on solid ground. The woman pointed to the horizon where the ruins of a sprawling city sat at the edge of a vast plain. She motioned down a wide valley filled with a patchwork of woods, hills, and fields. "Now, Megan travels past the ruins of the old capital of Talus, searching for proof."

Jon stared at her. "Proof of what?"

The woman's silvery eyes stared back. "Proof the prophecy is wrong. That neither of you is the Otherworlder." She stepped back, and everything around them drifted into swirls of white and blue and green. Then the colors faded until all that remained was a sea of dark mist again.

The mysterious woman nodded to Jon. "I must leave you now. For you will soon regain consciousness and you are in grave danger." With that, the woman drifted back into a dark mist.

Jon stared at the spot where she'd stood, alarmed at her statement and wondering what grave danger he might be in. Then his thoughts became muddled as a foggy haze spread through his consciousness. Unable to form a thought, all that remained was a vague anxiety, until that too faded into nothing.

Dellia barged through the door to Garris and Jon's room. She glanced around the bright and cheery space, flooded with sunlight from a row of arched windows on the two outside walls. Jon was nowhere to be found, but Garris was there, seated on a lavish and colorful canopy bed. He never looked up as she plowed into the room. He simply continued rubbing down a shiny throwing dagger, one of a raft of weapons and supplies he'd arranged on the sheets with care.

"It's all falling apart," she said.

Light glinted off the slender blade as he finished slipping it into a belt that lay on the bed. He glanced over at her. "You know, you and I never really talk anymore," he quipped as she paced across the sunlit floor.

"I told them off," Dellia said. "I said they needed to trust me. That I could handle it."

"That you could handle Jon?" Garris asked.

Dellia halted and nodded, then continued her pacing.

He resumed scooping up the narrow, silver blades from the bed and sliding them into the worn leather belt.

"I thought I could help Jon and serve the council at the same time, but now …" She shook her head. "The Rhanae have sent word, and if we're still here by tomorrow night, it'll all come crashing down."

Garris ceased his activity and looked thoughtful for a moment, then picked up his simple crossbow and began to slip off the bowstring. "I see. Well, first off, in my considered opinion, it's probably best not to tell off the council."

Dellia halted and glared at Garris. "Thanks. I kinda figured that one out on my own."

"Look, it's not all bad. If you help Jon get home, the council will be grateful, and none of this will matter. And if he's the Otherworlder and they capture him, the fact he trusts you will make you indispensable to the council."

It was disturbing to hear him propose Jon's capture in such a cold and casual manner. And even more distressing that he had conceded Jon might be the Otherworlder.

She lowered herself onto the chair opposite the opulent bed and studied him. "You know my father's story, right? What happened at Githeo?"

Garris paused for a moment, then nodded. "If you mean the awful choice he had to make, yeah, I know. Perhaps better than you."

Dellia's head dropped as the memories flooded back of years of taunting and humiliation. She could recall with the sharpness of yesterday the sense of pain and resentment in those who had lost family members because her father had failed to protect them.

"You never had to live with the consequences." Dellia raised her head and peered into Garris's face. "How could you know?"

Anger flared in his eyes. "Don't speak of things you know nothing about."

Startled by his outburst, she sat for a second, searching his eyes, wondering about the source of his pain.

Soon, he snapped back to his placid self. "What I know is that at Githeo, your father saved his wife and child."

"At the cost of many lives," Dellia shot back. "Lives of people we knew, who knew me. Lives he had a responsibility to protect."

Garris lowered his head, looking down at the sturdy crossbow in his hands. "People are hurting when they've lost a loved one. To say your father neglected his duty, to say you should have died instead—" He shook his head. "It's wrong. They never faced that choice."

She inhaled a deep breath of warm, dry air. "I have dedicated my life to proving I am not my father, to correcting his mistake. If Jon is the Otherworlder, then ..." She paused, reluctant to give voice to her fears. She stared into his face. "You don't think he really could be, do you?"

Garris sent Dellia an immediate shake of his head. "No."

"Just like that? No?"

"And if he was, I doubt I'd be here. Not because of some unreliable old prophecy, but because I've traveled this path before and where it leads is not any place I will ever return."

Garris was quite emphatic and his desire genuine. But if he felt so strongly, then why be here at all? Dellia watched him for a moment as she pondered the strength of his conviction, then asked, "What makes you so sure it's not him?"

He laid the crossbow down on the bed with care, stood, and wandered to one of the many arched windows along the wall. He leaned on the sturdy, brick windowsill, staring down into the sunlit avenue. For a moment, he lingered there, as the drone of conversation drifted up from the street below.

Then, he turned back toward Dellia and looked straight at her. "You can tell if I'm being truthful, right?"

"Some people are pretty good liars," she said, "but we could test it."

"How?"

"Tell me I'm the most beautiful woman in the world."

"You're the most beautiful woman in the world."

"Well, you're definitely telling the truth." She smiled.

He shook his head. "Oh, so this is you being serious?"

"Sorry," Dellia said, then adopted a more solemn attitude. "How do you know?"

Garris sauntered back to the bed and sat facing her, next to his well-used crossbow and quiver of arrows. And when he spoke, his voice was calm and quiet. "I was given this piece of metal, passed down hundreds of years, generation to generation, with a message: help the one who needs it find his way home." He leaned in toward her. "In that tower, Jon needed it. It was part of what he needed to get home. That's not a nebulous prophecy that may or may not occur and may or may not be about Jon. That was something real. It happened. I saw with my own two eyes."

Dellia had seen many things in her time as a protector, but nothing like that. Ancient prophecies were just that: legends of the past, things that happened long ago, or to distant people you never met. With eyes wide, she leaned in toward Garris. "You *saw* a prophecy being fulfilled?"

He nodded. "But here's the thing: How could Jon be the Otherworlder if I need to help him find his way home? If I succeed, then he wouldn't be here to be the Otherworlder." He leaned back as he finished.

She nodded. There was a certain logic in what he'd said. Even more, it agreed with her own conclusions about the prophecy and Jon. Yet, there was still more to Garris's story, something he wasn't saying. Or perhaps something he didn't want to say.

"So what did you mean about the path you traveled before?"

He averted his gaze, staring at the floor as he became still and quiet. "It's not important."

There was a deep-seated resentment that accompanied his words, something way down that he was struggling to master, and it stood at complete odds with his words. Dellia watched him for a moment, puzzling over it before she spoke. "There's a lot of anger there for something so unimportant."

"Oh," he shot back, "so now you're prying into *my* feelings?"

"Look, I get that you need time and space to deal with things on your own, but it's been fifteen years."

"So you think this is just something that happened in the past?"

"No. I'm trying to help. Whatever this is, it's eating you alive."

"Really. You want to help. Fine," Garris said, his words sharp and bitter. "Those who banished me left me unprotected by law. So it was only a matter of time before they came: old enemies with a grudge, young fools out to make a name for themselves, morons seeking the thrill of hunting a protector. They knew they could kill me, without consequence, so they came, a few at first, and then more and more, for so many years. So tell me, Dellia, how are you going to wash all that blood off these hands?" He thrust his palms out for her to see.

"Oh." She glanced at them, then looked down at the ground. He was right. She had stirred up something best left alone, and now nothing she said could erase his feelings of guilt and bitterness.

She looked back up, staring into his face. "I'm so sorry. I had no idea."

His irritation was still present, even as he grabbed up a cloth and his crossbow and buried himself in the work of cleaning it. As awful as Dellia felt, there were still parts of his story that weren't adding up. It was critical she learn as much as she could, and with Garris being so guarded, this might be her only chance.

"But that doesn't explain your apprehension. I don't need a gift to see this prophecy, Jon, all of it, has you rattled. Why?"

He remained intently focused on his work as he answered. "Let's just say the story of how I came to be exiled is a long and complicated one. And it involves the reason for the council's concern over this prophecy."

It took a moment for his words to sink in. His talk of the path he'd never follow again, his bitterness over his exile. They were all tied into what was happening with Jon right now. But she needed to hear him say it. "Are you saying ...?"

Garris ceased his cleaning, then looked up at Dellia. "Jon isn't the first one suspected of being the Otherworlder? Yeah, and my bet is, he won't be the last."

Jon awakened to a stale, dusty odor and the distant sound of muffled voices. Like a dream, the memory of Megan winding her way down a long-abandoned road through lush woods quickly faded, becoming a distant memory swallowed up in a groggy haze. His mind still mired in confusion, he raised his head and stared at the jagged shadows that rippled across the room. They stretched over the coffin before him, obscuring it and the large granite pedestal on which it rested.

A flush of adrenaline hit as he tried to reach out and realized his hands were tied. Panic took over as he thrashed and writhed, struggling against the leather straps that bound his hands and feet.

Jon halted and closed his eyes. This wasn't helping. He had to figure out what was happening, or why he'd been taken, or even where he was. He glanced up, above and behind his head, at the sunlight flashing across a crude staircase that descended from an open doorway above. Glancing around the small room, his gaze fell on a shelf carved out of the stone and lined with colorful pottery. It began just above the coffin and ran the length of the wall, disappearing into darkness.

Muffled voices echoed through the small cavern and he became still, straining to catch the words.

"I heard something. I'm not going down there," a woman's voice said.

His head whipped around, toward the source. There, down a hallway, barely visible at the edge of blackness, stood a pair of silhouettes conversing.

"You have to," a man's voice said. "We need something to plant on him."

"We should get him out of here," the woman said. "I'm telling you something's down there."

"No, that's not the plan. Our focus has to be her, not him. The guards will be here any second. Go."

The woman's silhouette straightened and crossed its arms.

Then came the man's voice again. "Fine, I'll go." He took a single step further into the darkness.

Then what Jon had assumed to be the outline of the wall moved, separating from the wall itself. Suddenly, it flew toward the two dark silhouettes.

The woman screamed, and the pair bolted toward Jon, their panic-stricken faces becoming visible as they hit the light.

The outline of an enormous figure hurtled after them. It burst from the shadows, becoming something new and terrifying: a red-haired monster, huge, dark, and sickly green, like some giant, savage, winged human. It bore down on them. Its bulging red eyes stared after them as saliva glistened off its canines. Massive muscles propelled it after the two, quickly overcoming them. It smashed the man in the back of his head with one of its enormous, heavily clawed hands.

The man tumbled to the ground with a thud.

The woman spun around and lunged for him.

The creature grabbed hold of her throat, lifted her up, and hurled her to the ground with a horrible crack. She lay in the dirt wheezing in pain and gasping for breath with the knee of the enormous creature pinning her as it knelt on her chest.

It grabbed hold of the unconscious man's arm and raised it to its mouth. It smiled down at the woman just before it sank its jagged teeth deep into his flesh.

Blood spattered everywhere. It splashed into the shadows and over the woman's face and body as the creature wrenched a huge chunk of meat out of the arm and began to wolf it down.

The woman tried to scream, but it only came out as a wheeze. She reached out for Jon, as the creature raised the arm for a second bite.

Desperate to reach the woman, Jon struggled and squirmed against his bindings.

The sound of footsteps approaching echoed down the staircase and the creature halted, the arm inches from its fangs. It glanced up at the noise, then glared at Jon with bulging red eyes.

Still struggling to free himself, his heart jumped as the creature rose and leered at him. He feared he would be next and was powerless to stop it. But the hulking monster just turned, reached down, and seized a leg from each of the man and woman. The man moaned and stirred as the red-haired abomination began to drag them off.

In a wild panic, the woman clawed at the ground, grasping for anything near. Her frantic face pleaded to Jon, and again she reached out to him.

"Jon, please, help me," her wheezing voice called out.

He freed his hands as the woman disappeared into the shadows.

A pair of soldiers dressed in deep blue burst into the cavern and hurtled down the stairs.

He untied his feet and lunged for the darkness, but the two soldiers snagged his arms. They began dragging him up the stairs as he wriggled and squirmed, trying to free himself.

Jon glanced back and forth between the guards. "We have to save her. We have to stop it." He tried to catch their attention, but they were determined to ignore him. "You're not listening." He thrashed again as his captors lugged him to the top of the steps. "You don't understand. It'll kill her. Let me go."

The men ignored his pleading cries and flailing as they dragged Jon through the door and into the light.

Chapter Eighteen

WITH HER DUTY

Clusters of people flowed by Garris as he hustled down the row of modest shops that bordered the lane. Head down and vigilant, he endeavored to remain inconspicuous, using the shuffling of shoes against the paving stones to guide his way.

What was it Elt had said? "I'm asking you to go to a place where you could be hunted like a dog." Given the present circumstances, he had to wonder if it was were merely a turn of phrase or a portent of some danger Elt foresaw. Because here he was, engaging in the most idiotic course of action possible, strolling busy streets, over half the city, out in the open, in a place where he was known. And if word of his presence spread, it would bring those who would hunt him as though he were a rabid dog.

But there was no point in dwelling on it. Dellia had let her charge wander off in a city where he knew nobody and could blunder into any unsavory part of town. That woman's head was in the wrong place. And her soft spot for the fellow was going to put them all at risk. So now, the only way he could help was to expose himself to discovery or arrest by wandering here and there, searching for Jon. Well, at least he blended in, or he would until he spoke and his accent betrayed his Shirdon upbringing.

As Garris approached a corner pottery shop, laughter erupted nearby. He lifted his head just enough to spot the source. Above the shop's colorful display of vases in orange and red and black lay one of the rooftop terraces so prevalent in this part of the city. There, buried in a crowd of brightly attired people, stood a woman. Decked out in jewels, and dressed in red, her henna-painted hand covered her mouth as she let out another laugh. It was just a wedding party. He scanned the crowd but found nothing.

Then, out of the corner of his eye, he caught sight of a figure in a dark blue cloak. He seemed to appear behind him as if materializing out of shadow. Garris returned his gaze forward, careful not to change his manner or pace.

As he rounded the corner, the cloaked figure came into view again at the edge of his vision. In a flash, it dodged back into shadow and disappeared. Garris took a deep breath as he doubled his pace. It figured. He was being followed. And by someone adept at it.

A narrow alley appeared ahead, at the corner of two shops. Careful to keep his footsteps silent, he hurried toward it, then ducked into the shadows of the cramped space. He slid up against the wall and stood motionless, slowing his breathing so he could better hear through the sounds from the street.

Seconds passed, and nothing appeared.

Garris slid over and peered around the corner, down the line of buildings that bordered the lane. No dark figure appeared, only clusters of people wandering the streets. As he pulled back from the corner, a low voice came from behind.

"Easy," a man said.

Garris stiffened as the tip of a blade poked him in the back. He glanced over his shoulder and there, behind him, was the darkest of blue cloaks, and beneath it, a figure obscured in the shadows.

He let out a slow breath. Hunted it would be.

He relaxed and slowly began to raise his hands. As he turned toward the man, he let out a low grumble of resignation.

In a flash, he spun the rest of the way around and slammed his arm down, smashing the hand. The knife flew from the man's grip where Garris snatched it out of the air. He smiled as he held the azure blue handle of a gracefully curved golden dagger to the man's gut.

"Not so quick," said the low voice.

Then came the prick of another blade. Garris glanced down to spot a second dagger, exactly like the first, poised at his groin. He relaxed and let out a slow sigh. Before the last of the breath had left his mouth, he lunged and thrust the hilt of his newly acquired blade downward. It smashed the hand and struck the knife with a clank, sending it spinning out of the man's grasp and rocketing into the dirt.

The man dove for it, but Garris grabbed his clothes, yanked him off the ground, and carried him backward, slamming him against the wall. He pinned him to the large, clay bricks, his feet dangling off the ground and the graceful curve of the blade now a hair's breadth from his throat.

Garris smiled. "Who are you?"

The man cleared his throat, and the head beneath the dark cloak made a tiny motion to Garris's left.

He followed the nod to yet another blade, and judging by the position, its tip was uncomfortably close to his jugular. He shook his head. "This is getting kinda repetitive."

"Yeah," said the deep voice, "but you have to admit, it's been fun."

"Sure, if assassination attempts are your idea of fun."

The cloaked figure dropped his blade and raised his hands. "I just want to talk ... and if it's a name you require, you may call me Cain."

Garris lowered the man, setting his feet back down on the dust and dirt of the dimly lit alley. He took a step backward into the shadows of the narrow space and eyed him with a sideways glance. From beneath the hood, the man's face was now visible. His black hair was short and wild and his dark skin leathery and scarred, but he appeared to be a local and his accent agreed.

Garris grunted. "Right, because Cain is such a fine Erdish name."

Cain visibly relaxed. "With remarks like that, it's no wonder everyone's out to kill you."

"What?"

"I wasn't sent to harm you but to warn you."

"Warn me?"

"That stunt you pulled in Durgun," Cain said, "your clumsy exploits in Talus, yesterday's wolf attack—they have not gone unnoticed."

"By who?"

"Brave souls out to make a name. Those wishing to curry favor. Mercenaries. Relatives of people you've killed. The Parishad here in Mundus, the Ruling Council of Meerdon. Shall I go on?"

Garris grimaced. It was an impressive list, and yet Cain hadn't even mentioned the worst—the assassins and warriors Kayleen would send whenever he set foot in Meerdon.

He calmed himself, attempting to hide his alarm and discouragement. With forced nonchalance, he shook his head. "So the same people that always want—" The implication hidden in Cain's words hit home. "Wait, you have spies in the council?"

Beneath the deep blue hood that shrouded Cain's scraggly face there appeared a crack of a smile. " 'Spy' is such a crude word. Let us just say we hear rumors, extremely reliable rumors."

"And extremely expensive, I imagine."

Cain's smile broadened. He stepped forward and slapped Garris's arm. "I see we understand one another."

Garris paused as his cautious side reemerged. Here he stood, in a dark alley with a total stranger, telling him exactly what he expected to hear. That alone was reason for suspicion.

He eyed Cain sideways. "Wait, why warn me? What's in it for you?"

The man's response was curt. "You ask a lot of questions for someone on the receiving end of a favor."

His answer was less than satisfying, and Garris turned to go.

Horses whinnied outside the alley, and Cain's head whipped over. Grabbing Garris's arm, he dragged him further into the shadows. Then he moved close, and his voice became a mere whisper.

"Truth is, I can't tell you, because I don't know. But whoever employed me has powerful connections because I was told to keep you safe at all costs."

Confused, Garris stared. "All costs?"

Cain nodded. "And that's proving to be difficult. And expensive."

Garris considered. He had no friends, much less powerful ones. That made Cain either the worst liar ever, making up ridiculous and implausible stories, or he was telling the truth. Given his ability to handle himself and inside knowledge of his life, the latter seemed the most plausible. Either way, his gut said he should take the threat seriously. And his gut was almost always right.

"So I have enemies, and they know I'm here." Garris shrugged. "What's your point? What do you suggest I do about it?"

"Wrap up your business here and leave," Cain said. "Quickly."

Troubled at the prospect, Garris stared. "Leave?"

"Yes. The longer you sit in one place, the riskier it is."

The disappointment cut more deeply than he'd have thought possible. Particularly given it was exactly what he expected, though he'd hoped a parting would be forced later rather than sooner. But then again, he and disappointment were well acquainted, and they seemed to become better chums every time he set foot in these accursed three realms. There was nothing new in this feeling that his life was a waste, that it would never amount to anything. It was just the way things were. And there was no point in being self-indulgent by dwelling on it or feeling sorry for himself.

"How soon?" Garris asked.

"Before nightfall, sooner if you can."

He closed his eyes. Well, that was it. With more time he might be able to complete his task and get Jon home, but if Cain could find him, he was exposed. And that gave him every reason to trust this stranger and his warning. He let out a long, slow breath and nodded.

Cain's gaze shot over, and the face in the shadow of the deep blue hood seemed to adopt a wary look as he peered into the street beyond the alley. Garris turned and followed his gaze, studying the sunlit avenue, but whatever had drawn the man's attention, it was beyond his ability to detect. He turned back, about to question Cain, but he'd vanished.

Garris shook his head and leaned back against the heavy bricks of the wall. There was no point dragging it out. This was over. He'd help Dellia find Jon, then at the nearest appropriate moment, he'd make his goodbyes. He lowered his head and let out an exasperated grumble. Then he turned and headed out of the shadows of the alley, back toward the sunlit streets of Mundus to continue the search for Jon.

Exhausted and frightened, Jon had given up fighting his captors as they dragged him down the bright, sunlit hall. They wrenched him forward by his sore arms and threw him to the ground. The stairs rushed toward his face, and he threw out his arms, catching his fall, his head almost striking the step.

He lay for a second, sprawled out, facedown on the floor.

A licking sound caught his attention, and Jon raised his head to find himself peering into the black-striped, orange-and-white face of a tiger. It licked again as the yellow eyes in its placid face stared at him, mere inches away.

Jon clambered to his hands and knees and scrambled backward, away from the cat. He froze, heart pounding, alert to its every move.

The tiger remained still, staring at him from the top of the steps, with a sea of purplish pink blooms behind it.

Just beyond the cat sat a sharp-looking man, watching him with keen interest as he sat upright on an ornate couch. His formal-looking dress of rich, golden tan and orange, his immaculate, tawny complexion, his perfect posture, and the throne-like seat on which he sat—they all added up to one thing. He was important. He was a leader. He was the one in charge.

Jon blurted out, "You have to send someone into the catacombs, there are two people—"

The man abruptly thrust out his palm, signaling him to cease. There was a clear sense of displeasure in his manner, and Jon stared for a moment as he motioned to one of the guards to speak.

"We found him in the catacombs," the guard said. "Apparently he asked Umata about them, then broke—"

"They'll die in there, there's something down—"

"Enough!" the man bellowed.

Jon shrank back away from the commanding voice.

A woman he hadn't noticed before stepped forward. She was beautiful, with skin the color of honey and black curls that cascaded over her shoulders. She was draped in gorgeous clothes of sunny yellow that blended down into a rich orange, and her dark eyes stared at Jon with a puzzling fascination. The man turned and watched her.

The tiger pulled itself to its feet and slunk over to Jon. He froze, cowering on hands and knees, heart pounding, as the beast stretched out its neck and smelled his face. He stiffened even more as the tiger's rough whiskers brushed against his skin, and with each sniff, he stifled a flinch as its hot breath blew across his face.

The tiger stayed there, examining him, for what seemed like an eternity before it pulled away. It rubbed its head against his shoulder as it passed, then circled around and glided up the stairs, leaping onto the couch next to the man.

As Jon rose to his feet, the woman took another step forward, then broke off her penetrating stare. Turning to the man, she granted him a subtle shake of her head.

The man seemed shocked. He glanced at Jon, then gazed sideways at the woman with his brow furrowed in a questioning look. She nodded, which appeared to end their secret exchange because the man turned his attention back to Jon.

This time, when he spoke, his words were soft and gentle. "I am sorry, this is my wife, Asina." He pointed to the woman and then himself. "I am Katal. May I ask your name?"

The change in tone and manner shocked him, and he just mumbled, "Jon."

It seemed as if a small gasp came from the woman and her eyes widened. The man must have heard it too because he glanced at her before returning his full attention to Jon.

"Go on," Katal said.

Still gripped by a sense of urgency and intimidated before these two, Jon's words stumbled out. "I was hit over the head in the temple. In the temple, not on the temple." He pointed to his head, then back the way he'd come. "You know, the place you go to worship, by Umata, I mean, I think, maybe. I don't know."

Katal shook his head and motioned Jon to slow down.

He nodded, then gulped and tried again. "I woke up in the catacombs, tied up. They were talking, two people, about planting something on me. It attacked them. It was huge and ugly and green. It took a bite out of the man's arm and dragged them off. It's going to kill them."

Katal took a deep breath and leaned back on the couch. He turned his head and stared at the tiger in contemplation as he stroked its orange and black fur. After a moment, he stopped and leaned forward, returning his attention to Jon.

"Let's say for a moment you're telling the truth. Then whatever you saw down there has had plenty of time to kill both of them."

"But she called out to me to help her. Please, her face ... You have to try."

Asina stepped forward, and a gentle look of concern graced her face. "What if they're dead and we rush in? More could die."

The thought made him shudder and his stomach twist in knots. He needed to help the woman, but what if it was his urging that caused more people to suffer the same grisly death? "So then ... what?" he said. "Do nothing?"

Asina smiled. "We will investigate. But we must be cautious so as not to lose more lives trying to save those whose foolishness has most likely already resulted in their deaths."

Relieved that they were at least going to do something, and too intimidated to press them further, Jon nodded.

Katal leaned forward in his seat. "Why did you ask Umata about the catacombs?"

"I need to enter them. There's something there I need, in order to get me and Megan home."

Asina's eyes widened again as she stepped back and stared with even greater intensity. Katal sent her another glance, then he returned his attention to Jon.

"I'm sorry. I know something about being far from home. But what you ask is not possible. The catacombs are sacred. Our most holy people are buried there, and many children."

His words were disheartening, despite the fact everything was as Garris had predicted. "So there's no way?"

There was a sympathy in Asina's eyes and in her voice. "I am sorry. My heart breaks for you, but what you ask we cannot do."

Jon lowered his head and stared at the pattern of sunlight on the polished floor. Garris was right. They would never let him in.

Asina stepped forward, and her soft fingers lifted Jon's chin. He look up into her beautiful, golden face, framed by the glow of bright sunlight, like a halo around her head. She moved to within inches of his face, and her voice became a whisper only he could hear.

"Be careful. There are dangers here beyond your imagining."

Dellia shielded her eyes from the bright, midday sun as she peered down the street, past the ornate entrance to the audience hall garden. There, hustling past a group of women, surveying his surroundings with a rapt intensity, approached Garris, alone. It had been a little concerning when she'd returned to find Jon was still out roaming the streets, and after a couple hours, that concern had grown enough for her to enlist Garris's aid in finding him.

They had decided that each would search half the city, but it was his idea to meet outside this impressive audience hall. It was one of the tallest landmarks in Mundus, making it visible from half the city. But now, as he approached, with no Jon, her concern turned into fear and alarm.

Garris shook his head as he spotted Dellia, signaling he'd had no luck.

As he pulled up in front of her, she heaved an exasperated sigh. "Where *is* he?"

"Maybe you should keep searching." He ceased his scanning and faced her. "I'll go to Gatia's house and see if he made it back."

She stared at him, considering his suggestion. His face remained as unreadable as always, but below the surface was a combination of disappointment, frustration, and disillusionment that he seemed to be struggling to contain. It hadn't been there when he left, and she wanted to ask about it. But having been chastised once already, she wasn't eager to take that approach again. It was silly really;

she knew what she knew whether she mentioned it or not. And as cool as men like Garris acted, they felt things as deeply as anyone, perhaps even more so. It was simply their instinct not to let it affect their outward behavior.

She was about to ask him about his search when she looked up, and there stood Jon, rounding the corner out of the garden entrance. Head down, oblivious to the world around him, he headed straight for them, strolling past a row of giant, blooming cacti interspersed with heavy succulents and dry, twisted shrubs.

Garris must have noticed her expression because he turned and peered down the street, watching Jon's approach. He glanced over at Dellia, and the two struck out for their friend.

As a gathering of pedestrians passed him, Jon looked up and spotted Garris and Dellia. Then, he smiled and hastened his pace. He rushed toward them, and the three met before a flower-edged walkway leading to a spacious manor.

Garris spoke before Dellia had a chance. "Where were you? Dellia got worried when you missed lunch. We've been searching the streets."

Jon simply shrugged and acted casual. "You know me. Same old, same old." He began counting off his misadventures on his fingers. "Got hit over the head, kidnapped, dragged into the catacombs. Had a mysterious woman show me a vision of Megan. Saw a creature eat part of a guy and drag two people off to snack on them later. Got captured by guards. Tossed in front of Katal and Asina ..." He dropped his hands and tilted his head. "I think she saved me. She let me go with a warning." A look of concern crossed his face. "Although it was kind of a disturbing warning, actually."

Dellia gawked at him for a second. "You haven't been gone that long!"

Garris gave him an annoyed look. "Okay, that's it. No more sightseeing for you."

Jon stared back with equal incredulity. "So the part about a guy being eaten didn't really just jump out at you two."

"You were serious about that?" Garris said.

Jon rolled his eyes. "Yeah, I know, it can be so hard to tell. What with all the jokes I make about people being eaten. ..." He nodded with his eyes wide. "Yeah, I'm serious."

Garris stepped out of the way of a couple holding hands as they passed, followed by two children quietly bickering. He turned, and the three began strolling down the street together, back toward Gatia's home.

"And you told Asina?" Dellia asked.

"Yeah. I opened with that. I begged Katal to help them. Asina said they'd investigate, but, guys ..." Jon halted and turned to the other two. "I just can't drop this. I can still hear the woman's voice begging me to save her."

His horror and remorse were palpable, and Dellia wanted to comfort him, to tell him it would be okay. But nothing could take back the terror he'd witnessed. She took a step forward and put a hand on his shoulder. "I'm so sorry."

Jon peered into Dellia's face. "Maybe you could help her. They won't let me go into the catacombs, but you work for the council. You could intercede."

She turned away, startled by the suggestion. Her instinct was to say yes. More than that, she needed to show Jon her desire to help him was genuine, but with everything that was going on with Kayleen and the council, there was no way. Struggling for the right way to tell him no, she began to stroll again down the warm, sunlit street, and the other two followed.

"I ... I can't do that." Dellia gave a small shake of her head. "I'm sorry. I'd be acting without the council's approval."

"Even to save someone?" Jon asked.

"I'd risk upsetting relations between the council and the

government here in Erden." She looked over into his pleading face, and the words slipped out. "And I'm already in enough trouble with the council."

It was the wrong thing to say. She hadn't wanted to drag her problems into this, and she hoped he'd let it pass.

Jon let out a sigh. Then, as they walked side by side down the peaceful lane, he glanced over at Dellia and said, "Because of me."

"It's not just that," she said, trying to change the topic. "I'd be asking them to violate their deeply held beliefs."

"Just like the council asked you to violate yours."

Surprised at his perceptiveness, she glanced over at him. "You understand, right?"

He stared ahead, looking thoughtful as he nodded his head. "I'm beginning to."

There was something ominous and troubling in Jon's words, even if she couldn't quite put her finger on what it was.

From behind came the growing sound of horses' hooves thundering against the paving stones. It echoed through the neighborhood as three riders with their faces covered shot past, dressed in leather and cobalt-blue uniforms. They were Aashbal, a kind of specialized military scout, trained to get in and out of dark and dangerous places and ferret out the nature of a threat. Perhaps this was a sign that the Rhanae were handling the situation.

Garris had been silent much of the time, staring at the brick road as if in deep contemplation. He glanced up as the three sleek, black horses clattered down the avenue, carrying their riders to the corner and around it.

As they disappeared out of sight, he gave voice to his thoughts. "I wonder if they were trying to frame you." He glanced at Jon. "Get you in trouble with the law, make it hard for you to enter the catacombs."

"That's what I thought," Jon said. "They were talking about

planting something on me, sending for the guards." He tilted his head and stared at Garris. "But how would they even know I wanted into the catacombs?"

The notion struck Dellia, causing her to recall something she'd forgotten in all the chaos. "Huh." She halted and turned to the other two. "When I was tracking you, I noticed a couple who might have been following you. Did you mention the catacombs to anyone?"

"Yeah," Jon said, "in the temple."

Garris stiffened, and anger flashed in his eyes. "What? Someone was tracking us, and you just mention this now?" He glared at her. "There are people out there who want to kill me."

"Sorry," Dellia said. "I was a bit preoccupied."

"Yeah." He sounded even more irritated. "Trying to figure out what to say to your one true."

Jon grabbed Garris's arm and barked out, "That's enough, okay?"

Garris peered down at Jon's hand on his arm, and Jon jerked it away. "Oh." He raised his eyes. "So that's how it is?"

Jon stepped back away from him.

"Jon, her heart lies with her duty, and with her job. She's never going home with you."

Dellia was incensed. "*She* is standing right here."

"Then tell him I'm wrong," Garris shot back.

She clammed up. As much as she resented his speaking for her, he was right. But what would be the point in saying so, particularly when he was so wrong about Jon? Whatever Jon imagined he felt for her, it was over. Her thoughtless indifference to his feelings had seen to that. And if any flicker remained, it would soon be forgotten once he was back in his world with Megan.

After all, it was Megan he'd waited years for. And it was Megan who was behind everything he was doing. So what if he'd stood up for her now? That was simply the kind of person he was. And as much as she needed nobody to stand up for her, it didn't mean she couldn't appreciate the gesture. It was sweet.

For a moment, they all stood around, not knowing what to say. Then Jon, who seemed particularly uncomfortable, began to amble once again down the warm, bright lane. Dellia then Garris followed, and the three strolled in quiet.

After a while, Jon spoke, as if compelled to break the clumsy silence. "So that's it? We do nothing?"

Dellia shook her head. "It's not nothing to let Katal and Asina handle it."

Garris snapped his fingers and halted. "Wait. Just because we can't go in the catacombs doesn't mean we can't help. I know someone who might be able to figure out what you saw. If we can do that, we could go to the Rhanae with hard information on a threat. Maybe even get a shot at helping."

With those final words, the small knot in Dellia's stomach returned. It was the tower all over again. "I like the idea," she said, "except the part about talking our way into the catacombs."

Jon stared at her with a questioning look, so she fumbled out an explanation. "I mean they're probably already dead."

Garris eyed her. "Why are you so opposed—"

"Let's do it," said Jon.

There was a finality in his enthusiastic response that seemed to settle the issue. Garris nodded and, armed with their new plan, he turned and began to lead the way through the city to this "someone" he claimed could give them answers.

Chapter Nineteen

DESIGNS OF THE VEROD

The gentle thumping told Jon that Pretaj had stopped behind him and was tapping his chin once more, something he seemed to do when thinking. It was like being back in the school library again, the way he and Garris and Dellia were all sprawled out in creaky, wooden chairs surrounding a circular table heaped with books and papers. Only, in so many ways, it wasn't like any college library he'd ever seen. It was far too cluttered with scribblings, scrolls, and stacks of books strewn across nearly every surface, and a handful even stacked on the floor.

Jon glanced over his shoulder at the strange man as he ceased his tapping and stood for a moment, immersed in thought. When Garris had introduced him, before he'd uttered a syllable, the man's appearance gave him away as a bit of an oddball. It wasn't the crook in his nose, or the bald spot on top, or even the long, thinning white hair, it was the wrinkled linen robe, bloodshot eyes, and disheveled appearance that lent the impression of one who spent too much time with his head in a book and not enough tending to his appearance.

Pretaj pivoted and stormed around a tree growing in the middle of the library, over to a ladder in front of one of the many bookshelves that packed each of the six walls. He scaled the rungs and ran his finger along a row of ancient-looking tomes, their spines littered with foreign scripts and indecipherable runes.

"You said it was big, with wings, red hair, large canines, and oversized, bulging red eyes?" Pretaj glanced at Jon over his shoulder.

Jon nodded.

Pretaj continued scanning, running his crooked finger across the row of books on the shelf below. He stopped again and peered at him over his shoulder. "And it took a bite out of his arm? While he was still alive?"

Jon nodded again.

Without selecting a book, Pretaj halted and clambered down. He shook his head as he strolled back toward the table, staring at the floor, appearing deep in thought. "Hmm. Unfortunately, that doesn't narrow it down much."

"Really?" Jon said, somewhat surprised. "There are lots of red-haired, red-eyed, winged creatures that go around eating people?"

Pretaj gave a vigorous shake of his head. "No. No. Hardly any."

Jon watched and waited for an explanation or at least some sign that the man realized he was waiting for elaboration.

Dellia wasn't as patient. "If there are hardly any, then doesn't that narrow it down?"

Jon made a frustrated motion toward her. "What *she* said."

"Oh. Yes. Right," Pretaj said. "Well, there are creatures with the gift of maya."

"Maya?" Jon asked.

Garris leaned over and spoke into his ear. "They can appear to change form."

Jon kept his focus on Pretaj. "How many? I mean, doesn't that narrow it down, too?"

Pretaj granted him a vigorous nod of his head. "Oh. Definitely. Yes. Yes. To the really bad ones."

Garris's calm stare matched his deadpan response. "As opposed to all the fluffy, gentle creatures that eat people?"

Pretaj perked up, seeming quite intrigued. He raced over and shoved his face near Garris's as he raised an eyebrow. "Oh, really? I'm not familiar with those."

Jon shook his head. "He's being sarcastic."

For a moment, Pretaj seemed disappointed, but he soon snapped back. He marched around the table, stopping next to a tall stand. He looked down at the brittle, faded old map of Meerdon on its surface as he tapped his chin. "Oh. Yes. Well, now if it was in its native form, then it would almost certainly be a Rakshasa."

Garris seized on the answer. "That's good. That's good. Let's assume that. How do we fight it?"

"Oh well, fighting it isn't the problem," Pretaj said. "Most can be killed by normal weapons … possibly. … Well, better use a brass dagger through the heart, just to be certain."

"If fighting it isn't the problem, what is?" Garris asked.

"Well, Rakshasa have the gift of maya." Pretaj acted as if it were common knowledge.

"Oh," Jon said, betraying his concern at the prospect of taking on a thing that could change form. His exclamation seemed to capture Pretaj's attention. He stared at him for a second, appearing puzzled, then stepped closer and cocked his head.

"Tell me," Pretaj said, "why who?"

"What?" Jon asked.

"Why not why?"

"Why what?"

"Why ask *who* is in the catacombs? Isn't it better to know *why*?"

Garris chimed in, "I think we figured if we knew who, it would tell us why."

"Hmm." Pretaj's interest seemed to intensify, and he marched over and shoved his face in Jon's.

Jon squirmed a bit in his chair, feeling conspicuous as Pretaj swung his head around with a puzzled expression, examining him from every angle.

Uncomfortable with Pretaj's intrusive examination, Jon let the curious examination lie.

Dellia seemed far more impatient. "Okay, then why is this Rakshasa in the catacombs?"

Pretaj halted but continued to stare at Jon, even as he turned his attention to Dellia. "Huh? Yes. Excellent question. Well, nobody's broken into the catacombs in decades. There's nothing there for a demon. All the souls have been released to Samsara."

"Samsara?" Jon asked, unfamiliar with the term.

Pretaj became animated at the question as if it were a favorite topic. "The endless cycle: birth, life, death, rebirth."

"What does that mean?" Jon asked.

Pretaj reached over and shoved several stacks of dusty, old books from the center of the table. He pointed to a painting on its surface that had previously been obscured. He ran his fingers along the outside of a circular image divided into six segments with intricate depictions of people and gardens and landscapes in each.

"Oh. Well. Life is a cycle, just as creation is a cycle, and history is a cycle. It repeats. Never the same, always repeating." Jon leaned forward, and Pretaj focused in on him, as if pleased to have such an interested audience. "You see, the oracles in Elore, they have it wrong. If you wish to know the future, you need only know the past. Because the past repeats."

"I mean, what does that mean about the catacombs?"

"Oh. … Well, that's the question, isn't it?" Pretaj said. "If there's nothing in the catacombs of interest, then why are they there?"

"They?" Jon cocked his head.

"Yes, excellent point," Pretaj said. "Glad you brought it up. First the two people, then the Rakshasa. Oh, and don't forget the Blood Wolves. It can't all be coincidence. What if they're all related?"

Dellia's and Garris's heads spun over, and they stared at one another.

"Oh Adi," Dellia said. "You don't think—"

"—it knows Jon wants to go there." Garris finished Dellia's thought.

"But how would it even know that?" Jon said.

As if struck by a sudden inspiration, Pretaj straightened and his head snapped around. "Oh ..." he said as he stared at Jon.

Reaching over, he snatched a magnifying glass from a nearby counter strewn with papers and rushed over. He palmed Jon's head and continued to speak as he squinted and peered through the glass at each of his eyes. "Ah. I should have seen it before. Your odd manner. Your odd look. You're from Prith."

Great, more words he didn't know.

"Another world," Pretaj said, as if he sensed Jon's confusion. "That's why they're interested in you. They think you could be the Otherworlder."

All the torturous contortions and confusing turns of the conversation fell away as Jon found a focus in the one topic that most concerned him.

"What do you know of the prophecy?" Dellia asked.

Pretaj stood back and shrugged his shoulders. "Like all prophecy, only what the Augury and council agree to make known." Pretaj straightened, standing tall and proud. "But it is not prophecy that concerns me, but history. History repeats, remember, and Jon is not the first to come."

"How do you know about that?" Garris shot back.

"What?" Pretaj said. "No. Hundreds of years ago, others came from Prith. And many demons appeared, and they fought them, and there was a great war."

Concerned at the serious turn the conversation had taken, and yet eager to hear more, Jon leaned forward.

Dellia seemed to take note of his interest, and alarm spread across her face. She rose from her chair, and there was a certain brusqueness in her manner and an urgency in her voice. "We need to talk to the Rhanae, let them know what we've learned."

He started to get up but sat back down as Pretaj leaned over the table. He placed his hands on its surface, among the clutter of books and papers, and eyed Jon with intense interest. "But there's more to know. For example, demons don't just appear spontaneously. They have to be summoned, and that requires power."

"So this is part of some plan?" Garris said.

Pretaj spun around to face him. "It seems likely. And if it was summoned, then why summon just one? There are likely other, possibly worse, demons in the catacombs."

Jon's interest turned to alarm. "Worse than eating people?"

Dellia stepped back, and her concern seemed to grow.

Pretaj turned back to Jon and smiled, seeming eager to explain. "Oh, yes. The most dangerous are the Bahkaana, demons with the gift of deception. They always appear at times of turmoil. They can see into men's hearts, their worst fears, their greatest desires, and they spread discontent and lies."

"Deception?" Jon said. "Why would people believe them?"

Pretaj leaned in even closer, eyeing Jon. "Oh, because they never lie."

Jon shook his head, baffled. "I don't understand."

"That's what makes them so dangerous. They twist truths into seductive lies. But they are always half-truths, and the part they leave out persuades people of the opposite of reality. They sway the greedy, the gullible, and those anxious for meaning in their lives with the illusion of truth. They make people believe their cause is just, even as they serve evil."

Garris eyed Dellia as she stood there, staring at Jon with her mouth covered and a look of worry on her face. Garris stood up, as if in a sudden hurry, and in a curt manner he said, "So, don't believe anything the demon says. Got it. And might I add … duh." He glanced at Dellia again. "Now, we should go."

He grabbed Jon's arm and hoisted him out of his seat with a creak. As he dragged him from the cluttered, circular table, Pretaj scooted in and took Jon's place. He snatched a book from the top of a stack, flipped it open, and began to page through. As Garris propelled Jon toward the door, Jon turned back, wanting to ask more about demons and the prophecy and past Otherworlders. But Garris seemed to be in some big rush all of a sudden.

"I'll go get some brass daggers and meet you at Gatia's house." Garris shoved him past a pair of bookshelves brimming with old tomes and out the door. "From there, we can go see the Rhanae."

Jon was about to object when Dellia grabbed him by the shoulders and escorted him away.

For the third time this day, Kayleen emerged from the tall, arched tunnel that led to the courtyard. It was more difficult than she had imagined. For fifteen years she had blunted her feelings of loss and loneliness by burying herself in her work. When the days ran together, burdened by a wounded heart and consumed with juggling numerous crises, she often pined for simpler days with more time on her hands. Yet now, without a lengthy list of political conundrums to focus on, there was nothing to distract her from the reality that there was nobody left in her life with whom she could share her burdens. And without something to occupy her mind and heart, her thoughts continually returned to the peril in which the council had placed Dellia.

She could still recall as if it were yesterday sending Garris to investigate a disturbance in the veil unlike any she had sensed before or since. It all seemed so innocent when it led to a confused young Erdish woman named Prisha. Then the mysteries began to multiply. They learned she was from another world, and Leanna saw the connection to prophecy. She brought her concerns to the council, and they sent her to investigate. Then came the discovery that something or someone powerful had sent Prisha to do things even she didn't understand. The Window of Rhina suddenly became unreliable, and communications with Garris erratic.

With their understanding and control of events crumbling, the council began to blame Garris, suspecting he had sided against them with the Otherworlder and was actively undermining their will. Only Garris knew what happened next, but she sensed a tear in the very fabric of the veil near them with something cold and destructive flooding through. Rumors of death and devastation spread, and later they found huge patches of land that had been leveled by whatever transpired. Unable to get a clear picture of what was unfolding or to use Garris to enforce their will, the council became frustrated and intolerant.

Then came the news that Leanna was dead and Prisha had vanished. Unable to recognize their part in causing the tragedy, the council blamed it all on Garris, imagining that he had turned against them and was shielding the Otherworlder. An idea that was unthinkable to anyone who knew him.

It had been sheer torture trying to defend her protector as events descended into chaos and the council became unhinged. Yet at least as a council member, she was at the center of events and held some sway and control. If not for her influence, the council would almost certainly have executed Garris for treason.

With Dellia, she was now powerless. All she could do was sit by and wait to see what disaster would befall her. It was imperative she find her way back onto the council.

So here she was, returning to the Shir Courtyard to do the only thing left for her to do: deal with a political problem—specifically, hers.

What she needed was to make a mental list of her options and envision the complex web of pros and cons for each. And for that, she needed a secluded spot. Fortunately, such a place had been part of the design of the courtyard—a hidden spot, known only to council leaders throughout history, a place of solitude to consider the problems of the day.

Kayleen slipped off the trail, across the rocky border, and around the line of dense, blooming shrubs that bordered the path. As she strolled down the row of greenery, laden with large, yellow blooms, the intoxicating fragrance drew her. So she stopped to inhale the sweet smell of one of the soft, golden flowers before coming to rest behind the impenetrable greenery on a large, slate boulder at the edge of a crystal pond. She slipped off her leather sandals and slid her feet into the cool, clear water, watching as the colorful fish darted around her toes.

No sooner had she settled herself and cleared her mind than Council Member Jiam's familiar voice approached on the path outside the dense line of greenery. It carried a hint of an Elorian accent, but aside from that it possessed a quality that was unmistakable.

At first, she couldn't make out what he was saying, but he was conversing with a woman whose voice was unfamiliar. As they neared, their words became clear.

"When did this happen?" Jiam asked.

"A few hours ago," the woman said.

"No courier is that fast."

"They used a war pigeon from Shirdon."

The footsteps halted, and Kayleen could almost picture Jiam's skeptical stare.

"What?" the woman said. "A Skri told them they needed one."

"A Skri?" Jiam said, his words sounding just as skeptical as Kayleen had imagined.

There was a brief pause.

"Fine," he said. "What do you mean you think they're dead?"

"They never left the catacombs. They knocked out Jon and

dragged him in there. Renash went to alert the guard. He watched and waited, and the guards came out with Jon, but Parun and Aasha never returned."

Kayleen's mind raced. *Jiam involved with a plot against Jon?* Of all the council members, he was the one she had most expected to come to her defense. Yet, he had remained silent when Idria dismissed her. Perhaps, all these years, his actions had not been aimed at supporting her. Perhaps they were born out of sympathy for the Verod, and her views simply happened to align with theirs. Kayleen leaned closer.

"Maybe Renash missed them?" Jiam said.

"No," was the woman's immediate reply.

"How long did he wait?"

"Hours."

"And they don't suspect Jon of being in the catacombs to raid them?" Jiam asked.

"Apparently not. They let him go."

There was another, longer pause. Careful not to make a sound, Kayleen slipped her feet from the crystal water and slid closer to the delicate yellow blooms of the shrubs, straining to hear.

Eventually came the woman's exasperated words. "Well, what would you have me do?"

"Look," Jiam shot back, "you wanted my help. Well, I'm telling you. Stop Jon from going home. It's a simple equation. The council is making an enemy of him, and an enemy of the council is a friend of the Verod. A friend who might serve as a rallying point for your cause."

"That's what Renash is trying to do. He thinks he can still prevent Jon from returning home. He said he had a plan."

"Okay, so what's this brilliant plan?"

An awkward moment of silence followed. "Um, he didn't say," the woman said.

"And you can't ask?" There was another, even longer pause, then Jiam's frustrated voice. "I knew it was a mistake to align myself with the Verod."

Kayleen remained motionless with her ear to the shrubs, staring into the water as the footsteps resumed and grew more distant. *The Verod?* She had always insisted the council was underestimating them. But a plot like this was far more brazen than she would have ever expected. In fact, it was treason, using a highly visible target. This just might be the information she needed.

The footsteps had become too distant to hear, so Kayleen pulled herself over and slid on her sandals. She rose from her perch near the flat, black rock but remained crouched down to avoid detection. With slow, careful steps, she crept to the end of the row of thick blossoms and greenery. She skirted the shrubs and popped up onto the path, heading the other direction from the footsteps.

Glancing back over her shoulder, she spotted Jiam walking away down the winding, stone path. He turned and caught sight of her, then granted her a nod of acknowledgment as she slipped through an archway and around a column to disappear from view.

Kayleen smiled. Yes, this information might be just what she needed—but now how to use it to get back on the council?

Dellia hurried along the sunny, stone streets and alleyways of Mundus, avoiding discussion, as she led Jon back to Gatia's home. Pretaj had speculated about a great many things that were unsettling, and she needed time to sort through them and make sense of her next move.

It was obvious Jon came from another world, but Prith wasn't supposed to be real. It was the fabled garden world from which they had all been banished back in an age when Meerdon had yet to be tamed. It was a myth, like Olympus or Elysium. To find out it may be real and Jon's home was disturbing.

Most unsettling of all, though, was that these demons may have been summoned to Mundus with the specific intent to stop Jon. So the last course of action he should take was to walk straight into their domain. Yet, his intense interest made it seem as if that was exactly what he wanted to do. And Garris was already out gathering weapons to do just that. It was insanity, and she had to stop it. Yet how could she claim to be helping Jon if her intent was to stand in his way?

Having arrived at Gatia's sprawling house, they rounded the corner, came through the gate, and stepped onto the narrow, sunlit path to the front door. None of the family appeared as they burst into the home and scurried up the wooden stairway. Dellia headed for her room, hoping Jon would go to his and give her some time to figure things out. Instead, he followed her through the arched entry and into young Aishi's room, the one Gatia had assigned to her.

He strolled to a petite chair next to a small, wooden dresser adorned with a crouching tiger cub painted across its drawers. Dellia snatched her bag and lay it across the giant pattern of a yellow desert flower stitched into the covers of the modest child's bed. Behind her, the chair creaked as Jon plopped down into it.

Upon rummaging through her worn pack, she gathered a pair of brass daggers, then held them up, looking them over. If only her duty were something as simple as fighting a demon. As terrifying as that would be, at least it would be straightforward.

This prophecy had the power to do far more harm than a few demons, and it was her duty to find out everything she could about it. But how was she going to do that after Jon was dead? He was barely equipped to deal with everyday life in this world, and the idea of him confronting a demon terrified her. The second that monster figured out he was defenseless and that she feared for him, it would use that to its advantage. Then how could she stop it from killing them both?

As Dellia looked over the daggers, she caught Jon's reflection on the shiny, brass surface. He was reaching out as if to offer her something.

She set the daggers on the bed next to her pack and swung around. He yanked his arm away and looked sheepish as he tried to hide the dragon coin she'd given him. A profound sadness came over her at the realization that it was probably his intent to return it.

Jon jammed his hand in his pocket and yanked it out, averting his eyes, glancing all around, like a child caught stealing sweets. His eyes rested on a small loop of bright, rose-colored string that lay on top of the little dresser. Snatching it from the surface, he leaned back in the chair and looped it through his fingers and thumbs, botching an attempt to play a simple child's game. After a moment he began to speak with a forced nonchalance.

"The Rhanae, they're some kind of rulers, right?"

Still burdened by a tumult of feelings, Dellia turned her back and returned to organizing the items in her pack. "Yeah, they rule all of Erden."

"Both of them?"

"Yes, they're co-rulers, wife and husband. It's the way in Erden."

"Hmm. That must be nice," Jon said, "to rule with someone you love."

His words touched a part of her she didn't often get to indulge. She had always had a fondness for the stories of the rulers of Erden. Often, she had imagined what it must be like to be a queen and rule with a husband you love. Something in his voice or the question itself melted away all her confusion, and Dellia turned and sat on the bed facing him.

Jon looked up from his clumsy fiddling and dropped the string in his lap. He gazed into her eyes as he sat upright in the undersized chair, listening with rapt attention.

"Before the Ephori, Talus was ruled by co-queens. The people of Erden saw the wisdom of two rulers but adopted it in their own way."

Dellia scooted a little closer. "You see, they believe we are all born only for one person. So we marry just once in each life. It made sense to them to adopt the idea of co-rulers but as wife and husband. They even wrote it in the Arashastra, their book of how to rule."

Jon stared into her eyes, as if his imagination was in a faraway place. "That's beautiful. ..."

A sudden wave of self-consciousness seemed to come over Jon, and he glanced away.

Dellia seized the opportunity to reach in and snatch the string from his lap.

His gaze shot up into her face, and she beamed a mischievous smile. She pulled the string tight, then looped it through her fingers, creating the most elaborate pattern of crisscrossing threads she knew how to make.

He smiled and shook his head as he rolled his eyes. Then his curiosity returned, and the tiny chair creaked as he leaned closer. "But does it work?"

Dellia had to think for a moment. The question had never really occurred to her. As she considered how Katal and Asina ruled, she nodded. "Yes. It gives them stability, and they govern wisely, as if all Erden were their children."

Without warning, Jon's disposition became cloudy, and he averted his gaze, staring at the floor at Dellia's feet. "They're never going to let me enter the catacombs, are they?"

She hesitated. This was the reason she'd rushed home, the reason she had been avoiding talking to him. It was a simple enough question but one she had hoped to evade.

Dellia dropped the string in her lap and hung her head for a moment before looking up into Jon's face. "Can I be honest with you?"

"We're friends, right?"

"I wish you didn't want in there."

His sympathetic gaze shot up and his eyes met hers. "I know. I've put you in such a terrible position, with the council and all."

"No, that's not what I mean. And besides, everything that's happened, they were all my decision."

"I know, but a friend wouldn't put you in that kind of position."

"You know what else friends wouldn't do?" Dellia picked up the colorful string from her lap and placed it back on the little dresser. "They wouldn't spend all their time worrying about their friend being eaten by demons or wolves."

Jon rolled his eyes again. "Tell me about it."

She dropped her head, staring at his feet. "You're no warrior, Jon. And you have no gift. And these are demons, for Adi's sake. Demons that will eat you. That's why I wish you didn't want in there." She lifted her gaze, staring up into his gentle face. "I'm worried about you. How can I ask the Rhanae to let you enter knowing it could mean your death?"

At her words, a sudden conflict entered Jon's heart. There was no way for her to know what it was about, but he was worried, and not about the catacombs or the demons. It was not worry over danger, but the concern of a friend.

Jon gave Dellia a warm smile that sent all her doubts and fears scurrying away. "I wish I could ask you to trust me, to have faith in me. But I can't, because you're right. I'm just an ordinary guy. Look, Dellia, don't worry about me. I'll find another way once the demons are gone." Jon gave a small nod of his head. "It's okay."

"And if the demons aren't the end of it?"

He smiled, and his disposition became more cheerful. "You know what else friends do? They sometimes talk about frivolous, unimportant things."

She smiled back, eager to embrace the change of mood. "Like what?"

He thought for a minute, then seemed to get an idea. "How

about this?" He smiled. "You know that journal we found in the tower?"

"What?" Dellia gawked. "What journal?"

"Sirra didn't tell you? I—"

A pair of guards burst through the arched entry into the room and clattered to a stop. They eyed Jon and Dellia, then one of them, dressed in a sharp, sky-blue uniform, faced Jon and said, "The Rhanae wish to see you. Right away."

Dellia blinked for a moment, puzzled and confused. She turned to Jon at the same time he turned to her, and the two stared at each other in bewilderment.

Chapter Twenty

AT THE STEPS OF THE TEMPLE

A man and woman raced by as the pair of guards in their sky-blue uniforms ushered Dellia down the warm yellow hall. The din of conversations grew louder as they approached the chaos of activity on the raised end of the room that served as a dais. She had seen a court in crisis before, and the surrounding bedlam added up to only one thing: something big and bad had just happened.

Jon seemed oddly unaware as he leaned over toward her and asked, "This book of how to rule?"

"The Arashastra?" She kept her focus on the dais. With his kurta of saffron and ocher, Katal was easy to spot. He stood poised and confident as he spoke to a group of city administrators. Dellia turned her attention to Asina, who was carrying on an animated discussion with Gatia and a small group of soldiers in their uniforms of varying shades of blue.

"Yeah, is it here?" Jon craned his neck to search the dais.

"Yes, up there." Dellia nodded off to the edge of the platform where an ornate pedestal held an enormous, gilded book.

"What is it? A bunch of laws?"

"No. More like guidance," she replied, her attention still on the couriers and soldiers scurrying here and there.

They approached the brightly lit dais and Dellia strained to hear through the clamor of activity and discussion, trying to catch any word of what might be happening.

"How does that work?" Jon asked.

"Not now." She motioned to him to cease his babbling.

They reached the base of the handful of steps and halted, waiting as Katal concluded his pressured discussion and hurried over. He raised his voice above the babel echoing through the hall.

"Jon, it seems you were right. Our investigation has not gone well. Gatia sent soldiers to check out the catacombs. The creature killed them as soon as they entered the temple. Now it sits in the open, and a crowd is forming."

"It killed your guards?" he said, seeming shocked.

As soon as she finished with the soldiers, Asina hurried over with her sari of lemon and tangerine flowing behind her. Katal watched her as she barged into the group with Gatia at her side. He returned his focus to Jon. "We must consider the possibility this is part of something larger. Many lives could be at risk."

Asina stared at Jon, and the concern in her eyes matched the apprehension in her voice. "We are trying to organize a defense against a foe we don't understand, whose plan we have yet to discover. We need to know what you know of this creature."

Jon was about to reply, but Dellia jumped in. "We spoke with Pretaj. He believes it may be a Rakshasa."

Asina and Katal exchanged a brief glance.

"A demon?" Katal said.

"If it's a demon, there may be more," said Asina.

"And we believe it was summoned for Jon," Dellia said.

"I see," said Asina.

A man passing by mentioned the Arashastra to his partner.

Jon swung his head around and banged into Dellia.

She looked over and he was staring up at the book. Here they were, with the two people who could grant him access to the catacombs and his way home, and what was he doing? Staring at a book. Then it hit her. He wasn't distracted, he'd simply given up. That's why he seemed more interested in a book than in talking his way into the catacombs. He'd given up because she'd asked him to.

A pang of guilt struck her. She had vowed to help Jon, and instead, here she was standing in his way. And not because it was her duty; on the contrary, only through helping him could she discover many things about Jon and the prophecy. No, she was standing in his way because she feared for him. Because he was right: she lacked faith in him. Dellia's small knot twisted at the realization of what she must do. She had done this; now she had to fix it.

"Rhanae," she said, "might I suggest that we clear the catacombs of these demons for you."

"This is not the council's concern," Asina said, "it is ours. We will handle it."

"I'm not asking as a protector. I'm asking as Dellia, whose friend Jon needs very badly to get into those catacombs."

Jon's head whipped around. "Dellia?"

"I see," said Asina, "an exchange."

"What?" Jon said.

"Still," said Katal, "we do not wish to doubt your ability, Dellia, but can we trust you to handle this on your own? Our people's lives would be in your hands."

"People's lives?" Jon said, sounding a bit like a stupefied parrot.

Dellia threw him a hurried gesture, signaling him to hold off. "It isn't just me. It is me and Jon and Garris. We will eliminate the threat and protect your people."

Asina and Katal sent each other another brief look.

"Protect people? Me?" Jon said. "That's a bad id—"

"Garris is with you?" Katal interrupted.

Dellia nodded.

Jon turned to Dellia. "Wait. Can we just talk ab—"

"Consider it done." Asina sounded relieved. "Clear the catacombs. Protect our people now. And later Jon can enter to find whatever he needs."

Asina's words were more a proclamation than agreement. Gatia grabbed ahold of their arms and ushered them away. Jon tried to say something over his shoulder, but Asina and Katal had already turned their backs, scurrying away into the cacophony of the platform.

Dellia watched with concern, unsure what had prompted Jon's apprehension. Was he still trying to protect her, or had she just made a colossal blunder? Either way, they were committed now. A demon sat in the temple, with who knows how many more in the catacombs, and now it was up to them to save the city.

Kayleen drew her ear closer to the heavy wooden door, straining to catch the sound of movement within. She raised her knuckles to give the door another rap, but it eased open, and Braye's face appeared in the crack. She shoved through, barging into his ostentatious chambers. Decked with ancient weapons and priceless works of art, they typified everything she disliked about his whole philosophy.

Those on the council were privileged to serve the people and should acknowledge that trust with prudence and humility. Instead, Braye saw the people as the ones who should be grateful for his wisdom and guidance. And his opulent surroundings were merely a just reward for his blinding brilliance. In truth, the only characteristic that set most of the council apart from the common man was a talent for cunning and manipulation. That and an overblown view of their own self-importance. How could it be so hard to see? Bending others to your will did not take talent, and it didn't make you important—it made you a tyrant.

Kayleen turned back to Braye, ignoring her surroundings. This was her chance to find a way back onto the council, so she turned to the task at hand. "Shut the door."

Braye sent her a confused look but complied and then turned

to face her.

"I just overheard something I'm sure I shouldn't have," Kayleen said.

He motioned to the rich brown interior of his chambers. "The walls are thick. I think it's safe to speak openly."

She gave a curt nod and in her normal voice said, "The Verod have sent three people to stop Jon from going home. Two of them were killed trying to frame him in the Andera Catacombs, but the third has a plan to stop him."

"Hmm." Braye turned away, appearing thoughtful as he strolled to an enormous map of Meerdon that covered most of one wall.

This was good; it was precisely the reaction she hoped for.

He stared at the map for a moment, stroking his chin, before he nodded and turned back to Kayleen. "I just received news from Mundus that confirms parts of your story. Where did you hear this?"

Kayleen stepped closer, playing the part of a colleague and confidant. "I overheard a conversation in the courtyard, but I couldn't see who it was."

"Go on," Braye prompted.

"Well, that's all, but it's enough." She stepped closer still. "We must take this to the council."

He stiffened, his brown eyes peering at her with a skeptical expression. "To what purpose?"

And there it was: her opening, her chance to show him a better way to handle this, one that would benefit everyone. Kayleen sent Braye her most earnest look. "If the Verod want him to stay, then we should be helping Jon. Doing so makes a friend of a potential enemy, denies the Verod their goal, and would end part of a threat to the council. What more elegant solution could we desire?"

"Do I need to remind you," Braye said, "you are no longer on the council? There is no 'we.' "

"Braye, this is the safest and most sure path." She rested a hand on his arm. "Don't let our disagreement over recent events cloud your judgment in such a crucial matter."

He gave her hand a gentle pat. "Your mishandling of this affair is not a factor in our decision." He faced the dark and detailed map again, staring at it as he stroked the salt-and-pepper stubble of his chin.

This was good. So far, he had not ruled out her suggestion and even seemed to be considering it.

Without tearing his eyes from the huge map, Braye said, "Have you considered that it might be rash to help Jon without understanding why the Verod want him to stay?"

"To serve as a rallying point for their cause."

He spun around and shot Kayleen a stare disturbing in its coldness. "In that case, there is a much safer and more direct way to end that possibility."

She stepped back. "What does that mean?"

He brushed her off with a wave of his hand. "That's not your concern anymore. In fact, none of this is."

She stood gawking at him in stunned silence as he turned and marched back toward the dark and heavy door.

"Is there no limit to what you'd do?" she asked.

He halted next to a massive bearskin rug and swung around, glowering at Kayleen. "This council has ensured peace and prosperity for centuries, and we have an obligation to pay whatever cost is necessary to continue to do so."

"So that's a yes?"

"Look, we're never going to agree on this. We never have. And, to be honest, that more than anything is why you are no longer involved. You do not have the vision to see what needs to be done to protect us."

Kayleen shrank back. He was talking about life and death as if every soul in the three realms were his to sacrifice. "You mean, I have some degree of moral conscience."

Braye crossed his arms and glared. "You always do that, Kayleen. You wrap yourself in this shroud of moral superiority at a time when what is needed is clarity of purpose and the strength to do whatever it takes. You're putting one man's life above the good of everyone. That's not a conscience, it's a distracting weakness that endangers us all."

She shook her head as she stared back. "Are you really so afraid of any ideas contrary to your own?"

Braye closed his eyes and shook his head as he lowered it.

It was over; she never had a chance. He was the only person with the influence to get her back on the council, but it appeared they had already decided on a much more radical and terrifying course. To tamper with a prophecy like that—it was impossible to know what harm might be done to all of Meerdon. Or even if their own actions might precipitate the very thing that had them running scared.

Braye lifted his head. He stepped forward, and there was a genuine note of fondness in his voice. "Look, you and I are old friends, so I will do you the courtesy of telling you this much: We received word from Mundus that Jon is there, and we have sent a detachment. If all goes as planned, they should have him in custody within the next few hours, and this matter will be settled."

Kayleen could only watch as the situation slipped beyond her grasp. A thousand questions tortured her mind about the myriad ways their plans could turn against them, the consequences to Meerdon, and the fate of Dellia and Jon and herself, but instead, she simply asked, "And what of the Verod and their plans?"

Braye's countenance took on that disturbing coldness again. "Perhaps we can have Dellia deal with that more discreetly once we have Jon in custody."

Shocked at his inference, she stood and stared as he marched back to the door.

"By doing what, exactly?" she said.

He flung open the substantial wooden door and motioned, showing her the way out.

"Good day, Kayleen. I appreciate you bringing this to my attention, and I will let the council know of your helpfulness in this matter. It will not go unnoticed."

The clang of a smith hammering out metal rang above the din of the crowded Mundus Market as Garris plopped down his coins on the rough surface of the weapon smith's table. How could he not be pleased? He had haggled an outrageous price for a set of finely crafted brass daggers. The weapons clanked as he scooped them up and jammed them into his bag, but as he turned to go, he nearly tripped over a young man, a boy really. Dressed in a kurta of various shades of deep blue, the boy paused for a moment as he hunched over, catching his breath. After a second, the youth straightened and eyed Garris.

He placed his hands together and granted Garris a deep bow, then reached down and touched his feet. "Shri Garris," the boy said between breaths.

Taken aback by the formality of his address and the fact that the boy knew his name, a simple "yes" was all Garris managed.

As if to remain unobtrusive, the boy leaned closer and in a hushed voice said, "I am a special envoy, sent by the Rhanae, with a message." Garris motioned him to continue. "Jon and Dellia are on their way to the temple to fight the demon; you must meet them there." The boy scanned the area as if afraid of being overheard, then added, "I was instructed to tell you one more thing."

Garris nodded.

"Try to pass unnoticed. It would be deeply unfortunate, for everyone, were you to be arrested."

Before Garris could say another word, the boy pivoted and sprinted off, darting through the legs of the customers that crowded the marketplace.

It was surreal, being treated like some kind of important dignitary rather than the outcast criminal he was. Garris mulled over the implications as he hurried to the temple. It meant the Rhanae knew him—by name, no less. And it meant they chose to send a messenger rather than arrest him. How he had merited a temporary pardon from someone as high up as a king or queen was a mystery. And there were too many possibilities to narrow it down: people he'd helped, long-lost relatives or friends in the Erden government, Dellia's influence, the Erdish distrust for the council ... it was impossible to guess.

Garris pushed through the colorful crowd that had gathered well back from the steps of the temple. Upon clearing the assemblage, he halted, staring upward along the gently sloping stairway and into the magnificent rows of sculpted columns that disappeared into shadow.

As he surveyed the striking stone edifice, he had the sudden impression of being watched. Movement flashed across the corner of his eye, and then came Cain's voice whispering in his ear. "You can't be here."

"Says who?"

"Rhan's brothers. They're here to kill you, right now."

"You mean they're here to *try*."

A knife tip jabbed into his back, and Garris glanced back over his shoulder, attempting to spot the blade. "Really, we're doing this again?"

"I can't have you spilling blood all over our streets. Gatia would have to hunt you down. That would be bad. For both of us." The tip of Cain's knife dug a little deeper. "They're minutes away. Now, let's go."

Garris began working his way back through the crowd. In

hushed tones, he spoke over his shoulder to Cain. "I can handle Rhan's family without bloodshed."

"Look, it's not just that. The council has sent soldiers. If they recognize you, they'll try to apprehend you, maybe even kill you."

"Dammit," Garris said, as he accepted the inevitable.

Despite having expected this moment to come, the disappointment was heavy. He had hoped to evade the forces against him awhile longer. Perhaps even long enough to see Jon home. But like an animal hunted by a pack of dogs, he could sense his enemies closing in, and if he wanted to end it on his terms, it had to end now.

Knife to his back, Garris worked his way to the edge of the throng. Then, they both halted as a murmur ran through the crowd. He glanced at the gathered people, every face transfixed on the mandapa. He turned and stared up the temple steps as the outline of a massive beast moved toward him.

A huge, deep-green monstrosity slunk out from the shadows. Jon's description couldn't truly capture the sense of malignant evil that exuded from what must be the Rakshasa. No wonder he had been shaken by his encounter. The abomination stared down at him, following him with huge, red eyes and bloodred hair. Blood dripped from its razor claws and long canines as it smiled and licked its twisted, blood-soaked lips.

Garris closed his eyes and sighed. It would be a risky enough proposition for all three of them, so there was no way he could leave Jon and Dellia to battle this hell spawn alone. If it meant he had to fight Rhan's family and evade Shirdon soldiers, so be it. Even with a hundred dogs on its trail, a cunning enough prey could escape. He could be that prey. He needed to do this one last thing.

"I can't," Garris said.

The dagger jabbed still deeper. "I must insist. Now go."

He started to move again. Searching for some way out as they cleared the crowd and skirted the backs of the assembly. Up ahead, with her back to them, Garris spotted a woman with a fuchsia wrap slung over her shoulder.

He glanced back and said, "Then can you at least give Jon and Dellia a message for me?"

"What?" Cain asked.

Garris lunged forward, away from the blade. He snatched the woman's wrap, spun about, and whipped it around Cain's blade. Jerking his hands away, he raised his arms and stepped back as the woman whirled around.

"Tell them you like stealing women's clothing," he said.

The woman glanced at him, then glared at Cain. She raised her fist and stepped toward him, prepared to smack him. The wrap dropped, revealing the blade, and the woman recoiled as Cain jammed it under his cloak.

From beneath his hood, cool anger flashed in Cain's eyes and he shoved Garris backward. "I'm trying to keep you out of trouble."

Garris smirked. "Aw, it's so nice to know you care."

"No. If you get caught or killed, I'm out a lot of money."

Garris stepped closer and motioned with his head to the substantial crowd gawking at the beast. "And that's more important to you than these people's lives?"

Cain glanced around, surveying the crowd, and somewhere beneath his dark cloak appeared the slightest hint of empathy. He stared up the steps at the Rakshasa, still peering down at them. "You know you're real annoying."

"I get that a lot," was Garris's monotone response.

Cain faced Garris. "You're not going to make this easy, are you?"

"Look, two people I know are about to face that thing alone. And you want me to abandon them merely because of an old enemy and a few soldiers?"

"I'm telling you, you won't get away."

"Look, I'm not going to debate this. Either you let me help Jon and Dellia fight that thing, or I fight you and then go fight the demon. Your choice."

Cain shook his head. "Fine, go get caught. I'm done helping you."

He snapped around and stormed away. Garris took a deep breath and looked over the crowd, this time alert for the outline of one of Rhan's brothers. Satisfied that he was in the clear, he dove back into the crowd, heading for the temple steps.

As the last of the spectators gave way, the three stepped into the open, and Dellia got her first good look at the beast. There, at the top of the wide, stone stairway, lurking in the shadows of row upon row of elaborate, carved pillars, stood the creature.

It was just as Jon had described: the deep red hair, the dark wings, and the veins covering its sickly green skin. Yet, what he could never have known was the cold disdain that gripped its heart. Blood smeared its face as its bulbous, red eyes stared down at something moving through the crowd, following it with a disturbing intensity.

Dellia shivered at the image of Jon alone in the cramped catacombs with that thing mere feet away. What was she thinking, talking him into a confrontation with that monstrosity? The claws of one hand were like a set of the sharpest daggers, and those canines were designed for rending flesh.

She brought herself up taller. No, she had decided to trust Jon, to have faith in him, and now was not the time to give in to fear. She glanced over at Jon and Gatia, and they stood mesmerized, gaping up at the demon with a mixture of terror and awe.

All of a sudden, its wings twitched, and it twisted around, peering down at them … at Jon in particular. Beneath its blackish green skin, powerful muscles rippled as it slunk forward toward them.

"The demon has flown all over," Gatia said, her attention still focused upward, "but it can't seem to leave the temple. Someone must have bound it."

The Rakshasa stooped over a body crumpled on the stone slab that formed the top step. It kept glancing down at Jon, as if to make sure he was watching. As it crouched over the head of the man, it raised a heavy paw and brought down a claw, slicing open the man's neck. The beast eyed Jon again as it reached down and let the blood pool in its cupped hand.

"I sent in guards," Gatia said, "and ..."

The dark demon lifted its palm to its crooked mouth and lapped up the blood.

Gatia raised herself up, proud and tall even as horror flashed across her face. "Oh Adi, it's eating them."

A disruption broke out near them as Garris shoved the rest of the way through the crowd to stand beside them. As if it had heard Gatia's words, the demon seized hold of the man's foot and wrenched it off. It began tearing it apart, wolfing down huge mouthfuls as if ravenous.

Jon's panic was intense, strong enough to grab Dellia's attention. At the spires, he had been frightened, but this was way beyond that.

"Guys, look at that thing. What if it eats more people because I failed?" He turned and peered into Dellia's face. "What part of anything I've ever said made you think I could do this?"

The Rakshasa made a guttural sound. Jon and Dellia broke off their conversation, and all eyes swung toward it. As they looked up at it, the beast transformed into Dellia and she found herself peering into her own likeness.

She glanced at Jon, and he stood frozen, staring at the thing in horror.

The Rakshasa returned his gaze, blood dripping from the corners of its mouth as it smiled and blinked its eyes.

"Okay," Jon said, "that does it. No way. No way."

Garris stepped into Jon's line of sight, and his voice remained calm and matter-of-fact. "The wolves, the tower ... how is this different?"

"Because lives depend on what I do," Jon said.

His fear was intense, but she'd seen him get past it before. He could do it again; she had faith in him. Dellia grabbed hold of his shoulders and looked into his eyes. "Then don't do it to save lives. Do it because it's your way home."

Jon pointed to the crowd. "I can't just forget those lives are in my hands."

She smiled and in a calm voice said, "I know you can do this."

Jon shook his head. "All the faith in the world isn't going to fix me, Dellia."

"Look, if anyone gets hurt, it's my fault, okay? I thought you could do this, so if you can't, it's on me."

His fear flared at her words. "No. No. That makes it worse. I can't put that on you."

She pulled her hands away from his shoulders and stepped back. What was he saying? That she couldn't help these people? Dellia looked over the crowd, then up at the demon. She looked into Jon's eyes again and in a calm voice said, "This is really simple, Jon. Either we fight for these people, or nobody does and they die."

Jon's eyes went wide. "I ... I ..."

Disappointment crept into her heart. "So, there's no part of you that cares enough about these people to fight for them?"

Her words struck him like an arrow. He was mortified, caught between shame and terror. He looked out over the crowd and his focus seemed to fall upon little Aishi with Chatin at her side, watching them with calm anticipation. His fear leaped, and the sharpness of it caused Dellia to gasp.

Jon turned back to her, on the verge of tears. "Don't you get it?

If I go, they die. Because they counted on me. That's how this works."

All she could do was stare. He had been so passionate when he talked of faith and trust, but they were just hollow words. Because when she had believed in him, he had rewarded her faith by leaving her to face the demon alone.

Dellia took another step backward. "You're right. Forget it. I don't even know why I'm trying to convince you. You're better off here, anyway. Garris and I will handle this."

She motioned to Garris, and the two swung around and headed up the rough temple steps. The Rakshasa slid backward, toward the rows of massive lion-shaped pillars.

Behind her, Jon's turmoil continued to build, and he yelled after them, "I can't let you go alone, and I can't go with you. What do I do?"

Dellia never looked back as she barked out, "Stay there. That's an order."

As they continued up the steps, Garris glanced over at her, his usual blank expression replaced by one of concern and surprise.

Dellia peered over her shoulder. Jon's eyes darted to Aishi, then the Rakshasa, then to her. His torment pulled at her heart. He closed his eyes and shook his head, and as if something had snapped, his shame vanished, and he called out, "Wait" as he sprinted up the steps to where they stood. "I'm coming with you."

"You're in no state," Dellia said. "It's dangerous enough without worrying about you."

"I can handle it," Jon said, but his fear and apprehension said otherwise.

"No. You were right." Suddenly, Dellia realized that this Jon, the one before her now, was the Jon she knew, the one that had entered the tower, the one that had fought the wolves, and her frustration and disappointment melted away.

"Look, I don't want you doing this because I guilted you into it." She cocked her head. "Or even because it's a way for you to get home. I want you to do this because you want to help these people."

Something in her words touched Jon, more deeply than she'd thought possible. He looked at her with a puzzled expression. "Why does it matter so much to you what my reasons are?"

Dellia stopped and stared, searching for an answer, but every explanation she could muster came back to one thing: She cared about Jon more than she should. It was pointless denying it. But she couldn't love him; that was impossible. Protectors don't have romantic entanglements. And perhaps this was why. Here she was, at the steps of the temple, with the fate of a city in her hands, and she was letting her feelings for one man distract her.

Dellia gave a subtle shake of her head. "You know, you're right." She motioned up the steps with her head. "Fine. Come on then. I don't know what I was thinking."

She whipped back around, and the three climbed the steps together as the Rakshasa slunk back into the shadows.

Chapter Twenty-One

THE ANDERA CATACOMBS

The nauseating sounds of the demon feeding drifted through the pillars of the open pavilion and down the stairs. Jon glanced over his shoulder at Aishi, watching from the crowd with Chatin by her side. His heart pounded in his ears as he fought the image of what the beast could do to her.

His head snapped forward as he tried to shove it out of his awareness. He couldn't think. He couldn't function. This was so much worse than his worst fear. It was as if he were back in that classroom, staring at the corpses of his friends and stepsister. A stepsister he had promised he would take care of. Only instead of a handful of students, it was thousands of people who would die by his actions.

His mouth dry and stuck in a haze of panic, Jon stumbled on the steps, then stumbled again. Only vaguely aware of Garris and Dellia staring back at him, he strived to appear calm as he waved them on.

He tried taking a deep breath, but it was as if he were paralyzed. He tried to tell himself he needed to do this for Aishi, but the tightness only worsened. Then Dellia's words drifted through his panicked haze, and he knew. He had to do as she urged and think only about finding a way home, and not just for himself. He closed his eyes and repeated the words that had helped him in the tower. *I have to be fearless ... for Megan.* His breathing slowed as he struggled to take his

345

thoughts from all those deaths he would cause from one careless action.

As they reached the top, the Rakshasa came into view. Far back down the rows of white, lion-shaped columns, it crouched over a cobalt-blue uniform. Guttural sounds and slurping carried through the peaceful pavilion as it feasted on the bloody flesh of a fallen man. A sudden sick feeling struck, and Jon averted his eyes. His breathing grew short, and his mind clouded again with the weight of all those lives that hung on his actions.

Jon glanced up at the sound of clinking metal. Ahead, Garris slipped three shiny brass daggers from his pack, then let it drop to the rock floor with a clank. The demon halted and glanced up before returning to the butchered corpse.

Garris passed one of the golden blades to Dellia, then held one out for Jon to take. He grabbed ahold of it without thinking. Trailing behind, he stared down at the cold, metal weapon in his white-knuckled hand.

His head shot up at the sound of swords being unsheathed. Dellia signaled to Garris, and the pair split apart. Poised and alert, eyes fixed on the demon, they slunk silently through the carved pillars to flank the beast on either side.

Jon slowed, only half-aware and unsure what to do.

The monster seemed to grow in stature as they moved through the lion-shaped columns. Dark and sickly green, it hunkered over the corpse as it watched and gorged itself with greedy abandon. Without lifting its face from its feast, it shifted its eyes from side to side, watching as Garris and Dellia came to a stop. Jon froze as the beast focused on him, staring with bulging, bloodshot eyes. Gore smeared its face, blood dripped from huge canines, as it twisted its mouth into a wicked smile. Then the beast vanished.

"What?" Jon nearly shouted as a collective gasp echoed up from the spectators below.

His gaze darted everywhere, searching the stone pavilion for the demon. He glanced at Dellia then Garris, hoping for some sign explaining what had just happened.

They both stood tense and poised, ready for anything.

Jon looked down at the sharp, brass dagger in his hand. Nobody said anything about disappearing.

"Stay alert," Dellia's voice rang out, reverberating through the ornate pavilion.

His head whipped up to meet her apprehensive stare.

All of a sudden, she darted for him.

A cry rose up from the crowd. Movement flashed out of nowhere, and Jon bolted upright as a razor claw slashed down from above.

Dellia flew out in front of him, her sword swinging up past him, clanging into the massive paw a hair's breadth from his neck. The blow wrenched the clawed hand backward but didn't break the skin.

The Rakshasa vanished again, leaving Jon frozen, his breathing short and quick.

"Jon," Dellia shouted, "you need to snap out of this now, or you're—"

A blur of fangs and claws burst into view, flying toward Dellia at blinding speed.

The mob shrieked.

She skated to the side and threw herself off-balance as she thrust out her dagger, slashing the clawed hand inches from disemboweling her. She caught herself on the sweeping horn of a sculpted lion as the demon blinked out of sight.

Moments later, a streak careened down on Jon from above as he stood frozen in a panicked fog.

His body wrenched as Garris slammed into him and jabbed his dagger upward, slashing the Rakshasa's paw. Pain shot through Jon's arm as he crashed down onto the cold, unforgiving ground.

Garris rolled and sprang to his feet.

Dellia turned her back to Jon, every fiber seeming alert as she crept backward past a stone feathered wing and up to Jon. She held her sword and dagger wide, protecting him as she whispered over her shoulder. "Stay close."

She lowered her weapons and closed her eyes. Her breathing became calm and regular, as if she were in some kind of trance.

Jon rubbed his shoulder and glanced over at Garris on the other side of him, slowly turning as he scanned the temple. The murmur from the assemblage below tapered to a stop as they all stared upward. The silence seemed to go on forever, Dellia motionless and Garris watchful with Jon protected between their backs.

A flash sped out of view as a gasp echoed up from the crowd. Jon swung around as the demon bore down on Garris. The warrior lunged forward with a heavy blow, but the beast vanished, and his blade caught only thin air. Garris stumbled forward, thrown off-balance.

The blur reappeared and slammed into his side. It vanished again as Garris was sent sprawling.

The Rakshasa blinked into view again, streaking across the stone pavilion and heading straight for Jon's unprotected side.

Dellia snapped out of her trance. She twisted around Jon, shoving him behind her as she thrust her sword out. Her blade sliced into the beast's side.

She struck with two more lightning slashes, and blood splashed across the rough stone floor, then vanished along with the demon.

The rumble of voices from the assemblage came to a sudden stop, and a tense silence followed as everyone waited and watched. Then, the Rakshasa reappeared, far down the lavish pavilion, between the two lion-shaped columns that marked the entrance to the catacombs. Blood oozed from several slashes and a deep gash in its side.

Its eyes bulged in a creepy stare as it swiped the deep wound with its hand and licked the blood from its paw. Its blood-drenched lips twisted into an amused smile as it turned and disappeared down the catacomb stairs.

"You okay?" Dellia called out.

"Yeah," replied Jon. "I'm fine."

She glared at him. "Not you. Garris."

Garris nodded, and they began walking toward the stairway where the demon had disappeared.

Garris motioned to it with his head. "Trap?" he asked.

"Trap." She said.

Jon stopped in his tracks. "What?"

Dellia drew a short sigh. "But it doesn't matter, we have to go."

Garris nodded.

Jon raced to catch up. "Into a trap?"

She placed a hand on Jon's chest and brought him to a halt. "Not you. After that performance, you're staying here."

He glanced down at the palm pressed to his chest, then into her eyes. "But this is my chance to—"

"I can't babysit you and fight a demon at the same time."

"That's not fair. This is my life."

"Yeah, the one I just had to save." Dellia lit a torch on a nearby lamp and handed it to Garris.

Jon looked back and forth between the two. "But—"

"You need to stop worrying about all those people out there"— Garris motioned to the crowd outside the temple—"and worry about us."

Jon nodded. "I can do that. I can." He turned to Dellia, his eyes imploring. "Dellia, please."

"No," she said.

"I'll do better. I promise. You can't—"

"Fine." She shook her head in exasperation. "But you stay

between Garris and me." She shoved her head in Jon's face. "You understand?"

He nodded.

She lit another torch, and the three descended the stairway into darkness.

The sounds of the crowd grew distant as Jon followed down the stone stairway. And as the last reminder of the onlookers dwindled in the distance, he found his terror easing. He could handle this. He had to.

They rounded the stairway past the coffin and wall where he had been tied up. Jon stared at the leather straps that had bound him, still lying on the floor.

Dellia halted before a massive blood splatter spread across the rocky ground. "Is this where the attack occurred?"

Jon nodded.

She crouched and swiped her finger across the dried blood caked on the limestone floor, then smelled it. She followed a heavy red streak with her eyes as it left the stain and traveled through a narrow passage.

Holding the torch out above it, she rose and followed for some distance down a rough, uneven hallway. A small gasp reverberated down the cramped passage as she halted before a dried pool of blood and spatters that sprayed across the rock walls and ceiling. Crusty, dried bits of blood-soaked clothing were scattered everywhere.

Dellia lifted her foot and nudged a small pile of shredded, bright-colored cloth coated with dried blood. Revulsion gnawed in the pit of Jon's stomach, and he averted his gaze.

Garris rested a hand on his shoulder. "They never had a chance."

His words were cold comfort as the haunting image returned of the woman pleading for him to save her.

When Jon looked back at Dellia, she stood eyeing him with a look of concern. But it quickly faded as she spun about and gingerly stepped around the blood, as if trying not to touch the stained ground.

They continued on, Dellia divining the way forward and Garris guarding the rear, while Jon obediently stayed between them. Watchful and wary, they forged downward, their light footsteps echoing down one low, cavernous passage after another. Torchlight flickered across rocky walls, often adorned with exquisite carvings. Passages broke into small chambers, little vaults full of jars, coffins, and statuary, their walls splashed with magnificent stonework, turning them into little temples.

The path often split into several branches, and at each, Dellia studied the tracks and listened with care, then selected one of the exits. Whenever she hesitated, Garris would chime in with confident advice, and they traveled deeper and deeper.

They stopped in a chamber containing two gilded coffins and an enormous statue of a monkey-headed man. Unlike many before, this one was a mess. Debris, bones, and wood were scattered across the ground.

With intense concentration, Dellia studied the litter surrounding her. She looked to Garris, but he just shrugged. After listening and scanning a while longer, she selected one of the passages and continued. A couple dozen more steps and Dellia halted at a pile of rubble below a crumbled opening in the wall.

"The tracks, they just vanish," she said.

Garris stood motionless, not paying full attention as he peered back the way they'd come. "Shh." He turned to Dellia, speaking in a whisper. "There's a man following us."

"A man?" she whispered back. "You mean a demon, right?"

"No, definitely a man."

"Okay, but the tracks stop?" She pointed down at the floor.

"Could they have gone in there?" He motioned to the rough, crumbled opening.

Dellia stepped forward and thrust her torch through the jagged hole, revealing a modest cave beyond with a rough, uneven floor. Garris joined her, staring into the dimly lit cavern.

Jon startled and recoiled backward as a massive, four-armed brute stepped into the passage ahead, blocking the way forward. His fear rushed back, and his breathing grew short as he eyed its sickly green skin covered with heavy veins. It hunched below the ceiling, brandishing a pair of massive swords with two of its muscular arms as it stared with bulging red eyes. It had to be another kind of demon.

He couldn't tear his eyes away even as he tapped Garris and Dellia on the shoulder.

The two glanced over, and when they spotted the demon, they whipped around and bolted upright.

"I smell a trap," Garris said.

The brute smashed the ceiling with one massive fist. The floor rumbled, dust fell from the roof, and rocks crumbled from the edge of the opening.

All three pivoted around, heading back the way they'd come, but the Rakshasa stepped out into the hallway, crouching below the ceiling, blocking their exit.

"Yup, trap," Dellia said.

Jon swung around, but the demon raised one of its four palms, and a ball of swarming insects materialized above it. The green monster hurled the ball, and it unwound into a stream of large, buzzing flies.

Dellia and Garris jumped back, plastering themselves against the wall.

Jon followed, but not quickly enough. He cried out in pain as the stream grazed his arm. When he pulled it back, the flies had blasted away the skin, leaving only a painful patch of raw flesh.

The stream turned and filled the air.

"I think we're being herded." Dellia nodded to the jagged opening.

The demon ahead charged at them.

"Agreed," said Garris, "but we have no choice."

As Jon stood staring at the four-armed demon, she shoved him through the crumbled hole, then followed. He whirled around. She was between him and the opening and began backing them both away.

Outside the hole, Garris dodged and kicked as the Rakshasa flew past. Then he dove through the opening and swung around.

The stream of insects roared through the jagged hole, headed for Dellia. She shoved Jon back and dodged out of the way as the Rakshasa flew into view, bearing down on Garris.

The four-armed beast outside the opening smashed the wall with all four fists. The ground shook as rock crumbled and fell, blocking their only exit.

The Rakshasa slammed Garris backward, then grabbed a large boulder and lobbed it over his head. Garris ducked as the enormous stone arced over the stream of flies.

The massive rock smashed through the floor behind him, disappearing into the ground, taking a hail of wood and stone with it.

Chunks of the floor in front of Dellia fell away, revealing that all three were standing on a false floor, just flat stone slabs held up by rotted old planks spanning a huge black pit.

Another boulder slammed through the ground and bits of the floor began to crumble and fall away into the dark hole. Garris bolted, sprinting away as the floor disintegrated behind him.

Dellia snapped around, tossed her torch, and dove for Jon. She slammed into his chest with a jarring blow that sent him hurtling backward onto solid ground, next to her torch.

Garris leaped as the ground under him collapsed. He missed

the edge and fell, then caught the ledge, dangling there by his fingertips.

Jon turned and stared in horror as the floor lurched under Dellia and she dropped a few inches. His heart leaped into his throat as it fell away and she disappeared into the seemingly bottomless pit.

He snatched up the torch and scrambled across the rocky floor on his hands and knees.

Garris heaved himself up over the edge and rolled onto a broad, rocky ledge while the Rakshasa barreled down upon him.

Jon reached the edge and peered over it. Dellia lay a dozen feet down, clinging to the rotted, broken remnants of an old wooden rung. Above her, nothing remained of the ladder, and below her, jutting from the wall, were the remnants of a few decrepit rungs, then nothing but darkness.

"Are you okay?" he shouted.

"Yeah," Dellia yelled back. She glanced down at the seemingly endless darkness below her, then up at Jon again. "But there's no way up or down."

The rickety board in her hand creaked and fractured, dropping an inch. He glanced around in sheer panic.

Across the pit, Garris leaped to his feet and danced out of the way. Banking off the cavern wall, he swung down as the Rakshasa careened toward him, then vanished.

Jon's gaze flew across the rocks, wood, and stones of the room, searching for anything he might use. Then, it struck him, and he froze, staring down at Dellia. "Do you have anything that belonged to your mother?"

She stared up at him, perplexed. "My ring, but—"

"I'm coming to get you. Grab me with your ring hand and then fall with me. Your *ring hand*, remember."

"No," she shouted. "Absolutely not. Don't you dare."

"Or what?"

Dellia looked down, then up at Jon's face, and a chilling calm came over her. "Or I'll let go."

In a frenzy, he glanced up, hoping for help.

Garris dodged the Rakshasa, and it deflected blow after blow with its claws as a river of flies swirled around them both and headed for Dellia.

As they approached, she swung aside and let go, grabbing the rung closer to the wall.

In a burst of buzzing, the flies scattered against the rock face, obliterating part of the rung. The swinging of her weight caused the rotted wood to creak and begin to give way.

Jon's pressured words rushed out. "I can save you. Please. Look into my heart and tell me if I'm sure I can do this."

"You're not at all sure," came Dellia's instant response. She glanced down, and he panicked.

"No. Wait." He threw out his hand. "Tell me this wouldn't cripple me. You know me. I can't ... oh god."

She looked at her hand clinging to what remained of the rung, and her expression became one of resignation. She was going to let go.

Jon reached out, desperation banishing every other thought. "No. No. No. No. No. I'm begging you. Dellia, please. Don't."

Garris cried out, and Jon's head shot up. The huge warrior was charging the Rakshasa, blood oozing from a gash on his side. The torrent of flies whirled past his head, then flew up to a point above the hole. They coiled there, over Dellia, like a rattlesnake ready to strike.

The wood she was clinging to fractured and broke away. She dropped a short distance and snagged the rung below with a sharp gasp.

She looked back up at Jon. "I can't let you sacrifice yourself. You're not at all sure."

"No. No." He pointed at her. "Remember the three rules? If you let go because your gift tells you I'm unsure, you'll hurt me. I'll never be the same." Jon's eyes locked onto Dellia's. "Don't listen to your gift. Listen to *me*. I can save you. Trust me."

She looked at the creaking plank, then back at him. "You're sure."

He nodded. "Yes. Absolutely."

"Okay. I trust you."

He glanced up at Garris as he took a deep breath and dove over the edge. Above, the coil of flies began to unwind, chasing him as he plummeted toward Dellia.

Jon reached for her and she grabbed his hand, the cold metal of her ring touching his skin. His weight yanked her from the rung, and she slung herself around him, clinging tightly.

He focused on the ring and concentrated, but nothing happened. He tried again, and still nothing.

Dellia buried her face in his chest as they plummeted down the ragged pit into darkness.

The wind whistled by as he closed his eyes. He focused all his attention on the smooth metal of the ring against his skin, his concentration intense.

Suddenly, his fall slowed, then halted. A shimmering scene materialized around him as if it were solid ground he was standing on. He found the moment when Sirra had stepped through the portal, then shook his head and snapped back, resuming his fall.

As he thrust his palm downward and willed it, a portal blinked into existence below them. He eyed the Rakshasa through the shimmering gateway and yanked the dagger from Dellia's hand.

They plunged through the portal and tumbled out the other end, headed for the demon.

Jon shoved her head down, hunkering below the stream.

The flies blasted through the gateway, rocketing over their heads to pummel the demon's face.

As the last of the insects streamed through, Jon sprang, leaping at the beast. With both hands, he plunged the dagger through its sickly green skin, partway into the creature's chest.

The beast's half-raw face looked down at the weapon sticking out of its chest and let out a low, disturbing moan.

Garris flew at the monster, kicking the dagger with all his might, plunging it deep into the Rakshasa's chest with a sickening thunk.

It staggered back to the edge and teetered there before falling slowly backward over the precipice and down into the seemingly bottomless pit.

Jon scurried to the edge. "Don't like it when people just pop out on top of you, do ya?" he yelled down into the hole.

Jon smiled, feeling quite full of himself. He turned to face Dellia, and his pride turned to contrition as he met her horrified gaze.

Aghast, she glanced at his hand, then the pit, then his hand again. Her mouth open, she stared into his face. "You can open portals?"

"Not ... exactly," Jon stammered back.

Her expression turned brittle. "That's a *gift*, Jon, in case there's any confusion."

"I know, but—"

"I was totally honest with you, and you kept this from me?" Her face turned red with anger. "After you made such a big deal out of being honest and telling the truth?"

"I didn't exactly lie. I just didn't tell—"

Dellia shoved her face inches from Jon's. "You're unbelievable. You're still playing games?" She pointed to herself. "This is my *life* we're talking about."

He glared back. "Yeah, the one I just saved."

Furious and red faced, she whirled around.

"Not the time, guys," Garris said.

She gave him a crisp nod, and her expression turned hard and cold.

In her reaction, Jon found the familiar pain of regret over words too hastily spoken. "Look, I'm sorry, that wasn't fair."

Dellia's eyes fixed on Jon, her icy stare unrelenting. She was waiting for something.

He turned away, trying to hide it from her, as he raised his palm and made a portal shimmer into existence. Without uttering a word, she marched around him and through the gateway into the hall beyond.

Jon stepped through into the cramped hallway outside the cave-in. Garris followed, and the portal crumbled into a colored rain.

All business, Dellia snapped around, glancing back the way they'd come, then forward again. She forged ahead, never looking back or saying a word.

Jon hung his head as the feeling returned that he'd put a distance between them that would never be bridged. Still, he had to clear the air. "Dellia?"

"What?" she half shouted back.

"We may have also, sort of … um … cleared the Recluse Tower."

Garris closed his eyes and shook his head in disbelief.

Dellia halted and swung around. A flash of anger lit up her eyes. "What?"

Jon shrank away from her withering gaze. "Well, you see … Garris and I were holding off the spiders, and these flying lizard things and this huge creature came up from below, and then—"

"You and Garris … held off the spiders that swarmed me?"

"Yeah, but, you know, there were, like, two of us. And only one of … you."

Jon stopped for a moment as Dellia glared.

He glanced away, and his nervous words poured out as he tried to fill the uncomfortable silence. "Thing is, see, I noticed they burned.

So I lit them on fire, and they fell, and I kinda sent them through this portal. And they fell from the sky, and just sort of splattered … all … over."

He had been using his hands to illustrate falling and splattering. He stopped when he glanced up at Dellia's angry expression.

"So you're telling me 'you' conquered the Recluse Tower?"

Jon stammered, "No. No. That's … that's not what I'm saying at all. It was—it was me *and* Garris." He motioned back and forth between Garris and himself. "Both of us."

She mumbled something about more lies, then spun around and focused her attention forward again.

With her back turned to them, Garris leaned in and whispered to Jon, "Quick tip: now might not be the best time to make her even more angry."

Jon paused, then leaned over and whispered back, "I thought I was doing okay. I mean, at least I don't have a dagger to my throat."

Dellia whipped around and shot him a blistering stare. She muttered something about the day not being over yet, then snapped back forward and continued.

Garris gaped at Jon as he shook his head.

They crept down magnificent halls lined with tombs and carvings. Passages wound through elaborate chambers adorned with coffins, shrines, and statuary. Dellia led the way with Jon and Garris following in uncomfortable silence.

She halted in one of the chambers, straining to hear a faint buzzing down one of the paths out of the room.

"Just in case anyone is interested," Garris said, "there's still someone following us."

She whirled around and glared. "I'm sure Jon has some other secret gift he's lying about that can deal with them."

Dellia swung back around and stepped quietly into the hall. Up ahead, on the left, an arched entry appeared. As they approached, the buzzing became louder.

A small, yet opulent sepulcher carved out of stone appeared through the doorway. Intricate carvings lined every wall, and a cloud of oversized flies swirled through the air high up in the space.

Soon, the massive brute came into view, standing full height, in front of a wall covered with recesses holding gold inlaid coffins. The beast smiled as it stood waiting. It stared at them with its bulbous eyes as two of its four heavily muscled arms brandished a pair of swords.

Garris pointed to a modest stone bench on the left. The seat had been smashed to rubble, and resting in the debris lay a small, gold box with an impression of three leaves arranged in a circle on its lid.

"Look," Garris said, "just like the tower. That must contain what you need."

At the mention of the tower, an annoyed look passed over Dellia's face.

Garris shouldered his crossbow and eyed her. "Ready?"

She raised her sword and granted him a crisp nod.

An arrow flew from the crossbow with a twang as the pair charged. The arrow whistled across the room but snapped with a crack as the demon deflected it with a sword.

Dellia and Garris flew at either side of the beast in a flurry of clanging metal that reverberated through the small space. He slashed and stabbed with devastating blows that sank deep into flesh. Dellia's blades whistled through the air in a blur, landing blow after blow. Flies swarmed, and wounds multiplied, covering the demon's body, but most were shallow and healed in seconds.

Jon stood frozen, trying to devise some kind of plan, but nothing came to mind. It was obvious Garris and Dellia were growing tired while the beast was not, and it was only a matter of time before it killed one or both of them.

The demon suddenly grabbed one of its swords with both hands and swung down on Garris. Their blades met with a loud clang, sending him hurtling backward where he tumbled to the ground.

The demon turned all its attention to Dellia.

Jon panicked and bolted. His palm shot forward, and a black portal materialized behind the monster.

Dellia's taut angry expression turned to alarm as the demon whipped around and faced Jon with its sword raised high to intercept him.

She seized the opening and jammed her sword through the beast's shoulder.

It roared in pain as it swung a huge blade down toward Jon's head.

He tried to swerve out of the way, but it was too late.

Dellia's dagger flew up to meet the sword, and she bowed under the weight of the blow. She twisted out of Jon's way as he hurtled past.

A painful kick in his rear sent him off-balance, and he stumbled into the portal.

In an instant, he was plummeting down the pit again, flailing his arms and legs, trying to keep from spinning. The rocky walls raced past as the light from the image above grew distant.

He thrust his palm out, aimed downward, and caused another portal to form underneath him. He shot through it and tumbled out onto the floor of the vault.

Dellia clutched for her sword, still in the beast's shoulder. It bashed her with a massive fist, and she was flung backward like a rag doll, slamming against the wall. It turned toward her, ready to charge.

The buzzing of flies sounded right behind Jon as he flew to his feet and raced at the demon. He thrust out his palm and opened another dark portal behind the creature.

At the last second, he ducked down, aiming for the beast's feet, but it reached down, snagged his clothes, and hoisted him aloft. Jon dangled there, a target for the stream of flies that raced at him.

The demon raised a sword, ready to plunge it into the helpless Jon, but once again Dellia's dagger flew up to block it.

Garris glanced at Jon and nodded.

He gulped and stiffened, bracing himself, then nodded back.

A black-haired stranger drenched in sweat barged around the corner into the room. He froze, his saucer eyes staring at the chaos.

Jon raised his finger to point at him, but Garris kicked hard, and a jarring blow ripped him from the demon's grasp and hurtled him back through the portal.

Jon tumbled down the dark pit, the walls and portal above whirling past. He thrust his palm again out and waited for the gateway above to swirl by, searching for the perfect split second. His head spun and his vision blurred as he plummeted downward.

He willed it, and a portal blinked into existence below him.

Jon plunged through and shot out across the rock floor of the vault, landing with his face staring at a pair of dark, leather boots. He looked up into a strange man's face, dripping with sweat, his dark eyes wide with panic.

Garris lunged for the metal box.

The black-haired stranger reached over Jon and snatched it from the rubble, leaving Garris grasping at thin air. Before Jon could react, the stranger dashed out of the room, clutching the shiny golden box to his chest.

The demon let out a deafening bellow and smashed Dellia aside. She flew through the air and plummeted to the ground as the brute stormed out of the room followed by a stream of flies.

Jon raced over to her.

As he helped her to her feet, she looked up into his face and said, "If he gets away, you'll lose any chance of getting home."

"He's a dead man," Garris said.

"We have to save him," Jon shouted.

Surprise flashed across Dellia's face as Jon snatched her torch from the ground and raced out of the room. Flames from the torch fluttered in the wind as he tore down countless hallways and vaults, with the sound of Dellia and Garris chasing behind. At first, he'd catch glimpses of the demon, then just the flies, and eventually all he could follow was the distant sound of buzzing echoing down the halls. His muscles ached, and his breathing grew labored, but Jon pushed on. That man had come because of him, and he couldn't let him die at the hands of that beast.

Heaving from exertion, Jon sprinted to the top of the steps. He tossed the torch aside as he sailed through the entrance and out onto the open spaces of the ornate temple.

Shielding his eyes, Jon raced down the row of lion-shaped pillars lit by the late-day sun behind him. He glanced back to see Garris and Dellia fly into the open after him.

The steps neared, and he slowed as the demon began to emerge from around the edge of the last column. It eyed Jon from the top of the steps as it hunkered over the black-haired stranger's lifeless body.

Behind it, a large crowd stared upward from the base of the gradually sloping stairway, the echoes of their fearful voices filling the pavilion.

Jon froze, unsure what to do next as Dellia and Garris halted at his side.

The demon raised itself up to full height and turned toward the group. Glancing over its shoulder, it surveyed the crowd, then raised its head and bellowed.

As if that were a command, the crowd became silent, all eyes turned upward, watching and waiting.

The beast faced the three and curled its lips into a wicked smile. Then it spoke, its voice loud and deep and dripping with disdain.

"So, the Otherworlder has come to stop me."

Gasps and hushed comments rumbled up from the onlookers as Jon stood there, stunned. Despite the warning of demons that deceived, he never imagined one *speaking*.

Dellia grabbed Jon's arm. "Don't believe him. He's afraid of you."

The demon glared at Dellia for a moment, then smiled. "So the witch continues to abuse her gift," it said in its low, gravelly voice, "just as your kind always do."

At the words the crowd drew silent again, as if stunned and waiting for her response.

Jon glanced at Dellia as her expression turned to one of horror.

"Don't listen to him," Garris said and began slinking out to flank the beast.

The demon continued to eye Dellia. "The same way you abuse your gift to betray Jon to your masters, while you tell yourself you're helping him."

Jon turned to Dellia, and she seemed even more horrified. She swung toward him as if wanting to explain.

Garris glared at her. "Why are you listening to this demon? Its only aim is to deceive."

The demon turned its attention to him. "Hmm. Am I deceiving you, or are you deceiving yourself? So desperate are you to give your life meaning that you'd help the one who could be the downfall of you all."

Jon stepped forward. "You're twisting the truth. Just because I'm from another world doesn't make me the Otherworlder."

At Jon's admission, a ripple of gasps and murmurs passed through the crowd at the base of the steps.

Aghast at their reaction, he stepped back.

A look of deep satisfaction filled the demon's face. "Ah, there's the fear." It stared at him with its bulging red eyes as it bellowed in a theatrical voice. "We have waited and prepared for you for a long time. Did you think we would not recognize you?"

"You're lying," Jon said.

The demon raised one of its huge palms as if presenting him to the crowd. "Ask the witch if I'm lying. You are Jon, the one and *only* Otherworlder."

A clamor swept through the crowd. The demon smiled again. "You can see the truth of the prophecy, can you not?"

"No. No, I can't," Jon said.

The demon raised all four arms and motioned to the crowd. "Then tell them all, did you come here to save these people?" It beamed a broad smile and shook its massive head. "No, you did not. That is not who you are."

"You're twisting the truth," Jon said.

"Am I?" The creature kicked the broken box at its feet. An evil smile filled its gruesome face as it extended a clenched fist toward Jon. Slowly, it opened the clawed hand to reveal a shiny gold leaf resting in its palm. It was just like the one in the tower. "Then kill me, and take this, Otherworlder, and prove that your only aim was to help yourself."

Jon jumped as an arrow shot through the demon's neck. He turned and stared at Garris.

Garris shrugged. "He just wouldn't shut up."

The demon broke off the arrow and slid it out of its neck. The wound closed and healed as it turned and stormed toward Garris.

Jon glanced around in a panic, scanning the pillared pavilion. This demon was impossible to defeat, but he had to find a way. There had to be something.

His gaze rested on the yali, and like lightning, the realization struck. "Protect," he mumbled.

He reached out and set a hand on the smooth surface of the carved lion's chest and concentrated. Time slowed, and the world froze with the demon's sword raised and only a handful of feet from Garris.

An image appeared, already moving at a blur. Jon focused on the yali, reaching back in time, farther and farther. Back through decade upon decade the shimmering image flew. Centuries passed, until it stopped at a scene of a young Elorian man carving one of the yali out of stone. He spun the image forward in time until there it was, the moment he had hoped for. He shook his head and snapped back, then everything started to move again.

Hand still on the yali, Jon closed his eyes, lowered his head, and chanted, "*Zinda mein aao or raksha karana.*"

A loud crackling sound halted the demon's advance. It swung around as the stone yali pulled itself from the pillar and transformed into a real-life lion with thick, golden fur, enormous amber wings, and dark gray horns.

The yali lowered its head and shoulders and began a slow, steady advance, stalking the demon.

Jon moved over to place a hand on the smooth surface of a second yali. He lowered his head and chanted again, "*Zinda mein aao or raksha karana.*"

The crowd gasped, and Jon's raised his head.

Dellia faced him, staring with a mixture of fear and awe as the second yali crackled and broke away from the stone pillar.

The demon leaped away, but the first yali pounced, propelling itself forward with its massive feathered wings in a gust of wind and dust.

It collided with the demon midair, and the pair fell like a stone, slamming into the ground with a deep thud and a burst of air.

The yali stared downward, its dagger-like teeth inches from the beast's face as it let out a deafening roar.

The demon slashed with its sword, and sparks flew as the blade glanced off the stone hard surface.

The green beast heaved the yali off and rose, but the second yali sprang and hurtled onto it, sinking its long, white teeth deep into the sickly green flesh of the creature's neck.

The demon let out a deafening roar of pain as the yali shook it. Then it began dragging the beast by its neck across the rough stone floor.

The demon glanced up at the first yali as it was lugged across the ground toward it. It looked over at Jon with an expression of anger and frustration before it burst into flames and vanished.

The gold metal fragment fell from the flames and clattered across the ground. Dellia watched with a wide-eyed look of shock and disbelief as the pair of yali strolled past her to either side of the steps and sat, tall and regal. Still in their living form, they stayed there like statues, peering out over the crowd.

Her eyes turned to the gold metal leaf still lying on the stones of the temple floor. She approached it like a frightened child, then picked it up with reverent care. Head still lowered, she returned to Jon.

Jon's heart fell. She couldn't even look at him.

"You can't believe that monster, Dellia," he said, hoping she'd look up at him and her reassuring face would tell him everything was okay. But when she did raise her head, the eyes that looked into his seemed distant and troubled.

"It wasn't lying, Jon. About any of it." She turned and trudged down the steps and into the crowd, never looking back.

Garris scooped up his bag and hurried over to Jon. He planted his firm hand on his shoulder and looked him in the eyes. "I can't be here." Garris turned and took a few steps down the stairway where Gatia met him and grabbed him by the arm. He turned back to Jon. "I ... I can't do this anymore, Jon. I'm sorry. I won't be back."

The words paralyzed him. The only thing that had allowed him to persevere were these two people who had stood by his side, and now, both had just abandoned him.

All he could do was watch as Gatia escorted Garris down the steps. He stopped at the bottom and surveyed the crowd then gave Gatia a nod before he pulled away. As if he were avoiding someone, he ducked down and hurried off, disappearing into the throng.

In a haze, Jon slowly descended the steps. As he approached, the crowd parted, and their fearful faces stared at him, as if more afraid of him than they had been of the demon. Isolated voices rang out as he trudged through the sea of faces.

"He killed a demon," a woman said.

A man yelled out, "He's the Otherworlder."

Then a voice rang above the others. "He's *evil.*"

Jon shivered at the accusation. The clamor grew, and he quickened his pace, trying to ignore their cries.

As he cleared the crowd, he glanced back, and they were following him. When he faced forward, a group of soldiers flew around a corner, moving at a run. Their eyes locked onto him, and they drew their swords, sprinting straight at him.

Jon halted and glanced around, searching for some avenue of escape. Then he realized what he needed to do. He raised his palm, aiming down a nearby alleyway, and willed a portal to appear. As it shimmered into existence, he bolted, sprinting down between the buildings. He ducked and dove through, leaving the temple and every awful thing that had happened there behind.

Chapter Twenty-Two

THE BLADE OF CAIN

The broad temple steps drifted by under Dellia, as in a daze, she trudged downward toward the murmuring crowd. Behind her stood Jon, amid the carnage of the temple. She could almost feel his stare on the back of her neck, but she no longer knew who it was that watched her from the top of the steps. She had seen power the likes of which she'd never imagined: bringing stone to life, creating portals as if it were child's play, and who knew what else he was capable of. In all of history, only a handful of people possessed more than one gift. And never two such powerful ones in the hands of one person, much less a soul so undisciplined.

She waded into the crowd of frightened onlookers, still staring upward at Jon. A sea of whispers, bright clothes, and stunned faces passed by, her mind clouded in a haze of confusion, her gut rebelling against her head. It couldn't be. Yet, Jon *was* the Otherworlder, no doubt remained. All her plans of helping him turned upside down, in a single moment, a single realization. Her life a mess, her hopes dashed, Kayleen's trust betrayed, she needed time to think, to work out what to do—but there was no time.

Dellia slipped into a nearby alley and stood for a moment, struggling to come to terms with it all. An image flashed into her memory of Jon's imploring face as she turned to leave him. A tension gripped her chest, and she felt as if she couldn't breathe. She set her hands on the heavy bricks of the wall and leaned forward into them, staring down at the hard, packed dirt as she struggled to fight back tears.

Her gaze was drawn to the edge of the fearful crowd staring up into the temple in shock and amazement. How could Jon, of all people, hurt them? Yet, that *was* the destiny of the Otherworlder. She shook her head. This couldn't be. It wasn't right.

Dellia peered around the corner at Jon, his face drawn and frightened as he trudged down the broad temple steps. Her whole being ached as her heart went out to him. He seemed devastated and so alone. She yearned to go to him, to reach out with her gift and touch his heart, and reassure herself that he was still the same man she thought she knew. But her gift was gone.

The urge struck to push down her tumult of emotions and harden her heart, for in doing so she knew she could restore her gift. And then she would know. No, that wasn't the answer; that was never the answer. She could never become one of those cold-blooded monsters who had excised their feelings to strengthen their gift.

She turned away as the tension returned at the idea of facing Jon and all he represented. She didn't need her gift to know he had a good heart and that he never wanted any of this. As she stared at the cold bricks under her hands, she cleared her head, then pushed away from the rough wall. None of that mattered now. All that mattered was that she finally knew who Jon was to the council and what that meant. She had a duty. *She could never be like her father.* Pulling herself up straight and tall, Dellia gathered her strength and mumbled under her breath, "My duty."

She turned down the dusty alley and began her march back to Gatia's home. At first, she moved slowly, her mind still in a fog, struggling to maintain her resolve. Then, her pace quickened, and she began going faster and faster as if chased by the phantoms of all those who might perish under the weight of the prophecy.

Soon she was in a blind race, flying down broad streets, around

370

corners, and through dimly lit alleys. Massive homesteads flew by, their families talking and laughing from yards and terraces, but none of it could penetrate the heaviness of her heart.

Dellia pushed down the street, whipping around the corner and through the simple gate into Gatia's lavish garden. She came to a sudden halt. Her breast heaved from exertion as she looked over at the small bench before the cool pond dotted with yellow lilies. It had only been this morning that she and Jon had sat there and talked, yet it seemed as if it were another lifetime. She faced forward and pushed the image out of her mind so she could resume her march.

Onto the porch and through the door she raced, then up the stairs, down the hall, and through the arched doorway to her room. She snatched up her bag and tossed it onto the small bed. Her heart pounded as she rifled through it and grabbed the Window of Rhina.

She raced down the hall to a lavish and colorful room and came to a stop before a wooden desk covered with ornate carvings. With trembling fingers, she placed the bar on its smooth surface. As she caught her breath, Dellia steeled herself. Then, she leaned over the bar and exhaled softly into it. She collapsed into a chair, staring into space as the mist formed and the image clarified.

Suddenly, Dellia snapped to attention. She had drifted off and was staring through the Window into Kayleen's sparse chambers.

Kayleen appeared, and concern flooded her face. She lowered herself into her simple wooden chair. "What's the matter?"

"It's …"

Kayleen's eyes became wide with alarm, and she blurted out, "What is it? What happened?"

"It's him. He's the one."

Her brow furrowed. "Jon?"

Dellia nodded. "What do I do?"

"Jon is the Otherworlder?"

Dellia nodded again.

Kayleen's puzzlement deepened. "But then why are you so …" A flash of recognition passed across her face, and she let out a small gasp. As if compelled, her hand flew to the long blue crystal of the pendant that dangled from her neck. "No. Don't tell me." She leaned back in her chair and stared at Dellia. "You love him, don't you?"

A sudden pang of horror struck. It was as if Kayleen had seen right through her, as if she knew she'd done the unthinkable. She'd always kept men at a distance, guarding against feeling anything, because more than anything she wanted to be a protector. But from the very start, something about Jon had made that impossible. He wasn't handsome or brave or charming. He was none of the things she ever thought could capture her heart. But he had, and there was no denying it any longer: she loved him.

Dellia lowered her eyes and nodded. "What do I do?"

Kayleen leaned in toward her. "Listen to me."

There was a passion in her voice that compelled Dellia to lift her eyes. "This is important. Are you listening?"

Dellia nodded again.

"Go to him. Protect him. Be with him. Don't let—"

The door opened behind her and Kayleen's head whipped around to spy Braye barging into her room. She snapped back forward with a startled look on her face. Her eyes met Dellia's, and in a commanding voice she said, "Don't let anything happen to him. Do you understand?"

The whole manner of her presentation made it feel as if the words were not an order from her superior but the heartfelt urging of a friend. Then it became clear—her friend Kayleen, the leader of the Ruling Council of Meerdon, was telling her to run away with Jon. The proposition struck with unexpected force, and her resolve began to crumble.

Braye strolled across the modest room to where Kayleen sat. "I thought I heard voices," he said. "I thought maybe it was Dellia."

He halted when he saw her face. He looked suspicious, surveying first Dellia, then Kayleen. "It's Jon, isn't it?"

Dellia sat silent for a moment, trying to find a way not to respond.

"Jon is the Otherworlder," Braye said.

She snapped out of it and composed herself. This was her duty. She adjusted her position, somehow becoming even more stiff and straight. "Yes, Councilman Braye."

"And there's no doubt?"

"There's little doubt."

"Hmm." He looked thoughtful for a moment as he stroked his chin. "Then do as Kayleen says. Don't let anything happen to him. Where is he headed?"

"Kanlu," Dellia said.

Kayleen glanced over her shoulder at Braye, then addressed Dellia. "I have to say, I had my doubts when I decided to let you handle this on your own. But I'm pleased to see they were unfounded."

It took Dellia a second to realize. Kayleen had covered for her. It was as she feared. Her actions had cost Kayleen her seat on the council. The thought sickened her, but Dellia simply smiled. "Oh. Yes. Thank you, Councilwoman."

Braye hesitated before saying, "Perhaps that was the best call. But now I need you to stay with him and make sure he reaches Kanlu. I can meet you there, and we can bring him in together."

Dellia's heart stopped. She hadn't thought far enough ahead to realize where this would all lead. The tension in her chest returned, and she opened her mouth to protest, but Kayleen jumped in. "No, I'll go."

Braye stepped back, eyeing Kayleen. "Hmm." He looked thoughtful for a moment as he stroked his chin some more. Then, his expression dissolved into a sort of self-satisfied look. "Yes. That might do nicely. It will give you a chance to prove what a good team you and Dellia make. I will gather some men to accompany you."

She appeared suspicious of his acquiescence. "I'd like to take my own detail," she said, "if you have no objection."

"Of course." Braye smiled and turned to go, but then halted and turned back. "But I'll assign a few more men, just in case."

Kayleen nodded.

He looked at Dellia, then Kayleen. "Good. It's time we ended this."

Kayleen's hand passed through the image, and it splashed down across the table and floor, then vaporized.

Dellia stared into space for a minute. It all seemed so unreal. She had just turned the Otherworlder in to the council. But she had also turned in a friend who trusted her and the man she loved. How could she ever face him again? How could she just pretend everything was fine? Dellia folded her arms on the smooth surface of the beautiful desk and buried her head in them.

As he dove out of the portal, Jon hit the ground, rolled, and sprang to his feet. He spun around to glimpse the crowd outside the darkened alley as the shimmering portal rippled in the gentle breeze. Then it disintegrated into a colored rain that scattered across the thick green leaves and delicate pink blooms of the bushes in the corner of Gatia's yard.

Voices rang through the neighborhood. Still in shock and terrified of capture by soldiers, Jon ducked down below the line of heavy shrubs that formed a hedge along the fence. He crouched there and waited and listened.

Footsteps echoed down the broad street, approaching at a flat-out run. He ducked down further and backed up into the dense, jade-colored greenery, hidden from view.

The footsteps sped past the fence behind him and whipped

around the corner. The gate slammed open as pounding feet dove through and down the path to the house.

Dellia appeared and came to a sudden halt. Even without a full view of her face, her state was unmistakable. Her manner was taut, her skin almost white, and she seemed distressed, panicked even.

She glanced away at the small bench in the corner, surrounded by vines of ruby, deep-throated flowers. He could picture her pained look as she stared. But when she turned back toward the house, it was worse than he could have ever imagined. Her face appeared pale and shocked, and the strain reflected in her eyes was heartrending. Jon gulped as Dellia steeled herself and then marched up the steps to the door and through it.

He lowered his eyes and shook his head as an insufferable heaviness sank into his heart. It had been painful enough to witness the horrified looks on the faces in the crowd and hear their accusations born out of fear. But seeing Dellia like this was more than he could bear. It didn't matter that it had never been his intention to hurt her. The fact remained, he was the source of her pain. And if there was one certainty in this whole mess, it was that things would only get worse.

Jon raised himself up and took a deep breath, standing straight. He couldn't be the cause of this.

He crept up the heavy brick steps, through the door, and into the house. Careful not to make any noise, he moved quickly through the colorful main room, past the kitchen, and up the stairs.

The sound of Dellia's distraught voice carried down the hall, but he dared not stop to listen. He slipped into his room, lifted his bag onto the bed, and filled it with the few loose items he'd left around the room.

Travel on the streets would be dangerous, and the image of a small alley outside the stables still lingered in his mind. So he snapped up his bag, slung it over his shoulder, and raised his palm. In a few moments, a glistening portal stood before him, with a view of the dark alley.

Jon stepped through to the sound of voices approaching on the street outside. He slipped up against the heavy brick wall as the portal disintegrated and splashed down to the dry, dusty ground.

A smiling couple with their arms around one another passed by only a few feet away. As their footsteps faded, Jon moved from the wall and peered around the corner the other way. The street was clear, and the dimness of dusk would help mask his identity. Head down, he darted around the corner and into the brick stables.

As Jon rushed over, Enna nickered, seeming glad to see him. He stroked her gorgeous, dappled-gray face as he gazed on her with fondness. After he led her out of the stall, he paused for a moment, resting his forehead against her warm flank. "It's just us now, girl." He grabbed a nearby blanket and threw it over her back, then located his saddle. Before long he had bridled and saddled Enna and worked his way out of town.

To his left, the red orb of the sun was disappearing below the horizon, and to his right, across the scrubby expanse, lay the mountains at the edge of the barren plains. All he had to do now was keep them on his right and he would soon find Elore, and within it, Kanlu.

Jon turned for one last look at Mundus as the enormous houses with their bright terraces and desert gardens grew distant behind him. An intolerable heaviness burdened his heart at the thought of leaving Dellia back there, never to see her again, but it was the right thing to do. He faced forward and spurred Enna onward, and she broke into a gallop, carrying him far northward toward the Chaldean Desert and away from Dellia, Garris, and all the pain he had caused.

Garris surveyed the crowd, trying to ignore the uneasy feeling rotting in his gut. Gatia eased her grip on his arm, eyeing him with caution as she escorted him down the steps of the holy temple. He grumbled under his breath. He wasn't in the habit of ignoring his instincts, but in this case, they were urging him to stay. And although the decision weighed upon him more than he had expected, only a moron would stick around knowing what was bound to come next.

Several ominous faces lurking in the crowd jumped out at him, confirming he'd already pushed his luck too far. In fact, because he'd dragged his feet, getting out of Mundus at all would be risky, and getting out without bloodshed a near impossibility.

He halted on the stone steps, scrutinizing the sea of murmuring faces, memorizing the location of everyone he recognized. Garris turned to Gatia and gave a crisp nod before he broke away and dove into the throng.

His head hunched down, he headed north along the steps, then swerved and headed back the other direction, hoping to throw off anyone attempting to follow his movements.

Above him, a field of shocked faces drifted past, all eyes fixed on Jon. Over the whispers of the crowd, individual voices rang out.

Behind Garris, a woman cried, "He killed a demon."

An elderly man just above Garris yelled, "He's the Other-worlder!"

Another voice farther back in the crowd said something about evil as Garris shook his head. These idiots knew nothing of Jon. They were letting their fear over some worthless prophecy drive them to turn on a man they had just witnessed saving their collective hides. "Complete insanity," he mumbled to himself.

As he reached the edge of the restless crowd, Garris ducked between two large buildings constructed of huge clay bricks. He straightened up and hurried down a dusty path between the two heavy walls. The sounds of the crowd faded behind him as he approached the next street.

The familiar faces of a pair of old enemies flashed by, searching the alley from the street beyond. They raced past, then a moment later they backed up and reappeared. The two heavily armed brutes stepped forward with folded arms. They stared at him with grim expressions as they blocked the narrow passage out of the alley.

Dust kicked in the air as Garris spun around and rushed back the other direction. Halfway down, three more unwelcome faces flew into view then stopped, blocking the passage back.

Garris backed up a few steps, dropped his pack, and drew his sword. He relaxed as he set the tip on the ground and leaned on it as if it were a walking stick. He donned a casual grin and yelled down the alley, "We're all friends here. No reason for any hostilities."

The alleyway was barely wide enough for the three burly men to fit through as they adopted grim expressions and began to strut toward him.

"Is that what you told Rhan before you killed him?" said the man in the center.

"I tried to take him in," Garris said, striving to remain casual.

"You protectors," the man continued. "Always bargin' into a fight that's not yours, takin' sides before you know what's what."

"He killed Jhohit's entire family," Garris protested.

"Yeah, but they were all bad people."

Garris startled. "Most of them were over sixty."

All three men stopped and drew their weapons.

As they brought them to the ready, Garris spotted his opening. He kicked the tip of his sword, scraping sand and dust from the ground and flinging it into two of the men's faces.

As they covered their eyes, he slammed one man's head into the hard clay of the wall. As the sword flipped up over his head, Garris snatched the hilt out of the air and brought it down on the second man's head with a crack. Still clutching the blade, he punched the third in the face, and all three men crumpled to the ground.

Garris swung around to meet the source of the footsteps

bearing down on him. He ducked and kicked his assailant as a sword whistled through the space his head used to occupy. Thrown off-balance by his own clumsy move, his assailant stumbled, so Garris slammed his foot into the man's side, sending him flying backward. Tossed through the air like an old shoe, he collided headfirst with the unforgiving bricks of the wall and toppled to the ground.

The last man growled under his breath and stormed toward Garris. All of a sudden, he stiffened and froze with a look of shock on his face. He fell toward Garris, plowing facefirst into the dust. And there behind him stood Cain, grinning from beneath the darkness of his hood.

Garris glared. "You let me take out all four, then you decide to help?"

"I wanted you to feel useful." Cain's smile broadened.

"I could have managed the last guy."

"I know. But what would be the point?"

Garris looked down at the man at Cain's feet. "You didn't have to kill him."

Holding out a dagger, Cain stepped forward, presenting it to Garris. "I didn't. It's coated with my own concoction. One nick or scratch and it paralyzes the victim. Mimics death. Take it. It might prove useful."

Garris sighed in exasperation, then granted him a quick bow before he took the dagger and slipped it into his boot holster.

"Particularly effective for a wife when trying to send the husband a message," Cain said.

"Wow," said Garris. "You're ... mean."

Cain grabbed ahold of his arm and escorted him down the alley, stepping around the unconscious bodies in their way. As he rounded the corner out of the cramped space, Garris smiled as Kyri came into sight. She stood before him, saddled and ready to ride. He mounted her, then urged her on, and she bolted to a gallop. He glanced back and there, next to Cain, stood Gatia waving goodbye.

The sound of hooves against the pavement echoed through the streets as he galloped down the nearly empty boulevard. Most of the residents prone to gaping at spectacles were back at the temple, but best to take no chances. He pulled his hood up, covering his face from the few natives gawking from the rooftops, windows, and terraces.

Garris caught a brief glimpse between two buildings as a water-like portal flashed into existence a block over. He slowed and craned his neck, searching for a spot with a better view.

Across a field between two homes, he found it, as he caught sight of a glistening gateway in the corner of Gatia's yard. Garris pulled Kyri to a stop and watched as his steed moved restlessly under him.

A man flew through the portal and sprang to his feet. When he turned around, it was Jon, staring at the shimmering image as it splashed down to the greenery of the garden.

An oppressive guilt nagged at him at the sight of Jon alone, but he had no choice. He was already under siege, and soon Kayleen's hirelings would come for him. So he had no choice but to betray his solemn vow and abandon his friend in his hour of need.

Garris began to turn Kyri south again, as voices rang out, followed by footsteps speeding down the street. He turned back as Dellia sprinted down the fence line, through the gate, and into the yard. She paused, staring at the bench in a corner, below a large tree, then resumed her flight, disappearing into the house.

Jon stood and stared after her for a moment, then straightened himself and marched up the porch and through the door after her.

Garris heaved a sigh of relief as his guilt eased. He'd been afraid Jon might wind up on his own, and it lifted his spirits to see the two back together. He completed Kyri's southward turn and urged her forward, racing toward the edge of town, satisfied that he had done all he could, and now Dellia would have to look after Jon alone.

Hours passed, night fell, and from below, the sounds of the family eating and conversing came and went. Still, Dellia sat in the dark, on the floor, propped against the lavish canopy bed, with her knees to her chest and her arms around them.

Eventually, a light came down the hall, and Gatia whisked through the doorway with a lantern in her hand.

She halted above her, staring down. "What are you doing in my room?"

Dellia never raised her head, continuing to gaze at the elaborate carving on the dresser in front of her. "I needed a place to contact the council. Couldn't use my room."

"Then, by all means, don't ask permission. Just barge in and use whatever you want."

Dellia couldn't answer or even look up.

"Wait," Gatia said. "You left the temple hours ago. Why are you still here?"

She tried to think of a thousand different ways not to answer, but the need to confide in someone won out, and she settled on the truth. She looked up into Gatia's face. "I can't face him."

"Can't—who? … Jon?" Gatia's eyes opened wide, and she slid down onto the floor next to her. "Oh, Dellia, what did you do?"

"I told the council he's the Otherworlder."

"Well, that's not exactly a mystery anymore. It happened in front of half the town. The council was going to find out, anyway."

Dellia stared at the floor. "Then why do I feel so dirty? I did my duty, Gatia. How can I feel so—"

Gatia's head whipped over. "Wait. Orders came through to detain Jon. I thought he was long gone … with you."

Dellia straightened and stared at Gatia for a moment before

bouncing to her feet. "He's not in his room?"

She flew out the door and down the hallway to Jon's room. She raced around the cramped space, half-panicked, searching for anything that might assure her he was still there.

"His bag. Where is his bag?"

"His bags are gone," Gatia replied.

"No. Not again."

Dellia raced out of the room, down the stairway, and out the front door with Gatia giving chase. Down the streets and around the corner she ran, racing into the stables.

In an instant, she spotted Ulka's sweet face, but no sign of Enna or Kyri. Gatia flew through the door as Dellia spun around in a panic, looking everywhere, as if Jon might be hidden somewhere in the shadows. "Enna's gone. I have to catch them."

"Them?" Gatia replied.

"He has to be with Garris, right?"

"No. I kept an eye on Garris as he left. He was alone."

Dellia froze and stared at her. "What?" she said, on the verge of tears. "Jon is out there?" She pointed north, across the barren planes. "In the Chaldean Desert? Alone?"

"I'm sorry," said Gatia.

"No. No way is he equipped for that. He'll die out there." Dellia's hand flew to her mouth as she imagined Jon lost in the burning desert, hunched over the dead body of Enna, with his skin cracked and burnt and on the threshold of death due to lack of water. "This is all my fault. I should have stayed with him. I could tell he was taking it hard."

Gatia stared at her with a puzzled expression. "You did just inform on him to the council."

The words barely registered through Dellia's panicked haze. She grabbed a saddle blanket and headed for Ulka. "I have to get to him before something happens."

DELLIA

"What can I do?" Gatia asked.

Dellia's words poured out. "Grab my things out of the room and bring them here. And lend me some supplies. I have to leave."

Gatia grabbed Dellia by the shoulder and granted her a deep nod. "Of course, and I'll make sure any search for Jon is fruitless."

The two exchanged a quick hug, then Gatia ran out of the stables. Dellia threw the saddle blanket over Ulka as she began her frantic preparations to leave.

Chapter Twenty-Three

CHALDEAN CROSSING

As the light faded and the city at dusk disappeared behind him, Garris turned his attention to one last nagging question before admitting defeat and heading home. Blood Wolves never appeared outside the Alundeer Mountains. So the riddle of where they came from, and how they got here, was of some significance. And not a matter he could, in good conscience, ride away and leave unanswered. It seemed unlikely the council would give Dellia the latitude necessary to deal with the situation properly. So it fell to him to play protector one last time, to do the job the council wouldn't let Dellia do, and find the answer.

When Garris arrived at the spires the moon was just rising, a huge orange orb drifting above the desolate skyline. With its light glinting off the enormous teeth behind him, Garris searched by torchlight until he found a set of tracks coming from the southeast. Tracking at night was a foolhardy exercise, but there was little helping it. He had to act now, under cover of darkness, before his adversaries caught up. So, for hours, Garris followed the almost imperceptible tracks in the hard-packed ground as the spires vanished behind him and the Malthayan Mountains loomed larger and larger before him.

The moon sat large and high in the night sky by the time Garris pulled Kyri to a stop at the feet of the mountains. He slipped from his horse and knelt on the barren ground, focused intently on the puzzle before him.

Garris ran his fingers over a set of paw prints in the dust and dirt. Then, he reached over and examined a few broken twigs that hung from a trampled clump of dry, crumbled brush. It was undoubtedly the same wolves he'd been tracking, so he lifted his head and followed the paw prints back with his eyes to a point some distance out from a rock wall.

He rose and strolled a short way to where the tracks began. A thought entered his mind, so he looked up, and there, right above his head, lay a ledge. He needed confirmation, so he crouched down, studying the first set of impressions that seemed to appear out of thin air.

From behind, a shadow of a hand seemed to stretch out from the darkness, reaching for his shoulder. Garris shot up and whipped out his blade as he spun around to face the shadowy figure. From beneath his deep blue hood, Cain's scraggly face glanced down at the dagger held to his stomach.

"Really? We're doing this again?" his deep voice said.

"I don't recall asking for an escort," Garris replied.

"Just doing my job. Which if you recall is protecting you." Cain knelt and touched one of the paw prints. "You tracking the wolves?"

Garris motioned to the mountains. "They had to come from somewhere."

"We've already tried to figure out where they came from. The tracks just start here as if the wolves appeared out of nowhere."

"Maybe that's what they wanted you to find."

Cain shook his head. "You're determined to make this difficult, aren't you?"

Garris motioned to a ledge atop the rock face. "See up there? There's a path. It winds up into the mountains." He motioned to the prints at his feet. "See these prints? They're less distinct and deeper. I think they jumped down off of that path. To throw you off."

Cain raised an eyebrow. "Awfully smart, these wolves."

Garris strolled to a nearby shrub and lashed his horse to it. Then, he located a crevice in the rocks above and used it to hoist himself up, climbing the rock wall.

Cain muttered half to himself, "All costs, my foot," then followed behind as Garris pulled himself up onto a small path. He reached down and helped Cain up, and the two set out in silence along the narrow pathway.

Garris tracked the wolves for quite some time, occasionally stopping to examine some disturbed rock, broken twig, or smudged print in the dust. He halted at the almost imperceptible sound of snarls drifting down from the ledge above.

Garris motioned to the rock wall that bordered the right-hand side of the path, indicating the source of the noise. Cain nodded, and Garris began climbing the wall, grabbing onto ledges, cracks, and crevices to propel himself upward. When no sound came behind him, he paused to glance down.

Cain met his gaze with a look of annoyance, but after a moment he shook his head and followed.

Garris reached the top and peered over the edge at a huge plateau. There, a half dozen Blood Wolves roamed the area, along with a couple of the same gangly, three-clawed creatures that had accompanied them at the spires. A crackling sound carried across the flat expanse from a pair of pillars opposite them. A sheet of swirling darkness appeared between them and a new wolf leaped through. It landed badly and yelped. The other wolves swung around and began circling it.

The wounded beast took a couple limping steps before the other half dozen Blood Wolves lunged for it. Their jaws snapped down on its throat and legs and began tugging and pulling. The desperate wolf struggled, unable to breathe, until one of the wolves eviscerated it, and its entrails spilled out. The attackers dropped the throat and legs and dove for the open belly, snarling and snapping, devouring the whimpering wolf as it tried to drag itself away.

Garris yanked his head back below the edge. He'd seen enough.

Cain followed, and Garris was signaling to him to head out when a sudden silence interrupted the yipping and snarling. Garris paused for a second, then pulled himself up to peek over the edge again. Four of the wolves had their heads back and noses high in the air. The other two swiveled around and locked their eyes onto Garris. They stared for a split second, then in unison, they tore off away from him and toward a small pathway in the rocks.

He glanced down at Cain. "They caught our scent. They're coming."

The two slid off the rock wall and onto the dirt path. Garris dove down the passage with Cain following on his heels. The two raced over rocks and around jagged walls as the dusty trail twisted and turned its way down the mountain.

Cain pulled a dagger and yelled up ahead as he ran, "I'll handle this. You go find Dellia. Warn her. She can get word to the council."

Garris shouted back over his shoulder, "You're going to take on a pack of Blood Wolves with just a dagger?"

"Well excuse me. I left my scimitar in my other clothes. Now go."

"*You* go. I'll stay."

"This is my duty," Cain yelled back. "Besides, paralyzing daggers, remember. And I have the gift of shadows."

"What if they're shadow creatures? They'll see through it."

"I guess I'll find out. Now go, save my horse."

The pair raced through a narrow passage between two tall rock walls. Cain glanced up, halted, and spun back the way they'd come, standing his ground with his dagger ready.

Garris halted and returned to grasp Cain's forearm, giving it a firm shake.

Cain grinned as he rushed the words out. "I'd say it was a

pleasure, but really you've been kind of a pain."

"Oh yeah, don't look the Blood Wolves in the eye."

Cain shook his head. "Make that a huge pain."

"Promise me we'll meet again, so I can show you just how big a pain I can be."

"It's a promise."

Garris whipped around and took off down the path, careening around twists and turns at breakneck speed. Barks, yips, and snarls mixed with the plaintive cries of the wounded broke out behind him, then receded.

The path disappeared below Garris as he raced off the edge, out into thin air. The horses flew by under him, then he hit the ground, rolled, and leaped up. He grabbed the reins of both his and Cain's horses and flew up onto Kyri's back.

As the two steeds surged to a gallop, he reached behind him and snatched the crossbow slung over his bags. The desolate terrain flew by at a dazzling speed as the two horses' hooves pummeled the ground.

Behind him, one after another, the three wolves leaped from the cliff, landed, and bounded after him. They rapidly gained on him, their amber eyes flashing against their dark red fur as the scrubby brush of the plains raced by around them.

Garris loaded an arrow into the crossbow and twisted around in the saddle. The horse heaved and jolted under him as he shouldered the bow and took careful aim. The arrow whistled from the bow and arced back behind him, straight into the skull of the lead wolf. It toppled, end over end, as the two behind it crashed into it and tumbled across the dry, hard ground with a string of sharp yelps.

One of the wolves whimpered and couldn't seem to drag itself upright. The other snapped around and leaped onto it. Garris raced away with the snarls and growls of the two wolves tearing each other apart receding behind him.

Miles drifted one into the other, the hours passing reluctantly as Dellia stared at the moonlit ground. The gentle thumping of Ulka's hooves carried through the chill night air as she followed Enna's tracks into the desert.

The hard, dusty ground, with little discernible trail, gave way to sandy terrain where hoofprints could be seen with ease. She tried not to think about what lay ahead; in fact, she tried not to think at all, afraid she would be unable to face what she must do. Yet, her mind could not let go of the image of Jon, scared and alone, descending the temple steps, trying to be brave as a world he barely knew turned against him.

Dellia lifted her head, staring out across the desolate landscape. Finally, there up ahead, sat Jon, alone, leaning against a small rock outcropping. Behind him, the desert spread out to the base of dark mountains that rose up to meet a star-filled sky. Jon never looked up, never noticed her, even as she grew closer.

Eventually, his worried expression became visible in the moonlight, as if the weight of the world were on his shoulders. He sat with arms crossed and knees pulled up to his chest, trying to ward off the cold as he shivered in the chill night air.

Dellia halted and lowered her head, holding back her jumble of emotions. After a moment, she took a deep breath and raised herself up taller in the saddle. As she urged Ulka forward, she whispered under her breath, "My duty," reminding herself of her responsibility to the council and to the people Jon was one day destined to hurt or kill.

She was nearly upon him when Jon's head whipped up at the sound of her approach. His gaze shot over, his eyes wide open, appearing frightened and abandoned. But when he spotted her, his face lit up, and a broad smile spread across it. For a moment, it seemed as if he was fighting back tears.

"You're alone," Dellia said.

Jon turned and glanced over his shoulder as he subtly brushed his eyes. "No. Enna is here with me."

She couldn't quite hide the shakiness in her voice as she said, "I left you. How could I do that?"

He gazed up at her with kindness. "Don't be upset with my friend Dellia. She doesn't deserve it."

She dismounted and crouched next to him. "You're shivering. Why didn't you light a fire?"

Jon glanced away, and a long pause followed before his reluctant response. "I don't know how."

Dellia returned to her horse and found a warm blanket. Upon returning to Jon, she draped it over his trembling shoulders. Then, she came around in front and rubbed his arms in an effort to warm him up.

She focused on her work, unable to look him in the eyes. "I'm not feeling like I've been much of a friend to you right now."

Another reluctant pause followed, then Jon's head dropped. "To be honest, I thought you were done with me, after all the lies I told."

She stopped and stared at him, wounded by his words. "I was mad at you, ya dummy. It doesn't mean I wanted you to run off into the desert alone and get yourself killed."

He glanced up at her and smiled. "Oh, so you *do* care."

Unable to smile back, she threw herself into her rubbing. "It's not funny. Why do you always have to be like that? Why can't you yell at me, or call me names. ..." She stopped her rubbing and looked him in the face. "Or hate me?"

Her voice cracked, and Jon looked up into her eyes as bewilderment and affection filled his face. When he spoke, his words were almost absentminded. "I could never hate you."

Dellia's heart nearly stopped. All she could do was stare.

Suddenly, the look of affection faded, and Jon glanced away, appearing self-conscious. "I owe you so much," he said as if trying to explain the moment away.

Dellia stopped her rubbing and sat down, facing Jon. "Oh, don't say that. You don't owe me anything." She forced a smile, but it was as if Jon could see right through her, as if he could see right into her heart. A sudden sadness filled his eyes. "What have I done to you? I've ruined your life. I wish you'd never met me."

Dellia's head whipped up. "I don't," she shot back. Jon seemed startled by her abruptness.

She stared for a moment, and a sudden compulsion forced the words out. "I need you to know something. To remember something for me." She placed her hands on his, much as she'd done when they first met. "We're friends, Jon. I will always be on your side. I can get angry or upset, but I care about you. I will always come back to that. That's my center. Remember that. Please. No matter what happens. Because the truth is I—" She averted her gaze. "I don't have a lot of friends."

He sat for a moment, seeming baffled by the sudden outpouring of affection. "That's crazy. Why would you say that?"

"Because it's true. Look at the way I treated you."

"No way. You're one of the easiest people I know to get along with."

She hung her head. "You're only saying that because I don't currently have a knife to your throat."

Jon smiled, but it slipped away when he saw that she was serious. "But I lied to you. I understand. I get it."

"No, you don't. Not completely."

He looked at her with a puzzled expression, seeming at a loss for words.

"Look, my people, my gift, it doesn't always work. Too many conflicting emotions, they mask it."

Jon spoke quietly to himself. "Like trying to hear a whisper on a crowded battlefield."

Dellia froze and stared at him. Those words were an ancient saying, known to only a few among her people. To hear them from the lips of someone foreign to her world was startling.

"How could you know that saying?"

Jon's response was matter-of-fact. "It was something Ellira said."

She sat for a moment, stunned and speechless. How could he know the source of the saying?

He seemed compelled to fill the awkward silence. "She told of those who tried to heighten their gift by excising emotion. She blamed it for their ruthlessness, and for giving your gift a bad name."

Dellia heard her voice say, "You can't possibly ..." Jon watched her, expectant, as if waiting for her to continue. "Right," she said, as she snapped out of it. "So ... I try not to hold back what I'm feeling. I express myself. Which, as you've seen, can be hard on friendships."

"No. You're just doing as Ellira taught. Because it helps with your gift. See, I told you, I understand. I get it."

She shook her head as she gawked at him again. "You constantly amaze me. How do you know that?"

"I read it in Ellira's journal. The one I found in the tower."

Now it was Dellia's turn to watch Jon as she waited for an explanation.

"Yeah, we found it at the top of the tower. I tried to tell you in Mundus."

He seemed to brace himself, as if waiting for a rebuke.

She lowered her head. This was not the act of someone prophesied to destroy a civilization. Finding that journal was a historic act of inspiration to her people and to her. But it also meant so much more. Dellia raised her head and peered into Jon's eyes.

"Then you really did save my life, didn't you?"

"Yeah, when you fell I opened a portal below you, sent you to safety."

For a moment she was at peace, her troubles banished by his gentle blue eyes.

Then it all came rushing back. She had a duty, no matter what she thought, no matter how she felt, no matter how kind or generous he may seem. Dellia tore her eyes from Jon's and looked out across the sandy, moonlit desert. She would never be with him. And no matter what may be in her heart, these few moments between them were all that would ever be.

Jon must have sensed her sadness. "No, that's a good thing. Why is that a sad thing?"

"I'm sorry. It's just ..." Hiding her face, Dellia stood up and strolled around behind Jon. She lifted the blanket from his shoulders and slung it around her own. "You're still shivering. Scoot forward."

He did, and Dellia slipped down behind him. Opening the blanket wide, she invited him inside. "Come here. You need to rest."

He leaned back against her side, his shivering body next to hers, as she wrapped the blanket around them both. Jon rested his head back on her shoulder. Moments passed with him gazing up at the thousands of stars that swept across the desert sky. His warm body next to her, her arm pulling him close. Then he pulled forward a little and turned to face her.

"Dellia," he said.

"Yeah," she replied.

Jon looked into her eyes. "Truth is, I didn't want you to find me. Look, I know in my heart this prophecy is wrong about me, but this world doesn't know that. I saw how people reacted. I can't stand the idea that this stain on me could hurt you."

Dellia stared back, and her heart filled with affection even as it became heavier.

He seemed to summon his courage. "You worked your whole

life to become who you are. Don't let me be the reason you lose that. It would break my heart. Please just leave. I'll find my own way home."

Dellia paused as a rush of emotions pulled her in different directions. He had left for her. He had risked his life to save her from pain. Yet the pain of what she must do to him tore at her. Dellia lowered her head, unable to look Jon in the eyes.

He glanced away, out across the barren desert at the outline of distant mountains against a star-filled sky. After a moment, he tried again. "Dellia, don't let me take you down with me."

She struggled to set aside her angst. If she were to make it through this, the only way would be to focus on the present and on protecting Jon, rather than a chain of events she could no longer change.

"No." Dellia raised her head and looked into his eyes. "I'm staying with you ... till the end."

"But why?"

She pulled him close, and he leaned into her side, resting his head back on her shoulder again. As her arm hugged him tight, she sighed. "Because you're not even going in the right direction."

Jon opened his eyes to the near darkness of just before dawn and the warmth of Dellia's leg under his cheek. Half-asleep, he gazed past her feet, across the flat, sandy terrain that stretched out to meet a dark, star-filled horizon.

His eyes turned upward, and Jon smiled as he gazed up into Dellia's peaceful face, framed by the thousands of specks of dim light in the predawn sky. He'd fallen asleep with his head on her shoulder. How it had drifted down to her leg, he wasn't quite sure, but it felt right to have her so close.

He rubbed his eyes and lifted his head from her lap just as a lizard darted through his line of sight. Slowly, he pulled himself up and removed the heavy blanket. Dellia never stirred, still asleep, still resting against the rock outcropping. Raising his arms over his head, he stretched as he admired the wispy, red clouds set against the deep blue sky, hanging over the glowing outline of faraway mountains.

Jon paused for a moment, gazing down at Dellia's serene face. It was a stark contrast to the the woman of the night before. At times she had been the same one he'd met that first day in the Illis Woods. And there were moments when he felt such a strong connection, and everything seemed right. Then, in an instant, she would turn cloudy and distraught, and it was difficult to shake the feeling that he was at the heart of her sadness. Often, he wanted to say something, or do something, and the only thing holding him back was the certainty that there were no good answers to the questions he wished to ask.

He wanted to stay and gaze at that face for hours, but Jon glanced away and took a deep breath. Dellia was right, he didn't even know which direction to go—but he couldn't bear seeing her distress and knowing he was the cause.

There was no getting away from her; she could track him down with ease, no matter where he went. But he needed to try, to give her one last chance, now that she knew of his concern, for her to walk away from all that surrounded him and go back to her world.

Jon gathered his belongings and prepared Enna to leave. Then, he took one last, long look at Dellia before he turned and led Enna away. Once he had put some distance between them, he mounted and urged her forward.

Enna seemed reluctant at first, throwing frequent glances backward, and it was difficult not to feel guilty for separating her from Ulka. Instead of abating, that guilt only grew with each gentle thud of her hooves in the sand. As they headed northward, the skyline grew brighter, and Dellia receded behind him, becoming a distant spot on the glowing horizon.

DELLIA

Eventually, Jon stopped and turned to take another last look. He slipped the eight-sided dragon coin out of his pocket and gazed at it for a moment. Guilt still nagged him, and all of a sudden, it felt like he was running away. A flush of shame overcame him, and he hung his head.

Dellia had decided to stay by his side until the end, and he wanted her with him. And in so many ways, the only time he felt at ease was when she was around. So why was he still running?

Then it hit him. It was fear. He was terrified that if he stayed, it would lead to telling Dellia of his feelings, and if he did that, it would be a repeat of what happened with Megan in the lab. Only with Dellia it would be so much worse, and with that realization came a truth: that he was never as much in love with Megan as he was with the idea of a life with her. With Dellia it was so much deeper and more profound, and he had been using his concern for her as an excuse, a way of avoiding that truth. He loved Dellia more than anyone he had ever loved in his life, and he was petrified of being rejected by her as he had been by Megan. So he had been running from her since the Talus Plains, and it was becoming a habit. One he couldn't bring himself to repeat again. This was not the answer.

He slid the coin back in his pocket and brought Enna around. Then, with no urging, she headed briskly back across the barren desert toward Dellia. Returning wasn't going to change anything, of course, but perhaps it was time to stop being afraid. To tell her how concerned he was and ask her what was wrong. As terrified as he was of the answers, at least then he wouldn't be leaving behind her back. If he left, it would be because they both agreed it was best.

Dellia grew closer as Enna trotted toward her. Then, a whistling sound cut the predawn silence, followed by a dull thunk.

Jon glanced down at an arrow sunk deep into his stomach. A sick feeling hit along with blinding pain. His hand flew up, holding his stomach. Blood oozed from the wound, running down over his fingers as he began to slide off of Enna.

He tipped over and tumbled to the ground, landing on his back, faceup, staring at the few remaining dim stars in the morning sky. The world around him became surreal as if he were drifting away. He closed his eyes, struggling to remain awake as his breathing became rough and raspy.

This was the end. A wound like this could bleed out in minutes. Even if he somehow reached Dellia, she couldn't save him now. A sudden cold took hold, and he began to shiver. All his indecision seemed so trivial. He was going to die, never having taken a chance, never having told Dellia how he felt.

Jon raised his head and opened his eyes, staring across the flat, sandy expanse at Dellia in the distance. She was still sleeping peacefully with her head resting on the rock outcropping. He reached out to her as his eyes closed and his body went limp.

Chapter Twenty-Four

LOST IN THE DESERT

The gentle thudding of hooves carried along the crisp dawn air from a dozen soldiers spread out down the dirt road behind her. Rocking gently in the saddle, Kayleen glanced back over her shoulder at the billowy charcoal clouds that crowded the predawn sky above Mount Karana. They shrouded her home in a darkness that extended from the Shir Courtyard, high on the plateau down the winding stairway to Shirdon, nestled at the base of the mountain.

She watched for a while as the lanterns in the city windows vanished behind rolling hills. A reminder of the life she needed to reclaim and the importance of the journey before her.

Kayleen faced forward again, toward the dark clouds above a deep red skyline. She used to travel this road with Garris as he left for missions. He would always make fun of her "foolish insistence on pestering him as I was leaving," and she would tease him for trying to get her in trouble with his mother Eejha for not seeing him off.

The last time she spoke to her sister Leanna was on this same road on a morning much like this one as she departed. Her sister had made herself an expert on The Prophecy of the Otherworlder. She'd become intrigued when she discovered ancient references to a prophecy the Augury knew nothing about.

When news of Prisha reached her, Leanna had brought her discovery to the council. Seeing her as a source of critical information, they sent her to meet Prisha. Kayleen had strenuously objected to sending an untrained civilian into such a threatening situation, but they were determined to "control events." She never saw Leanna again.

So here she was, following in her sister's footsteps, going to confront someone from another world. Now, as then, dark and hidden forces seemed drawn to Jon like a moth to a flame, and the possibility that she could be following in her sister Leanna's footsteps filled her with trepidation. Kayleen sighed. The only thing she could do now was to make sure she and Dellia didn't suffer the same fate as Garris or Leanna.

Far down the road, a group of carts and horses approached with lanterns still lit. No doubt farmers on their way to sell goods in the Shirdon Market. In front of her, Quirtus, the captain of the detail, kept a watchful eye on them. Calm and relaxed, he led the way down a thoroughfare that wound through the rolling hills, far into the distance. It was comforting to have a trusted ally with her, particularly given the troubling developments of the last few hours.

Attempting to go unnoticed, Kayleen glanced back at the clump of three rough men plodding along separately from the rest. The group stood out, each having the same red leather chest plate with a crude likeness of a flaming horse etched into the surface. They were the men Braye had assigned, and though they were not part of her usual detail, their reputation was well known. Of the two largest and most imposing, Grekor had to be the leader. It was apparent in the way the other two treated him. Pedrus grumbled and complained but never contradicted him, and the small and lithe Nikosh, with all his combative talk, avoided looking him in the eye.

Ever alert, Nikosh caught Kayleen eyeing him and returned a fleeting glance.

She faced forward again as Quirtus dropped back next to her. In a quiet voice he said, "You know, if you're trying to keep an eye on them, I'd suggest being a little less obvious."

Almost under her breath, Kayleen replied, "Why? They'll slit my throat in my sleep one way or the other."

Quirtus let out a low chuckle. "Well, don't be shy there, Kayleen, tell me what you really think."

She stared ahead as she mumbled, "You don't want to know what I really think."

He paused, and when she glanced over, his countenance appeared troubled. "Wait. You're serious."

She simply eyed him with a solemn expression.

"Listen, if something is going on that affects this mission or my men, you need to tell me. You owe me that."

A cart of produce bound for Shirdon rattled and creaked past, the light from its lantern casting long shadows across the hard-packed dirt road. Kayleen leaned in toward Quirtus and lowered her voice even more. "For one thing, my dagger is missing." She motioned to her empty scabbard with her eyes. "I had it when we met in Shirdon, but now it's gone."

As if to avoid drawing attention to the missing dagger, Quirtus returned his gaze ahead. "The onyx one, with the silver, dragon-claw pommel?"

"Yes. And the only contact I've had since are the men in this detail."

"It's very distinctive. Why take something so easily recognized?" He motioned toward the three riders with a subtle nod of his head. "You think one of them took it?"

"No ... well, yes. I mean, I don't know. The dagger is just the latest. It wasn't why I was watching them."

Quirtus looked back at the three men.

Nikosh seemed to notice him watching and adopted an almost imperceptible sneer.

Quirtus leaned over again and spoke quietly to Kayleen. "But something about them has you worried. What is it?"

She paused for a moment, reflecting on the question, trying to put her vague sense of unease into words. "This is my personal detail. All handpicked men. Ten of our best soldiers, along with Dellia and I. All to bring in one man." She motioned to the three outsiders with her eyes. "Do you really imagine those three extra men were necessary, that they'd make some kind of difference?"

"I guess I assumed they were here to keep an eye on us."

"Of course." She glanced again at the three imposing men. "But look at those men. They are not the soldiers you'd assign if insight and discretion were your aims. Those are men known for their ruthless efficiency. You don't assign those guys to merely watch. Or to protect a prisoner. You assign them when you want something distasteful done."

"Hmm. I see what you mean. But in that case, what about Tetch? He worries me more than those three."

"Who?" Kayleen said.

Quirtus motioned with his head to another man also riding separately. He was unfamiliar to her and unnoticed until now. Small, lean, and dark, with wild red hair, his eyes darted to catch every sound or movement, yet he appeared unusually calm. He threw Kayleen a quick glance, then his eyes shot away.

"Tetch," Quirtus said. "He wasn't one of the men you chose. He replaced Lanse. It was suggested I choose him for this unit." He leaned a little closer and lowered his voice. "And by 'suggest,' I mean given an ultimatum."

A hundred questions flooded Kayleen's awareness. "What happened to Lanse? Why wasn't I consulted? These are *my* men."

"It happened just before you were removed. Sorry. And it was made clear to me that these are not your men anymore."

She eyed Quirtus with surprise. "Oh. Does that mean you have some secret orders I'm not privy to?"

"No, no. The council was quite forceful in ensuring I follow your orders to the letter."

She stared for another long moment as she sifted through the implications. "Why do I find that the opposite of reassuring?"

Quirtus didn't answer; he simply kept his eyes on the glowing horizon.

Kayleen peeked over her shoulder again at the three imposing men, then faced forward. "One thing is clear. This whole situation has the council spooked. And when a group like that gets scared, they stop questioning and thinking clearly. They talk themselves into stories that make no sense. They chart a course that is reckless and dangerous. And that's when they hurt people."

Quietus shrugged. "If you say so. You're the politician. I'm just a soldier. I follow orders."

"I can't protect anyone if I'm outside the council. Not the people, or my friends, or even myself. If I'm to be any good to anyone, I must regain my position on the council. And to have any hope of doing that, I need this mission to go well." Kayleen stared right at him, making sure there was no misunderstanding. "So my orders are simple. We find a way to bring Jon in and deliver him to the council, no matter what may come."

Quirtus gave a quick nod of acknowledgment and spurred his horse on.

Dark clouds still hung above an orange and red sunrise as he pulled ahead, leading the way down the long road that wandered through the hillside and far into the distance. Somewhere on that horizon lay a rendezvous with Dellia and Jon that she must navigate with care. And to do that, she needed to account for every factor that might affect the outcome. There would be no rest or respite on this trip. She needed every second to plan and learn and, by any means necessary, discover what secret orders had been sent along with Grekor and his group.

It was a warning purchased at the cost of a man's life. The image of Cain standing alone against a pack of Blood Wolves haunted his imagination. So Garris rode hard, straight back to Gatia's house in Mundus. There, he scaled the heavy brick wall and slipped silently into the room he'd shared with Jon, only to discover it was empty. It wasn't entirely unexpected. If the reaction of the crowd outside the temple was any indication, Jon would not find the city welcoming for long. Still, it was not him but Dellia he needed to speak with, so he crept down the hall, only to find what he expected—Dellia was gone, too. Instead, Aishi lay sleeping peacefully in her room.

A hurried ride to the stables confirmed what he suspected: they'd already left. He "acquired" a lantern from within and made a quick survey of the surrounding area. That led to a lone set of familiar tracks headed cross-country to the north. It wasn't exactly the right direction, and it was only one set, but from the characteristic shape and size, it appeared to be Enna. After a short time, a second set of tracks joined them, and from their appearance, it had to be Ulka. That they hadn't started out together seemed strange, but it didn't matter as long as he was on Dellia's trail.

He struggled to stay awake those many sleepless hours. Wrapped in a blanket, Garris tracked the two by the light of the lantern, far out across the plains and into the desert. Slouching in the saddle, tired and haggard from the long journey in the cold night, Garris trudged on through sandy terrain until the small hours of the morning.

The sun had just barely risen above the mountains far across the sand to the east when Garris pulled Kyri to a stop in front of Dellia. As troubling as it was to find her with no Jon, the other signs were even more disturbing. Guilt seized him for leaving Jon alone, but he quickly suppressed it. This was no time to let sentimentality turn him into an idiot.

Garris dismounted and crouched before Dellia as she sat asleep against a rock outcropping. He scanned the sandy terrain and shook his head.

"I don't like it," he mumbled to himself.

Dellia's eyes fluttered open at the sound of his voice, and she stared, half-asleep. "Garris? I'm confused, I thought you were gone."

"It's not me you should be worried about." Garris looked around.

Her sleepy face appeared puzzled for a moment, then flashed with alarm. She looked down at her lap and patted it. Her eyes flew straight up, staring into Garris's face. "Where's Jon?"

Before he could utter a word, she bolted to her feet. He stood and crossed his arms, watching as her gaze flew all around like a wild woman's, scouring their camp.

She spotted Ulka standing alone. "He did it again. He left. He just—" Dellia stopped when she spied Enna a short distance away. "No. Enna is ... loose?" She spun around, searching everywhere, until she spotted the tracks heading north across the white sands. She followed them with her eyes. "He did leave, with Enna. ... But then why? ... Oh, no."

Garris stared at her. "I think you're up to speed now. So—"

Dellia tore off down the tracks at a sprint.

He shook his head as he mounted Kyri. She was letting her feelings get the best of her instead of using her head. Garris steered Kyri over to Enna, then followed her tracks back, passing Dellia with ease.

He stopped and flew off Kyri when he spotted a well-trodden patch of desert. He shook his head as he surveyed the area. Things were going from bad to worse. Resisting the urge to let his imagination get the best of him, Garris continued assessing the scene as Dellia raced up beside him.

Garris pointed to the tracks. "Hmm," he grunted. "He did leave, but he was headed back when—"

"He fell off his horse."

He crouched down, examining a depression in the sand most probably made by a falling body. "At least there's no blood."

Dellia stared at the spot, her eyes wide. "You know that doesn't mean anything. And where are the footprints?"

"Exactly what I was thinking. I see Enna's tracks coming and going, and where Jon hit the ground, but whether he walked away or was carried, there should be footprints." Garris stood and turned toward her. "Someone didn't want to be followed."

Dellia turned to face him. On the verge of hysteria, her words raced out. "Then how do we find him?"

Garris stepped back and put his hands up. He'd come to deliver an urgent message, not get dragged back into this whole mess. Sure, he wanted to help Jon. Way more than he should. He'd grown entirely too fond of the little twerp. And it was difficult to resist Dellia's pleading face, but he must. This was exactly the kind of disaster-filled misadventure that destroyed lives and got friends killed. Not this time.

"Whoa, whoa. What do you mean 'we'?"

"I thought …" Dellia stared. "Then why are you here?"

Garris looked into her scared face. "The wolf threat isn't over. I saw them gathering through a portal in the Malthayan Mountains south of Mundus. Could be hours, could be days or weeks, but something worse is coming. Much worse. You need to warn the council."

Having delivered his message and eager not to drag this out into some huge melodrama, Garris pivoted and mounted Kyri.

Dellia watched in apparent panic. "So you're just going to leave?"

He swung himself up on Kyri. "That's the plan."

"So Jon is gone. Who knows what happened to him … what *is*

happening to him. More wolves are coming, probably to kill him, with nothing to stop them. And you're just going to walk away?"

Garris swallowed the lump in his throat. "I told you, I'm not traveling this path again."

"But Jon is your friend. What about the message? What about your vow to help him?"

"That's my business, not yours."

"And Jon isn't your business?" Dellia said.

"Not anymore." He gave Kyri a gentle urging forward. His words sounded harsh and cold, and he hated telling her no, but he had to.

As Kyri carried him away, Dellia's desperate voice came from behind. "Wow. Here I was, thinking you were an honorable man. Someone who did what was right, no matter what. Boy, was I wrong. You're just a coward."

Her words stung and his guilt came rushing back. And with it, anger at Dellia's harsh words. He halted Kyri and turned back. "You don't know me. You don't know anything about me. This prophecy has taken everything important in my life and it turned me into someone you should hunt and kill, not beg for help. Someday, when someone you care about has been hurt or died because of you, then maybe you will have earned the right to sit in judgment of me."

Garris began to leave again but stopped and turned Kyri back to face her a second time. "And how dare you lecture me about doing what's right. I just told you wolves are coming that could threaten lives across an entire region, and all you care about is one man. I pray you never have to choose, but right now all I see is a girl who'd say anything to save someone she cares about, no matter who gets hurt or killed."

Dellia stared at him, stunned and speechless. After a moment, she recovered. "You're wrong, I care about every single life in Meerdon. And I care what happens to you."

"Really? So what happens when the council orders you to kill me?"

"Kayleen would never do that," Dellia said.

Garris couldn't suppress a scornful laugh. "You really do have no idea who you're working for."

She seemed shocked for a moment, then became even more adamant. "I would never kill you."

"That's real easy to say when you've never faced that choice."

She stood and stared as he brought Kyri around to leave again. He stopped with his back to Dellia as she spoke.

"You're right. I don't know what you've been through. But I do feel the scars of it. And I also know guilt, and regret, and remorse. They are all around me, in almost everyone. If you turn away from this, and something happens to Jon, or to Erden, or me, that guilt will be far worse than anything you're feeling now. It will haunt you. It will scar you forever. It will destroy you."

Garris remained staunch, staring ahead at the sun rising over the distant mountains. There was a ring of truth to her words, but neither they nor his desire to help nor his nagging guilt changed anything. He never uttered another word or peered back. He simply urged Kyri forward, and the sand kicked up beneath her hooves as she shot to a gallop, racing away across the sands of the Chaldean Desert.

A soft dripping sound pricked Jon's awareness as his thoughts swirled through a haze. His eyes opened but remained unfocused in the dark. Searing pain stabbed at his stomach, and his breath came in shuddering gasps as he lifted his head. He attempted to pull himself upright, but the movement brought searing agony, and he cried out, his breath coming in quick, wheezing gulps.

Jon's head slumped, and he tried to remain still as the pain eased and his eyes focused. Indistinct, blurry shapes became ropes that bound his chest. Below them, blood oozed from an arrow in his stomach. The dripping sound was his blood dribbling down to puddle on the damp stone floor beneath his feet. The ropes tied him to what felt like an enormous post behind him and lashed his wrists firmly to his sides.

Jon tried to struggle against his bindings. His head whipped up as crippling pain shot through his insides. He cried out, and his breathing became short and quick again. As his rapid gasps subsided, he slowly glanced around. Dim light flickered through an opening to his left, illuminating the small, damp cave of his captivity.

Footsteps approached, and the thudding of his heartbeat quickened in his ears as the outline of a rather small man appeared in the opening. He stood for a moment surveying Jon, his silhouette dark against the vague light. Jon remained as still as possible as the man strolled over. He was stout, and his gait and manner possessed a brusque and businesslike air as he seated himself on an overturned crate a short distance from Jon. As he drew a deep breath, the dim light from a nearby lantern threw shadows across his jowly face, giving him a menacing look that was at odds with his well-groomed gray hair and beard.

He turned his attention to Jon, staring up into his face with an amiable expression. "I must apologize, Jon. I had hoped we could reach some kind of understanding. Not that we'd be friends, mind you. I'm not delusional. But I had hoped you'd come to appreciate your situation and be reasonable."

His mind still in a haze, all Jon could manage was, "Huh? I don't understand. Why am I tied up?"

The small man scowled. "Don't change the subject, I'm explaining that arrow." He reached out and nearly touched it.

Jon winced. The pain tore at him again, and he cried out.

The small man leaned back, smiling at his torment. He waited for Jon's distress to ease, then said, "It was meant for your horse."

Sickened by the image of Enna with an arrow in her, Jon blurted out, "No. No. Not Enna! Why would you hurt Enna?"

Seeming intrigued by his distress, the small man said, "You're tied to a post with an arrow in your gut, and you're worried about a filthy beast of burden?" He cocked his head and eyed him for a moment, then his lips curled into an amused smile. "Interesting."

Still muddled and disoriented, Jon said, "What did you do to Enna? Why would you hurt her?"

"Don't worry. She's fine … for now. I was trying to take her down with that arrow. So I could capture you on foot. But I missed, and I'm afraid your wound is quite fatal."

"Fatal? You mean I'm going to die?"

"Well, yeah. In this situation, 'fatal' means 'resulting in death.' So, that is generally what I was getting at." The small man shook his head. "I heard you were smart, Jon. This is going to take much longer than I thought if I have to explain simple words like 'fatal.' "

"But why would you …" Jon's mind cleared enough to make sense of his situation. Nauseated, he let out a small gasp as a deep dread crept into his soul. "Oh no, you're going to torture me."

The small man's placid demeanor now seemed thoroughly disturbing. "Oh, I doubt torture will be necessary. That arrow is going to be painful enough, and if not I can just kill Enna."

The thought threw Jon into a panic. "No. No. No. You don't need to do any of this. I'll tell you whatever you want. Anything."

The small man beamed a satisfied smile. "You see? I had a hunch you'd see reason. Okay, let's start with who advised you and Megan to separate."

"I don't know. It wasn't my idea," Jon said, desperate to convince the man his desire to comply was genuine. "It must have been the ones who took her."

"Hmm. Well, okay, then where is Megan now?"

"What? Why do you want Megan? …" He gulped, and his

breathing deepened as the full scope of his predicament dawned on him. "Oh, no. You want to torture her."

"No," the man said, "I promise. She'll never feel a thing."

"Never feel ..." Jon shuddered. The desire to comply gave way to an impenetrable resolve. And with it, desperation and dread at the realization of what he would be forced to endure. Through trembling lips, his weak voice said, "I'm not telling you anything."

"Okay," said the small man, "but I hope you said your goodbyes to your horsie." Then he signaled to something or someone beyond the opening.

Almost in tears, Jon pleaded, "No, no, no. Please, don't hurt her." He struggled against his rough bindings, desperate to get free. He cried out as the arrow ripped at his insides. His breathing grew short and rapid once again, and he cast his gaze all around the dimly lit space, desperate for any avenue of escape. But as he scanned the rough, dank walls, his attention was drawn back to the small, creepy man, his demeanor now hard and harsh.

"Tell me what I want to know," he said, "and I'll remove the arrow and let you bleed out." In an instant, the small man's manner turned soft and gentle, and he motioned to Jon's wound and bindings. "Then all this suffering will be over. And Enna will be safe."

Unsure if he could endure what was coming, but certain he had to, Jon held back tears as his meek words eked out. "I can't help you hurt my friends. I'll never tell you anything."

The small man donned a sympathetic expression and shook his head. "I truly don't think you appreciate your predicament." He pointed to the arrow stuck in Jon's stomach. "Because of that arrow, any movement will be agonizing, and you really can't avoid moving. ..." His manner grew hard and menacing again as he reached out and grasped Jon's little finger, yanking on it to emphasize each word. "... if ... I ... do ... *this*."

On the last word, the small man wrenched Jon's finger. There was a sickening crack and jab of pain as the finger twisted backward into an unnatural position. He cried out, then gasped and shuddered and a second, searing pain shot through his gut.

"Don't worry," the small man said, "it's only dislocated. An important step for what comes next."

His words were like a whisper in a hurricane of agony. Jon's head became heavy as his thoughts swam through a debilitating nausea. The dark cavern and the small man seemed to grow distant and unreal before everything drifted away into darkness.

Chapter Twenty-Five

TO BE FREE AGAIN

Dellia needed to focus on the task before her, but how could she, when all her determination and optimism seemed to be drowning in a sea of endless sand? To lose him. To not know whether he'd been captured, or was injured, or even dead—it was torment. Yet she pushed forward, plodding through the hot desert for hours on end, staring at nothing but unending white sands, searching for any sign of Jon. Enna plodding alongside her, remaining a constant reminder that he was out there somewhere, lost and alone. And her every instinct was telling her something horrible had happened to him.

Having swept a vast area multiple times and checked every sheltered location she could recall, Dellia was forced to accept that there was nothing here to find. Not only had she failed to locate Jon, but she hadn't even seen one track or sign that might hint at where he'd gone. He had just vanished. So she did the only thing she could think to do and headed for Kanlu, in the forlorn hope he might have somehow made it there.

The journey to the city seemed to drag on forever as the endless white terrain gave way to vegetation, then rocky forested hills. Dellia spent the trip trying not to dwell on the most horrifying explanation of all: that tracks existed, and something or someone with the power to hide them had abducted Jon.

It all seemed so hopeless. What would she tell Kayleen when she arrived empty-handed? Even if she found Jon, how could she turn over the man she loved? But most of all, how had she let herself fall for him in the first place when it was forbidden? Yet the more she tried to talk herself out of her feelings, the worse they got. And the more disconnected she became from her gift.

Eventually, she arrived at a craggy hillside overlooking the southernmost tip of the city. Exhausted and spent, Dellia crouched next to Ulka and Enna, peering down the cliffside at the outskirts of Kanlu as it curved along the lakeside, disappearing out of sight behind the hills. Far below, slant-roofed houses lined the peaceful shoreline. Beyond them, quaint fishing boats spread out across crystal waters, almost to the horizon. And further inland, courtyards dotted the landscape, each surrounded by a collection of single-story build-ings and connected by a loose network of simple dirt roads.

At another time, she might have stopped to admire the tranquil beauty of the scene, but not today. Now, all that consumed her was the overwhelming magnitude of the task before her and the sheer hopelessness of her chances of finding Jon.

Soft footsteps and the gentle thumping of hooves drew her attention from the futility of scouring every nook and cranny of the city. A person and horse came to a stop behind her. So Dellia closed her eyes and calmed her despairing heart.

With practiced concentration, she reached out with what minute speck of her gift she could summon. She could often identify a person by their normal state of being. Some would feel impatient or angry all the time, while others might feel happy or serene. A tumult of conflicting emotions snuffed out the last shred of her ability as she recognized that unique brand of irritable cynicism.

Still crouched, Dellia closed her eyes. "I thought you'd be far from here by now."

"Couldn't," came Garris's voice from behind her.

"Hmm," she grumbled, trying to hide her anger at being aban-doned and her relief that he'd returned.

"Because you were wrong."

Dellia rose and turned to face him. He stood there with Kyri's reins in his hands, his expression placid and unreadable, but appearing as tired and spent as she felt.

She glanced down at the ground. "Then you came a long way to tell me something I already knew."

"I'm no coward."

She cringed, then looked up at him. "Garris—"

"But I am a hunted man." He barged ahead. "And there comes a point when you have to realize you've done all you can do. But I did make a promise … a promise to help Jon. And nothing is more important to me than my word."

"You were right. That's none of my business."

"So, perhaps I gave up too easily. See, I was out there headed home when I realized I've spent the last fifteen years training for something and I don't even know what. So I decided it's you."

"Me?" said Dellia.

"Yeah, you. Well, you and Jon. The council, and demons, and prophecies, and hundreds-of-year old promises—I don't trust any of it. And there's no way I'm going to risk my life for any of that."

Dellia glanced down and nodded her head.

"But right now, there are two people who need my help. That's simple. That I understand. People in trouble. People who fought by my side. So I'll stand by yours now. Until I can't any longer."

She stared. Garris seldom showed much emotion, yet the sincerity in his eyes was touching, and his sure and determined words were a desperately needed lifeline. Dellia struggled to maintain her composure. She had always striven to be strong and independent, but someone she deeply cared about was in trouble, and the relief that flooded in at knowing Garris would have her back was intense. She threw her arms around him and gave him a firm hug.

He went all stiff and glanced about like a cornered animal. He was clearly uncomfortable, and when she didn't let go after a second, he gave her a forced pat on the back. "Whoa there. Easy. I don't recall there being quite so much hugging when I trained as a protector."

Dellia let go and stepped back. Garris stood staring past her at the peaceful lakeside community below. Up until now, she had needed to stay strong, but with Garris here to share her burden, Dellia let all the bottled-up desperation and sadness race back.

"I can't find him," she said.

"I know," said Garris. "I've searched. It's not like someone covered their tracks. It's like they never existed."

"I don't know what to do. I'm grasping at straws. I came to Kanlu hoping he somehow made his way here."

Garris's confident face gazed into hers. "Look, we'll find him."

"How?"

"We'll *find* him." Garris was insistent.

"And then what? Because you were right. I can't put my feelings above the good of everyone. So if I find him, I'll have to—" Dellia stopped and shook her head. "I don't even know if I want to find him."

"I know," said Garris.

"But I have to. He could be—"

"I know," he repeated, his voice strong and reassuring. He smiled and put a hand on Dellia's shoulder. "Let's just start by searching Kanlu."

Dellia nodded, and the two began to lead the horses along a modest path that wound its way down through the sparse woods to the base of the cliffs. There among the trees at the outskirts of Kanlu lay a large stable surrounding a brick courtyard. They could shelter their horses there while they searched the city.

As they strolled along past twisted trees and scraggly brush, Garris eyed Dellia with a thoughtful expression. "Did you ever think that maybe something happens to Jon, in the future, to make him go bad? And the whole point of the prophecy is for us to get him home before then?"

Dellia peered down at the well-worn path as she mulled the concept over. Her words were as gloomy as her mood. "Or get him thrown in a deep dark dungeon so he'll never see home again."

He looked over at her, clearly taken aback. After a moment, he tried again. "Or to be there to stop him from going bad."

"Or maybe it's happening right now, and we'll have to kill him before he can do any harm."

"What?" Garris halted and stared. "Why would you say that?" He shook his head and resumed their stroll. "I'm trying to be positive here … work with me."

His reaction struck a chord, and she realized this was not the person she needed to be. If she was to stand any chance of finding Jon, she needed to stay positive.

Dellia glanced at Garris and forced a smile. "Then stop saying stupid things like 'Jon going bad.' I mean, can you even picture that?" She bugged her eyes and waved her hands in the air. "Evil Jon," she said, mocking Garris.

He smiled. "All right, all right. Point taken."

They turned a corner, and the stable came into full view before them. Garris pulled a scarf over his face, shielding his appearance from view. Dellia glanced over at him walking next to her. He was strong and capable, and he was putting his life on the line for no other reason than to help her and Jon. His words came back to her, how he saw his purpose now as standing by her. And for the first time in three days, she began to believe they might just find Jon after all.

Surrounded by the colorful flowers of an open sunlit field, Jon raised his face skyward, letting the bright sun warm his skin. His eyes followed a bird as it swooped by. A branch drifted into

existence just as the bird came to light upon it. Dellia took his hand. She turned Jon toward her as a bench formed behind him. She guided him down onto it, then came to rest next to him, under the sheltering branches of a giant, lone tree. The bench grew shorter until their shoulders touched. Dellia reached over, and her warm fingers curled around his. She tilted her head, and as she lay it on his shoulder, the fields and flowers drifted into the breeze and the landscape melted into the desert at night. Dellia's head still rested on his shoulder, but she lay curled up against him, her warm body clinging to his.

"Stay with me," she said.

She lifted her head, and her beautiful blue eyes stared deep into his. There he found a longing, something imploring him to stay. Behind her, falling stars shot through the darkness as a curtain of lights danced across the starlit sky.

"There's nothing but pain for you if you go," Dellia said. "Stay here, with me ..."

The images slipped away, drifting into darkness, and Jon was back in that place again. That poor, unfortunate soul was still there with him, lashed to a pole, with his head hanging down and his eyes closed. Indistinct words drifted from the pitiful man's mouth, and it was his own voice, but the words came from some far distant place.

"Stay here, with me, now and forever," the voice mumbled.

The man's eyes fluttered open, and dim light entered. An agonizing ache clawed at his mouth, and a throbbing pain pounded through his hand. He looked down at the horrid, blackened wound with a bloody arrow sticking out of the unfortunate fellow's stomach. As the floor came into focus, Jon once again choked back the urge to retch. Fingers and teeth lay in a pool of blood and vomit on the floor between the poor soul's feet. He tried to throw off the images of what had been done to that wretched man, but the memory wouldn't budge. It had been disturbing to watch, but he'd been unable to turn away.

From somewhere beyond the lighted passage came the small man's horrible voice. He had done this. He was the cause of all this pitiful man's pain and suffering.

"He refuses to say anything," the small man said.

"The Verod will be gravely disappointed," came a deeper voice.

"He's already a tortured man, and whatever he's afraid of, it's more terrifying than anything I could do."

"So," said the deep voice, "he hasn't even hinted where Megan might be?"

There was a short pause, then the small man's voice said, "And even if he did tell us, we couldn't trust anything he says. Right now, he'd say anything to make it stop."

"Then we'll just have to find Megan on our own. And if Jon is no longer of any—"

A sharp shout and clatter erupted, ending the discussion. A furious clanging of metal rang down the cavern walls. Thuds and guttural cries blended with the clashing of swords. A bloodcurdling scream was cut short, followed by a gut-wrenching cry, then silence.

Head still hanging, the pitiful man stared downward as the arrow turned to mist and then dissipated. The black wound and bruises on the poor soul's belly melted away as the blood, teeth, and disembodied fingers on the floor evaporated into mist. The miserable fellow was still lashed to a pole, but he was unharmed.

Jon shuddered and let out a quiet gasp as everything seemed to drift into focus again. He raised his head and peered out into the indistinct shapes of some cave, trying to stay in the moment. Out of the corner of his eye, he caught someone standing in a passageway.

"Oh, Adi," said a familiar voice. "What were they doing to you?"

Jon stared into space as a woman rushed over and sawed through the coarse bindings with her blade. Everything became confused and muddled again as the unfortunate man began to fall. The woman caught him, and he landed on his knees. She started to check the pitiful soul over as he stared into space, struggling to hang on.

She lifted his hand to examine it, and a sudden panic hit. Images of fingers being carved off flashed through his memory, and he yanked the hand away. The woman lifted his chin, trying to look at his face, but the agony of teeth cracking and breaking off clawed at his consciousness, and he shrank away from her touch.

But the woman was someone familiar; he remembered her clearly; he trusted her. Slowly, he turned his face to hers and looked up into her eyes.

He smiled and said, "Dellia? You came for me."

"No. No," the familiar voice said. "It's Rillen."

Confused, the man stared into space again, and Jon's voice said, "Rillen? Isn't that what I said?"

Nothing made sense. Jon peered down at his stomach and felt where the wound should be. He remembered being on Enna as the arrow cut through him. And he was here with it dripping blood. How could the man from a moment ago have the same wound? Jon raised his hand and wiggled his fingers. The remnants of the pain still throbbed in his hand from where the man's fingers had been severed, but the fingers he was watching now were his, alive and whole. He remembered every moment of panic and pain. He recalled it all with clarity. But how could that be? How could he feel someone else's pain or remember their panic?

The woman tried to catch his attention. "Jon," she said, "focus on my voice. What happened here?"

Jon struggled, trying to reconcile his thoughts and memories with the reality before him. "I—I don't know. ... I thought—I mean, I was sure ..." He focused on his fingers, still wiggling before him. "He cut them off. They were ..." He looked down and felt the stone floor at his feet. "On the ground"—he felt his mouth all over—"with the teeth ... but ..."

The woman looked thoughtful for a moment, then her eyes grew large as a look of recognition and horror came over her. She shook her head.

"Oh, no," said Rillen's voice. "Nobody would do that. It's ..." She shuddered. "It's unthinkable, and nobody has that power anymore."

"What?" said Jon.

"They tortured you?"

Through the haze, it all began to make sense. "Yes, torture. But Dellia took me somewhere safe."

"Long ago, in the many wars, there were a few with the gift of illusion, who would use it to make their victims experience"—she closed her eyes and shuddered again—"the unthinkable."

"Long ago?"

"It's illegal now," said Rillen's voice. "Rhina gave the council an artifact to punish the perpetrators. It visits their own torture on them over and over."

Jon shook his head, as if it might somehow clear away the cobwebs and confusion. If it was Rillen's voice, then it had to be. ... He looked her up and down. It was her forest-green robe, under her deep red leather armor. It was the same golden hair and deep blue eyes. Jon looked up into Rillen's concerned face.

"Rillen? Is it really you?"

She nodded.

"But how?"

"I'll explain later, but right now we have a problem. I killed two of them, but there were signs of more. It's only a matter of time before they return. We need to leave, now, and get as far from here as we can. Do you understand?"

Jon nodded.

Rillen wrapped her arm around him and hoisted him to his feet. "Where were you headed?"

"I have to get to Kanlu."

They began to move, but Jon staggered. The pain was dwindling now, but the nausea and trembling persisted. Still weak from his confinement, he stumbled as they shambled toward the door. Rillen caught him, her strong arms steadying him.

"Don't worry, Jon. I'll get you there."

His back to the wall, Garris peered out around the corner and down the street. There, at the end of the block, stood a building with a wide entrance between two large round windows. Above the door hung a white flag with the familiar red symbol for "wines." He turned to Dellia, leaning against the wall next to him. From beneath the dark scarf that obscured his face, he said, "A pub. A good place to ask around."

The two slipped around the corner and out onto the large, flat stones, hurrying down the street toward the pub. Garris scanned the passersby as they strolled among the quaint buildings with their sloping tiled roofs and broad open fronts. There was a certain tranquility in the symmetry of their architecture, their use of simple shapes and abundant open space. The whole city was built along the lake and surrounding hills, and it was a model of blending the man-made with the natural. In many ways, it suited the Elorian people, with their simple and reflective lifestyle.

Garris constantly scanned his surroundings as he scurried down the quiet lane. Regardless of his decision to stay, he was nervous about being here. His skin was darker and his eyes different from those of the natives, two facts his scarf couldn't hide. He remained as committed as ever to seeing this through, but the more he stood out, the sooner someone would recognize him, and the sooner he'd have no choice but to flee.

DELLIA

As they neared midstreet, two royal guards rounded the corner ahead. They were instantly recognizable in their sharp uniforms the color of unglazed pottery edged with the same purple that signified the imperial family. Uniforms of higher rank tended to have more extensive patches of purple, and the scant amount on these two told him they were common soldiers at the bottom.

The female guard stared right at Dellia, then pointed at her and stopped the man. He appeared surprised when he spotted Dellia but quickly turned sheepish as the woman marched on past him.

Garris controlled his instinct to hide, remaining as calm as he could. They'd been spotted. But really, they only seemed to be interested in Dellia. Then again, that wasn't any better. He glanced over at the broad opening of a windowless building next to them. It was the obvious place to lose them.

Dellia grabbed his arm, her grip firm and strong as she held him in place. "They're probably not interested in you," she said in a soft voice. "And if they are, please don't cause any trouble."

Garris spoke in a loud whisper. "You expect me to just stand there and let them arrest me?"

"I'll see to it no harm comes to you."

"You can't promise that."

"If I must," said Dellia, "I'll go behind the backs of the local authorities, or even the council." Garris stared at her, still unconvinced. "If I have to bust you out of jail myself, I will."

Garris grumbled under his breath. If she was so willing to break the rules later, then why be so unwilling to do it now? It was obvious it was just a gamble. She was hoping she'd never have to deliver on her promise, that she'd find some other way out. Frustrated by Dellia's naive insistence on playing by the rules, Garris relented. "Fine. Now shh."

He returned his attention to the pair. The man's short, black hair flew everywhere in the wildest-looking cowlick while the woman had a pair of narrow, black braids that cascaded to her shoulders then down the front of her uniform. Both of them were shorter than Dellia and thin, and there was a similarity in their appearance that went beyond their distinctive Elorian features.

As the guards drew closer, Garris could hear indistinct bickering, and as they grew nearer still, he could discern their hushed words.

The man said, "Elder sister, I think—"

"I told you to stop calling me that. We are on duty, Sitong."

"Yes, elder ... uh, I mean, yes, Simay."

As they approached, Sitong tugged on his sister's sleeve like a child trying to get her attention. "What are you doing?"

"We have orders."

"We could pretend we did not see her."

Simay shoved her brother forward. "Just go."

"But what if they do not want to be detained?"

"They can hear you," Simay whispered.

"I do not care," Sitong whispered back.

The two stopped in front of Dellia with Simay glaring at her brother. She tore her eyes from Sitong and smiled as she faced Dellia. After a quick bow, she addressed her with a curt and official-sounding tone.

"I am sorry for my partner's lack of professionalism, but if you are Dellia, we are under orders to detain you. Would you come with us, please?"

Garris sent Dellia a sideways glance and a mischievous smile. Just because Dellia wanted him to comply didn't mean he had to play nice. He pivoted to Simay and scowled as he rested his hand on the hilt of his sword. "And what if Dellia doesn't want to be detained?"

Sitong looked like a scared rabbit as he startled and prepared to bolt, but his sister grabbed his arm. He whirled around to address her. "I told you. Now what?"

Simay responded in a hurried whisper. "Not in front of the detainees."

Dellia turned to Garris. "Find him."

"I am sorry," said Simay, "our orders are to also detain whoever is with you."

"They probably think you're Jon," Dellia said.

Both guards looked puzzled.

"What is a Jon?" Sitong asked.

Dellia drew herself up, towering above the two guards in their sharp uniforms. "I'm on important business for the council. I can't afford this delay."

"Our orders come *directly* from the council," Simay replied.

Garris adjusted his grip on the hilt of his sword. "We could fight our way out," he said to Dellia as if the two guards weren't even there.

Simay remained staunch, but her brother looked suitably alarmed. He gulped and addressed Garris. "Wait, wait. There may be room for some compromise here."

Garris narrowed his eyes, glaring at Sitong. "What compromise? Either we're detained or we're not."

Dellia rolled her eyes. "Nobody's fighting here."

Garris leaned in toward her. "Geez. Ever hear of bluffing?"

Wide-eyed, Sitong leaned in toward his sister and in a quiet voice said, "I think he is bluffing."

Simay shook her head. "He just told us he is bluffing."

"Really?" Sitong leaned over toward Garris. "Um, you know it does not really work if you tell us you are bluffing."

Dellia became exasperated and glared at Garris. "Stop messing with the guards."

"You're no fun."

Dellia addressed Simay. "You two. I will make you a deal."

Sitong turned to his sister. "Are we allowed to make deals with detainees?"

Before Simay could answer, Dellia continued, "You are if one is a protector under orders from the council."

"What deal?" said Simay.

"We will come with you if you promise to get all the Kanlu guards to ask around about a stranger named Jon, then report back to us. It's imperative we find him, but if you promise to make every effort to find him for us, then we will be free to go with you."

"All right," Simay said, "it is a deal."

Sitong took out a rope and reached for Dellia's hands, preparing to bind them. Simay glared at her brother as she gave a slow shake of her head. Sitong averted his gaze as he stepped back and put the rope away. Simay rolled her eyes and shook her head. Then, she motioned for them to come along, and the four headed down the busy street together.

Garris gave an exasperated sigh. This turn of events was both unexpected and disturbing, but he had Dellia's word that she would set him free. And if that failed, he still had a trick or two that might get him out of this. Anyway, nothing could be done about it now. So he resumed scanning the streets as the two Elorian guards carted them off to jail.

Her head dropped as she nodded off, but the falling sensation jarred Kayleen immediately back awake, and her head jerked back up again. It was a distant echo of a simpler time. When a young girl used to talk her best friend into playing spy. He would trick the guards by creating a distraction, then they'd both sneak into Shir Keep to hide out and spy on the council meetings. To a young girl and her friend, it all seemed so exciting and dangerous. But now as she sat in the dark woods, outside the back of Grekor's tent, hoping to overhear something useful, she was plying those same skills on a purpose of a more serious and deadly nature.

DELLIA

This wasn't her first attempt at eavesdropping on the three. But so far, in four tries, all she'd gathered were a few cringe-worthy comments about her and some of the women and a lot of typical male bluster and posturing. So either there was nothing to be learned or they were deliberately not talking about it.

Still, giving up was not an option. Too much rested on navigating her way back onto the council through a situation fraught with unknowns. And the biggest one was what these three were doing here. So here she was, alone with no best friend, far from the rest of the unit, outside their tent, waiting for their return.

It had been a long vigil, and the lateness of the hour was catching up with her. It was only a matter of time before she fell asleep and risked being discovered when they returned. Kayleen adjusted her position and bit her lip, hoping the discomfort would help her stay awake just a little longer.

Buried under the croaking of toads and the hooting of an owl came hushed voices, carried on the damp night air. A far-off light moved toward her through the trees, and Kayleen sat a little straighter, facing the back of the tent.

"Finally," she muttered under her breath.

Light flooded the tent, creating shadows of the three men on its wide cloth surface as they filed through the entrance. Nikosh began to speak but was cut off by Grekor's low, ominous objection.

"Stop talking," he said.

Nikosh said, "But—"

"Now!" bellowed Grekor.

Moments passed, the tension thick in the air following Grekor's angry outburst. Then, the smaller shadow moved closer to the larger one, and Nikosh's brittle response spat through the strained silence. "Keep it up. We'll see how well you shout me down after I rip your tongue out."

His anger lay there for a moment before the third shadow

427

pointed at the smaller one's head. "You know there's a little vein in your head that kinda pops out when you get angry."

"Yeah," said Grekor, "you know, I could remove that for ya."

"Don't touch me." Nikosh's voice was even angrier and more indignant.

The larger shadow held up its hands and stepped back. "All right. All right. Take it easy. I'm just trying to follow orders."

"So am I," Nikosh said.

"Really? Because Braye was crystal clear: never discuss this." Grekor's emphatic statement halted the discussion, and Kayleen slowly leaned closer, straining to catch every word.

Then came Nikosh's voice, quieter than before. "Braye couldn't have anticipated her getting suspicious and snooping around."

"Of course he did," said Grekor. "Why do you think we're not discussing this?"

"She's the shrewdest member of the council. She sees patterns nobody else does. She'll figure this out."

"So what? Then we deal with her, just like we're gonna deal with him."

Kayleen stiffened in surprise.

Shock and surprise were evident in Pedrus's voice, too. "With a member of the council?"

"Seriously?" Nikosh said. "You can't be that thick. She commands this detail and Quirtus is on her side. That's ten against three, numskull."

"Even a pair of half-wits like you two must realize I'm not saying we have a big brawl with the entire detail." The larger shadow moved closer to the other two, and Grekor's voice grew quiet. "We do what we're known for; we figure a way to deal with her. We get the job done."

The smaller shadow nodded its head. "Deal with her, huh? Yeah, I can think of a few ways to deal with her."

Kayleen leaned away. She wasn't altogether sure what Nikosh was implying, but she was certain none of it was good.

"Look," said Grekor, "Jon's already been taken, and he thinks he's being rescued. Right now, he's headed straight into an ambush. Nothing in this world can stop that."

"Right," said Pedrus, "and we just have to be there when the trap closes."

The large shadow leaned back, and Grekor said, "What's important is that one way or another, it's over for this Jon fellow."

A silence followed, and Kayleen leaned closer once again, straining to hear.

"I suppose," Nikosh said.

Pedrus nodded and said, "Then it's a good thing we didn't talk about it."

The tone in his voice told Kayleen there was unlikely to be further discussion. So she rose and began to creep away. Her head shot up at a flapping noise from above. Earlier in her vigil, some large fowl had flown up to roost in the trees and her proximity had no doubt made them restless.

With her gaze focused upward, she never noticed the low branch as she passed a nearby sapling. It caught her in the neck, causing her to lose her balance and tip over backward. She landed with a thud and rustle of underbrush.

Her attention shot over to the tent.

The two larger shadows froze in place, and the smaller one cocked its head, listening. Not a sound issued from the tent, but as Kayleen scrambled to her feet, the largest shadow signaled to the smaller one.

As the small, lithe shadow crept to the door, Kayleen hurried off into the darkened forest. Suddenly she recalled how those young girl's spy adventures invariably ended. Kayleen's excitement would give them away. Then a frantic chase through the keep would ensue with Garris trying to trip up the guards while he berated her and swore he'd never let her talk him into it again. Oh, how she missed those days. Only this time, it was not merely lighthearted fun. The stakes were infinitely higher.

The croaking of toads masked the sounds of her movement as Kayleen scurried back toward the main camp, her mind already racing. It seemed as if the council, or at least Braye, had set a course every bit as misguided and perilous as she'd feared. Because now, it appeared that soldiers under her command were headed for a direct confrontation with a man who had survived the Recluse Tower.

Chapter Twenty-Six

ALONG THE PATHS OF KANLU

Perched high up in the corner of his crude prison cell, Garris clung to a small, jagged stone that protruded from the masonry. He glanced over his shoulder at the bright light coming through the barred window on the opposite wall.

With a small grunt, he yanked himself upward, planted his feet higher on the two walls of the corner, and pushed off, springing far out into space. He twisted around as he sailed through the air, then grabbed one of the bars and slammed into the opposite wall with as quiet a thump as he could manage.

As he dangled by one arm, Garris caught his breath for a moment. Then, with another soft grunt, he hoisted himself up to peer out between the cold, iron bars.

His face now bathed in bright sunlight, he squinted as he surveyed the world outside his dark prison cell. Inches below the window ledge ran a wide, stone walkway, and beyond that, dirt paths cut across a broad grass courtyard ringed by similar long, stone prison buildings.

Garris strained, listening for sounds of soldiers patrolling, but all that met his ears was the distant sound of people on the streets mixed with the chirping of songbirds. It seemed odd that no guards strolled the area, but then again, they could merely be out of sight.

As he hung by one hand, Garris turned his attention inward, feeling the cold, damp mortar that held the bar in place. It was sturdy.

431

So it would take some doing, but he could loosen the bar.

He grumbled under his breath. He wouldn't have to break out of this stupid cell if Dellia hadn't foolishly trusted those two numskulls with the mission to find Jon. This was idiotic. Rotting in prison rarely proved to be a productive use of time. Particularly not with his enemies closing in on him and someone as feeble as Jon out there lost and alone. This was rapidly deteriorating into one of his typical calamitous trips to Meerdon. Fortunately, from the look of it, the prison cell was merely a temporary setback.

His head whipped around to the sound of footsteps approaching, and Garris froze for a moment.

Endeavoring to remain as silent as possible, he pushed off from the wall and dropped to the floor. He stood up and brushed himself off, finishing up just as a guard rounded the corner.

The man stood there, glaring at Garris, attempting to appear imposing in his uniform of light brown edged with royal purple. "Stop whatever it is you are doing," he blustered.

No sooner had the words left his mouth than his head spun around at the sounds of an intense scuffle. The guard startled as a set of rigid fingers flashed out from behind the corner to jab him in the throat. His hands flew up, clutching his neck as he doubled over, wheezing and gasping. As Garris approached the iron bars of his cell, the hilt of a dagger slammed down on the guard's head with a thud, and he crumpled to the floor.

A slender woman rounded the corner, her face hidden under the hood of a long purple robe. One that didn't quite hide her out-of-place blond hair. With silent grace, she sheathed her weapon and approached the cell door. She stopped in front of Garris and paused for a moment. Then her head tilted, listening to the silence that hung in the cool, clammy air.

When she lowered her hood, he stared, shocked at the face glowering at him. "Rillen? What are you doing here?"

432

In an irritated tone, she said, "Breaking you out of prison, last I checked."

She whirled around and scooped up a large black iron key ring from the unconscious guard.

Surprised by her curt response, Garris said, "I thought you were following—"

"Yeah." Rillen began searching the numerous keys of the large ring. "A lot of people went to a lot of trouble to create that impression." She stopped and glared at him. "Thanks for messing that up."

"What did I do?"

Rillen stopped her fiddling again and moved a little closer. "You shouldn't be here," she insisted, then resumed her search.

"Excuse me. I was helping. Jon is missing, and Dellia is about to make a big mistake."

Rillen selected a large key and jammed it into the lock. She twisted it with a clank, followed by a low, metallic creak as she swung the cell door open.

When Garris didn't budge, she motioned, inviting him out.

He crossed his arms and stood taller. "I'm not going anywhere until I know what's going on."

Rillen shrugged her shoulders. "Fine. You can stay here and try to explain a bunch of unconscious guards." She motioned to the uniformed bodies strewn across the floor beyond the cell door. "Or you can come with me."

He suppressed a smile of admiration and instead just nodded. Then the two took off, with Rillen leading the way across the heavy stone room lined with empty cells.

"What about the council?" Garris said. "You know, the people you work for."

"What the council doesn't know can't hurt them."

"Um, I'm pretty sure that's not true."

They turned the corner and climbed a set of rough-hewn steps to a broad, crude hallway leading to other rooms and a door at the end. Garris slowed, distracted by the string of unconscious soldiers strewn down the path ahead. This time he couldn't suppress a smile of admiration. She had done all this without making a sound.

As he stepped over each body, Garris stared down, trying to recall their rank based on the varying splashes of rich purple on their uniforms of clay brown. "Wow. I'm impressed, but I'd appreciate knowing what I'm doing."

"Let's just say we need Dellia to do something. And I expect she'll refuse unless she knows you're out of here and safe."

"And who exactly is this 'we'?"

Rillen glanced over her shoulder. "If I say it's the Augury, will you stop with the questions?"

He jerked to a stop and folded his arms. "No. I'm not getting mixed up in any oracle nonsense again."

She eyed him as she shook her head. "Oh, Garris, you've been mixed up in oracle nonsense since you met Prisha." With that, Rillen spun around and took off again down the broad stone hallway.

"Prisha?" he said. It had been a long time since he'd heard that name. Elt avoided the subject, knowing it was a sore spot.

"Yeah, the first one suspected of being the Otherworlder. The one you helped."

"You mean the one I helped and got *banished* for my efforts."

They came to a halt as Rillen slid up next to a heavy wooden door. It made a small creaking noise as she slipped it open. Sunlight flooded through the crack as she peeped out into the grassy court-yard.

In a flash, she pulled back and closed the door, then raised her curved sword, ready to swing it down on whoever entered. "You can't blame Prisha, she knew nothing of the prophecy."

"I don't blame her. I blame the council and the Augury."

Rillen snapped back, "The Augury had never heard of The

Prophecy of the Otherworlder before that."

"Every oracle belongs to the Augury. You expect me to believe they had nothing to do with it?"

"It was hidden, even from the Augury. For reasons no one knows."

She put her ear to the door, listening as Garris mulled over her assertion. The Augury did seem particularly clueless when it came to this prophecy. And if some master plan was at work, it was a spectacularly disorganized and horrible one. Besides, arguing over ancient history was pretty much pointless at the moment.

"Okay, so I blame the council," Garris said. "But I'm not following beyond this door unless I know where we're going." He crossed his arms and stood firm once again.

Rillen replied in a monotone as if reciting her orders. "I am to get you out of town and hide you there. Then I'll find Dellia and tell her where you are."

Garris uncrossed his arms and stared. Was he to be taken out of harm's way like some little puppy dog that needed protecting? All of that guilt and anguish over leaving, all the debating and talking himself into returning—was it all to be for nothing?

"But what about helping Jon?"

"It's impossible," she said, this time seeming sympathetic. "It's too risky for you to be here."

"Then why go with you at all?"

Rillen put a hand on Garris's shoulder. "Look, you want to help Dellia and Jon, this is how you do it."

He drew a deep breath. Perhaps it was a blessing in disguise. After all, he never wanted to be here anyway. He nodded and said, "Okay."

Light spilled through the crack as Rillen slid the door open again and peeked out. Satisfied it was safe, she opened it further and motioned for Garris to follow as she slipped into the bright daylight.

He followed her out underneath an overhang where a wide stone pathway led around the outside of the courtyard. Rillen signaled him to be quiet, then led the way past several cell windows that bordered the path. She turned and scurried around a shrub, heading out onto one of the dirt paths that cut across the grassy middle.

As Garris rounded the corner, a flash of purple caught his eye. He glanced down and there, peeking out from beneath some dense, low branches, lay the hem of a uniform. No doubt some unconscious guard Rillen had hidden.

They hurried down a well-worn path surrounded by lush, green grass, but as they neared the far side, a voice rang out behind them. Garris glanced back as a uniformed woman knelt down over the body hidden in the greenery. She bolted upright and scanned the area, and when she spotted Garris, she pointed and began yelling.

"Perfect," he grumbled.

They turned in unison and shot forward, racing down the dirt pathway, away from the soldier. They hit the line of buildings on the far side and flew down between two of them, where the dirt path turned into a stone walkway.

A sea of brown and purple uniforms poured into the courtyard and headed toward them, their numbers becoming obscured by the narrowing view out between the two buildings.

Garris faced forward again, racing toward a line of shrubs at the end of the alley. He shook his head and yelled to Rillen, "Oracles, prophecies, the Augury ... how could that go wrong?"

The two hit the end of the alley and flew around the corner behind a low, stone building, following the row of dense bushes toward an opening farther down.

Behind them, a flurry of footsteps pounded the paving stones as uniformed soldiers careened around the corner, giving chase. Garris glanced back at their determined faces as Rillen slid through an opening in the hedge. The scraggly branches clawed at him as he followed her, diving through the shrubs and out onto the busy street beyond.

Bone tired and confined to a small, windowless room in a dark, stone building, Dellia's first thought was to sleep. But unable to set aside her torment over the fate of Jon, she wasted restless hours staring at the ceiling, the walls, the dark wooden dresser. She even spent a while studying the intricate jade inlay of a serpent-like wingless dragon that wound its way across the surface of a large screen in the corner. Yet, sleep never came, so she relented and, driven by nervousness, began pacing.

As time wore on with no word of Jon, her concern broadened, and an endless stream of questions plagued her. After arranging to meet her so she could deliver her charge, why would the council order her detained? Why did they blindfold her when bringing her here? Where was Simay? Had she organized the guards to search for Jon as she promised, and if so, why had there been no news? What if coming to Kanlu was a mistake, and Jon was elsewhere? What kind of mess had she gotten Garris into, and what was he going to do while unsupervised? The possible answers that flooded her mind only heightened her discomfort.

With time and no answers, the frequent glances at the sliding double door turned into staring at it, torturing herself as she studied the enchanting, windswept tree painted across its panels. It was only a matter of time before Kayleen came through that door, and she would have to admit her abject failure. Not only had she neglected to bring Jon with her as ordered, but she'd lost him entirely and, in fact, had no idea where he was. She had gambled she could convince Kayleen that Garris had been invaluable and should be let go, but it would be an uphill battle to bargain from a position of utter failure.

Dellia halted at the sound of muffled voices in the hall outside the room. Then, with a soft swishing sound, one of the doors slid open. A guard entered, followed by a figure in a familiar black hooded robe.

"We were under orders to detain her," the guard dressed in black said without looking up.

"Whose orders?" a familiar voice said. "The council? Perhaps it has escaped your attention, but you do not work for the council."

Dellia tilted her head, trying to peer under the hood, but the angle wasn't right.

The guard said, "But, sir—"

"This discussion is over," said the familiar voice. "I'm taking her with me. Do you understand?"

"Yes, Chenyu," the guard said and bowed his head in deference.

The robed figure pulled back his hood, and Tsaoshi's placid face gazed out at Dellia. She stood for a moment, stunned.

"You?" she said as she stared.

"Come, we must hurry." Tsaoshi whipped around and stormed out of the room.

Dellia puzzled for another breath, then raced after, out into a long broad hallway with ornate lanterns hung from the ceiling. The pair rushed down a corridor lined with pairs of sliding double doors, each adorned with elegant depictions of soaring landscapes, brightly colored flowers, or windswept trees.

"Wait," Dellia said, "where's Garris?"

"I do not know, precisely," Tsaoshi replied without looking back.

She grabbed his arm, yanking him to a halt as she yelled, "Stop!"

He gently pulled his arm away from her grasp and eyed her with calm sincerity.

Dellia stilled her anxiety. "I'm not going anywhere without Garris. It's my fault he's here. I made a promise."

Tsaoshi nodded. "I have arranged to free him and to take him somewhere safe. But he may have been safer in prison. And the longer he stays in Kanlu, the greater the peril." He placed a hand on her arm. "But he is safe for now. I give you my word."

Tsaoshi bowed his head, then whirled around and took off again.

Dellia charged after, struggling to catch up. "And exactly whose word am I taking?"

"I am Tsaoshi, as I told you."

"Why should I trust you? You deceived me."

He stopped a short distance from the door and turned to face Dellia. "I spoke only the truth. It is you who sought an oracle to deceive Jon. I merely made certain it was me." He gave a thoughtful nod of his head. "Then again, it is not for me to judge who deceived who. That is for our descendants to decide."

Surprised, she said, "Our descendants?"

"Yes, what is happening now is history, hundreds of years in the making."

Dellia took an unconscious step backward. "History?" she said as she stared. As she thought back over all she'd done in the past days, a flush of shame washed over her. She pictured her treatment of Jon, or her abuse of her gift, being recounted to future generations, and the prospect mortified her.

"Who are you?" Dellia said, still staring.

Hands at his sides, Tsaoshi gave a gentle bow. "I am Tsaoshi, the closest thing this era has to a Great Oracle." He motioned to his surroundings. "Here they call me Chenyu, though I have not yet attained enlightenment. So it is not a title to which I have earned the right."

Tsaoshi pivoted and took off at a brisk pace. Dellia followed, and the pair burst through an open door, flying out onto a stone path that wound its way through a vast, rectangular garden surrounded by long, single-story buildings. It was magnificent. Full-size trees, trained to twist and wind out over huge rock gardens, ponds, and waterfalls, all blended with an artist's eye to resemble a towering mountainside or peaceful grotto.

They raced along, accompanied by the quiet murmurs of a tiny brook that broke off from the path, snaking its way through the miniature landscape. Dellia slowed for a second, wondering at the spectacle.

The buildings were recognizable, too; she'd seen their stone walls of black and deep brown and their roofs of dark jade tile, but from the other side. This was the Augury, the mysterious glue that bound all oracles. It was said no oracle existed that did not belong, and those few bestowed with the Gift of Prophecy came here to study and perfect their craft.

"I don't believe you." Dellia eyed Tsaoshi. "I've never heard of you."

"Just as the council has protectors, the Augury has the Shou. Their purpose is to protect that which must be kept secret, and my identity is one of those secrets."

"I thought the Shou were a myth."

He smiled. "They will be gratified to learn they are doing an exemplary job of cultivating that belief."

She watched Tsaoshi with suspicion. "And you expect me to believe you work for them?"

"No. It does not work like that. The Shou protect prophecy. I *am* prophecy."

They raced past a small waterfall that rumbled as it cascaded down a rock wall. It spilled into a pond, over which an evergreen swept as it wound its way down from a cliff above.

As the roar faded, Dellia returned her attention to Tsaoshi. "What does that mean?"

"There is no time to explain the intricacies of the Augury, or why Wistra set it up as she did."

Dellia raced ahead and stopped at the garden entrance,

blocking Tsaoshi's way. She stared for a moment as customers wandered the busy market in the street beyond. As the murmur of shoppers haggling drifted over the garden wall behind her, she closed her eyes. She concentrated and reached out with what little of her gift her tired mind could summon.

In Tsaoshi, she found a serenity more profound than any she could recall. And her inner turmoil began to untangle in the presence of such a tranquil mind. It was impossible to tell if he was telling the truth, except that it seemed inconceivable that anyone could achieve such a peaceful state in a mind accustomed to lies.

Dellia stared in shock. "You're telling the truth."

Tsaoshi nodded.

A vague, sick feeling struck her. "History?"

"Yes. Choose your path wisely, Dellia. It will be remembered."

Too late, Dellia thought.

Tsaoshi slipped past her and out into the busy street.

She composed herself; whatever Tsaoshi wanted with her, it must be important. The Shou were a secret guarded with great diligence and care—so much so that even now, after his revelation, it was hard to believe they really existed. That he would divulge that secret to her in such a casual manner was surprising, and she could conceive of only a few explanations, none of them comforting.

Then, Dellia stiffened at another realization. She had sensed something else in that tranquil mind, a deep sympathy and concern. At first, she'd assumed it to be aimed at all humankind, simply a burden of his gift. But it was more than that. It was a reaction. The same one he'd had when he gazed at her in Talus, as she confronted him outside the stables.

And with that memory, Tsaoshi's puzzling words came back: "I wish I could tell you it is all going to be okay." A dread filled Dellia as she wondered if those words had been founded on a knowledge of things yet to come.

She shook her head and calmed herself. This was not the time or place to indulge in self-doubt. She took a deep breath and bolted after Tsaoshi, out into the busy Kanlu Market.

Tired and impatient, Jon stared down at the hand pressed against his chest, stopping him from moving forward. He glanced over at Rillen, holding him back with one hand as she peered around the branches of an evergreen that cascaded down from the rocks above.

Beyond its boughs lay a chaotic arrangement of rickety, run-down houses that was apparently the outskirts of Kanlu. It wasn't at all what he expected. Then again, why should this place be any less disorienting than the rest of this world?

She continued to scan the hovels for a moment, then removed her hand and motioned for him to follow.

Jon planted his feet and crossed his arms, refusing to move. He'd been trying for hours to talk reason into Rillen, but she'd remained intransigent, refusing to listen to his well-reasoned assessment. It was puzzling and frustrating, and if only he could just make her see. "You're not listening. I thought she was your friend."

"I listened. You needed to get to Kanlu ... your words, not mine." She motioned beyond the branches to the line of decrepit buildings connected by a jumble of worn streets. "Well, here we are." Rillen turned and hurried away toward one of the buildings.

Jon stood for a moment shaking his head. Was she deliberately being dense? He took a deep breath and rushed to follow.

Rillen raced up to the first corner and slammed her back up against the crumbling walls of a shabby old house. She peered around it and down the street at a few disparate groups of pedestrians conversing as they hung out on the deteriorating pavement.

In a loud whisper, Jon said, "I keep explaining. Dellia should have found whatever trail you used to track me. I'm telling you, if she

442

didn't, it means she's in trouble. We need to find her."

Rillen swung around and faced him. "There are many less sinister explanations for not finding you."

"Like what? She decided to chuck it all and move to Tahiti?"

Her face adopted the most perplexed expression. "What? No. Where?" She sent Jon an exasperated look, then dove around the corner, hustling down the street.

He shook his head. There she was, running off again. He rushed after her, the dilapidated old buildings flying by as the two quarreled.

"Look," said Rillen, "maybe she simply couldn't pick up your trail."

"Right. Because nothing's harder to track than a grown man being dragged across a wide-open desert."

They turned left at the first intersection and raced across a broad lane. Jon glanced over at a pair of children in rough, well-worn clothes playing some sort of game. Each had a string slung between two sticks, and they laughed as they whirled a large yo-yo-like top up and down and tossed it between them.

"Or maybe she decided to arrest someone," Rillen said.

"Like Garris? Yeah, why not arrest the guy following you around everywhere, helping you?"

As they reached the far side of the street, she halted and shoved her face inches from his. "Or perhaps she just finds you as aggravating as I do."

"Well, that's a given, but still she's—"

Rillen grabbed his shirt and yanked him into the darkness of a nearby alley, between two misshapen brick walls. She tilted her head and listened to the sound of approaching footsteps. Jon held his tongue until she let go and hurried away between the crumbling stonework.

He tried again as he chased after. "But still, Dellia is deadly serious about her duty."

"Perhaps her duty took her elsewhere."

"Like where? Tahiti?"

Rillen halted and faced Jon. "What is this obsession with this Tahiti place?"

He was about to answer when she stormed off a short distance and halted at the next corner.

He hustled to catch up. "And it doesn't bother you that in all your searching of the same area, you never once ran into Dellia. Doesn't that tell you something's happened to her?"

"No, it's a big desert."

Rillen glanced around the corner, then suddenly pulled back and reached over, shoving Jon up against the wall. She waited, and after a few moments, a woman wearing a torn, rust-colored tunic sauntered by on the street beyond.

Jon waited for her to pass before resuming. "And what about *your* duty? I thought you were searching for Megan. I thought she was this big, terrifying threat. Why send you after me?"

"Look, Megan obviously split from you to make it hard to capture you both. Dellia can only track one of you. So that's why I was brought in. But it's a big world, and Megan doesn't want to be found. So I was sent to find you."

"And yet, my captors didn't want to be found, and you found them."

Rillen peered around the corner again, then turned back to Jon and shook her head. "I don't remember you being this persistent and annoying."

"I'm sorry, have we met? Persistent and annoying is kinda my thing."

"Look, if it will ease your fears, once we find a hiding spot for you in Kanlu, I'll go search for Dellia myself."

"Thank you," Jon said, relieved by her promise.

Rillen peered around the corner again, then dove into the

street, muttering to herself, "If it makes you shut up, it'll be worth it."

As they crossed the wide avenue, Jon glanced up at the hillside, and there in the distance lay a neatly arranged collection of quaint, low-set buildings, looking like something out of a picture. He slowed and glanced around at the decrepit buildings that seemed to be everywhere. The contrast was stark and unmistakable, and suddenly it was clear: it wasn't the whole city that was in a state of disrepair, just this part.

Jon scanned the dirty, dingy buildings that seemed to be all around him. "So, why are we going through such a bad part of town?"

He stopped midstreet. Rillen's insistence they continue, her less than convincing answers, they were all part of a picture. A terrifying prospect dawned on him. "For that matter, why didn't we go through the front gate? You're a pro … tec … tor …"

He trailed off as he realized he probably didn't want to know the answer. He spun around, anxious to put some distance between him and this seedy part of town.

From the shadows, three large strangers silently stepped out in front of the alley. They were concealed by robes of reddish black and scarves that hid most of their faces. Chains and various pieces of armor were slung all over their bodies, and they bristled with knives, throwing stars and other assorted weapons.

Jon froze as they stood there, arms crossed, blocking the way back. He pivoted as three more heavily armed strangers in similar garb slid into position, obstructing the passage into the deteriorating alley ahead. He glanced to the right, where a third group of three huge men stood blocking the street in the other direction.

Jon's stomach knotted up. *This was a carefully laid trap.*

He and Rillen both turned to the left, toward their only remaining avenue of escape. But another four strangers came together, blocking the way further down a street lined with dirty old buildings.

He stumbled backward. They stood surrounded by a small army of vicious-looking strangers. He stared into Rillen's face. If this was a trap, then how could it have worked unless she was in on it? Yet, she appeared to be as alarmed as he felt.

Using slow, fluid movements, she shifted her stance, tightening her hands into fists held ready in front of her. Her focus seemed everywhere as she crouched, poised and ready, as if the moment were balanced on the edge of a knife. Jon's mind raced. At thirteen to two, they stood no chance. Panic welled within him, and he glanced at Rillen, hoping against hope that she knew some way out.

Chapter Twenty-Seven

IDENTITY CRISIS

Kayleen sat on a bedroll in her spacious yet spartan tent, staring out the open entrance at nothing. To keep a low profile, she'd chosen a large, picturesque garden area hidden by long, low buildings for their encampment. It was emblematic of a contradiction in the Elorian people that had always fascinated her. The buildings that surrounded it, like most structures in Elore, were perfectly symmetrical, every door and window designed with care to make the left half of the facade a reflection of the right. Even the buildings on either side of the garden were mirror images of one another. Yet, the garden enclosed within was an artwork of the natural. Grass, trees, rocks, and water all tastefully arranged to flow together, creating a place of peace and harmony.

She had positioned her tent with a view of the only entrance or egress to the area, a small wooden bridge that arched over a peaceful pond. Grekor and his two thugs-in-arms were involved in exactly the kind of foolhardy exploits that always blew up in everyone's faces. That meant bringing Jon in might be the only course that could protect everyone, and that required tact and finesse, not brute force and unbridled chaos. So, whatever fiasco Grekor or Tetch or anyone in the unit might be involved in, she was determined that it not happen without her knowing. Wherever they might be headed, she would spot them, coming or going.

The ceaseless watching and waiting were torturous, yet what

choice did she have? Her life, Dellia's life, and even the fate of the three realms could rest on what happened in these next few hours. So she sat and stared and waited.

The unending boredom had made her inattentive, and she startled at an unexpected burst of noise, jerking herself to attention. A harried Nikosh barged through the open flap, and she flew to her feet, all her senses focused on the lone intruder. He halted in front of her, hair disheveled, hunched over and gasping for breath.

Kayleen stepped back across the grassy floor.

He looked at her, eyes wide with alarm, and his words heaved out between gulps of air. "A disturbance … Kianlong Square … come … hurry."

She bolted past Nikosh, heading for the open entrance. But a sudden unease jerked her to a stop. She slowly lifted her head.

"Something's not right." She stared back at the exhausted soldier, striving to put her finger on it. "What were you doing at the square?"

Nikosh's response sputtered out between gasps for breath. "I wasn't … I saw people … fleeing."

Her concern grew, and Kayleen cocked her head, listening to the distant sounds of a woman laughing and children playing. "Those are not the sounds of people fleeing."

Nikosh's eyes widened even more. "There's no time for this. You need to come see for yourself."

Kayleen scrutinized him, studying the lines of his face. Then it hit her: This was not how Nikosh would react in a crisis. He'd be cool. Detached even.

She stepped back again. "Full sentences? A second ago you were gasping for air." She tensed. "You're lying."

He ceased his labored breathing and raised himself upright as his expression turned cold. With unnatural swiftness, he slipped out a dagger and flashed it at Kayleen. "You just couldn't make this easy, could ya?"

Kayleen tensed. She'd only have one chance to catch him off guard. She donned a terrified expression and put her hands out. "What are you going to do? Kill—"

She dove to Nikosh's right and thrust her arm up, deflecting the steel dagger. She swung her arm down, wrapping it around his, then whipped around, twisting his shoulder backward with a crack.

He spasmed and released the dagger. Kayleen shoved him with all her force, and as he lost his balance, she kicked him in the back. Nikosh hurtled to the ground as she dove out of the tent.

She flew out onto the base of the narrow bridge that sat between her and the entire unit. Tense and alert, she peered out across the encampment. Whatever Nikosh was up to, it was certain Grekor was behind it, and that meant he and Pedrus had to be lurking out there somewhere.

Kayleen stepped back and scanned the stone path that wound its way through rock groupings and over small bridges. But she found no sign of their red leather chest pieces embossed with that distinctive flaming horse. Every fiber of her being alert, she crept backward across the wooden slats of the bridge, searching the half dozen tents scattered across the lush, grassy areas of the encampment.

First Grekor, then Pedrus appeared out from behind one of the tents and approached her with the wariness of a predator cornering its prey.

"Listen," Grekor demanded, "we have orders, direct from the council. Now get out of our way."

Kayleen raised her voice, making sure it would carry throughout the entire camp. "Do those orders include attacking a member of the council?"

Nikosh stumbled out of the tent, rubbing his shoulder and swinging his arm, trying to work off the pain. As soon as he took in the situation, he froze, and the apprehension on his usually calm face was even more frightening than the two hulking men slinking toward her.

Grekor and Pedrus kept inching across the open ground toward Kayleen, alert and stalking. Pedrus slipped his hand around the hilt of his sword.

"We're on the same side," Grekor said. "Nikosh was supposed to lead you away so we could get out of here and complete our mission."

Quirtus appeared out of his tent at the back of the camp. Pedrus snapped around toward the noise and faced him, wagging his finger and shaking his head no. More and more of her soldiers appeared as Quirtus pulled his sword and stormed toward the two men.

Kayleen's heart jumped; this was about to turn bloody. She stared at Quirtus and put her hand out, signaling him to halt. Quirtus stopped and glanced around at the rest of the unit, then waved them off.

Kayleen returned her attention to the two men prowling toward her. "That presents a problem, you see. Because you killing Jon would prevent me from bringing him in. And those are my orders, direct from the council."

Nikosh turned to face Grekor. "Tell her."

"No," replied Grekor.

Pedrus slipped his sword out, brandishing it with practiced ease as he and Grekor continued slinking toward her.

Kayleen's breathing quickened. "Tell me what?"

"Get out of our way," Grekor demanded.

"No!" she replied.

"This is lunacy," Nikosh said, "*tell* her."

Pedrus threw him an angry glare. "Apparently, you haven't quite grasped the concept of secret orders."

Grekor glared at Nikosh, too. "I already have to explain you

450

attacking her. I don't want to have to explain how you blew the whole plan!"

Kayleen reached for her dagger. Her hand missed it, and she glanced down at the scabbard, still empty. She was unarmed against two of the most ruthless men in the three realms. She took a deep breath and readied herself, alert to every move of the two hulking warriors approaching the base of the bridge.

Kayleen raised herself up taller, trying to appear calm. "I agree. We are on the same side. We want the same thing. Stop this and we can talk."

"There's no time," Grekor said. "Lives depend on this. It may already be too late. Now move, or we will move you."

Nikosh darted in front of Kayleen, between her and the two hulking men. He spoke to her over his shoulder. "Our orders are not to kill Jon. They are to save him."

"What?" said Kayleen. "How?"

Grekor shot Nikosh a blistering stare and bellowed, "Shut up."

Pedrus dove for Kayleen, but Nikosh intercepted him and kicked him backward.

Nikosh turned to face Kayleen. "It's all part of a plan: Nab Jon, lead him into an ambush. Then we rescue him. He hates the resistance, loves the council. He becomes ... compliant."

Grekor halted a couple of arm's lengths from her and drew his huge sword as he eyed her with a hard scowl on his face. "Happy now? The ambush is real. The assassins are real. We had to make it as authentic as possible. So if we don't show, he dies."

"And if you're lying, I'm sentencing a man to death. A man I've sworn to bring in and protect."

"Protect?" said Pedrus. "With what those oracles say he'll do? I should be joining the assassins, but I got orders."

Grekor scowled at Pedrus.

"And I have mine," Kayleen said. "I will not fail. I *cannot* fail.

There's too much at stake."

Kayleen glanced back and forth between the two enormous brutes. They were already in striking range and the rest of the soldiers too far back, watching with apprehension from the stone paths and grassy patches of the serene garden. She had only moments to make a decision that would determine the fate of a man, herself, her friends, even the three realms. Any second, she would lose control, and with it, any chance of making that choice.

Dellia hurried along, following Tsaoshi down a narrow lane that wound along the banks of a peaceful river. Long, single-story houses with slanted roofs of curved, ceramic shingles crowded one side. While the occasional quaint, wooden bridge arched across the water on the other.

Any other time, she would have had no trouble keeping up. But she couldn't stop thinking about all the things Tsaoshi had told her. Things that, at the time, seemed to have no weight, coming from the mouth of an assumed impostor. But now, as she relived those moments, her heart grew more and more distressed. A physical threat she could handle, but apprehension over the prospect of an unknown and troubling future—that was like an anchor tugging at her soul.

Eventually, she had to know. "You say everything you've told me is the truth?"

"Yes," replied Tsaoshi.

Dellia slowed, weighed down by her troubled heart. "Outside the stables, why did you look at me like that? Why did you say you wished you could tell me it would be okay?"

He halted before the steps of a towering black temple and turned back to face Dellia. He closed his eyes and let out a sigh. It was as if his hurried pace had been an attempt to outrun the very question she now made him face.

After a moment, he opened his dark eyes and peered at her with the look of a concerned father.

She leaned away, struck by the answer implicit in his gentle gaze.

Tsaoshi lowered his head. "There are moments in history when everything changes, and the fate of humankind hangs in the balance."

"And this is one?"

He looked up and granted her a single, definitive nod. "Those moments are often difficult to see beyond because knowing too much changes them, changes all of history, all that will be."

"I don't understand."

"Those moments also have a life and a power all their own. Even if I knew exactly what happens, the people caught up in them, the things that happen to them, they are beyond anyone's ability to change."

Dellia's hand flew to her mouth.

Tsaoshi glanced away at the layers of the towerlike black temple next to him, his eyes as distant as his voice. "You cannot move two mountains, and a hundred roads between them will always lead to the other side." He returned his attention to Dellia.

She dropped her hand from her mouth. "Am I going to die?"

He shook his head. "I do not know. A much more powerful hand than mine is at work here, because most of the tree is shrouded in darkness. I can only see bits and pieces of a few branches."

He lowered his eyes again as if considering whether to reveal anything more. After a moment, he lifted his head. "I am not enlightened enough to see all the paths your fate may take, but I do know there is great pain for you in all of them."

Dellia stiffened. "If you can't see them, then how can you be so certain?"

As if coming to his senses, Tsaoshi gave a quick shake of his head and spat out a curt answer. "I cannot tell you. It could change things." He whirled around and raced off down the street, heading for the next bridge.

Dellia caught up, then dove in front of him and stopped. She stood firm in front of Tsaoshi, with her arms crossed, blocking his way. "If you don't tell me, I *will* change things."

Tsaoshi sighed again and stared up at Dellia as laughter drifted down from a couple dallying on the bridge behind him. "When we met in Talus, I could see it clearly. Jon is your one true love." He shook his head. "No greater love have I ever seen. Do you see now?"

Dellia took a step backward, shaking her head. "No. That can't be. He loves Megan."

Tsaoshi gave a quiet shake of his head. "Megan has a fate all her own. Perhaps more important than you, or Garris, or Jon. That fate has taken her far from here."

"I don't understand."

"She left so she and Jon would not be captured together. Aylun knew the risks. He convinced her. They have gone far from the reach of the council, searching for answers."

"Answers to what?"

"That is another story. One that has yet to be written."

Dellia stood there in stunned silence as Tsaoshi dove past her and took off again down the street. She snapped around and chased after him, her mind in a daze, not fully aware of the gentle sound of flowing water or the children running by on the street.

What had she done? She knew how she felt about Jon, but what Tsaoshi said could only mean one thing: Jon would eventually come to feel the same way. If only she could find him and tell him of her feelings. But she couldn't. Jon was still the one of the prophecy. His destiny remained as dark and troubling as ever. And she still had a duty. She could never follow in the footsteps of her father.

Tsaoshi led them around a corner and up onto one of the bridges. Dellia slowed, weighed down again by the burden of her troubled heart.

"It doesn't matter." She came to a stop and stared at the ground, struggling against her tears.

He stopped near the top of the bridge and turned to face her as a flat-bottomed boat skated along the surface of the water beneath them. She looked up into his face and, once again, found a gentle look of deep concern.

"Love always matters," Tsaoshi said.

"I have a duty. I must protect us all."

"I know, but to do your duty, you must keep him alive." He pointed behind him, across the bridge, the direction they had been going. "Go to him. Do as your heart bids. For at this moment, they are one and the same."

Her heart leaped. "You know where he is?"

"No. Not precisely. You must go to Kianlong Square. He will be drawn there. And it is there that you are destined to play your part. Many lives depend on this. You must go. Quickly."

With those few words, all the weight lifted from her soul and nothing else mattered. "He's here?"

"Yes. Now go. Run." He pointed again in the direction of the square and Dellia raced off across the bridge and into the streets. Just before she rounded the corner, out of sight, she halted and turned back to Tsaoshi, still watching from the bridge.

"Thank you," she called out, then ducked around the corner and down the streets of Kanlu, buoyed along by the prospect that Jon was okay and that soon she would see him again.

Jon froze and his mouth became dry as he stared at the three menacing strangers beyond Rillen. Garbed in an almost black shade of red, their bodies were laden with chains and assorted pieces of armor. Their faces obscured by scarves, they stood with arms crossed, blocking an alley that ran between the dirty walls of two run-down old homes.

Jon spun around. There was no way past the three in the street to the right or the three behind him. And four more dark strangers stood blocking the way further down a road lined with tired, patched-up buildings.

Jon's breathing quickened as he glanced here and there, searching for some opening in the heavily armed strangers all around them. They eyed him with cool determination, their bodies strewn with knives and whips and long, arced blades.

Rillen stood next to him. She remained crouched like a tiger, ready to pounce, her attention everywhere, with her tightened fists held ready in front of her.

He hesitated, unsure what was going on or whether to trust her. It seemed as if she had gone out of her way to lead him into a trap. Yet his only choice was to trust her and hope he was just misreading the situation.

Jon faced forward again and leaned over, whispering into Rillen's ear, "Tell me you can take on ten men."

"I can take on ten men," came her immediate reply.

Jon glanced all around. "You just said that because I told you to, didn't you?"

"Yup."

As the surrounding thugs began to advance, he brought himself up taller, and with as much conviction as he could muster, he bellowed, "You might want to think twice about angering Rillen here. She can take on ten men."

His words had no effect as the threatening figures continued their slow, steady march.

A burst of yelling and loud noises halted their advance, and they turned toward the sounds echoing down the dilapidated passage. A woman in a purple robe raced out of the alley and slammed into two of the men, shouldering them aside.

Garris followed, bashing the third along the paving stones. The woman stumbled across the dilapidated avenue, straight into the middle of the group.

The dark, ominous strangers stepped back, and Rillen sprang upright as the woman lurched to a stop. She raised her head, revealing a second Rillen staring straight into the face of the first.

Garris jerked to a stop, inches from colliding with his Rillen. He raised his head, then shot upright, his eyes shifting back and forth between the duplicate Rillens.

Jon just stared, trying to process a scene that made no sense on any level.

Garris looked at him and shook his head. "I'm not even going to ask."

Jon continued to stare in stunned silence. Two Rillens? Identical, down to the last detail? And Garris? He wasn't even supposed to be here. Was he real? Was anything real? Was he still back in the cave? But if Garris was real, maybe he knew.

"Is Enna okay?" Jon blurted out.

Garris looked puzzled but quickly became irked. "I'm fine, thanks for asking."

Ignoring the response, Jon continued to stare at him as he wait for reassurance.

"She's fine, okay? She's at the stables." Garris pointed. "At the edge of town." He shook his head. "Idiot," he grumbled under his breath.

Jon nodded. That was Garris, all right.

The surrounding strangers glanced at one another from beneath their scarved faces. Some shrugged, then one by one, they resumed their gradual progression, though slower and more hesitant than before.

The newly arrived Rillen glanced around at the many heavily

armed strangers closing in. She leaned back, speaking to Garris over her shoulder. "You know these are assassins, right?"

"Yup," he said.

She scanned the dark red strangers again, then eyed the other Rillen. "Does this kind of thing happen a lot?"

Garris shook his head and grumbled, "Way too often."

Jon stiffened. Assassins? Had this whole world gone completely nuts?

He brought himself up tall again and bellowed, "That's right, two of them. For those who can't do the math, that means they can take on twenty of you."

He turned his attention to the two Rillens. It was a puzzle that seemed to have no answer. How could there be two people who not only looked identical but had the exact same wardrobe? But if there couldn't be two Rillens, then one of them had to be a fake. A sudden notion piqued his curiosity and he reached out and grabbed the wrist of his Rillen, the one who it was now obvious was an impostor. "Can two play this game?"

Jon concentrated, and the world slowed, then dimmed. He pictured a moment in the cave, and a shimmering, translucent image appeared and slowed to a strange amber-skinned Elorian woman outside a passage, listening to his delirious mumbling in the cave beyond. She waved her hand down over herself and transformed into Rillen. He shook his head, and it all vanished, then the world around him brightened and began to stir again.

Just as the woman had done, Jon waved his hand down over his body as he concentrated on an image, and in an instant, he and Garris transformed into Rillens.

The assassins all halted and stepped back, staring.

Garris peered down at his now-female chest and scowled. His head shot up, and he glared at Jon as he growled under his breath.

Keeping track was becoming difficult, so Jon scanned each

Rillen and tried to memorize their true identities.

The real Rillen gawked at the other three with a shocked expression on her face. "I'm getting kind of freaked out here."

Jon glanced nervously at the surrounding assassins, then straightened. "That's right. There are four of us. That means we can take on forty."

The assassins all ignored him and began moving toward them again.

Another clatter erupted, and the assassins stopped as a woman flew out of the same alley. Something must have been chasing her because she stared over her shoulder as she slammed into the same two men Rillen had, bashing them out of the way. She stumbled to the center of the group, then snapped forward and screeched to a stop.

Jon's heart leaped. It was Dellia.

Her eyes went wide as she stood there, staring at the four Rillens before her. As if in a profound state of shock, she mumbled, "This is so wrong."

Relief flooded in as Jon stared at the face he had so desperately wanted to see. For countless hours they had traveled out of the desert and into the rocky terrain of Elore, and every step of that trip he had feared he was leaving her in peril. Yet here she was, standing in front of him. And as her questioning gaze met his, the danger surrounding them seemed to fade into unimportance.

Dellia straightened and alarm spread across her face as she scanned the threatening strangers all around.

Jon gathered his wits then puffed out his chest and shouted, "Yeah, that's right. There are five of us. That means—"

The assassins continued ignoring him, and all began drawing weapons.

He shook his head. "Oh, forget it."

Dellia eyed the four Rillens standing before her. "Which one of you is the real Rillen?"

Both Rillen and the impostor raised their hands.

"Okay, let's try this. Whose stupid idea was this?" Dellia motioned to the four Rillens.

The two with raised hands lowered them, as Jon raised his. Then the hesitant impostor raised her arm again.

Garris shook his head and popped the impostor Rillen in the face. She crumpled to the ground. As her body landed, it transformed into the same amber-skinned Elorian woman Jon had seen in the cave.

He passed his hand downward, and everyone turned back into themselves. They all stood for a moment poised and ready, throwing wary glances at the assassins surrounding them with their weapons drawn.

"What is this?" Dellia said.

"Ambush, I'm guessing," Garris replied.

"For who?"

"Jon," Rillen said. Dellia eyed Rillen, who shrugged. "He was surrounded and alone when we got here."

Dellia looked worried.

The assassins resumed closing in on the group.

Dellia eyed Garris and Rillen. "You have to get him out of here. I'll stay."

"I'm not leaving you," Garris shot back.

"I can take them. I trained against multiple protectors."

"Yeah," said Rillen, "four or five, not like a trizillion."

Another clatter erupted, this time all around them as three new men careened into the assassins on three sides. Two huge, burly soldiers on the left and right took out an assassin and began brawling with the others as a smaller, more lithe man struck from behind. It appeared to be some kind of coordinated attack because all three wore the same reddish leather armor with the ragged image of a flaming horse embossed on the surface.

When Dellia and Rillen spied them, they seemed relieved.

Jon looked around at the assassins on every side. He couldn't just run away and leave Dellia alone. He couldn't leave her unprotected. He wouldn't. There had to be some way to help.

He straightened. "I've got a plan."

Garris grumbled, "Hope it's better than the one that got you into this?"

"Hey. That wasn't my plan. I was being rescued."

Rillen looked at him in surprise. "By who?"

Jon peered down at the amber-skinned body on the ground. "Apparently, I have no idea."

Dellia glanced around at the heavily armed strangers moving in on them. "I count thirteen assassins. Is this your idea of a rescue?"

Jon stared at her. "Sure, pick on the guy who was just tortured for two days."

Dellia stopped and returned a wide-eyed expression of alarm. "Tortured?"

Jon caught Garris's eye and pointed at the alley ahead where three dark assassins were poised with weapons drawn, blocking the way. Garris nodded, then bellowed as he charged at them. Jon and Rillen flew after him.

Garris danced around their whistling swords, dodged a knife and a throwing star, and slammed two of them out of the way. As he flew into the alley, Rillen whipped around, and her foot smashed the third in the head, rocketing his skull to the crumbled pavement.

Jon followed, and as the three barreled down the decrepit alley, he checked back over his shoulder at Dellia disappearing on the street behind him. She braced herself and drew her dagger and sword. Stepping backward, she staved off four lightning blows from two assassins.

Jon faced ahead again and pushed to a sprint, driving out in front of the group. He passed his hand down and all three transformed into assassins, complete with deep red outfits, scarves, rusty chains, and gleaming weapons.

They rounded the corner out of the alley and flew into a stone avenue surrounding a long plaza. Jon screeched to a halt, scanning a grass-covered park, its length scattered with small trees smothered in pink blossoms.

He whipped around, glancing either way down a road lined with modest, well-kept homes. There, at either end, he spotted clusters of guards in uniforms of terra-cotta and royal purple, searching streets and houses.

Jon jumped up and down, waving his hands and yelling at the top of his lungs. Garris and Rillen joined him, their shouts echoing through the square.

The guards at both ends snapped around and spotted what appeared to be three assassins acting like crazy people. They pointed and shouted, then took off, charging down the lane toward them.

Jon pivoted his assassin-shaped body, heading back the way they'd come. Garris and Rillen surged toward the crude alley, but two assassins burst out of it and screeched to a halt as they came face to face with … themselves.

The four stood for a moment, stunned. Garris and Rillen dove at them, bludgeoning their look-alikes, who dropped like stones. The pair flew back into the dirty alley, with Jon close behind. As they raced down the decaying passage, Jon put on a burst of speed. He dashed out ahead and passed his hand down over them, and in an instant, the three switched back into themselves, then transformed into guards, just like the ones chasing them.

Jon peered ahead, anxious for any sign of Dellia. All of a sudden, she came into view in the street beyond, moving like a whirlwind: kicking, blocking, and slashing as she defended against three assassins.

He flew out of the alley, back into the midst of the brawl. Rillen and Garris followed, throwing themselves at the three assassins attacking Dellia.

Three of the surrounding assassins turned and charged the group.

Half a dozen more guards poured out of the alley, careening into the midst of the fight. They halted and expressions of alarm spread as they viewed the pandemonium they'd barged into.

The three charging assassins turned tail and raced off. Then, all the remaining assassins joined them, and every guard bolted after, pursuing them as they scattered into the dilapidated streets and dusty alleys.

The four stood and watched for a moment, then Jon passed his hand down over the group, and they all changed back into themselves.

Dellia spun around to face Jon. "This isn't over."

Garris nodded. "It's when you think they're defeated that assassins are at their most dangerous."

"I'll follow them," Rillen said. "You get as far from here as you can. Somewhere public."

Garris and Dellia looked at one another and in unison said, "The square," then took off in the opposite direction of the assassins. Jon barely had a moment to think, much less recover, before he turned and chased after.

Dellia and Garris flew around the corner and dove into an alley. Jon smiled as he raced after them into the disintegrating old passage. Moments ago, he had been convinced he was alone in a world that at every turn seemed determined to kill him. He knew all the reasons their parting had been for the best. But even as they clattered down a worn alleyway in a dirty part of town, chased by a pack of heavily armed assassins, he felt relieved, because the three of them were back together.

Chapter Twenty-Eight

REACHING OUT

Dellia whipped around the corner and slowed, waiting for Garris and Jon to catch up. As eager as she was to put distance between herself and the hired killers, it did no good to let her anxiety drive her to leave Jon behind in her haste. Dark, decaying stonework flew by as she focused on the footsteps of her companions behind her.

She took a deep breath, trying to still her terrified heart. In all those long hours scouring the desert, she had imagined finding Jon many times. She had pictured her apprehension melting away at the sight of his kind face, or the comfort of hearing his reassuring voice. What she had been utterly unprepared for, however, was to be greeted by illusion and ambush, or to hear stories of abduction and torture. And now, as she led the way down a dirty, run-down ally, evading assassins and soldiers alike, that sense of relief she had so often imagined was nowhere in sight.

The pace of the footsteps behind Dellia sped up, their thuds carrying down the crumbled old walls of the narrow alley. They told her that Jon had put on a burst of speed and was now close behind Garris.

"Where are we going?" Jon shouted.

"Kianlong Square," Dellia replied over her shoulder. "It's public and far from the assassins."

As he raced by her, he passed his hand down over them. In an instant, all three transformed into guards, complete with long, curved swords and authentic terra-cotta uniforms trimmed in royal purple.

Dellia nodded to Jon. It was a good idea. With guards and assassins on their tail, it would be better to look like one or the other, rather than appear as the ones both were after.

Jon was still staring back at her when they burst into the next street to see a body lying on the ground and a crowd gathered around it, gawking. Dellia halted, but Jon slipped on a pool of blood and stumbled forward. He tripped over the body and crashed to the stone pavement, landing with a breathy grunt.

The people gasped and stepped back, and murmurs flew through the onlookers.

Jon lay there for a moment, staring into the face of a guard with his neck slashed open and his blood draining onto the rough dirt and rock of the street.

Dellia hurried over and reached down to help Jon up, but he bolted backward, scrambling across the worn paving stones on his hands and knees. He continued to back away as he rose to his feet with his eyes wide.

The stunned crowd cleared around him, their eyes shifting between Jon and the lifeless body. Dellia peered at the face of the dead guard, then her gaze shot over to Jon. They looked identical.

Jon spun around and pushed through the crowd, as if simultaneously horrified and embarrassed by the scene.

Dellia's heart went out to him. He was trying so hard to handle a situation he was so ill equipped for. She hustled after him, and as she ran up alongside him, she hooked her arm around his, steadying him even as she hurried him along. At first, he shivered at her touch, then he seemed to calm, and the worry lines on his face relaxed.

Dellia let go and forged ahead, leading the way once again. The three sprinted along the park's edge past low benches and scattered trees laden with large pink blossoms. They flew around the corner, along the tranquil park, and down to the next intersection, where

Dellia dove into another alley.

Garris slowed and turned back to address Jon. "Can we not look like one of the two groups trying to kill each other here?"

Dellia glanced at Jon. "Tsaoshi? He has authority here."

Jon nodded and passed his hand down over the both of them. They returned to their original form, then Jon turned into Tsaoshi and Garris into a stranger.

Dellia led the way down streets and through alleys, one after the other. Houses slowly became longer and more ornate, and the courtyards visible between them, larger and more impressive. The dress of the people changed, too, from simple rough-spun tunics to long silken robes with bright patterns, gold trim, and elegant embroidery.

Dellia's focus remained single-minded. She had to get Jon to the square. Once there, he would be in a wide-open space. That would make it impossible to attack him and remain hidden, so she could spot any threat coming. Beyond that, she couldn't think. Tsaoshi had told her she had a part to play, and for now, she had to believe it was to protect Jon and keep him safe.

They sprinted around a corner, which Jon cut more closely than the others. He banged into someone in a long black robe. The stranger started to fall, but Jon stumbled and lurched forward to catch them. As he lifted the man back upright, he raised his head, and Jon found himself staring into the brown eyes of a startled Tsaoshi.

He stiffened, obviously bewildered for a moment as he gazed into his own face on a stranger. He spotted Garris, then Dellia, and an expression of comprehension came over him. The oracle returned his gaze to his look-alike and bowed. "You might not want to go around looking like someone so well known."

Jon passed his hand down over himself, and he and Garris changed back into themselves.

As Tsaoshi spotted Jon, he became even more agitated, and

there was an urgency in his voice. "You must come with me, to the square ... *now.*"

He took off toward the square. Jon must not have noticed Garris's disgusted expression because he turned and ran after. But as he passed Garris, the warrior reached out and snagged Jon's arm, jerking him to a stop.

"Why?" Garris demanded as he glared at Tsaoshi.

Tsaoshi stopped and faced him. "I do not precisely know why. Just hurry." He motioned for them to follow.

Garris remained still. "Typical. You know where you need to be, but not why."

"I have instructions. It is where Jon will find what he seeks."

"Instructions?" Jon asked. "From who?"

"Nobody knows for sure," Tsaoshi said.

Puzzled, Jon stared.

Garris scoffed. "An oracle following anonymous instructions, how reassuring."

Screams echoed down the street from the direction they were all going. All four startled and peered ahead, searching for the source of the noise.

Tsaoshi became even more agitated. "There is no time for this."

Garris crossed his arms and glared. The oracle blurted out a rushed explanation. "It is how the Augury works. Every few generations, a Great Oracle is discovered. What they see is never fully known. Who left these instructions I do not know. Someone very powerful has worked very hard to keep every part of it a secret, even from us."

Garris appeared disgusted. "Why should we trust an organization that can't even trust itself?"

Jon eyed him. "Do I have a choice? I have to find the oracle room."

Tsaoshi looked at Jon with a puzzled expression. "Oracle room?

There is no such place."

"See," said Garris, "he's useless. He doesn't have a clue."

Jon turned his attention to Tsaoshi. "What about Kita Pass? I have to answer the riddle of Kita Pass."

Dellia pointed in the direction they'd been headed. "Kita Pass? It leads up into the mountains from Kianlong Square."

Jon became animated and stared down the street where Dellia was pointing. Like a kid heading to a candy store, he said, "Then let's go."

Tsaoshi turned and led the way. Jon yanked his arm from Garris's grasp and took off, leaving him and Dellia behind.

The ground rumbled, and more screams emanated from down the street, the direction Jon was headed.

Dellia stared at his back as he rushed off, leaving her standing there. She had worried so much, and fought so hard, to get to Jon, and here he was running from her, yet again, as if all she had gone through meant nothing to him.

An irrational aggravation came over her, and she donned a sarcastic sweetness as she conversed with Jon's departing backside. "I'm happy to see you, too. Oh, you shouldn't have worried about me. I'm just glad you're okay."

Garris eyed her sideways. "What did you expect?"

She took off after Jon, still hurt by the sudden abandonment. Garris hustled after and pulled up alongside her. Dellia looked over at him. "It's just, I was so worried about him, and here he is charging off like nothing's happened."

"Can you blame him, when he's this close?"

"You're right. It's not like we're married or something."

He gave her a peculiar look. "That's not even close to what I said."

"And why is he always running away from me?"

"You do realize you might have to arrest—"

Garris halted as they rounded the corner.

There Jon stood with his back to them, frozen and staring, his outline framed by the chaos in the massive park that was Kianlong Square.

In the distance, across the lush grass and serene ponds, dead bodies, in all stages of decay, from skeletons to the newly deceased, jolted and jerked their way down Kita Pass. They became a river of corpses and skeletons skittering down the canyon and into the square. A handful of soldiers hacked and slashed in a losing battle to contain them as screaming residents fled and hid all across the massive park.

Dellia halted some distance behind Jon, stunned by the scene unfolding beyond him. Powerful necromancy was at work here, more powerful than anything she could have ever dreamed.

A boulder plummeted from the sky, landing uncomfortably close to Jon. It hit the ground with a boom and shattered, and he turned away, covering his eyes as dust and stone fragments flew everywhere. Dellia headed for him. She had to protect him. But how could she protect anyone from this?

Kayleen stood on the arching wooden bridge, staring into the serene waters below, wondering if she had made the right choice. She had chosen to trust Grekor when he said their orders were to save Jon from an ambush, and despite her deep reservations, she had let him and his two companions go. In the end, what had swayed her was not the sincerity in Nikosh's voice or her sense they were being truthful. What convinced her was that his claim was too conniving a subterfuge for those three lugs and precisely the kind of elaborate ruse she'd expect from Braye.

She jerked her head up at the sound of distant screams and yells drifting over the buildings that ringed the camp. Those cries were the echoes of something terrible unfolding. She closed her eyes and concentrated.

Her gift rarely proved useful. It might seem like the ability to sense disturbances in the veil would be indispensable, but nature and humankind constantly drew power from beyond the veil, and travel through portals punched holes right through it. Things were always happening beyond the borders of the world we knew. So her gift was like a constant noise in the back of her mind, like the crashing of waves near the ocean, or the singing of birds at sunrise.

Once in a long while, something big or unusual would grab her attention, such as when Prisha came, or when Jon and Megan arrived. Otherwise, the constant roar tended to go unnoticed, and it required focus to sort through the chatter. But as she concentrated, she shivered, and a chill ran through her soul. Right now, in the cliffs above the city, a gaping wound to somewhere dark and terrifying was bleeding unknown horrors into this world.

Kayleen swung around and sprinted across the bridge, headed for the street.

Ahead, a woman shouted as she dashed by, and as Kayleen neared the road, another flew past carrying a child. Kayleen stopped at the edge of the lane and snagged the arm of a man running across her path. He jerked to a stop, and his panic-stricken face whipped over, staring into hers.

As he struggled against her grip, Kayleen shouted at him, "What is it?"

"Creatures," the man said, "in Kianlong Square. So many. The dead and giants."

Kayleen let go, and the man raced off. She shuddered at the kind of power needed to cause a disruption of this scope. The kind normally found only in artifacts or … she didn't want to contemplate the alternatives. Right now, the details mattered little. People needed protecting, and she commanded thirteen soldiers she could bring to the aid of the city.

She spun around and sprinted back over the small arched bridge and down the stone pathway. It was impossible to tell what was occurring, but the chances were good it wasn't all just a colossal coincidence. Chances are it somehow involved Jon. Regardless, she needed to get Quirtus and gather the men.

She flew around an artfully arranged grouping of massive boulders and shot past a grove of sculpted trees that sprang from the rocky ground. Cutting across the grass, she dove into Quirtus's tent.

She came to an abrupt halt. There before her on the dimly lit grass, Quirtus lay facedown with her onyx dagger in his back, its dragon-claw pommel jutting into the air.

She stood for a moment, trying to comprehend the scene as a scream drifted along the breeze. She flew to his side and crouched, checking his breath, but he was dead. She let out a small gasp. "Oh no."

At the edge of her vision, an almost undetectable movement caused her to freeze. Without moving her head, she raised her eyes from the body and scanned her surroundings.

Her heart jumped as she spotted it. There in the shadows, a figure crouched, almost invisible against the pattern of dark and light. The dark outline lifted its hooded face, and she recognized the wild red hair of Tetch. His eyes shifted between her and the door, his expression cold and menacing.

His manner and voice remained calm as he said, "How inconvenient."

Kayleen shrank back away from him.

In a flash, Tetch snatched the dagger from Quirtus's blood-soaked back and brandished it.

With slow, careful movements, she rose from the ground.

"Your constant snooping is getting to be a real problem." Tetch glanced down at the body below him and smiled. "Well ... especially for poor Quirtus here."

Kayleen had one chance to catch him off guard. She stared and said, "I don't think you've thought this through, Tetch, what do you—"

She dove to his right and shot her arm up, deflecting his blade. She swung her arm down, but he dodged and twisted out of the way.

Kayleen lost her footing, and Tetch shoved her as she flew by. She stumbled and caught her balance as he slid over in front of the entrance.

She pivoted to face him, but he now stood blocking her only avenue of escape.

Still calm and unruffled by the exchange, Tetch looked at the onyx blade. "I had intended to use your dagger to frame you for killing Jon, but you had to go and make Quirtus suspicious, and he blundered into … things."

Nervous, Kayleen glanced at the exit behind him. "Quirtus always suspected you. Ever since he saw you and Braye talking."

"Nice try. I've never spoken to Braye."

"What are you going to do now, kill me?"

Tetch smiled. "Why would I want to do that? You're going to find Jon for me." He raised his ear, listening to the now-closer screams and yelling. "Besides, you're soon going to be far too busy with what-ever that is to worry about me." His smile broadened into a grin. "But you will find Jon. And when you do, and you are both too occupied to think of me, that's when I'll strike … and end you both."

Kayleen tilted her head to better catch the sound of voices approaching outside the tent.

Tetch kept his eyes fixed on her as he turned his head toward the noise and smiled. He gave a short bow and tossed the dagger toward her.

She caught it as he dove to the ground and rolled out under the back of the tent.

She stared down at the polished, black blade, its fresh blood streaking her hands. She looked down at the dead body on the ground, then over at the entrance as the voices grew closer.

Kayleen crouched and cringed as she stabbed the dagger back into Quirtus's back. She dove to the ground and rolled out the back of the tent, just as Tetch had done. As she rose to her feet, she quickly spat on her blood-streaked hands and rubbed them on the grass.

She crouched again and raced around the tent, then stood up as she circled behind the group of men approaching the entrance to Quirtus's tent.

"You, men," Kayleen nearly shouted, "come with me. There's a disturbance in Kianlong Square."

"We were just fetching Quirtus," said Alkis, one of her men.

"He's not there. I sent him on an errand. Now come."

Her heart pounding and gravely wounded by the death of an old friend, Kayleen snapped around. Without checking to see if the men would follow, she struck out for the exit. As much as she wanted to honor Quirtus, for he was an honorable man, right now, the fate of the living took precedence.

The moment she had been dreading was at hand. Events were coming to a head, and the course they took in the coming minutes might very well decide the fate of all. It pained her to the core to leave the body of her loyal companion facedown on the ground, but she dared not show the least sign of her sorrow or trauma.

As she marched off at a stiff clip, Kayleen choked back her tears and steadied her voice. Then she shouted over her shoulder, "Come. Now. That's an order!"

Dellia stood for a moment, staring past Jon's outline at the stiff, twisted corpses scrambling down the narrow mountain pass. A few guards yelled between them as they hacked and slashed in a losing battle to contain the rotted, decomposing bodies twitching and jerking their way onto the park. Dellia's pulse quickened at screams and cries for help. People were fleeing in every direction as guards hurried them off to safety.

Garris tore his eyes from the scene and nodded to Dellia. "Take care of him. I have to help." Then he raced off in the direction of Simay and Sitong, battling the horde far across the park.

Dellia moved toward Jon, who seemed mesmerized by the chaotic scene unfolding in the enormous square. She stopped at his side, watching with him.

Without turning, Jon said, "This is it, Dellia. The final piece, and then Megan and I can go home."

"What?" Dellia's fear jumped.

He turned to her, and they faced one another. He pointed at the swarm of gnarled bodies skittering across the square. "I knew it would be like this. Someone doesn't want me to leave." He smiled at her. "I don't know how, but I have to do this one last thing."

Dellia's heart pounded faster at what she feared Jon was implying. "You can't be seriously considering going up the pass with all that?" She pointed to Kita Pass and all the dead massing down it.

"I have to."

"But you'll never make it!"

Jon stepped closer and looked into her face. "Listen, Dellia, I've been so worried about you."

Her gift persisted in failing her, but his face spoke volumes. The surrounding chaos drifted into a haze as she lost herself in the affection in his soft eyes. "Me?" she heard herself say. "Why?"

"I knew something was wrong when you didn't find me. I was so afraid that they might have done something to you when they took me."

"They? Who? Why did they take you?"

"Information," said Jon. "I was tied up. It seemed like days. And

I know now, it was an illusion, but it felt so real. I had an arrow in my stomach. They kept asking where Megan was, over and over. They cut off my fingers. They pulled out my teeth."

Her stomach knotted, and her mind rebelled at the horror of what Jon must have endured. "Oh, Adi."

He smiled again. "But I made it because you were with me."

"I don't understand. I wasn't with you."

He glanced down just as Kayleen burst into view behind him at the edge of the park with almost a dozen Shirdon guards. She shouted a few orders, and they dove into the pandemonium.

Surprised by her sudden appearance, Dellia stiffened and stared.

"No. I know that now," Jon said. "I was probably hallucinating. But still, you got me through it." He raised his head, searching Dellia's face for her reaction.

She answered as she continued to watch Kayleen. "I know you've been through a lot, and—"

"I'm trying to tell you something, Dellia."

Her focus snapped back to him as she realized she wasn't paying attention to words that were not coming easily.

Jon reached out to take her hands. "I'm trying to tell you—"

Her heart jumped at the prospect of what she feared Jon was about to say. "Jon, please. Don't." Dellia pulled away from his touch. Then she shook her head and looked away at Kayleen again. "Not now."

He halted and dropped his hands. "But I may not get another chance."

She returned her focus to him as she struggled with what she knew she must do. Finally, she understood. This was the part she had to play. This was why Tsaoshi had said there would be pain for her here.

A profound sadness took hold, and Dellia tilted her head.

"There's something I have to do first."

"This minute?"

"Stay here, Jon." She was barely able to hold her composure. "Just for a moment. And when I'm done, you can tell me anything you want."

Her every instinct told her to reach out and grab hold of him. To melt into his arms and tell him everything that was in her heart. But she couldn't. Fate had cast a different role for her.

"But ..." Jon's eyes fixed on something behind her.

Dellia gazed into his face. "Just stay. Okay—"

His head whipped over, and a sudden boom echoed through the park. Alarm spread across his face, and he bolted toward the noise, leaving her standing alone.

Dellia closed her eyes. "Or not."

She took a deep breath and turned to watch as Jon zigzagged his way through the crowd of dead. He was putting himself in danger, and every fiber of her being wanted to run after him, to protect and watch out for him, but she was frozen by indecision. As Jon dove under a bench, she shook it off and braced herself. There was no point in mourning what might have been. This was her duty. She steeled herself, then marched off toward Kayleen.

Anger welled within her as she dove through the pack of stiff, jerking bodies.

The rotted and growling corpse of a woman flew at her.

She whipped out her sword and hacked down, putting all her frustration into the blow.

It severed the arm from the body, but the corpse turned and clawed at her anyway, clamping down on her wrist with the cold, dead fingers of its remaining hand. Its head lowered and mouth opened, preparing to take a bite.

The body of a man slammed into Dellia, wrenching her from the dead woman's grasp and sending her tumbling to the ground.

She drew her dagger with her free hand as she rolled over and sprang to her feet. Unleashing all her frustration, she whipped around and plunged the blade into the woman's forehead as her sword whistled through the air, taking off the man's head.

Her blades whirling in a frenzy, blinded by frustration, Dellia hacked a path straight for Kayleen as corpses fell around her like leaves before a hurricane.

She pushed through the guards surrounding Kayleen and stepped up to her. Her voice trembling, almost pleading, she said, "Kayleen, I can't do this."

Kayleen stared for a moment, apparently confused by the abrupt entrance. Then, a look of sympathy crossed her face, and she rested her hands on Dellia's arms. "You have to."

She looked straight into Kayleen's face. "I love him."

"Do you know Tetch?" Kayleen pointed to the chaos in the square. "He's out there somewhere, plotting to kill Jon. And he's not the only one. People are afraid of him. We have to take him in."

Kayleen's concern was genuine., and she could see the danger to Jon, but her heart rebelled at the idea of confronting him. How could she ever explain it? How could she ever make this right?

"It's our duty," Kayleen said.

Every instinct, every fiber of her being struggled against those words. Words she had repeated to herself so many times of late. Yet she understood the truth of them. It didn't matter how much her heart ached or how much it told her that what she was doing was wrong. Kayleen was right. She had sworn an oath. She had a duty to something greater than her herself.

Dellia closed her eyes as her anger and frustration drowned in a sea of anguish. She gave a small, sad nod.

Kayleen's warm fingers lifted her chin, and she stared into Dellia's eyes. "I will do everything I can to keep him safe."

Dellia pulled herself upright and pushed down her tumult of

emotions. Now only one thing mattered. She had only one mission, one goal: to apprehend Jon and bring him in. And there was no way she could face what she must do unless she hardened her heart. She readied her sword and dagger. It was time to put every ounce of skill she possessed to work.

She turned and marched off into the chaos of stiff, jerking corpses. Operating on instinct alone, she slashed and stabbed like a machine, kicking and punching with deadly efficiency as she headed straight for Jon.

Chapter Twenty-Nine

KITA PASS

As Jon gazed into her beautiful blue eyes, images of Megan and that moment of rejection in his lab flooded his mind. Fear gripped him over the prospect that Dellia might do the same. He swallowed hard and struggled to push back his demons. Summoning all his courage, Jon reached out to take her hands. "I'm trying to tell you—"

"Jon, please, don't." Dellia recoiled from his touch. She shook her head and stared off into the distance. "Not now."

Jon dropped his hands. Fear gripped him again at the realization that Dellia was on the verge of turning him down, just as Megan had done.

He shoved the thought aside and forged on. "But I may not get another chance."

A sudden and inexplicable sadness transformed Dellia, and she stared into Jon's eyes with a pitiful, anguished look. "There's something I have to do first."

"This minute?" Jon said, distressed that he wasn't being given a chance to voice the feelings he had struggled so hard to express.

"Stay here, Jon. Just for a moment. And when I'm done, you can tell me anything you want."

As he watched at her pained expression, his confusion only grew. It had taken all his resolve to face her like this and tell her how much he cared about her. Yet, she was shutting him down before he even had the chance. And the look in her eyes was heartbreaking. She was struggling. And he wanted desperately to do something, anything, to fix whatever it was. But he had no idea what he'd done wrong or what to do to make it better.

Jon stared at her. "But ..."

A harrowing scream cut through the chaos. His head whipped over, and his eyes fixed on a sparkle of ornate jewelry. It adorned a woman in a long purple robe, its gold trim shimmering in the late afternoon sun. At the edge of the park, she writhed and squirmed against a pair of guards as they struggled to keep her from storming into a horde of grisly, lurching corpses. She reached out in a blind panic, babbling and incoherent as she clawed at the air, frantic to get to something or someone.

Dellia gazed into Jon's face. "Just stay. Okay?"

His head swung around as he followed the woman's gaze to a young boy hidden under a bench carved of stone. Bones draped with rotted flesh twisted and scrambled by the young man's saucer eyes as he crouched there, frozen in terror, peering out from his meager shelter.

Jon's stomach knotted, and he flinched as another boulder slammed into the ground with a boom that resonated throughout the park. Dust and debris flew into the air, and the boy shrank away into the shadows as Jon bolted toward him.

He drove headlong in an all-out race. The last thing he needed now was to see a child torn to pieces or a mother lose her son. A horrid, fetid odor assaulted his senses as he ducked and dodged past one rigid, jerking body after another. The sounds of grumbling and moaning rose above the din of clanging swords and shouting.

Jon glanced back to find a swarm of corpses scrambling after him. Despite their twitching and stiff movement, they were gaining on him. His heart jumped at the prospect that he might now be in more trouble than the child he was struggling to reach.

He passed his hand over his face and body, and in an instant, the flesh of his hands turned dark and putrid, indistinguishable from the dead rampaging after him. It worked and they ignored him as he shouldered his way through a muddle of shambling bodies. He turned his attention forward, his eyes focused on the smooth, stone bench where the boy lay hiding.

The growling and snarls dissipated as Jon cleared the crowd, and his pursuers drifted off, having given up the chase. Trees and flowers and corpses of all kinds, in all states of decay, flew by as he pushed harder, and the chaos of fighting and screams grew distant behind him.

He ducked as he approached the bench and dove under, feet first. He waved his hand again and turned back into himself as he slid to a stop next to the boy.

The youngster gasped and skittered backward in a panic, cowering from him.

Jon smiled. "It's okay. It's okay. I'm going to get you out of—" He halted at the metallic clattering of a sword tumbling across a stone walkway. His gaze shot over as it slid to a stop, right outside the cover of the bench.

He looked up to see where it came from, and a short distance away stood Garris, fighting back-to-back with two of the men who had saved them at the ambush. He nodded to Jon and rejoined them, their blows raining down heavy and hard.

Unable to help, but unable to turn away, he watched as Garris's sword plummeted down on an attacking corpse. It sliced through its wrist, cleaving the hand from its arm. But the attacking dead showed no sign of pain. Its flesh was rotted through, just tattered muscle that should be incapable of moving its body. Yet the abomination redoubled its attack, animated by some hidden force.

With its remaining hand, the cadaver grabbed the wrist of the massive, red-leather-clad soldier standing behind Garris. It jerked its head down, burying its teeth in the uncovered part of the soldier's forearm. The soldier bellowed in pain.

His lithe partner dove for the corpse then stabbed it over and over like some crazed machine, but the animated carcass never slowed its assault.

Garris turned and swung his sword across with all his weight, severing the corpse's neck and barely missing the two men. The head flew away, and the body crumpled to the ground.

Jon jerked his eyes away and hid his face, trying to shove the horrifying scene from his mind.

After a moment, he returned his focus to the boy. "I'll get you out of here. Okay?"

Eyes wide and trembling, the boy nodded.

Jon scanned the pandemonium, searching for the boy's mother. He found her far across the park, still in a frantic haze, wailing and crying out as she struggled against her protectors.

He motioned to the dead just outside the bench. "I'm going to make us look like them. Then we can just walk through. Okay?"

The boy shrank back further, his eyes wide as he gave a vigorous shake of his head.

"But they won't bother us."

The boy shook his head again.

Jon pointed at the woman in her long purple robe, desperate to tear herself away from the pair of guards. "See those guards? Do you think they're afraid?"

The boy offered a gentle shake of his head.

"Do you think they are brave?"

The boy nodded.

"You're afraid, aren't you?"

The kid nodded vigorously.

Jon donned his most earnest expression. "Then you are braver than they are."

The boy's eyes flew wide.

"You see, being brave isn't being unafraid. It's doing what needs doing, even when you *are* afraid."

Jon thrust his arm out farther, pointing at the woman again. "Your mother needs you. Be brave. Come with me. Please."

Then came the boy's voice, tiny and trembling, but trying hard to sound grown up. "You will stay with me?"

"Yes, I will never leave you. You can count on it."

Jon offered his hand, and the boy reached out and wrapped his trembling fingers around it. He glanced up, and anxiety clutched at his chest as he viewed the dead raging everywhere, plunging along the ponds, by trees, and across paths.

He waved his hand, and in an instant, he and the boy took on the appearance of putrefied corpses. As Jon flew out from under the bench, he snatched the sword with one hand while he dragged the terrified boy behind him with the other.

After only a few steps, a firm hand seized Jon's arm. He spun around and raised his sword but stopped when he saw Garris's hand grasping his rotted-looking arm.

Jon looked down at his decaying body. "How did you spot me?"

His speech pressured and his tone sarcastic, Garris blurted out, "Yeah, how could I possibly spot a corpse wielding my sword?" He pointed back in the other direction to a group of guards with a middle-aged woman in their midst. "That's Kayleen over there. She's council leader, and those guards work for her. Dellia is with them, and that means odds are she's coming to arrest you."

Startled by the notion, Jon said, "But she would never do that. She was helping me."

"She's a soldier," Garris said, his words fading as he took off back toward the two men.

Jon's head reeled as he scanned the area. Garris had to be mistaken. Dellia couldn't. She wouldn't. Then, he caught sight of her as she shoved her way through the guards with her dagger and sword drawn. With an expression of intense determination, she began carving a path straight toward him.

Jon's breathing quickened, and he glanced down at the boy, then over at his mother. He tried to take off, but the hand clasping his wouldn't move. He looked down at the boy, standing there, frozen and trembling, his eyes wide, staring at the swarm of dead bodies skittering all around them.

Jon glanced back at Dellia and then the boy. "We have to go—"

A thunder of hooves pounded in his ears and he went rigid and frozen in alarm as a massive, decaying horse galloped right by his head. The boy stiffened as the horse swung around them, bashing bodies out of the way like they were toys. It charged out across the park, past Dellia, and barreled into the guards, scattering them and trampling one.

The remaining guards attacked it, but Dellia forged on, undeterred, with a look of hard resolve. Even now, as she hunted him, she was a glorious sight, a flurry of blades, kicks, and punches, toppling the dead before her like grain before a scythe.

Jon snapped out of it. She was now only a couple hundred feet away and closing in with alarming speed. He tugged on the tiny, white-knuckled hand grasping his, but the petrified boy still wouldn't budge. Jon looked over at Dellia, then down at the little man, then over at Dellia again. Waving his hand, he knelt on the grass before the young man as he transformed back into himself.

He placed a gentle hand on the frightened boy's decaying cheek. "It's okay. I will get you through this, but you have to come with me now. Be brave, okay? Your mother needs you."

The boy stared for a moment, then swallowed and nodded.

Jon waved his hand and changed back into one of the dead. He glanced back at Dellia, now only a couple dozen feet away. He took off again with the boy in tow, headed for the distraught mother.

Then Dellia's voice rang out, sharp and demanding. "Jon, stop."

He turned to face her, and it was like she had become a different person. Her posture was as stiff and unfeeling as the look she gave him.

"I'm sorry, but I have to take you in." Her expression and words were determined and strong.

She began a slow advance.

As he backed away from her, Jon yelled out, "Why, because you believe I could do all those things they say in the prophecy?"

"It doesn't matter what I believe."

"It does to me."

Dellia stopped inching forward and stood tall and proud. "I have a duty," she proclaimed.

Stunned, Jon halted and stammered, "And that's more important than ... I mean, I thought ... you and me ..." Unable to put his feelings into words, Jon just shook his head. "I guess I was just wrong."

It was as if he'd slapped her in the face. A hint of remorse cracked her harsh determination, and for a moment she seemed torn. "But you need protecting."

"Maybe." He shook his head again. "But I never thought I'd need protecting from you."

Dellia seemed crushed by his comment. As if to quell the struggle apparent in her eyes, she pulled herself up even taller, but when she spoke, her words were softer and more pleading. "Jon, please, don't make this harder than it already is."

He took a step backward. "I'm so sorry, Dellia, I have to get home."

In a flash, he snatched up the boy and bolted. Carrying him under one arm, he sprinted for the mother unhindered, cloaked by his illusory form.

Jon kept checking over his shoulder as Dellia stood for a moment, appearing to gather her resolve. Then she took off, chasing after him, but she lost ground, bogged down by the need to hack her way through waves of skittering dead.

As Jon raced up toward the woman, one of the two guards whipped around and flew at him, his gleaming sword whistling through the air.

By reflex alone, Jon snapped his blade up to intercept, right in front of his face. A loud clang rang out as the impact drove the weapon from his hand and sent him flying to the ground. He grasped for the sword as it clattered away.

He turned his eyes upward as the guard stepped toward him, his blade raised high over his head.

Jon passed his hand over himself and his charge, and they transformed back into their native form.

The guard's eyes flew wide as he stiffened and jerked his blade away. He stepped back, staring at the boy with a horrified expression.

Jon snatched his charge's hand and yanked him along as they scrambled across the ground on hands and knees. He scurried past the legs of both guards and popped up in front of the woman, hoisting her son up for her to see.

Relief flooded her face as she grabbed her boy and squeezed him tight. She rained kisses down on him at a feverish pace, then stopped and turned her gaze toward Jon, bowing her head in deep gratitude.

He shot his gaze back to Dellia, only a couple dozen feet away and plunging toward him with that same look of grim determination.

In a panic, he seized the woman in purple, still clutching her boy, and spun them around as fast as he could. As they whirled in circles, he passed his hand down over them and transformed himself into her and she into him.

Now disguised as the boy's mother, Jon pushed away from her, and as the guards fought and puzzled, he raced off, away from Dellia.

He glanced back over his shoulder as one of the soldiers motioned the other to stay. Then he glared at Jon and shook his head as he sprinted after. It was a dumb plan, and the confusion had only bought him a moment's lead.

Dellia slashed her way past the last two dead and barged past the remaining guard, coming to a halt in front of the woman, who still looked like Jon cradling a boy. After a moment's discussion, Dellia pivoted toward Jon, anger flashing in her beautiful eyes as she charged after him. Sure, he'd gotten away, but now he was being chased by two very angry people.

He pushed harder, trying to stay ahead as he watched his pursuers over his shoulder.

A sudden panic flooded Dellia's face, and she came to an abrupt halt, her arms reaching out to him.

Startled, he snapped back forward, puzzled at what could alarm her so. He gasped as he discovered he was hurtling toward a horde of snarling, moaning corpses and behind them an enormous decaying giant. The rotting giant stood three stories tall, with a massive boulder hoisted high above its head. He glared at Jon, and his feet thundered as he stepped forward and hurtled the enormous stone down at him.

Jon swerved as he poured on the speed, and the boulder arced over his head. He dove into a sea of putrid legs as it crashed into the ground right behind him with a thunderous boom.

Shattered fragments ripped through a dozen corpses above him. Bodies hurtled over him, blasted to the ground by the impact.

Jon rolled out of the way, coming to a stop right at the giant's decrepit feet. With a gasp, he stared up at the massive, dead brute looming above him. Horror gripped him as the rotted giant turned his festering eyes downward, staring straight at him.

He passed his hand down over himself, and his form changed to match the surrounding dead. The monstrosity's focus seemed to drift away and he began scanning the area. Breath heaving, Jon scrambled out of sight, hiding out behind the giant's massive feet.

Jon stared back toward Dellia, charging at him, blades flashing through the air and nearly upon him. In a panic, he cast his gaze everywhere, desperate for a path of escape. The thud of the giant's feet covered the shouting and mayhem of the park as his eyes fixed on the base of the pass where dead swarmed into the park. His racing heart thundered in his ears as he decided what he had to do.

Jon braced himself and tore off toward the pass, staggering and jerking like one of the putrefied dead. Never looking back, he dove through the crowd of corpses, becoming lost in the whirlwind of twitching, jolting bodies.

The stench was nearly intolerable. Snarls and growls came from every direction, almost drowning out the distant screams and yelling as Jon shouldered his way through the throng. He tried to glance back at Dellia, but bodies hurtled past, jolting, lurching, all around him, blocking his view behind a storm of animated death.

As he reached the other side, Jon searched everywhere, frantic to locate Dellia before she could spot him. He spotted her standing over the wounded guard, fighting like a possessed madwoman. Her movements were a blur as she fended off a host of dead and the attacks of the giant, reaching down to grab her. His heart jumped, and adrenaline shot through his body as he imagined what that giant would do to her.

He scanned the chaos around him and found Garris a short distance away, fighting at a feverish pace. Jon took off toward him, dashing through a sea of the dead in a desperate race. He jerked to a stop next to him as he passed his hand down and reverted back into himself. "I lost the sword."

Garris sent him an annoyed look. "You what?" he shouted as he slung his weapon down with brutal force, sinking it deep into the shredded thigh of a cadaver.

"Please, Garris, not now."

Between blows, he eyed Jon. "In my pack. There are daggers."

Jon spun around to Garris's back. The pack jerked up and down with each heavy blow as Jon flung it open. He reached inside and grabbed a short, curved blade.

Then, his eyes fell on the tiny, silver vial with an intricate pattern of vines etched into its surface. A sudden image flashed through his mind of Garris back on the Talus Plains. Jon jerked upright as he snatched it up and stared at it. The interment solution—Priyal's Pyre. He'd sprinkled it on the dead bodies.

Jon eyed Garris over the warrior's heavily muscled shoulder. "I have to rescue Dellia. I'll be back." He dashed off toward her with the vial still clutched in his fist.

Jon raised his hand, preparing to pass it down over himself and transform back into one of the raging deceased. He jerked his arm back down. No, that wouldn't do, he needed to attract their attention.

He poured on the speed, diving and dodging his way through the carcasses scrambling all around him. As he raced toward Dellia, a swarm of skittering bodies began to chase after him.

Ahead, beyond the bodies jerking across his path, Dellia leaped and tumbled. Her blows fell in blistering succession as she staved off an army of the dead and the giant's massive hands.

Jon thrust his dagger out in front of him with the blade forward. The sound of thundering feet grew closer as he gripped the weapon tightly in his sweaty palm and braced himself.

He drove the blade through the giant's massive calf. The impact wrenched his hand back and he winced in pain. As the beast reached down, Jon spun around, snatched the vial, and splashed a few drops across the gaping, bloodless wound.

The giant swiped at him with both hands, but Jon dodged out of the way. Vines sprang from the few drops on the giant's festering wound. They dug through the enormous brute's legs, reaching out to dive through the flesh of its grasping hands and trap them.

Jon ran through the giant's legs, coming within a few feet of Dellia as she battled corpses on every side. A horde of dead chased Jon through, only to become ensnared in the writhing mass of spreading vegetation.

Jon dodged around the giant's ankle and raced off back toward Garris. Vines grew and dug, tendrils reaching out, leaping from corpse to corpse, expanding, growing into a solid mass of dead flesh and living plant.

He glanced back at Dellia. She now stood in the midst of a writhing, squirming wall of vegetation. No longer battling the surrounding dead, she turned her attention to the living barrier and began hacking a path straight toward him.

He halted at Garris's side and shoved the vial in his face. "It isn't necromancy. It consumes death to spread life."

"Fascinating," Garris said, clearly not paying attention. "But you remember Kayleen?" He thrust out a finger, pointing to the opposite side of the park from Dellia. "She's headed our way with a bunch of soldiers."

"You don't get it!" Jon shouted over the snarls and growls.

Garris stared, perplexed.

"This stuff eats these things." Jon flung his arm out, pointing to the vine-covered giant.

Garris followed Jon's finger and straightened as he spotted the enormous brute at the center of a solid mass of vines and corpses.

Jon's gaze darted between Dellia on one side and Kayleen on the other, both headed toward him.

"Crossbow, now," he barked.

"You know you can't hit anything?" Garris slung the crossbow down off his shoulder and tossed it to Jon.

"Yeah." He shoved Garris forward, and the two began plowing their way toward the pass.

DELLIA

As Garris slashed and chopped a path in front of them, Jon sprinkled a drop on the dead chasing after them, and in seconds they too became enmeshed in a ball of spreading vegetation. He sprinkled a couple drops on the blade of the arrow, already loaded in the crossbow, then shouldered the weapon and aimed at Kayleen.

She halted, and alarm spread across her face. Jon swung the crossbow forward and fired well in front of her.

The weapon jerked in his hands as the arrow flew from the crossbow, slipping through the soft, rotted flesh of one corpse after another between Kayleen and the entrance to the pass.

Vines sprouted from the wounds. Tendrils reached out, spreading from one dead to another. The growing, twisting mass snagged corpses raging by, boring through flesh, jerking them to a halt, and spreading into a living wall that blocked Kayleen.

Jon skirted behind it, and Garris followed, headed away from Dellia and toward the entrance to the pass. Garris pushed ahead, kicking and shoving, his blade whipping through the air as he kept himself between Jon and the dense crowd of scrambling dead.

Jon snatched another arrow and sprinkled a drop on the blade. He pulled back the string as Garris had taught him and made a clumsy job of loading the arrow into the crossbow. He yanked it up to his shoulder and steadied it, trying not to become distracted by the emergence of new footsteps thundering down the pass ahead.

He fired, and the arrow leaped from the crossbow, nicking and piercing dead along a line between Dellia and the pass. Vines sprang from the wounds, spreading into a wall separating Dellia and Kayleen from him and Garris and from the base of Kita Pass.

Jon glanced forward at the dead streaming from the pass, just as another massive, rotting giant appeared, careening down the path toward the park.

"We need another arrow," Garris yelled over the booming of feet and the snarling of the dead.

Jon nodded and snatched another arrow.

Garris unleashed a barrage of devastating kicks and blows as Jon sprinkled the last drops from the vial on the blade of the arrow and jammed it into the crossbow. With the surrounding area cleared for the moment, Garris plunged the tip of his sword into the dirt and yanked the crossbow from Jon's grasp.

He whipped it up to his shoulder and fired while Jon jammed his dagger into the face of one rotting corpse after another. The arrow flew from the crossbow, arcing through the air and right into the eye of the giant. He tossed the crossbow back to Jon and snatched his sword from the dirt, redoubling his efforts.

Jon glanced behind them at the impenetrable wall of vines and bodies snaking toward them, threatening to ensnare them. Pods grew, becoming deep bloodred before they burst open into intense vermilion flowers. Ruby-red powder rained down, covering the jumble of vines and corpses spread back across the park. Violent flames began to sprout and spread far out behind them as Garris and Jon carved a path through the swarm at the base of the pass and headed up it.

Garris's sword whooshed through the air, hacking off limbs and heads. Jon's dagger slashed and stabbed in a fury of blows as they pushed their way up the narrow pass between two rock walls.

Ahead towered the giant, his head shrouded in layer upon layer of dense vines, weighing upon him until he teetered and began to fall forward.

Garris reached over and slammed both their backs to the wall as the vine-covered head of the massive, deceased brute plummeted down past them. It slammed into the ground a few feet away with a huge thunder and spray of wind and dust.

Jon glanced back as the vines enshrouding the giant's head dug through nearby twitching bodies like the tentacles of some morbid octopus. It grew and covered the pass, reaching out for them as the two surged ahead. Garris bent his effort forward, hacking through and clambering over the dead crowding the narrow space between the giant and the craggy walls of the pass.

A sudden, loud shriek rang down the passage, and a dark shadow passed overhead in another gust of wind and cloud of dust. Jon's gaze flew back toward it, and above the growth wrapping and digging across the fallen giant, he saw an enormous, decaying, pterodactyl-like creature swooping up out of the way. The flying monstrosity flapped its hole-ridden wings, and with another piercing shriek, it began a wide circle back through a sky littered with rising, flaming ash.

Jon stared in shock. "You've got to be kidding me."

Garris showed no sign of recognizing Jon's words, his entire being focused on pushing forward. His sword rushed through the air, hacking vines and heads as he scrambled over the bodies of the fallen.

The pair broke clear of the giant and forged their way up the pass. They cleaved through the dead or flung them back into the hungry vines as they charged through a seemingly endless river of putrid, shambling corpses.

Jon's arms burned and his breathing was labored as they rounded a bend into an open area where the path widened. He halted. Far up ahead, blocking their way, lay a swirling, black curtain of darkness between two gleaming metal rods at the edges of the canyon.

"A hole in the veil," Garris mumbled, half to himself.

It was beautiful and inexplicable, and as the first few flakes of violet flaming ash began to fall, Jon peered through them at the dark vortex blocking their way forward. It bore some resemblance to the phenomenon in his lab, though it was as if the bars were stretching it and warping its shape into a swirling vortex. Light from this side appeared to spread across the darkened, rocky ground beyond its liquid surface.

The sound of approaching wings and a deafening shriek from

behind yanked Jon out of his daze, just as another massive dead giant thundered through the dark, churning curtain. The brute let out a deep moan that reverberated down the rock walls surrounding them. They were trapped, with nothing left in the vial to use on the giant.

In a panic, Jon glanced backward, hoping for some avenue of escape, but a slithering wall of vines was winding its way up the pass behind them, consuming body after body and blocking their retreat. He snapped back forward. "We're trapped," Jon said.

As if attracted by the sound of his words, the giant's enormous rotted head swung around toward them. Still staring at them, it reached over and seized a massive boulder resting on a rock shelf nearby. It raised it high over its head as corpses appeared through the black curtain, one after another, twitching and jerking toward them.

Garris stepped forward, slinging his sword down, slashing through the bodies as they skittered toward him. "If you were gonna think of something, now would be the time."

"Me?" Jon said.

The animated corpse of the giant flung the boulder, but it fractured at the throw. Fragments careened into the side of the canyon, crashing through it. A hail of stones pelted them, and they both ducked and hid their faces.

Jon's head whipped forward, and he pointed at the newly collapsed wall. "He just made a new passage, what about that?"

"We don't know where it leads. We could wind up trapped," Garris countered.

Jon glanced back again, and his eyes locked onto the wriggling mass of body parts and vines. He ran back and grabbed hold of a vine-covered hand from the squirming mass. Grimacing, he hacked and sawed at the wrist until the hand tore free.

He ran back and held up the severed extremity as vines grew and twisted around and through it. "If I toss this can you hit it with the crossbow and send it through that flying thing?"

Garris held up the arrow. "Are you nuts? It's an arrow. It has hardly any weight."

"Oh yeah. Duh, physics. What if I hit that thing with this, can you pin it to it with the arrow?"

Forced to return his attention to the dead bearing down on them, Garris hacked and slashed as he shouted over his shoulder. "Don't be insulting. Can you actually hit it?"

As Garris's blade whooshed through the air, Jon readied himself, glancing back and forth between the airborne beast and the giant.

As the flying monstrosity neared them, Jon whipped the hand high out into the air. It arced through the flame-spattered sky behind them as tendrils plowed through its rotting flesh. Garris swung his crossbow up to his shoulder and fired with a gratifying twang.

The arrow sprang from the bow and hurtled through the falling flames. The severed hand hit the diving creature right as the arrow darted through it, pinning it to the chest of the beast.

Vines spread across the flying monstrosity's body and wings, digging through decomposed flesh with startling ferocity. They caught in the creature's hole-ridden wings, covering them as it streaked through the violet flamed ash. A bloodcurdling screech rang down the passage as the vine-covered beast hurtled overhead. The growth snared its wings, turning it into a projectile rocketing straight at the giant.

It hit with a deep thud, sending the brute staggering backward as the vines entangled the two. The giant stumbled, then toppled back through the black, swirling curtain. He slammed into one of the gleaming metal bars, and it bent and then broke under the decrepit giant's tremendous weight. The swirling vortex disintegrated into a black rain, leaving only the lower half of the giant wriggling in a shroud of vines.

The growth snaked out from the giant's legs, snaring the jerking, twitching dead all across the canyon. A wall of growth on either side slithered toward them. It threatened to overtake them and entangle them in an almost impenetrable barrier.

Garris lurched forward, hacking his way through scrambling corpses, headed for the mound of rubble at the opening of the new passage.

"We need to get out of here fast," he yelled back to Jon.

The two living walls crawled toward them, diving through decrepit flesh, ensnaring corpse upon corpse as the pair raced through the ever-shrinking space between them.

They reached the entrance and dove over the mound of rubble and into a narrow passage. Jon glanced back at the twitching dead, unable to clamber over the debris, just before vines pierced and overwhelmed them.

His heart hammering in his chest, Jon raced after Garris up a narrow passage that twisted and wound its way through solid rock. The pair jerked to a sudden halt as the left wall opened up to form a plateau overlooking all of Kianlong Park. Jon's breath heaved as he peered down at the panorama below.

Shouts and screams carried up from a wall of silent, violet flames that leaped stories high, engulfing most of the park. Underneath it, a carpet of bodies, vines, and bright-red blooms writhed and squirmed as it fed the vast inferno. Above it all, flaming ash whirled hundreds of feet into the late afternoon sky, drifting out across the entire city.

Jon stared for a moment until his eyes fell on Dellia. In a clearing below the fog of drifting flames, she stood, hacking with ferocity at a dwindling wall of burning bodies that separated her from the base of Kita Pass. It would not be long now before she cleaved her way through and came to arrest him.

As he watched her, bending all her effort at those few remaining bodies and vines, a profound sadness took hold. He had always understood that nothing could ever happen between them. So all he had hoped for was that she would be there to help him. And that when the time came to leave this world, he would stand before her and look into her eyes one last time as he said goodbye. But that was never to be. They had already said their goodbyes. And now, his only chance of getting home was to stop the one person he cared for most in this world from doing her duty.

Chapter Thirty

A LIFE WITHIN A DAY

The sounds of yelling and swords chopping carried up from Kianlong Square to the plateau where Garris stood staring down. Relieved to have survived the harrowing experience, his every muscle was sore and spent, and his breathing heaved from exertion. Yet, he was unable to tear his eyes from the woman.

The outline was obscured by an inferno of silent purple flames below and the flaming ash it sent swirling into the sky. Yet it was unmistakable. It was Kayleen. The woman who had sent so many to kill him. The sight of her fueled his hunger for justice. Not for himself, because in so many ways, he deserved her wrath, but for her fifteen-year vendetta, which had resulted in so many needless deaths. A burning anger welled within as he watched her bark out orders to Dellia and the small group of soldiers she commanded. She had to be stopped.

Garris averted his eyes. Now was not the time to get bogged down by the ghosts of his past. He turned back, focusing his attention on the pace of her detail, hacking and slashing their way through the living, squirming wall of vines and bodies that surrounded them. Their blades flashed with a purple flicker as they cleaved a path through the last several feet of the dwindling, tangled mess that separated them from the base of Kita Pass.

At the front stood Dellia. She was the finest protector he'd ever seen. Her two blades possessed a speed and precision that were unnatural, and her awareness of her surroundings was uncanny. Of all the people in this world, she was the last one he'd want pursuing him. Yet pursuing them she was. Only minutes behind, in fact, and the prospect of her delivering him to Kayleen was thoroughly disturbing.

Garris steeled his resolve. That was never going to happen. Especially with Jon a hair's breadth from his goal.

With a renewed sense of urgency, he turned to Jon, only to see an expression of utter despondency on his face as he watched the scene below. Then, Jon's eyes fell, and he stared at the precipice at his feet. Yet the sound of yelling and soldiers chopping continued unabated.

Garris shook his head. This was bad. They needed to be pushing forward, but it was obvious Jon was letting the situation with Dellia get the best of him. There wasn't enough time to indulge in this nonsense.

He turned to face Jon. "Whatever you're planning, it needs to happen fast."

Jon raised his head and stared at him, but his expression remained vacant and glazed over. Then he seemed to come out of it to a degree. "Okay. Yeah." His words were halfhearted, as if his mind and heart lay elsewhere.

Jon cast his gaze around the plateau, getting his bearings, and Garris joined him. Though the two nearest walls were solid rock, the remaining one appeared promising. Along the far wall lay a rectangular table of stone, with numerous slots carved into its surface. Near it, a large alcove held a round platform with three stone "teeth" clinging to the ceiling above it. They arched down, their tips surrounding the platform like a mixed-up version of the spires.

Still in a daze, Jon wandered over to it and granted it a halfhearted looking-over before giving up. "I have to solve the riddle of Kita Pass, but if this is a riddle, I don't get it."

Garris shook his head. Did he really need to spell this out? Was

Jon really so distracted he couldn't even grasp the gravity of their situation? He pointed down the pathway, the direction they'd come. "Any minute, Dellia is going to come up that pass, and any chance of you getting home will be gone."

Jon granted Garris an absentminded nod.

Garris grumbled under his breath. No, this was worse than he thought. Jon was too disheartened to care. He stepped closer. "Look, Kayleen is with her, and she hates me. She sent people to kill me. Chances are, if she catches me, she'll try to finish the job. So I'd really appreciate it if you'd stop moping around like some lovesick teenager and focus on our survival."

Seeming annoyed at Garris's goading, Jon glanced around. "There is no riddle here. What do you want me to do? I can't just miraculously find something that's not there."

"I expect you to try."

Jon folded his arms. "Fine." He gave the area another passing glance. "There. Happy? I got nothing."

Garris shook his head and turned away. Did he have to do everything himself? He strolled the area as he scrutinized every facet. "A riddle would have to be written, right?" As he passed the platform, a set of markings on the side caught his eye. "Writing." He strolled up and squatted before them. They appeared ancient, but still legible.

Garris glanced at Jon, catching his eye. "It's old. It says, 'It tugs and pulls with endless might and keeps us all down. It seems to come from nowhere, and yet it is all around.'"

That seemed to get Jon's attention, and he strolled over and examined the writing with Garris. "That's not much of a riddle. It's obviously gravity."

"Then that must be the answer."

"Okay, sure it's an answer, but I don't see how it helps me know what to do next."

Garris puzzled for a second, then looked up at Jon. "Well, the answer is here somewhere. So what is ... gra-vity?" he said, trying not to butcher the unfamiliar word.

Jon shook his head, as if boggled by the question. "I couldn't even begin to explain it. Even if it was perfectly understood. Newtonian physics, general relativity, string theory, they all look at it differently. For example, classical mechanics sees it as a field related to mass. One theory even views it as a sort of negative energy. ..."

Jon's eyes opened wide. His gaze shot down, and he stared at the surface of the table. "Negative energy. But that's not even close to ..."

The expression on Jon's face told Garris all he needed to know. He was onto something. Jon reached down and snatched a stack of black polished stone plates from the corner of the table. At his touch, a blue beam of light shot out from a glass sphere in the corner. He wiped off one of the plates and stared at his reflection in its dark, glossy surface.

"What?" Garris said.

Jon glanced back and forth between the plate and the surface of the table as a look of disbelief spread across his face. "This can't be."

"Care to explain?" Garris said.

"It's my laser table."

"Your whose-a what's-it?"

Jon placed a black plate in one of several slots below the path of the beam, and it deflected it. With a confidence that could only have been born of familiarity, he began jamming plates into slots all across the table, explaining as he went.

"It's impossible. This is something I was working on, in my world. But how could anyone in this world have known?"

As he slid in the last plate, the brilliant blue beam reflected off it, ricocheting here and there across the table. When it hit the final plate, it shot off the table and over to a small hole in the base of the circular platform.

A crackling sound issued from the round stone surface as a swirling black sphere formed in the center, between the teeth. Flaming ash drifting down from above bent into the perfectly round, water-like orb as the two stared at its complete blackness.

Garris stepped closer. "What is it? I've never seen anything like it." He glanced over at Jon, waiting for a response.

Jon took a small step back from the darkness as apprehension filled his face. "I have no idea."

Garris returned his attention to the dark ball. "Is it a portal? Does it lead to your world?"

"No, I don't think so. The medallion isn't complete yet."

"Are we supposed to go through it?"

Jon shook his head. "How am I supposed to know?" He glanced at Garris. "It's not exactly like the portal that got me here, or like Sirra's portals. But I've seen several kinds, and they all show you where you're going. This is pitch-black."

Garris's head whipped over toward the distant clatter of feet and voices echoing down the path.

Jon put out his palm toward Garris as he stared at the dark ball. "Don't rush me. I need to think for a—"

Garris seized Jon's outstretched arm and shoved hard. Jon stumbled forward and disappeared into the swirling darkness.

Jon stumbled to a stop, his footsteps echoing through the blackness of what sounded like a large hall. Outrage flared at Garris tossing him into unknown danger. It quickly dissipated, replaced by a dread of what might await him as he stood alone in the dark. His heart still thudded in his ears as he listened and waited for the next terrifying catastrophe to hit. Yet, all that met his ears was silence.

The compulsion to breathe became too much, and upon realizing he'd been holding his breath, Jon took a deep gulp of air. The smell and feel of it were different here, musty and dank, but also something foreign, a quality that defied description.

Satisfied that he was safe for the moment, Jon took a single, cautious step forward. He shielded his eyes from a warm light shining out from either wall of a large cavernous hallway. From beneath his hand, he peeked out at the source: a pair of shiny glass balls atop corroded metal staves resting in mounts on either crude wall.

Jon lowered his hand and took a few more tentative steps forward. Riddled with translucent, amethyst stalactites, the high ceiling sparkled with every move as light reflected off the facets of countless crystalline daggers.

Lumbering footsteps erupted from behind, and Jon glanced back as Garris fumbled forward, then caught his balance and straightened up. What irritation he still felt toward the big man evaporated at the realization he was no longer alone. Above the round stone platform behind him hovered a water-like sphere exactly like the one that had sent them here. Except the surface seemed to hold a distorted reflection of the plateau from which they'd come.

Garris stepped up next to Jon, and the two followed the polished, dark floor as it led down a long, broad hallway. Lining either wall were pairs of glass balls that lit up as they approached. Then, the hall turned and narrowed to a small, jagged passage, with what appeared to be a dark cavern beyond.

As they passed through into the dark cavity, a light seemed to spring from nowhere, filling an enormous stone hall with a soft glow. Enormous crystalline stalactites hung from the ceiling high above a broad, circular platform of stone centered in the room.

Jon gasped as across the hall, a small pedestal came into view with a dark, metallic box resting on its surface. Even from a distance, the impression of three leaves arranged in a circle was visible beneath the dust on its lid.

Their footsteps echoed through the enormous hall as they raced over to it. Then Jon gently opened the lid to reveal a leaf resting inside, just like the others. Only this one was formed of some dark, almost black metal, the likes of which he'd never seen.

Jon bent closer, examining its dark and delicate features. "This is it." With reverent care, he picked up the piece from inside the box. He slipped the medallion out of his shirt, and as he brought the dark leaf close, it flew out of his fingers and clanked into place. A bright blue aura surrounded the medallion as the last leaf fused into the whole, completing the pattern of three leaves arranged in a circle.

The blue glow unwound from its surface to form a wispy stream that snaked its way across the room. Jon and Garris followed the bright blue thread over to an indentation in the massive circular platform.

Jon looked at the medallion, then the hole. He held the medallion over the indentation, and it appeared to make a perfect match.

"I don't understand. ..." Jon said.

"Maybe it's a portal like the one before." Garris's eyes flew back and forth between medallion and indentation. "Maybe this is how you get home."

Jon recalled Isla's words: *"Find them … reassemble it … I can send you … home."* He eyed the indentation. "I don't think so. That's— that's not what she said. But … but I don't know."

Garris eyed him with a puzzled look. "Who is 'she'?"

Jon's head spun toward a distant clamor of voices and footsteps out in the passage, then back to the indentation.

He yanked the medallion away as he rushed out the words. "What if I'm wrong? What if this *is* how I get home? I can't just leave Megan. And I can't leave you here, either." He glanced again toward the clatter of rattling metal and marching footsteps approaching. "What about the soldiers and Kayleen? It's a death sentence."

"Don't worry about me. I vowed to get you home, and there's no way I'm going to let you stop this close."

Jon balked. There had to be another way. "Give me a minute. I can't just—"

In a flash, Garris yanked the medallion from Jon's grasp and slammed it onto the indentation with a clank.

Jon pivoted and glared at him. "Would you stop doing tha—"

The rumble of marching feet grew close and Jon tensed. Something better happen fast. He and Garris turned and faced the platform, staring in anticipation.

Jon tensed even more at a host of footsteps echoing through the chamber from soldiers bursting through the jagged passage and into the massive hall. The sound of swords being unsheathed and bows drawn joined the footsteps as grim soldiers filed both ways around the outside of the cave, surrounding Jon and Garris with weapons held at the ready.

Garris kept a wary eye on the menacing troops surrounding them as Jon's gaze flew between them and the platform, hoping in desperation for something to happen.

As the last of a dozen or so soldiers surrounded them, Jon raised his hands to give up. Garris glanced over at him with a peculiar look and rolled his eyes, as if he were doing something strange.

Jon eyed the doorway as first Kayleen, then Dellia walked through and stepped off to one side. He glanced over at the platform, and a sudden realization struck: if this wasn't his way home, then he still needed the medallion.

Jon lowered his hands and snatched it from its resting place on the platform. The moment he yanked it free, all the light vanished, leaving complete darkness.

Moments passed in utter blackness, broken only by the shuffle of feet and the sound of bowstrings being relaxed.

Then, a light sprang from the platform as a huge, ghostly image emerged from the darkness. It coalesced into a beautiful, glimmering likeness of a heavily branching tree that hovered over the platform.

Light from its fall-colored leaves of yellow and red danced across the rock walls and crystal ceiling. Every person in the hall stood staring, drawn in by its stunning intricacy and beauty.

As if from nowhere, a calming female voice filled the enormous cavern.

"The future is an infinite branching tree of possibilities, each determined by free will."

The translucent image of the tree faded into a full-length, glittering likeness of a serene, middle-aged Elorian woman. She possessed a quiet grace as she smiled down from above, and her voice was gentle and calming as she spoke.

"I am Wistra, the oracle of your prophecy, and I must beg your forgiveness, for you have been misled, and I have played my part. You see, I have known for most of my life that humankind will soon face extinction."

The image transformed into a massive horde of horrible, twisted creatures pouring over grassy hills. They raged through a small village, striking down any who fell in their path, crushing the fleeing men, women, and children under the hooves of their steeds. The sight was bloody and horrible, and Jon wanted to turn away in revulsion, but he couldn't.

As quickly as the gruesome scene had appeared, it vanished, and in its place was a much younger Wistra, her black hair blowing in a gentle breeze as she strolled along a high mountain path. Then, the glittering image shifted again, to her sitting cross-legged as she meditated in the stillness of dusk on a mountainside overlooking the white sands of a desert.

"So," the disembodied voice continued, "I have meditated for many long years as I wandered this land, searching for an answer." The translucent image faded back to the middle-aged Wistra's comforting face. "That answer is you," she said as she looked down at Jon. "You see, you are not the villain, Jon. You were destined to be one of our greatest leaders. The one sent to save us all."

His pulse quickened and his stomach twisted into knots at the mere idea of being the person of which this woman spoke. Yet, she had said his name. She knew who he was, and she knew he was here. And with that realization, the knots twisted even tighter.

The image transformed once more to that of an important-looking, bald-headed man speaking with Dellia in a darkened chamber.

Then to an image of Dellia sneaking up behind Jon and plunging her dagger deep into his back. He wanted to retch as he watched himself crumple over and his head crack into the ground. The compulsion to turn away clawed at him, but his eyes remained fixed on the scene, unable to tear them from his body lying there with a vacant expression in his eyes as his blood flowed onto the dirt.

"But had I written that prophecy, the council would have sent an assassin to prevent your rise, for such is their conviction in the superiority of their rule."

The glittering image shifted back to the calming visage of the middle-aged Wistra. As she smiled, light from her serene face flittered across the dark cavern walls. And with it, some of Jon's apprehension and revulsion eased.

"So I wrote only the truth that you would bring about a new age, knowing it would let the council spin their comforting web of lies."

The image dissolved once more, this time into one of a columned, marble chamber with a large, dark table in the center with people debating and arguing around it.

"By turning the world against you, I turned their thoughts to capture. Thus, their lies protected you, while I set you on the path that has brought you here."

The image shifted once again to a younger version of the oracle, prying a silver leaf from the medallion. Then to a shimmering scene of a small, silver box being placed in a bench in a tower.

"It was a path to prepare you through trials and cut years of pain and suffering from your rise. Yet, only you can lead us safely through the perilous events ahead to a time of peace and prosperity."

The translucent image faded back to the full-length likeness of the tranquil, middle-aged Wistra. Her manner remained calming and gentle like before, but her eyes held a disturbing sense of pity.

"Great power is often borne at great cost, and so there is one last trial. A vision. Not to prepare you, but to ease my conscience. A warning. So that if you accept this burden, you know the ultimate cost."

The image seemed to fade entirely, only to be replaced by a new image of Wistra standing over the medallion while it played the message they had all just watched. She bent over and touched the three leaves: first black, then gold, then silver, and the image before her vanished.

Wistra turned and smiled at Jon, her face framed by the glittering light shimmering off the stone walls behind her. She lingered for a moment, a tenderness in her gaze as her eyes seemed to focus directly on him. And for the briefest of moments, he had the sense of some undefinable connection between them. Then she bent down and snatched a small gold and red marble from the floor at her feet, and her image dissolved into blackness.

Darkness hung in the air as everyone stood motionless. As the light brightened, Jon glanced over at Dellia, standing next to Kayleen with a stunned expression on her face. The world unexpectedly began to slow and turn hazy. It was exactly like his gift, only this time he was not in control. This time someone or something else was making it happen. His gaze remained on Dellia, staring at her in puzzlement, as she and everything in the room ground to a stop, frozen in time.

In an instant, the world was torn from him, and he was thrust into another. It was far more disorienting than his gift, for he was no longer in the oracle room but a lone disembodied observer drifting down from high in a vast cavern. Unable to look around or affect what he was seeing, he could only watch as the scenes of a story unfolded from some other time and place.

A blistering ball floats high up in a massive cavern, shedding daylight across the ranks of two vast armies, casting deep shadows in every corner and crevice.

With Dellia on one side and Garris on the other, Jon stands on a broad pathway that winds its way along one side of a seemingly endless cave. He glances over and nods to Megan, standing in a pocket up along the wall. She smiles with affection and returns a nod that exudes confidence.

Behind them, the ranks of an enormous army stretch out down the path, row upon row of soldiers punctuated by glittering weapons and bright-colored banners.

Washing down the path toward them streams a sea of dark, twisted creatures of every imaginable shape and size: heavily muscled brutes alongside the wiry and thin, all manner of skin, scales, and fur in shades both bleak and ominous, razor tusks, horns and teeth, snarling, shrieking, and growling in a terrifying menagerie. They spread back, wave upon wave, as far as the eye can see.

Near the front, their huge, scale-covered leader glares at Jon with lizard-like, amber eyes. Sharp quills coat its back and skull, and it clings with massive arms to a wingless, black dragon. Blue streaks along its gnarled, serpent-like body ripple as it slithers down the path toward them.

As Jon returns the leader's penetrating stare, his face turns white. Apprehension saturates his expression, and he gulps as he endeavors to regain his calm.

As if sensing his fear, Dellia places her hand on his shoulder, watching him with worry etched on her beautiful features.

Jon turns to address the assembled forces. He takes a deep breath and scans the sea of frightened faces looking to him for encouragement.

Then, his voice booms out, strong and reassuring. "We have come together today, all of us, from all across Meerdon and beyond, not just to defend our territory or protect our way of life, but to fight for our very existence. The enemy we face now does not desire peace, nor will they ever accept coexistence. They seek nothing but to enslave us or wipe us from the face of this world."

Jon thrusts his arm out, pointing to the gnarled creatures surging toward them. "And we are all that stands between them and everything we care about, everything we love."

He straightens and points to the rocky ground below him. "Let history say that on this spot here today, we stood together as one people and shouted, 'No! We will not yield. This is our home, and it will never be yours. For we will fight to our last breath before we let you set one foot on our land.'"

The troops shout and raise their weapons high.

As if responding to Jon's words, the dragon rears its head and issues a disdainful snarl that rumbles down the enormous cavern.

As Jon turns back to face their foe, he drops the facade, and fear returns to his eyes. He grasps Garris's forearm and gives it a firm shake as he nods. Then, he smiles at Dellia, but it cannot hide the apprehension that fills the rest of his face.

The leader digs his claws into the black dragon's scales and yanks back. As the dragon twists to a stop, the enormous rider flings a dark blade at Jon with unearthly force.

Dellia steps in to deflect it, and it ricochets off her sword, but it is heavier than it appears and veers only slightly from its path. The razor hunk of metal nicks Jon's leg, then clatters down the rocky floor behind him as Jon gasps.

Dellia grabs his shoulder. "What's wrong?"

"I don't know. I feel … sick … wrong." He pulls a black marble out of his pocket and clenches it in his fist as a look of intense concentration comes over him. "My gift. I can't trigger it. It's gone."

Dellia turns as white as new snow.

In unison, the approaching army bellows a bloodcurdling shout that reverberates through the cavern as they break into a sprint, a swarm of frenzied creatures dashing toward them. Their racing footsteps rumble down the cavern as the dragon raises its massive head.

With a deafening bellow, the beast belches out air and spray. As it shoots from the dragon's mouth the spray freezes, turning to a volley of jagged ice daggers that arcs through the air toward Jon's front lines.

Wind whirls around Megan, whipping through her hair as she thrusts out her palm.

With a tremendous crash, the icy blades shatter on an invisible shield over Jon and the entire front line. Jagged fragments spatter from the barrier, ripping through the charging army, severing limbs and rending flesh from bone.

A few icy blades arch over the upper edge of Megan's shield to pepper the wall high above her. They shatter, sending razor fragments shooting into her back.

She cries out in agony as she's sent to her hands and knees, struggling against her torment as blood flows down her back.

Dellia and Garris glance at one another and charge into the front lines. Garris kicks and punches, his sword hurtling down, cleaving creatures in two. Dellia's blades whistle through the air, cutting down waves of opponents with blistering speed.

Creatures fall before them like wheat before a scythe, as the pair work together as an unstoppable machine, carving a path through the army and straight toward the dragon.

The front lines of the two armies collide in a cacophony of battle cries and clashing swords

Three enormous spiderlike creatures with long necks and human heads appear from the shadows high above, scurrying down the wall toward Megan.

Jon glances at them and goes white as he breaks into a sprint. Panic spreads across his face, compelling him as he's pushed into a frenzied dash.

The dragon raises its head and bellows again, straight down at Dellia and Garris.

From her hands and knees, Megan shoots out her blood-soaked hand in a burst of wind.

The violent volley of ice daggers blasts the invisible shield over Dellia and Garris. The daggers shatter with a rumble, spraying shards into the creatures all around them, tearing them to shreds.

Two of the spiders snag Megan's limbs and begin twisting them behind her. They yank at them, contorting them, wrapping them around each other in unnatural ways. The sound of popping cartilage and breaking bones mixes with Megan's desperate screams.

Jon races for her as the spiders pull and twist her body into a grotesque shape. Megan's screams stop as her broken and crushed body goes limp.

The shield falls, and Dellia is blasted to the ground as the last of the icy blades rips through her body.

She stumbles to her feet, her face raw and bloody. Gaping holes in the soft brown leather of her armor reveal huge gashes in her side and legs. Bleeding, staggering, but undeterred, she hurtles her dagger upward with tremendous force.

The leader tries to catch it but is too slow, and the blade shoots through his grasp and into his eye, plunging deep into his skull. The horrid beast slips from the dragon and crashes to the ground with a rattle of metal armor and weapons.

Garris throws all his weight behind his sword, sending it

hurtling down through the leader's neck, cleaving the head from its massive body. The disembodied skull tumbles across the ground, the dagger still protruding from its eye.

The dragon whips its tail.

Dellia leaps and rolls out of the way, but Garris is still recovering from the heavy blow that beheaded the leader. The dragon catches him full in the chest and flings him thirty feet through the air. He slams into the rock wall with a sickening crunch and tumbles to the ground, gasping for breath with blood trickling from his mouth.

With tremendous effort, Garris hoists himself upright. A spear hits his shoulder, then his arm, then two of them pierce his stomach. He falls to his knees, heaving, trying to draw breath as spear after spear lodge in his body.

Barely able to stand, Dellia pulls herself upright. With what fading strength she has, she lunges for the dragon's neck with her sword out.

The tip glances off the dark, metallic scales and slides up between them, plunging deep into the soft flesh of the dragon's throat.

She pushes forward with all her weight, ramming the sword up to the hilt. Dark red blood streams down her arm as she twists and rips the blade out.

Wounded and bleeding, its breath rasping through a slit in its neck, the enormous monster claws at Dellia.

She whips out a second dagger and spears its paw.

The dragon yanks her up by her blade. With its free paw, it grabs hold of her body and squeezes with a nauseating crackling of bones.

The dragon glares at Jon and flings Dellia's broken body a hundred feet to land like a rag doll, limp at his feet.

He picks up her savaged frame. Blood streams from everywhere as he cradles her in his arms and her last breath leaves her body.

DELLIA

Jon raises his head and bellows out an anguished cry. He glares at the dark dragon as it belches out breath and spray straight at him.

The pressure of its icy breath rips a gaping hole through the wound in its neck. As ice daggers hurtle toward Jon, the beast spasms in pain, its body flinging soldiers like ants as it writhes.

Ice shards slam into Jon, and the rumble of shouting and swords goes silent as the scene vanishes, leaving only darkness.

As suddenly as he'd been ripped from the world, Jon was thrust back, standing in the same enormous cavern he'd left.

Time still did not move, everything remaining eerily frozen. Garris standing next to him, the dozen soldiers surrounding them, even Dellia and Kayleen by the door—all stood like statues, staring with stunned looks at the space above the platform where the images of Wistra had been.

The only sign of life was Jon's own pressured breathing, reverberating through the cave as he stared over beyond Dellia, frozen in shock.

Slowly at first, the world began to move again, but Jon couldn't. He remained stuck back in that far distant scene, living through the slaughter of everyone he cared about, unable to push it out of his mind.

Crippled by horror, he stood frozen and staring past Dellia as everything around him returned to life.

Chapter Thirty-One

SHATTERED

Kayleen stood staring at the space above the platform where moments ago the oracle had revealed Jon's prophecy. Her mind reeled. This was the hand of Wistra? Revered by the Elorian people, her teachings were the foundation on which all prophecy was built. Others could glimpse what was to come, but she was the first to reach enlightenment, to understand the future with clarity. If this was her hand, then every word she uttered must be taken as absolute truth.

Kayleen tore her eyes from the empty space, scanning the large cavern. Everything she thought she knew was wrong. The entire landscape had shifted out from under her, and it was crucial that she get her bearings, fast. Her mind whirled like a dervish, weighing factors and repercussions.

The council's actions must have been foreseen, as was her role in them. In fact, Wistra would have known she would be here to witness this message. Which meant the message could be as much for her as for Jon. But then again, none of that mattered. The only thing that was clear was that Jon's role in all this was now paramount, and protecting him was her most crucial responsibility.

Kayleen's attention shot over to Dellia standing next to her. She knew Jon better than anyone else in this world, but she stood frozen, staring at him with a wide-eyed look of shock and dismay that was deeply disturbing. "Oh no," Dellia said in a voice that was weak and filled with misery.

Kayleen's gaze darted to Jon, standing near the platform, staring in her direction with his face contorted into an expression of abject horror. Guilt stabbed at her heart. The council under her leadership had spun the lie that made him a wanted man. And now he stood surrounded by a dozen of the most loyal and ruthless warriors in all of Meerdon. He was in mortal danger, and in no small part by her hand.

Her breathing became shallow and her heart raced as she scanned the unsettled soldiers surrounding Jon. Their backs to the cavern walls, they shifted nervously in place with a half dozen glittering weapons at the ready. The fate of her entire world hung on what happened next.

Then, her eyes were drawn to Garris, muscular and proud, his piercing eyes staring up at the platform. She had seen him before in Kianlong Square talking to Jon, but what part did he play in all this? For that matter, what was he doing here? Didn't he realize he was in mortal danger?

Garris lowered his eyes, and his gaze met Kayleen's. Hatred flashed across his rugged features. He whipped his crossbow up to his shoulder, aiming straight at her.

Kayleen froze. Her memory raced back to a time when Uncle Edan had taken two young children hunting for the first time. She had seen that same look of grim determination when Garris had a doe in his sights. He was going to kill her.

Her soldiers raised their weapons, and those near her shouldered their bows, aiming them directly at Garris. Panic struck. *He was going to get himself killed.*

She made a frantic motion to her men to lower their weapons. Guilt savaged her. She had been at the center of all the tragedy that had befallen that idealistic, young hunter. As the tips of their bows dropped, she smiled at Garris and opened her arms wide, inviting his arrow. After all that had gone between them, perhaps this would be the perfect poetic ending to their story.

Garris's hard expression turned to one of puzzlement, and the tip of his arrow drooped.

Behind him and Jon, a hooded figure slipped out between two of the guards. His head snapped up, and wild red hair flashed out from beneath his hood. His eyes shifted all around the room as he plunged forward and raised a pair of daggers aimed at Garris and Jon's backs.

Kayleen gasped as Tetch sprinted across the shiny black floor. She dove for the solder to her right, shouldering him out of the way as she grabbed the crossbow from his hands and pulled the trigger. The arrow whistled from the weapon with a twang.

Garris stood frozen and confused as the arrow shot over his shoulder. He whipped around to watch it plunge into Tetch's head, yanking him backward and sending him crashing to the ground.

Garris snapped back toward Kayleen, staring at her face with a look of profound bewilderment. He whipped his crossbow upward, aiming it at the ceiling crammed full of enormous, amethyst stalactites. The arrow darted from the bow, and all eyes turned upward. The arrow splintered with a snap as it hit a massive stalactite directly over the center of the platform. The enormous, crystalline dagger wobbled, then broke free with a loud crack and began hurtling downward.

Garris dove for Jon, jolting him out of his stunned daze and slamming him to the ground with an *oomph*. He threw himself over Jon as Kayleen covered her face, peering out between her fingers.

The massive crystal plunged into the platform and shattered with a thunderous crash, sending fragments shooting everywhere. As Kayleen's soldiers turned away and shielded their faces, Garris grabbed Jon's arm and yanked him from the ground.

A hail of fragments clattered across the walls and floor, peppering the bright cavern. They hit bodies and covered faces as Garris dragged Jon right past Kayleen and out through the entrance.

As they passed by, Dellia's meek voice let out a heartrending plea. "Jon, don't leave me."

Jon glanced back at her with a vacant look on his face as Garris lugged him down the corridor and around the bend. As they disappeared from view, Jon seemed to snap out of it enough to pass his hand down and transform the pair into two of her soldiers.

Kayleen glanced at Dellia only to find her staring at the passage where they had disappeared. Her expression fell into a sad, stunned sort of daze, and she seemed unaware of the shouting around her.

In a clatter of weapons and feet, Kayleen's soldiers began to race after Garris. Kayleen snapped to attention, afraid of what they might do if they caught them, or what Garris might do to escape.

"Stand down!" she shouted out.

Her only chance to protect Jon now was to get Dellia to go after them. Kayleen pivoted toward her and tugged on her arm. "Dellia, we need to go." But she showed no sign of hearing her words. "We need to go. Now ... Dellia!"

Shocked and bewildered, Garris glanced over his shoulder as the narrow cavern entrance disappeared around the corner. Kayleen was back in that cavern, and he'd had her in his sights. It was his chance for justice, just as Elt had predicted. And perhaps his only opportunity to end her fifteen-year vendetta. Yet he couldn't. Not because he had chosen a higher purpose, as Elt suggested, but because all he saw was that little girl he used to share sweets with when Eejha would take them to the Shirdon Market. He was too weak and pathetic. So now even more poor souls would die because he lacked the stomach to put an end to it.

Shouts erupted behind them, followed by the rattling of weapons and pounding of feet. Garris surged ahead, sprinting harder, dragging a dazed Jon down the rock hallway. A feeling grabbed the pit of his stomach, as if he were in a trap that had already been sprung, and the jaws were hurtling down on him. Watching behind him for signs of pursuit, he ran toward the portal, then shoved Jon through it.

The bright sun stung his eyes after the dim light of the cavern, and fresh air filled his lungs as he hustled Jon down the path. Around corners and along pathways that turned and twisted through the rocky canyon, he dragged a stunned Jon down Kita Pass toward Kianlong Square. The scene with Kayleen kept spinning through his mind. She could have ordered her men to kill him at any time, yet she didn't. She had even made herself an easy target. Yet shooting her would surely have gotten him killed. And when she had a bow in her hands, he had hesitated, and she could have killed him. Instead, she saved him from an assassin.

None of it made sense. Countless times, killers had died with her name on their lips. Warrior after warrior sent to kill him, with notes on their bodies containing the most vicious lies, scrawled out in her hand. Perhaps she needed him, or Jon. Perhaps she wanted an even more gruesome end for him. All that was certain was that she was a schemer, and somewhere in all this, there had to be a method to her madness.

As Garris flew around the corner into Kianlong Square, sheer chaos came into view, spread across the broad park. All sign of the vines and dead had vanished, replaced by physicians and attendants scurrying through a sea of unconscious and wounded. Garris grumbled under his breath. Every blasted solder and official in the city was out in full force, stopping strangers and asking questions. It was the last thing he needed.

He plowed ahead, all his concentration focused on evasion as he dodged and skirted his way through the crowd.

A young Talesh woman ahead called out a name—Kellon, or something—and flew up in front of him. Fear shone in her dark eyes and her breath heaved as she blocked his way. She blurted out a question about the whereabouts of Kayleen and the rest of her unit.

Someone bumped into Jon, and he seemed to come out of his daze. His eyes flew up, and he scanned the park, his expression like that of a scared rabbit.

Soldiers riddled with bite marks shuffled by. Here and there sat grizzled warriors with blood oozing from gaping wounds or missing flesh. And scattered all around were residents wailing and weeping over fallen friends and relatives.

Jon's head whipped over, and he stared at Garris as his daze turned to all-out panic. All of a sudden, he yanked his arm free and raced away across the park.

Still blocked by the woman, Garris pointed up the pass and told her Kayleen was coming. When he tried to shove past her, she grabbed his arm and hung on tight. He pushed her down and broke free, but it was too late—Jon was nowhere to be seen.

Garris bolted after him, evading and skirting his way to the edge of the square. As he cleared the crowd, his gaze shot all around, searching for Jon, but he was gone.

He raced down street after street, scanning everything, checking brick roads, dirt alleyways, and the doors and windows of an endless sea of long, low buildings, but it was hopeless. Jon was nowhere, and he couldn't stay and search. He was known here, and sooner or later he'd no longer be cloaked as one of Kayleen's soldiers. He'd return to his native form, and the whole city would be upon him.

Garris halted. Jon was smart and running scared, and that meant there could be only one place he would go. If he were even capable of making his way there, Jon would head for the stables. He cursed himself under his breath for pointing them out and telling him where he could find Enna.

Careful to evade the brown-and-purple-uniformed soldiers and officials, now on every street, Garris flew down broad avenues and around corners. But by the time he arrived at the small stables, Enna and Jon's equipment was gone.

As he stared down at the dirt floor, considering his next move, a set of hoofprints caught his eye. Of course. Enna's tracks were unique and easy to identify.

In a few minutes, he was on Kyri, hurtling down Jon's trail away from town. As he raced across the countryside, a realization hit: Perhaps this was the wrong course of action. He felt trapped, and so he was running. But Jon was on the right side of this, and they should fight back. Perhaps his perfect revenge lay in exposing Kayleen and the council's arrogant disregard for everything but themselves.

After a while, Garris transformed back to himself, but by the time he caught sight of Jon and heard the thundering of Enna's hooves, it was late in the day, and the sun had become a scarlet orb, drenching the sunset in red and deep yellow.

He spurred Kyri on, pushing her faster, striving to catch up to Enna. Orange light from the waning sun painted the grassy landscape with a strange copper glow as they hurtled across the hilltops with Garris chasing down a panicked Jon.

As he grew closer, he leaned forward, and above the pounding of hooves he yelled out, "Jon, we're safe, slow down."

Jon kept staring forward, his eyes fixed on the vibrant skyline, giving no sign he'd heard.

"Hey, slow down!" Garris bellowed louder.

It was clear Jon was more spooked than he'd realized, but nothing he had witnessed could account for this kind of reaction. Garris pushed Kyri again, and her hooves hammered the ground as she surged up next to Enna.

He reached over and snatched the leather reins out of Jon's hands. With care, he pulled back, bringing Enna to a stop. Then, he brought Kyri around and faced Jon. "Snap out of it. What in Hades happened to you back there?"

Jon closed his eyes and shuddered. Then his pale, terror-stricken face looked up at Garris. "I saw you die."

"What are you talking about? I'm right here."

"No. A vision. I saw how you die. Everyone, you, me, Dellia, Megan, everyone. And it's my fault."

Garris straightened up, sitting tall in the saddle as he stared at Jon with the crimson horizon glowing behind him. "Don't tell me you believe this oracle mumbo jumbo." He pointed back toward Kanlu. "We have to go back, confront Kayleen. She lied about the prophecy. She made everyone think you were dangerous."

Jon recoiled with a rapid shake of his head. "No. I've never seen anything so horrible, it was beyond my worst nightmare. I can't be responsible for that. It's too much. I'm going home."

"You heard the oracle. The future isn't written in stone. Besides, this whole seeing-the-future crap is a crock, you can't believe that nonsense."

"Just stop it," Jon blurted out, then his voice calmed. "Of course I believe it, and you do, too, or else why would you want me to go back?"

Garris struggled with what to say, the only sound the heavy breathing of their horses and the thumping of hooves as they moved restlessly in the lush, orange-lit grass.

He nodded. "Okay, let's say I believe. That means I believe the people of Meerdon need you. You can't just turn your back on them."

Jon stared, seeming shocked. "I needed you, and you left me the moment you found out I was the Otherworlder." He glanced away. "And I never blamed you for that. But how is this any different?"

"Because I was wrong, okay? And selfish. Don't be me. You're a better man than that."

Jon shook his head. "No. That's where you're wrong. When people depend on you, you help them. I just get them killed."

"You're just scared."

"You would be, too." Jon reached out and gently pried Enna's reins out of Garris's hand.

Frustration welled up within Garris. "So that's it. You turn and run like the scared little boy you are?"

Jon closed his eyes and bowed his head. He took a deep breath that seemed to calm him. And when he lifted his head, his soft eyes gazed into Garris's, and his words had a finality to them. "I'll never be able to thank you enough. You went with me into places no sane person would ever go. With no more reason than to help me. You've been more than a friend to me, and I'll miss you more than I can say. Goodbye, Garris."

Jon brought Enna around, then spurred her on, and she bolted off in a burst of thundering hooves. Kyri pawed the ground as Garris sat atop her, staring after Jon, unable to stop him as he raced off across the setting sun.

"Dammit," Garris grumbled.

Her eyes unfocused, Dellia stared off into the distance as the quiet thudding of hooves droned on for what seemed like forever. Images kept swirling through her mind: her talking to Braye, stabbing Jon in the back, his blood running into the dirt. But most horrendous of all was Wistra's calm voice proclaiming she was the assassin who would have murdered the one sent to save her people.

She wanted to rebel against it, to tell herself that it couldn't be. But that was a lie. Wistra was right. That was who she was. Her actions of the last weeks were undeniable proof. With the right lies, she would have killed Jon. Even knowing it would haunt her for the rest of her days. Unable to face the horror, Dellia withdrew into silence.

Eventually, the thudding came to a stop, and she stared down a winding path that led through lush fields and on into the deep red, glowing sunset. Dellia had been riding next to Kayleen as the company plodded along in quiet rumination. But for how long, she was not aware. Nor did it matter.

Kayleen leaned over, and her words broke the glum silence. "We're going to stop here for the night," she said in the quiet voice of a concerned friend.

The words rolled past Dellia, unable to pull her out of her haze, trapped as she was in a perpetual prison of her memories.

Kayleen closed her eyes and lowered her head. When she raised it, she looked up into Dellia's face, as if she wanted to say something but was stopping herself. Instead, she paused for a second, then swung down off her horse and wandered off toward her troops.

Dellia sat atop Ulka for a while, staring into the fading light of the red horizon. Finally, when she couldn't bear to be around anyone a second longer, she slipped down off her horse. And as the soldiers broke into somber activity, she trudged off the well-trodden path and down into a grassy ravine.

Finally sheltered from view, she slid down with her back against a large, gray boulder and stared off into space. As the sound of the soldiers making camp drifted over the embankment, quiet tears began to roll down her cheeks.

Dellia sniffled and raised her head, fighting back her feeling of hopelessness. This was not who she was. She pulled herself upright and swiped her cheeks, rubbing away the wetness. Adjusting her position, she pulled herself up even taller, forcing back her sorrow, endeavoring to sit tall and proud.

Anger swept through her veins. All she had ever wanted was to serve, and now that had been torn from her. Fate, the council, Wistra —they had all conspired against her. Taking away the one thing that mattered in her life. The one thing she had sacrificed everything for.

Her eyes fell on the delicate vine bracelet on her wrist. At the center of it all was him. None of this would have happened if she'd never met Jon. She yanked the bracelet over her hand and flung it into the grass.

The instant it disappeared, a stab of remorse pierced her soul. Her hand flew to her mouth. Not Jon; never Jon.

She leaped forward, scrambling across the grass on her hands and knees. Her tears returned as she pored through the green carpet in a frantic search, afraid she'd never find it in the fading light.

Desperation had set in when at last a glint of silver flashed among the greenery. She snatched the bracelet from the ground, and as she clutched it to her breast, her tears turned to sobs. She loved him, beyond words, beyond hope. And this was all she had left of her love. She dropped down in the long grass, clinging to the cherished memento as her sobs began to heave.

Then, the image came back, the one memory more haunting than all the rest. The one Dellia had shoved out of her mind but could no longer hold back. In the cavern, after Wistra's message, when the light came back, there was Jon's face, staring at her with such horror in his eyes. She had betrayed him, fully and completely, and she deserved every speck of his hatred. How could she have done that to her one, true love?

Dellia slipped the delicate silver bracelet over her wrist and pulled her knees to her chest. She had discarded her love with as little care as she had tossed away the bracelet. Unable to forget the vile things she'd done or all she had lost and unwilling to blunt the experience of it, she let the floodgates open. Sorrow and remorse washed over her, drenching her soul, and as she buried her head in her arms, her sobs became uncontrollable.

Painted orange by the setting sun, lush rolling hills flew by as Enna raced on at a full gallop. Though Jon was somewhat calmer after getting some distance from Kanlu, the horror of what he had witnessed there had burrowed its way into his soul. So he hurtled onward, as if somehow, with enough speed and distance, he could leave that horrible feeling behind.

After a while, Enna slowed of her own accord, and by the time the final sliver of the setting sun had disappeared over the horizon, Jon was plodding along in glum silence.

He slumped in the saddle, crushed by the burden of a world that was against him. All he had ever asked for was a simple life with few responsibilities. He needed that life in order to function, to cope. Yet here he was, at the center of a maelstrom, accused of being someone he knew in his heart of hearts could not be him. But worst of all was the knowledge that if he stayed, he would lead his friends to their deaths. It was that certainty, more than anything, that chased him on into the descending darkness.

When the outline of a grove of trees appeared to his left, Jon was finally ready to give up the race and let slumber blunt his pain for a while. So he veered off and headed toward the peaceful stand of trees.

He had no idea how he would find his way, but tomorrow the chase would begin again, and he would find Megan, and together they would make their way back to Isla. And there, in her cave, perhaps they would find their way home, and this nightmare would be over.

Under the sheltering branches of a modest grouping of white-barked trees, Jon slipped to the ground. He turned to go collect firewood but stopped himself and reached out to untie his small blanket roll. This time he wouldn't be such an idiot. He would do as Dellia had done in the Chaldean Desert and use his blanket to keep warm.

He fumbled with the tie, but in the dim light, he couldn't see what he was doing. Frustrated, Jon yanked at it, and it gave way, throwing him off-balance. He fell and sat down hard at Enna's feet.

As he sat there on the cold ground, remembrances of that night in the Chaldean Desert flooded back. It was the most contented he'd been in his life, under the stars with Dellia holding him close as the white sands spread out around them. And with those memories came an unbearable pain, as if part of him had been ripped away.

Now, more than ever, he needed her. He ached to see her face, to hear her voice, to be with her one last time. But that was not to be. There would be no last-minute arrival. No coming to his rescue, ever again. Quiet tears rolled down Jon's cheeks. He was alone now, more so than he had ever been in his life.

As he stared off into the faint glow of the horizon, a giant, dappled-gray head appeared in his face as Enna reached down and gave his shoulder a gentle nudge. It was as if she had heard his thoughts and wanted to let him know he was not alone.

Her dark eyes peered out from the outline of her head, and as Jon stared back, it seemed as if the massive beast could somehow sense his anguish. Despite himself, he let a short laugh escape. Then, he reached out and ran his hand down her warm muzzle, caressing its smoothness.

It had been Dellia's compassion that had led her to seek out a horse for him. Without her, he would have never had one at all, much less one as beautiful. And now in the final days of his journey, she was still here with him, helping him. He pictured Dellia's beautiful brown hair cascading down over soft brown leather as she handed him the reins. As he sat on the cold hard ground, with Enna's head under his hand, Jon realized he would never find another soul as kind and understanding as Dellia.

For Kayleen, the road from Kanlu was fraught with fear and guilt. Her fears over the course the council had set seemed so trivial now. A disturbance in the veil, an army of the dead—it was power beyond any she had ever witnessed. It was the stuff of old legends. Of gods and demons, and every child's nightmares. What if the oracle was right? What if this was just the start? How could her people survive? No army could fight that kind of power. That dread festered in her consciousness, clouding her every thought and action.

While the rest of the unit was setting up camp for the night, Dellia had vanished. And when she returned, the sight of her was shattering. She had been crying, and not just a little. To see a proud Talesh warrior so despondent and defeated was haunting, and doubly so because it was Kayleen's doing. So she tried to talk to Dellia, to convince her to go after Jon, that together they would both be safe. But at her first words, Dellia had turned away, refusing to look at her. And at the mere mention of Jon's name, she had shut down completely.

When Kayleen finally settled in for the night, it was not the fate of her world that consumed her but what she had done to her friend. Dellia had trusted her, and she had repaid that trust with suffering and pain—pain with which she was all too familiar. In the quiet of her tent, she lay awake tortured over the agony she had visited on her friend.

So she distracted herself, racking her brain in the forlorn hope of finding a way to salvage things when they arrived back in Shirdon. Yet, no matter how she looked at it or couched the facts in glittering rhetoric, it was impossible to argue that their mission had been anything but an abject failure. And with that failure came the inescapable truth that her life as a member of the council was over.

It was obvious Dellia was their best hope. Only she could reach Jon and bring him and the council together. But it was inevitable that the council would see him as a threat and Dellia as his accomplice. And, with no power to protect either, she feared what misery the council would heap on Dellia's already shattered spirit and what that would mean for her world.

Tired of lying awake in futile obsession, Kayleen rousted the troops well before dawn, insisting they get an early start. They broke camp and set out in the near darkness. As they rode on through the dreary, gray sunrise, the grassy hills grew steeper and more treacherous, and scattered rock outcroppings began to litter the landscape.

Kayleen stayed near the back, alongside Dellia. She was more responsive than the night before, but a troubling despondency seemed to have taken hold. She had never seen her like this before, and it prompted Kayleen to keep an even closer eye on her.

As they plodded along with the hazy sun barely visible through a layer of flat, gray clouds, the broad roadway turned and began snaking its way along a hillside above a winding, rocky canyon.

Kayleen glanced back again to check on Dellia, and she was staring into space, her normal state since the events of the day before. Then, her eyes seemed to lock onto something ahead, and she sat up tall and determined.

Kayleen spun around to see what had caught her attention, but all that lay ahead was another turn in the road and a sheer cliff that dropped down to a stony riverbed.

She whipped back around in time to see Dellia raise her heels and dig them into Ulka's sides. In a thunderous clatter of hooves, he shot to a gallop, carrying her straight for the edge.

Kayleen froze, unsure what was happening. Caught by surprise, the soldiers ahead halted and looked back as pounding hooves blasted between them, hurtling Dellia toward her death.

Kayleen snapped out of it and shouted, "Dellia!"

Dellia responded by leaning forward and spurring her steed on again. Ulka surged faster, his hooves pummeling the ground as the cliff raced closer.

Chaos broke out as horses flew to a gallop, carrying soldiers after Dellia. Kayleen spurred her horse on, but it was impossible to reach her in time.

Then it hit her. As she jostled in the saddle, Kayleen raised her fingers to her mouth and let out a piercing whistle that echoed through the countryside.

Ulka pulled up short, right at the brink, and in a second her soldiers were upon Dellia. Nikosh seized one arm while Pedrus grabbed the reins.

Kayleen pulled up in front of Dellia and flew down off her mount. She ran over and stared up at her expressionless face. "Dellia, what is wrong with you? If I didn't know you better, I'd say you were trying to kill yourself."

No sooner had the words left her mouth than she realized that was most probably what Dellia *was* trying to do. Some among her people saw suicide as noble, as the ultimate act of self-determination.

Kayleen's remorse rose up to consume her whole being. She had caused this, and she could never fix it. And in that moment, she knew precisely what course she must take when they arrived back in Shirdon.

Chapter Thirty-Two

TIDES OF TIME

Jon slept little that night, haunted by visions of horrific bloodshed and the slaughter of everyone he loved. When he did manage to drift off, he'd awaken frequently, and more than once he bolted awake crying out and shaking in a cold sweat. It was as if his spirit had been broken in that cave and nothing would ever be right again.

Unable to lie alone with his thoughts any longer, he arose just as the deep blue and red sky of predawn peeked through the branches of the small grove of trees. He shivered in the chill morning air as he packed up. Then, just as the rising sun painted the rolling hills with its deep yellow rays, he headed out alone.

He had no clue how he would find Megan, but finding her was paramount. He could not go home without her. Hence, his need for a plan was desperate, but this world was still foreign to him, and now, it appeared, he was a hunted man. Inquiring after her whereabouts would entail randomly poking his head into one place after another where he was at high risk of being attacked or arrested. So, with no solid plan, or indeed any plan whatsoever, he had turned his attention to Isla and home, in the hopes that along the way some epiphany would illuminate a clearer path forward.

Using the position of the sun and length of the shadows as a guide, Jon headed in what he estimated to be a south-southwesterly direction. He plodded along, hour after hour, the thud of hooves droning on ceaselessly across the pastoral landscape.

Each passing minute was torturous, with nothing to distract him from thoughts of how lost he was without his friends or the horrors he was destined to visit upon them should he fail to press onward. To make matters worse, he was nervous about being alone and startled time and again over imagined threats watching his every move.

The landscape turned rockier and more treacherous as what appeared to be noon approached. The sun rose higher, and light wispy clouds began to streak the blue sky. As he looked up at them, Jon heaved a soft sigh. Cirrus clouds were a worrisome sign and a possible warning that a warm front was headed his way. He was barely equipped to be out here at all, and the thought of being caught out in the open during a torrential downpour was more than he cared to contemplate.

As he traveled down a passage between two craggy hills, he craned his neck, staring up at the midday sun surrounded by feathery trails of white. With the yellow orb now high in the sky, trying to estimate the angle of the sun had become sheer guesswork.

He returned his eyes forward, staring at the tiny shadow of a massive rock outcropping that jutted into the passage. It was a foolish idea anyway, trying to use the sun and shadows to navigate, and as expected, it had fallen apart. Yet despite its being no surprise, the sheer futility of his situation was becoming intolerable.

Jon's head whipped up at a faint scraping sound, like the grinding of gravel beneath a shoe. In the narrow passage, it was impossible to locate the source.

He glanced up at the hilltops on either side. Then, he twisted around in the saddle and stared back past a large, old tree that hung over the gorge. His gaze lingered there, scanning the landscape as a pair of birds swooped down onto a jagged branch.

Enna came to an abrupt halt, jogging him in the saddle. Jon snapped forward and jumped at the sight of Rillen on horseback, waiting in silence for him behind the enormous rock outcropping.

He lurched backward and put out his palms, as if they could stop her. "Hey, I'm warning you. Stay back."

Rillen let out a small laugh. "Take it easy. If I wanted to hurt you, I could have done it while you were asleep."

"Wait, it's you." Jon glanced behind him. "You've been following me. You've had me jumping at every little thing all day."

She planted her hands on her hips and gave him a stern stare. "It wouldn't have been necessary if you'd have stayed with Garris. Why did you separate? It's not safe for you out here alone."

"Not safe for me? You must have missed the memo." He hung his head as sadness filled his heart. "Staying with me is a death sentence. I'm the most dangerous person in this whole messed-up world."

Rillen pulled closer and in a gentle voice said, "Well, if you don't mind, I'll risk accompanying you, at least for a while."

He pulled back and eyed her. He was desperate to have help and company, but this just didn't add up.

"Why?" he said with a mix of suspicion and curiosity.

She paused, apparently to contemplate her answer. Then she gave a small shrug. "Faith."

Jon stared, trying to figure out what the heck that meant.

She seemed to sense his puzzlement. "Faith in prophecy. Faith that this is where I need to be. Faith that if an oracle seven hundred years ago knew your name and said to help with whatever path you chose, then I need to help you."

Jon cocked his head. "Seven hundred years?"

"Seven hundred seventy-three, to be exact."

Her words made as much sense as anything else in this world, but they did little to quell his unease.

"Yeah, okay, but how do I know it's really you?" He turned his head, looking at Rillen sideways. "And why should I trust you? You work for the council."

She gave her head a small shake. "It's not that simple. My situation is … complicated. Sometimes to serve one master, you must serve another."

"What does that …" Jon trailed off as he realized it didn't matter. None of it mattered. "You know what? I don't even want to know anymore. I just want to find Megan and go home."

Rillen turned her eyes to the ground, seeming to contemplate his words. After a while, she took a deep breath and raised her head. "Megan is an impossibility."

"What does that mean?"

"If you poke around trying to find her, you'll get yourself arrested in a flash."

Jon shook his head. "I don't care about me."

"Then care about Megan. She has a destiny of her own. One of critical importance to all of us, and I won't lie. It is likely to place her in grave danger, but regardless of how perilous her path may be, you must let her follow it."

"But—"

"Besides." Rillen pointed at him. "You just said it yourself. Staying with you is a death sentence. You're the most dangerous person in the whole world."

Frustrated, he glared at her. "That's not what I meant."

"It doesn't matter what you meant. It's true. If you go around stirring up a lot of attention by trying to find her, you could reveal her location to others and put her in grave danger. The council is still after both of you, remember?"

"But I can't just abandon her."

Rillen's tone became more even tempered. "I'm not asking you to. I'm asking you to pass the burden for her safekeeping to me. After we part, I will find her and let her know where you are, and if it is her wish, I will accompany her and protect her wherever she may go."

Jon pointed in the direction he was headed. "So, just go merrily on my way home and leave her behind?"

Rillen startled and sat taller in the saddle. "See, that's what I'm talking about. You don't even have a clue where you're headed. You're pointing to the heart of Akolah."

He gave a frustrated grumble. "That's not the point."

She planted her hands on her hips again. "Fine. Yes. You go home, if that's the path you choose. But you need to let Megan find her own way." She shot him a piercing gaze. "She does not need you to rescue her."

It was one of those statements for which he had never found a good response. "I know. I know. Fine."

The conversation halted for a moment, the only sound the grinding of horses' hooves against the gravel of the rocky ravine.

Jon stared at the wispy clouds that streaked the crystal-blue sky as he tried to reconcile his jumble of feelings. As much of a relief as it was to have Rillen's help, the prospect of leaving Megan behind to struggle with her own peril was intensely uncomfortable. Yet, he knew in his heart Rillen was right. He had to trust her. Whereas he might never reach Megan, Rillen would have no trouble because it was her job, and nobody would question her doing it. So, he resigned himself to the fact that he had no choice.

After a moment, Rillen relaxed. "Twice now, you've said you're headed home. How?"

Jon pulled the medallion partway out of his shirt. "Isla promised if I assembled this, she'd get me home. So that's where I'm headed."

"Isla?" Rillen said, sounding puzzled by the name.

"Yeah, the dragon."

"You mean Islong?" Her eyes widened in surprise and wonder. "The dragon? Is that where Dellia found you?"

He nodded.

She adjusted her position in the saddle. "Well," she said, her manner becoming matter-of-fact, "there's no way I'm going into a dragon's lair, but I can get you there."

He lowered his head. The whole conversation was pointless. Rillen could do anything she wanted and he couldn't stop her. So he might as well be gracious about it and accept her help.

Jon lifted his head and nodded. "Thanks, but don't expect me to be decent company."

Rillen nodded back, and the thud of hooves resumed as the two headed on through the peaceful ravine in silence. He closed his eyes and felt the heaving of Enna beneath him. After a few minutes of following Rillen, the familiarity of the situation finally struck him.

He lifted his head and forced a smile as he stared down the path ahead. "So, should I be expecting an ambush when we get there?"

Garris turned Kyri around as he tried to get a handle on his frustration. Watching Jon ride away had only served as a reminder of how powerless he was to do anything about the injustice the council had visited upon them both. Sure, it would be easy enough to go after him, but what would be the point? He was headed home. Where he had always planned to go. And even if he did catch Jon, what was he supposed to do, kidnap him and drag him kicking and screaming back to people who would just as soon see him dead? As appealing as the idea might seem at the moment, Jon was a man ... sort of, and entitled to make his own mistakes. And without him, it would be pointless to confront Kayleen.

So Garris did the only thing he could: he headed home, away from Kanlu and this whole exercise in futility. To avoid Kayleen, he doubled back, traveling east, the opposite of the direction she would go. He skirted Kanlu and hugged the southern shoreline of Kinshai Lake. The quiet lapping of the water against the shore accompanied him as he watched the reflection of the city lights grow distant, then disappear into the gentle waves.

The feeling that he lay in a trap that had already been sprung traveled with him. So, after a few hours' sleep in the picturesque village of Chongji, Garris forged onward to the rugged Naichi Mountains. He headed south along their base, then through the white sands of the Chaldean Desert to the Neri. This time his pace was pressured but not frantic, and as the days passed, the futility of everything that had happened consumed his thoughts. He worried about Jon and feared for Dellia, but most of all, anger and frustration drove him onward.

By the time Garris found himself atop the enormous pillar of stone, he was seething. He had journeyed to a land that wanted him dead. He had gone into insane places. Risked death countless times, worried and agonized over keeping Jon safe, and all for nothing. And there was only one person to blame for sending him on this whole disaster of a journey.

The morning sun was peeking through several towering columns of rock in the distance as he stormed up to the front door of the crude little cabin made of pine logs.

He raised his hand to give the door a heavy knock, but before his knuckles hit, the door flew open, and there stood Elt, his scaly features glistening in the morning sun.

Garris wanted to bash that self-satisfied look off his lizard-man face, but he merely glared. "What the Hades, Elt? Why would you send me to help only to see it fall apart? It was pointless."

Elt remained calm and unruffled. "You're not mad at me. You're mad because you cared."

Garris could almost feel his blood boiling and that little vein on his head throbbing. "All right, yeah, I cared, and look what it got me. Thanks, Sensei. Lesson learned." He shoved his way past Elt and stormed into the cabin.

With care, his scaly mentor closed the door and turned to face him. "Would you really have stood with the Otherworlder again?"

Thrown by the question and wondering how Elt knew about Jon, he stared for a moment. Then, he shook his head. "I don't know."

Elt motioned to a rough-hewn chair at the small table, inviting Garris to sit. It scraped across the floor as Garris pulled it out, then rattled and creaked as he plopped down into it. He watched as Elt began to stroll around the crudely made table.

"I would have stood with Jon," Garris said.

"Why?" Elt cocked his head. "To be a hero? For fame and glory? To get your vengeance?"

"No," Garris shot back, aggravated by the inference, "because he's a friend. Because what's happening is wrong."

Elt beamed another one of those self-satisfied smiles as he seated himself in the chair opposite Garris. "Good, then my work is nearly done. But there's a story here that needs an ending, and it's not Jon's, and it's not Dellia's."

Garris glared at him. "For Adi's sake, it's like a sickness with you, you can't give a straight answer."

In a calm voice, Elt said, "Go back to the council, to the council chamber, and you'll have your answers. Answers to questions you didn't even know you had."

It was all he could manage to not leap over the table, grab Elt, and thrash some straight talk out of him. "Answers to questions I didn't even blah, blah, blah. You're insane. I'm learning from an insane person." Garris calmed himself and shook his head, striving to speak in a more reasonable tone. "Look, even if I wanted to, I'd never get close."

Accustomed to being on constant guard, his gaze flew over toward movement in the room beyond. He tensed, ready for anything.

Then, in the doorway behind Elt, an outline appeared of a slender woman wearing a simple linen robe. Garris bolted upright and stood there, gawking as she strolled into the room.

In his astonishment, the words sputtered out. "How did you get … how could you know … you and Elt?"

Behind Jon, the branches made a swishing sound as they swayed and bowed in the stiff breeze. Beneath billowy gray skies, gusts of wind whipped through the grass of the clearing before him like waves in a storm. He glanced over as Rillen stepped up to his side, then he looked out across the sea of dancing grass at the huge, dark hole in the cliffside. The entrance to Isla's lair beckoned to him, but he stood frozen, unable to take the first step.

The journey here had seemed slow and the days dark, his heart clouded and broken. He had to leave. This was not his world and never would be. But it was like a part of him died back in Kanlu, and the loss of it had haunted him this entire trip. He was no stranger to heartbreak, but this was pure torture, and instead of each day becoming easier, they had grown more difficult as his heart grew heavier.

Rillen had been great, guiding him unerringly through hills, across desolate plains, and into the forest. Always supportive, but never interfering, she had allowed him his silence. He had even begun to suspect she was biting her tongue, as if determined to let him find his own way.

Even now, as they gazed across the rustling grass at his destination, though she feared to be here, Rillen stood with him, watching in quiet.

Jon turned to her and peered into her eyes. "You made a promise to me, do you remember?"

Rillen's head whipped over and she stared with a look of exasperation. "Asking every few hours is really getting on my nerves, Jon."

"I know, but I need to hear you say it. It just feels wrong, leaving like this."

She calmed and put her hand on her heart. "I swear, on my honor, I will move heaven and earth to find Megan and, if it is her wish, to help her get home."

"And you promise."

"For crying out loud, Jon, I just swore on my honor. What do you want, a blood sacrifice?"

"Eww." He shook his head. "Wait, would that … no, you aren't serious—I mean, you wouldn't …"

"No." She wrinkled up her nose in disgust. "Oh, for Adi's sake."

Rillen shook it off and placed a hand on each of Jon's shoulders. "The council ordered me to find her. If I don't, it's over for me as a protector. They could even banish me. So your incessant nagging is just plain pointless."

"I guess so."

"She is with Aylun, and he will protect her with his last breath. Trust me. He takes this very seriously, and if anyone can keep her safe, it's him."

"So I can really do this? I can go?"

Her expression turned more earnest than he had yet seen. "Yes," she said with a confident nod.

Somehow, that final response calmed his worried heart more than all the reassurances that had preceded it. Jon turned again to the mouth of Isla's home and stared for a long while as stiff winds sent rustling waves through the long grasses of the clearing.

This was it. He was going home.

The urge for tears returned as Jon realized the part of the journey he dreaded most had come. A gust of wind tousled his hair as he came around to look one last time at Enna's beautiful, dapple-gray face.

"I've never had a horse before, and you saw me through so much." He pressed his forehead to her muzzle. "Goodbye, Enna. I'll miss you." She let out a quiet nicker as he held his head pressed to hers. Jon stepped back and handed the reins to Rillen. "Make sure she has a good life."

She nodded.

He eyed Rillen as tears came to his eyes. "Tell Dellia … tell her I love her more than anything in the world—no, more than anything in *two* worlds—and I will miss her … terribly … every day."

She seemed about to tear up as well, and it made it that much harder to maintain his composure.

Jon hesitated. Then, he quickly wiped away the wetness from his eyes. What good would it do now to tell Dellia what was in his heart? By the time she heard it, he would already be home. "Scratch that. Tell her … tell her that she saved me more times, and in more ways, than I can count. Tell her I could never forget her and that she will forever live in a special place in my heart."

Rillen nodded.

"Yeah. Tell her that."

Suddenly, she reached out and grabbed ahold of him, pulling him close in a firm hug. It caught him by surprise for a moment, but then he embraced her back.

When she let go, she seemed a little sad. "You're a special person, Jon. I wish your path had kept you here. This world needs more like you."

Her sincerity caught him off guard. He didn't want to break down completely in front of her. So he stepped back and gave a quick nod before he turned and marched off.

The rolling grasses whipped around him as the mouth of the lair drew closer. Images flashed through his memory of flying out of the cave, shielding his eyes from the glaring sun, frantic to find Megan. It was on this very spot that he'd raced off across the clearing after her. He recalled sitting in the forest, sure he was lost forever. Then Dellia came, and after that, it seemed as if his world would never be the same again.

545

Jon passed through the mouth of the cave and headed down the worn pathway, through the long, blue-streaked passage to the lair. As he traveled downward, the light grew dimmer, and the rumble of wind gusting across the mouth of the cave became distant. His footsteps echoed around him, carrying downward, as if announcing his arrival.

With each footfall his anxiety grew, so he distracted himself. In his mind's eye, he pictured Dellia back in her home on the Shir Plateau. She'd be staring out the window, angry at him for eluding her but glad to be done with him once and for all.

The light was almost gone when the ceiling opened up into the massive cavern. There, in near darkness, she lay, coiled in a circle with her head resting on her tail, watching him in silence.

Jon slowed. Isla was much bigger than he recalled, and her enormous steely eyes stared at him, following his tentative approach. He had forgotten how intimidating she was as the feeling of being easy prey returned.

As he grew near, she uncoiled some with a deep scraping sound and drift of dust. Without making a noise, she lifted her head high above him, then swooped down to within an arm's length of his face. She snorted, blowing back his clothes and hair and stirring up a cloud of dust all around him.

Unnerved by the proximity of the carnivore's sharp, jagged teeth, Jon eyed her as she let out a deep moan that seemed to hang in the air forever as it reverberated through the cavern.

"It is done?" Isla asked slowly, in that deep, breathy voice.

He pulled the medallion from his shirt and set it in his palms. His anxiety grew as he held it out for the dark, scaly monster to take. She stared at him, her hot breath blowing through his hair.

"Keep it."

Jon jerked upright. "What? I thought you needed it."

"No," she said, her reply nearly instantaneous.

For a moment, he stood gawking. "Then why did I go through all this?"

Jon could swear surprise passed over Isla's enormous face. "To prepare," she said, as if it should be obvious.

He stared, puzzled. "But what possible reason could *you* have for putting me through this?"

Isla moved her face a hair's breadth from Jon's. "Survival," she said, low and clear.

He stood for a moment, perplexed. What could that possibly mean?

Then, it dawned on him—Isla's fate somehow depended on him. That was insane. His anxiety turned to terror and dread. Jon struggled, fighting to remain calm and keep his thoughts lucid.

"No," he almost shouted. "I'm not this person everyone thinks I am. I'm no savior. I'm just a guy."

Isla issued a snort that sounded vaguely derisive, and her breath tossed Jon's hair back again.

He stood his ground, staring at the enormous beast, doing his best to feign bravery. "I'm sorry, but you promised." He thrust the medallion high into the air and demanded. "I put it back together; now you send me home."

She let out a low growl that reeked of disapproval. Then she rumbled to her feet in a cloud of dust. With the claw of her wing, she reached over to a mound of jewels and weapons.

A clatter of metal against metal echoed through the chamber as she dragged a full-length mirror from its depths. It was reminiscent of the one behind the portal when Jon arrived. His anxiety inched higher as she swung it over and placed it on the ground before him.

She swept her wing above it with a stiff gust of wind and a swirl of dust. A soft light filled the cavern as a glow ran across the mirror. When that glow vanished, a small, irregular mass appeared hovering in front of its reflective surface.

His anxiety mushroomed as he peered into the fluid, whirling blob. It was just like the one in his lab.

Isla's focus remained fixed on the mass, staring at it as it spun and grew.

An unexpected wave of guilt washed over Jon, and he turned his head, eyeing the enormous face of the dragon. "I can't stay. I can't watch them all die."

Isla's gaze shifted from the spinning mass to him, and she gave a small nod of agreement. "Yes ... better ... not to see."

Startled by her response, he stared. Then a flush of irritation took over, and he glared. "Really? Sarcasm? From a dragon?"

Isla's brow furrowed, and she tilted her head, like a dog puzzled by a strange sound.

He stiffened and gasped. She was serious. What did she know that he didn't?

An image from the oracle room flashed through his memory. The enormous army deep below the earth, spreading back wave after wave. What if that army wasn't there because of anything he'd done? What if they would come anyway? Humankind would soon face extinction. Those were Wistra's words.

His heart pounding, Jon turned away, staring into the irregular patch of darkness. Isla did the same, and they both watched as it whirled and expanded.

He began to tremble. This wasn't his world. He wasn't a hero. They were wrong about him. He knew it in his heart of hearts. Whatever happened, he was powerless to stop it. And Isla was right: all staying would accomplish would be watching every single person he loved die.

Jon lowered his head. "Look, I just want to go home."

Dust began to whirl into the mass as it swirled and pulsated.

Isla turned and stared at him. Then, with a low, breathy voice that reverberated through the cavern, she said, "To ... what?"

DELLIA

At the question, his anxiety blew out to unbearable proportions, and Jon's head whipped over. He took a step back. And as he stood, staring at the dragon, trying to stumble out an answer, his clothes began to pull from his body, drawn toward the growing mass.

Dellia gazed out the small window of her home at the rolling gray skies that stretched out over the hills of Erden as far as the eye could see. The breeze through the window blew through her hair and loose, linen robe. She had put away her leather armor forever and donned a peplos she had made for herself, secured at her shoulders with a pair of silver, leaf-shaped broaches.

A soft rap on her door couldn't pull Dellia out of the depths of her grief. The trip home had been unbearable. And rather than her guilt and shame subsiding, it had only grown worse. Her whole life she had been proud of her integrity and worked hard to serve and protect with honor. In a moment, it had all been ripped away. She hated what she had done and what she had become. But most of all, she hated the fact that she hated herself. She wanted it to be over, but it never would be.

The soft rapping came a third time, then the door creaked open, and someone, a woman from the sound of it, crept inside. With quiet, graceful steps, she strolled over next to Dellia and stood with her at the window.

"I know you want to be alone," came Ceree's voice, "but there are matters I must discuss with you."

Dellia stood motionless, staring out the window. She used to hang on every word, look forward to every mission, every order. But now Ceree's words were hollow, and nothing the council said or wanted mattered anymore.

When Dellia failed to respond, Ceree forged ahead. "Kayleen has argued that she was responsible for everything that happened in

Kanlu. She is being detained while the council considers charges of treason."

Dellia knew she should feel something for her. She wanted to. It was in her nature to be empathetic. But Kayleen had had so many chances to tell her the truth, and instead, she'd lied, even ordering Dellia to violate her beliefs.

"She betrayed me," was all she could bring herself to say.

Ceree continued, "I asked that I be the one to break the news: you now report to Braye."

Anger jolted Dellia out of her daze. The scene of Braye convincing her to assassinate Jon was seared into her memory. A wave of outrage and remorse tore at her, as if Braye had already drenched her hands in Jon's blood.

Her head whipped over, and she glared at Ceree. "Braye can rot in Tartarus." Then her sorrow rushed back as she realized he had not acted alone. "You *all* can." She hung her head. "Me, too, for that matter."

When she looked up again, there was sympathy and concern in Ceree's deep brown eyes, and for a moment, Dellia wanted to collapse into a heap and pour her heart out. But Ceree was one of those who had done this. Surrounded by people she had known her entire adult life, Dellia had never felt so alone.

"You don't understand," Ceree said. "The Verod has used this crisis to gather support. They are marching on Shirdon as we speak."

All Dellia could do was stare in disbelief. The council had used and manipulated her. They had put their own interests above the truth, above all of Meerdon ... and now they wanted her to protect them?

"What?" Her eyes began to well with tears. "You expect me to continue to play this role you cast for me?"

"Dellia, please, we have sent more soldiers than we can spare to meet them. We *need* you. I have asked that you be the one to stand guard in the courtyard and protect the entrance to Shir Keep."

"Protect the council? Why would I do that?"

Fear flashed in Ceree's eyes. "Because you know the Verod. They hate us. They won't want anyone left to oppose them. They won't hesitate to butcher all of us, Kayleen included. The council may be flawed, but the Verod are worse. You know this."

The truth of Ceree's words struck her to the core. Many on the council had kept her at arm's length, and she'd always thought they were simply nervous around her gift. But those she knew had been friends, and regardless of what they may have done, they did not deserve a gruesome death.

Yet, what Ceree asked was impossible. For her to stand alone against an entire army? It was suicide. And with that thought, the answer came to her. She brought herself up taller and turned to stare out the window once again.

"Perhaps you are right. Perhaps this is the end I deserve."

Ceree seemed stunned. She moved around in front of Dellia and peered into her face with a look of surprise. "What does that mean?"

Dellia raised her chin, and some small speck of pride returned. She would defend the courtyard, and she would fight with everything she had to stop them. But she would not kill a single Verod. She would not shed blood for the council. Never again. And when she became too weak to fight, she would fall. And this nightmare would be over.

She gave a slow nod. "Fine. I will play the villain this one last time. I'll stand at the courtyard until this role is played out."

Ceree reached out as if to place a hand on Dellia's shoulder, then seemed to reconsider and pulled it back. She opened her mouth but closed it without uttering a word. Then she turned and walked from the room, leaving Dellia staring out the window at the gray skies over the hills of Erden.

Chapter Thirty-Three

DISAPPEAR

There she stood before him, the last person Garris would have expected to find in Elt's little abode. A host of questions spun through his mind. How did she know this place existed? How did she get here? What could possibly bring one of the Ephori to this cluttered log cabin?

Sirra nodded to Elt and faced Garris. "I'll get you to Dellia's home on the Shir Plateau."

He stood for a moment, staring at her.

She stepped up next to Elt. "Garris, please. All my daughter ever wanted was to serve, and now she could be found guilty of treason."

He glanced away. The prospect was disturbing. Dellia was one of the most genuine, caring people he'd ever met, and she had become a friend. But making it from the protector's homes to the council chamber would require a miracle. The barracks sat just off the courtyard, so soldiers were always strolling through the gardens near the entrance to the keep. The massive wooden doors into Shir Keep were barred, with guards posted inside and out. And any time of day or night, soldiers were stationed to patrol the corridors.

Yet, how could he abandon Dellia? She was the closest thing he'd had to a brother in arms in fifteen years. He couldn't leave her behind. He was all too familiar with what happened when the council decreed someone guilty of treason. Images of her being banished and becoming an outcast from the world she loved nagged at him.

Garris took a deep breath and stared out the small window at the rock spires of the Neri jutting up from the canyon floor. "Just like I was." He returned his gaze to Sirra and nodded agreement.

Then, he eyed Elt, and the desire rushed back to wipe that smug look off his face. He glared at him as his frustration returned. "Sure, why not, but if this ends the way the last trip did, I'll come back and beat some straight answers out of your scaly, Skri hide."

Elt flashed an amused smile. "I'd like to see you try."

Garris grimaced as the urge to punch someone hit. He shoved his head closer, glaring at Elt as he growled.

His heart pounding, Jon clung to the edge of the dark, metallic scales, his fingers digging between them as the sunlit, billowy clouds raced by below. Frightened, cold, and exposed, his mind was drawn back to that evening in Sirra's home when he and Dellia had sat side by side, bathing in the warmth of the fire. "People don't ride dragons" she had said. "trying to ride one, that would be extremely foolish." So here he was being just such a fool. Only "foolish" didn't really come close to covering it. This was outright madness, hurtling through the skies, clinging to the neck of a beast that was never designed to be ridden and who made it clear the very idea was an affront.

Jon squinted from the glare of the late afternoon sun, watching as they raced up behind a flock of birds, far below. The air here was warmer than on the ground, but he still shivered as the wind whistled around him.

Or perhaps it wasn't the cold that made him shiver but the fact he was racing toward a situation that terrified him more than any dragon—risking almost certain rejection again by baring his soul to a woman. A prospect made many times more frightening by her habit of unexpectedly attacking him.

In her lair, Isla had waved away his portal home, leaving only the full-length mirror behind it. Then she used the same mirror to locate Dellia in what appeared to be a picturesque garden of some kind, and the beast seemed to know exactly where it was.

Isla spread her enormous wings wide and flapped one more time with a tremendous surge. Jon yanked himself tighter to her scales as she pulled in her wings and stretched out her neck, then banked and dove for the clouds below.

The wind roared past, whipping his hair and clothes back as he careened downward, clinging to the dragon's neck. A sudden weightless feeling wormed its way through his stomach as he plunged through the flock of birds. One slammed into his arm and almost ripped his hand from the rigid scales.

The clouds rushed up, then they plummeted into them, and he lost sight of everything as they disappeared into a rush of billowing mist.

Beneath stormy gray skies, Dellia stood scanning the myriad plants and trees of the enormous Shir Courtyard. Even though her heart and soul were as dark as the sky above, she was able to find some small solace in the knowledge that this would be her last vigil.

No matter what approach the Verod might take to the keep, from this vantage point she would hear and move to intercept. Once there, she would put every ounce of her expertise to work, trying to keep them back. But she would not harm them. She was skilled, and so her death would not be swift. It would be arduous and brutal and bloody, and she would die in agonizing pain. Even so, she must face it, for it was a more noble ending than she deserved.

By all accounts, the Verod remained many hours away. So unless they sent scouts ahead, she had a long struggle ahead of her to maintain her resolve. She stood at attention and stilled herself, listening to the near quiet, broken only by the distant sound of thunder rolling across the hills. A light rain began to fall across the immaculate plants and tree as Dellia took another deep breath and scanned the pathways and arched entrances to the courtyard.

Far off in the distance, a massive object plummeted out of the clouds. Her eyes shot over, watching it scream downward, dragging a piece of the cloud cover with it.

Suddenly, a pair of enormous wings opened wide. Dellia startled and gasped as the object became recognizable. It swooped up and leveled off. Then, with a flap of its massive wings, it turned and headed off to the side, around Shirdon.

Having never seen a dragon before, she stood mesmerized by the sight of the majestic beast swimming through the rolling dark skies. She squinted through the drizzle, and as it grew nearer it became clear that its head was aimed in her direction, its eyes scanning the courtyard, searching for something.

Dellia gasped again as the dragon's eyes locked onto *her*. Then it banked and headed straight toward her. With a tremendous flap of its wings, it propelled itself forward, hurtling at her with terrifying speed.

She tensed and readied herself, calming her pounding heart. If the dragon was here for her, she would give it the fight of its life.

As it reached the courtyard, the enormous beast spread its wings wide again and stalled over the far edge of the circular garden. Dellia raised her sword, gripping the hilt with both hands as the massive dragon hung there in the air for a second, proud and majestic.

The beast dropped into the courtyard opposite Dellia. It landed with a deep thud that seemed to shake the very foundations of the keep.

Dellia began cautiously stepping forward, closing in on the monster, alert and ready for its attack. The beast pulled in its wings and bent its head down near the ground, its eyes never leaving her as she stalked toward it.

She halted, frozen in shock, as Jon appeared from behind the dragon's massive head, slipping from its neck and dropping to the ground. He landed some distance down the broad stone path from her, in front of a large archway between two columns.

A stab of pain pierced her heart as she remembered her childhood dream of a man appearing on the back of a dragon to swooping down and rescue her. She knew she had betrayed all of Meerdon, but it crushed her soul that fate had dealt her such a cruel perversion. "It had to be a dragon," she mumbled.

The beast leaped back into the skies with a huge flap of its wings and a blast of wind that whipped back Dellia's hair. It flapped a couple more times as it soared up toward the peak of Mount Karana.

Dellia turned to face Jon, but the instant their eyes met, her calm shattered. A dragon she could confront, an army of the Verod she could handle, but she could never face Jon, not after what she'd done.

The urge to turn and run compelled her. Then in an instant, it came to her, the perfect symmetry of it all. This was her chance to gain some small grain of redemption.

She fought back her tears and pulled herself up tall and proud. She raised her sword high and charged Jon as he approached. Her footsteps clattered against the rocks as she stormed down the path past trees and flowers, her weapon ready to strike.

Startled, he yanked out his sword and whipped it up to meet hers. Dellia swung her blade down, but he deflected her halfhearted blow.

"Fight me," Dellia cried out, her anger not able to hide her desperation. "You have to fight me."

Jon's eyes flew wide, and he stared at her through the drizzle. "What?" he said.

Dellia swung her blade down a second time, but Jon deflected it with ease. She began trembling as sorrow and remorse took over, and from some place deep inside, the words poured out.

"I've spent my whole life training to be a protector. I set aside everything I wanted for myself." She swung again, but this time the blow never came close. She let the blade drop to her side. "All I ever wanted was to help people, to make a difference." She thrust out her hand, motioning to Jon. "Instead, I betrayed the one sent to save us all."

He stared with a shocked look on his face. "You just put your faith in the wrong people."

"No." Dellia gave her head a brisk shake. "I knew what I was doing. I knew in my soul it was wrong, but I did it anyway. I always thought evil was done by bigger-than-life monsters with black hearts and twisted souls. It's not." She stared at him and pointed to herself. "This is what evil looks like. It's done by people like me, who lie, and hurt, and use other people and tell themselves it's for the greater good. I am evil, Jon."

Dellia charged again, this time her blow driving him back as the rain mixed with her tears.

He shook his head as he fended off her blows. "No. I know your heart."

"History will call me the villain. Parents will tell their children stories of the evil protector who betrayed the one who came here to save us. I can't live with that. Give me this one last chance to redeem myself. Please. Defeat me. Fulfill the prophecy. Become the person I need you to be."

Dellia renewed her attack, blow after blow, their swords clanging through the courtyard, driving Jon back to the wall under an overhang, out of the rain. Overwhelmed by guilt and frustration, she leaped as she whipped out her dagger. She thrust the weapon forward, pinning him to the wall with her blade to his throat.

Jon's eyes went wide, but his words remained calm. "Then give the story a different ending. I didn't come back for the prophecy, or the council, or your people. I came back because I was standing at a portal, and all I had to do was step through and I'd be home. And then I realized, it wouldn't be home because it wouldn't have you." He became even more calm, and he shook his head. "I can't live in a world without you."

Dellia stepped back. She dropped her dagger, and it clattered across the ground. Water dripped off her hair and ran down her clothes as she stared into Jon's pleading face.

His eyes began to well with tears. "Dellia, listen, please. I have nowhere to go." He took a step closer, and she moved back. "Save me. Make this a story about a man who fell madly in love with his protector, and how she made him a better person."

Still trembling, she stood staring, her heart breaking at the sight of the man she loved standing before her, soaked from the rain and looking so lost and alone. She wanted to take him in her arms, to tell him it would be okay. To do anything to ease his suffering.

In that moment, all her pain and conflict melted away, and with it, her gift came rushing back. And for the first time, she felt Jon's love, simple and pure and overwhelming. He loved her. After everything she had done, he loved her, desperately and completely.

She took a step forward and reached out.

Like a frightened child, he jumped backward and banged his head against the jagged stones of the wall. He winced and reached back to rub his wounded scalp.

Dellia cocked her head and smiled, and Jon smiled back. Then, she threw her arms around him, pulled him close, and pressed her lips to his. He went stiff, but after a moment he relaxed. Then, he leaned into her and wrapped his arms around her, holding her tight.

She stayed there for what seemed like forever, letting the feeling wash over her like the rain until she couldn't tell where her love stopped and his began.

Then Jon seemed to stiffen in her arms.

Dellia opened her eyes and pulled back to peer at his face. He was focused on something behind her with an alarming look of apprehension in his eyes. With slow, cautious movement, she turned, half expecting to see a contingent of Verod, but there behind her was the last person she expected to find—her mother. Sirra stood watching them in silence, with her head cocked and her tears mingling with the rain. Dellia had rarely seen her mother so moved and contented.

As the pair of them stood gawking, Sirra stepped out of the rain.

Jon took a few tentative steps toward her, and when he grew close, Sirra sniffled and threw her arms around him. "Bless you."

Her mother motioned to her, and Dellia flew over, embracing them both. When Sirra let go, she sniffled again as she straightened and stepped back.

She stared for a moment, her eyes taking in her daughter. "I'm afraid Tsaoshi was never there to see either of you. He came to see me. To tell me I needed to be here, now, at this time." Sirra smiled, and her gaze drifted to Jon's face. "Adi bless you, I never thought I'd see it. Could you kiss her again?"

His embarrassment was complete. Dellia covered her mouth, stifling the urge to laugh as he sputtered, "Right now? I'm not ... with an audience ... I mean, I'm just—"

Hoping to put an end to his unease, Dellia threw her arms around Jon and kissed him again. His self-consciousness only grew, but he never resisted; instead, he gave in to her completely.

After another long moment, Sirra said, "I didn't come straight here. I picked up someone on the way."

Footsteps approached and stopped beside her mother, but Dellia couldn't bring herself to pull away. After so many dark days, she never wanted this kiss to end.

DELLIA

A man cleared his throat, and when that didn't interrupt them, he said, "Damn, I miss all the good parts."

Startled by the sound of Garris's voice, Dellia broke off their embrace, and the pair swung around to face him. Though his expression never gave it away, he was a little uncomfortable. Dellia wanted to ease his discomfort, but since it would be against the three rules to give it away, she simply smiled and said, "Yeah, dragon boy here brought his dragon."

Jon beamed and added, "What good is a dragon if you can't use her to impress the ladies?"

Garris shook his head. "Charming, but you all realize this"—he wagged his finger in their general direction—"what you were doing … well, let's just say Kayleen wouldn't be a fan."

The mention of Kayleen soured Dellia's mood, and her mind turned to more practical matters. This was not the place to be standing around talking. But they had nowhere else to go.

She eyed the pair. "Garris. Mom. I am so glad you're here, but I need to speak to Jon alone, please."

Jon became anxious at the suggestion. His insecurity was sweet and endearing, but she didn't want to prolong it. So Dellia took Jon's hand and, with gentle care, guided him across the brick walkway to a curved bench along the wall.

It was one of her favorite spots. Sheltered by stone walls on either side and a roof above, it had a scenic view of the keep and, above it, Mount Karana towering up into the dark, rolling clouds. She set Jon down and rested beside him, watching as the patter of warm rain caressed a patch of butter-yellow flowers.

Dellia turned toward Jon and took both of his hands into hers. She gazed into his eyes. "Everything I thought was so important turned out to be so wrong. Everything I worked for is gone. There's nothing tying me here … tying *us* here."

"What are you saying?"

Dellia let go of Jon's hand and looked down. "We could disappear." When she looked back up into his face, his eyes were glassy as if he were swept up in her dream. Encouraged, she became even more animated. "We could be free of all this." She pointed to the keep. "The prophecy, the council, all of it. We could just go. Follow where the rivers flow. All would be ours to find." Caught by Jon's hesitancy, she slowed. "You know, find someplace far away, a place where we could be ... happy."

As if waking from a dream, Jon's expression fell, and he gave a small shake of his head. "Don't say that."

Dellia stared. "What?

"All I've ever wanted was a simple life with few—"

"Then go away with me." She became animated again. "Right now. We could be anyplace else ..." She glanced over toward Shir Keep and shook her head. "Not here."

"And then what?" Jon glanced away.

Dellia moved closer and pressed her body against his as she leaned her head on his shoulder. "Just be together, you and me."

He smiled, but it couldn't hide his sadness. "I wish it were that simple."

"It could be." She lifted her head from his shoulder and peered into his face. "Don't you want to be with me?"

Jon was hurt by the question, but he simply smiled. "More than anything I've ever wanted. But I want to be with the real you, not a fantasy."

"This is the real me."

This time, Jon took one of Dellia's hands into his. And as he gazed into her eyes, he gave a gentle shake of his head. "No, it's not. I know right now you think it is. But you spent your whole life becoming who you are. You can't just flip a switch and become a different person." He let go of her hand and looked away across the peaceful garden, his eyes focused on the towering mountain beyond. "You can't just be simple and ordinary. I don't think you'd ever truly be happy."

"What about your world? We could go there. Prith is supposed to be a paradise."

He startled at the suggestion, then shook his head. "No. It's not. Things don't work there like they do here. I never had a gift until I came here. Which means going there would probably take away yours." He placed his hand on her cheek. "It would take away what makes you *you*. And that would break my heart."

Dellia lowered her head, the patter of rain surrounding her as she watched the droplets roll down the yellow petals of a flower. As much as she was desperate to be done with this whole part of her life, it was pointless resisting the wisdom of his words. Jon was right … about all of it.

"So what then?"

Jon became troubled and uncertain, but he put on a brave face and smiled. "We find an answer."

Reluctant to even mention the subject, Dellia hesitated. Then, she glanced down and in a timid voice said, "What about the prophecy?"

He shuddered, and an unexpected horror filled his heart. He turned white, his gaze shot away, and he stared at the bricks of the floor. He looked as if he would be sick as he stammered out, "I can't … I just …"

Startled and concerned by his reaction, she said, "Look, I know you're scared." She placed her hand on his chest. "I can feel it."

He calmed a little at her touch, but he stared at her wide-eyed and said, "I'm not scared for me. It's you. I saw you die. And if I choose this, I'm choosing for you to die. You and Garris, both of you, horribly."

Dellia shrugged. "And if you don't, maybe I die tomorrow, an even worse death."

Garris stepped out from behind the wall, making his eavesdropping apparent. He spoke as he strolled over to where they sat. "Dellia and I, the day we started training as protectors, we knew our deaths would probably be violent and horrible. That's not a choice you can make for us. It's already done. All you can do is help us put that death off for as long as you can."

Jon swallowed and shook his head, as if in a daze. "I won't do it. For a hundred reasons, me being in charge of anything is a horrible idea."

His reaction was extreme, beyond all reason. And yet it was understandable. It was the same reaction he'd had as he recounted the events of his childhood. He had taken charge of a classroom back then to protect his friends and stepsister, and now he felt responsible for their deaths. How could she ask him to take on an even greater responsibility? So she relented. "Okay, okay."

He looked into her eyes. "All I want is a home here with you."

"Then that's where I belong. My duty lies with you now."

Jon eyed Garris. "I can't ask you to—"

"I promised someone a long time ago I'd help you find your way home," said Garris. "Could be I took that a bit too literal. And I know a little something about what it's like not to have a home." Garris sent Jon a crisp nod of his head. "What do you say we make a home here for you, together?"

Jon stood. "Then whatever we do, we do together." He thrust out his hand, palm down, as if the act contained some special meaning.

Puzzled, Dellia said, "What are you doing?"

"I was putting my hand out so we could all put our hands in together."

Garris's brow furrowed. "Why?"

"It's a gesture. You know, that we're forming a pact. Don't you? …" He yanked his hand away. "Never mind, the moment's passed."

DELLIA

The gentle sound of raindrops slowed to a stop as Dellia stood, and the three headed back toward Sirra. After a handful of steps, she came to a halt. "Oh yeah, I almost forgot, the Verod are closing in on the city."

It was her mother's turn to make her eavesdropping apparent. Sirra stepped out from the shadows. "No doubt taking advantage of rumors of Jon's coming as an opportunity to strike."

His anxiety mushroomed. "Then it's starting already." His voice reflected his panic. "People getting hurt because of me."

Sirra stared at him and shook her head. "The Verod have wanted to take on the council since long before you arrived."

"Then I guess I have to stop them from hurting anyone."

Surprised and puzzled, Dellia stared at Jon as he turned to face her. "And you need to be doing good. And Garris was obviously destined for greater things. And I need to set this prophecy nonsense to rest."

"And what about the wolves?" Dellia said.

"An army of them is massing outside Mundus," Garris informed them.

Even without her gift, she could tell what Jon was feeling; his exasperation was palpable. "Oh sure. Why not? Because things weren't messy enough." Dellia and Garris stared at Jon, waiting for him to elaborate. After a moment, he became uncomfortable. "Look, I haven't got it all completely figured out, but I may have an idea. A sort of a plan. For all of it. Well, except the wolves, I need to think about that."

Dellia glanced at Garris. "So just how afraid should we be?"

Garris nodded his head. "Terrified."

Without giving either of them the slightest glance, Jon rolled his eyes and turned to address Dellia's mother. "Sirra, can you open a portal to the Ephori? I need to talk to you ... and to them."

Sirra nodded and smiled.

Chapter Thirty-Four

MESSAGE OF THE ORACLE

Dellia's hair was still wet from the rain, but the ground was dry, and the air smelled different. She looked behind her, and a gust of wind sent ripples across the liquid surface of the portal as Garris stepped through. A second gust hit, sending deeper ripples along the surface before the image of the dark and damp Shir Courtyard blew away in a colored mist.

She raised her head and looked around. They had arrived on the street before Commander Prian's home in the modest capital city of Egina. The weather here was brisk, and the fading sun shone down between billowy clouds, its rays warm against her skin after the gray, rainy skies of Shirdon.

Dellia continued to survey the area, taking in the familiar sights and sounds while her mother rushed off toward the commander's simple clay home. Sirra hurried around back and vanished into Prian's private courtyard.

While they watched and waited for her return, Dellia relaxed, and as she bathed in her newfound love and contentment, her gift blossomed. For the first time in weeks, she felt whole again, and her gift reached out to all those around her. Garris was at peace and enjoying the excursion. Her mother's happiness and sense of fulfillment were still palpable, and though Jon was troubled and worried, he was determined.

Dellia glanced over at him, still sopping wet and deep in contemplation but happy. It all seemed so unreal. He was hers. And he was standing so close and loved her with such a passion.

As she watched him stare away at the house, she understood for the first time her mother's misgivings over what she'd given up to become a protector. As fulfilling as that former life had been, it was pale by comparison to the warmth and sense of completeness that enveloped her right now.

After a couple minutes, her mother returned with the commander in tow. Her name, like her black hair and brown skin, gave away her Erdish roots, but Prian was every bit a woman of Talus: strong, intelligent, compassionate, and outspoken. She had an intuitive grasp of battle strategy that was uncanny, and her commanding presence and empathy for her men had proven time and again that she was an ideal commander.

As they approached, she overheard Sirra ordering Prian to call the Ephori to an urgent meeting. They most often met in an open square in the middle of the city. But she had told Prian to bring them to the Theater of Laminus, a small amphitheater in the hills above the city. It made sense if her goal was to avoid notice and prevent eavesdropping.

Prian smiled and nodded to Dellia before rushing off. Egina was only an hour's ride from her childhood home, so she and Prian had grown up together. And with limited peers near Egina, they had spent many an hour sparring and training together.

The commander's home stood next to the stables and barracks, and within minutes, four pairs of horses had galloped off. As each one left, a twinge of anxiety struck because she understood who the runners were bringing, and the idea of facing them was unsettling.

After a while, a small, square carriage rattled up, ready to convey the four out of the city. And with it came a sense of dread at the realization she had no idea what he planned to do with the Ephori, but it had now reached the point of no return. He had summoned the rulers of Erden as if they were servants to come at his beck and call, and nothing could stop what was going to happen next.

The carriage occasionally jumped and jolted as they rumbled along the streets and pathways of Egina. Dellia stared out the window at the jumble of clay houses and shops, both small and large, crammed along the hillsides. But Jon never noticed. He sat next to her, head down in deep concentration.

By the time they were rattling past the outskirts, the sun was setting, and the breeze had settled considerably. The same could not be said for Dellia, since her concern only continued to grow. She loved Jon, and he possessed so many great qualities: he was kind, and loyal, and smart, and articulate. But the truth was, he had no experience with this kind of thing, and he was planning to meet with people who ate, drank, and breathed politics. What's more, she hadn't the slightest idea what he intended to do or say, which led to her imagining all manner of things he might come up with that would make their situation worse.

After a time, the silence and worry became too much, and Dellia turned and gazed into Jon's gentle face. "So, care to let us in on your plan?" She pointed back and forth between Garris and herself. "Or are we to just stand by and do nothing?"

As if he was waking from a dream, the glassy fog disappeared from Jon's eyes, and he looked over at her. "Plan," he said, then hesitated. "Uh, to … to win."

Uncomfortable with the level of detail in Jon's "plan," Dellia waited with patience for him to elaborate.

After a long moment of discomfort, he put his hand on hers. "I have learned many things, from you, from Garris, from your mother, and I intend to use every bit of it."

"To do what?"

He paused for a moment, then sighed. "Look, I've decided to fight for us, for all of us, to make us a home. And if there's one thing

I've learned—from your mother, actually—it's that I'm not going to fight halfway."

Dellia considered for a moment. "Then can you at least tell me why you asked to see the Ephori? They are among the toughest groups to sway. What is it you think you're going to accomplish?"

At her skepticism, Jon's anxiety blew out to overwhelming levels, and she realized her questions weren't helping. What's more, his every reaction told her that Jon didn't know what he was going to do and was insecure about letting on. It was a state of affairs not entirely unfamiliar to her, having worked with the council for so many years. So she decided to be true to her word and put her faith in Jon and his ability to figure it out as he went. However, it was too late; the question was out there, and his anxiety only grew as he struggled for an answer.

After several moments, Garris bailed him out. "I only want to know one thing. Are we going to confront the council?"

Jon was quick to answer. "Since they are at the center of all this, yeah, that's the goal."

"Then I'm in." Garris gave a crisp nod.

And that was that. The rest of the trip Garris rode on in silence, as he always did, and Dellia left Jon to think and plan.

When they arrived at the theater, Jon insisted that he face the Ephori alone. This was undoubtedly a mistake, but having given her word, Dellia deemed it important to demonstrate her trust in him. So, she moved off to the side of the theater and watched from the shadows while Garris stayed near the road and kept an eye out for intruders.

Jon ran off alone to "try something," he said, and a short time later, he joined Sirra on the stage.

From her vantage point, off to the side of the rows of carved stone seats, Dellia had a clear view of the entire small amphitheater. Sheltered from notice, she gazed at Jon and her mother. Their faces lit by the flaming cauldrons that ringed the theater, they stood side by side on the modest, circular stage.

Before them, under the gentle rustling leaves of several huge, old trees, sat three of the Ephori, dressed in the simple robes of her people. On the left were the proud and muscular Ukrit and Nomusa, with the sturdy and beautiful Saneya next to them.

The five Ephori were all older, like her mother, having been elected from those of her people who had proven to be exemplary spouses and parents, capable warriors, and bright strategists.

Dellia surveyed the patient look on all three faces. An expression that did little to betray their irritation or their true nature, for they were all skeptical, perceptive, and intolerant of foolishness. Not one of them would be gentle with Jon, and they would not be an easy group to sway.

Behind him, the red crescent of the moon peeked out from behind the billowy clouds that rolled across the night sky. Apparently eager to speak, he glanced at Sirra and, with a tiny bob of his head, motioned to the three seated before them. Her hair swaying in the light breeze, her mother sent Jon an almost imperceptible shake of her head. She was waiting for the last to arrive.

Only a short time before, Dellia had decided to be true to her word, to put her faith in Jon and trust that he would find a way through. But now, as he stood on the stage, her concern had blossomed into fear and dread. Not only did he have no plan, but he was no statesman. And while he hid it well, he was entirely too anxious, more so than any in his audience.

Movement drew her eyes to the entrance where Commander Prian appeared with Urana, the last of the five. Prian guided her over to the flat stone seat next to Ukrit. As Urana sat, the commander turned to go, but her mother motioned to her and spoke out.

"You may stay, Commander. What we have to present is news of critical importance to all our people."

In a flash, Saneya stood and turned to Sirra, and the tone of her voice did little to hide her irritation. "Are you now deciding when we are called to assemble, as well as what is important to our people and who may hear it?"

Forever slow to anger, her mother bowed in deference. "Apologies, Saneya." Her words were soft and gracious. "But I think, in the end, you will agree." She motioned to Jon. "You see, this is Jon. The one of whom I have spoken."

The four passed startled looks among themselves as Saneya seated herself. Sirra walked off toward the seats, leaving Jon frightened and alone on the stage.

It was all Dellia could manage not to rush up there to stand with him and lend her support. But Jon had insisted, and even if she didn't understand why, she had accepted that he wanted to handle this alone.

The whispers and surprised looks continued as Sirra seated herself beside Urana. Then, Ukrit stood and addressed her mother. "He is scrawny. Are we to believe he conquered the Recluse Tower and gave us Ellira's journal?"

To Dellia's surprise, he took no offense whatsoever. Instead, he calmed considerably, then granted them a simple bow, and when he spoke, it was like the voice of a different person.

"Do not judge me by this frail body that stands before you, but by this heart, which out of love and respect desires only that you know the truth."

Dellia's jaw dropped, and she stared. Her love had just delivered the familiar words with such strength and passion that her heart went out to him. And in that moment, she realized, she could not have fallen for a better man.

His words were met with startled looks as Ukrit sat.

Saneya spoke next, without standing. "We appreciate what you have done for our people. But you do yourself no favors, coming here and quoting Ellira to us." She gave a disapproving shake of her head. "You are not one of us."

As he stepped forward, Jon bowed his head, and when he spoke, it was from his soul. "I am just paying homage to a heart which she opened to me in the pages of her journal. If I am at fault, it is only for recognizing the truth when she revealed it to me."

Then came Urana's turn. She stood and faced Jon. "Strong words. But it is clear they are designed to gain favor, and we have heard many words before."

Urana sat, and Jon stood alone on the stage for a moment, pondering what to say. When he looked up, he addressed the entire group. "Then I ask, if any among you has the gift, look into my heart now and tell me if it is not filled with love and admiration for your people. And a desire only that you should know the truth."

Saneya stood, and as the branches swayed and her hair and loose robe billowed in the breeze, she stared at Jon in deep concentration.

Dellia needed no effort; to her, his heart was an open book. Her hand flew to her mouth, and tears came to her eyes. No wonder he calmed in the face of them. He felt a profound sense of connection to these five before him. As much trepidation as Jon was suffering through right now, he was also gratified to be addressing those whom he appreciated and respected. It was as if he were facing family. As if they were *his* people because ... they were *her* people.

As Saneya stared, a puzzled expression filled her face, and she tilted her head. "I do not know how you can have such a deep love and admiration for a people you barely know." She turned to the other members. "But it is as he says."

Nomusa smiled at Saneya, then he rose, standing with her. "So tell us then, what are these truths you came here to reveal?"

Jon stepped forward again as they all sat. He removed the medallion from around his neck and held it out, dangling it by its chain. "The truth that you have been deceived by a council who has no respect for the truth or for your beliefs."

Sirra smiled at him and gave a nod of approval while the other four passed whispers and nods of agreement among themselves.

Jon placed the medallion on the stage before him and touched first the black, then the gold, then the silver leaf. Then, a ghostly image of a heavily branching tree materialized, filling the entire stage. Much larger than before, it towered as tall as the surrounding trees, with the red moon peeking through its shimmering branches.

Above the crowd, a gentle gust of wind rustled through the leaves of the trees as a calming female voice seemed to come from nowhere. "The future is an infinite branching tree of possibilities, each determined by free will."

Dellia let out a small gasp. To use the medallion like this was completely unexpected and utterly brilliant. Admiration filled her heart as the image transformed and the voice continued.

"I am Wistra, the oracle of your prophecy, and I must beg for your forgiveness. For you have been misled. …"

It was the same long dining table in the same large house as the last time Jon had visited Gatia. But no laughter met him from the kitchen; it was still and dark. And the only light in the room came from a few flat candles floating in a bowl of water near the elephant-headed statue.

Jon lowered his head and smiled. He was different, too. The last time he'd been here, he had been drowning in hurt and rejection. But this time he was euphoric, and it all went back to those two words. He recalled with clarity the inexorable pull of the portal a mere few feet in front of him, his clothes and hair drawn toward it. He had been desperate and terrified when he told Isla he just wanted to go home. Then she spoke those two words, "To what?"

He had always understood that home was not a bunch of buildings, or a place on the map. Or even a job, because jobs come and go. What makes a home are the people, the relationships, family. In a split second, Isla's two words had cut through all his angst and confusion, and he realized Dellia had become the most important relationship in his life. One he could no longer live without. And in that moment, he knew he had to do everything in his power to win her heart. And it wasn't just her, but also his friendship with Garris, and even Megan: they had all become his family, and they were here, in this world, not beyond that portal.

After that, the decision to stay had come with surprising ease. And sure, he'd miss his home, and his car … oh man how he missed that car … and television, and phones, and texting Megan to ask where the heck she was, and his friends at work: Nichole, Ryan, and others. But he would trade all of it in a heartbeat for the chance to be with Dellia forever.

Even before she asked, he knew that her role as protector and her home mattered far more to her than his job and home had ever mattered to him. So he couldn't ask her to leave this world she loved so much. He had to be the one to stay. So he had gone to her. And it felt awkward and stupid, and his words were clumsy and scatterbrained, and she attacked him, which seemed like a bad sign—but then she kissed him.

He was still trying to puzzle out how it could ever happen that someone like Dellia had kissed someone like him. It was impossible and amazing and heart stopping. Yet, at the same time, it was nerve-racking because it could all still come whirling apart. He needed to unravel this one last knot and find a way to be with her in peace.

The meeting with the Ephori had been harrowing, but in the end it had succeeded beyond expectations. A long road lay ahead with much to do and few hours to do it in. The prospect that each step might be equally as arduous filled his heart with dread. But to be with Dellia was worth facing any ordeal or bearing any tribulation this world might heap upon him.

Aishi had awoken upon his arrival and insisted on seeing him. Gatia had forbidden it and sent her back to bed. But no sooner had her mother left than the mischievous little girl had snuck down the staircase and plopped down across from him at the large dining table. Jon considered sending her back to bed himself, but didn't deem it his place.

Her dark eyes scrutinized him as she swung her legs. Then she smiled. "Where is the one who likes you?"

"Dellia?" Jon asked.

Aishi gave a vigorous nod of her head.

"She is near, but there are some things a person must do on their own."

She puzzled for a long moment. "Why?"

He donned a solemn look. "If I want to be taken seriously, I have to stand on my own and not be seen to take my strength from her." He smirked as he leaned over the table and whispered, "Even if the truth is I would never have the strength to do this without her."

Aishi grinned back as her innocent eyes regarded Jon from across the wooden table. Suddenly, she became all too serious for a little girl. She leaned over the surface and whispered, "Something's wrong with your aura. It—"

Footsteps from outside cut her short, and her head whipped around. She sprang from the table and raced back up the steps in a patter of bare feet. As she rounded the corner out of sight, the door swung open with a thud, and Gatia, with her metal bow and azure-blue uniform, marched through the doorway.

Behind her trailed Asina and Katal, their clothes of tan, yellow, and orange even more colorful and impressive up close. No sooner did Katal step into the house than he spied Jon at the table and stopped.

He pointed at him as he barked out orders to Gatia. "Arrest him." He faced Jon. "We went to a lot of trouble to see you and your friends safely out of here, precisely to avoid being put in this position."

Asina seemed calmer and more sympathetic. "I'm sorry, Jon, but we are compelled to do this. You must understand. You know the prophecy, what it means."

Startled and a little panicked at the unexpected greeting, he stood and smiled as Gatia marched around the table. As she reached him, he clapped his hands together and gave a slow, deep bow. While he did it as a sign of respect, he also needed time to think.

As Jon straightened, he blurted out, "I regret putting you in this position, Rhanae. But with all due respect, I understand the prophecy better than you."

Katal seemed startled by the claim, but Asina remained gracious. "We cannot risk putting ourselves in the middle of this. It could destroy a delicate relationship with the council."

Katal motioned to Gatia, and she grabbed Jon's arm, her grip firmer than he expected. Afraid he wouldn't have time to make his case, Jon rushed out the words as she hauled him toward the end of the table.

"That is precisely why I am here. Hear me out. Give me a chance to help you understand your role in history."

Katal straightened at the mention of history. Asina motioned to Gatia, and she halted but kept a tight grasp on Jon's arm.

Taking advantage of their reaction, he leaned across the table, pulling against Gatia's grip. Now was his chance to make his case.

"Look, I can still recall that crowd at the temple steps, what they said about me. Don't you want to know what would compel me to return?"

Asina looked to Katal, her eyes questioning, asking him to listen. He relented and motioned for them to sit. All four moved to the table and seated themselves, Katal and Asina facing Jon, with Gatia next to him, poised and ready to act.

Jon waited for them to settle in their seats. Then, he took a deep breath. "I have information I want you to spread, as far and wide as possible. Preferably tonight."

All three were taken aback.

Asina shook her head. "What could possibly be so important that we would risk taking sides with you?"

Jon bowed his head as he searched for the right words, then lifted his gaze to hers. "The truth has no sides. And I think once you know it, you will be driven to do what is best for your people." Katal seemed about to object, but Jon barged ahead. "Just hear what I have to say. No ... what *Wistra* has to say."

He slipped the medallion out of his shirt.

Katal shot upright in his seat. "I ... I've seen this before, in an old tome on artifacts, in Pretaj's library." With great care, he lifted the medallion from Jon's hand. "This was lost hundreds of years ago. Where did you get it?"

"It's a long story. Longer than we have time for. But it wasn't lost. Wistra arranged for me to have it."

With his eyes wide, Katal stared at the three leaves arranged in a circle. With slow gentleness, he placed the medallion in the center of the large table. With delicate care, he first pressed the black leaf, then the gold, then the silver.

The small, bright image of a heavily branching tree formed in the center of the table, reaching up to the timbers above. Light from its ghostly leaves of red and yellow sparkled and danced across the walls and ceiling as the three watched in wonder.

Then a soothing female voice surrounded them, resonating throughout the room.

"The future is an infinite branching tree of possibilities. ..."

DELLIA

Garris stepped through the portal to a hillside with a sweeping view of the moonlight glimmering on the tributaries of the Baihu River as they meandered their way through the streets of Kanlu. His last visit to the city had involved prison time because he let Dellia talk him into walking into the heart of the city. This time her mother had arranged a more prudent arrival—in a dark, secluded spot, just outside the imperial palace grounds.

He scanned his surroundings for any sign they might have been spotted. Light peeked over the walls from the well-lit courtyard within. But, from the houses along the hillside overlooking the city, to the river valley below, all lay dark and quiet, with most of the town now deep in slumber.

As the portal drifted away in the gentle night breeze, Garris eyed Sirra and in a hushed voice said, "I don't get it. You can't open a portal to a place you haven't been recently, or am I wrong?"

Jon chimed in. "Yeah, I had to picture the destination clearly in my head to make it work."

Sirra looked at all of their faces and sighed. "A few weeks ago, an oracle came to me. He asked me to take him to the Recluse Tower, and after we'd gone, he said I needed to visit four other places." Sirra motioned to the scenic view of rivers winding through the darkened city below. "This is one." She stared into Dellia's eyes. "I didn't ask why, and he warned me it could lead to your death if I told anyone."

Dellia nodded. "Is that what those mysterious visits to Shirdon were about?"

Sirra nodded.

While they'd been talking, Jon had been scanning the hills above the palace, then his eyes seemed to rest on one particular dark spot on the hillside. After a moment, he noticed Garris watching and jerked his eyes away, returning his focus to the group.

"Where does the emperor sleep?" he asked.

Garris pointed to the wall next to him. "In the palace."

Jon shot him an annoyed expression that seemed impatient for elaboration.

Garris motioned to the park beyond the wall. "The other side of this wall are the palace grounds. Across them and up the steps is the palace."

"Sounds simple enough."

"It's not." Dellia sounded alarmed. "Some of the best fighters in Elore guard the palace. And they take the emperor's safety very seriously. They'll kill intruders without hesitation."

Jon lowered his head for a moment as if spinning some intricate plot, then he raised it. "Well, I have to reach the emperor, so here goes."

Garris stared in surprise. "What? You're insane. Did you not hear Dellia?"

Jon shrugged off the warning. "I've got this."

Garris motioned to Dellia. "They'll know Dellia. She can get you in."

"No. I have a plan. I can do this." Jon thrust his palm out at them and said, "Stay here" as if they were dogs he could order about. Then he slipped off around the wall.

Dellia stood gawking for a moment. Then she shook her head and made a hurried move to follow. But as she passed, Sirra grabbed her arm and yanked her to a stop. "I know you want to protect him, but what he needs from you right now is to have faith in him."

Dellia shook her head. "He's no warrior. He could die."

"Neither were you, and you never would have become one if I hadn't let you take risks and learn to stand on your own two feet."

Garris butted in. "I'll slip inside. I'll follow Jon. He'll never know I'm there."

Sirra nodded.

"What?" Dellia said. "So it's okay if Garris goes, but not if I do?"

Sirra smiled at her daughter. "You have a power over him that Garris never will."

Dellia shook her head and stared at Sirra in apparent bewilderment.

Sirra sighed. "Jon is a good man, and he has a good heart, but he is not the kind of leader the oracle spoke of. You have the power to make him want to live up to your belief in him. Or you can treat him like a child." Sirra put her hand on Dellia's arm. "So it comes down to this: Do you want to help him become everything he can be, or do you want what he becomes to be in *spite* of you?"

Dellia stood taller and crossed her arms. "You don't know what you're talking about. Jon knows who he is. That's one of the things I love about him."

"Oh, Dellia, he's a man."

"What does that have to do with anything?"

Garris set a hand on each of their shoulders and looked them in the eyes. "Look, while you two stand around exchanging pointless nonsense, I'm going to look out for Jon."

Dellia threw up her hands. "Fine. You go. But I'm telling you, you better keep him safe."

Garris nodded and slinked off around the corner. He bounded up a tree, then dove over the palace wall and landed behind a building. After hurrying down an alley, he came to the opening and scanned the long parklike palace grounds with its artfully crafted landscape, but Jon was nowhere in sight. Perhaps he wasn't here yet. Garris crept over to a clump of bushes and peered out at the broad entrance.

A sudden gust of wind swirled around him, and he whipped around, trying to catch where it came from. A thud followed, and movement caught his eye. He snapped back toward it, and there was Jon, racing up the center of the palace grounds in plain view of every blasted guard in the place.

Keeping to the shadows, Garris ducked and sprinted along the edge, trying to keep pace with Jon. He dodged in and out of porches and bushes as he watched Jon fly straight up the wide-open middle. It was like he wanted to get caught. Was this his idea of a plan?

Shouting, followed by rattling weapons and racing footsteps, erupted from behind, and Jon pushed harder. He looked up, and his eyes locked onto a pair of imperial guards armed with long spears standing at the top of the palace steps.

Garris tensed. They were the emperor's best.

At the sound of Jon's approach, the two whipped their spears forward, the metal tips glistening in the light from the hanging lanterns that lined the walkways on all sides.

The guards spotted Jon and plunged down the stairs in a clatter of footsteps. To Garris's surprise, Jon pushed faster, heading straight at them.

Garris raced alongside, watching as his friend hurtled forward toward his doom. What was he thinking? Even if he survived, he would never reach the emperor.

The guards hit the bottom of the steps and in unison shouted, "Halt!"

Jon flew to a stop and froze with his arms up, a mere couple of feet from the tips of their razor-sharp spears.

Garris dove behind some bushes, his heart pounding as he watched from a short distance away. He hunkered there, frozen by indecision, unsure whether to act now before the bloodshed began or sit tight and pray for divine intervention. For a smart guy, this was a thoroughly stupid, lame-brained, and moronic plan.

One by one, a dozen guards raced up around Jon, the tips of their spears ringing him as he stood frozen with the look of a scared rabbit.

A sinking feeling hit, the kind that always accompanies a

runaway strategic disaster. Jon would be fine as long as he remained motionless, but if he ran or made any sudden movements, they would run him through before he took two steps. And Garris was too far away to do a blasted thing about it.

At the top of the steps, a man appeared in a purple robe with a golden dragon embroidered on the front. It was Emperor Shaosheng himself. A woman strolled up to his side—the woman from Kianlong Square, the one whose boy Jon had rescued. Standing on the palace grounds dressed in her long, gold-trimmed robe in shades of purple, she suddenly became familiar: this was the Empress Tsaoyan.

She took one look at Jon and shouted, "Do not harm him."

Suddenly, his strategy made some semblance of sense. The boy he'd rescued was the emperor's son. Then it hit Garris. Jon had no inkling of who he'd saved. This wasn't his plan, this was a miraculous fluke.

The emperor strolled down the steps toward Jon. "How is it you managed to infiltrate the palace grounds?" he bellowed.

Jon appeared flustered. "I didn't exactly infiltrate anything."

The emperor glared. "Explain your presence here immediately, or your visit will be short-lived."

Jon motioned back over his shoulder. "A friend brought me."

Garris glanced over where he had indicated only to spot a dark form springing from the palace walls with a tremendous whoosh. It pushed its way up high into the night sky, then soared down over them until it blocked out most of the stars and moon. It hovered motionless above the group for a moment, then set down behind Jon with a deep thud and a burst of air.

Garris stood mesmerized. It was a dragon, for crying out loud. The beast sat there, so close its low breath rumbled in his ears. It pulled in its wings and lowered its head over the soldiers, positioning it right above Jon.

Garris smiled. He had assumed Dellia was joking when she said

Jon had brought a dragon, but this was astounding. It was far closer than he'd ever been to a dragon. The beast's dark metallic scales shimmered in the moonlight as its tail whipped across the entire width of the courtyard. Now *this* was a plan.

Light from the glowing lanterns glinted off the dragon's huge bright eyes as it scanned the group, its gaze resting on the empress. Then, it let out a deep, resonant moan that reverberated through the palace grounds.

As if awakening from a daze, one by one the soldiers planted their spears at their sides, dropped to one knee, and snapped their heads down, bowing before the enormous beast.

Then, the emperor and empress dropped to one knee as well and lowered their heads with the rest.

"Islong, forgive us," the emperor said. "We did not mean to anger. Whatever you desire, just name it."

Then, in the slowest, deepest, and most breathy voice imaginable, the dragon spoke. "Listen … and decide," she said, her words echoing down the courtyard.

Jon slipped the medallion out of his shirt. He held it up high, and his voice was strong and clear as he spoke to the whole group. "I am Jon, the Otherworlder. Islong gave this to me as part of a bargain. Assemble it, and she would send me home." He glanced up at the dragon. "She was wise, for in so doing, I came to realize this world *is* my home." He lowered his head, his gaze resting on the empress as his voice became softer. "But what you have been told about me is a lie. And before I can be welcome in this world, I must correct that lie. So I come to you with a truth and a bargain."

Islong leaped into the air with a flap of her enormous wings that blew back everyone's clothes and hair. She flapped a few more times, propelling herself upward into the night.

As everyone stared, Jon set the medallion on the grass. He reached out and touched the black leaf, then the gold, then the silver.

A ghostly image of a tree formed in the center of the palace grounds, towering into the night, many stories high, tall enough for the entire city to see. Light from it glittered along the rocky hills and rivers banks scattered with houses.

Then, a calming voice boomed out across the night, echoing down the streets and alleys of the entire city.

"The future is an infinite branching tree of possibilities, each determined by free will."

The tree faded, replaced by a full-length image of a simple Elorian woman, and when she smiled her manner was gentle and serene.

Garris looked up, and as the scene continued, lanterns appeared in houses across the hillside and into the river valley as the people came out of their homes to watch.

"I am Wistra, the oracle of your prophecy, and I must beg for your forgiveness. For you have been misled, and I have played my part."

Her stomach twisted and turned as Dellia stood with her eyes clamped shut, unwilling to view the image of her murdering Jon for the third time. As she tried to tune out Wistra's voice, Jon's fingers sought out hers, intertwining with them.

"It never happened, Dellia," came his voice whispering in her ear.

At his touch, she calmed and was at last able to open her eyes. She glanced over at Jon, standing next to her in the grass-covered valley. He stood gazing at her with such grave concern and affection. He smiled, and as his eyes met hers, she suddenly felt foolish.

She had been so caught up in her own guilt and shame, she'd ignored Jon's discomfort. Though he was good at putting on a brave face, he was a nervous wreck. In fact, it was amazing he could function at all, yet somehow, he was the one comforting *her*.

Jon turned his gaze upward, staring up at the full-length image of Wistra, shimmering in the darkness of night, her head almost clearing the surrounding hills.

Dellia glanced at Garris, on the other side of Jon, then turned her eyes to the modest-looking Verod leader, dressed in a dark red kameez. A man accompanied her on either side, and all three stood with their necks craned upward, eyes transfixed on the ghostly oracle towering above them.

Dellia gazed out across the valley at the couple hundred Verod gathered around numerous dying fires, staring up in stunned silence.

She moved closer, yielding to Jon's yearning for the comfort of her body next to his. His tension eased as she leaned into him. He slipped his arm around her and pulled her close, and for the first time that night, it felt like she was part of what was happening. She was making a difference. Because she made a difference to him.

"Great power can come at a great cost," the disembodied voice boomed out across the valley, "and so there is one last trial. A vision, not to prepare you, but to ease my conscience. A warning, so that if you accept this burden, you know the ultimate cost."

Colored light from the image played across the grass of the hillside and valley as Wistra reached down. She touched three leaves on the medallion at her feet, and the image vanished.

His hand still clinging to hers, Jon turned to face the smoldering fires spread out across the valley. As all eyes turned to him, he gazed at Dellia and smiled. Then he stepped forward, and his voice bellowed out, loud and clear, carrying down the entire valley.

"I am Jon, the one to whom Wistra was speaking. I am the Otherworlder, and I am sympathetic to your plight. I have learned, firsthand, what the council is capable of." He glanced over at the Verod leader. "But your situation is more precarious than you know. Because the council has sent an overwhelming force to intercept and crush you."

Grumbling and discussion broke out among those gathered around the fires of the camp. Jon spoke louder, trying to make himself heard above the din.

"We can help you, but in return, I need fighters."

"A couple dozen should do," Garris belted out.

"Anyone trained in combat," Dellia added.

As murmurs and discussion broke out around the campfires, the Verod leader and her two men turned their attention to Jon.

"Why not join us?" the bright-eyed man on the left said. "Lead us, and you can command whoever you want."

He shook his head. "I have no desire to lead anything. And I have problems of my own I must deal with. So I cannot follow anyone."

The woman gave a respectful nod of her head and motioned to the men standing around the fires, gathered in groups, talking. "These men are free to help you. We do not own them."

Dellia bowed her head. "Thank you."

She motioned to Garris to go, and he and Sirra headed off into the camp.

Garris wandered from fire to fire, talking to each group, assessing capabilities and selecting the best fighters. Jon was insistent that the caliber of the recruits didn't matter, but experience had taught Garris that anything could happen, and the stronger the group, the less room there'd be for calamity to strike. And the less the chance it would result in injury or death.

It wasn't until midway through that a new possibility reared its head. Here at one of the many fires stood a woman who seemed typical of what he'd seen so far. By contrast, the two men with her bore many scars, were well equipped, and carried themselves with a bearing and sense of respect typical of highly disciplined soldiers. These two were not typical resistance fighters.

The babble of discussion drifted through the darkened valley as Garris gazed down at the dying embers of a campfire, mulling over the difficult decision—to accept the two best candidates he'd seen so far or turn them away on the possibly unfounded suspicion they were planted here to undermine the Verod.

He looked up into the dark brown eyes of the sturdy Erdish woman. "We would be honored to have your sword arm with us." He pointed to Sirra. "If you would please follow that woman over there, I would be most grateful."

Garris turned to the other two sturdy men standing at attention. "I appreciate your enthusiasm, but I am sorry, I cannot use you."

The two men glanced at one another with questioning looks.

Garris seized the opportunity to snap around and march off before either could object. As he headed away, he scanned the valley littered with piles of fading embers. Off to the side, Sirra was leading a couple dozen fighters to the next campfire. So he picked the clump of tents beyond and headed for it.

As he strutted across the grassy field, a flash of wavy red hair flew through his field of vision. He spun around and stared at a woman shuffling away, off to the side, between the backs of two tents.

"Megan!" he called out.

The woman never slowed or showed any sign of having heard.

Garris raced up behind her. "It's you, isn't it?"

The woman froze for a moment. Then she turned to reveal her smiling face. "You were the one with Jon, right?"

Astonished to find her here, he stared for a second and nodded. "What are you doing here?"

Megan pointed in the direction she was going. "Sorry, I was in a hurry. I was headed to meet Aylun ... you know, the guy who was with me. We were looking into something important."

Garris motioned her to follow. "You have to come with me. Jon has been worried about you."

She gazed up at Jon, standing beside Dellia, and slowly shook her head. "It doesn't look like that to me."

Garris puzzled for a moment. This wasn't the reaction he was expecting. "Is something wrong?"

Megan snapped her attention back to Garris and gave a crisp shake of her head. "No. I guess I'm just surprised to see them together like that." She paused for a moment, then sighed. "Whatever is going on here, it sounds important. I don't want to interfere with it."

"Interfere?" Garris stared, puzzling over her response.

She pointed over her shoulder again. "We went to Lanessa. We fou—"

"You?" Garris straightened in surprise. Lanessa was the lost city. Cut off from the world with the fall of the capital city of Katapa. Any trip there was an insane act of suicide. "You went to Lanessa? Are you kidding me?"

"We found something there. It's incredibly important that we follow up on it, and we don't have much time. I ... I can't stay."

Megan swung around and hurried away.

After a few steps, Garris shouted after her. "So what exactly am I supposed to tell Jon?"

She froze again. The quiet discussions of a sea of Verod gathered around the many waning fires droned on as Megan slowly turned and walked back to Garris.

She sent him a warm smile. "What we found in Lanessa." Megan pointed again to Jon and Dellia. "It said that this, what's happening here—it's important." After a moment, she returned her gaze to Garris. "This is where Jon belongs. Here, with you and that woman. I have answers of my own I have to find. They might amount to nothing, or they could change everything. The thing is, if I let Jon get dragged into that, it could put an end to all he is trying to do here. He doesn't need that. He doesn't need me." A sudden certainty transformed

Megan, and she brought herself up taller. "I won't become the reason he fails. Don't tell him you saw me. Please."

"Are you serious?"

Megan peered into Garris's face. "Yes, completely serious. Promise you won't tell him."

"You're asking me—"

"Please, it's important to both of us." She shook her head. "Don't tell him."

Garris stared, dumbfounded. There was obviously a lot that this woman was not saying, and it seemed wrong to keep her presence here from Jon. Yet her desire to not disrupt her friend's plans seemed both heartfelt and sensible. If she were to show up now, it could raise many questions and throw a wrench into events just as they were gaining momentum. At a loss for a reason to turn her down, and not entirely sure he should, Garris simply shrugged. "Okay. If it's that important."

Megan clamped her arms to her sides and gave a deep bow of thanks. She raised her head and stared into his face with a solemn expression. "You give your word."

Garris nodded.

"Thank you." Megan bowed again, then spun around and raced off into the darkness.

For a time, Dellia stood with Jon's hand in hers, staring out across the grassy encampment. She sensed his nervousness returning, so she slipped her arm around him and pulled him close, as he had done with her. He was warm, and she could sense the profound comfort her touch brought. So she stayed there with him, watching as Garris and Sirra worked their way from fire to fire.

After a while, the modest-looking Erdish leader in her deep red kameez moved out in front of them. She stared into Jon's face, catching his attention. "Tell me, how can you help us?"

Dellia pointed at Sirra. "My mother can open a portal to a clearing in the woods south of Shirdon, behind the soldiers, with them heading away from you."

Jon jumped in. "But I need you to delay any action until tomorrow afternoon."

The leader seemed taken aback. "But we must act quickly. The council is in chaos. They are afraid and leaderless and their forces spread too thin. Now is the time to strike—we will never get another chance like this."

"If you can wait," Jon said, "I can assure you their forces will be even more depleted and the council in even greater disarray later in the day."

"You can promise this?" the woman said. "You give your word?"

"I give you my word."

Sirra and Garris appeared with over thirty men and women following them. He approached Jon like a kid with a new toy. "It went better than expected."

"There were many we had to turn down," Sirra added.

Garris glanced back at the group behind him. "These here are more than capable."

Jon looked over the crowd. "And they understand that they are not to harm anyone?"

Sirra nodded.

Dellia stepped forward, addressing the leader. "There's a lot to be done and next to no time to do it in. We need everyone to break camp immediately. We need to move within the hour."

The group that had followed Sirra and Garris left, hurrying back to their tents to pack up. The woman whirled around, and her two men accompanied her as she began to move throughout the camp.

Jon turned to Dellia. Behind her, the leaders moved from fire to fire in the grassy valley, and when they reached each one, it became a hive of frenetic activity as people began to break camp.

He smiled at her. "A few sparkly lights, an authoritative tone in your voice, the illusion you have a clue what you're doing, and presto, you're a savior."

Garris shook his head and glanced at Dellia. "I can slap him for you if you'd like."

"Oh, please do." Dellia grinned.

He gave Jon a sharp slap on the back of the head.

Dellia laughed while Jon winced and rubbed his scalp. "Remind me again why I hang out with you guys."

Dellia motioned to Garris. "Obviously, it's our charm."

Jon smiled and glanced at the camp scattered across the gentle rolling valley behind him. "Well, all the pieces are falling into place. Now if we can just pull this off."

Dellia became serious. So far it had been all talk, but what Jon was contemplating next was crazy and insane and highly likely to get someone hurt.

Dellia stared into his eyes. "Are you sure this is what you want?"

"I've never been more sure of anything in my life." He stepped forward and hugged Dellia. His anxiety eased as he clung to her, so she leaned her head against his chest. And as they embraced, the quiet valley behind them continued to transform into a chaos of activity.

Chapter Thirty-Five

THE WAY HOME

The cool night breeze whipped through her hair as Dellia glanced over to her left. Between the houses, glimpses flew past of the edge of the plateau and beyond it the watch lights of the peaceful city of Shirdon nestled in the dark forests at the base of the mountain.

Dellia pulled back just a little on Ulka's reins to slow her while leaning forward to make it appear as if she were pushing faster. It was a crazy plan. So many things could go wrong. Not the least of which was galloping through dark streets at night. But it was too late to start having doubts now.

Out ahead of her, Jon pushed Kaala faster, and his beautiful black stallion put on a burst of speed, hurtling down the narrow street.

Only a few soldiers remained stationed outside the long stone barracks as he burst into the square in a clatter of hooves. The soldiers snapped to attention, startled by Jon careening past the pit fires.

As loudly as she could, Dellia shouted out, "Stop. Now."

The soldiers' heads whipped around as Ulka thundered into the open.

Dellia pulled Ulka to a halt next to one of the leaping flames and turned him toward the barracks as soldiers burst out of it. "Gather everyone. It's the Otherworlder. We have to catch him."

As the soldiers shouted and sprinted for the stables, Dellia whipped Ulka around and galloped off after Jon.

She pushed her horse hard, racing down the moonlit street as it curved clockwise through the rows of buildings between the edge of the plateau and Shir Courtyard.

When she hit the plaza before the gates of the keep, Jon was already disappearing at the other end. Dellia pulled herself closer to Ulka's neck and leaned forward, speeding by the flickering torches that lined the keep walls. Ulka's hooves pounded the pavement as she raced past rows of darkened homes. Dellia's own house flew by, then the long stairway that wound its way down the mountainside to Shirdon.

She was closing in on Jon fast when the square before the barracks came into view a second time. Only this time, it was jammed with soldiers on horseback moving restlessly around the blazing fire pits.

As the clatter of Kaala's hooves bore down on them, the soldiers whirled around and spotted Jon. In a chaos of movement, they swung their steeds toward him and charged out of the square like a stampeding herd, barreling straight at him.

Jon whipped his head back, watching her.

Dellia kept her focus on him and the soldiers, waiting for the perfect split second, then jabbed out her right elbow just as Jon had described.

He whipped Kaala to his right and shot down the paved alley between two homes.

Dellia plunged down the pavement behind him.

The hooves of several soldiers' horses rounded the corner behind her, their pounding blending with hers and Jon's, echoing down the narrow alleyway.

He shot out from between the buildings at the other end. He swerved left, then right. Then he flew down the cobblestones and out under an archway, careening into the open spaces of the darkened Shir Courtyard gardens.

594

A split in the path lay up ahead, so Dellia jabbed out her left elbow and tucked in her right.

As if on cue, Jon's gaze snapped back, then forward. He veered to the left and tore down the stone pathway past dimly lit flowers, trees, and plants. He barreled through a large archway, and Dellia lost sight of him again. It was amazing how well he was doing, but visions of him plowing Kaala into a dozen soldiers argued with her faith in him.

Dellia blew through the archway and out into the plaza before the massive doors to Shir Keep, where the council would be safely locked in hiding. Jon's handsome, black steed spun restlessly in place, the torchlight gleaming off his shiny coat while Jon stared at Dellia, waiting for guidance.

She thrust out her left elbow, and Jon whipped Kaala around and tore off counterclockwise, breaking for the ramp down the plateau to the city below.

Soldiers on horseback by the dozen thundered down the cross-street toward Jon, and he pushed faster, racing right by them and down the dark ramp.

Dellia pushed Ulka harder, plowing into the herd of horses pouring in behind Jon. She whipped Ulka left and drove down the ramp.

The wide roadway seemed to go on forever into the darkness. The chill night air whistled by, blowing back Dellia's hair and clothes. Hooves thundered all around her as she weaved her way down through the soldiers' horses to the front of the group.

The city loomed closer and the treetops, distant at first, grew larger until she plunged into an ocean of foliage. Ahead of her, Kaala galloped downward surrounded by the tall, dark trees.

Dellia thrust out her right elbow and tucked in her left.

As Jon hit the bottom of the ramp, a split in the road flew closer. He glanced back, then whipped his stallion around a sharp corner, headed back into the forest, racing past Dellia on her right.

She tore around the corner after him to the sight of dozens of horses, careening down the bottom of the ramp, seconds behind her. Their hooves chased her into the night as she raced behind Jon down the path.

She followed only a few horse lengths behind as Kaala swerved left and right, hurtling through the tall pines and down the pathway into the dark night.

Dellia whipped around a corner to the sight of the massive spires looming ahead, their polished, white teeth jutting far into the moonlit night.

Jon pushed his dark charge harder, and Kaala flew up onto the platform.

Dellia followed, chased by a small army.

As she landed on the platform, the portal crackled open above her with a second moon visible through it, near the first.

Soldiers by the dozen chased her up onto the massive circular stone in a clatter of many hooves.

Kaala thundered across the platform and plunged off the other side.

As she approached the edge, Dellia slowed Ulka. Then she pulled him to a stop and looked down at Jon, positioned amid the bows and spears of more than a dozen Verod poised on the ground.

Soldier after soldier pulled to a stop around her, their horses whinnying and prancing in place as more poured up onto the platform.

Dellia stared down, feigning surprise at the trap, trying to appear uncertain. As the hooves leaping onto the platform behind her slowed to a stop, she whipped out her spire stone and slammed it onto the symbol on the spire.

As the portal began to fall, Dellia urged Ulka forward. He plunged off the platform, just clearing it as the shimmering gateway passed over the soldiers, and they vanished, sent far south and west to the Illis Woods.

Cheering broke out among the Verod surrounding Jon. Then the ones on the far side of the platform, and all around, joined in.

Dellia breathed a sigh of relief and faced Jon. "That worked better than I thought."

He shot her a mischievous smile. "Don't seem so surprised. I mean, eventually one of my plans had to work."

"There may be a few soldiers left, but if that didn't roust them, we should be okay."

Dellia looked up at the plateau, towering above them in the moonlit sky. With the soldiers no longer present in force, they stood a chance of getting to the council without bloodshed. But with the gates still barred from the inside, their options for getting in were way too limited.

She scanned the side of the mountain, fearful of what might be happening. Because somewhere up there in the dark night, Garris was risking life and limb, and now it all rested on him.

Garris dangled for a moment, hanging by one arm, with his fingers clinging to a cold crevice in the moonlit cliff face. With a quiet grunt, he hoisted himself up and grabbed onto the ledge above.

The rock was covered in a layer of loose dust and rubble, and his hand slipped away. He lurched downward in a rain of dirt and debris then yanked to a stop, swinging there by his fingertips.

Garris glanced down at the pebbles skittering along the massive drop down the dark face of Mount Karana to the rocks far below. He closed his eyes and let out a long slow breath.

He opened them, staring downward at the gently swaying treetops while he repeated to himself that this was his idea. When Jon had been moaning about having no way to get past the doors of the keep, he had piped up and cheerfully volunteered to get them inside. Now, as he dangled in space, with only a few tenuous finger-holds between him and a gruesome death, he made a mental note that this is what you get for being an optimist.

Still, if he managed to get only a few moments alone with Kayleen, to confront her, it would be worth it.

Garris glanced up at the light from the window, still many body-lengths above him and to his left. He braced himself and let out an even louder grunt as he hoisted himself up and over toward the window. He grabbed onto the same ledge, only this time, with the rubble cleared away, his grip held.

And so it went. Foothold by foothold, handhold by handhold, he worked his way from ledge to crack to crevice, over and up, until at last both hands rested on the sill of the lighted opening carved in the side of the mountain.

Garris yanked his body up into the window, then heaved himself across the small table before it and tumbled to the floor. He rose to his feet and dusted himself off, but when he raised his head, he froze as his gaze met Kayleen's.

She sat in the corner of her typically unremarkable chambers, watching him in quiet. Light from a small lantern on the plain, wooden table next to her flickered across the rough-hewn white walls with veins of the pale purple swirling through them. It highlighted the warm glow of her familiar blond hair and striking features as she gawked at him in astonishment and disbelief.

Garris tensed, and his hand flew to the hilt of his sword, unsure what to expect.

As if coming out of a daze, Kayleen rose to her feet. She stared at him for a long moment.

He looked down at the dirt and grime coating his armor and muscles, trying to figure out what the heck she was staring at.

Then, she flew at him and flung her arms around him. The

force of her embrace threw him backward into the edge of the small table. Her weight pressed against him, bending him back, until he was forced to put his hand on the surface to brace himself. She stayed there for a long time, hugging him tightly.

Shocked, Garris stared down at her as she let go.

She gazed up into his face. "I missed you so much. I can't believe you're here." Tears came to her eyes. "I thought I'd never …" She stepped back and hid her face as she composed herself and wiped away the wetness.

Confused beyond the point of coherence, Garris sputtered, "But … you … hate me."

Kayleen shook her head as she peered into his eyes. "Never."

"But … those were your words. You said, 'I hate you.' To me. I remember … I was there."

A flush of shame crossed her face, and her head dropped. "I said a lot of things. Things I thought you needed to hear."

Astonished and angered, he glowered at her. "I needed to hear my best friend tell me she hates me? Are you insane?"

Kayleen stepped closer and raised her eyes again to his. "They voted to banish you, and I was—"

"You said it was *you* who made sure they banished *me* and to never come back."

She appeared to choke up for a moment, then reached out to Garris, but he recoiled. "I lied." She dropped her hand. "I'm so sorry. I'm so terribly sorry. I wanted you to believe there was nothing left for you here. I was afraid you'd come back and they'd kill you. So I made sure there was nothing to come back to."

Garris's head spun. "You blamed me for Leanna, and for failing you, and the council, and the whole blasted three realms."

Kayleen shook her head, seeming horrified. "I've known you my whole life. I know that whatever happened, you did your best. How could you think I blamed you?"

He shook his head. As if the movement might somehow scatter away his confusion. His anger began to seethe. "Because you said, and I quote, 'and that's all your fault.' That's pretty darn hard to misconstrue."

Kayleen swallowed and turned her head away as her eyes welled once more with tears. "I know. I know. I was awful and terrible—I cried for months after that. I still can't think about it …"

As she stood there looking dejected, Garris's eyes were drawn to the silver chain around her neck. And as he stared, all the confusion melted away, leaving only shock.

"Holy crap. You're telling the truth." He reached out with gentle care and palmed the long blue crystal. "You wouldn't wear a necklace given to you by someone you hate."

Kayleen put her hand on his. "Passed down from your mother. Eejha gave it to you to give to the one you'd marry. But the day you went to train as a protector, you realized you'd never marry, so you gave it to me."

Garris jerked his hand away and stepped back. "Why didn't you just tell me the truth?"

"That the council had turned against you? That the whole world blamed you? That your dreams of doing great things were over? How could I do that to you?" She peered into his face. "I was afraid it would kill you. I thought it was better if you blamed me."

His outrage flared. "That is so … you … I just …" Garris calmed himself as he glared. "Did it ever, for one second, occur to you to tell the truth? Did it ever enter your warped little mind that I could have handled it if I knew my best friend had my back?"

"I always had your back."

"No, you stabbed me in it." Garris turned and stared out the window at the dark Talus landscape, his breath angry and short.

He watched out of the corner of his eye as Kayleen moved up next to him and silent tears began to flow down her cheeks. He ignored her as she reached out for him, then pulled her hand back. She looked down at her feet. "You can't forgive me, can you?"

He kept staring out the window as he slowed his breathing and calmed himself. "Forgive you? Are you ..." Garris turned to face Kayleen. "I almost killed you."

As he spoke the words, his anger returned, and he struggled again to regain his calm. "But look, right now I need your help. And it would be the easiest thing in the world to stand here and tell you I forgive you. But that would be a lie. Honestly, I don't think I'll ever forgive you for what you put me through. Fifteen years, Kayleen. Fifteen years of thinking you betrayed me. That you were sending people to kill me."

Shock flashed across her face. "Kill you? Oh no." Her look of shock turned to one of horror, and she stumbled back and fell down into the chair behind her. She looked up into his face with a pitiful, hurt expression on her tear-streaked face. "You thought I was capable of that?"

Stunned at the implications, Garris gave a rapid shake of his head. It was clear she wasn't lying, but if Kayleen wasn't the one sending people to kill him, then what in blazes was going on?

Garris shoved all his confusion and anger down deep. "This is not the time for this."

Kayleen straightened and acted dutiful. "Of course." She brushed away her tears as she stood up. "You need my help? What do you need? Anything."

"I need to get Jon and Dellia into the council chamber to address the council."

"They're together? With you?" She gave him a deep bow. "Yes. Of course. I can get you in."

Kayleen turned the corner out of her chambers and led the way down the polished, marble hallway, headed for the Shir Keep entrance. Carved through the solid stone of the mountain, giant swirls of pale mauve and ivory streaked with blue gray lay beneath the torches that lined their path.

A sudden déjà vu struck her at the familiar cadence of Garris's footsteps behind her and her heart soared. Kayleen glanced back at him to assure herself that it was true, he was really there.

Even though helping Garris was outright treason, this moment, now, felt more right than anything she'd done in years. It was true, she had no inkling of what Jon intended to do, but it didn't matter. She trusted Garris and Dellia with her whole being, and if they believed in him, then she believed in him, too.

As they passed a guard patrolling the hallway, he gave Garris a suspicious glance. So Kayleen snapped around and ordered him to accompany them.

As all three marched down the hallway, Kayleen glanced back again at Garris. Though he tried hard to control it, his mood had always been as easy to read as any book. And right now every line on his face said he was still hurt and angry and upset. The council was bound to find her guilty of treason. Dellia would never speak to her again, and what troubled her more than any of that was that she had earned Garris's contempt.

Her mind raced back to that idealistic young man on a bench under a tree in the Shir Courtyard. It was a moment she had replayed thousands of times over the decades. She had been devastated when Garris said he was going off to train as a protector. But it was all forgotten in a moment when he told her how sorry he was and that their friendship was as close as he would ever get to having a wife. Then he'd placed the necklace around her neck and kissed her. Their first, last, and only kiss. Then he left. She lost her best friend, and her life was never the same.

Kayleen glanced back again, and the contrast was heartrending.

That younger Garris was full of life, and joy, and ambition, and full of himself. The one that followed her now seemed a sad and broken imitation.

When they reached the keep entrance, Kayleen shot the guards posted on either side of the door a stern stare and informed them Garris would now stand guard. Then, she ordered them to hand over their weapons. They seemed shocked, and she expected them to resist, to claim that she had been removed as council leader and didn't have the authority. Yet to her surprise, they all complied without threat or persuasion.

After Garris collected the weapons, she pointed to the elegantly appointed visitor hall and ordered all three to go inside and await further orders. Once they were in the room, Garris hoisted the sturdy wooden bar off the keep doors and carried it over to the visitor hall. Once there, he jammed it against the door, ensuring none of them could get out. Heaving against its substantial weight, he swung open one side of the massive keep door and stepped out into the crisp, night air.

Kayleen followed, and as she walked away, she turned back to take one last look at the keep towering into the starry sky. She could never go back. Not only had she taken the blame for everything that had happened and was sure to be found guilty of treason, but now, she was willfully aiding fugitives in infiltrating the keep. If she ever allowed herself to be caught after this, they would hang her, or worse. And yet, the prospect never gave her a moment's pause.

Dellia glared as she approached and spat out her cold, angry greeting. "Kayleen."

It hurt to be met by such deep hatred in one she considered to be like a daughter. But right now, the one that consumed her thoughts was Garris. She turned to face him.

"I am so sorry for everything. I know that words can never repair what I've done. And I have no right to ask forgiveness."

Garris never moved or even flinched. He just stood there, his piercing eyes staring at her with cold indifference.

Kayleen bowed her head as a sadness struck more profound than she'd believed possible. It was over. There would be no forgiveness for her, not from Dellia and especially not from Garris. She was a homeless fugitive and now a friendless one.

She gave a single nod, then raised her head. "There is nothing left for me here."

She stared at the three, trying to memorize their faces. "You will not see me again." She glanced first at Dellia, then at Garris. "I love you both, more than I can express, and I have made so many mistakes. I only hope that someday you will find it in your hearts to forgive me."

For a moment, Garris seemed torn, and a fleeting hope sprang in her heart that he might try to stop her. But when no objection came, she turned her gaze to Jon. He seemed unremarkable. And yet, Garris and Dellia were ready to accompany him as he confronted the council. It was impossible to guess what he intended to do, but it was just as difficult to see how it could go well.

Kayleen smiled. "Good luck, Jon. I hope you have more success with the council than I have."

She turned and took a few steps away, then swung back to face him. "Be careful of Braye, he is devious, self-serving, and dangerous. It is he that was behind the ambush in Kanlu."

Jon nodded to her.

She walked several more steps away before pivoting back again. "And it was the Verod that dragged you into the catacombs in Mundus and tried to frame you. And there's something going on with Ceree and Rillen. And watch out for Idria. I think there is more going on with her than meets the eye."

The look of concentration on Jon's face told her he was struggling to commit to memory all she was telling him.

Kayleen paused for a moment, trying to come up with anything else that might be of use to Jon. But when nothing offered itself, she turned and walked off into the night, certain she'd never see Garris or Dellia again.

Jon followed Dellia down the bright hallway lined with flaming torches. Schemes, ideas, and fragments of speeches swirled through his mind as they twisted and wound their way through a sea of whirling white and pale-purple hallways. There were no seams or segments in the architecture as if its makers had carved the keep straight into the mountainside.

A bit panicked at what he might face at his destination, Jon attempted to organize his chaotic thoughts. He systematically categorized and worked through strategies and scenarios. But it soon became apparent that with no inkling of who these people were or what they might do, he had no basis for deciding which course of action would be best.

He glanced back at Garris following behind, scanning and alert as he brought up the rear. With his head still craned back behind him, Jon almost bumped into Dellia as she stopped some distance from an open door.

She turned to face him and pointed to the entry. "This is where the council will be. It's where they stay when there's an imminent threat."

He eyed the open passage. The last few hours had been a whirlwind, talking to leaders of all three realms. With each of them, he had some notion who he was dealing with. But as he stared at the doorway, the pit in his stomach grew. Everything came down to this moment, and here he stood, staring at his destination, with no real clue what to expect or what he intended to do.

He was about to face the brightest political minds in this world.

How could he hope to accomplish anything? And with countless ways this could go wrong, all he had managed to assemble were far too many half-baked ideas.

He turned back to Dellia. The torchlight cast a warm glow on her face as Jon gazed into her eyes. "Well, this is it."

She took his hand and lifted it up to her lips, clasping it between her hands. "You're trembling."

Jon hung his head. "I'm not a brave man, Dellia."

She lifted his chin and peered into his eyes. "It's not too late. We could still leave here and never come back."

He shook his head and smiled. "I would face anything for you."

"What are you going to do?"

"I don't know exactly. I wish I did." Jon slipped his hand out of hers and brushed Dellia's cheek. "I have only one thought, one goal: to find my way home … to you."

She smiled and hugged him, holding him tight. When she released him, he stepped back and stared at the doorway once again.

"Well, I managed to fool everyone so far. If I can pull this off, it will be a performance worthy of an Academy Award."

Jon motioned to the door, inviting his companions to take the lead. If Dellia was right, guards would be posted on either side of the door, and they'd need to be dealt with.

It seemed as if she wanted to say more, but as Garris slunk off, she turned and hurried after. The two acted in tandem, ducking through the doorway with quick, silent movements.

Jon took a deep breath to calm himself, then followed close behind. The sounds of a scuffle lasted only a second, but he ignored them and strolled through the doorway into a modest room carved from soft, yellow-streaked marble.

He stopped and faced the eight members slouched around the square, granite table. He eyed them across its gleaming, azure surface streaked with gold and black as they snapped to attention.

DELLIA

The man from the oracle's message, the one Dellia had called Braye, leaped to his feet. The remaining members sat surveying Jon with shocked expressions lit by a pair of sunstones in the corners, shining up from the polished stone floor.

Braye glared at him. "How did you get in here?"

"I walked," said Jon in as calm a voice as he could muster.

"Guards!"

Striving to appear relaxed, Jon listened, straining to catch any sign of a response as Braye's command echoed down the long marble halls. No distant clatter of metal or running feet met his ears. There was nothing but the quiet sounds of the two guards behind him, with Dellia and Garris holding knives to their backs.

"Guards!" Braye yelled again, this time louder.

When no reply met his cries, he glared at Jon. "Where are all the guards? What have you done with them?"

Jon summoned a casual smile. "I have things I must discuss with you, and I figured they'd interfere, so I sent them away."

A woman rose. Her dark brown hair was woven into a single long braid and worn over the shoulder exactly as Dellia had described. Ceree flashed a warm smile and bowed deeply. "You must be Jon."

He gave a curt bow in return and faced the remaining members. "You lied about me and turned your people against me. So I'm here to tell you what's going to happen."

A woman whose short silver hair and oddly pale blue eyes gave her away as Idria sprang to her feet. "This is treason. We are the rightful rulers of Meerdon. You have no right to come here making demands. Especially not in response to one little lie."

Brisk footsteps marched through the entry, and Jon whipped around as Kayleen charged past Dellia and Garris. They both stared in shock as she stormed across the floor, around Jon and up in front of the table. Her manner appeared brusque and her expression determined as she glared at the group across the colorful council table.

The surprised members gawked at Kayleen as she spat out her forceful words. "You arrogant flock of cowards. Rightful rulers? By whose decree? Your own? Most of you are only fit to rule because you'd fail at anything decent or honest."

With a hard eye, she glared at Idria, who took an almost imperceptible step backward. "You lie constantly. The Kirwan accords, ambassador Rotus, the Setlanders, the list goes on and on and on." She brought herself up taller and glared at the group with ferocity. "You tell the people one thing to pacify them while you plot to do the exact opposite, all the while lying to yourselves that it's necessary to further the cause of good."

Kayleen paused to scan the members, her expression brimming with righteous indignation. "You even lie about your lies, telling yourself it's 'just politics' or 'the way things must be done.' It is malicious deceit, and you know it. And those lies destroy lives … not that you care."

She glowered, letting the council members stew. Then, she motioned to Jon. "Jon here never harmed any of you. He has done no wrong. Yet, before he even arrived, you planted a lie in a calculated plot to destroy him." Kayleen stood up taller. "I saw Wistra herself prophesy that he is here to prevent the end of all humankind." She wagged a finger at the sheepish members. "He is here to save all you pompous idiots."

She paused, staring at the council members, letting her claim sink in. "So how did you repay him? You kidnapped and tortured him. Well, actions have consequences, my friends." She leaned over the table and motioned to Jon again. "And he stands here before you now to deliver yours. I saw him single-handedly decimate a massive army of the dead while evading a protector and my entire detail. You have no clue who you're trifling with. And if you value your pitiful lives, you will sit down, shut up, and listen to what he has to say."

Kayleen stepped back and turned to face Jon. Stunned, he just stared at her. It was as if he were seeing her for the first time. She was a force to be reckoned with, and she was on his side. This modest-looking woman had just rendered his audience speechless and given him the opening he needed to press for the most ambitious of his schemes.

After smiling and bowing to him in a gracious manner, Kayleen withdrew and motioned for Jon to retake the floor.

He stepped forward, eyeing the council members across the deep blue surface streaked with gold and black. He raised the gleaming metal medallion aloft where all could see it. Striving to match Kayleen's masterful delivery, he spoke in as strong and confident a voice as he could muster.

"This medallion contains Wistra's true prophecy, in her own words. In it, she exposes your lie and how you put all of Meerdon at risk. I have visited all three realms this night and played her message to the Ephori, the Rhanae, and the emperor. They all know of your treachery, and any support you may have had among them is gone. By tomorrow, every soul in the three realms will know you have betrayed them. And, as we speak, the Verod marches on you with a small army." Jon leaned forward. "And I have made sure your forces cannot stop them."

Braye leaned forward. "So what do you propose? That we hand power over to you? You know nothing of how to govern."

"No. I have no desire to rule. But I do know how you're going to fix this." He took a deep breath as he scanned the council members. "You're going to hand power back to the three realms. They will govern themselves: their own army, their own government, their own laws."

A woman who matched Dellia's description of Aapri spoke up. "They will never agree to this. They need us."

Jon gave his best imitation of a derisive laugh. "Oh, they have *already* agreed to this." He adopted a more assertive tone. "In fact, I speak for them now."

"But they are incapable of governing themselves," Braye said.

"You are wrong," Jon insisted. "They are far more capable of ruling themselves than you are. I have seen it, firsthand."

Ceree stood and addressed Jon, her words tinged with genuine concern. "They warred for centuries before the council. It was formed to put an end to their ceaseless conflict."

With no idea whether to trust her words, he looked to Kayleen, hoping for some help.

She gave an almost imperceptible nod of her head, an affirmation that Ceree spoke the truth.

His plan was unraveling. But it was too late to turn back now; he was committed. Jon faltered, standing there speechless like some bumbling idiot while the whole council stared. After a moment of silence, Kayleen gave a subtle motion of her head, urging him to continue.

Jon forged ahead. "Then, to ensure peace between the realms," he improvised, "the council will stay. Yeah ... uh ... stay, but it will have limits. Strict limits ... on its power. To make sure the three realms continue to rule themselves."

"This is nonsense," Braye declared. "Who will decide on these limits? You?"

Kayleen approached Jon. She leaned in toward him, her back to the council members crowded around the granite table. Her voice became a whisper only Jon, Dellia, and Garris could hear. "Jon, it used to be as you describe. The council existed only to foster cooperation. But over time they seized more and more control. It may take time, but they will do so again."

He pondered for a moment, then a notion hit him. "Okay," he whispered back, "but what if each realm had a vote on the council?"

"You mean members appointed by the three realms?"

Jon nodded.

Kayleen considered it for a moment. "That's good. That might work. They would never vote for the council to seize their power." She stood in quiet contemplation for a moment, then gave a subtle nod of her head toward the council members. "What about them? They have influence. Removing them will make you many powerful enemies. Enemies you cannot afford."

"But they lied," Jon whispered. "Soon, everyone will know that."

"Then they will lie some more to cover their lie. And their supporters will believe it. They are too emotionally invested not to."

Jon sighed, then paused for a moment to think. "Keep your enemies closer."

"What?" said Kayleen.

"An old saying. Keep your friends close, but your enemies closer."

Her brow furrowed. "That sounds like an extraordinarily dangerous proposition."

It didn't matter; the path forward was clear now, and it all made sense. Jon raised his head and stared at Kayleen. "I have an idea."

He stepped around her to face the council again. "Here's what you are going to do." He paused and eyed the council members. Once again trying to mimic Kayleen's forceful delivery, he said, "The council will remain, but it will have an entirely new set of members." Jon held up two fingers. "Each of the three realms will appoint two of their people to vote on it."

He motioned to those assembled before him. "You members of the old council will remain, and you will meet and debate as you always have." He switched cadence, striving to emphasize each word with strength and clarity. "But you will *not* make *law*. Instead, you will appoint two of your number to argue and vote on the new council."

Jon stepped forward, glaring at each of the council members, endeavoring to be clear and forceful. "This reformed council will serve at the pleasure of the three realms. It will have no power unless *all* members of *all three realms unanimously* agree to grant it that power. It is the three realms that will determine the council's limits."

He stopped and stepped back, trying to appear confident as he scanned the skeptical faces crowded around the council table. Moments passed as he watched and waited for their reaction.

"That is only eight members," said Idria's crisp voice. "You need an odd number to avoid a stalemate."

Braye scoffed. "You have just proven you don't have the wisdom to even talk about such matters. You've created a council with no leader. And it will fail because it has no guidance and no vision."

"And you were that leader?" Jon asked.

"Yes." Braye puffed out his chest.

Ceree pointed to Kayleen. "No. Kayleen was."

"Well, yeah," Braye said, "but I advised and guided her."

All of a sudden, Kayleen jumped in. "Jon will lead." She pointed at him. "It must be so. It is his vision."

Horrified, Jon stared at Kayleen for a moment. In desperation and panic, he thrust out his finger and pointed back at her. "No, not me. Kayleen, she will lead."

She turned to him, speaking openly and in a calm voice. "Jon, I cannot. If this is to work, people will need someone to look to, someone with a vision, someone to trust."

He panicked. This was his worst nightmare. He needed to do something, anything. His eyes shot over to Kayleen. "Then … then represent me. Advise me. Sit on the council and argue for me."

She froze for a moment. Her gaze darted over to Garris, as if begging for his reaction, but he stood there in an unresponsive stupor. Her eyes flew to Dellia, but after a second with no sign from either, she returned her gaze to Jon.

"I can't, Jon. I can't ask—"

"No." Dellia snapped out of her daze. "She will do it."

Kayleen tilted her head and stared at her with a bewildered expression. After a moment, she faced Jon and nodded.

He glanced at Dellia and Garris as the tension in his chest eased. This wasn't even close to the plan. Yet it so neatly solved everything. He loved Dellia immensely. He had given up his world for her in the hopes of making a home with her here. This would let her continue to be a protector while he stayed nearby. And it could return Garris to a role for which he was so obviously suited. More than anything, it would put him in the best position he could imagine to find Megan and help her get home. It all made sense. And as much as the thought of being in charge panicked him, he could do this. He could be a figurehead and let Kayleen make all the real decisions.

After a second of his allies staring on with stunned looks, Jon spun around and faced the council again. "One more thing. Dellia and Garris will remain as protectors for as long as they choose, and they will both answer only to me."

He stared straight at Braye, endeavoring to appear resolute in the face of the councilman's defiant expression. "Are we agreed, or do I leave you to fend for yourselves with no army, the Verod coming, and the three realms in revolt?"

One by one, the members nodded reluctant agreement, except Braye. He stepped forward. "This is insanity. I will not allow a sniveling child to undo all that the council—"

Idria stepped forward, stabbed him in the side, and twisted the blade.

Braye groaned and crumpled to the ground. His breathing labored, he lay there clutching his wound with blood rushing over his fingers.

Idria plucked a shiny dark stone from her pocket. Holding it with two of her blood-soaked fingers, she thrust it up high. Through the red gore smeared across its surface, the three lines glowed orange as she spewed her cold, unemotional words at Jon. "You annoying little insect. You have no idea the forces you're trifling with. The wolves and demons were a mere test to expose your gift." She threw him a disgusted look and shook her head. "And you foolishly obliged. You are a danger to all, and this ignorant meddling of yours cannot be allowed to continue. Now, witness the power of Syvis."

Idria shot her palm out at Kayleen, and in an instant she was frozen in place. Her expression turned to panic as red smoke swirled up from her feet and engulfed her. Then she crumbled to dust.

Dellia dove for a stunned Jon. She grabbed his wrist and began dragging him toward the door.

An unbridled fury flashed in Garris's eyes, and he threw himself at Idria.

She thrust her palm out before him, and he froze midleap.

Jon lunged for Garris, lurching Dellia to a stop.

Anger seethed on Garris's face as red smoke twisted up from the floor to enshroud him. Then he too disintegrated into dust.

Dellia bolted for Idria, and she raised her palm again.

Jon panicked as Dellia became a statue. His hand flew down to the hilt of his sword. He concentrated, and as a red vortex enveloped Dellia's feet, the world slowed and froze.

His heart hammered in his ears as a shimmering scene of a blacksmith at a forge appeared, overlaid on the marble chamber. He had stopped the catastrophe, but he couldn't stay in this image forever. He had to do something.

His eyes fell on the stone clutched in Idria's fingers. He dashed over and was shocked to find he could pry it from her fingers.

He concentrated again, this time on the stone, and the scene melted into a new one, deep and ancient, and moving at a blur. Jon closed his eyes and focused, trying to find the stone's maker, and the scene slowed to an altar that seemed deep below the earth.

A massive dark creature, its skin shiny and wet, hunkered over the stone as it chanted in some cryptic language full of groans and guttural noises.

Glowing lava smoldered around the rock ledge where the creature growled and jammed a dark blade through its paw. Blood flowed down the tip and onto the stone. Three lines glowed red through the dark, thick blood coating the surface.

A sudden searing pain hit Jon, as if his guts were burning from the inside out and his skin blistering and peeling from his body. A crushing pressure slammed him to the floor, as if he were buried under tons of rock in the deepest depths of the ocean.

Writhing and convulsing on the ground, he struggled to remain conscious. He managed to shake his head, and in an instant, he flashed up off the floor, back to where he'd stood when reality froze.

As the world began to move again, he fell to one knee, gasping and trembling.

No longer frozen, Dellia raced over to his side and helped him up. "What's wrong? Are you okay?"

Jon's head flew up and his back arched in a sudden shudder of pain. And there, inlaid in the ceiling over the council table, lay three huge stone leaves arranged in a circle: one nearly silver gray, one golden tan, and the third deep black.

In a voice so soft only he and Dellia could hear, Jon said, "This was always going to happen."

As he regained his footing and mastered his pain, a burning sensation shot through his eyes, and Jon clamped them shut. In a flash, it eased, so he opened them.

Dellia stumbled backward with a look of fear and shock on her face. "Your eyes. They're yellow, like the Blood Wolves."

A strange feeling of immense and ancient power coursed through Jon's veins and, with it, an insatiable anger. Anger at the chaos, imbalance, and cruelty of a world entirely out of control. And a contempt and intolerance for those foolish enough to deny the justice and wisdom of his will. Jon glanced down at its source—the stone still clutched in his hand.

A sudden burst of understanding flooded his mind. And for an instant, the meaning of the veil revealed itself with crystal clarity. This world that seemed so real and tangible was but a mere illusion, a curtain. And beyond it lay reality upon reality: entire universes of pure power, love, and evil, places of dark and twisted creatures, of delicacy and infinite beauty, worlds of nothingness, and of godlike beings, and the creative will behind it all.

In a flash, the knowledge was gone, and Jon's anger flared anew. A fury consumed him, rooted in something he couldn't quite place, a rage both seductive and satisfying, yet he knew in his heart it was wrong and evil.

This stone in his fingers was a conduit to a power beyond the veil, something terrible and all-consuming. The power to create or destroy, to force order out of chaos, to eradicate anarchy. The power to bend the world and everyone in it into conformity, to eliminate defiance and reshape this world into any form he saw fit.

A compulsion to yield to that power overwhelmed him, but he struggled back, rebelling against it, clinging to his identity.

The lines on the stone glowed bright yellow.

With an expression of horror on her face, Idria looked at the stone in Jon's hand, then at her fingers, as if checking to see if it was truly gone.

He needed to do something before this obsession overwhelmed him and nothing remained of his true self. Jon thrust the stone high in the air, and his voice boomed out, fierce and bitter, as if it wasn't even his own. "No one should have power like this."

The entire room stared as the stone in his fingers crumbled to dust, then blew away in a gust of wind.

The burning in his eyes abated and Dellia's anxiety seemed to ease as she studied his face.

Jon nodded at the pile of debris that had been his friend. It swirled from the shiny yellow floor in a whirlwind of blue dust that coalesced back into Garris.

He nodded again, and the second pile whirled up from the floor like a blue tornado and reassembled back into Kayleen.

He waved his hand in Braye's direction, and the blood and wound vanished, and he was whole again.

Jon struggled to control his rage, his voice bellowing out, "Are we agreed?"

Idria lurched toward him and shouted out, "You insignificant little—"

"Enough!" Jon shouted. And with a flick of his wrist, she was gone.

He struggled again, this time managing to regain some degree of composure. His words became more controlled and measured as he eyed the remaining council members. "Are ... we ... agreed?"

Every single member, including Braye, stood wide-eyed as they nodded their heads in ready agreement.

"Then, send orders to your army that they now report to Kayleen and me, as heads of the new council." His eyes burned again as he glared and snarled out the words. "Agreed?"

Again, every single member of the council nodded enthusiastic agreement.

With tremendous effort, Jon managed to retain his composure while he staggered to the door and out into the hall. But as soon as he rounded the corner, out of view, he threw his back against the cold, polished stone of the wall, leaning on it to remain upright.

Dellia and Garris rushed to his side, and Jon's words came out between winces of pain. "Don't worry, I ... didn't kill her. I just sent her ... far away."

Dellia forced a smile and gazed into Jon's eyes. "I wasn't worried."

He stared into hers and smiled back. "I can't believe that worked."

He winced again and clutched his hands as a wave of blinding pain hit. His weight fell on Dellia, and she pushed back, keeping him upright, her concern evident in her every look and action.

"I don't know what's wrong." Jon tried to stand on his own.

She threaded her arm under his and around his shoulder, propping him up. She felt warm against him as she stared into his eyes. "Stay with me. Please."

Jon's eyes burned for a third time, and he gasped in pain. Understanding flooded his awareness again and he could see how the laws of physics to which he had clung, the rules he'd used to make sense of his world, were not immutable. They shifted and flowed from one universe to the next. How millennia ago, like currents in a stream, those rules had conspired to bear the seeds of burgeoning life from his home world to a planet called Thera and to this unique patch of dust on it called Meerdon, and in so doing they had altered the fate of two worlds.

Then he saw his own experiment. All it would have taken was one small miscalibration to create modulation, and that tiny perturbation could result in drawing vast amounts of power from beyond the veil. That energy had to be the fuel behind the disaster in his lab. His own naivety and arrogance had brought him here.

A terrifying new insight hit, and Jon struggled through his pain. He raised his head and gazed at Dellia. "I can see things with such clarity, but I don't know if it will last. I need you to remember something for me."

She nodded.

"The invasion Wistra saw. It is all but inevitable. I see it now, Dellia. It will kill you all. We have to stop it. Remember that, please. We have to stop it."

Then in an instant, images of a place far away flashed through his mind's eye, visions of a dark, swirling portal and of a bloodred army moving down a narrow rock passage.

"It's one of the hordes." Jon shuddered. "Wolves, hundreds of them, they're on the move."

Jon pulled himself upright and fought back his dizziness and pain. With Dellia's help, he stumbled over to Kayleen. "Can you handle things for me here?"

"Of course." She gave a single nod.

"Make sure the military leaders understand. And inform the Verod of our agreement. It should satisfy them, or at least send them back to complain to their own leaders." Kayleen nodded again. "And one more thing. I need Sirra, fast."

She spun around and hurried off down the hall.

Jon stepped back and faced Dellia. "I have to stop the wolves. You and Garris should stay here. This is going to get bad."

"That's not happening." She glanced at Garris, and his face was stern and resolute as he nodded agreement. "We're your protectors now. We are both coming."

Jon couldn't help but let out a small laugh, even as he shuddered in pain. "I just knew this protector thing was going to go to your heads."

"You're welcome," said Garris.

He placed a hand each on Garris's and Dellia's shoulders and looked them in the eye. "Thank you both."

He lost his balance and his hands slipped. Dellia grabbed hold of his wrist, wrapped his arm around her shoulder, and helped him over to the wall. He slumped against it and closed his eyes, trying to remain lucid while he waited.

At the sound of footsteps, Jon opened his eyes to find Kayleen approaching with Sirra.

He dragged himself up, and Dellia helped him stumble up to her. "I have no right to ask, but we need to get to Mundus right away."

"You have every right to ask," Sirra said. "We are family now, and allies. Of course I will take you."

She thrust her palm out, pointing it down the smooth marble hallway, and a shimmering liquid portal formed. Torchlight glimmered on its surface while through it lay the predawn lane and gardens before Gatia's estate. Sirra eyed the destination with care, then stepped through. Once she arrived safely on the streets of Mundus, she turned back and motioned through the portal for them to follow.

Chapter Thirty-Six

SHE IS EVERYTHING

As Jon straggled out of the portal, the warm, dry air of the plains of Erden hit him, a shocking contrast to the coolness of Shir Keep. He winced again in scorching pain as he stepped up next to Sirra and stared back at the shining wet surface of the portal. There, like a reflection on water, stood Dellia and Garris, still in the marble hallway. Garris snatched one of the torches that lined the walls and its flickering light danced across the portal's water-like surface.

As the two stepped through to join him, Jon steadied himself and surveyed the brick streets of Mundus. A swath of stars burned its way across the predawn sky, hanging over the palatial homes, gardens, and terraces that lined either side of the dark and deserted street.

Dellia turned to face the wooden gate into the small garden before Gatia's sprawling home, now dark in slumber. She eyed Jon and motioned to the pathway. "You should speak to Gatia first."

Still weak and barely holding it together, he just nodded and stepped up to take his place at Dellia's side. She slipped her arm through his and clung to it tightly. Then, she lifted him up, lending him her support.

With Sirra and Garris following, the two shambled through the gate and down the path. As they passed the pond, Jon glanced over at the shimmer of stars reflected on its still waters, broken only by the dark lilies that dotted its calm surface.

Another wave of blistering pain hit as they mounted the steps, and Dellia hoisted Jon upright and dragged him up to the door.

The sound of Dellia knocking reverberated down the empty streets, followed by a muffled rummaging from inside.

After a few moments, an out-of-breath Gatia slipped open the door and peeked out. She startled at seeing the four standing on her doorstep.

Aishi appeared at her side, staring up from underneath her mother's arm. She spied Jon, and her eyes bugged as she stepped back behind her mother, peering out from around her.

Gatia focused on Dellia's mother, addressing her first. "I am honored, Sirra. Though I must admit, I'm surprised to find all of you here."

In pain, and his mind still touched by an anger and impatience that was not his own, Jon blurted out, "There's no time for niceties. Several hundred Blood Wolves are headed here from the southeast. We will deal with them, but I need your guards ready to handle any stragglers that get through."

Gatia balked. "I don't have the authority. Besides, what do you think you four are going to do against—"

"Do not quarrel with me." Jon's voice bellowed out as his eyes burned once again.

Gatia's eyes flew wide, and she stepped back, almost stumbling over her daughter.

A crippling pain struck, and Jon doubled over. With great effort, he managed to calm himself. "Forgive me. I'm not myself."

Dellia reached out and placed her hand on Gatia's arm. "Please, Gatia." Her manner was soft and gentle. "And send a runner to the Rhanae." She turned her eyes toward Jon. "And let them know that the new council leader of Meerdon has ordered it."

Gatia's eyes widened even more as she stared at Jon. "The new … Yes, Dellia, I will see to it."

She looked down at little Aishi and nodded her head. "Run."

DELLIA

The girl bolted off, racing down the path as fast as her small legs could carry her. As she sprinted out of the yard and down the street, Gatia placed her hands together and bowed deeply. Then she too dashed off.

Jon faced the other three. "There's something we need at the Temple of Knowledge."

Too preoccupied with managing his impatience and pain, he paid little attention as Dellia helped him out of the yard, down the long street, around the corner, and up another street to the base of the temple. Still grimacing with each searing wave, Jon turned off the brick avenue and mounted the temple steps.

As he reached the top, he slowed and put his hand out, placing it on the cool, smooth surface of one of the yali's enormous chests. Jon closed his eyes and concentrated, trying to recall the second chant he had heard in his vision. *"Sabhee zinda aao or raksha karana."*

An abrupt crackling sound broke the silence, echoing through the columns of the pavilion and down the dark, empty streets. As expected, another followed, then another, as one by one, a yali broke free from each pillar and transformed into living winged lions.

After they freed themselves, each majestic creature strolled down the rows of pillars toward the broad temple steps. The first pair came up to sit on either side of the group.

Dellia reached out and ran her hand through the thick amber fur and down the enormous feathered wings. As the first light of dawn brightened the sky, the yali raised their gray-horned heads and stared out into the fading night.

Struggling to remain poised through the pain, Jon glanced at his friends on either side. "Long ago, these protected the city. Now they will do so again." He motioned to a group of yali prowling down the ornate pavilion. "They are our army."

Jon shivered again as a new wave of pain swept his body. As it subsided, he opened his arms wide and motioned his "soldiers" forward as he willed them to accompany him.

With a powerful thrust of their wings and a rush of wind, the pair of yali on either side leaped to the night sky.

As they descended the steps, Jon's three companions craned their necks, staring upward, watching each of the remaining beasts spread their wings wide and take flight, soaring out over their heads.

"It's truly amazing." Dellia tore her gaze from the sight above and eyed Jon. "But they are a little more than a dozen against hundreds of wolves."

Jon gave a small shake of his head. "The wolves won't be interested in the yali. They'll be after me."

As they reached the bottom and turned down the street, the last of the yali sprang from the top of the steps, pushing upward to join the pride, drifting and circling through the starlit sky. The four allies strolled abreast down the abandoned streets as yali swooped and soared in the air above them.

Soon, lights began to flicker on in the massive estates that lined the street. Through windows, both lighted and darkened, faces appeared. Light from Garris's torch danced in the eyes of residents watching and whispering as they passed.

"I can destroy the wolves." Jon pointed above. "With the help of the yali." He glanced both ways at his friends. "I need all of you to guard me and keep any that might get through from reaching me."

As they reached the edge of the plains, a sea of amber eyes almost as broad as the city itself met them, bobbing far out across the dim glow of the dawn horizon.

Jon's heart pounded faster in his ears. Through shudders of pain, he gulped and halted. His breathing grew short as his companions stopped and turned to face him. Above them, yali soared through the air as Jon gazed upon the faces of these people who had become his friends. He shook his head. "Guys, this is my burden. They are here for me, not you."

Garris rolled his eyes. "Yeah, I'll just stand by and watch the council leader get eaten. I just got pardoned—are you trying to get me banished again?"

While the attempt to brush off his concern was touching, this was more grave than any threat Jon had faced so far. "This is serious. I'm terrified something might happen to you guys." His eyes met first Dellia's, then Sirra's, then Garris's. "To any of you."

Garris sighed, then thrust his hand out, palm down. "Together. Right?"

Without hesitation, Dellia placed her hand on Garris's and said, "Together."

Then her mother smiled and set her hand on the others. They all eyed Jon and waited. He shook his head and wracked his brain, searching for some way to keep them out of it. Then a wave of pain hit, and his will to resist crumbled.

Jon stuck out his hand and rested it on theirs. "Okay, together."

They all pulled in their hands, and Jon forged ahead into the wasteland. As he strode out onto the plains, he spread his arms wide and waved forward, and as he willed it, the yali soared out across the barren plains ahead of him.

They thrust their enormous wings back, propelling them far ahead, then spread them wide, drifting out along the desolate landscape toward the sea of bright amber eyes.

As Jon headed out to meet the Blood Wolves, Sirra took up a position behind him, her dagger in hand. The torch no longer necessary in the brightening dawn light, Garris tossed it aside and drifted out to the left as he readied his crossbow. Dellia caught Jon's eye, then nodded to him before she spread out to the right.

As Jon dragged himself on, pushing through the flashes of fiery pain, the scattered lights of the city became distant behind them. As the eyes grew closer, the gangly creatures from the spires became visible, interspersed with the wolves. With their unnaturally long, sticklike arms, they ambled along on their curved, razor claws, as the wolves weaved in and out around them. As the mass of wolves and creatures became clearer, the rumble of vicious snarls and growls grew louder, carrying far out across the barren terrain.

Jon closed his eyes and spread his arms wide again, this time calling upon the power he had gathered from the stone's creator. A wave of crippling pain and pressure hit, and he stumbled and nearly fell.

He opened his eyes and pulled himself back upright as a glowing yellow whirlwind formed in front of him. Rubble and dust swirled up from the ground, creating a tiny amber dust devil.

As the yali reached the wolves, they ripped pairs of bobbing eyes from the ground and dragged them far up into the sky. Then they flung the bloodred bodies back into the remaining horde. Distant yelps and cries of pain rose above the whistling of the whirlwind as wolf upon wolf plummeted to the ground.

Jon grimaced though clawing pain that continued to grow with the expanding whirlwind, as it became a small tornado of yellow, glowing dust and debris several stories high.

His resolve began to crumble as the wolves and creatures grew closer, and their overwhelming numbers became visible in the growing light of dawn. He slowed as he stared at the sea of bloodred fur and snarling white teeth, trotting toward him across the dimly lit plains at dawn.

At the far distant edges, the wolves broke into a run, curving around to come up behind them and surround them.

Jon winced and cried out between gasps. "The pain is back. It's getting bad. I don't know if I can do this."

"We should go back," Dellia yelled above the roar of the vortex.

Garris sent her an annoyed look. "It's too late, we all do this or we all die."

Jon braced himself against the pain and pushed harder. As the wolves closed in, the yali followed, forming a ring between the edge of the pack and the group of four. They swooped and dove all around the now-massive vortex, yanking wolves and creatures from the ground at the front and flinging them far back across the plains.

As the group waded into the sea of threatening teeth and angry amber eyes, Jon willed it, and the yali abruptly changed strategy. They dove down, yanking wolves from the ground in midstride. With a whoosh and powerful thrust of their massive wings, they dragged the snarling beasts high into the sky. Then they twisted and dove again as they flung the creatures into the roaring vortex.

Electricity crackled as each hit the whirling yellow wall of dust and wind and were snatched away, swept up into the sky where they disintegrated in a shower of sparks.

Surrounded by wolves racing at them, the group came to a halt.

Garris jammed a batch of arrows into the ground, dropped to one knee, and began firing into the wolves as they came screaming at him, felling anything the yali missed.

Dellia waded into the chaos as beast after beast flew at her. The yali snatched many of them out of the air before they reached her. Others she blocked and kicked, stabbed, slashed, and beheaded, as bodies crashed, left and right, piling up around her.

Jon glanced back. "Sirra!" he yelled. He winced as she paused from assisting Dellia to glance at him. Jon motioned to the vortex with his head. "A portal."

Sirra thrust her palm out, and a portal formed behind them, with the other end high above at the edge of the vortex.

Jon willed it again, and the yali near her began diving down to rip wolves and creatures from the ground and fling them into the shimmering gateway right in front of Sirra.

The bloodred beasts tumbled out the other end, hurtling into the whirlwind with a loud crackle and spray of sparks.

He struggled to remain conscious through waves of pain as the full brunt of the attack came to bear. He dropped to his knees, and everything became a blur, surrounded by a sea of angry, snarling teeth and fur pouring toward them as if it would never end.

The yellow, glowing hurricane twisted and rumbled. Yali rose and plummeted. They jerked wolves and creatures from the ground, causing yelps and cries of pain. Garris's crossbow string twanged time and again. Arrows whistled through the air, downing wolf upon wolf. Bodies tumbled across the ground. Dellia's blades whirled around her, as carcasses thudded to the earth. And above it all, creatures and wolves tumbled through the sky like rag dolls, crackling with light and sound as they were swept away into the screaming vortex.

As the attackers thinned, the yali roamed farther and farther back toward Mundus, plucking stragglers from the ground, dragging them high into the sky to fling them into the roaring tornado.

Jon leaned on the ground, the pain unbearable, as a yali tossed the last remaining wolf into the whirlwind. He summoned his final bit of resolve and cried out in agony as he slammed his fist to the ground, picturing the portal he had seen in his vision. A bright yellow arc flashed through the deep blue sky far out in the distance, striking the dark portal somewhere in the mountains.

The vortex dissipated as the yali drifted through the sky back toward Mundus, leaving only a sea of carcasses strewn across the scrub and dust of the barren, dark landscape.

Jon clutched his hands as every muscle in his body spasmed in pain. A loud crack pierced the warm air as Jon slumped into a heap.

Dellia rushed over and threw her arm over his shoulder as he lay hunched on the ground.

He turned his head to gaze up at her, and his words eked out through winces of pain. "The gate is destroyed. It's over."

As Dellia peered down at him, concern flooded every line of her face. She reached out and with great gentleness helped him up. Then, she slipped her arms around him, her warm embrace holding him tight.

Jon stayed there, leaning on her for support while she caressed his back, as if comforting a child. At her touch, his agony eased, and he calmed as the twitches of pain subsided.

After a while, he let go and stepped back. "Can we go home now?" he pleaded as he stood trembling.

Dellia took a deep breath and joined the others, surveying the dark and desolate plains scattered with broken and twisted remains. The sun was just peeking over the horizon as she turned to Jon and gave a quiet nod.

Having had no sleep in over a day, Garris was spent when they arrived back in Shirdon. He stepped through the portal from the carcass-strewn plains of Erden with thoughts of collapsing into a bed, but apparently rest was not part of the plan. No sooner had they arrived than Kayleen ferried Jon, Dellia, and him away and presented them each with several copies of an official-looking document to sign. It bore the signatures of the eight remaining council members, and its pages spelled out the changes in the council and its leadership.

Along with that, it carried orders to all protectors and military personnel to respect the new chain of command. It didn't seem like much of a change for them since they all still reported to Kayleen. Except now, according to this little piece of paper, Jon possessed the power to override Kayleen, and Garris and Dellia's word was to be taken as having come from Jon. It pleased Garris to no end that he could override Kayleen. Images of taunting her with it filled his mind, greatly improving his mood.

A brief exchange followed, during which the more Kayleen talked, the more anxious Jon seemed to get. It ended with them both deciding he had done enough for one day, and his presence was not required until tomorrow.

As they strolled out to the square before the keep, the topic turned to what to do next. Dellia seemed flustered and, with an obvious dollop of reluctance, told Jon he could stay at her house. The Talesh people had always been a bit more relaxed about such things. Even so, it was clear Dellia was more than a little uncomfortable with the idea of it becoming known she shared a home with one who had not vowed to share her life.

Sirra came to Dellia's rescue by offering her guesthouse until homes for Garris and Jon could be arranged.

Jon seemed acutely sensitive to Dellia's discomfort and more than eager to please. So he readily agreed.

Staying at Sirra's home would be like a vacation after what they'd been through, and it was a luxury compared to that cramped log cabin in the Neri. So Garris was eager to agree as well.

Despite it all seeming settled, Dellia insisted on a private discussion with Jon, over who knew what? This time, Garris decided that perhaps eavesdropping might be in bad taste. Besides, he'd probably get caught. After their brief talk, Dellia and Jon both seemed insufferably pleased with themselves and with life in general.

They made preparations to leave, but before they could go, the Verod leaders arrived and spent a fair amount of time in a spirited discussion with Kayleen and Jon. But with the power to address their grievances no longer residing in the council, they disbanded and left. Only then did Garris depart, Sirra taking him and Jon back to her home while Dellia stayed in Shirdon.

Sirra's gift, like most, was unique to only one realm. It was also rare, with only two people in all of Talus possessing it. Like all gifts, it came with a drawback. Sirra had overused hers, and while only a few had ever died from the strain, she was suffering from headaches and exhaustion. So she retired to sleep it off while Garris found something to eat, and he and Jon gulped down their first meal in a day. Jon disappeared shortly after, leaving Garris to clean up.

Sunset was nearing as he wandered out onto the porch to find Jon sitting there, staring out across the grassy expanse. He plopped down at his side and stared with him at some horses grazing in the distance, set before the pale blue of distant mountains.

It would have been nice to stay and relax, but Jon apparently had other ideas. Without removing his eyes from the scene, he said, "Well, I really stuck your foot in it, didn't I?"

Being generally overtired, Garris considered lying and telling him it was okay, but Jon didn't deserve that; he deserved the truth.

"Yeah, I don't really know if I have the kind of faith and belief it takes to be a protector anymore." Garris looked down at the step below his feet and shook his head. "Heck, I'm not sure I ever did."

Jon didn't speak for a while, and there seemed a vague tension in the air. Eventually, he said the words Garris had been avoiding. "You're going to leave, aren't you?"

Garris turned his head and eyed Jon. What could he say? In his banishment, the one hope he'd dared not indulge, even as he clung to it, was his desire to return to Shirdon. He missed his home and his mother, Eejha. And Jon had striven so hard to pull off this miracle and bring him out of exile. How could he tell him the truth?

Jon seemed to sense the answer. "What happened to the whole 'together' thing? I thought we were in this together."

Garris returned his gaze forward, watching a distant foal rub its head against its mother's neck. "Look, I appreciate what you're trying to do here, making a home for me and all. But Shirdon hasn't been my home for a long time. I don't know if I can go back to that place and that life."

Jon seemed to panic at his words. "No. No. No. You don't understand. Megan is still out there, who knows where? And with the council gone, there's no reason for her to run. I have to find her and help her get home, and I need your help."

Garris paused for a moment. In the Verod camp, he had made a promise not to mention anything to Jon about Megan. However, circumstances had changed, and it seemed like a bad idea to let him run off now half-cocked. He had to say something, but he would honor his word as best he could by keeping the details to himself.

He took a deep breath and closed his eyes. "I saw Megan last night."

Jon's head whipped around, and he glared. "You saw her, and you didn't say anything?"

"If you recall, you were a bit preoccupied with overthrowing the council and all." Garris turned away and stared into the distance. "Besides, she made me promise not to tell."

"Then we have to leave. Tomorrow. To go get her."

Astounded by the idiocy of the concept, Garris glanced over at him and shook his head. "You really don't get this whole council leader, protector thing. The whole point of having protectors is so you don't rummage all over the countryside risking your life."

"Well, that's not going to work for me."

"Look, she saw the prophecy. She knows you were recruiting soldiers. In a few days, word will reach every corner of Meerdon that you are council leader."

Jon stiffened and stared. "Oh, thanks. That doesn't make me panicky at all."

"Point is, it's smarter to wait for her to come to you. What happens if you leave, and she comes to Shirdon while you're gallivanting around?"

His attempts to reason with Jon seemed to only make him more agitated. Jon thrust out his hand and pointed away from the mountains. "I can't just sit there in Shirdon and do nothing."

Attempting to counter the animated display, Garris spoke in a slow and calm voice. "For the next few days, you're going to be far too busy to leave. And I need to see my mother, who I haven't seen in fifteen years."

Jon seemed startled by the concept and calmed considerably. "Oh. Yeah. You should do that."

"Well, thanks for your permission."

Jon looked at him with earnest eyes. "The thing is, I'm responsible for Megan being in this mess, and I can't just walk away from that."

Garris paused. Nobody would go to Lanessa unless they deemed their goal more valuable than their life. That Megan would do so meant whatever she was pursuing was as important as she said. Yet, he'd already broken his word by telling Jon he saw her. He couldn't compound his lapse by letting on that she was most likely off on some mission. He had to dissuade Jon from going at all or else go in his stead.

Garris took a deep breath. "Look. She was unharmed and surrounded by good people. I'm sure she'll be fine, and we can send runners to look for her. If they find her, they can even escort her back to Shirdon."

Jon sighed in resignation. "I suppose it couldn't hurt to stay put for a few days."

"A week. And if she doesn't show, Dellia and I will personally go find her, and we *will* return her."

Jon considered for a while, then gave a reluctant nod of agreement.

The pair returned their attention to the red skyline, staring out across the plains as a band of horses trotted off across the landscape.

After a while, the opening became too tempting. Garris turned to Jon. "And by the way, that's not even close to where Shirdon is."

Jon shook his head in apparent disbelief. "Well, that wasn't the point of the conversation, now was it?"

"Don't go getting all snippy. I'm just saying, a council leader ought to have a bit better sense of direction is all."

Jon shook his head in dismay and grumbled under his breath.

"Maybe if you're going to be like this, you *should* leave."

Garris flashed a sickly sweet smile. "See we're in agreement."

Jon buried his head in his arms.

Not done with his goading, Garris said, "What? I thought you were always saying I should talk more."

Jon lifted his head just enough to speak. "I take it back. I take it all back."

"You know, a council leader ought to be a bit more decisive, too. I'm just saying."

Jon buried his head again and groaned. Then he mumbled into his arms, "It's been too long of a day for this."

It was the first few minutes Kayleen had had to herself since the events of a day ago when Jon had taken on the council. It was morning, and he was to arrive any minute, so she had only a short time to relax. Yet, instead of relaxing in the warm sun of the courtyard, she found herself drawn back to the familiar white marble of the council hall, staring down at the spot where the Stone of Syvis no longer rested.

Many disturbing questions stirred in the recess of her mind. The power to use the stone was thought to be lost. Yet, the orderly and methodical Idria had used it as if it were second nature. And in their contact with the stone, both she and Jon had seemed altered, their expressions and words foreign to their usual pattern of action and speech.

The changed version of Jon had destroyed the stone with ease, then wielded power over life and death. A thing no mere human could do. Yet her heart told her he was as human as any person she had ever met. There was a pattern to all of it—to the stone, to Idria, and to Jon's power. She could feel it. Somewhere in the back of her mind, it struggled to form. Yet, the nature of that pattern eluded her.

DELLIA

A long breath sounded at Kayleen's side. She startled and glanced over to see Dellia. She had slipped into the hall unnoticed, then walked the entire length of the polished marble floor, around the council table, and through the arch to stand right next to her, all without making a sound.

It was the first time Dellia had come this close to her since meeting Jon. Kayleen waited as her discomfort mounted, ready for whatever recrimination she would heap upon her already guilty conscience.

"Would you really have walked away?" came Dellia's voice.

"I did." Kayleen stared down at the swirls of white in the shiny, smooth surface of the floor. "At least for a few minutes."

"What made you come back?"

Kayleen looked over at Dellia beside her. "You and Garris." Dellia turned her head and looked at Kayleen with a puzzled expression. "I was afraid Jon would fail, and I knew how much he meant to the two of you. So I came back to help him succeed. For you."

"But what you said in there, they weren't just words. You were frustrated and angry."

Kayleen nodded. "Sometimes it feels like I've spent a lifetime fighting against one deception after another."

Dellia seemed perturbed by her response. She stared for a moment, her eyes becoming sharp and piercing. "And yet, you lied to me and got me to betray my beliefs with such ease. Help me understand how you could do that. How you can sleep at night."

Kayleen turned away, her focus on the place where the stone had once rested. Uncle Edan had raised her to own up to her mistakes and not hide behind excuses. Yet Dellia was direct in asking for one.

"It was my duty." Kayleen glanced over.

Dellia pulled back. An unexpected look of shock overcame her and her eyes flashed back and forth across the large open space as if searching for some other, hidden answer.

Kayleen's guilt flared again as she realized she'd touched a nerve. Eager to distract Dellia from her discomfort, she continued. "I guess I told myself the biggest lie of all. That if I went along with their deceptions, I could change things, that I could protect you and Garris."

Dellia seemed incredulous. "But you are council leader."

"I can't lead where the council won't follow. That's something Jon may soon learn."

Dellia gave an immediate shake of her head. "No, he won't." Kayleen eyed her as she puzzled over the abrupt response. "You've done a terrible thing to Jon. The last thing he ever wanted was the power you placed in his hands."

Kayleen's guilt flared anew, and she shook her head. "I'm sorry. I didn't know. At least not until I saw his reaction. And by then it was too late."

"He isn't built for this. So you're going to help him. That's the only reason I insisted you stay." Dellia placed a gentle hand on Kayleen's shoulder. "He needs you, and that means I need you."

A little choked up at her heartfelt admission, Kayleen bowed her head in acknowledgment and contrition. "I understand."

Dellia looked into her down-turned face, trying to catch her gaze. "I can't just decide to forget the past or make myself forgive you." Kayleen raised her head and stared into Dellia's eyes. "But this is a new day. For all of us. And if you do your best to protect Jon, to help him, I will be forever grateful."

Anxious to prove herself, Kayleen nodded. "I have already met with all the military leaders, protectors, and ambassadors to explain the changes in the council and organize their concerns. I assumed you two would take the next couple days for yourselves. But after, I will meet with Jon so I understand his position. And when the new council convenes, I will be prepared to argue on his behalf."

Dellia's eyes widened in surprise. "You talked to all those people since yesterday?"

"It had to be done fast, to quell rumors. And ..." Kayleen stopped herself and glanced away. Unable to give voice to the one thing that had burdened her heart most in the last few days.

"What?" Dellia stared with a look of concern.

Despite her attempt to maintain her composure, a quiet tear rolled down Kayleen's cheek. "This has to work, Dellia. I need to redeem myself. I have to. ..."

Dellia reached over and hugged her. As she stepped back, her hands remained on Kayleen's shoulders as she gazed into her face. "Is this about ... you know who?"

Kayleen turned away as her breathing grew short, and her heart pounded. She knew. Of course, Dellia knew. How could she not? But it was so rare for her to let on.

Kayleen quickly wiped away her tear. "I never thought he'd be back. And I'd made my peace with that. But now that he's here ..." She hesitated, unable to explain further.

Dellia turned away and looked at the empty cushion where the stone had once lain. "It's always been about him, hasn't it?"

Kayleen's head whipped over, and she stared at Dellia in embarrassment.

"Did you ever really want to be council leader?"

After a moment, when the shock had subsided, Kayleen shook her head. "No. Not really."

It was a carefully hidden secret, never revealed to a living soul. Now, the relief at having someone to share it with was intense, and fresh tears rolled down Kayleen's cheeks. "But he hates me. He absolutely hates me. He thinks I sent people to kill him."

Dellia seemed touched, yet troubled. She took Kayleen's hand in hers. "Tell him."

"How could I?"

"How could it make things worse?"

"I said terrible, awful things to him. He won't forgive me."

Dellia glanced over at the sound of footsteps echoing through the chamber. "Tell him."

She turned and raced off into the arms of her love.

Kayleen gazed at the entwined pair near the dark council table. She had lost Garris twice. When he joined the protectors, she had fled to Kanlu, and many dark months followed as she tried to get over the missing piece of her soul. Eventually, an oracle who had been unable to see her fate gave her some simple advice: look into her heart and if she believed Garris was her one true love, then don't give up. With those few words, all the pieces fell into place and suddenly she had a plan. The next five years, she devoted herself, spending every waking moment studying and training for the chance to become a council member, for the chance to once again be near Garris every day.

As Kayleen watched Jon and Dellia, she whispered to herself, "I will find my way back to him, and when I do, I will never lose him again."

Dellia awoke to the sound of a bird chirping outside her window and a sense of peace and contentment she could not recall having had for a long, long time. She looked up at the warm, yellow ceiling of her home as she stretched and wiped the sleep from her eyes.

Then, she propped herself up in bed and gazed at Jon as he stared out her window. Watching him, she could imagine the warmth of the sun's first golden rays against his skin as the curtains billowed and danced in the light breeze. He was happy and at peace, and it did her heart good to see him more relaxed than she had ever known him to be.

A sudden mischievous urge hit, and she smiled. "You know, protectors aren't supposed to have romantic entanglements."

Jon chuckled under his breath. "Oh, a forbidden tryst. I like it."

"And they're *definitely* not supposed to marry the head of the council."

"I think we're safe, seeing as how all the council members were at the wedding." Jon turned around and smiled at her. "I loved the simplicity and honesty of the ceremony."

"Marriage has always been a simple affair for my people. It is for us to stand before the world and let them know I am yours." Dellia sent him a coy look. "And that you, and all you own, now belongs to me."

Quite pleased with herself, she granted him a demure smile.

Jon's eyes bugged. "All I own?"

"You said you liked tradition. In ancient times you would have gone back to the barracks to fight and train, and the home and children would have been mine."

Dellia rose and wrapped the bedsheet around her, draping it over one shoulder and securing it with a simple leaf-shaped broach she snatched from a stand near the bed.

Jon looked her up and down.

She bathed in the feeling as a sudden wave of awe washed over him and he froze. She had taken his breath away.

"You look like a goddess. I married a goddess."

Not done toying with him, Dellia granted Jon another mischievous smile. "Are you sure you don't want me to shave my head? I would, for you."

Jon startled at the idea and blurted out, "No. You're perfect the way you are."

"It would make it easier to sneak into the men's barracks to see you."

"Okay, okay. So maybe some traditions aren't all they're cracked up to be."

Jon turned back to stare out the window. Dellia sighed as she watched him. She knew she shouldn't manipulate his emotions, but he loved her so, and it was just too easy.

A smile came to her lips as she strolled up from behind and slipped her arms around him. She pressed herself against his back, his skin warm against her body, as she let his passion engulf her.

"I love how you feel." Dellia rested her head on his shoulder. "You look preoccupied, almost troubled, but you're feeling such warmth and happiness and love."

Jon curled his arms around hers. "I was just thinking about the future. What the oracle said about what's coming."

"Jon, don't—"

"No, it's not bad. I was just thinking about how I'm just a guy who stumbled into this world. And how I don't know its rules, or its customs, or its culture, or its people. I'm not strong, or brave, or a warrior like you. How could I be this great leader of this prophecy?"

"But you are," Dellia said, though she didn't care in the slightest who he was, as long as he was hers.

"No, that's just it. I can't be. I mean, I get that there's this big threat we have to stop, and we will. But to be a leader, to bring about a new age ... and that's when it hit me. I'm just a fluke, a fulcrum, something that everyone can point to and say, 'That's when everything changed.' " Jon turned his head just enough to catch her eye. "Dellia, this prophecy, it's never really been all about me. It's always been as much about you as me. It's the only way any of this makes sense."

The sentiment was beautiful and charming, yet at the same time a bit sad and troubling because he really couldn't see how strong and capable he was. But the feeling flittered away the instant it came. He was here, with her, and always would be, and nothing could ever tarnish how perfect and right this moment felt.

She kissed Jon's neck, then rested her head back on his shoulder, watching out the window with him. "Have I ever told you I love the way you think?"

DELLIA

He turned around and kissed her. Behind him, the curtains still billowed and danced in the breeze, as birds flew across the rising sun, signaling the start of a new day.